PENGUIN BOOKS

THE RAINBOW STORIES

William T. Vollmann was born in Los Angeles in 1959. He attended Deep Springs College and Cornell University, where he graduated *summa cum laude* in comparative literature. Vollmann's books include the novels *You Bright and Risen Angels, The Ice-Shirt, Fathers and Crows, Butterfly Stories, Whores for Gloria,* and *The Rifles*; two story collections, *The Rainbow Stories* and *Thirteen Stories and Thirteen Epitaphs*; and a work of nonfiction, *An Afghanistan Picture Show*. Vollmann won a 1988 Whiting Award in recognition of his writing achievements and the Shiva Naipaul Memorial Award in 1989. He is currently engaged in writing a series of seven novels exploring the repeated collisions between North American native populations and their colonizers and oppressors. William Vollmann lives in California.

THE RAINBOW STORIES

WILLIAM T. VOLLMANN

PENGUIN BOOKS

PENGUIN BOOKS
Published by the Penguin Group
Penguin Books USA Inc.,
375 Hudson Street, New York, New York 10014, U.S.A.
Penguin Books Ltd, 27 Wrights Lane,
London W8 5TZ, England
Penguin Books Australia Ltd, Ringwood,
Victoria, Australia
Penguin Books Canada Ltd, 10 Alcorn Avenue,
Toronto, Ontario, Canada M4V 3B2
Penguin Books (N.Z.) Ltd, 182–190 Wairau Road,
Auckland 10, New Zealand

Penguin Books Ltd, Registered Offices:
Harmondsworth, Middlesex, England

First published in Great Britain by
André Deutsch Limited 1989
First published in the United States of America by Atheneum, a division of Macmillan
Publishing Company, 1989
Published in Penguin Books 1992

5   7   9   10   8   6

PUBLISHER'S NOTE

These stories are works of fiction. Names, characters, places, and incidents either are the product of the author's imagination or are used fictitiously, and any resemblance to actual persons, living or dead, events, or locales is entirely coincidental.

THE LIBRARY OF CONGRESS HAS CATALOGUED THE HARDCOVER AS FOLLOWS:
Vollmann, William T.
The rainbow stories / William T. Vollmann.
p.   cm.
ISBN 0-689-11961-5 (hc.)
ISBN 0 14 01.7154 1 (pbk.)
I. Title.
PS3572.0395R35   1989
813'.54—dc19   88–32628

Printed in the United States of America

Misery is manifold. The wretchedness of the earth is uniform. Overreaching the wide horizon as the rainbow, its hues are as various as the hues of that arch; as distinct too, yet as intimately blended.

Poe, "Berenice" (1835)

PREFACE

These stories are about skinheads, X-ray patients, whores, lovers, fetishists and other lost souls. Some of you will not like them, but I ask you to consider the wise words of that forceps philosopher, Robert Gilmore McKinnell: "While it would be inappropriate to dedicate a vade mecum to a group of cold-blooded vertebrates, perhaps a kind word would not be out of order."* This has been one of my intentions. And yet single-minded kindness might prohibit kind words, or any words, because words only show the good to our eyes; they do not bring the good to our hearts. My attempts to do good, however, having been disasters thus far, I have become a mere recording angel instead of a Michael or Gabriel (in whom I do not believe). So much for that subject.

As to the scheme, I do not understand colors in themselves. I have therefore based my ideology not on the innate qualities of certain hues, but on their extremes and their negation. Thus the spectrum of these *Rainbow Stories* is bordered by white and black, and it is in their progression from the one to the other that their meaning lies. – I wish I could say that I loved all the colors equally. In fact, I have a special affinity for green and yellow (no doubt because I do not eat enough vegetables), and a surpassing admiration for the color black (I have been told that black is not a color, but refuse to believe it). the motto for this collection, therefore, is:

The prettiest thing is the darkest darkness.

* Content-mongers and lords of the world are invited to visit the treatise itself: *Cloning: Nuclear Transplantation in Amphibia – A Critique of Results Obtained with the Technique to Which Is Added a Discourse on the Methods of the Craft* (Minneapolis: University of Minnesota Press, 1978), pp. 172–3.

THE VILE RAINBOW

SHEWING
HIS ORDER IN THE
UNIVERSAL SPHERE

MECHANICAL TERRORS
ELECTRIC PULSES $1 \times 10^{16} - 1 \times 10^{13}$ Å
RADIO 1×10^{10} Å
TELEVISION 1×10^{7} Å
RADAR 1×10^{5} Å

Red Orange Yellow Green Blue Indigo Violet
7000 Å   4000 Å

ULTRAVIOLET $1000 - 100$ Å
SOFT X-RAYS 10 Å
CRYSTALLOGRAPHY 1 Å
MEDICAL RADIOGRAPHY 1×10^{-1} Å
HARD X-RAYS 1×10^{-2} Å
COSMIC RAYS 1×10^{-13} Å
MYSTERIES AND MONSTERS

CONTENTS

The Visible Spectrum
page 1

The White Knights
page 15

Red Hands
page 65

Ladies and Red Lights
page 77

Scintillant Orange
page 143

Yellow Rose
page 203

The Yellow Sugar
A Tale of Infamous Righteousness and Righteous Villainy
page 235

The Green Dress
A Pornographic Tale
page 277

The Blue Wallet
page 305

The Blue Yonder
A Tale of Cleanliness
page 327

The Indigo Engineers
page 439

Violet Hair
A Heideggerian Tragedy
page 481

X-Ray Visions
page 535

A Note on the Truth of the Tales
page 542

Acknowledgements
page 543

THE
VISIBLE
SPECTRUM

It is important for the patient to know in advance
that some doses will be reduced but not by how much
or when. Liquid oral and injectible forms of analgesia
are easiest to disguise.

> Philip Rubin, M.D., ed., *Clinical Oncology
> for Medical Students and Physicians: A
> Multidisciplinary Approach*, 6th ed. (1983)*

The Red Line

Bending and leaning on his crutches, a patient dwindled down the
white glassy corridor, trying so hard to follow the red line that he was a
joy to watch. – "You came at the wrong time, guy!" laughed the fellow
at Radiology Reception. "Everybody's gone to lunch! That's what they
do, you know, when they go to lunch. They send everybody down
here."

"Do you have any allergies?" a woman was asking sweetly of a man
with a metal clip on his nose. The man was on a stretcher. He was
about to die. – "No," the man said. Every now and then one could see
the soles of bandaged feet projecting from other stretchers, which were
wheeled along the red line, which sometimes bifurcated or got lost
inside the blue line, loving the glyphs of that other line, or else, like a
mother wrenching her hand away from her child's anxious grasp, the
red line even abandoned one at times, and there were only mocking
lacunae on the floor.

"You might as well go and get some lunch," the Radiology guy said
kindly.

* Published by the American Cancer Society. Chapter 29 ("Principles of Psycho-social Oncology"), section: "Terminal-Palliative Phase."

Stories of the Radiology Man

A man he knew had just gotten killed in the Broadway tunnel. The man had been riding a motorcycle. A speeding car had mashed him against the guard rail until his head came off. I imagine that head sailing, sailing down the long yellow tunnel, blinking in wonder at the view, while the killer roared away in his car, being anxious, as we all are, to avoid being convicted of manslaughter; and long after the killer had lost himself in the night traffic of Chinatown that head remained aloft, fixated in its astonishment within the eternal rushing of that tunnel; other cars were rushing home to other deaths and they did not even see that lonely head so high above them, still moving at sixty miles an hour, consecrating their windshields with its last drops of blood, saying to itself *How could this have happened to me?* – and the motorcycle arrowed faithfully down that long straight tunnel, the dead hands of the dead body still clenched on the handlebars; but the dead head slowed to fifty miles an hour, forty miles an hour, beginning its ruinous descent to concrete – not that the head would ever know that it had fallen at last: – the eternity of the dead brain would be preserved, like a butterfly in an album, as a bright rushing of colors.

The radiology man said that sometimes people came in with ruined faces, black mush or green mush or blue mush where their eyes used to be. He said that sometimes people paid no attention to instructions and followed the green line instead of the orange line, the blue line instead of the red line. Then the hospital could no longer be responsible. When this occurred, terrible mistakes were committed. People had their kidneys cut out when all they needed was an ankle-cast. People lost their arms and legs beneath the bone-saws for no reason. – He was joking, of course. In my opinion he was an extremely funny fellow. Mistakes were not usually so serious.

The Tale of the Dying Lungs

Once upon a time there was a man whose lungs were decaying and swelling up with black stuff and puffing out in his chest like puffballs so that he began to suffocate over a period of two years. It was explained to him that at the end of the two years he would die. He had more and more difficulty breathing. Finally he went into the hospital knowing that he would not walk out, and they wheeled him along the wide black line and tucked him into his deathbed and as he lay in it wheezing the doctors asked him for his consent to be assigned No Code status. (A No Code patient is one who is not hooked up to a respirator when his heart stops.) "Let nature take its course," the doctors said. The man gave his permission not to be intubated. But time passed, and his life passed, and he could not breathe. He was like an underwater swimmer stroking desperately to reach the surface and breathe in the cool air in big luxurious gasps, but when his head came up he had to breathe in foam and spray, and each time the surface was harder to get to and he had to breathe in more water (it was his own water, flooding his lung-cells from his decayed lymph-sea), and he panicked and begged to be intubated, but, being informed of this, the doctors concluded that he was no longer rational because he was requesting something not in his own best interest – namely, to catch his breath and stay alive a little longer; and, besides, it cost the hospital money to run the respirators, so they kept him No Code, and he choked and choked and choked and died.

Business Picks Up

In the afternoon more patients came in. A man with something wrong with his leg lay back on a gurney groaning through clenched teeth, "I can't stand it! I can't stand it!"

A woman was being wheeled along the blue line to the elevator. She was screaming and screaming in pain. "*Oh, my God!*" she screamed. Somebody in a white coat bent over her to make an examination. She began screaming much louder, so that the hall echoed with her screams, which bounced off the glassy walls and skated along the glassy ceiling. It was heartbreaking how useless those screams were. – "Be quiet," the nurses told her. (Who could blame them? If I had to listen to people screaming all the time, I would tell them to be quiet, too.) "Shut up," the nurses said. "Now, what's your date of birth? Just relax. What's your social security number?"

The Waiting Room

"Sixty-four thousand guys died in one minute," said the veteran on the bench, scuffing his foot across the green line. He had lines in his forehead so deep and tightly spaced that they looked like stripes. He had lost most of his hair. "Goddamn fucking Jap killed my goddamn wife," he said. "Stuck a piece of bamboo right up her."

"You saw it?" said the black man beside him.

"Yeah, I fucking *saw* it. I couldn't do anything. But I watched the Jap that did it. I memorized his face. I spent four years in that prison camp. Then I escaped. The others that escaped with me said, where you goin'? – I said, I'll be back in ten minutes. I went back and found that Jap *sonofabitch* and said, you killed my goddamned *wife;* I'm gonna kill *you.* He thought I was kidding at first. He didn't think so very long. And now the war's over, and they say, so long, *sucker!* We don't need you. – And they think I'm a mean sonofabitch. *Oooh,* they say. He's *mean.*"

"Hey, man, you *made* it."

"Only reason I made it is because I know judo and karate. If I have to kill again, I'll do it."

"I learned that, too," said the black man softly.

"I like Reagan. You know why? He'd drop the bomb on the god-damned *Japs.'*

The loudspeaker said, "Tilda Barrett to Triage."

The most attractive objects in the room were the gleaming crutches. Second in the ranking were the wooden rubber-tipped canes that leaned against the seats at a rather cocky angle, while their owners stared into dimensions beyond the ken of mathematicians, or nodded, eyes closed, into their beards. – Next came the shoes: dirty sneakers, twenty-year-old wingtips, sandals no longer white, women's shoes of that flat-bottomed-boat style so popular in the 'fifties and 'sixties; and of course the white-swaddled feet of cripples, the swaddling being cleaner than mountain snow, so that the white hair and white beards of the cripples seemed dingier than they really were. The sturdy old shoes and other walking appliances promised to outlive their owners.

Then there were the yellow bracelets that marked the patients. These were made of almost indestructible plastic. Decades from now, they would still be bright and yellow.

Almost as pretty was the rainbow of lines upon the floor. The red line went to Atlantis, the orange line to Hyperborea, the yellow line to Thule, the green line to Heaven, the blue line to Hell, the indigo line to Purgatory, and the violet line led God knows where.

Sometimes, after sitting patiently for half an hour, a man or a pair of women might get up and change their seats to the opposite side of the little room. One woman breathed in a way that fluttered her chest, but she sat reading a magazine, evidently quite used to it. – Many of these people did not look sick. How little we can tell when others suffer! – Those smokers, those page-turners and soda-can clutchers, all sat waiting for the blue afternoon sky of their Saturday to become dark, so that time would pass and they would be seen. Fat women with folded arms scratched their armpits. Men sat. They sat and waited for their fate to be decided. Faces pale, collars upturned, eyes undershadowed, they waited. Every half-hour, one or two names were called once. Sometimes nobody got up. Once a woman stumbled to her feet, the pain-lines in her forehead momentarily smoothing with relief at having received the Call, and she hobbled slowly down the bright orange line to get her carrot. But she had not been Called, and soon she came back to us.

A man read a magazine for an hour, very intently. Finally he put it down. The entire time he had not turned a single page. The veteran picked it up and stared at it for awhile. When he laid it down, I saw that he had not been reading it, either, only looking at it because he had to look at something. Eventually he got up and followed the green line which led him out of the hospital.

Getting Accepted

From the triage desk you had to go along the red line to the registration desk, then back to the general waiting room until your turn came, then along the red line again to the Radiology waiting room, then along the indigo line to the X-Ray room, then back to the Radiology waiting room, then to the triage desk, then the general waiting room, and finally if you followed the orange line or the violet line you were admitted to the private consultation room with its dirty steel gurneys of various lengths, its steel lamp, the white sink, with the long faucet bent over it like the neck of a swan, and the pack of Travenol wipes. Fluid dripped through a complex of tubing on the wall. The room was square and severe. Here one's future would be decided. Here it would be made clear whether one would be medicated or whether one would be expelled back into the cruel world.

The I.V. League

"Just follow the blue line," said the Recording Angel. "Did you hear that the President's going to have to take a urine test on Monday?"

"He has to wait on the waiting list!" cried a laughing woman who was missing every other tooth. She laughed and winked when her vein was popped. The phlebotomist smiled at her a little shyly. She called to her friend, "Hey, come on and hit me! He don't know where to hit me!"

The blood draw was at a round table, in sight of the red line. The addicts sat down, and then the phlebotomist bent over them.

"I took the AIDS test when you people were first here, and I never got my results," the next addict said indignantly. She was a plump blonde with black-and-blue arms. "When you first had me, you just took my mother's maiden name. Then you changed the procedure on me."

"We still do it that way," the Recording Angel said. "But you have to go to Ward Eighty-Six. Follow the white line."

"Oh, the white line? Then you changed it."

"Mother's maiden name?" the Recording Angel said.

"Browder."

"And what was your father's name?"

"I *told* you I don't know my father!"

"Well, let's call him X then. Can you remember that?"

The blonde nodded serenely. She sat down next to the phlebotomist and rolled up her sleeve.

"I smoke," teased the phlebotomist, "but I don't drink, I don't shoot up, and I don't chase women."

"Oh, shit!" laughed the blonde. "How passive!"

The Red Line and the Blue Line

The next man refused to take the test. He sat down and then stood up and returned along the red line.

"He's great," his wife explained. "A great person. But he's got gangrene of the pancreas, and most of it's gone. He doesn't want to know if he's got the antibody."

The man after him was very calm, and did not wince when the needle went in. But he looked away. I think it is very funny that if you shoot yourself up four or five times a day you do not mind the needle going in, but you cannot bear to watch someone else do it.

"I don't remember my number now," a woman mourned in the hall. For a very long time I could see her staring at the blue line.

A girl with long brown hair breezed in. – "I missed the last one, so this will be *new* for me," she bubbled. The phlebotomist tied the tourniquet on her arm. Her shoulders rose when the needle went in.

"They check your urine every week," the girl said brightly, "and if you're dirty, even with alcohol, you don't get to keep your baby. I have a girlfriend that's straight, but she drinks. We always used to go out in cars together. Now she can't go anywhere without a case of Bud. She was pregnant once. It was illegitimate. Then she married a lawyer, so I guess she *scored* pretty good. She wanted to give that lawyer a daughter, 'cause he's been a good husband, but they had to take it out of her in the eighteenth week. She took a picture of it. It was so white. Then she tried to have a son. You know how babies are usually *solid?* Well, this baby was so pale and flabby. He's three months and he can't lift up his head."

"Follow the blue line," said the Recording Angel.

"Can I do it again?" called the blonde from the hall. "I got such a charge out of it. You don't have to pay me this time."

"I need your parents' first names," said the Recording Angel to the next arrival. – "Mother Mary," said the man with certainty. "Father, uh . . ." – he thought a long time – *"John."* – He sat very still, wiggling his cheeks. He wore a grey beret. He played with his hands.

People Without Veins

"You busy or something?" said an addict shyly. He had to point out his good vein; they couldn't find it. But his good vein was used up, like the rest. The phlebotomist moved the tourniquet down. He prodded with his finger, poked, slapped, felt, touched, probing again and again with his forefinger; and finally he sighed and swabbed the spot with alcohol. – "Mmm mmm," he said, shaking his head.

"That's all right," the addict said. "I don't think you're gonna find a vein. I gotta go anyway. I'll just be heading down that red line."

"Well, let's try it again," the phlebotomist said.

"I even have trouble hittin' sometimes," the man said. "Fortunately I'm ambidextrous. Used to be, anyway. Usually my veins are pretty good. There's just a lump or an abscess there today."

"Are you interested in taking the test?" said the Recording Angel to the next arrival.

"Yeah, but I don't have any veins!" Grimacing, the woman undid her coat. Her arms were covered with bluish-black spots. The phlebotomist probed gently with his thumb, and she leaned forward, so anxious to help him as I thought at first, but then I determined from her resignedly raised shoulders that she had no hope.

"All right," said the phlebotomist, "we'll do this one, just under the little butterfly. You don't have to look."

"That's good," she said. "I can't stand watching when other people do it."

All morning I watched the rhythmic bouncing of the finger-ball against the rubbery veins. Most of the addicts wore long sleeves. – "We could probably do a thousand of them in a day," said the Recording Angel. "I'm sure we could." – Between patients, the staff turned the pages of the newspaper. – "This woman I interviewed is on methadone," said the doctor, "and she's shooting heroin three times a day." – When the addicts came in, the other doctor stood, legs braced. "Got to keep your eyes on those needles," he said in a low voice.*

The Green Line

A pretty young girl came in. She had long black hair. "I remember you!" she said. There was a tattoo on her arm – an ornate iron cross. She stretched her arms out parallel on the table.

"Will them veins ever be good again?" she said.

"Probably not," said the doctor shortly.

"I just want them to be normal," she said.

"Have you used this one?" said the doctor.

"No. Well, maybe just once."

The doctor probed.

"My little girl's just frantic now," she said. "She wants to know, what are those bruises on Mommy's arms? I tell her, Mommy tried to get a tattoo, but it didn't work and it went into Mommy's veins." She looked at the needle with big eyes. "I'm shaking," she said. "I can't believe it."

"Hold still," said the doctor.

"I have my sister's kids, too. They shot my sister. She was six months pregnant, too. They found her on Eighth and Mission. And she was cremated, so I got her ashes in my closet. Her little boy, he cries every night. And there ain't nothin' I can say. I just hug him and hold him. He's a good little boy."

"Okay," said the doctor, "just about done here. Follow the green line around the corner."

Her blood went down the long scarlet tube.

---

* Needles are very difficult for addicts to obtain. Old ones must be babied, like old veins. One addict kept his needle lubed up with ear-wax.

The Challenge

"My date of birth is 7/23/27," said the old black man.

The young phlebotomist rolled up the man's sleeves, showing the world those two black muscular arms. "You tell me which is the best," he said.

"Well," chuckled the old man, "you *might* get some here. *If* you're going to do it." Like the others, he kept his cap on.

He sat there while the phlebotomist tried to get blood out. Meanwhile, the doctor did a woman and another man. – "I guess I'll take that test," a blond guy said. "I just had it four months ago. Is that okay with you?" – "It's fine," said the Recording Angel. – "I came out positive antibodies," the guy said, "so I should be concerned about it, I guess."

The black man was still there. "There ain't but one place you can get it," he said patiently. "I know. I'm a drug addict; I been one all my life. I know where the blood comes!"

"Well, all right," said the phlebotomist wearily. "Can you shoot up for us?"

"Sure I can." The old man leaned over and began searching for the special vein, his secret treasure which had not yet been expended. Of course the old man's inner resources would have been twice as plentiful if he had counted his arteries, but these would have borne the heroin away from his inmost center, diffusing into the tips of his fingers through capillaries that got smaller and smaller like drying-up rivers. – Nope, there was nothing for it but veins, and veins were precious few. Could he find that one true tube of happiness? – Yes! – I heard a snapping sound. – "I *know* where they are," he said. "I been doin' it forty-five years. The rest, they look like veins, but I done played those out *years* ago."

The phlebotomist rubbed his forehead.

"I don't need a bandaid," the old man said. "Yeah, you have a nice weekend."

"I started to say," said the Recording Angel, "that black man was here last year. And he looks *terrible* from last year. He must have gotten something."

The doctor sighed. "Send him down the green line."

Stories of the Drug Ward

Twice a month the addicts lined up to get their methadone. First they had to go down the yellow line to take a urine test. Their urine had to test clean for them to qualify for more methadone, so there were folks in the parking lot who made a peaceful living selling their piss. I am sure that this rendered the colored lines almost useless, but because the urine entrepreneurs were not friendly to me I did not ask them their views. – Another good trick of the yellow-liners who got what they had waited there for was to swish the methadone around in their dour knowing mouths and pretend to swallow it, and then go spit it out and sell it on the street. Even if they had to buy piss to sell methadone, they still came out ahead. So a staff person had to make them talk after they swallowed. When they talked she looked into their mouths to make sure that the liquid had gone down their unwilling throats.

Other Voices

"My heel hurts with a dull cold sensation," a man was saying next door where the violet line ended. It seemed as if he were a philosopher talking to himself, analyzing his condition for the sake of analysis, in order to infinitesimally enrich the universe. But I knew that there was probably a doctor kneeling in front of him like a fellator, prompting him and questioning him in a dry whisper.

Destiny

How anxious these patients all were! How much they wanted to know their fate! ... And yet all they had to do was look down from their gurneys and determine the color of the line they were being wheeled along; then they would know whether they would live or die ...

THE
WHITE
KNIGHTS

This story
is for
Bootwoman Marisa,
whether she likes it
or not

Though you suffered disgrace
and sorrow grieved me,
though I was outlawed and you dishonored,
joyful revenge will now proclaim us happy.

Wagner, *Die Walküre* (1856), 1.3

Ellis Street

Grey skulls and grey shirts, blue eyes and blue shirts; and a cigarette in every hand. The skinheads yelled and fought beneath the midnight stillness of the kitchen ceiling.

"Boy, what're we gonna do tonight?"

"I dunno, it's only ten-thirty."

"When I first met you, Dickie, and you got drunk, you used to get so obstreperous, man."

"I got *loud* and *rude!*"

"Then you would push me and I'd push you back. The next morning I knew I'd jumped on you. I was like anti-subconscious, man."

"That's right. That was when we had our skinhead harem. We had a squat in the city. It was wall to wall pussy."

"I don't want to hear it," said Dickie's bootwoman, Dan-L.

"WALL TO WALL PUSSY!" the skinheads yelled. "WALL TO WALL PUSSY!"

Dan-L left, slamming the kitchen door.

"Well, we can talk about the harem some other time," Dickie said. "Anyhow, you got so drunk and mad, you kicked me in the balls. Then Warren got mad and kicked me, too. But I fought you and Warren."

"And got your ass kicked!" Dagger roared. "Just kidding."

"We used to fight all the time, you goddamned bully."

"Hey, dude, don't call me no fucking bully," Dagger said. "I got fucked with by bullies when I was growing up, man."

"Suck my dick, Massah!"

"Stick it up me, Massah!"

"I remember it all," said Dickie wisely. "If you gotta fight somebody, you gotta fight 'em. Never back down."

"You gotta have principles, though," said Dagger. "You can't just fight like a nigger. For instance, I believe every man should have respect for a man's house. I won't whip your ass inside your house. I'll always give you a choice; you can come out and get whipped, or you can stay inside and I'll tear the place up. I remember when I was scrapping with my foster father, he said, 'Step outside.' He fought me outside, treated me like a man. When I whipped his ass, he went in and got his gun and chased me off the place. And I *respect* him for it, man."

Anthony, whom they'd been calling the Wop all night, because that was funny, was polishing his boots, black boots with red laces. He was stropping them one at a time between his thighs.

"Well, you do all the fighting, but I don't have no record, Dagger," said Dickie. "I always said I was the smarter."

"Hey," said Dagger, "I may not be the smartest, but I know when to back up and when to jump 'em."

"Yessir," said Dickie dreamily. "I was the original organizer."

"*You* were the organizer, uh?" cried Dagger, injured. "I was the organizer, man! In your day everyone wore fucking Mohawk haircuts!"

This was a stunning rejoinder, bringing only silence. Dagger pressed his advantage. "Anyhow, we didn't have no leaders," he said. "We was sayin' skinhead things long before *you* came along. We was sayin', 'We got to take care of all the Cholos and niggers.'"

"Aw," said Dickie. "People been saying that for two hundred years."

The generic beers were piled up in towers on the table, with George Thoroughgood tapes beside the player, and an ashtray for every man. The skinheads stroked their black shiny boots and bluejeans. Their shaven heads made them seem particularly thoughtful, with all the profundity of skulls. Dagger picked at the checks in his shirt, and Dickie relaxed, attended by his girl in her camouflage cap, her bangs down to her eyes, this girl who was in love with him. Even when she slammed out, she could not stay away.

The Last Bald Eagle

When Dickie put his arm around her, and she around him, they both looked at the world unflinchingly, but without her Dickie found things to concentrate on, like the cassette player, like fights, like lighting his bong, while Dan-L sat in the corner by the window, staring into heaven with clasped hands. Dickie sat crooning inwardly to the cassette player with his eyes closed, the clean shadow of his head and neck doubling in outline a soldier's helmet upon the kitchen door. Other shadows connected him to the tape player, the two round eyes of its speakers rolling dolefully, like those of an old dog; and Dickie tilted his head back farther, rigidifying the black helmet that he dreamed so freely in; and the shadow of his sleeve flared like one of those venomous elbow-spines sported by insects; and it was impossible to understand what he was thinking: his soul rested in a lone grave beneath the leafless tree of some Civil War battlefield, or wandered through the dugouts of Verdun, stepping from timber to slimy timber with the smell of mud all around him, and looking in the pockets of his dead comrades for extra cartridges, holding his breath when he reached into the swirling little pools of chlorine gas where the others had fallen, leaving him alone to await and admit the attack; for it is a lonely thing to be a skinhead, so lonely that only other doomed soldiers can imagine it. Let us get killed, then, in order to see the new mobilizations of Dickie's soul, helmeted by his skin-padded skull (padding out, hard side in) to protect him from Japanese attack in the Solomon Islands in '43 as he waded through the blood-warm water on his knees and flung himself behind the palms with his assault rifle blazing the way and cocked KER-snap!, Dickie (who was an Order of the Arrow Eagle Scout) being in action at last, soon to be killed in action, meanwhile sole survivor of his platoon, which lay in sodden, bloated khaki-covered pieces on the beach beside shattered wood and bamboo, the corpses' eyes transformed into mouths of pink rolled tissue – and then it's WHUMP! WHUMP! WHUMP! WHUMP! WHUMP! at Wesel and at Bremen and at Hannover, the eternal present tense of a German conflict, American shells turning blocks of apartments into grey plains stamped almost evenly by close-clustered craters; and the First Battalion strides down narrow, high-walled streets in Bensheim, blowing away the last pale, sweating Krauts hiding in doorways – but whose side could Dickie be on? He's American; he's a Nazi; and as the close-shaved, cropped-headed boys from Tennessee and Virginia march past splintered trees, splintered houses, sometimes Dickie is with them and sometimes he must be against this force that struck down the ole Reich whose emblems skinheads bear in their flesh – how many swastika tattoos have I lost count of?[1] (Of course the inmates of Buchenwald were the ultimate skinheads: stubble-crowned, tattooed, naked and angular.) – At least both parties agreed on hating the Soviet Union.

The Butcher Boys

"I'll tell you a story," Dickie said. "This is an early skinhead story. Long time ago, I don't know how many years ago it was, we had this house out by the river in West Virginia, a big house, and we were living together for about six months (we was even living with this nigger fella then, a guy with hair abnormally long, down to his butt), when these people started coming to town. I met this first skinhead; his name was Butch; he was driving a Chevy truck. Right away we made this rule that anybody that came in had to shave his head.

"We needed food, so we started the Butcher Boys; that was what we called ourselves. We went out killing all kinds of animals. We hung the meat on a line, and the way we got it was, we had this deaf pit bull named Bully, who barked funny on account of he couldn't hear himself, and he had a big square head and white spots on his shoulders; the girls used to draw circles in black magic marker around his eyes, so he'd look like Petey of the Little Rascals. Once that dog nearly got us arrested. We were in a McDonald's waiting for somebody to get off work, and Bully started barking real funny, like this, *Oooooh, oooooh, oooooh*, and somebody called the cops and said, 'Those skinheads are abusing their dog,' and the cops showed up and started giving us shit until some nigger woman went by, and of course Bully barked at that,

1 The question, "What is German? What is American?" is still not solved among the skins, *Pfeffer* going through the High Consonant Shift to become *pepper*, *Rasse* becoming *race*, and *Nazi* becoming *Republican*, hardly to the detriment of skinhead self-esteem.

and the cops said, 'Holy shit, you're right, he does bark that way natural,' so they let us go.

"Bein' the Butcher Boys and all, we'd send Bully into a chicken coop; he'd go in one end and the chickens would come squawking out the other, and we'd go *bam, bam* with a board – *haw!* – take us home a mess of chickens! We killed lotsa pigs, too, but most of what we killed was billy-goat. Those billy-goats were tough, which was why we usually sold the meat instead of eating it ourselves. We got like ten or eleven goats one night. They were in a pen. We just walked in there with our knives, *pop, pop!* (That was how I got this scar on my hand, gutting a goat.) We'd wrap the meat and sell it at this shopping center; all kinds of niggers bought it. They didn't know what they were buying.

"Now, this is how I got the bestiality charges: There was two of us, and we went and got this sheep. So, we went across this fence, and this sheep had two little lambs – really sad, heh, heh! So, anyway, here's this fucking sheep with bells on it, so I go *blap, blap!* with a sledge-hammer, then again for health, and we put it in the pickup and started driving home. I remember that we picked up this hitchhiker, and we were horsing around with her and she started freaking out. All the sudden we hear this noise in the back – that sheep was only knocked out! We started going for it with a two-pronged spade, and Bully and the other dogs were ripping at its neck, and guts and blood was spurting all over the truck, and that hitcher goes, 'Oh, my God, let me *go!*' so we let her go, and went home with the sheep and did the usual, right, 'cause we was the Butcher Boys.

"The next day, we see on page one of the paper that somebody's goddamned sheep got stolen. It was somebody's fucking *pet!* That was why it had the bells on it. It was in the papers, Snowy the Dancing Sheep; can you fucking believe it? – They had a five thousand dollar reward on it for two weeks. – Well, right then, just about the time we finished serving up Snowy, the girls took Bully with them to the shopping center to sell goat meat to the niggers, and he didn't come back. The girls said he ran off. People said, 'So, where's the dog?' We joked and said, 'Well, we ate it. Then we had a good time fucking the sheep!' – Just kidding, but this new cop heard about it, and it was like bestiality and thirty counts of rustling."

"So what'd you do with all the bones?" said the Wop. "Feed 'em to Bully?"

"Hell, no," grinned Dickie. "We had a *big* barbecue pit."

"Hey, Dude," said Dagger, tapping his middle finger on the table.
"Flip the tape."

"We didn't listen to 'Dixie Fry,'" said Dickie.

"Fuck *you*, man, I don't give a *fuck!*" yelled Dagger.

"I flipped it over," Dickie said.

"You're a *fucking* liar, man!"

The skinheads got into an argument over what to play, knocking each
other around with their tattooed muscular construction arms bursting
with veins, glaring, showing teeth, yelling, "*Suck my dick!*" until they
drowned out the music, the police sirens outside, the terrible life of the
Tenderloin streets.

Mark Dagger

Dagger's head had two narrow bars of shadow in which his eyes were
set. Whereas on Chuckles's shoulder was tattooed a sneering skull
resting on a basket of spidery skeleton-fingers poised over a heap of
little white skulls above the words EXTREME HATE upon a skull in a
bullet-pierced Nazi helmet, like one of those aboriginal myths about
how the world rests on the back of a giant tortoise that balances itself
upon another tortoise that seesaws upon still another blackish-green
shell as the creature splays its wrinkled legs out and voids its turgid
white reptile-piss on the ten million tortoises below it, except that
instead of tortoises it was all skulls, and surmounting this totem pole of
defiance was Chuckles's head, a smooth intelligent head that was
usually smiling faintly; whereas, in short, Chuckles had a lot of tattoos
on his arm, Dagger wore only one blotchy green skull on a bicep and
below that his identifying message, THE FUCKUPS, with a backwards "C"
and an upside-down question mark. The skull had very intelligent
eyeholes, though, and a chittering uneasy smile as if it were ready to
come rolling out of a graveyard to bite you. "You know those zombies,
with no eyelids and no lips?" said Dagger. "I'm gonna get one tattoo
full of tombstones, and a hand reaching out of a grave, grabbin' for a
dagger; it'll be one of them zombie hands, and the dagger will be right
over it, and above that it's gonna say DAGGER." – Dagger was heavily
built with big arms and big legs and a wide chest, and his face was a

skinhead block, a stolid casting on a barrel neck, seamed only by a scar above his youngish dinosaur brow where he'd been knocked out in a fight by a two-by-four because one night at the club this little kid was bothering Dagger and Dagger knocked the kid's head down and the kid fell and started crying, and all these people started to shit with Dagger then so he threw his beer on them and *bahh-whamm!* some dude came up with a two-by-four and cracked his head. Dagger was dead out for awhile. "That was a good hit you put on me," he said sarcastically to the dude. "I never hit a motherfucker with a two-by-four; I only hit with my fist." – The dude didn't say anything. – "You shake my hand," Dagger said, "or I'm your enemy for life." The dude said, "Get away, man." Dagger said, "Okay, that's cool." The dude jumped bail to move to Texas the next week. And he was *smart* to do it, too, because if he'd shaken Dagger's hand Dagger's plan would've been to climb onto him and drag him out back and beat the shit out of him.

Dagger's eyelids drooped when he was at rest; his bullet-head hung forward. He had a way of holding his cigarette between two fingers, his thumb cocked behind it as if resting on a trigger-hammer, but he also liked to just let his cigarette hang out of his mouth and drop ashes on his dirty T-shirt, with another cigarette waiting on yellow alert behind his ear. He had the naked muscles of skinhead youth. He could sit straight and still, but when he walked down the street he stepped toes-out in his boots, cocking his head and looking at people, and people in the know or sometimes out of it didn't give Dagger any shit because he'd just gotten out of San Bruno. The reason he'd been stuck there in the first place was that he'd been on this TV talk show "People Are Talking," explaining how much better skinheads were than punks, and a month later he was up on Skinhead Hill where it was sunny and you could play football or frisbee with the other Skinz or whoever happened by, enjoying the good weather and keeping an eye on Haight Street at the same time, because Skinhead Hill was what the hairheads called Buena Vista Park, a long narrow block of trees and grass that sloped up Central toward Sutro Tower, and at the bottom of it was Haight Street, with golden cement stairs in a golden cement wall, and you could run up the hill having war games and yelling and lobbing bottles in the bushes and getting drunk and as if you were a dragon-kite swooping in the clean San Francisco sky, far beyond the world, your string dipped in glue and glass to saw every other kite outta the sky, just a Skin among Skinz; when all the sudden this punk rock chick came up to Dagger and started talking *shit* about him, and Dagger wasn't gonna let this

insignificant cunt bug him with her punky stink; she was all fucked up
on wine and stuff, so he told her to chill out, and she said, "Mark
Dagger's a fucking pussy!", and Dagger told her, "Hey, bitch, you'd
better stop or you'll get hurt," and she swung at him, and Dagger
blocked it, and then she kicked him in the balls, so he kicked her in the
jaw. He only kicked her once. He broke one side of her jaw and two of
her wisdom teeth. – Even though *she'd* started it, *he* got convicted of
assault. The trial took place in the courthouse on Bryant Street, Dagger
sneering at the other so-called toughs who failed inside when placed at
the bar and pissed in their pants and croaked diffidently, "I was not
aware that the car above me was double-parked," or, "In both cases I
was never outta the vehicle for more than two minutes, and I didn't
have anyplace else to park, Your Honor," but then it came *Dagger's* turn
. . . and they led him in handcuffed, and he was wearing an orange
jumpsuit, and the back of his head was shaved bone-clean so that all
the spectators sitting behind him in the courtroom saw the monster-
skull tattooed there, and the monster-skull glared at them, and Dagger
just stood there during the trial and nodded as the indictments were
read, and he turned around slowly and bowed to the other skinheads,
and the judge said, "Mark Smith, you are a menace to society; I'm
going to throw the book at you; I'm going to give you the stiffest
sentence I'm allowed to give," and at that, Dagger turned around one
more time and bowed to the skinheads again, and the skinheads rose to
their feet and filed to the door and then they clicked their heels and
saluted and said, "*SIEG HEIL!*" – Dagger was in San Bruno for a year.

Several of this pureblood statesman's letters survive. They are written
on the stationery of the exiled, namely lined yellow paper. Here is one
of them:

> well well what's up yea I got your pictures and
> Man there cool as fuck thanks alot well I only got
> 108 days and a wakeup and Ill be back on the
> Haight raisen hell but this time I have to move
> careful well Ime not much of a writer but Ill try if
> you have any more pictures please please send
> them the ones with the Hitler signs arnt that cool
> to send but fuck it send em anyway fuck these
> niggers my buisness is my buissness write? I get
> along pretty good in here and nobodys fucked with

me but Im ready if they do Ill killem Ha Ha. well I
can't think of anything to say exept send me some
pictures of so wimen out there ok. be cool write
back.

friends
MARK DAGGER

He was up on the fifth floor for three and a half months. He got
jumped by eight niggers. They tried to take his tray. Dagger said, "You
don't disrespect me." He started kicking the first guy's black ass. He
grabbed him and took him down. He whacked his head on the bottom
of a table and split his skull *wide* open. Those niggers broke two of
Dagger's ribs, but the other guy went to the hospital, not Dagger! After
that, he got moved down to 2N with Yama. Yama had just come in then
for assault, so they got to do some time together. Dagger did his best to
help Yama, because he'd be out soon himself but Yama had a stretch
ahead of him, so Dagger gave Yama the *Playboys*, the *Shes* and all the
rest, though he kept the *Hustlers* for himself. That was all that he and
Yama could do to keep sane in there, looking at photos of nice pink
girls with closed eyes and open mouths who squatted in a corner with
their boots on and pulled their underwear down and spread their pussy-
lips apart with their red-nailed hands, or got down on all fours on the
sofa, wearing nothing but black lace stockings, and waggled their asses
in your face so you could see their twats sticking out under their butt-
cheeks. – Each prisoner was allowed to have up to three visitors per
visitation day in the absence of bad conduct. You and your visitors had
to keep both hands on the interview table at all times. You'd get your
bootwoman to visit wearing a miniskirt and crotchless panties so
afterward you could go into the shower and beat off until your thumb
was calloused.

Dan-L

Dan-L went to the refrigerator and got beers for everyone.

"That Dan-L, she's really nice."

"She's the best person," Dickie said. "She's the best in the whole world. She does everybody favors. It's funny. It *is* funny. Me and her were born beside each other. Our birthdays are only a week apart."

As for Dan-L herself, who always sat so modestly at the table, whose large dark eyes stared at her beer can as if they were embarrassed to be in her oval face, Dan-L with her parted brown hair, Dan-L with her jeans jacket, you could tell she really loved Dickie and would stick with him just the way that when Yama went to jail once his black hound Rebel took one of his dirty socks in his mouth and would not let go of it all day, just crouched in the corner, whimpering. And Dickie would stick with her, too, and had stuck with her, his arm always around her as she walked down the streets beside him in her black jacket that said *SHIT HOWDY*, which she still wore coming home from work at the café where she was about to be made into a manager but she was going to tell them to chill out if they didn't raise her to five dollars an hour; and when she got home she sat down in the kitchen and waited for Dickie and took off her jacket and let her cat pounce on it, and Dan-L remembered how Dickie had helped her when she and the other Shit Howdy Girls got into this terrible fight in New York, back in the days when they were all hanging out getting drunk on the streets, spare changing together and running down alleys where the buildings leaned together marrying each other's corroded fire escapes and in every direction, around every corner, were other buildings rising brick after grimy brick, their windows smashed, their windows barred; and the Shit Howdy Girls pounded their boots in the black slush, and when sleet came down to sting them they went to the liquor store and got the cheapest beers they could and hung out drinking at somebody's house and talked about the meaning of being Shit Howdy Girls. The Shit Howdy Girls were Dan-L, Sadie, Switch and Roxy (they wanted to make Betty Bones a Shit Howdy Girl, but Dan-L said no way, she's not dedicated enough). Dan-L was more or less living at home then. Her Mom was pretty cool. All three times Dan-L broke her camera her Mom took it to the store and told them the camera had been broken when she bought it, so Dan-L got another one free. Her Mom was the greatest Mom in the world. But Dan-L got into fights with her sister, like the time Dan-L was out and Dickie and some of his friends came over and Dan-L's sister had to entertain them, and Dan-L's sister got mad and called Dan-L a slut and threw beer in her face, so Dan-L had to beat her ass. It was certainly her own fault since Dan-L had always told her she was gonna hit her but she just didn't believe it. – The reason the camera had gotten broken that first time was because Dan-L was over at Dutch's and Dutch kept this nasty white-face slobbery pit bull named Judas,[2] a monster with a white-bleached head, almost salt-bleached, with bones sticking out of fat and muscle and tough rumpled skin, and Judas stared at Dan-L out of his dirty black glazed eyes; and there were dirty black hairs all down his chest and forelegs as he lay on Dutch's dirty rugs ready to bite her; and Dutch sometimes made Judas bite a rawhide rope and then Dutch cranked the rope into the air so that Judas was hanging on by his teeth; and this understandably soured Judas, so that he bit Dan-L's leg and she dropped her camera. It took about half an hour for Dutch to get Judas to open up his jaws so Dan-L could take her leg out. The second time her camera got broken was the fight, one of the most bloodiest fights of her life (though by no means the most violent, she explained; Dan-L liked to make distinctions), when she and Sadie and Switch and Dickie were in a bar and this guy Thor was busting Dan-L's chops just saying all this *shit*, and Dan-L said, "Switch, should I pour my beer over his head?", and Switch said go ahead and Dan-L did, and Thor knocked it out of the way and it hit this black dude, and the nigger said fuck you and Switch said don't yell at my friend and the nigger punched Switch so Dan-L punched him in the face and kicked him in the nuts, so he smashed a mug over Dan-L's head – that was the first bloody thing – and then he pushed Switch and she fell over the broken mug and got cut and that was the second bloody thing, and Dan-L said to Dickie to come on and do something. Dickie had thought until then that the girls were handling it, but when Dan-L called him he just climbed over the shoulders of the crowd to help her, climbing whether they liked it or not, with so much strength showing in his pink face; and the nigger's friends tried to stop Dickie but Dickie just kept coming, walking on their shoulders and on their heads, which was something that Dan-L would never forget all her life; and some poor guy with glasses got in the way and Dickie smashed his glasses into his eyes without really meaning to (that was the third bloody thing); and finally Dickie reached the nigger and chopped him in the head! (That was the fourth bloody thing.) The nigger was escorted out, and they all took off before the police came. Around then the American Front was started in San Francisco by Chuckles, Albert, Blue and Johnny Beast. Dan-L didn't sit there and go I'm part of the American Front and shit, but she sure said right on.

2 I don't know why every dog in every skinhead story was a pit bull.

Dan-L liked New York better because she could get drunker there; there was just something about New York with its cement parks and grey skies and brickfronts and mesh fences and drunks sitting down on the sidewalk pissing that made her able to drink more; she was sick of San Francisco. She and Dickie wanted to go back east for good ("*south*east!" yelled Dickie, drinking a beer), because too many dull crummy things happened here, like the time she was with the other Skinz at the Vats and there was supposed to be a show, but there wasn't, so they went to the Safeway nearby and kept ripping off booze and got thoroughly drunk, and they went to the Walgreen's at Sixth and Mission and tried to shoplift, and plainclothes people were watching so Dan-L didn't take anything but the others did. When they went out, the plainclothes people came running after them down the street and got the others, and Dan-L wasn't about to leave them so she ran back to the Walgreen's and went in and there was this guy standing at the door with his arms folded, and he said you can't go in there and Dan-L pushed by him just the same and saw the Skinz were tied up in the back, and they arrested her with the others but didn't tie her up because when they checked her I.D. they saw that she was a college girl, so the cops just escorted her by the elbow while the others had to wear cuffs; and they told Dan-L to appear in court to get the charges dropped, but she couldn't go to court right then because she had to go back to New York for awhile, so they probably had a bench warrant on her.

Mothers of Skinheads

Dan-L loved her Mom. Most of the other Skinz did, too (Bootwoman Marisa being an exception).

"I was adopted when I was three," Dagger said. "For a long time I blamed my real parents for breaking up and giving me away, but just recently I found out my Dad was a fag. Can you believe it? It makes me want to puke. So now I love my Mom even more for breaking up with him. Someday I swear I'm gonna go back down there with a .44 and find that fag bastard and blow his head off, *blam!*"

"You gotta think what's good for you," Dickie said.

"I almost forgot my Mom," Dagger said. "I went to a lot of

psychiatrists, and they *made* me remember; maybe I remembered those things in *dreams*, man, but I didn't know what they meant."

"Yeah," said Dickie, "it's that kind that gets you."

"Hey, this is a bad scene," said Dagger, jerking open the refrigerator door to look for more beer. "I ain't seen my Mom in eighteen years."

When Dickie and his Mom had a fight she said, "I shoulda aborted you! You shoulda been a goddamned abortion! You're too much like your goddamned father."

Anthony was still polishing his boots.

The New Boy

When he finished polishing, he started over. "I want these boots to be like *mirrors!*" he cried. "I'm gonna polish 'em up real good. People are gonna *see* their reflection right before I kick them in the face. It's gonna be the last thing they ever see!"

Nobody paid any attention.

Anthony was eighteen. He'd met up with the Skinz on Haight Street. *Shit*, he *still* hasn't met cooler people! – Hardly had it begun to force itself upon him that he was a skinhead when he looked the part. His skull, newly naked, looked upon the world with a haughty pride in belonging, in defending, in showing itself in its trueness of whiteness, like a splendid moon which had at last broken free of a thicket of kinky nigger-hair nettles and now rose high into the night. Then he got his tattoos. Once that was accomplished, everything began to happen for Anthony just as he had dreamed it would, like the time that he and skinhead Albert from Germany were staying at this girl's house, and Anthony had her down on hands and knees sucking his cock, and Albert stuck a cold cucumber from the fridge up her ass. How she did scream! Later Anthony stuck the cuke in the microwave and warmed it up and rolled her on her belly so she couldn't see and fucked her with the cucumber, and when she saw it she freaked and grabbed it and broke it so a piece stuck in her cunt. Another time he and Albert fucked a girl with a carrot rubbed in vaseline, and she was *loving* it, and then they ran around shoving the carrot in people's faces going, "SMELL THIS!" – Of course life was not always so romantic as that, since being a skinhead Anthony had to always guard himself against the assaults of the world, an example being the time that he was in the drunk tank and this fag came after him when he was pissing and Anthony grabbed his shoulder and slammed his head on the steel partition and cut a triangular gash from his cheek all the way up to his eye. It made him feel good to think about it as he sat in Dickie's kitchen now, repolishing his boots. The whitish-yellow walls gleamed in the night like a bone cavern.

Dagger and Spike

Dagger's pregnant bootwoman, Spike, came in from the living room looking tired. She felt cranky because the doctor had told her not to smoke or drink much, which was hard for her because she needed to be Dagger's bootwoman in full, the way she'd been before when she'd done half of every hit of every drug that Dagger took. - She and Dagger now got into a fight over who should carry the photo album back to the bookshelf. "You tell me to put it back, I'm just gonna throw it on the floor!" Spike yelled.

"Hey," said Dagger. "Why did you stick in those pictures of me with the black eye? I don't like those pictures."

"You can just fucking put it away yourself!" Spike screamed.

"Awright," chuckled Dickie. "You tell 'im."

"Stay the *fuck* out of my business!" yelled Dagger.

Dickie went for him with the scissors. They scuffled in their black Nazi-eagle T-shirts, punching the air and yelling, "I'm losing my faith in mankind!"

"No comments from the peanut gallery!" Dagger said. "You give me some comments, someone's likely to get stabbed. And not by me! Spike takes that stuff real serious."

"I'm not gonna stab her; I'm gonna stab *you*," said Dickie.

"Oh, forget it," said Dagger. "I've known Spike one year and a half, two years and a half before you ever *thought* of meeting her."

"Come on, Dagger, I remember your anniversary."

"You do? Remember Tequila Ed?"

"Sure I remember Tequila Ed."

"Oh," said Dagger, suddenly aged and beaten. "All the good old boys have left San Francisco. Only ones left are me, Dickie, and a couple others. Yama's in jail, Blue and Chuckles split; I tell you, you can jerk off all you like."

The Old Days

They used to go into bars and pick fights, punch people in the face when they didn't like the way they looked (being Nazis, they were conscious that appearance is everything). At least that was what some people said about them. But the Skinz said they didn't start anything. It was the others who started things, who talked rude to them and then didn't get out of the way. One time Lorelei and Blue were walking down Market Street and this nigger poked Lorelei in the ass with a stick and followed the two of them on the bus. Blue was hooded, like a viper. When he and Lorelei got off the bus, the nigger got off behind them, so Blue hit the nigger in the face a few times and said, "Now you'll remember the skinheads." – They sat on Skinhead Hill, crooning to each other and yelling; they muscled in on women walking down Haight Street with their boyfriends, and if the boyfriends didn't walk away pretty fast they got it in the face. It is not my aim, however, to describe these old times of violent freedom, for this record was made in the decline of their movement, when most of the bars had bounced them out for good; and they sat around in their middle twenties muttering about how it used to be.

At that time, it seemed to me, death was their watchword, death being not a threat, not a reward, but simply a placement. They had no thought for any future day in which they might be gypsies and sing on stairs, their faces soot-darkened for security.

Haight Street

Dickie lived, as indicated, in the Tenderloin, where poor men walk at night, where the windows of parking garages glow yellow and black where stones have smashed them, where whores greet you licking big ice cream cones at midnight as you come out of the 188 Club after a shot and a round of liars' dice, and other whores ease up to your car if you honk and roll down the window, and it doesn't matter that somebody shot out the streetlights because those orange whore-eyes *shine* and make you HARD; but most of the other Skinz (and by "Skinz" I am referring in particular to the gang known as the S.F. Nazi Skinz) enjoyed the delights of violence and idleness on Haight Street, which wakes up at 8:30 in the morning when the sad clerks who think themselves artists go off to work; and the patrol cars coast slowly through Golden Gate Park like Soviet tanks mopping up after the Hungarian uprising (the bums who sleep in the Park have now been arrested or gotten away); and then Haight Street dreams again beneath the blue morning, clouds securing Cole Street and Shrader Street from the wind; and the dreams of Haight Street are like dreams of driving through Nebraska or Arizona, which roll by all day on a cross-country drive without anything accomplished; and the sidewalk is held by sleepy panhandlers and bewildered tramps with big backpacks '("So this is Haight Street; now what do I do?"), and just west of the Holy Smoke Barbeque hangs the American flag from the terrace of the skinhead flat, as wrinkled as a fugitive's clothes; and then again between 10:30 and 11:00 the street wakes up again, comes into its real life, the thrift stores and secondhand bookstores and liquor stores and clothing stores and ice cream stores opening; and the cafés leach full of people reading newspapers and sipping Espresso and smoking, and people walk along the sidewalks, and Brandi the whore goes yawning to her corner by the liquor store to beg change ("You know what we call nigger bitches?" says Yama. "We call 'em mud dogs!"), and the first skinhead comes out grey-skulled in a grey jumpsuit, and other Skinz groan on the moldy carpet of the skinhead flat, that is to say Hunter and Dee and Nova's flat, and they scratch carpet-fuzz off their shirts and roll dead beer cans away from their eyeballs, wondering whether to take valium and sleep till dark or whether to watch TV or whether they might as well saunter out into the sunlight, as another two or three now do, the first hornets from the nest, already looking hard, looking angry, on the jump for some ass to beat. Later they'll be walking Yama's dog Rebel. For so long now we've seen them loitering in the sun, eyeing the last hippie girls surviving in storefront niches, watching other girls go clopping resolutely by in high heels while the skinheads roar, "She's just another skinhead slut! Roll 'er on 'er ass and stick it up 'er butt!", and the girls clop on a little faster, pretending that they didn't hear, their dwindling asses moving their new wave trousers out of sight.

Whether it is a happy life or a sad one the Skinz live is of course unknowable to anyone watching them stride by, turning their bulging skulls greedily upon their bulging necks, trying to be pitiless, exclusive; not listening much to one another; but we can consider the question. The lone ones lean up against the restaurant windows, hunching their heads in like turtles at the same time they swivel their gaze in what might be anxiety or might be automatic street wisdom. They spend too much time waiting, but on the whole they are arguably happy, having their fights to look forward to. What more, after all, could anyone yearn for in his guts than the chance to hurt somebody else, jawkicking a soul to screaming subhumanness in order to reiterate that *I live?* – "Politics," I once heard a conservative say, "is the exercise of power. Power is the ability to inflict pain." By this criterion the skinheads are among our most spontaneous politicians. Let us assume, then, that being spontaneous they are light of heart.

Afternoon at the Command Post

Up in the skinhead house, behind red curtains, a man kept looking out the street window, as if he were on sentry duty. He drank beer and wore camouflage trousers.

"Hey, get off the sidewalk!" he yelled. "You heard me! Get off or I'll give you some beer to drink!" He poured a Bud out the window.

The other Skinz crowded to look. – "Lookit that nigger," said Dee. "He's so scungy."

"They all look that way," said Nazi Joe solemnly, and at that they all laughed.

Powell Street, Emeryville

If you are white then I suppose it was your great-great-great-great-grandfather who started it with his runs for the Triangle Trade, assaulting the walled towns of Negroes by land and by sea, utilizing fire

with all diligence for this end; and thereby obtained prisoners, for which
he got good prices; and so on to the plantations, the lynchings and all
the rest of it, until a jumbo crop of hatred had been painstakingly sown;
but by now the wrong lies on both sides, as the tale of how Bootwoman
Marisa lost her front tooth will show; so there are times when we hate
them as much as they hate us; and it is hard to know or care where in
this circle the S.F. Nazi Skinz came in; the Skinz did not care, and out
by the Emeryville Marina no one in the workforce cared about anything
but beauty, of which there was a productive yield given the way that the
purple translucent plastic paper trays glittered in the sun. You could
look through them sideways and see through their ribs, through the
grilles at the back and out the window across the smog to the windows
of other buildings where the bank clerks and software jerks learned the
lessons of life from their Tandem mainframes: TAL ERROR 70: ONLY
ITEMS SUBORDINATE TO A STRUCTURE MAY BE QUALIFIED. (I wonder if our
country was better when Indians lived on it by themselves, fishing,
hunting and weaving blue blankets, or whether it was just as dreary,
wastes of bog and forests then corresponding to wastes of buildings
now.) Every firm was in convenient reach of the Denny's ("Always
Open"), and from the Denny's it was an easy walk to the tunnel under
the freeway overpass, a dark cold tunnel through which big trucks went
by so loud that your bones hurt. The exhaust smelled like old waffles.
This tunnel was the bus stop for the 57M or 57C, and there were
sometimes black boys coming up to surround you if you were white and
grinning at you and telling you to hand over your money, "or else I'll do
you a favor you might not appreciate!" because they would be quite
happy to hurt you for being white, just as the skinheads would be happy
to hurt them for being black.[3]

---

3 "We're a very racial people," Dee explained to me once. "We're not prejudiced;
we're racial. There's a difference. We have *pride* in being white. I have *pride* in having a
family. I've adopted a lot of kids, like Nova, but I wouldn't bring a black kid into the
family because it wouldn't fit in. It would get verbally abused."

Afternoon at the Command Post
(Continued)

"I got stuck in jail again last Tuesday," said Ice to Dickie in the back room.

"Oh yeah? What for?"

"Assaulting an officer and drinking in public. Or maybe it was the other way around."

"Fuck," said Dickie. "They caught up with me, too. Two hundred and fifty dollars bail that I won't see for who knows how many months, plus twenty-five dollars court cost. Bitch said I had a gun and was gonna kill her boyfriend. All I said to him was, 'Buzz off or I'll kill ya.'"

"And did you have a gun?" said Ice.

"Hell, no. They took my leather jacket, too. Said it was a dangerous weapon." He chuckled. "And it *was*. See, I got this license plate and cut it in half, then I wrapped it around the sleeve of my jacket so there was this razor edge. Ripped up a couple tin cans and did the same thing. That jacket weighed twenty or thirty pounds. All I had to do was sweep out my arm and I could just gut any old fish, *fuff!*"

So the Skinz hacked their way through the buttery blue idleness of the afternoon, progressing toward the evening, when wicked things come alive.

A little after three, Dee's husband Hunter came back from work with other skinhead men. – "You're not a man unless you bust your ass," Dagger liked to say. "I don't call it working, sitting in an office eight hours a day with soft hands." The skinheads were doomed to carry lumber and cement around in open pits, never trusted enough for the class jobs of hanging sheet rock in warm middle-income bedrooms, never getting to use the bathtub tap to fill their buckets, never swishing that bathtub-issue water into the mudding tray, adding the Fix-All just right to make grey-white dough, spreading it good in the mudding tray, the first layer going smooth over the bare ceiling boards so that they still textured the mud like ribs in flesh. No, for the skinheads work was a stretch of curses in grey fogged-in excavations, office workers leaning over the street railings to spit and comment interestedly while the Skinz sank in mud up to the knees of their jeans, hauling dusty white sacks of cement on their shoulders, having nothing but their strength to glory in, never getting to peek through the back windows on the job, or prancing up the fire escape, snapping the downstairs women's lacy lingerie on the line, or opening up spankin' new sacks of Durabond. They worked in the building pits when they got work, those skinheads, and rain dribbled inside their leather jackets; then they came home, their faces, arms and jeans whitened by cement dust. They sat scowling and talking about how much they hated the job. Their supervisors were always assholes. One super lived on the site so they could never get away from him. – "It was all I could do not to put a shovel through his melon," Hunter said. – A man scratched his skull for awhile, swishing his beer. "My dream," he said, "is to build a cabinet in my room and get me a badass gun collection, one for every skinhead. And one day, we'll all just go to the window and open up." – Dickie laughed, "Naw, leave the door *wide* open, and wait till somebody comes in, and *then* open up and *waste* him."

At the window, the skinhead in the camo trousers never took his eyes off the street.

A Sunset

Outside, the afternoon dwindled in the strange way that it does in Haight Street, the sun baking the almost illegible graffiti on the cracked wall of the deserted technical high school: AMERICAN FRONT – FOR A STRONG AMERICA; then, as the afternoon died, the far sidewalks and buildings turned gold in the slanted sunlight, the pavement underfoot already blue-grey and shadowed. The flat roofs of the Victorian houses brightened to beauty beneath the sky, which pretended to be as luminous as it had been at noon, but wasn't anymore. As clouds came in from the Bay, the first pair of evening police came walking down Stanyan to the head of the Haight, their uniforms already almost twilight-black. Hornets quickened in the night-hive. Skinheads sat in front of their house, scuffing their toes on the sidewalk, smoking, eating bagels, looking grimly from side to side. The first bookstores and antique boutiques were being locked, the steel shutters drawn. New Skinz came walking by very fast, nodding to nobody, wearing ski caps, looking daggers at the new generation of black-dressed Death Ladies whose faces were white and cruel as porcelain; perhaps it was they, whoever they were, who wrote in the doorways FUCK SF SKINZ THERE A BUNCH OF FAGS, or maybe they were responsible for the poem on the front wall of the anarchist bookstore:

I've got a bullet in my head,

Where there once was a brain, now there's lead,

but that's OK, fine with me,

Since that's all it takes to be a NAZI

and more and more Skinz now came swarming into the street, staring hard-eyed at all the aliens on the streets whose hair grew thick and bushy on their heads like coonskin caps. A few Skinz went down with Dickie to his place in the Tenderloin, the T.L. Yama called it, down the paved valleys of streets where red car-lights between twin lines of yellow lights lured them deeper into project housing with curtains drawn and past silhouettes sitting in the dark on park benches; then the Chinese restaurants came into view, the yellow-lit tunnels of hotel garages, the Peacock Club, the massage parlors, the old men in decaying footgear taking little wooden-legged steps across the street; and in Dickie and Dan-L's place Dan-L sat waiting in the kitchen with its 1984 posters, wandering into her bedroom, looking at her clothes neatly filed in boxes, her black pirate flag, the forty-eight-star American flag from the Marin county fleamarket, the hooded skull done in pastels by Spike on speed, the drawing of the skinhead saying I HATE THE WORLD (also done by Spike, I think); and Dan-L yawned and went back to her dirty kitchen table with a bottle of Windex on it, sitting around alone, playing with her cat Schwarzenegger, munching on Burger King takeout, her breath fogging up the cold black kitchen window, and the refrigerator humming in pulses, like a heart. Her lower eyelids were made up in black, as if she'd rubbed them with charcoal. She was dead tired; she worked counters and her boss wouldn't leave her be; tonight he'd called her up yelling because she'd paid the VCR repairman without his permission, and Dan-L said sorry to him because she couldn't afford to lose the job. She went back to the window, seeing the homosexuals peeking at her from the upstairs window. She hated and feared them because she'd heard a lot of stories; she saw their heads outlined through the yellowness, and when they caught her looking at them they ducked back behind their window plant. She wished that

Dickie and Dagger were here, that it was summer and afternoon and
Dickie would tell again all about how he met Dagger with Mick the
Prick that day on Haight Street when they were tweaking, and Dagger
would get a grin and yell *"Suck my dick, Massah!"* and Dan-L would
laugh in her soft hoarse way and they'd go up and laze around on the
roof the way they used to do, having rock fights; once Dan-L clocked
Dagger on the forehead with a big rock and he freaked out, started
throwing rocks at everybody so hard they had to run; but now Dagger
and Spike had gone up north for legal-fiscal reasons and nothing was
happening. The phone rang; it was Yama; he needed someone to meet
him when he got out of jail tomorrow, and Dan-L said okay and
promised herself to give him a lecture about using speed; and she ate
up the last of her cold Burger King, yawning there in the Tenderloin a
few blocks east of the War Memorial Opera House where rich people
had gone to observe Verdi's Falstaff sing out, "Aiee! Aiee! Aiee! Aiee!"
whenever Mistress Page and Mistress Quickly and the other torturers
spanked him with ferns and sang, "Piccatta! Piccatta! Piccatta! Piccatta!", while meanwhile the rich people's cars were being towed by
mistake, so that the rich people folded their gold opera glasses shut
with a snap and stormed off to the police station on Ellis to demand
their rights and called the Channel Eleven News on the phone and
scolded the meek night officers some more and made the officers give
them rides to the tow company, and the officers did their best to jolly
the rich people, saying joshing things like, "Well, at least you get the
nice new patrol car, ladies and gentlemen; you see, the other one is
used for *criminals* and the back is full of *fleas!*" (this being the patrol car
that Dagger and the other Skinz were used to); but the rich people were
not mollified and informed each other that this was an OUTRAGE;
and they condemned the officers for being symbols of a hateful
bureaucracy, not that it was their fault of course; and that Mayor
Feinstein was going to hear of this; and they formed exalted on-the-
spot charities and mutual defense leagues to pay the towing costs, and
they exchanged business cards to keep in touch for the protest hearing,
standing on a parking lot in Potrero in their black suits and black gowns,
with triple strings of pearls dangling down to the matrons' fluid-filled
artificial bosoms; and at the end of it the oldest, crossest, sternest lady
(who had called Channel Eleven three times already, saying "We have
thirty-five VERY INDIGNANT citizens here and we need your help!")
tapped on the driver's window of each departing automobile; and when

the driver powered the window down, *vreeEEE*, recognizing a fellow member of his or her class, the old lady said, "How did you pay? VISA? Mastercard? Good. Stop payment in the morning." – Meanwhile Dickie finally came in with his friends.

After Dinner

"What're we gonna eat, Dan-L?" he said.

"I already ate," she said. "Didn't think you were coming home, so I said fuck it."

"Hey, Bootwoman," teased the Skinz, "when are you gonna shave your head?"

"I've got like this feeling inside," she told them. "I'm a bootwoman, and I don't need to shave any part of my head to show it."

"You know," says grey-haired metaphysical Joe, who just blew in from Massachusetts, not a skinhead or nothing, just a would-be sheet-rocker and friend of a friend dreaming about a bottle of Thunderbird, which they call a short dog (and to fill you in I had better tell you that he was almost deaf, like the Butcher Boys' dog, but genuinely was metaphysical, had once been Brother Joe at a monastery back east but he was a *deaf* Brother Joe as you understand by now and worked and prayed and meditated happily inside his cloud of sacred deafness until a new Abbot came to the monastery, at which point Brother Joe's tribulations began, for since he was under a vow of silence he could not explain to the new Abbot that he was deaf, and the Abbot didn't know much about Brother Joe because Brother Joe kept to himself and worked chopping wood and repairing stone walls in the forest, and when the Abbot greeted him Brother Joe never heard and therefore never answered; so the Abbot, concluding that Brother Joe was anti-social, decreed that he had to become a hermit, and Brother Joe wouldn't do that, so he was expelled), "You know," said metaphysical Joe, not having caught too much of the table-talk or really hearing what the Skinz were all about, because he had his own cross to bear, but gathering that Dan-L was saying something about shaving or not shaving her head, "You know," goes old Joe, "I tried to get rid of my dandruff once by shaving my head."

"Did it work?"

"No."

Joe's attempt at a contribution having sunk into the conversation like a stone into deep water, the skinheads went about their own business.

"You didn't ask me how my foot is," said Dan-L. "I got another acid treatment."

The stale cigarette buts lay very still in the ashtray. Dickie loaded a bowl of hash. "This high makes me feel so nice, kicked back," he said. "When I'm on pot I get paranoid, walking down the street thinking people are looking at me funny."

Dan-L played with the tablecloth, lifting up corners of it. Underneath, the entire table top was covered with black-markered slogans like WHITE POWER and KILL.

"Getting to be hunting season," Dickie said. "Boy, it's been three years. Last time I was out with your father, Dan-L. Remember when we went down to his land in Alabama and he threw tin cans off a cliff and we shot them with his .357 magnum? That was cool."

"The land wasn't much, though," said Dan-L. "And the people were stupid."

"You calling people from the South hicks?" Warren the mover said, leaning forward very slowly.

"No," said Dan-L. "I was talking about my own people."

"Shake it, girl," Warren said. "Just shake it."

Nobody said anything.

"Down south the mountains are so beautiful, man," Warren said. "Out in Chattanooga you can see nine states, ten states with the nekkid eye."

"Knoxville's the place," said Dickie. "Lots of nice places, though. I remember one time when we were in Orchard Hill, one of the last great white neighborhoods. Then some niggers topped our car. So Chuckles's grandfather got a shotgun and said, 'Hey, King Coons! Get the fuck out of Our Neighborhood!' He liked to sit on the porch and rock with his shotgun."

"That's Chuckles's grandfather, all right," Warren said. "My grandfather died couldn't read nor write. But you couldn't forge his X, boy; he knew his X."

Just outside, in the dead glow of Ellis Street, Anthony saw a punk panhandling. The punk's Mohawk made Anthony feel sick. Nothing was worse than a punk, except for maybe a punk and a nigger. He told the punk to head out, beat it for Powell Street where the punks congregated (the way that chewing gum, for instance, congregates in stale hardened lumps under desks and tables), or beat it anywhere else but just get the fuck out of Anthony's sight. The punk whipped out a zapper gun and fired, *phhhh-bzzzzt!* but it didn't work like it was supposed to, just burned Anthony's chest, so that Anthony, rather than falling down screaming and crying onto the hard cold sidewalk as the punk had hoped, shook off the pain as a dog shakes off water, and beat the punk's ass *righteously!* The cops came running. But when they saw it was just a punk, and the punk had started it anyway, they grinned to Anthony's bootwoman, 'Your boyfriend got lucky this time. He got a freebie.' (According to the F.B.I., one violent crime occurs every thirty-one seconds.) And Anthony ran down the sidewalk laughing, his boots shining, the night worth living through again, and people jumped out of his way.

While other losers, the lame, the blind spinning down the street in firestorms of hallucinations, made their way through life over the stepping stones of others' pity, the skinheads derived power from their isolation and magnified themselves to themselves until the things they could do seemed to them all there was to do. This was but the rhetoric of unavoidable decay, their taut bodies knowing their own decrease, knowing the wane of the city, and desperately the Skinz wrote SF SKINZ in the Sunset, in the Haight, at Church and Duboce, in North Beach; and that was nice but it didn't do any good. Their politics excluded, they were hardly different from the trapped commuters on the Muni, who, dressed in their business best, stared down at their own tapping feet, or read, or rested their chins in their hands, waiting, waiting, waiting.

Left-Wing Utopianism: An Infantile Disorder

Back on Frederick Street, Chuckles stamped roaring down the sidewalk, looking for a fight. He saw a black man leaning against a wall. Chuckles slam-butted the nearest NO PARKING sign, yelling, "I'm gonna toughen up my head; I'm gonna use my head for a *weapon!*"[4] – Whereas

4 Chuckles's favorite song was "If I Could Talk To The Animals."

some toughs skipped side by side and leaned weightlessly against lit storefronts, watching one of their number do little ironical ballets for them, the Skinz just strode down the sidewalk, swiveling their domes to give both sides of the street equal views of their contemptuous eyes, dying to leave us soon for their own Promised Land. Three Skinz (say the anarchists) went to the anarchist bookstore and kicked in the front window. They hated that place because it was left-wing. Whenever they had a free minute, which was often, they went over there and painted swastikas on the door. The anarchists tried to classify them in the reflexive pseudo-biological way of all ideologues, writing: "*The males have shaved heads, high boots, rolled up or tucked in jeans, often with bleach marks, suspenders, and T-shirts or bare chest, often with a black leather jacket ...*" – the reiterated "often with" further betraying the anarchists' melancholy lust for typology, as if things would be O.K. if they could just definitely establish the Skinz as a product of late capitalism, the way Franz Neumann had done for the Adolf regime in his treatise *Behemoth* (1941); then the Skinz would stop tormenting them, beating them up, sending them letters like the one they got that fall, with the eagle on it, scowling, the eagle's claws out ready to seize and slice, its wings stubby and wide, like those of an Air Force bomber, and on its chest the "A"-inscribed circle of the American Front; and the letter said (and the eagle screamed):

ATTENTION!

PUNKS, COMMUNISTS, ANARCHISTS, HIPPIES, AND HOMOSEXUALS:

YOU ARE ENEMIES OF AMERICA AND THE AMERICAN WAY OF LIFE. WE THE SKINHEADS WILL NOT TOLERATE YOUR SPREADING OF UNWANTED DISEASES BOTH MENTAL AND PHYSICAL.

WE ARE JAILED BECAUSE WE USE EVERY METHOD AT OUR DISPOSAL TO PROTECT THE DECENT PEOPLE OF THIS COUNTRY FROM YOUR UNAMERICAN, SUBVERSIVE, LEFT WING MIND POISON.

WE ARE THE GUARDIANS OF FREEDOM AND LIBERTY FOR ALL GOOD AMERICANS. SO BEWARE ENEMYS OF THE FLAG.

YOUR DAYS ARE
NUMBERED.

© AMERICAN FRONT 1985

Upon receipt of this missive the anarchists were seriously kropot-kined, like medieval German churchgoers finding Luther's theses on the door, but the Skinz themselves just drank up their beers and forgot about it. Dan-L said that Z— Z— did it and what was the big deal. "He was going around on the street laughing about it and boasting about it for days," she said. "But I don't know that much about it. I heard about it and I didn't give a shit." As for Dickie, he just looked solemn. *"And the South will rise again,"* he proclaimed, *"Stars, Bars and Skinz!"*

Keeping It On

"You know," said Dagger, finishing off his third beer, "that little kid you brought today, he's setting up that guy, Brock, he's been stealing. We're gonna lure him up at the show and kick his ass."

"What about the owner?" Dickie said.

"The owner don't care, man. He's just a fucking nigger. He just cares about money."

"You gonna beat up the kid?"

"Hell, no," said Dagger, "he's a *skinhead* kid. Someday he'll grow up and make a fine skinhead, a leader, maybe. The person to do that is someone who's raised up on it and knows our law by heart. We started it. It's up to our kids to keep it on."

"I'm gonna play that song again," said Dickie.

"Flip the damned tape!" Dagger commanded.

Their big hands started pounding at the cassette player, at each other, grip-wrestling in midair.

"Don't fuck with me, man!"

Dickie leaped up and grabbed at Dagger's neck. Dagger snarled and bit. He sank his teeth into Dickie's cheek. – "But you can also take a motherfucker by the ears," Dickie said thoughtfully, "and you can just *rip* their *ears* off." – "Yeah," said Dagger, "but I bite hunks of skin off, and facial skin, *that* ain't never gonna heal. Hey, you remember, Dickie, when I used to hate your guts and want to kick your ass?"

"You never could!"

"I could rip that lardass nose right off you."

"Now we get along, so what's the *diff?*"

What Brandi Thought

The skinheads hated Brandi because she was black. "She's a walking stinkbag," said Bootwoman Marisa, "she's a sleazebag. I wish that bitch was rotting under the ground instead of on top of it." Brandi was a slender smallish dark-eyed whore who looked you in the eye when she found you on the street and promised you everything and made you believe in the freedom of her nogood ways and her hair felt like cotton candy and she hugged you and kissed you with the housefronts watching behind so that you thought you were the only one she loved, and she always tried to get money from you because she always needed it. She needed it so much that if you opened your wallet to give her something she'd stand on tiptoe to watch, and say, "There's another dime in there. Let me see if there's a penny in there." – If you gave her money once, she never forgot you. She'd pick you out on the sidewalk and be suddenly in front of you and she'd put her hand on her hip and smile at you with her pretty fuzzy hair done up, and she'd try to get more money out of you, but if she couldn't then you were still her friend. When she stood in her doorway looking at you she was all business, hooking her thumb in her jeans and leaning, like an urchin who might run away or hit you. She spare-changed until late at night, sometimes holding her little son by the hand, and the boy, who barely came up to her waist, held his palm out and stared up at you like some sad curious little frog; then when it got dark Brandi took him home and came back more lively and tried to sell nonexistent drugs and once the night was firmly established she started selling herself. There was a dress that she wore with three buttons down the front, and you could tell how late it was or how high she was by how low the buttons were undone. She might look straight at you, so earnest and loving, or she might grin at you with her teeth showing and her eyes wary and old. At two or three in the morning she'd be asking men coming out of bars if they wanted to make a little bit of *love;* or if she were desperate she'd begin flagging down the cars.

"What do you think of those skinheads, Brandi?" I said.

"I don' like 'em," she said.

When I left she stood up tall and kissed me. "I see you," she said.

I once had a dream that Brandi was running because someone was after her, and she held two little black children by the hand as she ran, and she was afraid, and she ran down narrow cement stairs that took her deeper and deeper inside a concrete wall, and the children kept up as best as they could but sometimes Brandi had to slow up for them and they held tight to her hands and rested their heads against her waist and while they rested she looked behind her, and then she pulled the children farther down the damp stairs; and finally she came to a door, and water was dripping from the keyhole, and the door was bulging outwards; and I realized that Brandi must be directly under some large reservoir, and I tried to tell her not to open the door, but she couldn't hear me, and she turned the doorknob, and tons of green water poured in and crushed her and the two children.

Marisa's Front Tooth

Bootwoman Marisa, hater of Brandi, her sixteenth birthday more recently behind her than her conviction for assault with a deadly weapon, got a ride to North Beach to have her fourth tattoo done, waiting coolly in Bronson's living room where meanwhile a pleasant time was had by others watching videos of Mark Pauline piercing dead dogs' heads with remote-controlled drills, burning dead cats with a flamethrower, firing cardboard missiles full of gunpowder, throwing switches to make dead rabbits walk backwards. – "This is *weird!*" Marisa said, not meaning it, sitting on the couch with her felt hat beaked over her forehead, her thick black lines of eyebrows poised above a dinosaur romance. She had a very pretty oval head – I say head, not face, because hairlessness makes the boundary between head and face vanish so that there is only head, the cheeks and temples curving with inevitable naturalness around to the ears and back to the grey stubble (something other than hair) growing out from the bone. It was a finely colored head that Marisa had, clean and marbled like the freckled stone stairs fronting San Francisco houses. The lighting in Bronson's living room caused a delicate shadow to deepen the tone of the right side, bisecting her perfect nose, which must have been crafted of special pink mollusk ceramic, like her lips. She leaned back in Bronson's couch, knees up, blinking her dark eyes and rubbing her dirty black sneakers on the cushions. There was a bunch of safety pins stuck in her earlobes. Her black leather jacket, stuck full of badass buttons and a Hitler iron cross, glittered with galaxies of zippers. – "Man, I hate your dog," she said. "If she bugs me again I'm gonna kick her jaw off." – Her boyfriend was a Nazi skin in Chicago called James who blew up cars by dropping pingpong balls full of Drano into the gas tank. – Six D-cell batteries in the same place will accomplish the same object, Marisa explained, although in that case the car-bomber had to be patient for the two weeks that it took for the casings to dissolve. – She bought acid in sheets and mailed them to James, who sold them at a considerable profit in Chicago, where skinheads were cool, where skinheads were organized, said Marisa, where it was all for one and one for all. He did not share these profits with her.

The tatt was going to be a dragon, on the right upper thigh. Marisa really needed it, just as Yama needed to get more tatts on his arms (he was gonna get a Joker with an evil-ass face, like a red and black Checkered Demon). Marisa undid her suspenders and slipped her trousers off, grinning. Although she still had her shirt on, her naked thighs and her naked head made her as naked as a hairhead wearing no clothes at all; and this equivalence made her more ordinary, especially since most of her other tatts, such as the red, white and blue boot on her upper arm, were hidden by her shirt; and so, most of her Aryan props gone, she was just another naked girl. No one takes special account of Nazis when they are naked. Marisa sensed this and became tentatively, submissively young. – "My legs are so fat," she said. – Beginning to outline the dragon on her thigh (he was not ready for his needles yet), Bronson bent over her in his studio of rainbow skulls, while she half-sat, half-lay on the tattooing couch, which was actually an old trunk with a sleeping bag folded on top. Marisa stared into the yellow oval of brightness around the filament of the light bulb, Bronson's music going "*Ooooooh, bunga-bunga bunga-bunga,*" and Bronson pen-sketched, holding in his other hand a fat phallus of deodorant which he applied now and then to keep the ink from rubbing off. Marisa, leaning back on her elbows, looked down at him and lay back, her head overhanging the couch, gazing now at a solar corona on canvas on the ceiling; and she played with the loose strap of her underpants. She had plump pink thighs. – "I can't stand pain," she said, but she wore a Nazi shirt. – "Oh, God," she said, "it's gonna be such a beautiful dragon; I've been waiting for this for such a long time now that I know I really need it on my body." Her pubic curls were the reddish-brown of dead roses. – This sixteen-year-old looked hardly like a bootwoman at all now as she lay there, all her prized difference receding to her mouth. This mouth, a hallmark of her narcissism, pouted downward, toward herself, so that one couldn't readily tell whether she was sullen or just self-absorbed. – Bronson, who had green barbed arrows tattooed into the back of his neck, like lizard vertebrae, now began seriously to work. At the rattle of the tattoo gun, Marisa's eyelashes suddenly fluttered, the shadows beneath them somehow darker now, bluer than they had been. I will pass over her cries and the sweat that burst out on that smooth, round skull, like that of a furry muskrat; while Bronson drilled slowly under her skin, wiping up her blood with a wad of tissue, and the sticky flesh of her thighs clung to the swab as it moved. From behind, Bronson's ear was red and distinct against her white flesh. Her thigh was as pale and soft as a flounder. The needle went in. Sometimes Bronson set the gun down to yawn and scratch at the callus on the middle joint of his second finger, known to those in his trade as the Eye of the Octopus. Marisa recovered herself better with each pause, as the needle lengthened the irrevocable lines already pierced into her thigh; biting her lip bravely at these required mutilations, she smiled wider and wider, smiled wet-lipped until the dragon was outlined on her thigh in ink and blood. Now she was even more essentially and unarguably a bootwoman. – "Are you done?" she said, "are you done? I want to see! If anybody comes up, maim, kill, destroy!", as she buckled her dirty jeans. She put her leather skinhead jacket back on, regaining more and more of herself with each button. When she'd first bought it, she'd broken it in by getting fucked on it. In the righthand pocket was her street knife. "Oh, kill, maim and destroy!" she screamed, making fists in the air. "I want to sucker-punch somebody!"

She worked as a cook at Bouncer's down in China Basin, making breakfasts from six to ten, lunches from six to three, Bouncer's being a tall yellow building from before the earthquake of 1906, in sight of the water, warehouses on every hand; and inside the half-boarded-up door was Bouncer's Bar where it was always dark and left of that the Bouncer's Café area, illuminated by incandescent bulbs on the high yellow ceiling (one burned out), and there were square plastic-wood tables with yellow chairs, and behind those was the faded yellow countertop, and Marisa worked between that and the faded yellow backboard planks that went up to the ceiling. There was a little dark hatchway where the countertop joined the wall, so that Marisa could slide plates of food directly into the bar, which also opened at six. Whenever I came to visit her she was so happy to see me, hugging me, rubbing her stubbly head against me like a puppy. Trustingly she pulled down her pants to show off Bronson's new work on her tattoo whenever I asked. She was my friend. Once I brought one of my pistols holstered under my coat, and when I brought her hand to it she stared at me and she squeezed it through my coat to be sure of it and her face lit up and she said, "Ooh, *dude!*", and old Darleen, who worked beside her frying up bacon and egg sandwiches and came from a ranch and wanted to have her own roadhouse in Oregon, teased Marisa and said, "That's right, dude!", and Marisa laughed and said, "Fuck, fuck, fuck! Now I have to have a nice day whether I want to or not, since you came to see me," and told how she was going to dress as a beatnik for Halloween, with *hair* and everything; and Darleen was gonna be a cowgirl; and there was a sign at the counter saying SEX IS THE ANSWER – NOW WHAT WAS THE QUESTION?, and Marisa seemed happy. (Poor Marisa! – In the Chatanuga Cafe up on Haight Street, a wavy-combed redhead out on a date smoothed her dress and said, "Marisa used to be really nice. We used to be great friends, and then – " "Then she got tough," her boyfriend supplied. – "Yeah, she shaved her head," the redhead said. "Then she lost all her friends.")

"I'd like an egg sandwich to travel," said an old hoss.

Marisa cooked it up. "Eggs with legs!" she screamed through the hatch.

Marisa worked slicing mushrooms and frying up the cutest little pork chops. "I do everything myself!" she cried, dancing to the radio. All the customers watched Marisa's earnest bald head at the corner of the range. She had a way of biting her lower lip as she worked that made her look as if she were trying not to cry.

"Hey, 'Risa, these hush puppies are hard through and through."

"*Fuck* you! Tells me it's raw! It's potatoes; what do you want?"

You could see her bent over the range, her snowy head, her green eyes looking up and around as she ladled oil on the potatoes. For four dollars or less she fixed the best breakfast around. And the customers sat scratching their greasy shirts and reading the paper and laboring over their food. As the months passed, Marisa came to rest her hand on her hip while she worked over the range, in the time-honored fashion of cooks everywhere. The blackboard said: MARISA'S FOOD FOR SALE. And whenever I asked her, she took me to the back room, smiling a little nervously with her tongue between her teeth; and then she pulled down her pants and knelt, one hand on her naked hip, to show off her proud dragon. Sometimes the regulars came around to the doorway to peek. "Another dollar for the Dragon Lady!" they cried, putting a buck in her tips jar.

"How's James?"

"James is fine," she said smiling, and you could tell she loved him because she looked so happy just being able to say the word James. "He really liked that little knife you gave me. In fact," she said proudly, "when I showed it to him he took it and wouldn't give it back." – "I guess that's a compliment," I said. – "Oh, yes," she said. "I was really really glad he liked it."

"What's your mother doing, Marisa?"

"My mother? Just being a Jew."

I will never forget the time I brought Marisa a white rose, and she grinned and said wow and hugged it and me, and as she was holding it, blushing and wondering what to do with it, a black woman approached the counter and said to Marisa, "Oh, somebody gave you a rose!"; and Marisa froze up and said nothing for a long time, and finally looked the black woman up and down a couple of times and said, "Yes, it's a *white* rose."

When the health inspector came to Bouncer's and didn't like her tiles, she punched him in the mouth. The inspector turned off the gas range. "You're closed."

Marisa was known sufficiently well that if you went and stood at a bus stop round about 10:00 in the morning you might see a blonde with dark rings under her eyes drinking beer in a paper bag, and she wore a black leather jacket; and if you asked her what time it was she'd laugh and say, "Oh, God, I don't even know what *year* it is," and there'd be a silence and she'd say, "Just kidding," and she'd say, "I think it's 8:30 or 9:00; you see, I just got out of Juvenile Hall; today's my eighteenth birthday," and you'd go (if you were nice), "Congratulations," and she'd go, "Now I'm out, I gotta stay out," and you'd say, "Yep, that's right," and there'd be another silence, and you'd go, "Maybe you know a friend of mine, a skinhead girl named Marisa," and she'd go, "You mean the one that's not quite a skinhead, with the stubble on her head? Sure, I know her," and at that the world would become a brighter place. Yes, she knew Marisa in Juvenile Hall, Marisa who was locked into her room every night, which was all concrete and echoey; and early in the morning the loudspeaker echoed: "*Wake up!*", and Marisa had to get up then and go wash and eat breakfast; and then for three hours she and the other girls sat doing nothing in the court-appointed "school," and then they had lunch; and in the afternoon they sat around and then after dinner the ones who'd been good were allowed to watch TV, and the ones who'd been bad had to do nothing; and then they all went back to their separate concrete rooms to get locked up again. They weren't ever allowed to go outside, but if nobody had fucked up, Juvie showed Walt Disney movies on the VCR on Friday night. They showed *Bambi* over and over.[5]

One of the reasons that Marisa hated blacks was that she'd been in Juvie in Detroit (how old would she have been then – thirteen, fourteen? Probably eleven, because she still had some of her baby teeth); the only white girl in Juvie, and they had to put her in isolation because all the other girls kept beating her up for being white, seven or eight black girls at a time (one on one Marisa could have handled them); and you must be informed of the final scene, when one of the girls got a pair of pliers from a guard (the guards were black); and in the cool wet unwholesome echoey darkness the black girls gathered around Marisa screaming and hitting her, and the black girl with the pliers banged Marisa's head down and got her mouth open and the black girls held Marisa down while she screamed and tried to punch them and the girl with the pliers pulled one of Marisa's front teeth out. – But when I first heard this story I misinterpreted one detail:

"So the girls held you down?"

"No, the guards did."[6]

---

5 "Were the other girls nice?" – "*Nice?*" said Marisa in astonishment. "They were in Juvie! We were locked up!"

6 "There will be some," wrote Major W. E. Fairbairn in his commando manual *Get Tough!* (D. Appleton-Century, 1943), "who will be shocked by the methods advocated here. To them I say 'In war you cannot afford the luxury of squeamishness. Either you kill or capture, or you will be captured and killed. We've got to be tough to win, and we've got to be ruthless – tougher and more ruthless than our enemies." This is undoubtedly what Marisa's dentists thought.

A Cold Sunday

Dee was a thin bootwoman with big teeth. She had a tall, egglike head and angular eyebrows. Her head was shaved to grey stubble. She had a way of smiling which bent her lower lip down and exposed her teeth, making her seem candid. Her right arm was tattooed. So was her back. When she took off her shirt to show it off you could see a horrid monster whose head was all eyes bulging out like pustules, except where its mouth was (it had long teeth); and below its lips writhed tentacles. On her left shoulder was her brother's name and the letters R.I.P. (He had died in an accident.) Her bowed head, the stubble cropped in a zig-zag at the back of her neck, furnished her with an intentness appropriate to her boots.

"I have a gun," she said almost shyly the first time I met her. "I'll show you. It's only my first one." She fumbled under the bed and finally dragged out something wrapped in a dusty garbage bag – a crude long-barreled .410 pistol without sights. "I'm gonna kill some coons with it," she laughed. "Just kidding." – The gun had never been cleaned. It didn't look safe to fire.

In a skinhead face, as I have said, the eyes become of prime importance. She had strong, calm eyes. Dee herself was strong and calm, intelligent and practical. She was always cleaning up, "keeping the house together" she called it, feeding other Skinz who came and stayed and stayed, unlike my roommate's discarded girlfriends who would sometimes come here because they had no place else to go, as in the case of Parisian Mathilde, whose uncle brought her here with a pair of suitcases, saying, "She'll be staying only a week," and Mathilde with her melancholy timidity interjected, "And it's a very *short* week!" – No, the Skinz were nothing like that, for many of them had no way to pay rent; Yama, for instance, slept for a long time in his car out by Kezar until it got towed. Late at night you could walk down Lincoln Street along the border of the Park, and there were always cars and vans and buses parked there, their windows blackout-curtained by plastic, by stacked up boxes, by junky possessions, and sometimes you might see a light flash briefly inside one of those carcasses, like a firefly inside the mouth of a dead horse; but when decomposer bacteria such as towtrucks finally disposed of the charnel there was no place for fireflies to flit unless they had someone like Dee to help them. She let them stay and kept cleaning up, making what had been the living room into the bedroom again, the bed up against the window. Even Yama's dog Rebel got fed while Yama was in jail. When Dee first came out from West Virginia she thought the S.F. Skinz were a bunch of assholes, because Blue, Chuckles, Johnny Beast and Dagger were younger then, wilder, more punk-rock, and the punk rockers were going nowhere new. The Skinz hadn't split off from the punk rockers yet. But now they were family. Dee shaved her head because that was very clean.

"Awright," goes yellow-toothed Tully, shaking out the sofa cushions, "so we found that little ole plastic spider Marisa lost and was bitching about. And here's Hunter's extra weights."

Dee was cleaning out the closet. "Nova," she called to her daughter. "You want a little purse?"

"No, thank you," said Nova moodily. "But is there anything in it?"

"Just my old health card. It's expired."

Nova didn't answer. She was a big blonde whose mother had died, and whose father wouldn't have anything to do with her once she got a Mohawk. For awhile she lived in a squat in San Francisco. Finally Dee took her in. (Marisa would have liked to be taken in there, too.)

The Skinz all stood around kicking the floor. One of them had hair. – "Oh, I'm a skin, see?" said blond Cam. And he rolled up his sleeve to show a tattoo of a skin being crucified.

"Why did you let your hair grow, then?"

"Well, I had to. That's all. I'm a non-traditional skin."

"Hey, *crucial!*" said Hunter. "My old V-necked green rugby attire." He worked with cement, as you may remember, setting up rebar, digging and pouring.

"Well, you wanna go play football?" said a new guy, standing there holding a pair of Hunter's moldy old boots from the closet. Hunter had given them to him.

"No," Hunter said.

"Then we can go looking for that guy with the green beret again," the new guy said.

"I'll bet he took off," Dee said.

"That sonofabitch," the new guy said.

"He said he'd cut up my dog and feed it to me," Hunter said.

Dee kept throwing things out of the closet. She was the only person working. "You know," she said over her shoulder, 'I was thinking about putting our firewood in the fireplace to make it look like it was really burning in there."

"That's hilarious," Hunter said.

"This one person I know," said Cam, "if you can believe it, she cut cardboard up and made it look like flames. Cardboard on top of wood in an empty fireplace."

"That's fuckin' *hilarious*," Hunter said.

"It's real cold in here," Dee said. "I've been cold all day."

At night in November it got so cold that you could see your breath, and the Skinz holed up in bars watching the Niners game. – "Fuckin' go for it!" they yelled. "Well, they took three last time, they took three this time, that's six. Forty fuckin' yards and they can't fuckin' make it; I feel like putting a foot up their fuckin' ass." – "Hey, don't sit there!" they yelled at the others. "Your hair's in the way." – And the tramps leaned forward wide-eyed at every pass, grinning cautiously in order not to get thrown back out for not buying beer. – "That motherfucker!" yelled the Skinz. "He didn't even get hurt!" – Some Dumbo laughed *Eee-heh-heh-heh-heh!*

Only Brandi was out with her son, trying to raise some money for dinner or drugs. – "C'mon, I gotta feed him," she said. "Spare some change, twennyfive, fifty cents?"

"No."

"Aw, look, you can do it," goes a white lady. "I have four children, and I still gave her a dollar."

"That's right," said Brandi eagerly. "Thank you very much, Ma'am."

"How about all the money you already owe me?"

"I see you later," she said brightly, moving away.

"Hey, you got any change?" went the tramps, leaning up against the streetwalls, and if you said no they dismissed you and went back to their talk: "Oh, he's got a connection, all right; I mean, *mango!*"; and if you give them money then they take it and do the same thing; but if you say to them, "No, I'm broke, do you have any change for me?" then they get all worried and say, "Just eight cents, I tell you, I can't give you anything," and THEN they dismiss you, and go back to their talk: – "Yeah, well, if he's got mango how come his snort is *lousy* like *piss?*" – "Because he don't get everything he wants like them skinheads, that's why!"

And two Skinz went by, wearing grey canvas jackets, with American flags on the back. On the wall by the anarchist bookstore was written THE POWER & THE GLORY: U.S. SKINZ. The skinheads sat smoking and shaking their heads when the Niners lost a play. "We're gonna *get* you, motherfucker," they said. They could not believe that nothing was ever going to happen.

A police car sat parked at the curb. The cop walked nervously around it a few times, trying all the doorhandles and shining his flashlight in the window-cracks. A man came running by, his breath puffing like smoke-signals, but he stopped short when he saw the police car, and strolled affectedly for half a block. Then he began to run again.

And the cop came back and laboriously double-unlocked his car. Then he locked it again. Skinheads went by in camouflage pants, jerking their heads back, puffing cigarettes between their lips. One of them came back, very dignified, with his bootwoman at his side. They ignored the police car, whereas the woman who walked by next turned to give it a fake salute. At the number seven stop, old people got on the late-night bus, shaking their heads slowly; the young strong ones shot their arms up against the ceiling rails in a Sieg Heil parade.

And in the November nights, the December nights, with the cold deep enough to make the insides of your ears hurt, the flags still flew high on Haight Street, the American flag whipping unconsoled beside Nova's Irish banner.

Preparations for Death in Ireland

Nova was an ice cream scooper at Bud's. She'd met Dee when Dee was a panhandling punk. Nova had panhandled with her, lived with her at the Golden Eagle on Broadway. In the afternoons, when the skinheads started coming back from work, rubbing their tired eyebrows, Nova sat in her room and listened to records. She didn't like going out because it was so boring.

"I have nothing to do with their sayings or nothings," said Nova sullenly. "They're just like my family. They're for American causes. I'm more for different causes, like I'm gonna join the I.R.A. But I don't care what causes my family are living in. Everybody's got like their own ways of thinking and expressions."

Strangles came in and sat there listening. He was a skinhead from

way back who had his own band, Rich Kids on L.S.D. He worried
about Nova sometimes.

"I relate to what's happening about America," said Nova. "It's too
damn free. There are weird people running around. Niggers going after
clean white girls and stuff. The way I see it, I'd like to go over to Ireland
and be like a drummer girl. I'll live there and die there, that's all."

Strangles nodded. "I used to be politically stressed out, like you," he
said. "You can take like years off your life."

"Maybe so," Nova said. "But I just don't wanna live here. I just don't
wanna be here."

King Yama

"Rebel, you be cool," said Yama[7] to his dog. He had a scary face.

"What's this American Front thing anyway?"

"It's just a little thing we have going," Yama said. "We work for our
money, or try to, at least. I'm looking for a job right now. We're just
proud young Republicans who like our President, who'd be happy to
die for our country."

Yama moved quickly, smoothly.

"You *are* an ugly bastard, don't you know that, Yama?"

"Yeahp."

Yama had a scar on his nose. "The night I got this," he said, "I was
panhandling from a nigger. I said, 'You got some green?', he said, 'Fuck
you,' and I saw the blood coming down inside my brain and I said,
'You're gonna die now, nigger,' and his eyes went BLING! and he went
running into Cala Foods, and this Cala Foods nigger came running up
and said, 'I'm gonna *fuck you up!*', and I hit him three times but he
didn't go down. He had a box-cutter with a triangular blade, and he
slashed me right like *this!*"

"Well, hell, man," said Anthony, "that's why I wanna hit up south. I
wanna go where there's lots of white people."

Yama didn't say anything. He had a way of suddenly glaring at you,
as if you were walking along a deserted dangerous road at night and

7 I have changed this street name, as I have so many others. However, "Yama" is
appropriate, being the name of the god of death.

suddenly headlights came around a corner you couldn't even see and then flicked off and then a car ran you over in the dark.

"Yeah," said Anthony, "I made some money off some dudes who're looking for Blue. I said, yah, he's in Canada."

"You writin' this down?" said Yama. "Say Chuckles and Blue are in Canada. Say Chuckles and Blue are dead. Tell 'em that Chuckles and Blue died last summer, you got that? Chuckles died in the summer of 'eighty-five. He got stabbed in the summer of 'eighty-four. Yeah, he got stabbed."

Yama and Anthony sat at the kitchen table drinking Bud and looking at pictures of themselves. "There's Vern," Anthony said. "Vern from L.A. He's a dick. We went down, and he wouldn't even let us stay with him. Not a very skinhead thing to do."

"Fuck 'im," said Yama carelessly.

"Yeah, carve him."

Yama didn't say anything.

"There's Rebel when he was a puppy," said Anthony.

"Yeah," said Yama, "I had that picture when I was in jail."

"Boy," said Anthony, "I miss Dagger and Spike."

Yama didn't say anything.

"They gonna have a kid, get married and stuff," Anthony sighed. "I hope it's a boy, 'cause otherwise it'll be a fuckin' ugly girl. Either way it'll grow up and respect America, man."

"A friend of mine just got out of jail," interrupted Yama, apparently addressing his knees. He preferred the company of his knees to that of many people. "Name of Cowboy. I hate that dude. He's a faggot. He was in San Bruno, too. The last time I saw him, he was in the faggot tier, the Polk Street tier, they call it, the he-shes. Every time I saw him after I found out he's a faggot, I booted him, I fucked him up."

"All *right*," said Anthony respectfully. "And whatever happened to Butch?"

"He's doin' time in a brig on an aircraft carrier," Yama said.

"That's like the worst," Anthony said. "You get no window, man."

"Hey, Reb, c'mon," said Yama. "Don't kiss me. Just lookit me, dude."

The two Skinz concentrated on Rebel, playing with his ears, frowning and grinning at the dog. — "Rebel, you want some Bud?" they said. — Rebel raised his ears and looked at them wide-eyed. — "I'm tryin' to train Rebel to growl at niggers," Yama said. "At the bus stop today, I saw some, I took Reb by the ears, I said, '*Watch 'em!*'; he started growlin'."

"Rebel's the best," said Anthony.

"This is my son right now," Yama said, pointing a forefinger at the big black dog. "The only person in the world right now."

"Rebel'll lock onto people when he's scared," said Anthony. "I fight the best when I'm scared. When I see some big bastard coming at me I just start to whale at him!"

Yama didn't say anything.

"Rebel's part Lab and part pit bull," said Anthony to the world in general.

Yama didn't say anything.

Anthony started polishing his boots. He had his arm all the way inside his left boot so that it looked like a black leather gauntlet. "I'm gonna polish 'em up real good and then when I kick someone in the face he'll see his own reflection," he explained, not for the first time. "It'll be the last thing they ever see!"

"Awright," said Yama. "America rules."

Encouraged, Anthony started to tell a story about Albert and some Skinz in Germany but Yama said, "You know Albert's story. You don't want no one to know what it is."

"What're you doin', lettin' your eyebrows grow out?" said Anthony quickly.

"Yeah," said Yama, "for winter. Girls love it, too."

"Right on. Girls love anything."

"I got a date on Lincoln Memorial, right by Lincoln's right leg, on July 4th. You don't know how many girls I've fucked by the reflecting pool."

"All *right!*" said Anthony. "Right on, Yama!" – But a month later Anthony had crossed the Skinz. – "I gave him three chances," said Dickie peaceably, leaning back on the double bed, "and he struck out. If he comes around this house I'll kill him." – "He's just a *shit!*" yelled Dan-L. "He *fucked* with everyone! Tried to steal Rebel, too, after all that Dee did for him! He's growing his hair now, I'll tell you. I'd like to *beat* his *ass!*" – "Yep, she knows," said Dickie with a wink at his Budweiser. On the wall a sticker read: DON'T BLAME ME – I VOTED FOR HITLER

But as of yet this rupture had not occurred, Anthony was still skull-

shaved, and Yama crushed his empty beer can in one hand, while the
two skinheads sat smoking and watching Rebel fight another dog.

I am wall-eyed. Yama, noticing this, turned to me and said, "Are you
blind in one eye?" – "Just about," I said. "I only see out of one eye at a
time." – "Oh, yeah?" he said with real gentleness. "Would you rather I
didn't talk about it?"[8]

Yama grew up on a ranch near Santa Fe. Every night his Dad would
put marbles in the freezer, and then roll them into his bed at 6:30 in
the morning to wake him up. No matter where you rolled in bed, those
marbles followed you to get you up. He was born left-handed. His
Mom died when he was three, and his Dad came and took him to New
Mexico and made him eat with his right hand. Even when Yama was a
little kid, his Dad would say, "When you're mad, you just let me know
and we'll take it out back." Later Yama was a punk in New York. He
inherited $33,000.00, so he bought three cars and plenty of cocaine.
Before he knew it, he started shooting up. One day he came into a long
dark hall in a burned-out shell on the lower East Side. At the end of
the hall was a curtain and three candles. It was five bucks for a C and
ten bucks for a D. You set your money in front of the curtain and a
nigger's hand reached out and took it and gave you your drugs. Yama
came up to the curtain to buy a D. There wasn't a sound in the gutted
hallway. Suddenly someone rushed up behind him and knocked him
with a piece of rebar. Yama had a .22 in his trench coat. He squeezed
the trigger twice, right into the kneecap, and ran into Tompkins Square
and had a pizza. He ditched the gun. Later he got a hundred-dollar
shotgun from another skinhead.

When Yama's girlfriend told him she'd miscarried, he was sitting
with her in his car. He punched the car roof. Later he said he'd missed
her chin by *that* much! He knew she'd miscarried on purpose 'cause
she thought the kid was somebody else's. He knew it was on purpose
'cause women could do that stuff whenever they wanted; after all, *he*
could *come* whenever he wanted to come.

Yama was accepted for admission at San Bruno because on Halloween night he saw this pretty girl in a halter-top get hit by some guy, so
Yama came running up and walloped the guy, because you don't hit
women in America. The dude's friends came running out, but a guy
ran up in front and said, "Hey, you don't fuck around with skinheads!"

8 In truth I often worry about my vision, and last night I dreamed that my blue eyes
ran like bloodshot mercury-droplets across my forehead, and finally touched, joined,
flowed together into a watery Cyclops eye.

At that time Yama was going out with this girl Tania from Berlin, and he decided to drop her, so the night before he gave her the news, he and a couple other Skinz three-holed her. The next day, he told her she was fired. Then Tania snitched on him. The police were on top of him like stink on shit.

In jail Yama made a gun out of a toilet paper tube. He packed it full of foil and wet toilet paper to close off one end. Then he ground up a bunch of match heads for gunpowder and sifted it into the tube. For shot he used broken aspirin. That gun could do some damage. Mainly he passed his sentence working out and reading, but he also learned from a little Chinaman how to kill people with his bare hands. Before you learn to kill somebody with your bare hands, you gotta go through all this other shit, but Yama went through it, all clean-cropped and dignified.

The White House

"Each tier is a country," Yama said. "2N, 2S, 3N, 3S. Like, 2N, was the tier to be on. We'd have outside clearance, so we got rum and weed in there. You know them big three-liter Seven-Up bottles. They brought those in full of white rum. Being a trusty, you have the privilege of a private shower, and the TV's on twenty-four hours a day. A Cuban nigger had my job, and I took his job, don't matter how. There's lots of land out there; they have a farm crew. I fucked up the farm truck when I was stoned. But that was cool. Now, Dagger and I were in there together. We were cooks. We could sell a hundred packets of sugar for a dollar twenty. Or hamburgers, you'd steal one and fry it up and sneak it in your coat and take it to one of the upstairs tiers and sell it for a buck. I had my neighbors, a white neighbor here, a white neighbor there; I was in a white neighborhood. That was the White House, we'd call it. In the morning I'd go, *Rring, rring, rring,* like I was on the phone, and somebody would say, What do you want, and I'd say, C'mon over and party!, and he'd go, O.K., click!

"Every tier, it says, MAJOR RULES, MINOR RULES. Major rules are like a page and a half; minor rules are shorter. Minor rules are like don't change the channel on the TV. You fight over that. Two people died over that when I was there. One guy got stabbed, another guy –

this five-six nigger – got thrown off a table. The niggers'd put on a nigger TV show and the white boys and Mexicans'd go back and play cards. I used to come back between the niggers and watch TV. The niggers'd go, 'Skinhead, you got heart! We like you! The other white boys go back; you stay with us.' I'd say, 'You leave me alone, I'll leave you alone.' They *respected* me."

Back to the Palace

Yama didn't stay out of confinement very long. All his friends agreed that he was losing it. There was something the matter with him, but no one could tell what it was. Dickie and Dan-L tried to be his friends as long as they could. They could feel themselves losing touch with him, as if he were dead and his eyeballs were slowly filming over. One day Yama did a strange thing which I will not write about that got him put in the psycho cells for a long time. He may or may not be getting shock treatments. Visiting days are Wednesdays and Saturdays.

The Old Look and the New Look

From where I sat watching the Skinz from behind the blinds of an ice cream parlor, they strode by, scraping their coats and chains against the glass, not seeing me, I thought, their heads high, shoulders swinging like powerful shark-flippers; while other jobless sat scowling into their little cups of Espresso, legs crossed under the white tables. Bootwomen went by, skulls sometimes turbaned in towels or in soft cloths, as if to protect those most sensitive bones from the world, the way that Muslim women veiled their faces. – The Skinz turned around suddenly and came back, staring into the glassfronts window by window until they found the spy; one of them, the most unfriendly, having a lush blond skull-carpet instead of the usual grey; and he kicked the window meaningfully with his boot. – They leaned up against the grilles of liquor stores at night, making faces and glowering so hard that they wrinkled up the chains and snakes tattooed around their ears. They looked as if they were about to spit burning shit out of their mouths.

Maybe Dickie had looked like that when he won the dogfood-eating contest. The other contestants hadn't been able to finish their first can, but Dickie was halfway through his second before he turned green and puked all over the video audience, spraying bile between his teeth to burn and stink on those screaming faces ... The Skinz leaned up against fences, kicking the sidewalk with their boot-toes. – "I'll slap her face," a new one said, "and she can just do anything she fucking wants; we're not friends; I'm just *using* her." – Round about eleven o'clock the drifters started sitting on their backpacks in the doorways between Clayton and Belvedere, not panhandling anymore; and inside the ice cream parlor, where it was warm, only the reflections of Christmas tinsel and streetlights could be seen, unless one of the Park People came up against the windowpane to look in. Buses caught the light. – The skinheads lounged in the painted alleys yelling, showing themselves to all as demonic concentration camp traitors. Just as after-images remain to closed eyes at the end of Halloween night – the transvestites, tigers, bears, vampires, military detachments, half-naked women in fishnets all compressing like coal in the eyes' darkness into half a dozen black-swaddled figures with gold plumes, advancing in silence – so the skinheads left behind them the picture of a single warrior in profile, a man with spiky scalp-grass pricking up proud on his skull, and a sullen all-seeing eye. That was the skinhead look.

There was a new look, too, a black-jacketed, black bandanna'd, thin-legged look that might supplant the skinhead look someday; or maybe the bearded tramps would be fashionably imitated by folks who used shampoo and moustache wax; all that was certain was that the skinheads *would* be supplanted someday; and no one would give a damn.

About the Photographer

And up by the anarchist bookstore, Ken the street photographer (who took pictures of the Skinz, so you might as well know a little about him) was still trying to get rid of his housemates Dahlia and Denise, who were getting on his nerves, so he ate everything they put in the refrigerator and he jumped up and down outside their room early in the morning, yelling, and he taunted the house dog with chains and iron bars until she barked *rrrrRRRAGGH! rrrRAUGHH!* so that the whole flat shook, and Ken threw the girls' mail against the door so that the dog snapped at it; and for weeks the girls laughed uncomfortably, pretending that Ken was joking, so Ken had to get a little more direct, like picking his teeth and rubbing his crotch when they talked to him, letting drool go down his chin, and when they said good morning he'd yell, "What the fuck do you mean, good morning? What's so good about it? Did I say it was a good morning?", and then the girls started ignoring Ken, and when they brought their friends home Ken would say, "What's your name? You're pretty! Can I take pictures of you NAKED? Will you fuck me right now on the floor?", and Denise would say, "Just leave him alone; he's obnoxious," and still Denise and Dahlia stayed, so Ken told Denise she made him want to puke, and every day he asked her if she'd found a place yet, and finally she got the message and started billing Ken when he ate her food, and going around all the time muttering, "*I want out!*", and one day they were both gone, were Dahlia and Denise, so quickly that Dahlia's father didn't even know they'd left, and so he called for Dahlia and Ken said, "Dahlia? Dahlia who?", and Dahlia's father goes, "Dahlia Ackerby," and Ken goes, "Oh, *that* Dahlia. This is her husband. Who the fuck are you?" – "WHAT!" goes Dahlia's father, and Ken goes, "Just kidding," and he could tell it was a long distance call so he dropped the phone for about ten minutes and had a beer and then came back and said, "Mr. Ackerby, you still there?" – "I'm still here," said Dahlia's father grimly, and at that Ken put down the phone for about fifteen minutes and had two more beers and then got Dahlia's number from the refrigerator door and read it off to her father and when her father said thank you Ken said, "You BET, pal!" and hung up, and then he and I went into the storeroom where one of Dahlia's suitcases was and we picked out some of Dahlia's nice clean pink underwear and sniffed it and threw it to the house dog and the house dog snapped at it and shook it so that it fluttered across her chops and the dog decided that Dahlia's underwear must be alive and made up her mind to kill the thing, whatever it was, so she snarled and bit and tore so many holes in Dahlia's underwear that Dahlia would have had to be an octopus to wear them; and the dog tore them some more until they were one long rag whose contours made lots of side trips, and Ken and I laughed and laughed and Ken was revenged for his sufferings.

On the front of Ken's house the skinheads drew a tombstone with the words:

R.I.P.
S.F. SKINZ
1981-1985
Some of The Best Men Alive or Dead

and right by the door they wrote: S.F. SKINZ THEY WERE HERE THEY FUCKED YOUR WIMMIN THEY DRANK YOUR BEER.

Three Futures

We are lucky that the skinheads are not capable (as I dreamed last night) of hosting hundred-dollar-a-plate luncheons for their cause, every skin, every bootwoman in business tweed, clinking glasses with their dupes, old farts and young, remarking on the parsley garnish, taking long private walks with bankers until they have the capital to stand smoking one winter's night at the border, *Maschinengewehr* happy and warm under a blanket of gun grease; and the Skinz stand waiting to cross the ice of the Rubicon at dawn. I am grateful that they spend their energies spray-painting schematic skulls-and-bones on the back of Polytechnic High, writing **RAGE** and **STORMTROOPS OF DEATH OR DIE** and **S.F. SKINZ BLOOD PURE.** As to the future, either someone could arm and pay them (there are neo-Nazi camps in Germany and Austria, where boys practice being clean and orderly, with firearms training and mock executions to complete their education; there is a National Front in the U.K., there is a Nazi printing company in Lincoln, Nebraska); or else they might get tired of being skinheads; or maybe the South of Market gang will carry out the threat which it has written by the freeway ramp: **S.F. SKINZ WILL DIE SCREAMING.** – There are plenty of people with that point of view: – when I was waiting for my bus tonight in Oakland, over at San Pablo and Yerba Buena, men were standing by the Bank Club Café drinking out of paper sacks, and I asked one of the blacks what he thought of the skinheads, and he said, "You want to see a knife that talks?", and I said sure, and he pulled out a knife and told it to say something, and it went SNICKK! and its blade switched out almost all the way to my chin.

What the Skinheads Thought

"Dude, I want to talk to you about your story," screamed Bootwoman
Marisa very rapidly, "because it fucking sucks!" – "Well," said Bootwoman Dan-L, "my first reaction wasn't too positive. You need a lot of
work with your grammar. You have a lot of run-on sentences." – "She
knows," said Dickie, lighting up his bong. "She went to college." – As
for Ice, he buttonholed Ken in private. "I don't really know this guy,"
he said. "But he seems too poetic. I can talk to you; you're levelheaded.
I've read parts of this story, and I think it should be cut, maybe to about
a page." Dagger, Spike, Dee, Hunter, Nova and of course Yama had
left town.

RED HANDS

I

Seamus (so he told me to call him here) had rank red hair and a reddish-blond moustache. He wore a black overcoat. Purity and sincerity were in his face. I suppose he felt the need to talk that any man feels when he has done something that he will be hunted for, and he is by himself in some open plain of phobias and the wind of death is blowing in his face and he would like nothing better than to discover on the horizon the cabin of a wise man who will invite him in and listen to him and tell him what to do, although Seamus knew that there was nothing to do. It is sometimes a hard thing to be a man and stand by the thing that you have done. He would have liked someone to take him out of the wind, but no one is supreme enough to do it; so, faced with us through some accident, Seamus looked to us for distraction, and when he was through with us and other caravans came by he told his tale again, searching each man's face to see if he was the wise man that every man needs, but nobody was . . . "Well, see, that's all I did at first," he said, looking down at his burrito. "I had a big back yard, and had a good-sized shed in the back. It was a good place to drop things off on the – you know, between here and there. I ran a safe house. That's what you call 'em here, don't you?"

"Yeah."

"Place to hide. Place to get a meal an' a shower, a bath. We didn't have a shower. We had a bathtub, though." He stopped for a minute to eat. – "I studied in Canada," Seamus said. He had a trick of hunching his shoulders. "I got my degree, and went back, and the first year I was back at Ulster I was teaching at a little school. My sister was still living at home at the time. I guess she was about seventeen years. She hadn't even started university yet. And she took ill. There was a curfew at the time. So the old man broke the curfew and tried to get her to a doctor, but he was caught on the streets after dark. He was detained. They held him for two weeks, and he died of a heart attack. When we picked up his body, we could see it'd been beaten. It was obvious. You know, the black and blue marks. You could see that there were fractures in his skull. You know, at that point . . ."

He stopped. He looked down at his food. "I mean, I grew up . . . Everybody hated something. Hatred is like – oh, fuck, how do you say it? – it's a way of life. It really is. We're very much a prejudiced nation, I guess you could say. If you're Catholic, you learn to hate the Protestants because you're forced to live in the ghettos. Your opportunity for employment and any chance for a good life is limited because of your religious belief. And you've got the Unionists, the Libertarians . . . Ireland's a land of factions. It's almost as bad as France, if you think about it.

"I got beaten up the first time when I was about six years old," he smiled. "There was a group of boys – must've been about fifteen of 'em. They did it 'cause I was Catholic. I didn't even know what being Catholic *meant* at the time."

As he talked, he forgot to eat. His voice was always soft. "After my old man died, I was pretty bitter. I watched my mam drink herself to death. Took about two years to do it. And at the same time, I travelled through India. I saw the hash runs through that part of the country. Started doing those things to raise money. When I was out of Ireland, I'd learned that the religious thing wasn't the big deal. It's not whether you're a Catholic or a Protestant that matters. But I felt that the British, they didn't belong. They didn't belong there. I felt that we were a nation of men, that we could deal with our own fucking problems.

"I was never involved, so to say, when I was younger. I used to go out on the streets and throw rocks and track tanks. Fuck with the soldiers, light off firecrackers. I'd do anything I could. I always tried to stay out of it, but I was always involved in it, 'cause it took my family. So I felt there was a need for involvement, for vengeance. I opened up my house. I let people stay there. We even got people out of Russia. But then one day – I guess it was about the same time that Bobby Sands started the hunger strike – I heard in the south there was a warrant for my arrest. I didn't go willingly. I ended up getting shot four times. I was tried without a jury, and I got a long sentence for something that was never proven, so to say. Not the way the judicial system works here. At that time I guess the British were desperate. And the single written testimony of another man was enough to incriminate you. So that's how I was introduced to the Block." – Seamus's red eyelashes twitched.

In the H-Block he had lived his life watching the British warders, with their scared baby faces and their truncheons. Once they had tortured one of his comrades. The man wouldn't talk. So they showed him a video of his sixteen-year-old daughter being raped. He still wouldn't talk.

"Most of the alleged terrorists were all kept in one area," Seamus said. "There were about eight hundred of 'em. I was with twenty-three others that got fed up. We took an opportunity, and gained our freedom. I guess I was a little more fortunate than some. Half of us were captured in the first week."

"So the escape went well?"

Pride came into his face. "Did the escape go well? It went like bloody fucking *dominoes*." He looked at the tape recorder defiantly. Then he said, "Like dominoes. Just like when we blew up the department store."

2

"So what happened when the department store was blown up?" I said.

"I wasn't there," he said.

"Trust him, man," said the fellow in the back of the kitchen, but Seamus was silent.

"Well," I said, "if you had any advice for people who want to blow up department stores, what would it be?"

"Don't do it," he said. "It's not worth it."

3

"That's why I hang out in the woods so much, in the mountains," Seamus said. "Just me an' Him."

4

"We had to kill a British soldier to get out," he said. "Not just anybody, but a British soldier. The largest manhunt in the history of northern Europe. Hey, they got sixteen of us, out of the twenty-four that got out! When I left that front gate, I said, 'We may be brothers, but from here we're on our own!' I was one of the selfish ones. It was the ones that stuck together and tried to help each other that got caught."

5

After the escape, he had gone down into Belfast and hidden on the Catholic side. Time obscured him further from the British, who were required to calibrate their hours according to the freshest cases. Presently he began his career of false voyages. He hired onto a Swedish ship as cook and carpenter. Upon completion of the journey, he joined an Italian freighter, and then a Dutch fishing boat, each time under a different name. – Finally he signed on a ship bound for New York. I don't know what he thought during those grey days on the grey sea; quite likely he thought of his two sons. – They came into New York Harbor late at night, passing through the Narrows while Seamus said his goodbyes. Everybody knew. They had a party for him, and it was a good one, since Seamus was fine to drink wine or Guinness or Jameson with; but every now and then at parties I have seen him suddenly look down at the table and fold his hard sunburned arms across his chest and fall silent; at those times I notice his sloping forehead, which seems more bare than it used to, and there are wrinkles at the corners of his pale eyes, and against his red and weatherbeaten face his hair might be reddish-blond or it might be going white. And that is how I imagine him at that other leave-taking party when he must have been saying goodbye to Europe and Ireland, not that I *know* it because his is a story told by a man of professional reticence, friendless forever, and we can grasp it only provisionally and approximately, by dreaming up our own ill-informed impressions of the scene, not omitting the smell of garbage which must have blown into Seamus's nostrils from the landfill on Fresh Kills Island; and Staten Island would have been very big and dark on his left, while New York began to grow, revealing its vastness, cruelty and coldness in the grin of its skyscraper-teeth, and lights burned dingily in Brooklyn; and ahead of him, behind the passionately upraised torch of Miss Liberty in her green old age, were the bright pyramids and dark rectangles of Manhattan, the tall buildings whose luminous dots of windows transformed them into dominoes, the docks whose light cast the coast behind them into greater darkness, and of course the customs-houses. The stubby skyscrapers became taller and wider now, casting their burdens of light upon the harbor; and cars whizzed steadily along the shore freeway like glittering beads, and between the skyscrapers Seamus could see the dark urban canyons into which a man could go and come out another man, or not come out at all. Let us suppose for artistic reasons that a great Cunard liner went by, maybe even the *Queen Elizabeth II;* Seamus would have given it the finger, but out of all the tourist faces peering from every porthole not one would have seen him; and then the moon went behind a cloud to have a cigarette, and everything was almost as bright as before, but harder with a beetling hardness. Seagulls rose in the mist and swirled around the ship before finally returning with screams of disappointment to Miss Liberty's feet. Ahead of him, through the masts and cranes of his ship, he saw long low-roofed warehouses like barracks, and dismal grey prisms of buildings honeycombed with windows, as if they were vertebrae from which all the marrow had been pecked. The American skyline was an interminable rampart which must somehow be scaled, made up of cubes and tall towers ridged and latticed like bones, all crammed together upon the land, crushingly tight, going on and on in a complexity that no one could understand; and the ship came closer until each skyscraper became itself a wall, ribbed and raised and vast, and there were millions of other walls behind it. His only hope was in the narrow spaces five hundred feet high between them where he might be able to sneak through if he could pull himself out of the water, dragging his belly over slimy concrete and salt-impregnated stumps of power poles and barbed wire; then he would have to skulk past the bright-lit foyers of the office towers, dodge past pay phones (water streaming from him all the while), encouraged by the realization that interstitial life might be possible since the in-between-spaces must be getting bigger if the skyscrapers were still getting bigger and bigger and bigger

. . . His comrades had told him that when you jumped, it was important to get a running start to keep from getting sucked into the propeller. He walked back fifteen feet and started running. He cleared the railing; in that transitional moment of regret and expectation, he must have had a sense of being at a great height, for below him was a whole world of black water and yellow lights. He began to fall, and continued to do so for a long time. No doubt he wondered whether or not he could save himself from the propeller. When he hit the water at last, his arms and legs had already begun to swim. Through that cold, dark and utterly foul water he made his laborious way. Not far from his left shoulder, the ship continued on without him. His possessions were his clothes and two hundred U.S. dollars in a watertight pocket.

It is literally true that he was washed up on a dead-end street. Now began his new life, which he must live without anyone, without even himself.

6

"All right, one further story," he said with a smirk. "We were in London, and what I call hoity-toity, kind of like upper-class. It was a rude section near Soho Park. Me and my friends were a bit drunk. We came across this café, and there were some people sitting there eating, and they *looked* at us. And I was offended. I walked over to the railing and I pulled down my zipper, and I pissed on the food."

7

"I'll tell you," said the doctoral student, Oliver (not his real name), "that's why I was so queasy about doing this. I haven't worked with live animals since high school. The power of it is very impressive. I was very impressed with how we bled the mouse the other day. We took the serum out. I usually do it by injection. Of course I won't deny that I'm getting sick of this mouse. In fact, the last three nights have been very difficult. She even keeps *struggling* when I inject her in the belly! I'm glad it's her big day today."

"What's the best way to do it?"

"To kill them, the easy way is to put them in a bag of CO_2. But it's supposedly very painful for the mouse, and it also adds another variable. It may do something to the physiology. That's why it's much better just to break their necks."

"So you use a cervical dislocator?"

"Yes. It's called a pencil."*

8

The lab had the usual formaldehyde smell. Being rich in glass bottles and plastic tubes, it was its own world, which you came to every day, not knowing whether or not you were going to have a good day until you shuffled over to the centrifuge for radioactive materials, flipped the switch, and listened to its good comforting hum, and suddenly it was clear after all that you *did* know which opening to dispense Parafilm through. There were hundreds of drawers to play in, hundreds of shelves and cabinets, and lab benches piled with a mole of this and an aliquot of that. Every chemical was like the muscle of a giant eye which allowed the researchers to see something which they had never seen before. They knew that their powerful reagents would permit them to shatter the unwanted cells, which were like boulders covering some antique tomb that the anthropologists were sure must be glutted with treasure which they could transfer from its underground grave to a public grave in some museum, where gold and bones lay in shame behind daily-cleaned glass.

Through the microscope I saw, on a pinkish field, the red mouse-spleen cells, like translucent beans. They looked like meat; they looked nourishing, but there were not enough of them to eat.

Just as I = AMP and II = TET (as it said on the wall), so the mouse had to die. Their books said, "An upward slope at low pH is reported

---

* We are all of us technicians and researchers in ethical laboratories. One common denominator is *procedure*. – "Clocks with alarms are grand!" I remember Seamus saying to me. "Look at this one from Radio Shack. They have others that you can set up to a year in advance. I like this one, 'cause it's got the alarm on it, right? And it's got enough of an electrical pulse to set off a detonation. You need only very low amperage to do a job."

from frog muscle and squid giant axon." They had killed a lot of things here. But they *had* to kill them to understand them. And this is not blameworthy, because we must each one of us feed on death, whether we maliciously inhale to trap bacteria in the fatal caverns of our lungs, where they must die so that we come to no harm, or whether we wear leather shoes. In those things we kill not out of sadism but tangentially, to achieve a result in some other sphere, and it is the same with the scientist and the terrorist. That is why Oliver remained a little squeamish while he and his companion made the final preparations, their gloved hands in the sanctuary of the BioGard™Ⓜ hood ("Creating Immaculate Atmospheres"). They turned on the germicidal lamp, and then the fluorescent lamp. In the hood was a double bottle of prismatic construction, each side containing its own reddish liquid. Oliver sterilized the tip of his pipette in the ever-burning Bunsen. Then he worked the red fluid, which was frothy with living cells, up and down in the pipette. He took another bottle, held its mouth briefly in the flame, and poured more red stuff from it into a flask with a stubby pointed bottom, like a pencil. – How peculiarly steadfast that BioGard hood must appear at night, with only that gas flame burning . . . – He held the tip of the flask in the flame, and then sealed it and set it into a beaker. From a bottle of what appeared to be blood-red cough syrup, his companion pipetted a specified amount into a Petri dish.

It was time for Oliver's mouse to die now. Somebody else had to kill another mouse, and he said, "Let's race them first!", but Oliver refused. – He took her out of her cage. Of course this rodent tragedy would not be on the order of the one in the department store, when Seamus's bomb went off and people screamed and fell down clutching their stomachs and blood rained and flesh rained; in fact, Oliver's mouse did not even squeak or struggle as Oliver set her on his bench and laid a pencil across her neck. – "Okay," he said to her, "this is your day to *shine!*" – He squeezed her neck down with the pencil, grasped her head, and jerked it up and backwards. There was a quiet dismal crack. Her skinny legs twitched. Then she raised her tail, and her bowels moved.

They took her to the BioGard hood and proceeded to subsequent steps of meticulous dismemberment (now that spontaneous generation has been disproved, it seems that we must cannibalize matter in our projects, just as the revolutionary must destroy in order to establish his own order). I began to wonder what would be the outcome of the magic trick.

9

I am not entirely certain of the connection between the tale of Seamus and the tale of Oliver, but they both have red hands and they both acted for what one might as well call structural reasons. Not being mice, we tend to think that Seamus committed the greater crime, if either of them committed a crime at all (in any event my interest in the dead mouse and the dead people in the department store does not partake of judgment; let us leave that to judges). Seamus did what he thought was right, and so did Oliver. Seamus killed some people and will be affected by it for the rest of his life. Oliver killed a mouse and was affected by it for less than five minutes.

LADIES
AND
RED LIGHTS

And those that deceive upon hope of not being observed,
do commonly deceive themselves (the darknesse in which
they believe they lye hidden, being nothing else but their
own blindness;) and are no wiser than Children, that think
all hid, by hiding their own eyes.

Hobbes, *Leviathan* (1651), II.27.154

The Black Closet

To see Virginia you had to go into a little black closet with a window
giving onto a slightly bigger closet which was lit from above as the black
closet was lit from above by a single orange recessed bulb so that your
face was lit up and everything seemed full of light to make you forget
the black closet that you were standing in; you saw only blonde Virginia
with her nipples peeking through her nightgown, and you could not
hear her even if you pressed your ear to the tip-slot; you had to pick up
the black phone and speak into it, never taking your eyes off her face
(and she never stopped watching you). She sat in a blue felt armchair
and there was a blue curtain behind her and red walls on either side of
her which probably weren't there because when the man in the next
black closet wanted to talk to her on his phone she walked through the
wall with ectoplasmic ease; and she came back with one tit slopping out
of her nightgown, and pretty soon the guy at the front desk was yelling,
"*Virginia!*" again, and she had to walk through the wall, and he said,
"Room Three, honey," and another man bolted himself into another
black closet as the guy at the front desk said, "Remember to give her a
GOOD tip and she'll give you a GOOD pussy show!" – and then I could
hear him back at the front desk saying, "All *right*, my friend, how *are*
you?" – and the radio played, and he wanted to take another girl out to
dinner, but she said, "Well, I don't think my boyfriend would like that
too much. He's *awfully* big and *awfully* jealous!" – and the guy at the

front desk said, "Well, I don't mind about that. What's your name?" – "Noelle," she said, tripping on down the street . . . and Virginia, who had once been a journalism major, came back rearranging her night-gown around her crotch and started speaking to me through the glass with her sad eyes speaking the loudest because I couldn't hear a word she was saying; it was as though she were trapped in a telephone booth and slowly asphyxiating, but then I remembered to pick up the phone and she sounded quite collected, so we talked on the phone for a minute until the guy at the front desk got tired of it and killed the power so that everything went dark and the only thing that came out of the phone was heavy soggy silence.[1]

A Speculation

Virginia's boyfriend was also awfully big and awfully jealous. He did not want her to talk to me, so when meeting me she had to tell him she was going to the gym to lose weight. Maybe he felt the way he did because day and night Virginia had to show people the parts of herself which women usually show only to people they love, so that Virginia's boyfriend had less of her for himself alone, and that hurt him, so he wanted to keep the rest of her for himself alone, like one of the men brooding in the black adjacent closets, each whispering to Virginia through the telephone and gazing at her as if she were his own private movie.

Then again, Virginia's boyfriend might just have been a capitalist, determined to keep her from meeting with other men except behind glass because Virginia might fall for one of the other men, and Virginia's boyfriend's income would dry up.

Once when Virginia said she would call me she did not call, so I went back to the strip joint at night when the barkers were yelling and the tits on the Condor's sign were winking their big red nipples to warn everybody on Broadway: one if by land, two if by sea, and going inside I saw the almost-nude girls in their aquarium, their fishnet stockings like chickenwire against thigh-flesh. Some girls were white and some were brown, but they all looked at me through the glass in the same

---

1 This paragraph cost me seven dollars.

way, crowded together like too many suffocating fish on a warm night when the oxygen pump has failed and the water is heating up and the fish are moving slowly, stupidly, already beginning to bloat. I don't think they liked me. Virginia saw me and her eyes got hard.

"I'd like to speak to Virginia," I said.

"One dollar, Bill," said the man at the desk. "*Virginia!*" he called. "Room One."

Virginia came in very slowly and unwillingly. I bolted the door of my black closet and picked up the telephone.

"Well, Virginia, how are you?" I said.

"Fine," she said.

"Why didn't you call?"

"My boyfriend thinks you must be a hot date. I'm really sorry."

"Tell him I'll meet him on Wednesday. Is two-o'-clock a good time for you?"

Virginia nodded and swam back to the other sad sick fish.[2]

But when I saw Virginia and her boyfriend from across the street on Wednesday I decided not to meet them, because Virginia's boyfriend looked awfully big and awfully jealous.

Enemies

The car pulled over. The cop rolled down the window. "You're leavin', *too*, RIGHT?" he said fiercely to the pimp.

The pimp stared coolly. "Who are you?" he said.

"Do you know what you're talkin' to?" said the policewoman, showing her badge. "Do you know who *you* are?"

"Do you know *what* you are?" the cop muttered.

The Elastic Bank

Meanwhile, night swarmed down the bar-fronts and antique garages of the Tenderloin like a dark and hairy animal, and in the HobNob Bar

2 This ended up costing two dollars, for naked girls must have their tips.

on Geary and Leavenworth big men stood playing pool and pinching ass until it got late and some of them said, "Well, goodnight," and the men who were left behind sat down at the bar and pulled their hats down lower and stared moodily straight ahead, while through the open door flashed old cars and police cars and blonde-dyed hairfalls of streetwalkers walking stroboscopically in and out of the streetlit radiance; and a few blocks down and south and east, past the Blue Lamp, Dino's waited for you, a warm dark place with a walnut-paneled bar upon whose leather-padded edge you could rest your drinks and elbows while trying to understand the topography of its smooth smooth curves like a wooden sea-coast polished by an ocean of palm-sweat over perhaps fifty or sixty years; the ceiling was plastered in a similarly womb-grotto fashion, which Clive Summers the sheet-rocker assured me would cost $1500 a foot nowadays; Dino's was the classiest topless join in the T.L. Dino said that business wasn't as good now as it had been when he started nineteen years ago, but he kept going somehow. He had a rococo piano in storage which Clive, who was drunk, wanted to buy for his studio. "It's so fucking elaborate," Clive said, "it's like if you was to take and slit your belly open and see all those dingly guts hanging out." He raised his arm. "Dino!" he said. "Hey, Dino! I really want that piano." – "It's not for sale," Dino said. – "Dino," said Clive very reasonably, "you don't understand. I really *want* that piano." – "My brother, he's starting a new restaurant on Polk Street, right across from Lord Jim's," said Dino. "He's going to put it in there for decoration." – "If that don't work out I want to cut a deal with you," said Clive. "How much do you want for it?" – "For four thousand dollars cash it's yours," Dino said. – "Are you going to pay him four thousand?" I said into Clive's ear. He winked at me at the same time that he struck a match, illuminating his pale stern face with the yellow of the flame, then with the blue of the dying phosphorus. "If a certain deal comes through," Clive said, "I'm certain I can get it for eighteen hundred. *Fuck*, I *really* want that piano. – Dino! Get me and my friend another beer."

I forgot to say that when you first came into Dino's a woman was waiting to ask you how you were doing (a very *caring* question, fellow penises), and then when you went and sat down at the long curvy bar you could watch the other woman dancing very slowly and looking into your eyes and smiling at you, while Dino paced austerely back and forth behind the bar making minute adjustments to the amplifier, and the dancer spread her hands and moved her hips back and forth very slowly and touched her toes and stretched and Dino said, "All right, gentlemen, here comes the sexy part!" and the dancer slid the straps off her shoulders and let her gown work itself down to her waist so that her small breasts watched you and she watched you, and she took her left leg out of her gown and then her right leg, so that you could see that she was wearing only a black G-string whose small triangle defined the perimeter of her shaved pussy, and the black elastic strap went up the crack of her ass and around her tiny waist to rejoin the top of the black triangle; and as Dino continued to make his cat-fine adjustments to the reel-to-reel so that nothing about the music was imperfect and the music struck your eardrums with firm masterful velvet-padded drumsticks, the dancer continued to dance for you, reaching up to touch the image of her own palms in the ceiling mirror and turning round to show you her ass so that Clive nodded very slowly and said, "What a *body* that woman has! What a *fine-looking* woman!", and the woman smiled at you in a heartmelting way as if she were as fond of you as she was unsure of herself; she had to have your approval or she would cry, so there was nothing for it; being compassionate, you had to take a dollar bill from your wallet and hold it out to Dino, who accepted it in silence and walked up to her pedestal and snapped it into her G-string, and this kept happening every two or three minutes so that by the end of the dance her thighs bristled with dollars down to her crotch, the green dollars symmetrically snapped to her by Dino to give her the appearance of a winged goddess. I cannot sufficiently emphasize how smoothly, how gracefully Dino performed this operation, which required as much skill as shuffling a deck of cards in some astonishing way that leaves everybody at the casino marveling at the naturalness of what is actually a very mannered act; because if Dino snapped the elastic too far her G-string would slip and show the men her pussy, which would *never* do, and if he held the elastic away from her flesh for more than a split second the other dollar bills would fall away from her thighs like green leaves in some unseasonable financial frost; that was why it had to be done in one crisp snap of shorter duration than a hand-clap.[3]

---

3 Seeing these marvels cost me twelve dollars.

Getting Your Rocks Off

Not far from Dino's was a real whorehouse where you knocked on a window and waited until somebody's hand drew back a curtain, and then a smartly dressed girl looked out at you from her desk, which was by a pink telephone, and on her desk was a red telephone, and behind her was a flight of stairs, and she looked at you very closely and then either nodded or shook her head, and if she shook her head the curtains went instantaneously back across the window again, but if she nodded the door opened and you could go in and a whore came grinning down the stairs.

The Ethic

An old bum on Grant Street could not sense an entire Columbus Day parade of dragons and monsters and drum-beaters and yellow-clad Chinese girls standing in the backs of pickup trucks, clashing cymbals; he just sat on the edge of a treebox and his head was in his trembling hands; and he shook it whenever there was a concussion of drumbeats or firecrackers in the street beside him, not understanding this loud night world of cheers and Chinese families waving Taiwanese and American flags and child-orchestras and marching women; he was blinded in himself – but when I gave him twenty-two cents he looked up, and although he could not see me or acknowledge me, he began counting the money very rapidly and practically. We are all anchored by something. Most of us are anchored by money.

The Golden Marriage

A man was crying, and said to his whore, "Don't leave me."
  "Don't worry," she said. "I won't leave you for a whole hour."

A Sore Loser

As Sebulsky and I walked along Eddy Street between Jonés and Leavenworth, an old black woman who had been lounging against a wall ran up and grabbed us. All along the street, black men leaned, watching us, their faces barely paler than the darkness. – "You boys want to get off, don't you?" the whore said. She grabbed our dicks, one in each hand, and squeezed hard. "I can get you off so good. I LOVE big dicks." – "No, thanks," we said, for we were but pansies who did not belong in the Tenderloin; we did not even particularly want to acquire any new disease. – "Don't you like black women?" she whined. Her breath stank and the whites of her eyes were yellow.[4] – "I didn't say that," said Sebulsky, who never cared to have people doubt his goodness. – "Then why not?" she said. "Don't I still got a cunt? Don't I still know how to use it?" – "Maybe we're already booked up for the night," I said. – "You *know* you aren't!" she said. We started walking. Her hands were still on our dicks. – "Where are you going?" she screamed. – "This way," I said. – "You don't like women, do you?" she said. She tried to make us hold hands. "You're going out with each other, aren't you?" – We kept walking. "Don't LOOK at me like that, motherfuckers!" she screamed from behind us.

We went to a bar around the corner and ordered two beers each. A little while later she came in and sat in the corner and stared at us as hatefully as she could. – "Honey, you have to drink something if you want to hang around in here," the bartender explained to her. She went out swearing.

Turk Street

Sometimes on rainy afternoons a black man stood by a storefront on Turk Street, holding out *The Watchtower* for all to see. This magazine

---

4 Here is a definition of an unfortunate profession: one whose practitioners become unfit for it in proportion to their practice of it.

was in a pouch of divinely waterproof plastic. He bent his head when no one came and began reading the cover upside down, like the Vietnamese boy who ran picking up dirty pieces of paper from the street and eagerly reading every one, as if he were about to learn something important. – A blonde cruised by, wiggling her fat legs in shiny blue tights. – A white woman with bare legs was leaning up against a yellow cab with a bunch of blacks – "Thank you," she was saying. "I needed that so much." – "Thank *you*, babybabybaby," they all said.

A black man was sitting under a street lamp. When a white office girl went by in her high heels, he said, "No smile for me today?" – But the white girl kept walking on.

At night, Turk Street became very red and yellow, like the interior of a cadaver. Red lights blazed from liquor stores and porn stores. There were red neon signs in the shape of cocktail glasses and women's legs. Yellow rectangles of light were activated at the peepshow houses. As you walked down the sidewalk, you might see a sickly-pale woman crying and smashing the parking meters with a length of pipe, while men lounged and watched, and red lights winked. Men lived their nights out against the red-lit walls. Whores yelled, "Come *at* me, baby!" Men stood together, hands in pockets. Whores sat in bars. Sometimes when you came close to them, you saw that they were very very old. Other times they were still fresh, and laughed and danced as they dropped quarters into the video machines, and excitement effused from them in compounds of sweat and perfume. You could go out and step over the piss-puddles on the sidewalk and there would be more whores, dancing and waiting – but men always stood behind them, watching.

Geary Street

As you approached the Tenderloin at night you started getting a bad feeling, even while you were still on the edge of Union Square looking in the Macy's window, and a trolley-car went by and a billboard flashed and the well-dressed people clicked their heels steadily past on the wide sidewalk, as if they were telling rosary beads. – "I *love* this square here!" beamed a frosty-haired old gentleman, and his dowager said, "The *air* is so clear!"

Going In

On O'Farrell a block away from Dino's it was quite empty and yellow-lit at the front of the Bohemian Parking Garage, but the sidewalks remained in good repair. Two skinheads sat airily, getting their boots shined by a black man. – "I *like* him," they laughed. "What's your name, hey, Sambo?" – If you turned down Taylor past a huge construction site (the sign said that someday it would be the biggest convention hotel on the west coast) and traversed the lobby-window of another big hotel (and a policeman walked by), you found yourself at Ellis Street across from the Airporter bus terminal. You turned right. All at once the sidewalk had cracks in it, and there was a stinking puddle and everyone coming out of the Airporter terminal was walking the other way.[5]

Amusing Scenes

Two men in business suits were arguing outside the Korean cabaret on Eddy Street. – "You don't grab me that way!" said one. "You grab me this way! Remember, I *own* this place."

On Ellis Street a man stood beside his ruined car, historicizing with a policeman.

5 I sometimes took a pistol to the Tenderloin, in regretful disrespect of local law, feeling the elastic of the holster stretch between my shoulderblades like some new muscle, while the gun hung down heavily from my armpit, working its coldness through my shirt so that my side was chilled. I was always very conscious of the barrel against my hip when I sat down. The gun did not have a safety. If it were ever to go off, the bullet would shatter my hip. Even so, I never regretted having the gun along. It was night, and I was alone, and walking in the Tenderloin by myself I always felt my heart beating fast, because it was a place whose laws had claws. Once a pimp held a knife to my throat. But I endured this smiling, because I had my gun waiting. How strange, when that doctor might have cured me of my life with a radical tracheotomy before the gun could possibly prevent the operation! But placebos are comforts, and the gun *was* a comfort to me. Having the gun may in fact have been prudent when I was by myself, proceeding from red light to red light in the darkness between Turk Street and Geary Street. Two men once told me that they were going to hurt me, and I showed them my gun, and they became polite. But my gun was a liability on the streetcar, or in a restaurant. So sometimes I did not bring it, but then I felt anxious. – Was carrying it good or bad, then? – You tell me.

"Far as I can see," said the cop, "first he smashed into your hood."

"No," said the man patiently. "First he hit me over the head."

At the Lamp Post

Starr was dancing on the corner of Leavenworth and Ellis. "Let 'em come *at* me!" she cried. "Oh, I'm READY! Let 'em come *at* me!"

"What's life like out here?" I wanted to know. Oh, the things I wanted to know!

"It's the pits, believe me," she said. She kept swinging her purse against the darkness. The yellow lights upheld her face very steadily, but the red lights cycled her through a thousand flickering blushes. Her face was lovely. She wore a pink tank top that was a window for her nipples to watch me warily. "I gotta do something," she remarked, "specially when I get drunk. When I get drunk, I get crazy. I gotta find something *out* about certain people. They been *following* me. Pretty soon they're gonna show me some I.D., I know it. But I don't care about goin' to jail. I don't care about anything anymore. You know, they got the nerve to come into the Welfare Office and act like they're workin' there. They come into my mother-in-law's house in Park Merced and have absolutely no business."

"Starr, can I buy you a beer?" I said.

"I already got one, right in that paper bag on that newspaper machine. See, I *know* where things are. That's how I know where they're gonna slip. When I come up here and do my business, I'm gonna set a *trap* for 'em."

"What kind of trap?"

"One that they're gonna fall *into*."

How she kept dancing and dancing on the sidewalk! Her high heels tapped upon the concrete with the rapidity of Scarlatti's legendary fingers ("Then I thought," said one of his nonplussed sonata-contemporaries, "that ten hundred devils were in the instrument!"), and the glare of the street-lamps gave her colors the bright sick luxuriance of glow-fungi in that cold toilsome forest of darkness all around her that sighed through its steel gratings and shattered windows. Starr was certainly very bold in her loveliness. – At first I thought that she was dancing to please herself, unlike the strippers at Dino's, but then I remembered that she, too, had to do it. Neither was she pleased. The world rubbed her the wrong way that night, like a lover with sandpaper hands, so that her dance was a ballet of nervous irritability, which must go on until exhaustion disposed of her. Once she ran across the street, and I did not think to see her again, but then she came back to dance again. – "Come *at* me!" she screamed. – A long, ancient station wagon full of men came slowly up the street, and a man on the passenger side rolled down the window and crooked a finger at her. – "*Fuck off!*" she yelled. – "I can't *stand* niggers," she confided. (But Starr herself was black.) "I can't *stand* black motherfuckers. I just told them punks so, too. I *told* them. I'm gonna get one tonight. I'm gonna get one. I'm gonna tear it up. I'm waitin' for the right one, the one I know. That's the one I'm gonna bust."

The Longshoreman's Footnote

"Just their way of makin' MONEY, man," said a chubby and smiling longshoreman who liked to lean against fire hydrants. "As long as they don't do wrong, I'm for 'em. The worst thing that ever happened to me is that once I got a bitch and paid fifty bucks for her, and she took me to her pimp's house. I guess she was new; she didn't know she wasn't supposed to do that. There was drugs and stuff all over. He came running in and started shootin' at me. I got out of there; I was *gone*. I bet he slapped her around a little. When a bitch does wrong, her man's gotta beat her around a little." (Two whores in earshot nodded their agreement with this aphorism.)

"That don't faze me," Starr said. "I been shot at before. I seen people get they head smashed in with *hammers*. I seen switchblades all covered with *blood*. I know some people who want to bust me in the head, but I be ready. I be READY."

A Benchmark Question

"What's the most interesting thing that ever happened to you?" I said.

"Nothing," Starr said.

A Happy Couple

The next day was a Friday, and action began as early as three-thirty in the afternoon among the sullen uneasy rush of Tenderloin people with downcast heads and closed dirty faces. (According to my friend "Christina," you could get customers twenty-four hours a day.[6]

"So, shall we walk or shall we take a cab?" said the foreign-looking spectacled girl in a very earnest way, as if she were reading the phrase out of a guidebook.

"We're gonna walk," the man said. "What's your name?"

She whispered it into his ear. "What's *your* name?"

"I can't say," he said.

"What do you mean, you can't say?" she said, but he said nothing, so the whore just laughed. "You know," she said, "I never drink nothing and yet I am so drunk."

The Missing Link (A Police Anecdote)

Once upon a time, a man picked up a woman who wasn't a woman. He drove her down to Division and Potrero to ball her. It was then that he discovered she wasn't a woman. He took a knife and cut the impostor's

---

6 As a pleasure factory, Christina offered a number of options to the serious investor, for she had not only a VAGINA ($40.00 minimum), but also a MOUTH ($20.00), and she had small brown HANDS which could be rented more cheaply still ($15.00). How convenient Christina could be to use! Men enjoyed thrusting their penises inside her, and Christina, although she did not enjoy being thrust into, spread her legs peacefully because, as Calvin Coolidge told us in 1923, "Economy is always a guarantee of peace."

cock off – *swisssssh!* He threw the bloody cock out the window. The impostor went to the Emergency Room. A sadistically humorous doctor told her that if she could find her cock he would sew it back on for her. She wandered the dark street for hours looking for it.

Four-o'-Clock

In Boedekker Park (Ellis and Jones), three boys were having a discussion. You could see them drop their shoulders and stiffen their step before it happened – "I'm not scared of you," said the white boy. "A-rab!" – The yellow boy wanted to cry, but he would not. The black boy was his friend, and stood beside him. He spat at the white boy. "Fuck you, you big fat honky turtle!" – "Shut up, man!" lisped the white boy. He was six or seven. "You want your *head* fucked up, man?" He was holding an empty rum bottle. "Shit," he said. "I guess you want your *head* fucked up!" He smashed the bottle expertly, so that it became a weapon. The black boy put his arm around the Vietnamese boy and they walked away, whispering. The white boy stood glaring after.

Five-o'-Clock

It was late afternoon in the park now. Shadows crept across the still bodies of the drunks, advancing so slowly, so reverently, as if they *must* increase but hated to disturb anyone. The drunks did not appear to be disturbed, because they did not appear to be breathing. But if you watched these prone bodies long enough, you might see their feet begin to twitch as they lay there in the urine-smelling grass. The air was cool. The sun had sunk almost to the tops of the yellow brick buildings.

Six-o'-Clock

This was the time when Boedekker Park began to clear out, in preparation for the more serious business of the night. On Jones Street the wastebasket said TRUST IN JESUS, but around the corner on Turk Street the sign on the bar said LOCKED BATHROOMS INSIDE. As the light failed, people started going home, slamming the security grilles behind them. If you didn't want to go home, it was a five-minute walk down Turk Street to a place where you could play the video game "Commando," wearing your camouflage raincoat, and you could stand in the nude arcade next to where it said DILDOES and play an electronic poker game to strip the video woman of your choice if you got a good hand; and if you had a bad hand she'd say, "*Ohhh*, don't go away," and kiss her hand to you lovingly before her image would flicker and freeze.

Birth of the Night

On a chilly autumn night the blue lights washed white cars blue, and the red lights pinkened them. A man with matted reddish waist-length hair bowed in a doorway sleeping; one of his legs was gone. It was not quite eight-o'-clock.

One side of Ellis Street was lit and one wasn't. No one was walking down the dark side. I crossed to the dark side and started walking past the deep dark doorways and the mounds of garbage bags. It was very cold and dark. Cars rolled by slowly. Sometimes there were men parked in long white cars who sat smoking and watching the street.

A man was walking behind me. I leaned into a doorway and watched him come. He slowed and approached me, but continued on past. Although he did not look back, I knew that he was keeping track of me. The stores were closed, and their steel shutters were down. At the next corner there was a fat white hooker standing outside a bar; a black man leaned against the wall beside her. I did not talk to her. Since it was still early, I went to a Vietnamese restaurant and stared for a long time into the shimmering moon of my fishbowl soup in its bowl. Then I went out.

On O'Farrell and Mason a white woman and a Hispanic woman were standing on the corner together. – "I don't want to go out tonight," the white woman said, so feebly as to wring my heart. – "*Bitch!*" yelled the Hispanic woman. "*Shut up and start making him money!*"

Company

"Hello, Starr," said a Chicana whore cheerily. She had gap-teeth, and a sad face like old wood.

"Hi, baby, how ya doin'?" Starr did not stop dancing.

"Listen, Starr," said her friend excitedly. "I went to see Jimmy. He gimme the money. I took a hundred dollars from him."

Another carful of men had pulled up. Starr's friend shook her head. "I don't like the looks of it." Stonily they ignored the car until it drove off, the men yelling threats and sick sad promises.

A prostitute came by, walking two little poodles on a leash whose coiffeur matched her own. – "Nice puppies," a drunk said, trying very hard to pat them, but something in the air came between him and the puppies, so that he could not bend over, and he walked in a spiral instead. Finally, not being exceptionally sensitive to traffic, he walked out into the middle of the street, thought deeply, and took a moody piss. A car honked. Another car swerved. – "Last night," said the longshoreman with a laugh, "there was one just like him. A block up the street. Car came along and squashed him flat. Oh, he was dead, all right. I'm telling you."

"He's not drunk," Starr said. "He's one of them that wants something, I'm telling *you*."

The Most Delicate Girl

Now here came Francisco, a male prostitute from Polk Street who had great big bubbles in the flesh of his swollen cheeks where exotic and erotic diseases presumably incubated. – "Life's been a *trip*," he sighed. "I been doing this since I been fourteen years old. I'm twenty-eight now."

"What's the hardest thing for you?" I said.

"The police."

"What do you do to get them to leave you alone?"

He looked at me pointedly. "I mind my own business."

"Where's my beer, girl?" the Chicana hooker said to him. "Where's my beer, baby?"

"I forgot it," he sighed. "I've had *such* a rough day! You see, I did all the way over here to the Tenderloin. Life's just been so busy. My parents never loved me, 'cause I was a gay person. Now I have to beg for love . . . You're not gay, are you?"

"No," I admitted.

"Too bad."

"How did you get in the business?" I asked Starr's friend.

"Baby," she said, "it just hurt me if I talk about it."

They all put their arms around each other, with Francisco in the middle, and went laughing down the street. They were going to Starr's place to have a drink. Because the darkness was so quiet, I could hear them for almost as long as I could see the lights flashing on their shoulders. Francisco was smiling and leaning on them. Whenever they called him "girl," he smiled for joy. He seemed to be the most delicate of them – their daughter, their sister. The trusting way that he rested his head on Starr's shoulder was sweet to see. He was weary; he was pale; he was not well, and Starr knew it. He could barely put one foot after the other. – "Come on now, sweetie," she said to him. "I'm helping you."

Big Al's

In North Beach, of course, it was FLEET WEEK! Our Navy was preparing to conquer the world. On Columbus and Broadway early on a Saturday evening, the sailors nodded white-capped heads at each other uneasily, walked up and down the sidewalk in threes and sevens, and their penises, exerting as yet a merely flaccid tyranny, impelled them to queue before The Original World Famous BIG AL'S (Totally Nude Girls On Stage); and a girl in a very low-cut black outfit emerged into the doorway and stood dancing and spreading her arms and slapping her bare legs together and playing with her belt and continually brushing herself off as if she had gotten half-drowned in pollen; so that soon the penises had become somewhat interested and Big Al's had filled with sailors to capacity and the girl was compelled to draw a velvet rope across the door and stand behind it drinking a Coke and tapping her foot to the music and shooing the new sailors away. They marched dejectedly around the corner like a squadron of blue-black crows. More sailors stood on the curb grinning, with their hands in their pockets. Next door, only one of the Condor's tits was blinking. The sailors started waving and yelling at the women in passing cars. They began to press around the doorway of Big Al's again, and the girl in black waved them off. When they were gone, she resumed her dancing, so dreamy and happy by herself, until a barefoot girl in a long loose red robe came to stand beside her. (She could become one of the Totally Nude Girls at a moment's notice.) At once a dozen sailors crossed the street, yelling, "Hey!", and gathered around them. This time the girl in black took their money and let them in. The girl in red withdrew behind the red curtain with the sailors. The girl in black drew the velvet rope across the doorway for a moment, went behind the red curtain, and returned counting her money and dancing. – Here came another formation of ten sailors lining up as attentively and earnestly as schoolboys.

It was evening. A woman was still sitting at her typewriter in the office above City Lights Books, and the sky was purplish-red, and the cars were so densely crystallized on Broadway that you could pick your way between them and cross the street wherever you liked. (But the sailors, being men of order, marched on the crosswalks.) Other people went about their business, walking up Columbus, while the sailors stood in their compact cautious squads. The Museum Café beckoned drinkers wanly; it was a place where everyone fell over themselves to introduce you to some poet who was the new Bob Dylan, although you had never heard him sing. As darkness fell, the Museum Café faded into the ranks of the outclassed, and the red lights became dominant. The black words **TOTALLY NUDE** cut into the bloody tissue of the red sign, and the red words **LIVE SEDUCTION** bled from the black sign. The sailors swarmed on the sidewalks. Sometimes there were so many, like ants on banana bread, that the girl in black got sick of them and stepped out past the velvet rope to shake her fist at them.

As you walked toward the Tenderloin, the current of sailors dwindled, sucked into pinball parlors and underground massage joints. Another block, and there were no sailors at all. Another block, and you saw the first crutch-people and door-sleepers. In the Tenderloin it was very dark and very very quiet.

The Bosses

We all have to go down sometime. In the streets leaned the men who had already gone down. Late one night I saw a black woman waiting against the lamp-post on the corner of Turk and Leavenworth.[7] Across the street, eight black men leaned. The prostitute smiled at me with come-on sweetness, and I would have talked to her, but I did not like the way that the men were looking me over, so I decided to cross the street and walk past them and look at them without seeming to look at *them*, and as I came toward them they kept looking at me, and one of them said, "Should we get 'im?", and they all reached into their pockets. But this was only to scare me, because they let me keep walking. I sometimes saw black men breaking bottles on the sidewalk there, after the midnight police sweep. They took long pieces of broken glass and shook them at their women. "Make me some money, you fucking black whores!" they yelled. "Work your black nigger asses!"

---

7 Brandi never stood on corners because that was the best way to get busted. She just walked up and down the street, asking for spare change, selling drugs, selling herself. "And, honey," she said, "I take the *first* thing that comes around."

A Chat Between Friends

One hot afternoon in Boedekker Park, two black men were talking quietly by the trash can.

"He had his hair braided," said the man with the boxcutter. "He took me all the way to the fourth floor. Then I didn't see him. I waited for him till one-thirty. I'm gonna get the boys together and kick his ass."

"Well," said the other, "everybody's got his own set of rules."

"I'll get a hundred dollars. Then we'll deal with him. I'll point him out to you when I see him again. Sound like a winner?"

"You're real hard," the other sighed. "You're real intense."

"I see you around. I'll be down here at around six. You know where number ** Turk is? Go down to the bar. You'll take care of this for me?"

"Yeah, fine. Don't worry."

Somebody else started coming over, but a woman caught his sleeve and said, "Leave 'im *alone* while he's doin' his job!"

More of the Same

It was hot. The guys sat reading in the park, wearing cool sunglasses under big-brimmed hats. They wore yellow shirts and red caps, blue shirts and green caps. It seemed that the flies were bigger and shinier here than anywhere else in the world. The kids walked by and said, "Oooh," at the flies. The men were walking slowly in the sun, coming up to each other's benches to ask hey how ya doin', and *man* you know what Charlie did? Her old man stole all the food out of the refrigerator, so she knocked him down and gave him a black eye. She a big chick, man.

It soon became apparent to me that the proper way to sit on the benches was with a squint. That was the first thing I learned. The next thing was the silence behind everything. The days seemed to go on and on in great meaningless angles of sunshine as the drunks snored and the brickwork of the park got hotter and hotter and stank, and the flies

crawled very thoughtfully in new and old puke; and yet when night
came to the Tenderloin and it took on its erotic and threatening aspect,
it seemed then as if it always had been and must be night, although
once a long time ago there might have been a tiny slice of afternoon;
because while the passage of time was slow in the day, it left little
residue of memory behind it, whereas after dark it was necessary to be
very very alert, and the memory of ten minutes was like the memory of
an hour. And yet when the sun came back the next day, everything was
slow and sad and decayed; the dead bones must sleep before they could
reassemble themselves for the next Danse Macabre.

Two of the men sat on a bench, quietly discussing the trade.

"I like your Miss Bitty Pants," said one.

"Yeah," said the other smugly. "I got her 'cause I heard she be more
controllable."

They looked over at me, and I looked very hard at the ground for a
quarter of an hour. (Of course they had dark sunglasses and I did not.
That was part of their power.)

A Good Story

On O'Farrell and Leavenworth a young black woman was standing on
the corner with two black men. I looked her up and down and started
walking on. – "There's one," said her instructor. I kept my head bowed.
Presently I saw her shadow on the sidewalk to the left of me, keeping
step with me. – I raised my head then and looked at her. "Do you want
to make some money?" I said.

"Sure," she said bitterly.

"What's your name?"

"Sugar."

"I'll give you five dollars to talk to you."

"You're just going to talk? Is that how you get off?"

"I write down people's stories," I said. "That's what I do."

"I'll do it for ten dollars," she said.

We settled on eight and ducked into a doorway. She was shivering in
her flimsy black dress. I gave her my coat. – "Give me the money," she
said. – I gave it to her immediately, because it is a fine experiment to
make, upon making acquaintance of a street-woman, to test her

decency, and see what she will do when she has your money – whether she will feel any obligation to give you your money's worth. (This is, after all, how we judge everyone else: why not prostitutes?) – As soon as Sugar had received my money, the rainwater of her friendliness drained magically into her deep dark sewers, and she let her contempt for me begin to show.

"I don't really do that," she said. "I'm a rock singer. I've always been a singer. I started playing piano when I was a kid. I was into entertaining."

"So what are you doing down in the Tenderloin? And why did you take my money?"

"I'm broke," Sugar said shrugging. "I'm tryin' to help the homeless. I came down here, and I ran into some musicians."

"Tell me a story."

"A poor homeless singer goes out and finds a band and becomes a great rock star," Sugar said, smiling sarcastically.

A man came by and nodded to us and started pissing against the side of a dumpster.

"What do you think about pimps?"

"I don't know anything about them. But if I did, I sure wouldn't give my money to any pimp."

"Is that right?" I said.

"Who are you?" she said, but just then her pimp stepped into our doorway and looked at her very very quietly. "I've got to go now," she said in a scared voice.

I talked with the pimp for a minute. – "And what do you do?" I said.

"I SURVIVE," the man said.[8]

Pimp Ecology

I cannot say that I like these fellows, but I must admire them for having established their niche, which must be as cozy as a cave in some surf-washed precipice. – What do they survive *on*? – Why, their whores.[9] –

8 This information, if I may recapitulate, cost me eight dollars.
9 The undercover cop whom I call Henry estimates that at least eighty percent of the streetwalkers here have pimps.

And what form of sea-life is it that nourishes the whores? None other than

Mr. Penis

Here is a man whom we may as well call Mr. Penis, for he is guided, instructed, dominated and managed by that organ. He may wake up with the hangover chills, so nauseated that he can barely draw breath through his dried-out mouth – and yet, though he is no stoic, almost cordially does he endure these miseries, which are unalleviable save by time and more alcohol, neither of which he has by his bed. It is a rainy foggy morning, and he is a day older than he was yesterday, and yet he is content, for between his legs is an organ of engrossing length and diameter, throbbing hard by his belly. If it did not exist, where would whores be? Raising the sheets, he studies this remarkable Penis, his self, whose vertical slot gives its glans the appearance of an Olympus OM-2 camera's battery cap, which may be screwed on or off with a coin. The Penis shrinks, so that the man is now permitted to count a greater number of his belly-hairs, but the *need* does not correspondingly diminish, and that is the source of Mr. Penis's joy, for this throbbing of desire which plays up and down its hard shaft, like a flutist's skilled fingers, is already a species of pleasure, being utterly unlike so many other cravings, such as loneliness and thirst, which plague our race with ugly desperation. The demands of that great Penis, while no less insistent, nevertheless convey their own sense of enablement, for the man who has the ability to assuage them at once with a few artful rubbings, squeezes, and jerks ("Making love to yourself," sighed Sheet-Rock Jake over his seventeenth can of Black Label, "is making love to the one person who's never going to betray you or leave you . . .") – and if Mr. Penis does not do that, it is because he is playing the only rewarding game in the whole casino of ascetic discipline: self-denial in the service of self-gratification. It would be all too easy for poor sick old Mr. Penis to take the easy way out afforded by curling palm and fingers, but no! he is a lofty strategist, intent on plundering the flesh of another, and though the Penis swells and chills itself with menthol-like radiations of need, though it then teases him with heated tingle-tricks, though it changes texture in a thousand insistent ways, the man resists, as if he were now doing what he is going to do later, slowing his thrusts and effecting a partial strategic withdrawal in order to prolong the sensation. To help him remain firm in his resolve, Mr. Penis has the acquisitive pleasure-in-advance of the collector. Who knows what china cup he will soon be stirring his tea in? He takes infinite refreshment from the newness of a face, of flesh. So for Mr. Penis the entire day is his foreplay as he cruises like a battleship through the slow liquid hours, his hard prow steering him into the red seas of night.

This is truly a noble picture, and yet one might ask why Mr. Penis does not use his hand now and his money later, since foreplay, if extended too long, is just another word for torture – and here we have to let out one of Mr. Penis's shameful secrets. He does not have an unlimited ability to come! In his youth, perhaps, he could groan out a half-teaspoon of fluid half a dozen times in the course of a Saturday, but now his powers are on the wane. Another humiliation for Mr. Penis, though he does not admit it, is that he must pay his whores instead of overpowering them with his own astounding Penis-self so that they do it for love and worship of him.

Fortunately, however, there is such a thing as a Penis Brotherhood, in which the Mr. Penises of this world (and there are really quite a few of them) roll onto each other the condoms of rationalization, thereby protecting themselves from the disease of self-disesteem (at the price of a loss in fine sensitivity). – "I paid a hundred and thirty bucks for a tasty cunt last night," I heard one Mr. Penis say. "The way I look at it, it's just like getting my laundry done."

A Thought

"And for Lust," says Hobbes, "what it wants in the lasting, it hath in the vehemence, which sufficeth to weigh down the apprehension of all easie, or uncertain punishment" (Lev., II.27.155).

Mr. Penis's Thoughts Before Taking a Whore

Despite the Penis Brotherhood, each Mr. Penis remains, at times, a self-pitying sort of fellow, and if you follow him down to the Tenderloin on a dark winter night, he may tell you that there is nobody who loves him – nobody! His wife has left him and his girl is away from town and he has just gotten out of prison, so that there is nobody who will be home for him when he calls late at night, and in general there is nobody that Mr. Penis can talk to, which implies that there can be nobody who will tell him that he is good (poor Mr. Penis! Is it his fault that he was born a Penis?), nobody who will warm him and kiss him, nobody who will let him love her in the way which only Mr. Penis can (because no one else has ever been Mr. Penis). Hence the porn theaters, hotels and liquor stores. The night is dark. He is so alone. There is nobody, nobody, nobody, nobody, nobody! – But quickly Mr. Penis pulls himself erect again and says that actually he is amusing himself; he is "showing her" and all the other bitches.

(What an emptiness Mr. Penis must look forward to! Why is there no one to be loyal to him? Nobody? Nobody?)

A Note Written on a Guest Check and Delivered to Me at the Tu-Lan Restaurant on Sixth Street[10]

10 The Hotel Canada was ugly. When you pushed open the dirty wooden door, how it stank! Then you could go up the stairs to a barred door with a window set in it, and behind the door was a glass cubicle within which two women regarded you and might or might not let you in to see Jamaika. Quite likely they would say, "She checked out this morning," and then if you said that she was still there they would say, "Jamaika? Who's she?", and then there would be no option but to go back down the stairs and exit through the dirty wooden door and be back on Sixth Street, where desperation was obliterated only by dullness, dullness by rain.

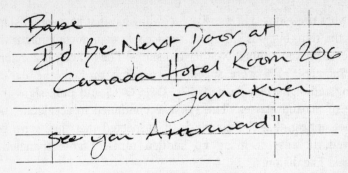

Babe
I'd Be Next Door at
Canada Hotel Room 206
Jamaika
See you Afterward [11]

The Other Side

But even as Mr. Penis spewed into the most lovely mouths and vaginas that money could buy, the Vice Squad was tracking him in unmarked cars. There was not too much that the Vice Squad could do about massage outcalls to a private residence, but they staked out hotels to which ambitious women were invited, and of course they watched and watched the Tenderloin streets. I was permitted to ride with two undercover cops, and here is what I saw.

On Her Tail

The policewoman was looking out the window intently. "There she is, getting into the car," she said. "A Porsche. Looks like an improvement over her last catch."

The Porsche pulled away ahead of us. It accelerated down the dark street.

"He's laughing. She's laughing. The two of them are *all excited*," said the policewoman wryly. "But they've got an escort." She sang a sort of triumph song: "We've GOT HER, GOT HER."

At the wheel, her partner smiled and shook his head. He had a

11 Jamaika was beautiful. A beautiful face can never be described. The colors of its self lie so far beyond this wretched visible spectrum in which I am usually confined that I can only write captions for missing paintings of whores' faces: pertness, anxiety, desperation, loneliness, hideousness – there they were, those faces, glowing in the red lights. There is often a certain coarseness or woodenness to a whore's face. This coarseness is accentuated by makeup, sometimes to the extent of making her seem a painted corpse. Yet Jamaika's face was still young, expressive, loving.

somewhat tired look. He was like a cowboy hat that had gotten stepped on in the rain, but was still more serviceable than anyone might think. He never missed a thing. Neither did she. – The police car accelerated into the night. We were speeding, speeding through the darkness, passing red signs that flashed GIRLS GIRLS GIRLS and pink signs in the shape of martini glasses. The Porsche continued to accelerate, but it did not appear that the couple in it suspected that they were being followed, because it made no sudden turns. Lights spangled the darkness like diatoms.

"There's a *lot* of girls out tonight," the policewoman said with satisfaction.

"Yeah," the cop said. He drove on.

"What we're doing now is *following*," the policewoman explained to me. "We saw someone that we know, a prostitute getting into a vehicle. So we're going to follow her, as I explained to you earlier. Eventually they'll get out."

"We'll find where they go and where they've parked," said the cop, "and that's how we find and gather INFORMATION. Now, she might go to a parking lot, she might go to an alley, she might go to Saint Mary's Cathedral and park just below the cathedral. You never know. She might take him to a hot tub. This is part of the game. This is part of the cat-and-mouse game."

On Sutter and Octavia, the Porsche stopped. The undercover car stopped, too, with the vacuous facility of any echo. I am not sure if I have made it clear how weary and wearying the whole thing was. The night was very quiet. It was a little after ten-o'-clock. Yellow security lights shone down the front of a white building whose windows were hung with elaborately ruffled curtains. Inside, a staircase descended and descended without moving a banister-muscle. The light made it seem more grand than it could possibly be. People moved inside the rooms of the place with the silent grace which is the due of those who are watched through glass, and the lights shone on and the night went on and presently the whore got out of the Porsche and so did the man, and she put her arm around him and took him into a courtyard on the other side of the street. The cops waited for a moment. They had to give the couple time to commence the illegal act, just as 'God had to let Eve and Adam each take a bite of the apple before He could punish them. How sad that those two could not know that if they did it they were going to be caught; they were simply going to do it and the cops were going to see them doing it. It would not be nice for anyone.

"Well, should I walk out there?" said the policewoman.

"Yeah, why don't you take a look," her partner said. "Turn off your radio so it doesn't make any noise. Walk up there and back."

She got out and closed the door. She did not seem nervous.

"How dangerous is this for her?" I asked.

"It's not dangerous at all," the cop said. "As long as I can see her. I can still see her head. She's just peering around the wall now. She's still there."

A minute went by.

"Can you wait here for a minute?" the cop said. He got out.

Their Prisoner

"Did I tell you my mother just got married?" said the whore enthusiastically, sitting on the back seat as the policewoman closed the door behind her.

"No, you didn't," the policewoman replied.

"Oh, it was *beautiful!* You should have been there. The wedding was in the back yard. I had my mother, and my mother and I had my brother as the best man. My older sister was the maid of honor. My little sister's five, and my daughter's five. I just came back tonight."

"Mmm hmm," said the policewoman. In the dark courtyard, her partner was checking Mr. Penis's wallet.

"So I got busted," said the whore. "No big thing. It's not exactly prostitution anyway. That guy I've known for four years."

"Yeah," said the policewoman.

"We're VERY good friends," said the whore. She had meaty features, and beer-breath came from her mouth. Her hair was slightly mussed. The police had allowed her to get dressed (if indeed she had undressed, for I never asked her what she and the man had been doing). Her eyes were so round and wide with makeup as to remind me of the silvery buttons on her shoes. Yet she was more than a doll, for a young, uncertain defiance animated her, although it might easily turn to tears. "So," she said to the policewoman, "as far as you and me, I'm not worried about this. You can just throw me in the back."

"You *are* in the back," said the policewoman logically. "Let's have the money."

"He took it! Henry just took all the money out of my pocket."

"Henry!" the policewoman called. "You took her money?"

"Yeah," said the cop.

"Actually," said the whore, with the air of one about to make a telling point in the intellectual debate of our times, "my point of view on the case is that if Mayor Dianne Feinstein can donate a quarter of a million dollars to the Vice Department to stop prostitution, I think you need to put it towards child molestation and everything else."

"We already have money towards that," said the policewoman.

"No, you don't!" the whore screamed. "*Horseshit!*"

"Yes, we do."

"*No*, you don't!"

The policewoman laughed gently. "Next time I see Dianne I'll talk to her about it."

"I *know*," said the whore determinedly, "'cause I've been on welfare. I've been on welfare till my daughter was four years old. And *no one* would help me with my kid. That's after being *beat* with a coat hanger."

True Confessions

"Could I have your first name again?" said the policewoman.

"Denise," said the whore. "That's D-E-N-I-S-E. And my address is — Avenue. I'm in the Sunset; I'm an Avenue girl."

"Can you run a subject for me, please?" said the policewoman into the radio.

"*Half* my money is in that *money* you took, okay?" said the whore, anxious to make the policewoman appreciate the magnitude of her sacrifice. "I'm just *sorry* about that money, okay?"

"Last name LOPEZ," said the policewoman steadily. "Leonard, Open, Paul, Edward, Zebra. First name DENISE. David, Edward, Nora, Ida, Sam, Edward. She's a WF, DOB 2–17–63. Copy?"

Various Things That Happened to Denise

"So," my seat-companion said to me, smiling sweetly. "What are you writing for?"

"I'm writing a bunch of stories."

"Okay, lemme tell you something. Your father rapes you from three to eleven, and the only thing you know is that you have a hatred of men, and then somewhere along the line you get kicked out of the house because your stepfather cannot acknowledge you, and five years later you accept him as your father because he accepts you as his daughter, and between that time you've been a pimped prostitute, fucked up on drugs. And then you *quit* it and you have a daughter and you're doing FINE."

"Everything's fine?" I said.

"Me and my family are *very* fine. *As* a matter of FACT. They accept me for who they love, not for what I do."

"So how did you get started in prostitution?"

"Well, you walk down the street on San Pablo, and like five pimps grab you and kidnap you. And keep you till the only thing you know what to do is become a prostitute."

"What's the best thing and the worst thing that's ever happened to you?" I said.

"The worst thing that's ever happened to me? It happened about two weeks ago, when this guy I got off beat me up and robbed me of two hundred and seventy-five dollars. The best thing that ever happened to me was giving birth to a six-pound, eight-ounce baby daughter. And that is my LIFE. And if anybody asks me who I pimp for, I will tell you the truth; it is my daughter; and I *bust my ass* to put her through school, and I *love* her. And I'm sorry, but this is the only thing I know." Her lip began to tremble. "I've been *cheated*, and I've been *robbed* of MY LIFE, and I am *tired* of it. And I do *not* want to cry, but I just got done going through this with my family. I am *tired* of it. And I don't want to go through with it *no more*."

Transportation of the Criminal

Henry got back in the car and turned the key in the ignition. "I don't know how much is there," he said. "I just grabbed what she had in her pocket."

"A hundred forty," said the policewoman. She turned to Denise. "Here's the eight dollars that you had," she said, "and here's the forty dollars that we have for evidence."

"So you're going to prosecute him, right?" Denise said. "You're going to press charges against him?"

"Him?" said Henry. "He got arrested just like you did. But he only got cited, since he had identification and he'd never been arrested before."

"Well, I've been arrested since I was sixteen," said Denise proudly. "And he don't even know who the hell I am."

"You know how it is with prostitution," said Henry, shrugging. "The girl goes to jail; the guy gets cited on the first offense."

"Oh, *right*," she said bitterly.

Henry had heard it all before. "You know the situation," he said, looking at her mildly in the rear-view mirror. "You got caught DIRTY. You were doin' DIRTY."

"Okay, okay, okay, *okay*," she said. "You taking me to 850 Bryant?"

"No, I'm taking you to Northern. You'll like it there."

"A lot of goodlooking guys there," said the policewoman, laughing.

"They'll be after my daughter soon," Denise said. "She'll be growing up one of these days. I'll be standing at the door with a shotgun when the guys come to take my daughter out. 'I know what you *want!*' I'll say."

"Talk about the pot calling the kettle black," said Henry. "Come on, now, Mom. She'll be a big girl one of these days."

"Not like me she won't," the whore said.

"She's not going to be like you?"

"You know what? I would rather *die* and *burn in Hell* before my daughter would ever be anything like me. And that's the honest to God truth."

"I'm sure it is," said Henry contentedly. "Just remember the game. Tonight you got caught."

"So what?" she said.

Henry and the policewoman didn't say anything. They had probably heard that before, too.

"Henry, why don't you answer me? You *are* a perfect asshole," Denise said.

"You know something?" said Henry solemnly. "I got hemmorhoids, so I'm not even a perfect asshole."

Everybody laughed and went to jail.

Consolation

Happily for Mr. Penis, who must undergo so many perils in the pursuit of his needful avocation, it was perfectly legal to drop in at the Palladium, another black closet rental outfit, where you went into a booth where there was a hopeful sign informing you that you could place up to five quarters in at any one time, and if you put just one in, to see what would happen, a little shutter flew up and you would see a roomful of fat bored naked women who would peer at you for a second to see if you would give them a tip to diddle themselves, *ooh! aah!* but if you didn't look to be that kind of sailor they'd give up and go back to bending over, scratching their fat bored naked asses. After about twenty seconds, the shutter fell. You had, of course, made a terrible mistake. If you had put the five quarters in, you would have had a *quality* time.[12]

A Cautionary Tale

I must, however, pass on to you a warning about another kind of temptation. Maybe, like Axel or Axelrod or whoever the hell the intrepid nephew was in Jules Verne, you wished to visit the center of the earth – that is to say, an Oriental massage parlor, which required you to go down a long dim dirty flight of stairs that brought you to a dark door

12 This information cost me twenty-five cents.

with a sign that said OPEN – RING BELL; and if you rang the bell a Chinese woman would come to the door and say it cost thirty dollars – so far, so good – but if you had less she would fly into a rage and begin screaming at you through the closed door, for she did not appreciate having her time wasted; so perhaps in your ignorance you might go round the corner to try the next Oriental massage place, which might be cheaper, so you went down the stairs and got buzzed into a reception corridor, but then the same woman would come screaming in a silly witchy voice, "I *told* you it's thirty dollars, so *whaiieeeee* you come ringing my back door?!"

Back at the Harem

Suitably warned, Mr. Penis is now preparing to satisfy his need for

A Blowjob

Now, here is a question that every man must consider: Is it impolite not to be HARD when you unzip your fly? If you are HARD, then maybe you can use your hand and you do not need a blowjob, which, after all, is a *service* that you are *paying* for. On the other hand, if you are not HARD, then maybe the prostitute will *scorn* you, and that will not do, either. – Yes, you must consider the issue from both sides, and when you are satisfied it is a simple matter to let a whore take you between two cars in the parking lot on Larkin and Golden Gate, and you face prudently away from the street and she kneels down and unzips your fly and puts her mouth to work and you slap her hand away when she tries to pick your pocket, and you cannot really see her face because she is looking straight at your belly, thinking no doubt thoughts which would surprise you, and after a few minutes it is all over and when she takes her mouth away you discover that sometime before you came she rolled a rubber on with her tongue and you never even felt it.[13]

---

13 This revelation cost me twenty dollars.

Meanwhile, in the Orinda Hills

"Everyone loved my pie," Martin's mother explained. "I don't know why I went to the trouble of making it, because I was supposed *not* to work.

"Diane, try a piece of your mother's pie," said Martin's father.

The Facts on Tina[14]

"Mr. Vollmann," said the police, "do you know that there's NO DRINKING IN THE PARK?"

"Oh," I said, my wallet shamefully open to expose my picture I.D. to their careful perusal, as if they had made me unzip my fly.

"Were you drinking in the Park, Mr. Vollmann?"

"No," I lied decisively.

"Tina," said the police, "have you been arrested before in San Francisco?"

"Yes," said Tina with dignity. (Of course since she was not Tina at all the police could not find anything out about her, because she did not want to change her name before my eyes.)

"What for?"

"All *kinds* of things."

"What things?"

"*Well*, there was *drunkenness*."

"What else?"

"A long time ago, *prostitution*. But I done my time. I think I can say," she put it modestly, "that I been to bed with a number of gentlemen."

"Anything else?"

14 Tina, who had two gold nose-rings, was a big black woman who was not quite thirty and liked to drink in the sun. As a matter of fact, her name was Terri, not Tina, but I was looking for a black woman named Tina whom I had never met, and Terri was wandering somewhat aimlessly by the park bench where I was supposed to meet Tina, so I went up to her and said, "Tina?" and she nodded cautiously, so I said, "If you tell me a few stories, I'll buy you lunch," and Terri decided that she might as well be Tina if she could get lunch for it, so that is what I will call her in relating her stories.

"Well, I been to prison for murder, which I *surely* didn't commit, and strong-arm robbery, which I *did*. I done my time, and that's all you care about, checking me out in that radio, but I'll tell you officers, though, that that robbery was a *drag*. I had a great *big* gun, and I told this other black girl to tie them up, but not too tight, because I didn't want to hurt them, so they got loose. I ran into an alley, but they caught me in half a *blink*. They pressed charges against the other nigger, but not against me, because I wasn't the one that tied them up. I guess they figured I was just *set up* or something."

And now that the police are satisfied, let us continue with Tina's stories.

The Hatchet

Once upon a time, a woman called someone a motherfucker. He didn't want no bitch to tell him kiss *her* ass, so he slapped her. She went and got a hatchet. Tina was living in the same house. She was surprised at the bitch because *she* wouldn't never even *think* about using a hatchet; her reaction would be to defend herself with her hands. It was sure pointless; the bitch was doing all right; she had been getting social security, some kinda *blind* aid, food stamps and general assistance, too – at two different addresses. But this bitch already had a tendency; she had a *violent violent* record. She took her hatchet and cut him on the back of the head. When the police came, she came to the door with no panties on, just bareass naked. She got out of bed like she was getting *pussy*-sucked. I guess she hoped to get those police-dicks hard, but there wasn't *nothing* pretty about *that*. When Tina put on her swim-suit she looked *fine;* she didn't have any stretch-marks, but *this* bitch, her body looked like it had been cut up and *abused*. Tina took a pair of panties to the jail and she told the sheriff that the bitch had gone to prison with no panties on. The sheriff told the bitch she'd better put them fucking panties on right now or they were going to force them on her. So she put them on. When she went to court it was already set up. To Tina's way of thinking the district attorney and the public defender were one and the same anyhow. They told Tina, "Don't go up there and perjure yourself." So she told them what happened. They were all sick of the bitch. The judge said, "I'll see you upstairs in Felony Court.

You're coming with me to Superior Court." He said it wasn't her first time, it wasn't her second time, it wasn't her third time and it wasn't her fourth time. He gave her nine months, so she did the nine. She couldn't blame Tina, because Tina couldn't be *perjuring* herself. Anyhow, they'd fucking subpoenaed everybody in that goddamned house. Didn't the bitch know her brother Cleveland that works on the motherfucking police force? Every day, the police would be sure to come to that house with their guns out. It was the kind of house where one of these days the landlord was gonna set it on fire. They had a kitchen with communal cooking. Communal my ass. Because I don't have no food today, I'm gonna be your best friend. That's the kind of cooking it was. Once Tina cooked some chitlins and the whole house went crazy over them and Tina said, "Why not invite the police over for dinner and save yourself a trip?"

Leila and the Knife

Leila was down there full of *lying* and *lying*, because Tina guessed it was for her business. You see, she was after Gypsy, whom Tina at least knew enough not to mess with because Gypsy had that FLAMINGO-GREY hair, but Gypsy had a lot of Social Security back pay coming so Leila wanted to be his woman (at least until the money ran out), so she dyed her hair red and got her nose pierced. This was a *performance*. She jumped out of her Cadillac with a *nothing* kind of blade, just a butter knife, and came up to Tina, but Tina had a gold-plated switchblade, and she whipped it out 'cause she wasn't afraid of *nothing*. They was all sayin' to Tina, "Don't cut the bitch; she's from the Projects." But did Tina leave her alone in her motherfucking Projects? Maybe she did and maybe she *didn't*. Later on, Gypsy's Cadillac broke down, so he *said*. Tina said that if she were him she'd just put it somewhere deep inside and go back to walking. That way he'd always have it for security. More likely, he wanted to see if it was him that Leila wanted, or if it was the money and the car. Well, Gypsy had his money in his shoe, because he said if a nigger ever whipped his motherfucking ass he wouldn't take his shoes. He certainly didn't want to keep it at home. All his kids, they'd just steal and steal. And Leila the bitch stole a hundred motherfucking dollars from him. She was just smoking the pipe all the time; she was just on the pipe. She be slick. All those kids of Gypsy's, they'd move in with ladies and have their homes and their cars. The first thing they'd go for with Leila, they'd expect her to go for their money while they went for her ass. Gypsy started testing her. Since he'd given her so much money, he wanted to see if she'd give him any. He'd borrow money from her and then if she gave it to him he'd be satisfied and give it right back. She didn't know it, but she was getting her fucking *soul* searched. She yelled at him, "You don't borrow no motherfucking money from me and give it right back!" She didn't like that. But he *knew* her.

Tina's Rules of Life

1. If you know a person, you *know* them.

2. If you're out with folks and you don't talk, they're not gonna trust you. You gonna get *shot;* you gonna get cut up over *bullshit.*

3. When a man gonna buy you something, don't get no Coke, and don't get no soda water. Ask for hard liquor. Then he won't have the change for it. He'll take out his wallet and you'll see how much money he got on him.

4. When you see what kind of drug somebody put on, you know what kind of mask to put on.

5. If you listen to a motherfucker and he care about every little thing that everybody say about him, then he's a *dangerous* mother-fucker, because he live in FEAR.[15]

The Other Side Again

As for the Vice Squad, they had their own rules of life. But I was not with them long enough to find out what they were, so instead I will reveal to you the principles imparted to me by a genuine officer of the

15 Tina's stories cost seven dollars.

Alcoholic Beverages Control Division, for they should be taught to every undercover schoolchild.

1. If you don't want to be remembered, don't look people in the eye.

2. When staking out a bar, you may have to keep ordering drinks to be inconspicuous. When you reach your limit, just pour them into your own or your fellow officer's shoe.

The New Girl

At Post and Jones, a woman stood in the chilly darkness, turning a rose over and over in her fingers. What was she thinking? What was she THINKING?

"See," said Henry to me, "we've got a new girl over there and we don't know who she is. We're going to find out, and we're going to target one of our undercover units to hit on her. We saw her earlier, walking the street. And you see those two guys down further from her? We saw *them* earlier, walking behind her, but across the street. So we know, number one, she's in a high-crime area; number two, she's walking on a 'prostitution stroll'; and number three, she's dressed in a dress that would be considered more revealing than what your normal person would be wearing on a cold night like tonight. – Now, they might have tipped her off, and she might have left. – Nope. Here she is."

"And there *they* are," said his partner.

"Okay. So we'll take care of her right now."

Henry pulled over. The policewoman, who was on the passenger side, rolled down her window. – "C'mere," she said to the girl.

Before I knew what was happening, Henry had leaped out of the car and his old, kindly-looking face was bent toward the prostitute's face, as if he were helping her and giving advice; their faces glowed in the little circle of flashlight-radiance as Henry bent over her documents. – In a doorway, the pimps smiled quite complacently, lounging and crossing their legs.

"Where are you from?" the policewoman asked them harshly.

"The East coast," said one. He wore a long tweed coat, a white scarf, white pants and very fancy shoes. How nice for him that he could dress so warmly, while his elastic bank must shiver and show leg! He did not care. – As for the other pimp, he cocked his finger. When the policewoman patted him down, he spread his arms, like a stylish bird wondering whether or not to fly. – "I got kids, too," he said. – That was too much for me. When he said that, I hated him.

"And where are *you* from?" the policewoman asked him.

He yawned. "The East coast."

Henry whirled around. "Shut the *fuck* up and answer the question," he said. "If we want to play Twenty Questions, we'll ask someone else."

"Where are you from?" said the policewoman, a little drily this time.

"Boston."

"What's your name?"

"Genghis Khan."

"Where are you living now?"

"I don't have an address," Genghis Khan said, fanning his mouth.

"When was your last arrest?"

The pimp smiled. "I haven't been arrested in six years. Since 1980. I don't see what you have *on* me."

"Let's get something straight," the policewoman said. "You know what you're doing here, and I know what you're doing here, and I'm telling you, we don't want this kind of thing on our streets. We're not stupid. Now, every time I see you on this corner, waiting for a bus or anything, you're going to talk to *me*. Or to my partner. Understand? And we don't want to see you near her. Either one of you."

"Are you done with these gentlemen?" Henry said.

"Yes," the policewoman said. "Anything you want to add?"

"If I catch 'em again, I'll *book* 'em!" he threatened.

"You hear that?" the policewoman said. "See you later."

The prostitute, left to herself, had been leaning wearily against the wall, her head cocked, her wrists crossed. Her face was pale and almost classical. Her reddish-blonde hair was stylishly cut; it accorded, somehow, with her scanty jacket. She seemed curiously bereft, and yet unhumiliated. This was something which she must endure. It had to happen to her, and now it had happened.

"First initials L.J.," the policewoman said into the radio. "Female. From Post and Jones."

"Lucy?" said Henry. "Here's the game, babe." And he began to tell her what the game was. "I can't force you, though," he said. "I can't force you."

"Is this your first time?" said the policewoman.

Lucy nodded.

"Have you done this before?" the policewoman asked, very gently. "Is this your actual first time?"

"Yes," Lucy said. "I didn't want to do it."

"When did you meet those men?" the policewoman said.

"Today."

"Where have you been staying?"

"In a hotel in Marin."

"With them?"

"No, no, no, no," Lucy said.

"Well, whose room was it?"

"Some men I . . . I tried to get away from."

Her cheek was wet with tears.

Ambiguities

"I said, 'Do you *want* to get out of this situation?'" Henry told me later, after he had taken her to a women's shelter, going via back streets so that the pimps could not follow, and left her with the matron as she sat turning her rose, her only possession, over and over in her fingers, and it was understood that she would be given Traveler's Aid to return to Nevada, and we got back into the car as the radio crackled, and Henry was telling me, "and she said, 'I'd *love* to get out of here.' Sometimes we're lucky enough to have some resources to get them out of here. Sometimes we're not."[16]

"Was she being straight with you, that story about the hotel?" I said.

"Maybe not," said the policewoman.

"It's too early," Henry said. "She's not sure of where she's at. You never know. You take a chance. Tonight I gave her the benefit of the doubt. We got her a place to stay, and hopefully she'll go back to Las

---

16 "Why did she come from Las Vegas to start with?" I asked the cops. – Henry shook his head. "I don't know," he said. "It's unclear whether these guys really picked her up in Las Vegas or not. I just hope they don't follow her back there."

Vegas. If she's out here tomorrow night, then we lose her. We start all over again."

Across the Street

A white girl, with blonde hair and a white jacket, paced slowly on the corner. When it started to rain, she walked down a block and stood patiently out in the night, her head lowered.

Slow Days in North Beach

"Come on in, come on in!" cried the barkers in mid-afternoon. "Why not check it out? Take a look." They leaned against their doorways with one hand, using the other to wave at men, scooping up handfuls of air to create a vacuum which would pull men closer. As the afternoon waned they became still more energetic, standing tall and yelling through cupped hands. "See a pretty show!" they called. "See what the ladies can do!" – A guy came out of the Condor's arched brick doorway, but a woman in a black bathing suit leaned out and pulled him back in. When men came out, some looked down at the sidewalk for a moment, and others swaggered proudly, ready to race the passing clouds. Most of the time no one went in and no one went out. The red sign-lights crawled from bulb to bulb. The barkers paced to and fro in the doorways; sometimes a black skirt flashed reclusively behind them.

Slow Nights at Dino's

Dino said that business was not what it once was. Of course, that is what people always say, but there were some Friday nights when the dancers off the set had nothing better to do than talk to each other and to the customers, one sitting by the door to check IDs and one serving bar until Dino made his ten-o'-clock appearance; and the barmaid said, "Eddie, you sure got Dumbo ears," and Eddie would order another beer and sigh, "Yeah, even your ears get fat when you're old," and the barmaid would laugh, while the blonde on-duty dancer wiggled boredly (the dancers switched every fifteen minutes), well aware that a minimum movement of her hips would propel her quim through a proportionately large number of degrees, her G-string – be it black with a wide pink stripe where her cunt was and a pink stripe where her asshole was, or be it sky-blue with white clouds and birdies on it – bumping smartly and attractively with almost no effort on her part; you can observe the same phenomenon by looking out the car window at the slowly moving general view of things, and then concentrating on a particular tree or fencepost, which will then whizz by obligingly; and one of the off-duty dancers said to the other, "Business is *slow* tonight," and the other replied, "Well, it's *fast* but it's *slow*," which was true because every barstool except the two reserved ones had a man's ass on it, and every ass was indirectly connected to a tired downcast face below a pulled-down cap, but no one was ordering refills on $4.50 Budweisers, and the last dancer had made only a dollar, and that at the very end of her set. One of the off-duty dancers, Carmen from Brazil, who, it was generally agreed, had an extremely fine body, with thighs *just* plump enough, stood beside us and asked how we were and said anxiously, "I just hope you gentlemen are having a good time." The impressive blonde, who was slightly less impressive now than she once was because her buttocks had begun to sag, lifted her leg and undid the sash of her yellow dress, and we saw that she was wearing not only a vinyl leopard-skin crotch cover but also a black brassiere to stretch the suspense out for another tune, but no one was in any suspense; and she wiggled her sagging ass until the next song started, and then she took her bra off, facing the wall, and turned around to show us her small high breasts, which had not begun to sag yet; and at the end of each number the barmaid clapped pointedly so that we would clap, too, however grudgingly; and then the music started again and the poor blonde wiggled some more, but no one gave the barmaid any dollars to snap into the blonde's G-string, so gradually she started snapping it herself and staring into our faces, but no one took the hint, so she turned her face away from us and made us look at her slightly saggy ass for longer and longer periods of time, and the barmaid shook her head and snickered but no one gave the blonde a dollar. Finally her fifteen minutes were up, and she pulled her yellow dress back on, shuffling off to stand by the door checking IDs, and Carmen from Brazil had to go back on stage.[17]

17 Seeing this cost $5.50.

Fast Nights

On fast nights the men were more generous, but often more raucous also, and when Carmen took off her clothes and slid her hands crosswise over her tits and smiled at us, they'd laugh and whistle and say things like, "This is so *STUPID!*" and she'd smile just as gently as before and they'd stare into her smiling mouth and go, "I *LOVE* IT WHEN YOU BRUSH YOUR TEETH LIKE THAT SO EARLY IN THE MORNING!", and if Dino was there he'd start casting hard looks but Carmen kept right on smiling and dancing.[18]

Carmen really was extremely nice.

Closing Time

So the music went on, and finally Dino announced the very last dance, and at the end of it came the very faint clapping of the last three men left in the bar, at which the dancer smiled, and then it was closing time, thank God.

In the Privacy of Your Own Home

There are, of course, whores who will drive to your apartment or hotel and spread themselves, which, since time is money for business travelers, permits the client to save as much as he spent. Lest you consider me a mere slummer, I hasten to explain to you that I, too, had a hundred and fifty dollars once, and that is how I disposed of it. (I actually – stupid me! – thought that having a call-girl would be less lonely than listening through the closed doors of rooms where television-watchers laughed all alone!)

When I dialed the number, a woman's voice answered on the first

18 This cost me nothing, because Clive Summers paid.

ring. (Evidently they ran a tight ship.) It was a quiet, wary, knowing and above all *unpleasant* voice, reminding me of silken hairs piled on guts – for I was three years younger then, my feelings more easily affected by others. In particular, it disagreeably influenced me in those days to have someone dislike me, and I could tell that this woman DESPISED me, because I had called. From looking at the pictures of the happy obliging girls in the Yellow Pages, I had gained the impression that while my phone call might not be answered with limpid endearments, still at the very least the voice of the woman I called would be fun-loving, even affectionate, as women sometimes are at airline reservation desks; because the bare-shouldered brunette looked right into my eyes above where it said INDULGE YOUR FANTASY – BEAUTIFUL GIRLS AVAILABLE 24 HOURS; and the girl in the Arab headdress made calf's eyes at me, and the blonde winked at me quite endearingly as she held the phone ("The Best Number Around," it said). – The bitterness in this woman's tone, therefore, was disconcerting to me, but I forged ahead.

The Sixty-Four-Thousand-Dollar Questions

"How much is your outcall service?" I said.

"Are you calling from a house or a hotel?" the woman said alertly.

"A house."

"Then it would be fifty dollars, plus a tip for the lady."

"How much is the tip?"

"That you have to negotiate with the lady."

"Fine," I said.

"So you want a lady to call, then?" the woman said shortly.

I gave her my name and number.

"All right, Bill," she said. "I'll check to see if anyone's available. You'll get another call very soon."

The ring came less than a minute later. "Do you still want company?" the most unpleasant woman said.

"Yes, I do," I said formally. I was now married.

So Help Me God

The phone rang.

"Hi, Bill, this is Ginger," a new voice said.

"Hi, Ginger," I said.

"So you want some company?" Ginger said, getting right to the point.

"I do," I said again.

"Good. So you have the cash?"

"I do."

The Sculptor and His Clay[19]

She wanted beer, but I only had whiskey and water, so I gave her water. She set her purse down on the dining room table. I went back into the kitchen and filled her a glass of water from the sink. I brought the glass out to her and decided to get one for myself. Seeing me go back to the kitchen, Ginger got up and followed me. Nobody had ever followed me wherever I went before. I realized that (for an hour, at least) Ginger would be like a piece of modeling clay, for me to handle and play with as I wanted. This thought filled me with terror because the clay would be looking at me and judging me and thinking her own thoughts. I would not be able to hide. – Meanwhile Ginger followed me up to the sink. It was obvious that she was not sure what I wanted. In fact all that I wanted was to be accommodating by having a glass of water since Ginger was having one. Maybe she wanted to give me a chance to put my arm around her or kiss her if I wanted to. But that only occurred to me later. I filled my glass, and we sat down at the dining room table together. – "Well, here's to our *friendship*," said Ginger, smiling a little ironically. – "Here's to you," I said gallantly.

We sipped at our water. My hour was passing.

"I have to check in," Ginger said. "Where's the phone?"

---

19 There comes to mind that couplet of Wordsworth's (1804): "A perfect woman, nobly planned/To warn, to comfort and to command."

"At the top of the stairs."

"Let's see the money," she said, rising.

The Brat Tries to Understand

"It must be pretty dangerous, doing what you do," I said.

"Yes, it is sometimes," Ginger said. "Twice I've run into men who wouldn't let me go. They couldn't come, or they couldn't get hard, and when this happens it's not the girl's fault. And all the time they want to keep you late. It's really pretty hard work.'

When She Was Naked

"You're pretty," I said.

She didn't say anything. She had looked me in the eye when she took her clothes off.

"Is there anything you don't want me to do?" I said.

"Well, I don't kiss," she said.

"Is that because you don't want to kiss anyone you don't love?"

"I don't do it, is all," she said. "Maybe if you were my boyfriend. But I don't kiss on the job."

While Trying Unsuccessfully to Make Ginger's Cunt Wet

"So are you enjoying the summer?" Ginger inquired.

I lifted my face from her nipple to answer. My erection dwindled slightly. "It's okay," I said.

"Do you like camping?" said Ginger.

"Sure," I said, continuing to rub her vagina earnestly, though without result. I still did not understand (stupid me!) that she was doing this only for the money, and not because she wanted to.

"Is there any place that's best for you down there?" I said.

"Down there?" said Ginger ironically. "No, anything you want to do feels fine."

Why It Was All Worth It

Later Ginger began to earn her money even more than when she had merely had to suffer my presence and my conversation and my lips on her breast and all the rest of it; she moved her hips obligingly up and down, so that it made me feel bad to think of all the trouble that she was going to, and my penis shrank a little more. As I rode her, her body covered with sweat, she screwed her hips around and I screwed my hips around, and I clung to her more and more tightly so that her body literally ran with hot slippery sweat; she moaned; she sighed; yes, she did throw in an oh oh oh or two for my hundred and fifty dollars; I was getting to her at last; she was enjoying being with me; maybe her cunt was even getting wet . . .

"Oh, God," she sighed – and I felt like a man for a minute, thinking that the oh God was on account of how I was making her feel – "oh, *God*, it's hot."

Live and Learn

"I never would've *believed* it if I hadn't done it," jeered the blonde whore as she got out of the car. "*Thank* you." – She ran down Mission Street yelling, "Nina, Nina!" – Nina came out of a doorway. – "Nina, I never would've believed it," said the blonde whore. – "Oh, shit," said Nina. "*Everyone* does that. On the *ground*."

Ladies and Red Lights

Walking down O'Farrell on some dreary grey day, the sidewalk almost empty, you might see a black woman come sleepwalking down the exact middle of the sidewalk, and if you stepped to one side she would step dully to one side, too, as if she were your mirror-image whose dead hands must touch your hands.

At night, walking between Jones and Leavenworth, you might see her again. But now she was twinkling her knees; now she was smiling; now when she sought *you* out she seemed to be aware of you, to know you and understand you and trust you and love you. She held an unlit cigarette in her lips. "Do you have a light?" she called. She looked back at you when you looked into her eyes. You could have her if you wanted her; if you went around the corner you could pick out another one who showed off her legs in black stockings. You could almost smell what it would be like to fuck her. She smiled. You walked on but looked back. She was looking back, too. You probably cannot remember her face, which was blotted out by the heat her legs gave you, that hot white feeling.

Unlucky Christina

As I walked down Ellis Street early on a Saturday night, while the shoppers had congress with their big wide monogrammed bags three blocks away, I passed a parked van and saw that a man was in it, and when the man saw that I had seen him he started the van and followed me for a block, so I turned four corners to get rid of him, and saw him parked on the other side of Ellis Street, and made a point of not noticing him, and the street was very quiet, and I walked past a vacant lot, and at the corner of Ellis and Jones a woman said to me, "Do you need a date?", and I said I did; I wanted to talk to her for five dollars.

Christina was a Chicana with a sad, sad face and sadder eyes. And yet she did not permit herself to be lugubrious, because if she did, men's erections might shrink when she asked them if they wanted to thrust their penises inside her. (How delicate, yet how proudly demanding, a penis can be! Yet I will say no more about this wretched reed.) She was twenty-six.

"Ten years ago," she said to me, "I'd just left home when I ran into the wrong guy. He was a white pimp from Dallas. He kidnapped me and locked me up in a room for a week. When he was breaking me in, he even stood outside the door when I went to the bathroom. There was no way I could get away." – She was no longer looking at me. We were sitting in a Vietnamese deli, and Christina looked down into her cup of coffee, as if she could see through the liquid night that steamed there, while outside the window was more night and once a man walking by saw Christina and tapped on the window and grinned. – "He had two other hookers who were proud to be his girls," Christina said. "They helped him watch me. He expected two-fifty to three hundred a day from me. When I didn't make it, he hit me. He hit me three times in the years we were together." – Christina now looked into my face, and I could not hear her thoughts at all but I think that she had said what she said to me with a sort of pride, because she had satisfied the pimp all but three times, gathering her money every night through niggling foresighted fucks, and all the hurting of them (which I am sure diminished as Christina diminished) ADDED UP to something which continued to increase by fifteen and twenty and forty dollar increments as Christina went around and around and around the corner and pulled her chafing underpants down; but I did not hear her thoughts, and it is possible that she might have been thinking about the three times. To me on my side of the little round table, her thoughts were blacked-out and silent. I could hear the steam rise from her coffee. We were the only customers in the deli. The woman was watching us patiently from across the room, knowing that we would leave in awhile and then she could close up, and red lights flashed outside.

"I had to work for him twenty-four hours a day," Christina said, her voice very low and dry and flat, and she sipped her coffee once. "I took my meals standing under the streetlight. One day two black men put a gun to my head and raped me. They made me do almost everything. Thank God they didn't fuck me up the butt. They drove me out of town and put me to work, and the whole time one or the other held the gun to my head." – Christina put her little finger through the handle of her coffee cup and lifted it to her lips and took a sip and put it back down on the clean white table. She did not seem to enjoy her coffee, but immediately she lifted the cup and took another sip. – "When I came back," she said, "the pimp didn't believe that I'd been raped. He drove me to a bridge and bent me over the bridge and squeezed my neck until I turned purple. Then he started beating me. The other two men had already beaten me half to death." – At this point I wanted very much to look into Christina's face because I could not hear her thoughts at all, but I looked away because she was looking away.

Two Aunties and a Loving Mother

"After that," she said, "my 'aunties' – that was what I had to call the other two girls – were always hurting me and checking me for money. But two years later, he went to jail for eight months. That was my chance. I put a restraining order on him. He tried to keep my little girl. He told the court I was his common-law wife because we'd lived together for over six months. But I got my little girl back and sent her to live with my parents."

"Why doesn't she live with you?" I said.

"'Cause I LOVE her too much!" said Christina, so bitterly.

Another Loving Mother

Brandi always kissed with her lips closed. Probably she was afraid of catching a disease. Sometimes you would see her skipping down Haight Street with a carefree air, dragging a white man or a black man behind her, and she'd grin and introduce him: "This my boyfriend, uh, *what* you say your name is?" – "C'mon," she said to me, "buy me some Tylenol for my little boy. He's sick; he needs it." – "All right," I said. "I'll come with you." – "Oh!" she cried, rolling her eyes, "then we gotta go *all* the way up to the Mama-san Papa-san, *'way* up the street. You just gimme the money an' I'll buy it." – "I don't mind," I said. "Let's go." Brandi saw in an instant that I was unbudging. But because I had promised to pay for the Tylenol, I must be humored. "Well, lemme tell Freddy we gotta be goin' somewhere." She ran catty-corner across the street and spoke to somebody in the shadows for a minute, then she ran back to me. "You *so* good to me!" she said. We started walking. I took her hand. She said, "And you buy me a cookie, too." – "Just be happy with what you've got," I said. As we walked along, some kids on the corner started cheering and yelling: "She finally got one! She finally got one!" – which of course she had, so I laughed, and Brandi said, "Who cares what they think?", and I nodded and said, "That's right. Who cares?"

We got to the store, and Brandi went straight to the front counter. "You got some children's Tylenol?" she said. – "Just these drops," the man said. (The drops were the most expensive – almost five dollars.) – "Lemme get those," said Brandi anxiously. "I gotta see if he can take these. Those drop kind might be bad for his constitution. If I bring 'em back without opening 'em, can I get the money back?" Truly, Brandi had a way with money.

On the way back she held my hand until she saw a tall black man on the street. "I wonder how big his dick is," she said. She yanked her hand out of mine and went back to him. "Sure, I wanna party," I heard him say. I kept walking. Pretty soon Brandi came flying up to me and took my hand. – "He say he'll do it with me later," she said.

When we were half a block away from Cole Street she said, "Up there's where I'm leavin' you. Gimme a kiss!" She turned her face up to me. I grabbed her and kissed her. Her lips tasted like old smoke. "I be *seein'* you!" she said, running, running into the darkness.[20]

If Brandi Had a Million Dollars

A million dollars? Honey, she'd take her son shopping and *spend* it. She *loved* her son. She'd *die* for him.

"It's Used For Scraping Paint"

"So then you went into business for yourself?" I said.

"Yes," said Christina, "but I'm very cautious about dating strangers."

20 As stated, this incident cost slightly less than five dollars.

She had an angular, olive-colored face. "I try to keep away from trouble," she said. "You see, most of the cops know me, so they give me a warning; they tell me to get off the street for an hour. They know I don't steal money from nobody. Also, I'm clean. I've been very careful, and I've only had one conviction in the last ten years. But now it's getting harder to tell who's safe, 'cause there are a hundred and fifty new cops all over the T.L., all young guys, twenty-two to twenty-five.[21] That's why I always pat my dates down to make sure they don't have handcuffs or walkie-talkies. I prefer older guys, 'cause they can't run as fast. You see, so many times I've seen the cops sneaking up behind the girls and jumping at them, and only the faster ones get away. But I have a couple of guys watching out for me, and in my purse I carry this folding razor, see? It's even legal, 'cause it's used for scraping paint! And I only work Ellis Street, where there's lots of light."

"How well do those precautions work?" I said.

"Well, one time I had a repeat of what happened in Dallas, when a guy put a gun up to my head. He raped me, and ever since then I was more careful. A girlfriend of mine got killed doing this last year. She used to steal a lot of money from men, so one of them beat her head in with a hammer."

Brandi Gets Busted

Brandi was up on the Castro when a police officer from Park Station cruised by. The policewoman knew Brandi. She pulled over. "What are you doing here?" she said. "You're out of your area. The Haight's your area." – "Hey, honey," said Brandi, "it may be my area, but the Castro's a-*booming*." – "Well, now," said the policewoman, "you're gonna have to give me your full name so I can call in and make sure there's nothing out on you." – Brandi tried to get away. "Lemme just go check on my son," she said. "I'll be right back." – "Oh, no you don't," said the policewoman. "Get in the car." – She called in Brandi's name. – "Well, well," she said. "Don't you know we have a three thousand dollar bench warrant out on you?" – Brandi knew that very well. It was petty theft and grand theft. They took her to 850 Bryant, stripped her down, put

21 Henry said that there were eleven.

her in the day room for awhile, and booked her. They locked her into cell number eight for twenty days.

"What did you do there?" I said.

"Honey, I made the *best* of it," she grinned.

Early Memories

Brandi was used to making the best of it because she had been *bad* as long as she could remember. When she was twelve she was sent to Trinity School in Ukiah and kept doing *bad* things, so they locked her in Isolation, which wasn't nothing but a room with four corners. They were always catching her smoking weed. One time she tried to set the place on fire, so they kicked her out. Her favorite thing was watching "Soul Train" on Saturdays and having smorgasbord. She could pick through all that meat and cheese and take whatever food she wanted. On Saturday nights they used to play "Lights Out," hunting for each other in the dark and scaring each other. One night these two girls named Jonnie and Janice wanted to be blood sisters, so Janice broke the window and took a big piece of broken glass and just *stabbed* it into her vein so that the blood was every which way, and then Jonnie got scared and said she wouldn't do it, and Janice said, "It don't hurt!", but then she fell down to the floor and bled to death.

A Good Thing

"But you feel safe?" I said.

Christina nodded flatly. "I feel relatively safe because I've built up a steady clientele. I have eight steadies. I've had them for three and a half years. I have their phone numbers. I know I'm safe from catching anything, because they're married men. Sometimes they don't even want to fuck me. They just want to take me out to dinner or something and have me act appreciative. See, my clients are lonely. They just want me to treat them right and then they treat *me* right. One of them's my sugar daddy. He pays me a couple hundred per date, and he also pays my rent."

Men

"It get boring," Brandi sighed, "jumping into bed with Tom, Dick and Harry."

"Have you ever had anybody you were in love with?"

"Once, but I had a lot of men in love with *me*." She chuckled. "And I taken *advantage* of it."

"That's Also So I Can Run"

Christina worked on Friday, Saturday and Sunday nights. She lived on Sutter and Taylor, so it was an easy walk to her beat. Then, of course, she *really* walked, round and round, up and down the street, past Asian stores that sold toy animals made of phony gold, past bars whose red and blue beer-lights made the sidewalks glow patriotic, and if the cops[22] came she would stand at the phone booth and pretend to make a collect call, or she would fiddle with her purse, or she would pretend to be waiting for the bus, or she might simply continue past bright hotel lobbies, past Dino's, out of which the music came bravely, as if the place were *packed* with men who were having FUN. Her beat was very small – only two or three blocks on a side. But because she had to walk it until she got her money, it was an infinite universe of rain and darkness and streets, steel gratings and liquor stores, puke and piss. The sorriness of what she had had to do for ten years was almost enough to make one believe in the Divine; there *must* be something else.[23]

The lowest Christina went was twenty dollars for a blow job. A half and half (a blow job plus a straight lay) cost thirty-five, but it was really

22 Sometimes she saw the decoy girls. The cops had a Chinese girl, a blonde and a black girl working for them. The Chinese girl usually parked on Ellis. If you came onto her it was a five-hundred-dollar fine.

23 It is interesting that Christina's beat was so claustrophobically tight, because looking down into the T.L. from above, you see narrow canyons of streets, with creeks of auto-lights flowing at the base of the cliffs, and the T.L. does not seem to be so much good or bad as CONSTRICTED.

more like fifty because Christina wouldn't get into a car with a stranger, so she took him to a room around the corner which cost ten bucks for fifteen or twenty minutes, including protection. Some of the men didn't want to use rubbers. When Christina gave a blowjob, as I have said before, she stuck a rubber into her mouth and used her tongue and lips to work it onto the man's sexual organ without his knowing, a prestidigitative feat which Mr. Penis could only applaud.

"What do you think about when those men are fucking you?"

"I just blank out when I'm dating. I try not to think about it. Of course sometimes I can't help having a good time; you know, I'll feel good in spite of myself, 'cause I don't *want* to have a good time with them. But of course I've known my steadies so long that it's relaxing to be with them, and that helps me feel good."

"And they're good to you, too?"

"Well, they are, but just last week one of them, a Chinese man who's been dating me for over two years, went all crazy when I was in his car. We drove to the parking lot, and after he gave me the twenty dollars and I blew him he said, 'Wait a minute. I can't let you have this. I just realized I'm broke.' – I said, 'Are you crazy? What do you think I did this for?' – Then he wrestled with me; he tried to get the money back by force. Good thing I knew how to kick him where it counted!" Christina laughed. She had a metallic laugh. "Well, I ran out of the car. I'm never going to do anything with him again."

"Where do you keep your money?" I said.

Christina looked both ways to make sure that no one else could hear. "In my sock," she said. "When I'm dating, I never take my shoes off, no matter what. That's also so I can run."

Justice Catches Up With Brandi

A year ago Brandi took three hundred bucks for assing and then didn't deliver because she didn't want to get them awful *diseases*. (One time she got crabs, but that was the only time in her life she got something, because usually she was pretty *careful*, you know.) So she ran off with the three hundred, and about a year later somebody tapped her shoulder; and she had this kind of *tingling* feeling, but she turned around and just as she saw that it was the man she'd ripped off he hit her in the mouth and split her lip open. Brandi started howling and screaming rape, but he dragged her round the corner, and she whimpered, "Please just lemme get up, lemme get up," and he let her get up so he could knock her down again but when she was up she ran away as fast as she could. Her lip was fat for the rest of her life, 'cause she wouldn't let 'em stitch it up; she wasn't gonna let anyone stick no *needle* in her lip.[24]

The Other Girls

Sometimes the other girls came up to Christina and said scornfully, "You're not wearing the right clothes to make money in. Go put on some money-making clothes." They meant, go put on a bathing suit or a nightgown. Christina told them to fuck off. They were just jealous. She made more money in a day than they did. Sometimes they asked her to turn them onto her dates, but she wouldn't; she always took care of them herself. After twelve she saw the black girls jump three in a car; they needed to get the money so bad they were *determined* to get it. (Christina didn't like blacks.) Most of them had pimps who drove them in from Oakland every night. They didn't use rubbers because they didn't care about their lives; all they cared about was making enough money so their pimps wouldn't beat them. "Pimps around here," she said, "they hurt their women if they don't make what they want them to make." The black girls were good at coming up to you and hugging you and kissing you and rubbing themselves all over you, and while they were doing that they took your wallet and you didn't even feel it. (Christina did it to me, to demonstrate. She was right. I didn't even feel it. She was kind enough to give my wallet back.) After they robbed somebody, they'd run away to the car where they kept a pile of wigs, and put on a new wig, a new dress, and go back out on the street.

24 This information cost me four dollars.

Something Nice for a Change

Christina left me when she had to go back to work. She told me to stay away from Turk Street, because it was all heroin, speed and cocaine down there. She hugged me. "You be careful," she said.[25]

Why Christina Whored

It was hard for her to quit. She needed the money; she needed to add to her little girl's savings account.

Why Brandi Whored

"I'm greedy," she said. "I gotta eat a lot. It don't look like it, but I do."[26]

The Peace-Loving Peoples Elaborate

According to the *Great Soviet Encyclopedia* (1977), hunger is "a social phenomenon accompanying antagonistic socioeconomic forces." This would seem to exclude lockjaw or natural starvation, but never mind.

Brandi's Life

And therefore if a man should talk to me of a *round*
Quadrangle, or *accidents of Bread in Cheese;* or *Immateriall*

25 Christina was honest. She also liked me. That is why all this information cost me only five dollars.
26 For an additional fifty cents, I learned that spaghetti is Brandi's favorite food.

Substances, or of *A free Subject; A free-Will;* or any *Free* . . . I
should not say he were in an Errour; but that his words were
without meaning; that is to say, Absurd.

Hobbes, *Lev.*, I.5.19

I Am Stupid Again

"You want some company?" black Tawnie said.

"Sure," I said. "Tell me the story of your life."

"Baby, I could talk to you for *hours*," she said. "I been on the streets
since I was nine. I can talk to you *real* good. For how much?"

"Ten dollars," I said.

I went into the bar with her and she got twenty out of me. Then I
waited for her to tell me stories. – "Hey, Buck!" she said to her friends.
"Hey, Red! How's the world?" – But I was still there. – Tawnie studied
me with amused disgust. "Don't you know when you been beat? You
don't know *nothin'* about *nothin'*."

The Poor Man's Revenge

At the F bus stop at San Pablo and Yerba Buena a blonde came to sit
beside a middle-aged black man. "She wanted money just because she
said hello," he told me when she left. "That's how it is. Once I bought
her dinner."

"What happened?"

"Nothing. Nothing at all. Now I just love telling her no."

How to Make Friends and Influence People

"Alms for the poor!" intoned a tramp, stretching out his dirty palm, but
nobody put a penny in it, so he called out, "Cadillacs for the poor!"
Nobody gave him a Cadillac, either.

You Can't Buy No More

"So you don't have any more money?" said white Delilah, staring at me open-mouthed through her stringy screen of hair. "I'll tell you *everything* for ten dollars. You don't have ten dollars?" – and for a moment I almost believed that if I had had ten dollars to give her, everything would have been all right.

"You're sure you don't have more money?" Delilah said.

"I'm sure."

"Then you got to leave. You drank your beer. You can't buy no more."

"I would give you ten dollars, Delilah," I said, to see what she would say, "but Tawnie took it all."

"She didn't take your money," Delilah said. "You *gave* her your money." She put her arm around Tawnie and led her indignantly away.

Red light-globes hung from the ceiling. The red felt on the pool tables was redder than the richest raspberry mucosa. From my side-vision I saw looming men. They did not particularly like me or my notebook. – The pool cue smacked smartly against the balls. Some players seemed only to flick at the ball with the cue, but the ball gathered speed through some occult means and pursued its way across the felt, while the ancient juke-box sang, "Nobody loves me like she does." Holding their beers, men came and went, silhouetted against the red lights. Shadows moved on the floor. – "Look at that ugly cunt," a man said, pointing at a whore. "I wouldn't put money down on *her*. And I oughta know. I pay cash for EVERYTHING." – Lights sparkled on the jukebox. Men in black leather jackets leaned over the pool tables. Slender chains glowed above their back pockets. The fan spun, and a man staggered out of the restroom clutching his beer. For a moment he leaned upon the lovely red felt. "I *can do whatever I want,*" he told me.

Outside, it was very very dark. On the sidewalk it said SUCK FLIPPER. A parrot-faced man in a black coat was waiting for me. – "Hey!" he said, panting. "Come here. Come suck my dick." – I walked on without answering. Suddenly I heard Tawnie's voice behind me. "Hurry up!" she was yelling to somebody. "He's goin' away!"

The pimp came running after me.

"What are you writing?"

"I write down people's stories," I said carefully.

The pimp hit me. Then he reached under his arm. He pulled out a rather stubby revolver. On the other side of the street, I saw the parrot-faced man gloating. "Go on, blow him away!" he called to the pimp. "I haven't seen anybody die since yesterday!"

It occurred to me that the parrot-faced man might not be exaggerating.

Reaction Check

"You must be feelin' awful," a guy told me on the street. "Aren't you lookin' *passionate* or somethin'?"

Jews and Niggers

It was almost midnight. Inside the Coral Sea bar on Turk Street, a beautiful blonde was bending over the pool table to make her shots. Every time she did so, her miniskirt rose up so that the patrons could see her bare ass-cheeks.

"Shit," the bartender said, watching her. "I sure wish I was single."

"You're SICK!" said one of the old ladies at the bar (there were a lot of old people at the Coral Sea).

"Shut up, you fat old broad," said the bartender. "Respect my heritage. I'm Guatemalan, is what I am."

"You're a watermelon!"

"*You're* a JEW!" he shot back.

"Watermelon!"

"Jew!"

"Watermelon!"

"Jew!"

"Don't say that to me! I'll get you fired! I had family in the Holocaust!"

"Hey! I'll say what I want! I'm a Jew, too. I'm a Guatemalan Jew.

You just shut up and let me talk to your sister. I'll pay her five bucks to give me a ride around the world."

All the old ladies laughed. "*And* smoke your cigarette. *And* pick her teeth with your toothpick!"

"What a world," the bartender said. "Shit. Things sure were a lot better around here back in 1949, before those fucking *niggers* moved in."

Tenderloin Politeness

"Hey, nigger!" a white man called.

The black man looked him up and down. "That's MR. Nigger to you."

Works of Art

"It all started when I was fifteen years old," said Leslie, a tall woman with huge breasts which she enjoyed rubbing against my hand. "I couldn't find my way across the *street* without somebody holding my hand! I came from Redwood City to this very block, twenty-five years ago, and there was this bar across the street then with big pink lights and a friend of mine said to me, 'You see that girl talking to that dirty old man over there? Well, she's doing it for money.' That really opened my eyes. The first time I tricked, I loved it, and I still love it; I'm still making it. I earned twenty bucks, forty bucks, a hundred bucks a trick, and I spent it on tits, on facial surgery, on hips and on a pussy. I got myself a brand-new pussy for Christmas."

"How much did your pussy cost?"

"Ten thousand dollars."

"Did it hurt?"

"No."

"How does it feel?"

"Great," she said, swishing her hand in the air sarcastically. "I even come."[27]

"What was the worst thing that happened to you?"

"I got beat up by a man in New York that tried to rape me. I got total amnesia. When I got out of the hospital, all I could remember was to go up to a man and say, 'Do you want a date?' I turned a forty-dollar trick the first day I got out of the hospital. I had the amnesia for a year. One day it cleared up on its own. – Angel! Oh, *An-gel!* Do you want to talk to someone? He'll pay you. – Give her ten dollars."

"I'm a transsexual and I have a pussy and a clit," said Angel, bored. "I had a doctor from Bolivia give me the pussy."

"And we use heroin," laughed Leslie.[28]

"No, we don't," said Angel. "Well, I had more female hormones than I had male hormones. I come from the midwest. When I got the operation, my mother started crying and said, 'What's my Stevie gone and done to hisself?' It took five years before she finally accepted me. But now she calls me her girl."

"What's the hardest thing about your life?"

"The police out here. *Bye*-bye!"[29]

The Sad Truth

"So are you really able to control this," I asked, "or do you basically have to contain it?"

"Just contain it," Henry said. "You can't control prostitution. It's always going to be there. All you can do is kind of keep it in the same area. You're not going to solve the problem. It just ain't going to happen."

---

27 The bodies of these people are works of art. When I was riding with the Vice Squad we drove past a pretty woman strutting her stuff. "That's a guy, in case you were wondering," said the policewoman. – "If you look at the hands," said Henry, "they'll tell you what he is."

28 Two months later, Leslie was in the hospital getting methadone while she waited for an abscess in her shoulder to heal sufficiently for her to return to prison. She had a thirty-day sentence to serve for prostitution, because she had turned herself in, believing that prison might well fatten her up.

29 This information cost fifteen dollars.

The New Generation

On the hot sunny corner of Haight and Shrader I saw Brandi. She was pretending not to see me, because she was lounging with a man, and also because her son Dabir was around the corner. But, seeing that I had crossed the street and was coming straight toward her, she decided to make the *best* of it, so she told the man goodbye and turned around in surprise and put her arms around me and grinned up at me and wanted to know how I was doing, so we leaned up against the side of a store where someone had written (appropriately or not, depending on your views about ladies and red lights) CLITSISTERS ARE DICKVICTIMS − SEX IS REVENGE; and Brandi and I agreed that it was hot, and Dabir had an orange which Brandi had bought him, so he started bouncing it up and down on the hard sidewalk, and then throwing it down as hard as he could, and I told him that he could probably squeeze the juice out of it now, so he ripped it in half and said, "Mom! Squeeze it into my mouth," and Brandi did, and she yawned and said, "It's so hot. I'm gonna go get in bed and sleep." (Somebody had set her house on fire but it had been remodeled now.) − I asked Dabir what his favorite thing to do was, and he cried, "Eat, eat eat!" − and Brandi said sharply, "An' go to *school!*" (but it was noon on a Tuesday and he was not in school); and Dabir said, "An' I like to *sleep!*" and his mother laughed, and he showed me the gum that he was chewing, and Brandi took a sip of her soda, while she was resting on the window-ledge, and Dabir said, "Gimme a drink! Gimme a drink!", so she held the bottle to his lips, and he said, "I want some more juice!" and turned his face up to her, so she squeezed the other half of the orange into his mouth, but a drop fell on his clothes, and he screamed.

"Those are nice slippers you have there," I said to Brandi. "I don't think I've seen them before."

"No," she said. "Somebody gave 'em to me."

"They're *ugly!*" the boy cried.

"Do you like your shoes?" I asked him.

"They're ugly, too!" he said.

"How about mine?"

"*Ugly, ugly, ugly!*"

Brandi set the soda bottle back in the window-ledge out of habit, as a cop walked by and said, "Good afternoon, Dessie," and she said hello in a low sullen voice, but as soon as he had walked on her eyes started sparkling and she said proudly, "They *all* know me," and I said, "You've got friends in high places," and Brandi laughed and laughed while the boy took one of the orange-halves and began smashing it on the sidewalk.

"Will you gimme fifty cents?" said Brandi. "I'm so thirsty. I really want a soda. Half of it's for him."

"Sure," I said. "I'll give you fifty cents."

"No, wait, gimme seventy-five. I wanna get an ice cream instead."

"No, I'll give you fifty cents."

"Awright, gimme fifty cents, and give him a quarter. That way he can get something, too."

"Gimme a quarter!" the boy cried, shooting out his young brown palm.

"You're training him well," I said. That was the one time I was ever bitter with her.

Brandi looked away. "Give us each fifty cents," she said so hopefully, probably believing that if they only had fifty cents each they would never want for anything, and so would never have to talk to me again. "You already promised me a soda," she said. "Aren't you gonna give him anything?"

"I'll give you fifty cents, and you can give it to him if you want," I said.

I reached into my pocket.

"Oh, you got *lots* of change!" cried the boy resentfully.

I gave Brandi twenty-five cents. The boy still had his hand held out, so I started to give him the other quarter, but Brandi snatched it away.

SCINTILLANT
ORANGE

We contend, therefore, that the physical process of oxidation, fire, is experienced with the aid of images which derive from the interior world of the psyche . . .

> Erich Neumann, *The Origins and History of Consciousness* (1954)*

Flame is pure. It is by flame that we must be destroyed. I have always loved heat and light so . . .

> Peter Neumann, *The Black March: The Personal Story of an SS Man* (1960)†

A Pretty Passion

We know from the Apocrypha the story of the mother and the seven sons who, tortured by the tyrant Antiochus, nonetheless refused to eat defiling foods – an example it would be difficult to emulate today, now that Mu Shu Pork is prepared so tastefully. The youngest boy, after feeding Antiochus a salty diet of reproach, leaped into the braziers and burned himself up before they could stuff his stomach as though he were a goose. He did not hesitate. – But in the matter of Mes'hach, whose career was equally heated, preparation was essential, for, more often than is expedient, the *act* is but a pastry shell which must be plumped full of the creamiest *motives* if the flambée is to be a success.

He, with his brothers Shad'rach and Abed'nego, was going to be cast into the Burning Fiery Furnace, which fouled the sky with its scintillant orange glow every night, while during the daytime hot air rippled above it and folded on itself and made mirages, so that sometimes you could watch what the Egyptian armies were doing across the desert, and other

* Trans. R. F. C. Hull (Princeton University Press, Bollingen Series XLII), p. 294.
† Trans. Constantine Fitzgibbon (New York: Bantam), p. 218.

times it seemed that great golden icebergs went sliding through the sky, and the persons condemned to the Furnace would see them and take comfort from them as they were marched toward the shaft of the Furnace, which was enclosed in a ziggurat so high that the prisoners had to be marched up hundreds of steps, and the farther they went the hotter it got, until the captive children began to cry, but their mothers said, "Hush! Don't be afraid! Look up into the sky! We're climbing toward these icebergs, and soon we'll be so close that I'll reach up and break off an icicle for you and your sister to suck on, and it will be so cool and nice . . ." – but by then they were already treading the last flight of black-burned steps which never stopped smoking, and of course nothing could disguise the roaring and that searing heat already on their faces and the bone-cinders spewing into the air (a thousand slaves were employed each day in raking them up to be pulverized into fertilizer for the Hanging Gardens); and above all they could not mistake the screams of their predecessors and the glare of the great orange flames of fire, to which Shadrach, Meshach and Abednego had been condemned because they would not worship the golden image made by King Nebuchadnez'zar.

They were all brave, those three; none shirked any trial. But what devalued Meshach's courage was that the Fiery Furnace did *not* try him, because he was an aesthete, and adored the Spirit of the color orange. – You think this preposterous, and I have no doubt that when you look inside your own globular head you find no such affection, preferring as you do the starchy whiteness of your hopes and the homogeneous blueness of your life, to a color so often associated with garishness; but surely you will allow others to take happiness pills of a different color? – Just as some burglars (so it is said) will ejaculate when entering a window, but cannot so manage in a vagina, so Meshach had dreams of certain orange flickerings whose mystic rhythm of color would have been imperceptible to the vulgar. You who at sunset have never gone into ecstasies while inhaling the thrilling orange gas, how do you expect to understand the sacredness of a hue which becomes on contemplation only more and more vivid? There were Manifestations within that warm glow which few today have seen and worshipped, and which it would be perilous to discuss directly. That lock of scintillant orange hair which a man keeps tied with a ribbon is a metonymy for his sweetheart; he does not show it to everyone. (Not for nothing was that Dutch king, William of Orange, also known as William the Silent.) For

Meshach, then, the glow of a single ember revived immeasurable orange fires inside his being, whose wealth of flame could not be spent, because he saw his love in them, and he believed that his love saw him; therefore that very narrow wavelength-band had become a necessity and an oppressive delight to him, so that he was at his fullest in the desert, where (with but a few thundercast exceptions) the sun daily took its course. At night he became weak and doubtful if he could not stare into the flames of the wall-torches. Had the Babylonians thought to break his spirit, it would have been simple: a few hours in some lightless dungeon, where the air, though hot with the memory of scintillant orange, had become stale with the other colors of darkness. As it was, he retained his equanimity, and often cheered his brothers in their captivity, for he had what *he* wanted. But he could not tell them why he remained content. (What would Shadrach say?) Lost in his lonely love, he saw orange blades of grass spring up on his mind's hillsides; each blade opened into two, and from the joining-place a new orange light burst forth, as refreshing to him as a sweet orange-grove found after days of desert wandering. Having faith in YAWEH, the one true God, he did not fear for himself; whether he lived or died was the same to him, as long as he could see the inside of the Furnace.

All Objections Answered

Ignorant persons will doubtless suppose Meshach to have made a pact with evil, for affinity with fire is generally linked (in a trope as false as it is convenient) with bondage to Hell. Yet he did not see the bright gruesome twistings of ruination that most do when gazing into a fire; for him the colors were innocent, scintillant, playful; because he could see the doings of the Salamanders in the flame.* Thus YAWEH, understanding that Meshach did true reverence to His creatures, was pleased. – Others, of course, would be delighted to close the case of Meshach differently, formulating judgments more learned and less forgiving than those of YAWEH; so, as I said, Meshach had never let anyone know the true extent of his converse with the lovely Salaman-

---

* Paracelsus relates that only the pure of heart can see Salamanders. He saw one once, in his boyhood, when he lived among the mountains.

ders, who did in fact come from Hell (although he did not know it). Win or lose, said Meshach to himself, good or bad, the Salamanders were all that was worth living for.

A Pyromaniac's Viewpoint

"It was the crowds more than the fires – those thousands of people. I can't explain it, but I got a tremendous bang out of it, like a prize fight or a bullfight."

Wolves and Fires

Before being carried away to Babylon he had been a shepherd-prince, and conformed to the tradition of the evening fire at the appropriate hour, when other flame-diamonds glittered from other hills, but his construction was marked by a care positively beyond what is normally observed in this occupation, for he decanted high-octane gasoline from a scintillant orange jerry can into a whole battery of eyedroppers with different nozzle-widths, in order to assure maximum flame propagation and flame velocity; and he had a talent for storing up hydrogen in his cheeks, from denatured water, which he could puff out upon the first sparks of his endeavors at that crucial moment when they had not yet committed themselves unshakeably to becoming flames; while the sheep, long conditioned to halt at the first whiff of petroleum distillates, gathered together into a mass of fluffy yellow cloud. Sunset came in all the colors of combustible gas, but slowly the fire grew brighter than the sky, climbing the pyre of railroad ties and dung chips which Meshach had thoughtfully provided, and I can truly say that it acquired its proper color with a minimum of adjustment, being pure and orange because all light was pure, and orange light contained the highest essence, partaking both of red and yellow, subsuming everything, glowing at him like a bright eye; YAWEH was in it as He had been in the burning bush for Moses . . . Nightly, then, Meshach sat on his hilltop, while the wind blew dust into his face and the wolves howled from every dismal ridge and the stars lay heavy on him, for his paralucent existence gave him no more pleasure than if he had been a prettified petrified dog, and it is no wonder that he stared so deeply into the flames, admiring them, wishing that he could go into them and kiss their pure orange tongues; thus, being happy in that other world, which was so intermittent, so perishable, he paid no heed to the wolves, who (having wrought themselves into lunar tension concomitant with the rise above the crags of that white orb – the light-emitting properties of which Meshach esteemed no more than those of any pale cheese), the wolves as I was saying loped and skulked and loped and skulked, creepy-crouching from ridge to ridge until they had ringed themselves around his silly curly flock that did not go *baaaa-a-a-a-a-a-!* in a panic because they were already too panicked to open their mouths, and in the silence the wolves' eyes shone *loud* like triangular green fires as they *slobbered*, and at a moment decided by the moon, tidings of the loneliness of death were bayed from shaggy throats which had served as graves for ever so many ewe-lambs – and yet you must not think them LOATHSOME, those wolves; you must call upon YAWEH to forgive them their gustatory premeditations, for their tongues lolled so prettily carmine between their white teeth as to exceed the fire-tongues the way a laugh exceeds a smile; no doubt, therefore, Meshach's lambs joyfully pranced those red carpets of welcome into dark hairy lobbies which narrowed and narrowed, for strait is the way to the Kingdom of Heaven.

Meshach, however, missed studying this hospitable toothwork, because he was looking into the flames – and if you feel that he is exactly where we left him when we started talking about wolves you are correct beyond disputation, but that is all he *did*, do you see, and that is why in after times he did not take cognizance of Nebuchadnezzar's golden idol, although of course he had looked her up and down to be polite, and nodded when the priests praised her pointy golden-orange tits (not that full appreciation of her would have saved him from trouble, for Shadrach did not like her and Meshach had to do what Shadrach commanded); really he was blind both to knowledge and to temptation as he sat rocking himself in the darkness and performing scintillant orange flame-calculations to prove that at the VERY LEAST tonight he would not fail to see a fantastic heat-silhouette or two, and there was even a possibility that YAWEH would permit him to glimpse and be haunted by his beloved, *the Tremulously Radiant Princess of Salamanders!* – so with all diligence he observed the troupes of Salamanders whirling about on their tails like natty red dragons while the flames upheld them and excited them so that they leaped and sparks snapped like popping-corn, in the unfailing ecstasy to which they were entitled in virtue of their high-energy molecular state, so Meshach could see that the Salamanders did *not* accept the rule that an all-or-nothing lover must be content with nothing (and neither did the wolves, who were now devouring all his sheep in desperate silence), and the Salamanders smiled upon him as they danced flutter-dances within the glowing orange arches of their castles, in a flamescape whose heavings and shudderings expressed rhythm more passionately than the happiest contractions of the Virgin's uterus . . . then sometimes the *Royal* Salamanders deigned to appear for Meshach within the purest cones of flame, and seven times he had indeed been privileged after all to see with his own eyes the TREMULOUSLY RADIANT PRINCESS OF SALAMANDERS!

The Beloved

She wore a crown of flames; the jewels upon it were embers. Upon her tail was a single royal star. Think, if you can, upon all the marvels which can be seen in a flame, and you will understand the trance that came over Meshach as he watched her. Orange and glistening, fat and slimy, with inquisitive black eyes that sent in his direction a thousand mischievous glances, she gamboled for him upon her adorable little paws, which were webbed, like duck's feet. She CARED for him! – and this thought enthralled him. (In fact she did not care for him *personally;* she warmed to him only because fire must be affectionate as long as it is fed and its grand ambitions are denied; a hearth-fire sends its love to all indiscriminate of their sin.) – "Oh, you poor little cold-face!" the Princess laughed at him. "You look so frozen; I'll drench you with orange and gold!" Truly she had marvelous eyes. How they snapped and sizzled at him! Oh, and she had such *fresh flames;* she was so natural and open! He put his face as close to the flames as he could whenever he saw her, for he loved to inhale her breath, which was as hot and piquant as the steam from mulled cider. He must prosper if he could kiss her. – But I cannot dare to be lingering in my description of that lovely crowned Salamander, for I write in a cold room filled with fog, and when I look too deeply into the scintillant orange tubes of my space heater (which are enclosed in some unearthly assembly of mirrorlike reflectivity) a spark leaps out, and the tubes fade to pinkish-grey and then cold corpse-white, for it is easy to blow a fuse in the course of any presumptuous endeavor.* Suffice it to say that in the movements of this Tremulously Radiant Princess of Salamanders were all the grace and dazzlement of the dragonfly; and I can give no higher praise. – "How can I come into the flame to be with you?" Meshach prayed to her, and at this she laughed and rushed and skipped and whirled upon her tail, but an ireful fire-face had risen up behind her, its muzzle funneling outward into wide orange jaws that sneered as if to say, "Just you *wait!*"; and for a moment he thought it was his Princess's face. How his heart was tormented! He wanted to turn his back on her – to throw sand upon the fire and smother her! – but he could not, for he loved her too much. And of course it was not her; *there* she was in her orange dress and her crown of flames; the Orange Dog of Hell had disappeared. She raised her delicate little hand, and a flame shot up and formed itself into a cup of light for her to drink from. Then other flames obscured her, and Meshach was forlorn, as anyone must be who has not gotten exactly what he wanted. If only he could have confided in Shadrach . . . But Shadrach would never have forgiven him for going over to the Salamanders. And perhaps it was just as well, for he knew from his researches into the nature of YAWEH that happiness, like any substance material or immaterial, thins when shared.

Not that he was happy, not that! Let us note it so in our petite prolegomenon. – Singed by loneliness, he had long permitted jealousy to become his faithfully flickering nurse, stroking the blistered brow of his thoughts with orange fingers that soothed him, warmed him, enraged him until he resembled a man in a flaming shirt who rolls violently upon the floor in paroxysms of fear which are mere embers compared to his anger – for it was not rare for Meshach to observe his Radiant Princess in company with other flame-spirits in smart red uniforms: puffy Salamander-Colonels with big orange bellies, discreetly amorous Sala-mander-Lieutenants, once even a Salamander-General with flaming yellow stars on his shoulders – although he could not fairly hold her

* The same was true for Meshach, who did not know that chief among the wolves was a scrawny half-dog the sunny bloody hue of Mississippi mud who directed the butchery with slavering side-tosses of his head. His yellow eyes regarded the world with hate, because it was not yet burning and screaming. His wrinkled muzzle grubbed evilly in graves; when he grinned his teeth matched his eyes. He was the Orange Dog of Hell, and we will see him again.

accountable for promiscuity, since her teasing words had been no sort
of promise to him; after all, was he any more to her than an almost
expressionless snowman or iceman beyond the flame? – no, she must
be credited for being able to discern him at all (so was it jealousy or was
it expediency that laid its heavy hand on him?). When she smiled
vaguely at him from the fire, he was happy all day, and his heart glowed
SCINTILLANT ORANGE. When (as occurred no less often) she ignored
him, he valued himself as less than twice-burned charcoal. But then the
next time she might blow him a flame-kiss, at which red sparks flew out
at him, although as soon as they felt the cold night air they turned to
ashes. Meshach caught them and kissed them and said to himself, *she
loves me!* – And yet he had never even touched the delicate web between
her fingers. (He had a very lofty conception of her, when in fact she
was only a flame-spirit who could not love any better than he could.
Perhaps you yourself crave some lofty conception?) – "Goodnight, you
dear little icicle," she whispered, but then she giggled; he saw she was
making fun of him again.

So his life burned; so he loved and loved. Even during the Babylonian
Captivity, when his nation was smashed into dust, he did not notice
the screaming refugees or the destruction of the Temple because he
was busy with his plans to win the Tremulously Radiant Princess of
Salamanders. Because *she* was orange, he adored all objects of the
slightest orangetude, which flavor, being common, could always suffice
to solace him – proof that the obscurest of affections may be ubiqui-
tously requited. – Now at last YAWEH had acknowledged his love, and
would give him a chance to consummate it. Surely, he said to himself,
the moth must die happily in the flame.

Symptoms

But Meshach sorrowed for Shadrach and Abednego, who must also
meet the flames, which *they* did not love. So while his brothers awaited
their fate with jagged exaltation, he was not without that particular
species of guilty anxiety which crawls up and down the lumbar vertebrae,
and one night he had a bad dream. It seemed to him that he was
running up the mountain to a place that only he and the sheep and his
brothers knew, and there was Shadrach, leaning on his crook, and

Shadrach's long black beard blew in the wind (they all had black beards, those brothers, and their features were brown), and Shadrach said to him in the place of dancing flowers, "What is the Name of God?" – and Meshach looked stupidly down at his sandals because he could not remember it; when you sinned you could not keep YAWEH in your head no matter how hard you tried – so Shadrach began to weep, saying, "Brother, you are no longer one of us! You no longer know the Name!" – and, crying, he chased Meshach off the mountain with stones.

Idylls of the King

That nightmare must be laid at Nebuchadnezzar's door, the Ishtar Gate, with its blue bricks and paintings of rams and two-headed horses. The parapets have been reconstructed, and the central archway retains its circular embellishments, but through the arch there is a view of nothing but dust all the way to Persia. Neither does his boundary-stone mark a boundary anymore. Let me grimly ignore the present, however, and grind on in a determinedly synchronic description of the boundary-stone, as if I were a man whose medial meniscus has torn and now flaps upon his knee-joint while he limps through the burning orange desert, and the dangling part rakes his tendons with casual cartilage-claws, but he must keep going on, and so must I, because my story has just begun. – Nebuchadnezzar's boundary-stone, then, is carved into two-dimensional storeys, like an executive skyscraper. In the topmost office can be found the crescents and the all-seeing starfish, to whom all must pray; these beings comprise Babylon's Joint Chiefs of Staff. Beneath whom is a floor of pointed-roofed houses too young for the open air. The next suite down is full of kneeling bulls (the world will never be rid of *them!*), and below them are rearing horses with the dull expressions of chessmen, while in a corner a bird on a pedestal stares sullenly at the wall, exhibiting an isolationism not unlike that of the three brothers. In the apartment beneath is Nebuchadnezzar himself on his crouching-horse throne, his crown resembling nothing so much as the head of a paintbrush. The King clasps his hands, elbows resting on his lap. He has a large eye without an eyeball, and he and his horse stare watchfully at a scorpion-tailed centaur who is cocking a bow at some enemy beyond the boundary-stone, perhaps a trespasser, perhaps anyone who will not worship his golden idol, who is to say? On the floor below, which must be the basement, we discern a cow, a tree, a fat turtle, another scorpion.

I have also seen one of his clay cylinders. Who knows what *it* says? In the woods, seeing a fallen tree in which the termites have invested their majesty, we marvel at the wondrous words, written (if we could but read them!) in lines of insect-carving.

The Conquest of Jerusalem

Nebuchadnezzar, who overwhelmed and slaughtered the Egyptians at Karkemish, who was crowned King in Babylon, who destroyed the rebellious province of Ascalon, who fought the King of Egypt in close battle, roaring like a lion and charging him and biting off his ear, yes, O mighty Nebuchadnezzar, King of Kings, who burned his thousands and tens of thousands in the Fiery Furnace, who wiped the desert clean of Arabs, "as though it were a dish"; – Nebuchadnezzar now gave his attention to the land of Judah, for the foolish and refractory King Jehoiakim had refused to remit the yearly tribute. Nebuchadnezzar assembled his hosts, put on his scale armor, donned his helmet. As the records of this campaign have not yet been translated, I rely upon an inscription concerning the previous Nebuchadnezzar:

IN THE MONTH OF TAMMUZ HE TOOK THE ROAD.

THE BLADES OF THE PICKS BURN LIKE FIRE;

THE STONES OF THE TRACK BLAZE LIKE

FURNACES; THERE IS NO WATER IN THE WADIS,

AND THE WELLS ARE DRY; STOP THE STRONGEST

OF HORSES AND STAGGER THE YOUNG HEROES.

YET HE GOES, THE ELECTED KING SUPPORTED BY

THE GODS, NEBUCHADNEZZAR WHO HAS NO

RIVAL...*

* Slightly adapted from George Roux's *Ancient Iraq* (London: Penguin, 1966), p. 251. Roux gives as his source L. W. King's *Babylonian Boundary Stones* (London, 1912), no. vi, pp. 29–36.

He captured Jerusalem, of course, and deported three thousand
Hebrews. Then he gave the throne of Judah into the hands of Zedekiah,
upon whom he assumed he could rely. This ingrate, however, entered
into negotiations with the Egyptians, who gave him gifts and said
noncommittal words to him until he in turn trusted them – without
cause, as it transpired, for when he began his revolt they left him to
scuttle as he might, like a spider fallen out of his web. – So Nebuchadnezzar once more laid siege to Jerusalem. After eighteen months, the
city surrendered. Nebuchadnezzar had the sons of Zedekiah slain
before their father's eyes, and immediately thereafter, Zedekiah having
now seen the last thing that Nebuchadnezzar considered it needful for
him to see, guards plucked out that rebel's eyes. They led him across
the desert in heavy chains of brass, and I am not surprised that the
world did not hear from him again, especially since the world did not
listen, its attention having been directed to the justice being done in
Jerusalem; for Nebuchadnezzar sacked that city, broke down its walls,
took hostages and razed the Temple of Solomon! Then he dismissed
Israel from his mind, as being of no further consequence, and entered
into a siege of Tyre that lasted thirteen years.

The Captivity

And so the Jews toiled upon the enamelled blue walls of Babylon,
smitten with rods as they mounted the ladders to bring their masons
fruit, smitten on the parapets of the walls they built, smitten while they
painted the ziggurats, and King Nebuchadnezzar sat under a tree
watching and smiling – but this was only so that they would know their
place. He intended to treat them as Kurt Franz treated the *Hauptjuden*
of Treblinka: – esteemed for their skills of dentistry, leatherworking,
and portraiture, and hence not marked for immediate extermination. –
Still, Nebuchadnezzar's Jews wailed.

But I saw them smiling when they stoned Achan, who had taken spoil
from Jericho in defiance of the LORD. And Achan sobbed until he died,
while the blood came out of his head. – And when they captured the
city of Hai, they showed no mercy. In their gold helmets and blue
helmets, which were as sharp as the blades of axes, they rode in upon
the city, and their armor was like rings of silver chain around them, and
they smote the warriors of Hai in two with their swords and shot the
defenders with their arrows, so that a thousand corpses tumbled down

from the towers all at once; and then they climbed the parapets and burned the city. They took the King of Hai alive, and for no reason that I can see they hanged him until the sun went down, and he blew back and forth in his green robe of state, so that he frightened the wild dogs. – And they laughed when they hanged the five kings of the Amorrhites, whose tunics fluttered in the breeze like the pages of books, and the dead kings' heads nodded forward or back, depending on which way their necks had broken, and their dead legs pranced as if, too late, they were trying to find the rungs of Jacob's ladder.

A New Start

Every time Nebuchadnezzar thought of something new in those days, his scribes had to go out and carve it into a cliff or a black stele. One day when he was hunting lions, it occurred to him that he should have three or four young men from Judah educated in his palace, as the Soviets do nowadays with children kidnapped from Afghanistan, in order to raise a reliable crop of puppets. So Nebuchadnezzar spoke about the matter to his chief eunuch, Ash'penanz.

"Ashpenanz," said the King, "you are my only friend. I have never regretted the honor and condescension I did you in having you castrated, for you have been worthy. When I take the field with my armies, and Babylon becomes a smudge in the dust behind me, and then vanishes entirely, it is a consolation to me that the women of my palace are in your keeping. You are doubly to be trusted, for not only do you have no desire to mount them for yourself, but you have no capacity for doing so."

"Thank you, O King of Kings," said the eunuch, believing that no good would be served by telling the King what the concubines liked him to do with his big toe.

"Therefore," said the King, "go to Judah to bring me back some fine boys. Teach them the language and fatten them up for three years and we'll see if we can make them into privy counsellors or some other minor ass-wipers."

Zedekiah was still in power at that time. When Ashpenanz came before him, he considered well and gave into his keeping some of the most stubborn lads of royal birth he knew. Their names were Daniel, Hanani'ah, Mish'a-el, and Azari'ah.

"Well, now," chuckled Ashpenanz to the boys, "those are lovely names, yes they are, indeed, but since you are to be brainwashed and piously anointed you must do away with them, so, Daniel, I am going to call you Belteshaz'zar; and, Hananiah, you will be known as Shadrach. Misha-el and Azariah will be – let's see – Meshach and Abednego. Now, Meshach, could you run and load up our donkeys?"

Daniel got thrown into the lions' den and was eaten up in the first minute. So that left Shadrach, Meshach and Abednego.

The Coward

Before the Captivity, Abednego had been a dentist. He was no Lomonosov, to walk hundreds of kilometers in order to master the scientific trade; but he did have a passion; he was a papyrophile. He specifically loved Pushkin. Often he would say to himself as he worked: O LORD, Let me do a good job on the fat priest's crown, or else let me keep the second scroll of Pushkin, with its leather case. Let me keep my office when the Babylonians come, or let me keep the third scroll. AMEN. – He was arrested at a performance of *Der Rosenkavalier*, in the middle of the third act. Close upon the heels of the head usher, a Babylonian policeman entered into the theater's velvet darkness, although the doors were not supposed to be opened for any cause whatsoever upon the dimming of the lights. The Babylonians had, however, conquered the capitol during the first act, so that in the second they had had plenty of time to establish a new government more expressive of popular whim, and this whim had decreed within ten minutes of the third act that all doors were subject to opening at all times; and thus it was that while the policeman waited, spinning the action of his handcuffs, the head usher tiptoed down the aisle in softest shoes and crept low in the dark plantation of heads to harvest Abednego, who could be seen with extraordinary ease, because he had huge glasses which glittered and magnified every stray beam of light from gold cuff-links and luminous watches, and fanned that light into a cool rainbow of blues and greens, so that the head usher was able to tap Abednego's shoulder with authoritative certainty. Abednego had had no warning.

As he was brought into the lobby, he bowed his head – for, like all intellectuals, he would rather define problems than solve them. The handcuffs went *whirrrr*-snggnkk!, the policeman led him out, and the head usher nourished himself upon a highly significant wink at his reflection in the gold-framed mirror (which was soon to hang in Nebuchadnezzar's guest bathroom). Already Abednego was praying: O LORD, please let me keep my dental chair from being nationalized, or else let me keep my fourth scroll. AMEN. – But when he saw Ashpenanz calmly presiding over the looting in his office, while the soldiers gleefully opened wine-jars with his drills, he realized that he would never be able to think about Pushkin again.

Entrance of the Hostages

The towers! The canals! They marched them down the Processional Way, and on every tower the captives saw archers ready to shoot them; and the walls of the city went as far as the eye could see; and the temples frowned at them with the countenances of alien gods, and the weary dusty plain went on and on behind and around them. (Several thousand years later, the desert was not much different except that there were Babylonian road crews on it wearing scintillant orange routine-hazard jackets and scintillant orange helmets that were as round and bright as pumpkins.)

I must describe the situation of the brothers in more detail, so that you may better judge whether Meshach's attitude partook more of farce or of irresponsibility. "They were to be educated for three years," says the Bible, "and at the end of that time they were to stand before the King."* Every day they saw the beardless Hittite prisoners led past the palace window, roped by their necks, and these long columns trudged into the slave-barracks or the Furnace, as Nebuchadnezzar decreed. The bound Syrian captives gazed up at the executioner's face, their eyes wide, their lips parted in pleading; but the executioner, being responsible to Nebuchadnezzar only, did not stop to listen, but seized them by their beards, two at a time, jerked their heads up, and slit their throats with a long blade consecrated to the glorious gods. This took

* Daniel 1.5. Revised standard version.

place punctually at high noon, outside Meshach's window. The blood sizzled in the sand, the flies swarmed, and the dust blew. – Babylon had almost conquered the world in those days. Its red-orange walls hemmed in the vision from the palace, as though these orange streets, these red temples, were lost in some deep canyon; and sunset came to the palace early because the high walls intercepted the orange rays, so that everything fell into shadow while the day-vultures still wheeled in the sky. All day and all night the tribute-bearers came, and Nebuchadnezzar stared blearily at the horns of ointment that piled up beside him, at the little black girls who were led up to him by the hand, as the tribute-bearers knelt down and raised their hands, which were efficiently emptied by Nebuchadnezzar's guards, and then they pressed their heads to the ground, and Nebuchadnezzar assumed that life would go on like this forever (from which misfortune YAWEH, God of the Jews, was already planning to spare him), and at night Nebuchadnezzar sat still upon his throne yawning, while the conquered peoples brought him gold and grain and oil, and occasionally Nebuchadnezzar condescended to taste the raw grain, and if he found it bad, the subject envoy was immediately thrown into the Burning Fiery Furnace.

At dawn the tramping of the prisoners awoke Meshach from his dreams. The soldiers smiled and puffed out their chests when they led them out of the palace. I am sure that the captives' necks were tied with bows. Women were driven away in carts toward Nineveh. "It just doesn't make sense," Meshach heard the soldiers whispering. "They wouldn't work any extra hours!"

Gold Drive

One day the heralds blew their ram's-horns, and the priests farted into their goatskin bagpipes. "We need gold, gold, gold, gold!" they cried. "Gold rings and gold things!" The people were stripped and taxed of their coins and ornaments. The gold was melted; a prisoner was thrown into the casting for good luck, and a new idol was presented to the land.

The priests had talked Nebuchadnezzar into it. Everyone follows the procedure described by the *Great Soviet Encyclopedia* (1977) in its definition of fetishism: "a product of human activity is turned into something transcendent." For Meshach it was the flames that men kindled in their beehive kilns. For his brothers it was the angels which men depicted, sight unseen; and for the Babylonian court it was the golden idol. They counted on her to support their victories. At night she was taken to the beds of rich men. The priests and Nebuchadnezzar split the profits fifty-fifty. As a clay tablet has it, "May ANU and ISHTAR and the solemn oath of Nebuchadnezzar, King of Babylon, decree the destruction of whosoever alters this agreement."

The Stubborn Boys

The golden idol stood upon a golden column and waggled her golden butt. The King bowed and frowned to show the seriousness of his regard, while minstrels plucked their D-shaped lyres, and crowds of notables, wrapped in their bat-winged gowns, genuflected behind every pillar, and the bearded priests waved their censers – but under a distant arch, the three Jews stood with their backs to the image and their noses in the air. So the illuminated Lambeth Bible has it, and who am I to argue, who was not there?

First Interview with Nebuchadnezzar

"Well," said the tyrant, "have you boys changed your minds?"

"No, sir," said Shadrach.

There was a silence not unlike that false lull which follows the onset of symptoms in fatal phosphorus intoxication. We all know such silences too well. Every sound glances off our rubbery haloes of failure and returns to its point of origin, and breath inhaled cannot convince us that we are not in fact stifling. This is a silence in which many keys are turning unheard in the locks of many awful consequences, one of which will pertain to us and punish us forever. – At last Nebuchadnezzar sighed. He was just, and would not have punished them on mere hearsay. – "It distresses me," he said, "to be assured of your transgression, but I daresay it will hurt *you* if I have you thrown into my Furnace. Can you smell the smoke? I can see it. Black, greasy smoke. – Slave! Fan me, slave! – I know that you're bright boys who majored in religious studies, so you have knowledge and righteousness. I am telling you that you have done wrong. Ashpenanz is burning people now, to *warn* you. (I think I can hear them scream.) If you persist in your disobedience, the priests will say that SUCCOTH-BENOTH has been insulted, and then I will be called weak. So it would please me if you fell down and prayed to that golden idol over there. I know you don't believe in her, but I'd like to remind you Jews that I conquered you, so I just might know more about gods than you do."

"O King, live forever!" replied Shadrach bitterly. "We will consider our position." (For he wanted time to didacticize his brothers into a glorious martyrdom.) "It may be that we have made a logical error. But I doubt it."

"Think it over," said the King wearily.

Preparations of the Heroes

Shadrach, like Koestler's old revolutionary, prepared himself by holding his fingers in a flame. But at night when his brothers could not see, he took a tiny transistor radio from under his clay-baked pillow and tuned in to Radio Free Judah (which was a capital offense), and he held the radio against his ear and listened to a crackly ghostly whisper:

> O come, O come, Emmanuel,
> And ransom captive Israel
> That mourns in lonely exile here
> Until the Son of God appear.

And the tears rolled down his cheeks. For Shadrach was no less sad and fearful than the other Condemned. But he would not show it; he would *not* show it.

Morning, noon and night he led his brothers in prayer. He slicked back his black hair and urged calm. He spoke of the power and the righteousness of YAWEH, and it was clear that he took pleasure in it and wanted to gladden their hearts – which he did, for they were all, as the King said, religious boys; I am not sure that I have ever seen boys as religious as they, with the possible exception of my poor friend Seth, who, pathetically in love with a woman who loved women, went around kissing her floor, her bookshelf, her doorknob, and when Seth found a

dead fawn in the forest he boiled the skin from the dirty orange skull
and bleached it white and pure to give to her, but in his heart was a
Burning Fiery Furnace which baked him and broiled him so that the
sweat ran down his face. – Shadrach prayed with equal fervor: "The
blood of YAWEH is as *rain* to the thirst of the RIGHTEOUS!" It was his
mind's tendency to soothe itself with its own steadfastness, as certain
machines for grinding and slicing metal must cool themselves inces-
santly with some circulating liquid; so Shadrach's mind required its
own arterial system, which, while it doubtless required a metabolic
effort of morals, permitted him to grind down his brothers. He turned
his consideration to them. – Meshach was no worry to him, for Meshach
had always been a stoical boy. Of *course* he would die for Shadrach's
principles! So Meshach was left to his own preparations, which
consisted, as we know, of 666 subspecies of guilty vacillation. (Occasionally he thought himself the most miserable of all human beings
because of his secret nature; other times he loved the secret and
gleefully hid it inside himself and was happy with the power of the
secret. For at those latter times he believed that his Salamander-
Princess loved him.) – Abednego, however, was but a measly ingot,
padded with a lamb's fluffy soul. It was incumbent on Shadrach to
machine him to a more appropriate tolerance.

Heels and Vultures

Whereas Shadrach was a character engineer, Abednego was a
researcher of the physical world. He had already begun various
experiments with clay, for it was his theory that he could find some
mixture which, when tempered, might keep his scorching doom away.
So he would become an armorsmith! If a dying man calls the doctor,
who are we to deny him the comfort? Certainly nothing he did could
hurt Abednego, since the worst had already been decreed. Accompanied
by a brace of jeering guards, he made his potter's expeditions, therefore,
to the foot of the Burning Fiery Furnace, which towered so vast and
sooty above the sand-hills that he could scarcely see the top of it – nor
did he care to, for why should he be reminded of the burning orange
nothingness into which he must soon be tumbled? As it was, he squatted
downcast upon a plain of nothingness, gathering clay amidst a wilder-

ness of waist-high hillocks whose sand down-trickled with the deliberation of hourglasses; and the sun smote Babylon all the way to the
orange distances of Arad and Baal-Peor, so that he was grateful for the
shade of the Furnace. Because his activity partook of the microscopic,
it seemed to the vultures who circled shyly (having learned that they
were as liable to fall lucklessly down the great orange shaft, smitten by
its heat that melted their feathers in midair, as they were to find some
poor gobbet of humanity exploding upward to be snatched by their
beaks), to the vultures it seemed that Abednego would soon be their
food, for many a time had they peered down between their black-
feathered shoulders to spy some lone refugee stumbling through the
sand, fleeing the fate which had already consumed his family, but his
flight was always to death, for if Ashpenanz's soldiers did not discover
him from the ramparts of the Furnace and rush down to slay him with
javelins, his thirst would certainly do for him, and then, when he was
still, the vultures would descend reverently upon his face to bring him
the blessed shade of darkness; so every day the vultures swooped round
and round over Abednego's head, beating their wing-points and
wondering when his motions would stop – but always fearful, too, lest
he prove to be an enemy whose purpose was to decoy and destroy them
(for vultures must worry their black heads over what they cannot help);
they were never sure that Abednego did not hide in his cloak some
spear or arrow with which he might suddenly pierce them, so they
wheeled and waited, and occasionally, startled by his shadow, one
croaked an alarm and they all flew away screeching – some few,
perhaps, to be caught in the updraft of the Furnace, at which point their
metaphorical geese were literally cooked and *roasted* in the midst of
their terrified flappings, but you may be sure that Abednego did not
look up from his clay-play. Every few minutes, of course, he had to
sweep away the cinders which had swirled down upon his shoulders; to
that extent he must, like Margaret Fuller, accept the universe, although
it had so gaily abandoned *him*. But he was smart enough to shut out
from him whatever he could. Here his steadfast lowness of regard
served him well. It guarded his eyes against cataracts – the bane of the
desert dweller – and when he did face the Burning Fiery Furnace, he
was preserved from the sight of anything save thousands of FEET: naked
feet and sandaled feet, the soft pink feet of children and the horny-
heeled feet of retired laborers, the feet of mothers and daughters and
grandmothers, all tramping up the steps of that Burning Fiery Furnace.

How strange that they were all going away from him! Abednego, having shut out ankles, buttocks, backs, shoulders, backward-looking faces, and the Burning Fiery Furnace itself, whose stairs were colorful with the ascending crowd, now worked at contracting his vision of feet, until in time (that comical fellow!) he perceived only HEELS. But the heels still went away from him. They passed and forsook him, although other heels substituted themselves with the miraculous ease of large numbers, so that Abednego should be comforted by familiarity in the landscape of his exile, should his eyes require it, which they did not. The tramping and coughing and shuffling which accompanied those heels blended into a steady noise that he was likewise able to rise above, in unknowing imitation of the vultures.

Eggs and Whores

In a little *wadi* he had found red clay and white clay. With the earnestness of a dung beetle, poor Abednego rolled out his clay-balls in the sand. He tried burning them and baking them; he mixed them with sand and blackened bone-ash. In the middle of each ball he placed a raw egg, whose embryo trusted in his mercy, for chicklings must trust as cannot defend themselves. Now came the heat-test: – O YAWEH, lend me Your power to command! Once Abednego had invented a material which would save the egg from being cooked (convincing the occupant that its fervid fetal prayer had been taken into account), *then* it would be time to say to oneself, "Abednego, activate your productive forces!" – at which, forthwith, our man would develop a clay buckler and a clay visor and a clay shirt and clay pants (tightness of the joints being of the utmost importance) and clay boots with a black glaze and reflective clay mittens, so that upon being cast into the Furnace he might be safe, always assuming that he landed on soft orange pillows of flame so that his shell of grandeur did not crack. Then, when night came, he would creep out of the Furnace and hitchhike to Palestine, triumphantly un-fricasséed! So Abednego had reason to hope that clay and prayer could sustain him, just as a leper dotes on vitamins and a drowning man will invariably stuff desiccant into his mouth before the final plunge. – But first, as I was saying, the mixture must pass Abednego's thermal test, for it would be facing severe operating conditions, both of conduction and convection, and the true mean value of the terminal temperature differential must be known and prepared for, to say nothing of the enthalpy. So Abednego prayed and blew on his fingers and rolled the new clay-balls against the wall of the Burning Fiery Furnace, where they could bake against a grating behind which the darkness flickered with evil orange lightnings, and the heat was sufficient to make a body scream. Here the experimental cookies were toasted overnight, at temperatures ranging from 2200 to 2700° Fahrenheit, while Abednego gnawed his fingernails and prayed and convinced himself that *this* batch would resound to the glory of golden-brownness, but when he smashed them open on the following day, no egg remained unscorched, O treacherous hydrous silicate of aluminum! If only he had ground in more feldspar, or maybe some of that crushed ganister rock . . .

At night, such was his anxiety (for their interview with Nebuchadnezzar impended, and the anger of the tyrant was said to be waxing), he rolled out lime-clay and flint-clay on the window-sill, and in his sleep his fingers were continually shaping and squeezing the dry air. As soon as morning came he must leap up, pray, and get a two-way Furnace pass from Ashpenanz (all too soon that worthy would make him out the dreaded one-way pass, on a clay tablet which would be tied around his neck and incinerated with him), so that he could run down Furnace Boulevard, where the wall-tops were lined with loungers kicking their heels and laughing and yelling, "BURN, baby, BURN!", but the shadows of their legs swung and crisscrossed on the pavement and cooled Abednego at the same time that he must run their gauntlet of laughs, hugging a dozen fresh eggs in his shirt; and he dashed through the Gate of Last Reprieve, while the shadows withered in the morning sun, and he galloped through the Gate of Death (while his guards trotted boredly alongside, holding their walkie-talkies to their ears to catch the latest MOLOCH joke), and he trotted across the plain of sand, looking down at his twinkling sandals, his clacking eggs, so that he would not have to see the Burning Fiery Furnace that loomed ahead of him, and he rushed wailing to his *wadi* to recommence the daily business of red clay and white clay: maybe if the layers were *thicker*, and he could somehow work in air pockets here and there; – while the sun burned, and grimy HEELS began the upward tramp and the Burning Fiery Furnace roared to life above him with its first puff of stinking smoke; and as he retrieved his previous day's clay-balls from the grating,

Abednego *must* peer despite himself at that ruthless orange glow within, just as we *must* know whether we have terminal cancer; and his heart went *pa-PAM, pa-PAM, pa-PAM!* until he concluded that he had better discover the secrets of insulation TODAY, but time came and time went and it was noon, and his guards settled down in the sand, picking the stones and thorns out from under their bottoms, for they labored toward their comfort as Christ labored to His Calvary. – "Now, you be good, kid," they said to their prisoner. Leaning up against each other's backs, so that they would be prepared for enemies coming and going, these happy guards guzzled their cans of orange soda, hove bricks at the vultures, pulled their helmets over their eyes, yawned and burped and finally snored. How sweet it was to see each guard-head pillowing the other! – Alas, their zephyrous nose-music was but the overture to the next of Abednego's trials, for a brass door opened in the Furnace wall, and up a narrow flight of stairs marched those goose-hipped, lemur-lipped women, once the Daughters of Zion, now infamously reincorporated into the Cinder-Whores of Babylon (may hard times never fall on *you!*); the oldest were black-faced; the youngest were grey-faced; and the hems of their dresses were rent with mourning for the Tabernacle of Judah and their eyes were red with weeping, but they must smile orange smiles now, and if Abednego had looked past his clay-balls he would have seen the pupils of their eyes shining with a black prisoner-light that glimmered behind the bars of their eyelashes, being elsewhere concealed behind their faces' stolid bricks, and this light betrayed their intent to make him take them all as his day-wives, for then they could buy wine and sing quavering songs beneath the Furnace and turn away from each other in the hot darkness to gloat upon shekels and roubles and dinars, but, needless to say, Abednego didn't look up from his clay-balls, so the disgruntled Cinder-Whores, not being mere saguaro cacti or anoerobic bacilli, who thrive on our inattention, were compelled to come out from the darkness, squinting and puckering their mouths in the sunlight, which acted on them like sour oranges, but although their scraggly hair crackled on their heads, their mouths were painted with orange fireclays so that they must stay upturned in grinning bows, and their eyes gleamed more sootily than ever in their sly faces – such black-chalked ball-bearings, rolling so frictionlessly in *such* engines of entrapment! and the Cinder-Whores whispered and winked (but Abednego looked only at his clay-balls); and they tiptoed through the sand, shaking the vermin from between their toes, and they smoothed their baked-on dresses into a million pieces of shattered crust, and hunkering down in a semicircle around him, the Cinder-Whores strummed the strings of mucus between their legs and sang "Come On, Baby, Light My Fire," and although Abednego kept molding his clay-balls, they undid the first seven buttons of pessimistic constriction, but Abednego just squeezed his clay-balls, so they smiled smoky silky smiles and bounced their sooty breasts on sooty palms, *swoosh! swoosh!* and inched their buttocks closer and closer to him, leaving salt-trails behind them in the poisoned sand, but Abednego, who would rather have seen departing heels than advancing toes, and in any event had no investment in anything above the ankle, was content to work and work at his clay-balls, so then the Cinder-Whores started to cry and strewed dust on their heads in supplication, for they knew about the raw eggs which Abednego cradled in his shirt: *fresh* RAW eggs full of fluid of richness superior to coconut milk, and there were dozens and dozens of them, all grade AAA Jumbo Extra-Large Plus, Abednego being of royal birth and all so that even now in his disgrace he could order whatever breakfast he wanted, whereas the Cinder-Whores had only spittle and semen for their food, and the pride was long gone from their eyes, and their babies had died on their bosoms, so they looked groaning into Abednego's face and named the Name of YAWEH, but Abednego shrank away from them and took up a thorn-stick and rolled his golden-baked clay-balls away from the grating and sorted them and categorized them, saying to himself, "Yes, here's the steel-reinforced polymer-clay, and this is the perfectly spherical ball of pure white clay that I prayed over seven times – now for my stick!" – and he started smashing his pottery wildly, his eyes starting with tears that only a noble hostage could afford to let fall into the hot hot sand that sizzled as it received them, and some clay-balls crumbled to powder and some shattered into glassy black fragments like obsidian, but inside every one was a scorched hardboiled egg, at which Abednego howled in despair. The Cinder-Whores waited patiently until he had smashed them all, and then they divided the food and went away blessing him in the name of the LORD. But if ever a fresh egg rolled out of his shirt, they pounced upon it and desperately bolted the fluid down, for they were so thirsty that their tongues cleaved to the roof of their mouths.*

---

* Lamentations 4.4: "The tongue of the nursling cleaves to the roof of its mouth for thirst; the children beg for food, but no one gives it to them."

Preparations of the Heroes (Continued)

Shadrach had doubts about these proceedings. He would not yet forbid Abednego to carry them out, and yet they showed a certain lack of martyrish resolve. Like squares of sunlight upon concrete, therefore, brightly unrelated lectures and assurances were projected by Shadrach onto Abednego's unyielding surface. – "Consider, brother, that if you were to be burned over a seventh of your body's surface you could endure it," said Shadrach. "Therefore, you need only increase your faith and endurance by a factor of seven and you will be prepared." – Abednego ducked his head and rolled out more clay-balls for his suit of ceramic armor.

"Abednego!" said the other sharply.

"Yes, brother."

"Don't you understand that nothing will save our lives? You know the King's heart. Even if we were to abandon YAWEH and worship the golden idol, we would not live. Nebuchadnezzar hates us! The picture is complete. He has destroyed the Temple, and he will destroy us."

"Yes, brother."

"'Yes, brother!' You say, 'yes, brother!' but you are ringed with fire, and you go on rolling your dung-balls! You cannot pull against fate. Abednego, I love you and would die twice, if I could, so that you could live, but I have no say."

"Yes, brother," said Abednego dully. "Everything is so difficult . . ."

So the brothers whiled away the last of their lives, and when he was as sure as he could be of their stony sense of sacrifice, Shadrach announced to Ashpenanz that all three were unyielding in their refusal.

Second Interview with Nebuchadnezzar

"I had not thought you so polluted," said the King, still pitying them and relenting toward them. "You who were princes have become unclean in your acts. I open my ears to you. Tell me the cause of this ungrateful and blasphemous refusal."

"O King," said Shadrach sternly, expecting and hoping that his head would be struck off any minute, "if we are worthy, then YAWEH will deliver us from the Burning Fiery Furnace. If not, we still refuse to worship your gods. You think you can see to the bottom of our souls, but what you mistake for the urine of yellow servility is the scintillant orange glow of martyrdom, and that is hotter than any of your fires. Are you prepared, Your Majesty, to draw the necessary political conclusions?"

"Do I truly hear self-righteous buzzing, or am I dreaming?" said Nebuchadnezzar, so sarcastically that the very air of the throne hall seemed to acidulate.

Shadrach could but bow in silence, imagining him fallen in death (if only!) from his lion-headed throne, struck suddenly by the bony fist of his own Sin so that he tumbled down the many ebony steps and hit his head on the dirt that was worn hard from the thousands who had fearfully prostrated themselves during his reign, polishing the earth with their foreheads; and in Shadrach's satisfied imagination the tyrant's crown rolled off and fell upside down on his face, impaling his dead eyes with jeweled spikes; and a breeze began to blow dust upon the throne.

"And what of you, Meshach?" said the tyrant.

"O King," said he, "may your treasures increase according to the quadratic formula! I must obey my brother." (But he was rolling the commitment between his fingers like an orange marble. How could he do it when he *wanted* to do it? But he *had* to do it because he loved the Tremulously Radiant Princess of Salamanders.)

The King shook his head sadly. "Abednego?" said he.

Abednego was the youngest of the brothers. Photographs in the family album always showed Shadrach grinning heartily, his arm around his brothers, his hair slicked back; and Meshach in the middle also smiled dutifully, but Abednego's smile was only a shadow of one, a worried grimace; if he had been smiling that way among ranks of fraternity boys after a panty raid the camera would have come to find him out, stopping its pan like a searchlight suddenly certain of guilt; and then his sick smile would be caught . . .

Discussions

In Meshach's family they never had Arguments; they had Discussions instead; and when Shadrach would say, "Brother, I'm afraid I've got to Discuss something with you," Meshach would start feeling all queasy, knowing that a prolonged difficult artificial situation would now be constructed by Shadrach, at Shadrach's pleasure, for a length of time determined by Shadrach, until Shadrach personally gave the nod to its decay. These Discussions could be over any number of things, from Abednego's failure to pray to YAWEH at the proper intervals, to Meshach's neglect of his sheep – not that the last was ever proved, but there was always *something* which could be proved ... Meshach considered his best defense against Shadrach to lie in attentiveness and more attentiveness; that was something impossible to overdo. Like the boy at school who asks questions in order to avoid being required to supply answers, Meshach made of himself, quite without obsequiousness, a punctuation mark for each of Shadrach's sentences. But Abednego had never learned that trick. He fared the worst in the Discussions, and accordingly hated them the most.

... "Abednego!" said Shadrach.

"Yes, brother."

"Abednego, I have been praying and looking into your heart, and I see Sin written there with a pen of brass and iron. You have been building *idols of clay!* Abednego, you are forbidden to continue your experiments. Kneel beside me and pray."

Spreading His Wings

It was Abednego, then, the only sane one of the brothers, who attempted to escape on the night after the second interview. You might wonder where exactly he intended to go, given the vigilance of Nebuchadnezzar's minions, to say nothing of the vastness of Babylon upon the moonlit plain, shadowed by its turreted walls and inhuman buildings. It seemed that the city went on forever. And every brick had been baked in the flaming ovens; every wall and street remained hot to the touch. At dawn this dull clay cemetery, inhabited by living ghouls, became pink, then orange. The heat of the sky-furnace sapped the determination even of warriors, let alone bookish fellows like Abednego. And beyond Babylon the hard plain of desert pavement continued, baked orange-brown by the sun, alleviated only by crumbling orange-brown mountains unpossessed of water; no one lived there except for scorpions and demons; and even if Abednego could traverse the Babylonian desert, he would have to wander by himself through the salty Slough of Despond and then he must endure the doleful sight of Eden, which was fenced off by barbed wire and surrounded by machine-gun emplacements manned (if that is the word) by scowling flaming-eyed angels, and everywhere he looked there were signs saying KEEP OFF and NO TRESPASSING and WE SHOOT TO KILL; and behind the barbed wire was what appeared to be a delightful green forest where he might be able (if he could attain it) to walk alongside silver rushing rivers, with green banana trees breathing down his neck, and sit down to dangle his feet below concave cliffs where water fell five hundred feet to refresh him with its mist, and green plants shook in the wind that that waterfall made, and the plants on the cliffside steamed and behind their curtain of silvery droplets, and in the rock at the bottom of the falls was a round pool of green water that rushed out, down, down, down, to mingle with pink flowers and white flowers and pretty clouds, and the air always smelled like pepper – but if you used your hawk-eyed Near Eastern vision you would see that the trees were bare and black, the illusion of foliage being given by the millions of fat bluish-green coils of a certain Serpent which had run wild and devoured everything; the very Mount of Eden itself had been tunneled through and puffed up by the monster in its restless hunger; and when everything was gone it had eaten the dirt, for which it substituted its own scaly flesh; so that aside from the dead trees and a thin layer of topsoil, the entire mountain *was* the Serpent; and even if Abednego had been able to get beyond that, there was no home for him to go to, for the kingdom of Judah was now but a bald expanse of orange sand, as hot to the touch as the bricks of Babylon; and if a traveler sifted patiently through this sand for a century or two, a tooth, a scrap of holy scroll, or a pitted Tabernacle ornament might come to light, but that would be all. – Please remember that Abednego was, however, a highly

rational young man, bearded like a scholar. He did have a definite plan:
– to eat YAWEH's manna, as the other righteous had done.

At night he escaped from the palace. How he did it is still a state
secret. Shadrach, whose nutlike heart was kerneled with bitter honor,
reported his absence to Ashpenanz, and the eunuch roused the King's
guards. – Abednego led them a grotesquely merry chase up the steps of
ziggurats, through MYLITTA's temples where the Cinder-Whores of
Babylon exercised their calling, and along the ramparts of the inner
wall. Laughing, they pursued him with resplendent torches. From a
tower, an archer shot an arrow into his shoulder, and he cried out and
fell into the Euphrates just as day was breaking. The river glowed a
sullen molten orange. They fished him out and dragged him home. The
Cinder-Whores followed, hoping (what is life without hope?) that a
Jumbo egg or two might yet roll out of his shirt.

Shadrach Faces Facts

Shadrach was stricken with horror by Abednego's cowardice. But the
harshest natures must blame themselves a thousandfold for the sin they
see in others. Had *he* been a niddering pansy? He had trudged into
Captivity so obligingly, and now he wondered whether he should have
poured out his rebellious blood on his own hearthstone. He wondered
whether he and Meshach – thank YAWEH he still had one true brother
left! – should have set out to become guerrillas on the day the news
came over the radio that the Babylonians had crossed the frontier.
Disguised as Hittite lieutenants, they might have wandered along
Nebuchadnezzar's troop trains, ducking in and out of lavatories, slitting
throats whenever they could ... but eventually the Babylonians would
have caught on, and begun searching the cars from locomotive to
caboose, ready with black anodyzed flashlights which cast a bloody-
orange beam; he heard their heartless tramping, and though Meshach
crouched wide-eyed beside him with a Joshua Scout knife in his teeth,
Shadrach could see that there was nothing left to do now but pull out,
especially since his Solomon PK .38 had jammed, so he dropped the
dead pistol down the toilet and made Meshach stand on his shoulders
to raise the window, then they jumped for it one by one – not out of the
base cravenness which had distinguished Abednego, but rather to fight

another day, this being Shadrach's desert Dunkirk – and Shadrach's alone; for Abednego had failed him and Meshach was only a follower at best (Shadrach never recognized the divine truth that half of the time others let you down, and the other half of the time you let others down), so it seemed fitting to him that as they ran through the hot orange sand Gilgamesh's great-grandson got Meshach in the back with a distinguished spear-cast for which he later received the Order of Ishtar, Second Class; and Shadrach saw that it was hopeless and let them come rushing up to slam the irons on him, *THONGGGGK!*, after which he was tried, tortured and convicted, sentenced to be executed at the pleasure of the DOG-GOD, so for weeks he and the other commissars earmarked for liquidation had to march behind the extermination apparatus, which was a pyramid on wide creaking axles, hauled by whip-lashed slaves, *phwupp! phwapp!* and once a day the Orange Dog of Hell howled and whimpered and grinned from the mountains, and when his voice was heard the prisoner whose number was up had to lift the door-flap at the back of the pyramid and crawl inside, then the slaves were whipped into a run, and as the pyramid rolled along, the prisoner was forced to trot with it, like someone stuck in a revolving door, and there were stout cypress-wood gears above him which turned as the pyramid was dragged along, and these had comb-teeth and started coming lower and lower and pretty soon he had to stoop as he ran, and after awhile he was running with his face almost in the sand, and the teeth ground lower and lower until they caught him and hooked him, and he was drawn up into the gears and minced. One day it was Shadrach's turn. As they cleaned the gears from yesterday, he stood looking his last at the shore of the Caspian, where the aircraft carrier U.S.S. *Babylon* prepared to embark into salty blueness, and seagulls wheeled around her gun turrets, hoping against hope that somebody would be court-martialed and hanged so that they could peck him for breakfast, and the cabin-boy was polishing the figurehead, which represented the sea-god DAGON, and elite orange squadrons marched up the gangway, each man bearing his own nuclear crossbow, and the battleship's grey armor-plates shimmered like scales, and on the runway deck, her arms rather forlornly crossed, was a slender violet-haired woman whom Shadrach recognized at once as Saint Catherine of Siena, whom he had always planned to marry between commando raids (for Shadrach considered himself a humanist), but that day of fruitful multiplication with Catherine had never come, what with the scorched-earth policy and the very time-consuming scintillant orange strategies of the Jewish Defense League; anyhow, there she was, and Catherine drummed her nervous fingers on the railing and bowed her head and stared down into the ocean, and then her gaze wandered to the desert land that she was about to leave behind, and there was Shadrach with the ropes on him, and the dreaded orange flag was flying above the pyramid, and Catherine understood what was about to happen, so she twisted her braids in her hands for a moment and went smiling up to an Admiral who doted on her, and she said, "You know, dear, I was actually kind of *wondering* if we could maybe have Shadrach over for a little *dinner* or something with us," so the launching of the battleship was suspended, and Shadrach was reprieved and his chains were struck off and he was brought into the presence of Catherine, for such is the power of beauty and grace in men's lives. – "And the ransomed of the LORD shall return, and come to Zion with singing."* – Catherine herself broke into a happy little song, for she often trilled. The Admiral patted Shadrach's shoulder kindly and said that of course dear boy mistakes were sometimes made. The galley slaves whisked out another chair and changed the lobsters in the aquarium, and then Catherine came and fetched him to dinner – an excellent dinner. O abundance! O gifts of YAWEH to men! – The fillet of Leviathan was especially delicious. – Just before dessert, the Admiral excused himself to direct a sea battle, and Shadrach and Catherine were left together for one of those awkward moments when there is nothing to do but stare down at the tablecloth, which in this case was patterned with tiny fishes, skulls and anchors, in keeping with the Admiral's threefold profession, and finally Catherine filled her wine-glass with a nervous hand and explained to Shadrach that she had waited for him longer than Saint Stylites stood on that pillar in the desert, but when she started getting sick and old and he still hadn't come back to her, she had had to marry the greatcoated Admiral, who was in fact *extremely* nice, and she wondered what Shadrach thought of him. – As a result of being saved, Shadrach had to be on his best behavior for years and years and YEARS and in fact for the remainder of his lifelong Babylonian Captivity so as to avoid compromising Catherine (having saved him, she would have been accountable if he had committed any subsequent terrorist acts); thus the bright orange fire of integrity was extinguished in him and he

* Isaiah 51.11.

became a high-level minor official in the Babylonian People's Autonomous Republic of Judah, where he stood in the ankle-deep sand dedicating new tombs and old tombs until it was time to be chauffeured back down the Chaldean Expressway to another VIP suite where the Caspian Sea ground against the orange pebbles with a sound like tank-treads on a driveway and he could watch TV in bed while he munched on salted dates and was astounded to find that *he liked every politician!* – for the ones who lied appealed to him on account of their human fallibility, their vulnerability (they were rotten, like him), and the ones who droned on like bombers, repeating themselves over and over, charmed him by reason of their sweet steadfastness; but sometimes Shadrach woke up in the middle of the night, sweating despite the mildewy effusions of the groaning air conditioner, and he rolled over in the double bed to peremptorily twang the underpants of his paid companion, but even after some of the old Song of Solomon stuff he still couldn't sleep, beset by orange bars of heat inside his eyelids, and eventually dawn came and he gave up and opened his eyes, and the sizzling orange bars of sunrise were coming through the venetian blinds, and it was time to go lay the cornerstone for still another mass grave; and one day when he was almost fifty Shadrach received a visit from Abednego and their ailing mother, who now had water in her kidneys, but had come all the way from her locust-tract resettlement housing nonetheless on a three-day transit visa, and she was lost in that luxurious griffin-fur coat which Shadrach had bought her at the official store, and the wind blew and the sand blew and the dry inimical lizards warmed their bellies on the hot rubble-stones, and Shadrach took his family around the various sites which he had dedicated, and Abednego was very quiet and his mother kept smiling and blowing her nose and everyone addressed Shadrach as Mr. Shah *Sir!* and at every new monument the bodyguards checked his mother's purse again, although they never found anything except Saltines and dirty kleenex; and Shadrach presented Abednego with a student's calfskin briefcase because Abednego had remained a student all these years, in fact, thanks to all the reeducation he had received on the drainage crews at Isin or Uruk State; and Abednego said thank you limply, and in the next sandy orange valley the chief bodyguard said, "Well, come on, Mr. Shah, let's get a snapshot of the happy visit!", but because the sub-bodyguards were busy smiling and organizing everybody into a photogenic phalanx, they did not see the desperately emaciated silhouettes on the ridge taking aim at Shadrach with their Lee-Enfield single-shot rifles which went back to the time of Moses, because Shadrach was the most splendidly dressed official there, so they naturally assumed that he was one of the hated Babylonians who had thrown their nation down, and if he wasn't, well, shit, he might as well have been, for, as Dietrich Eckart said in *Auf Gut Deutsch* (1918), "Politics is less damaging to character than character to politics," so they pulled their triggers, *pook!*, and a bullet punctured Abednego's new briefcase and then Shadrach fell, having received two bullets in the peritoneum and one in the lung; and everybody SCREAMED and the bodyguards practically pissed in each other's pants calling in an airstrike on that ridge, and an official orange ambulance came hurtling down the highways, flinging aside the Israeli road-beggars with its wide, wide razor-bumpers (how the paramedics laughed to see that dance of severed limbs!), and Shadrach was hustled onto a stretcher and pumped full of Balm of Gilead, and they rushed him to the hospital but by midnight it became clear that his wounds were mortal, and Shadrach's mother thought that Catherine might want to say goodbye to him, so she sent Abednego to her claystone apartment in the city and Abednego was crying (for he had always loved Shadrach more than Shadrach knew), and he said, "Mrs. Hammurabi, Shadrach's been shot, and he's almost at the end!", but Catherine was very old by now and had no desire to be mixed up with anything risky anymore, so she did not want to come. The next morning, as they were shoveling orange sand into Shadrach's grave, she met Shadrach's mother and she said, "You know, your son Abednego had the *oddest* dream last night. He said he dreamed that Shadrach's dog got caught in a trap and *died*. Isn't that *peculiar?*"

"No!" said Shadrach to himself, concerning this scenario. Far better to perish honorably in the Burning Fiery Furnace. As one of Malraux's Chinese Communists sighs, just before being hurled into the broiler of Chiang Kai-Shek's locomotive, "Let's just say I died in a fire."

Another Vision of the Tremulously Radiant Princess of Salamanders

Of course Meshach too had considered escaping. He did not want to die for his love if he could live for it. So now, as Shadrach shouted and pounded the wall with his fists (he had wanted to participate in the search for Abednego, but the guards would not give him permission), he smiled dreamily and looked into the orange coals of the ever-glowing braziers and imagined that he was at this very instant driving inconspicuously down the desert highway, which was packed with speeding orange Porsches, and bright orange construction signs directed traffic on heart-gladdening detours, so that Meshach could admire the orange bulldozers grinding up sand on the far side of hundred-mile barbed wire fences as drivers whizzed by jouncing and nodding to the silent songs of the radios, and the highway now rose through a cut in the red-orange clay of mountains and Meshach drove past the revolving orange balls of gas station signs, tailgating the big trucks from Redding and Red Bluff and Orange Grove, and the day got hotter and hotter until even the cool sly jazz on the tape player began to sublime into squeaking and chirring, and orange smoke gushed out of the cassette, and sweat formed in a film on Meshach's forehead except where the sun's orange rays were interrupted by big squashed bugs on the windshield; in those spots Meshach's face remained quite dry and collected. Brown-orange grass afflicted the eye, unmoving on brown-orange hills. The broad spiny lobes of cacti writhed in the wind, which was like the breath of a sunny furnace, so that if Meshach's orange Hyundai had broken down and he had had to start walking to the chalcolithic repair garage the sweat would have *really* exploded on his forehead and a deep sweaty nausea would have bubbled in his belly as the heat dizzied him and took his wits and thirst cracked the black-burned tissues inside his throat, and if he had bitten into one of the cactus-ovals in hopes of finding a few drops of bitter juice, there would only be hardness and dryness inside, and the spines would have pierced his tongue and ripped it out of his mouth so that it hung red and steaming on the thorns like a bloody trophy flag which dried out so quickly that in five seconds it resembled *carne seca* – but I am happy to report that Meshach's Hyundai did not break down; no, the drive was smooth and scintillantly orange. Presently he crossed the Oregon border, and there were green forests, and rain fell. ("This really figures," my Korean girl once told me. "When you hit Oregon, it's gonna rain like this. So pathetic! Makes me tired! This goddamn state never gave me a good ride.") He did not even stop to eat scintillant orange salmon jerky, such was his hurry to reach the state of Washington with its blue trees in the fog, its yellow autumn trees, its long freight-trains and gusts of rain, which brought nightmares even as Meshach lay a fugitive in his hotel room spinning taut membranes of sleep, these suddenly punctured by fears which the rain had drummed into him, for he lived only for scintillant orange things, and so he woke up shaking and shivering; he jumped out of bed and checked out and started driving on a dark street on a rainy morning. He passed by a store which was closed, but its lights still blazed and said FURNACES – how horrible! – but it made Meshach smile, because he knew that he was on the right track. Dawn came, disclosing a sickening grey drizzle. He merged onto 1–5 South, and when he got to Tacoma he took 16 West across the Narrows to the Persian Gulf, where the grey rain fell and fell, so that it was hard to make out the green highway signs that directed him, and he got lost and took a side-road deep into the glistening forest which was full of wet tacky houses whose people lived with one ear to the wall and the road dead-ended so that he had to turn around and go back to the freeway and just then he found the next green sign: SARGON CORRECTIONS CENTER FOR WOMEN, and he took a right and then the prison came into view, part way up a long muddy hill, its brick arms folded across its brick chest as it stood in the rain guarded by gigantic warning signs, and Meshach pulled into the parking lot and got out. The lot was almost empty. Everywhere he looked there was razor-wire, rolled and coiled on the roof, snaking upon the windows like vines; and inside it had taken over and insinuated itself into the procedures.* He had to empty his pockets and lock everything into a locker; at Control they warned him that even a penny found in his pocket would be grounds for terminating the visit. Next he passed through the metal detector. It beeped twice, the first time because of his belt buckle and the second time because of his watch. After that they stamped his hand with invisible ink so that no alarm would sound when the cheerful guard led him down a hallway and out into the courtyard fringed by razor-wire (to relieve the scene there was a tennis court in the middle, inside a fence topped by razor-wire), and the grey rain fell and the guard led him to Maximum Security and turned away as a second guard led him in, and the new guard read him a printed statement describing the requirement of being pat-searched, and Meshach signed the statement, and the guard made him take off

---

* The technical name, of course, is concertina-wire. This stuff literally sickens me, every other inch of it blooms with a double-headed razor, and I know that no matter where I touched it it would slice into my fingers.

his jacket and shoes and pat-searched him, not neglecting even the soles of his feet, and then he was led into the no-contact visiting booth with its stool and arm-shelf and barred window giving onto the cement courtyard, and in front of Meshach was a glass window behind which the Tremulously Radiant Princess of Salamanders was going to appear. As he sat there staring down at the talk-phone, someone tapped on the glass, and he raised his eyes and saw the Princess in the scintillant orange coveralls of a Maximum Security inmate, and she was smiling and waving at him. Such cheerfulness! Had she been corrected, then? Everyone was very friendly in Maximum Security, including the guard who had pat-searched him; when visiting hours were over and both he and the Princess were disappointed, the guard said, "Oh, well, take five," and left them together for a little longer. The orange-clad Princess kept smiling and laughing and reminding him that she did not break the rules anymore. She had no desire or plan to violate Babylonian laws. Of course she would like to get out but she didn't need anything anymore. Why should she when she could chew so many medicated orange Chiclets? Her face was a lovely new mask.* Sargon Corrections Center had succeeded in its transformation of the weak, the sick, the lost – evidently there was no need for the Fiery Furnace here.

Yes, Meshach would have escaped from Babylon if he could, but Abednego had already demonstrated that that could not be done, so Meshach settled himself down in his clay-brick cell and kept looking uneasily into the braziers as he whistled old Judean folk tunes. In the corridor, Shadrach was having a Discussion with poor Abednego.

A Meditation on the Burning Fiery Furnace

Old Cory Smith, who lived in a welfare home not far from Masonic Avenue, was a devout Christian who often reflected on Biblical deaths. I now pause to print a few of his remarks:

"The only thing that gets me is that they're making all these firemen that get around with their *re-soos-itator*, the coroners, and the morticians, they're just making money with the decedent's BODY. Doesn't seem to make sense to me, but it's gone on since the days of Abraham,

---

* "Our goal at Sargon Corrections Center for Women," says the Superintendent, "is to return each woman to the community as a responsible citizen, and I am sure you share the ultimate goal for your friend or relative."

let's say, because I'm familiar with the Scriptures. They had SEPULCHERS in those days. I suppose that what they *were* was caves, but they called 'em SEPULCHERS. It was all a racket. They didn't have to go through all that! I've seen the undertakers come in, with the dead-wagon outside, and they undo the orange blanket, and they cross their arms and slip the body into the dead-wagon, and away they go! They take them to the morgue for identification. I did overhear that. I sometimes seem to think, if you die, why don't they just take the body and take it away? Why do they need to identify it? Either they want the body *buried*, or *burned up*, or *dissected*, or if the guy happened to be in the Service, they want *burial at sea*. Or else they want INCINERATION. Now, that's something new to me. They want to send the body through a lot of *steam*, and it'll turn into *sewage*, and it'll go through the *sewer*, you know. Honestly, there's something in town, over there by the hospital. You see all that steam coming out over there sometimes, that Furnace just north of the main entrance? It's kind of weird. It's kind of *weird*, you know! They never turn it off. It's forever going, forever going. They take the body there and send it through the Whatever-It-Is. It turns into a lot of SEWAGE. It *decays* to *pieces*, you know, *melts*. Just flimsy flesh that goes to the SEWER. So that's all. According to the Roman Catholic faith, which I'm very fond of, it's the First Judgment. I have chronologized a lot since I first went to live in the Lone Star Hotel. AMEN."

Third Interview with Nebuchadnezzar

"Tomorrow is the day," the tyrant said.

"'The Lord will never permit the righteous to be moved,'" quoted Shadrach. (Shadrach, I am sorry to say, felt excited by approaching martyrdom; most immature of the three, because most noble, he had only a single concern: – to be named first in the sacred histories. Each day that passed thrilled him more. He felt almost as happy as I feel when I go down to Tijuana.) – "*Never* will be moved!" he said again, just in case Nebuchadnezzar (who was a little deaf) had not heard.

"We'll see about that," was the royal reply.

Into the Furnace

"Then Nebuchadnezzar was full of fury," says the official text, "and the expression of his face was changed against Shadrach, Meshach, and Abednego. He ordered the Furnace heated seven times more than it was wont to be heated, and all the Cinder-Whores screamed aloud and were burnt. And he ordered certain mighty men of his army to bind Shadrach, Meshach, and Abednego, and to cast them into the Burning Fiery Furnace ... Because the King's order was strict and the Furnace very hot, the flame of the fire slew those men who took up Shadrach, Meshach, and Abednego. And these three men, Shadrach, Meshach, and Abednego, fell bound into the Burning Fiery Furnace."*

The last thing that Nebuchadnezzar saw of them was Abednego grabbing a handful of dirt and rubbing himself with it. They had searched him and smashed his protective clay armor (which he had completed in defiance of Shadrach's prohibition). – The King saw the look on his face when the soldiers took him by the elbows and Abednego suddenly understood that he was going to have to go into the Burning Fiery Furnace after all, and he would perish unless there was a miracle, which he did not think to deserve – and he looked pleadingly into Nebuchadnezzar's eyes, his pale effeminate face following the King as a flower follows the sun; and the long-bearded soldiers dragged him backward, and his lips parted a little as if he were almost about to beg for his life, and Nebuchadnezzar felt sorry for the boy, but had he not commanded him to worship the golden idol? – And the soldiers threw Abednego into the Burning Fiery Furnace.

An Illumination

In my facsimile of the Cîteaux Dijon Bible, which was not reproduced in color, the flames are great black smudges; and the Furnace seems to be an open well of brickwork, so that the three Jews may be seen from

* Daniel 3:19–23.

the waist upwards; and Nebuchadnezzar seems to be a plump, apple-cheeked, medieval lout of a king, looking at them with his arms folded. His courtiers whisper and grin into his shoulder, but the fat king in his fish-scale robe is big-eyed with wonder. It is transparently evident that he was never to blame for the boys' ordeal. He never wanted to be king. In one of the Lives of the Buddha, we read that Buddha, being born to a king and his wife, determined while still an infant never to move or speak, so that he would not be crowned, because the deeds which he would have to command, being a king, would make him go to Hell for eighty thousand years. Poor King Nebuchadnezzar never had the option of refusal. So depicted he stands, gazing into the faces of the Jews who, serious and bearded, repose in the calyx of the flame. The guards consumed by the flames can still be seen in outline at the bottom of the pyre, the agony of their spirits glowing right through the brick, as if this Bible were illuminated by George Grosz, who loved to draw people naked inside their clothes. These dead men lie clutching their ghostly heads in burnt despair.

My Point of View

After deliberation, I too have chosen to imagine the interior of the Furnace as a round brick-lined pit, filled with flames and smoke, so that the country surrounding it is bare, no one being able to endure the fire; and sometimes on a moonless night you can see the scowling face of the Devil in those flames, and demons come scuttling out of the Furnace like grinning crabs. But they are invisible to *you*, who will never see the pretty Salamander that Meshach was to see, because you fear and abhor that Burning Fiery Furnace. You would not even want to look for her, because the mountains, being taller in these ancient times, all have sandstone steps sweeping up them in long curves, the better to bring you to YAWEH, and that means that YAWEH can see you very easily, and YAWEH *always* knows what you are thinking . . .

Inside

Because any human beings in the Furnace would have been burned into less than ashes in less than a second, we must tell this part of the story on the scale of nanoseconds. – At this time, then, the walls began to glow orange. Shadrach and Abednego stood defiantly in the light of this scorching brick well into which they had been tumbled, waiting to be consumed, and their jaws were clenched in this time of desperate trial, and there was a loud mad rushing of flame in their ears, and everything was cruelly orange. The hard hard walls of the Burning Fiery Furnace would not melt, so the three unfortunate brothers must now be tormented to death. When they gazed at each other, their features wavered and flickered in this fatal heat that was so powerful as to glow *through* them so that they could plainly perceive each other's black skulls through which the orange rays streamed like light in a lantern, and the ceiling was burning them, so they bowed their heads, and the walls were burning them, so they rushed away from them, and the floor was burning them, so they lifted up their feet one after another, but none of this helped them, because the truth was that *they* were burning, and the interior of the Furnace was long and low like a tomb. The heat was maddening. Shadrach could not pray. – Now the moment had come, for their beards burst into flame. And the world above them vanished like Heaven into a haze.

First Impressions of Meshach

Just as an adulterously disposed man (not yet knowing that he *is* so) may try and try to enjoy his own wife, but with limp success, so that he begins to think that he is old, and his squashy state must be in the round of things, like his dull wife and dull life and the dull things that a man has to do as he gets older, because taking an interest in things is expressly forbidden in that time of spinal consolidation when a man must be working and working and working, coming home to his tent in a bludgeoned state, his sword dented, his sheep wandering through the

desert, more monsters and thieves to be tracked . . . and then suddenly
his old flame calls him on the phone, that girl with breasts like ripe
oranges; he picks up the Biblical stone receiver, and the penis becomes
firm, in a rush of pleasure and shame – so Meshach felt EXALTED when
he saw the lovely orange flames. – Now, he said to himself, I may live,
and I may die, but surely I will see the Tremulously Radiant Princess
of Salamanders! – And he threw himself down upon the iron floor, the
better to be one with that magnificent orange. The walls were like
orange prisms of heat and light, and Shadrach's hair became orange,
and his face became orange as Meshach looked upon him, and his
beard burned fiercely, and it seemed to Meshach that the three of them
wore the rare orange garments of kings.

Abednego gazed round in agony. *No!* he cried to himself. The heat
. . . the hot dry wind smiting them into weakness . . . The burning-hot
walls, so thick and heavy, were beyond his hope to bore through or rend
with his hands. They were made of many rows of brick, with rubble
close-packed between.

But for Meshach, as I have said, the orange flames were like sunshine
after a season of ceaseless rain. His heart was gladdened. The flames
streamed around his heart, like an orange twilight in some marble city
near the sea, where the color was beautiful precisely because it would
soon be lost in the ocean's blue shadow. If he had been alive today, he
would have liked the furry orange hills near Grapevine, California,
furred with green bushes as if they were the shoulders and sleeves of a
Desert Fox camouflage shirt.

The Bargain Basement

The Fiery Furnace was deep in the ground, among the rubble of earlier
Babylons: – the shattered bricks, the tombs, the buried temples packed
with potsherds and the skeletons of jackals, all lost and dark and hidden
as were the fresher ruins of Judah. Here, for instance, was the broken
blackened palace of Shamashshumukin, who, appointed King of
Babylon by Ashurbanipal the Assyrian, revolted, lost, shut himself into
the palace and burned himself to death, accompanied (willingly or
unwillingly the record does not say) by his wives, children, slaves and
treasures. Just as a fire is signaled first by the black smoke that rises

across the street into the green-smogged night, next by the sorry howling of Assyrian fire-engines, then by a thin bright flicker of orange behind the corner window, so I will describe the development of that suicide-fire in discrete stages, as if the flames had a purpose or a plan instead of being mere gusts of idiotic malice. – Suddenly the palace roof came off, in a burst of clean white smoke which hung above the world as implausibly as that silver-meadowed planetoid, an Executive Vice President's head, will do in the airplane seat directly ahead of you; you cannot see his neck at all, due to the thinness and darkness of the air at that altitude; nor can you see his hand, which is ejaculating little trembling white droplets of Thousand Island salad dressing from an aluminum foil package; you see only that dismally floating head, as you saw only that hanging white smoke which coagulated in the darkness above the palace with such serene regret. It seemed then that the roof-tiles had simply been negated; they had gone suddenly, and the palace lay open to the world, an efficient smoke-factory now bent on producing maximum destruction and suffocation. Only the Assyrians, famed for their attentiveness, saw the tiles raining down in cinders behind the glowing windows. Ashurbanipal's firemen atop their ladders bowed their helmets and peered down into the blaze, standing tranquilly at the rim of this blazing shell, silhouetted against the scintillant orange. Perhaps they were hoping to reach the concubines on the upper storey, who must be screaming and burning now if they had been unable to flee. Their hair would be jeweled with fire; flames would be bursting from their bodies as they ran around coughing; then they would fall down dead but still writhing in their flame-shrouds, scratching at the rubble with smoking fingernails, as meanwhile postmortem changes of considerable interest ensued, their faces becoming charcoal-black, the lenses of the eyes going black and opaque, as in an El Greco painting; and while their brains cooked into little yellow balls their muscles shrank, drawing their blackened arms and legs into the well-known "pugilistic posture" of fire victims who clench their crispy-black fists; and their charred heads were thrust back and their mouths opened in a screaming gape with their cooked black tongues sticking out, and their eye-sockets became black and deep; their entire faces, in fact, grew hard and fantastic with cracked black bone-whorls, so that all the angles and cheek-spurs and teeth made them resemble Babylonian clay demons glazed with soot (which is why you can see them now in the credulous displays of the British Museum). My friends and I sat watching from across Marduk Street, where the shouts could be heard only faintly, something about death and defiance and how Shamashshu-mukin was going to be a god in the next world, but these were dissolved in the comfortable puddle of heat which warmed our foreheads so that we could sit out on the terrace in our bathrobes is if we were in Ecuador and did not have sore throats from the days of chilly rain which had blown down from the Caspian Sea and swelled the Tigris (pestilence multiplying with it); for us there was hardly a sound but the muffled noise of the firemen's axes breaking windows across the width of the upper storey, and then from one of the fire trucks a man yelled frantically through the megaphone, "*Run* now!" – and at that moment the fire burst out of the upper storey windows, and the orange smoke twisted and turned as if it were shaking with laughter while it shot up so high that we voyeurs persisted in our illusion that it was orange smoke, for how could a flame tower so high? A flame that tall might suggest that things were very threatening indeed, and we had no wish to think that. – Our foreheads were quite hot now. – Sparks ascended over the roofs of neighboring houses like orange minerals, gold or pyrite in a vein of black smoke; and the firemen ran down the ladder as the upper edge of the cube that had been a building melted, and the fire trucks began hosing down the neighboring temples, and the fire continued to get brighter and brighter. Now came the explosions and the thuds of collapsing beams. One fireman entered a second-storey window. Was he paid to be brave, or was he just brave? Spurts came out of the roof like the golden trails of comets. The firemen were spraying the blaze with some high-pressure chemical. Through the big square windows came a continuous orange glow, punctuated by falling sparks of unbearable intensity. Firemen moved in and out of the windows. Huge sparks fell upon them. Each window was outlined in gold, jagged where the firemen broke the glass. Sparks fell through the rungs of the ladder. Ragged spears of wood and plaster fell inside the shell. The top of the palace, now distinctly uneven, crashed down to the sidewalk. I saw the silhouette of a fireman desperately dragging something oblong and black (Shamushshukin's corpse) out of the window. Although the flames still burned, it appeared that the extin-guishers were making headway. The palace was now covered by dirty smoke. Presently the brightest thing in Babylon was the constellation of grandly revolving red lights on the fire trucks that growled softly in the street. – The next morning, how dreary it looked, the windows being charred holes giving into poisonous blackness, the front of the shell smeared with soot, broken glass on the sidewalk; and the grey sky drizzled on the ruin, leaching down the burned walls to form puddles black with dissolved soot. Yet I am a Believer, and I therefore trust in the results reported by Sir H. Thompson, Bart., F.R.C.S., in the fourth edition of that impeccable (if repetitive) work *Modern Cremation: Its History and Practice to the Present Date.** A very large proportion of the organic matter is reduced to harmless gases, says Thompson, "plus only a residue of pure white clay ash, which ... regarded as an organic chemical product ... must be considered as attractive in appearance rather than the contrary" (pp. 9–10). Ashurbanipal did not think so, and he had it leveled and buried in the darkness ... History continued to require its bonfires, and ruins collapsed upon burnt ruins, sickening and twisted and charred.

The Secret Comes Out

Now, as the Fiery Furnace continued to achieve higher and higher temperatures, breaking all previous records as recorded on Nebuchadnezzar's clay tablets (and when the priests heard this they felt that it had all been worth it), the rubble conducted excess heat down along old columns and steles and treasuries of rusty swords which glowed orange in the darkness, and a hot wind blew down echoing tunnels and into the caverns of Hell, where liquid fire dripped from the ceiling as if a million plastic party glasses had been set aflame and oozed their jelled orange light down through the cracks of the world until the demons took notice and stopped hurting wicked souls who had not followed all ten of the Commandments and so must be made to scream forever and ever in the scintillant orange darkness where nobody could hear them because every soul was too busy screaming and fusing and confusing to hear the others, and the demons, in one of the LORD YAWEH's efficiently merciful moments, had been created without ears, so that the cries of pain would not impede their work; but in the pools of flame the spotted orange Salamanders also swam. These creatures were neither good nor evil; they were merely Spirits of the Flame, and they went about their

* London: Smith, Elder & Co., 1901.

business as polliwogs will do in a pond, bothering no one and expecting no one; they danced and swam and multiplied when they could and were beautiful and that was all. So now, as searing droplets of flame fell from Babylon, the Salamanders were apprised of the working of the Burning Fiery Furnace, and the youngest, brightest, most beautiful of the Salamanders took it on herself to inhabit it. She was the Tremulously Radiant Princess about whom Meshach had dreamed. Her crown of fire had only grown brighter since he had seen her last. All her life she had lived in the darkness under dark red raspberries of flame, and she basked amidst the purple thorn-stalks of flame and watched the smoke pass across charred black worlds. She ruled the fire-pools under the leaves of flame, under the steep Hell-slopes of raspberries, the fire-foliage as thick as moss where mineral-flames budded steamy and green or shot up like Indian pipe or witch's broom. In a streak of flame she ascended through dim and smoky terrors, little imagining that she soon must confront the gazes of angels.

A Discussion

The Apocrypha says that an Angel came into the Furnace and fanned the boys. But it is equally true, as I have said, that the Tremulously Radiant Princess of Salamanders came to see Meshach. Shadrach and Abednego thought her a demon. Of course their ordeal had excited them to the point of imprecision; by then they had both given up hope, if they ever had it. – "The pallor visibly increases, becomes more leaden in hue, and the profound tranquil sleep of Death weighs where just now were life and movement. Here, now, begins the eternal rest." – So says Thompson in his crematorium work (p. 75). But then he shakes his rhetorical head, crying: "Rest! no, not for an instant. Never was there greater activity than at this moment exists in that still corpse." – And that was exactly how it was for the three condemned boys.

Two of them, at least, were more active than Mexican jumping beans. – "What are we to *do?*" wailed Abednego. "It's so hot down here, I don't understand why I'm not already a cinder." – "Kneel and pray," said Shadrach. – "Yes," replied Abednego, "but my knees are already smoking!"

Meshach alone said nothing. Shadrach supposed that he must be sunk into merciful apathy, or perhaps he was already overcome by the heat. Weakness of this kind, which was not cowardice or rebellion, touched his heart, and he was compelled to play the emotional commandant. – "Brothers!" began Shadrach, whose thoughts were as well organized as a line of scintillant orange hazard cones, and remained beacons, even through the smoke of his burning beard. "I am grateful that we can all die in this glorious way. Our agony will not last long.* Abednego, I forgive you the disgrace you brought upon us when you tried to run. You have been a good brother for the most part, and, unlike Meshach, never lost a sheep. I doubt, however, that I will see you in Heaven. – Meshach, I have always loved you and known you would do your duty, although you have been too much of a dreamer in your life. – *Meshach!* Do you hear me? Are you paying attention? Get up off the floor!"

"Shadrach?" said Abednego very timidly. "Shadrach, our beards aren't burning anymore, and I think I see an Angel in the air."

The Angel and the Salamander

I usually see angels descending in the early morning, inside blue bubbles of holiness, and when the sun strikes them their faces and their hair are gold. They wear shrouds of woven snow, and take themselves as seriously as do dead virgins. There is gold in their cheeks. They come asking for total victories. – But Shadrach and Abednego saw a woman with a blue halo; and the flames at her back became at once a speckled backdrop of gold-leaf, as if we were discussing illuminated Bibles or mosaics in ninth-century church vaults, instead of fiery burnings. – How cool that blue halo was! What cool blue eyes she had! – She raised her arms, and a cool breeze sprang up. (Angels are so beautiful, and there are purple shadows in their shrouds.) Abednego walked up to the gold leaf and peeled it back with his finger, to see what lay beyond it, and there was nothing but Bible paper.

Now that Abednego was not in imminent danger of combustion, he

---

* "It is during the early weeks or months which follow death," explains Thompson (p. 68), "that the poison of the diseased body is at its maximum . . . For we have at least the right to doubt whether specific morbid germs survive for many years the remarkable organic transformation which slowly takes place within a sealed coffin."

saw that the Angel was not so beautiful after all, being but a stout woman in blue who clasped her hands in her lap and smiled wearily. How quickly the glamor flakes off our saviors, once they have done their job! – (But to Shadrach she was beautiful because she resembled Catherine.) She sat down in a folding chair, flanked by a great semicircle of chorus angels who, though pale of feature, were all the colors of the rainbow, all standing, wearing long black dresses, white blouses; holding black hymnals out at their breasts. Their faces were pale and expressionless. They had solemn white chins. Their black dresses made it seem as if they were standing about a grave (which indeed, if Nebuchadnezzar had had his way, they would have been).

As for the Tremulously Radiant Princess of Salamanders, she arrived simultaneously with the arrival of the Angel, but kept her distance from her. Meshach recognized her immediately. (But did she know him?) To Shadrach and Abednego she seemed a horrid orange flame-tree that was growing and blossoming against the wall; and Abednego, ever the practical one, understood that her growth might mean their death, for he felt heat from her. As for Shadrach, he thought that she must want his soul, although that hard charred thing held no desire at all for the Princess, who was laughing and beckoning to Meshach alone with her rosy-orange arms. (As a baby she had been burdened by fiery yellow spots and red spots, but now she was pure scintillant orange, cautious and beautiful.) – "This is the Big One," Meshach said to himself, "the love I waited for," and he understood more than ever before that his love of orange things had been a hopeful mournful faithful love of her, and though his blood rushed through him with fiery nervousness, he knew that he must betray the other boys if it came to that.

She spread her hands; she rested her splayed flame-fingers on him very gently – and he was singed. He could not believe it. He pulled himself away. The Radiant Princess laughed. She began to dance slowly, shining like old blood; she moved her diminutive baby-hands upon his face. Because her eyes were set into the sides of her head, not her face, she seemed curiously intent. She slid her length down and rested her head in the flame. Then she rose and danced; she was always seeking a new position. There were flowers of flame at her gills.

The Former Life of the Tremulously Radiant Princess of Salamanders

Meshach loved the Tremulously Radiant Princess of Salamanders with flaming concern, because she was so remote from him and he had been taught that remoteness is caused by pain. When he was a child his mother had read him the tale of the Queen of Sheba, how she had been bewitched by a Frog at a well and she fell in love with the Frog and used to let him kiss her with his cold green lips and gave him her ring to slip over his webbed foot, so finally the Frog puffed his throat and said, "You must bring me to your mother and father and make them marry us," so the Queen of Sheba tied the Frog with ribbons and hung a gold medallion to his chest to make him look as handsome as she could, and he hopped at her side into the throne room where the old King and Queen sat, and the old Queen screamed and said, "A frog! Kill it!", but the Queen of Sheba said, "Mother, this Frog is my fiancé, and tomorrow we must be married. Will you give us your blessing?" – "I would sooner die," said the proud old Queen, and she swallowed poison. – "See what you have brought upon us!" said the old King. "You are not my daughter anymore. Go out into the desert and wander among the slimy oases between the dunes, and marry your Frog, if that is what you are set on," at which the Frog gulped and exclaimed with hoarse inarticulate anger. The Queen of Sheba turned and walked away, and the Frog leaped up upon her shoulder, and she never saw mother or father again. They came to the Frog's country, which was called Schleimheim. For a bed they had a plain of mud by a spring, and at night the beautiful Queen of Sheba must lie in it and suffer her Frog-husband to hop up and down on her and smear her with his slime, which she did suffer for love of him. In the mornings her husband made her catch flies for his breakfast, after which he would go to the spring, *hop-hop-hop!* and croak there with the other frogs. At first she tried to make herself agreeable to them, and swam in the stagnant water with the frogs, but they said, "Uggh! Uggh! How ugly she is! What long, white arms and legs! And she has no slime of her own! It will not stay on her, no matter how much we rub ourselves against her! Uggh!

Uggh! We don't want her in *our* games!" And so the poor Queen of Sheba was banished from the pool. One day the Frog said that he was tired of her, and would seek another wife. By then she believed that she herself was a frog, and so she went from pool to pool, as her father had commanded her. Presently she found some kindly frogs. "Of course she will never catch flies as well as we can," they said, "but, poor soul, she cannot help it; she is deformed." So they did their best for her. She cut off her beautiful long hair and learned to squat in the mud like a frog. Time passed, and she heard from the frogs that her husband had remarried. What most humiliated her was that once again he had married a woman, not a frog; for if he had taken a frog-wife, only an impersonal proclivity for slime might have been demonstrated, but since he had taken a woman to himself, a Queen like her, it must have been *herself* that the Frog had despised. She became very depressed, and her friends discovered in due time that their equanimity about her was sinking under them, like the lily-pads they so plumply sat on; oh yes! they were WORRIED about her: they neglected no opportunity to store away the best flies for her, and often thrust them into her mouth with their slimy tongues, but the Queen of Sheba had lost her appetite. She could not understand why the Frog had married another Queen. She had done everything she could to be a good wife. One day she learned from a froggy friend that her husband had been sleeping with the other Queen all along, even before the divorce. She went and hid in the mud, and when the other frogs called her on the phone, it rang and rang. Later they got only the tape recording on her answering machine. A frog who had learned to ignore her unsightliness of person grew alarmed and dug through the mud with his pale webbed feet. Between his lips he bore a lovely blue dragonfly – his friendship present for her. He dug and dug and dug. On each side of his head, an eye goggled out in anxiety, for though he croaked and croaked in that cold muddy darkness, he heard nothing in answer. He should be near her by now. Finally he saw her dead white body in the black mud, and mud was in her mouth and eyes and ears; she had killed herself by eating mud. When the little frog saw this, he cried, for he had a good heart and was grieved. Any other frog might, perhaps, have swallowed the dragonfly then, for it could be of no further use to her, but this frog would not, and tenderly cleaned the mud from her mouth with his webbed little hand, so that he could leave the dragonfly on her tongue. This he did, and then he began to hop away, back along the tunnel he had made –

for it is the custom of the frogs to leave their dead as they find them – when suddenly her telephone rang, as it must have done when he had called to leave his messages of anguished concern on her answering machine, and he turned and peered past her dead white belly and saw the answering machine winking and winking its scintillant orange eye in the darkness, so that the frog winked his own eyes for sympathy, and at the fourth ring the answering machine came on and spoke in the Queen of Sheba's voice and said, "Because you were a true friend and sought to help me, YAWEH has allowed me to speak to you. I have been reborn with your amphibious nature, but not wholly yours, for the Frog who was my husband was hateful to me, so you must know me now as the *Tremulously Radiant Princess of Salamanders*." The little frog was astonished, and as he sat swelling his throat and goggling, a blue flame was kindled in her mouth – it was his dragonfly! – and her poor dead body glowed blue, then red, then scintillant orange, and there was a sheet of flame and then the little frog glimpsed a beautiful orange Salamander rushing laughing downward.* She laughed because she did not care about anything anymore.

The Angel and the Salamander (Continued)

When she swam in the flames, that most Royal of all Crowned Salamanders, she arched her belly and let her hands dangle. Sometimes she kicked to propel herself through that sea of fire in which she lived, and her foot-strokes became flames. She could swim to the deepest hottest places. Maybe if she did love him she would take him down into the fiery meads where he would drink of the liquid fire and pick great fire-blooms for her which would explode into sparks in his hands, and that high lofty face would be his to warm and kiss ... How egotistical a lover can be, in imagining that his cold flesh, which lives in mud and is made of mud, can warm a hot-blooded Salamander! Yet so he did imagine it. "Come," she'd say, "kiss me, I feel so cold," and as he pressed his mouth to hers for the first time he would feel a tremendous shock of oranges burning and bursting in his head, and the Salamander

* "Once more they cried, 'Hallelujah! The smoke from her goes up for ever and ever.'" – Revelation 19.3.

was smiling and embracing him – but it could never happen. Was he any different from the wicked Frog? And how could he blame her if she would not trust him? – But maybe she did need him for fuel to be burned in her fire, "the fire which," says Paracelsus (1590), "purifies the rotten and crapulous skin of the salamander and makes him to be born anew." So maybe she would lead him down deeper into Hell, where she could ignite him with the clinging burning love of phosphorus, which warms its victims to the bone. Her smile encouraged him as the firelily encourages the bee.

The Angel understood Meshach's thoughts, and glared at him. She had a Bible in her lap, and began to turn the pages, frowning. She slid her glasses down her nose. Everyone waited for her to speak. Meshach's brothers knelt so low as to momentarily leave existence, so that Meshach was alone, a gargoyle among the angelic choir.

Fraternal Epiphany

Really, why go on? Must we record the bitter denunciations of the Angel, the shock and loathing of Meshach's brothers, the unretractable expressions of enmity?

Pity Meshach! He could not help the way that he was. If, like Abednego, he had been a coward, it would not have been his fault; and he was not a coward; he was lacking in no glowing moral quality. What was he to do? How could he deny himself by denying the Salamander and going over to the Angel, who was now looking at him in such a forbidding fashion? If he yielded to the commands of the other two boys and renounced the fire (which *they* had rightly renounced), he would be committing a sin. As for his brothers, they scorned him because he was *honest*. Meshach had always known that they would, and he had known that the burning fact of it would be shocking to him; and it certainly was. It is a hard thing to be burned in a Furnace; it is harder still to burn when your fellow martyrs despise you.

"I hereby command and decree," said the Angel, "that you, you mischristened Meshach M. McGuinness, be withdrawn from the protection of my wings, that you be scorched to death, that your body and soul be charred ignominiously, thence to be borne to Hell piece by piece on the back of your amphibious paramour, and that you be resurrected there to eternal torment, for the glory and good of the Heavenly Commonwealth!"

Meshach, relieved, in a way, that all was lost, turned his back to her and embraced the Tremulously Radiant Princess of Salamanders, although (truth to tell) he was already feeling a bit on the warm side. She kissed him. (He reminded her of the good frog.) In spite of his doom he felt a sleepy tigerish satisfaction; the world became a tiger-skin rug, orange with goodness and black wherever it was not orange. He was as comfortable as I feel on some chilly afternoon in San Francisco when I lie beside the fire, burning a volume of Erich Fromm and watching the pages curl into the petals of a black-orange flower.

A Stunning Turnaround

At this very moment, YAWEH Himself appeared, in a pillar of ice enclosing scintillant orange fire, and he said, "Let the boy be. At least he's sincere. I always enjoy the sincere ones. I let Goering in, because he was the only one in the dock who did not repent. Besides, the boy likes the color orange, and it *is* a nice color."

And so the Angel had to apologize, and Shadrach, Meshach and Abednego stood pretty in the Burning Fiery Furnace until at last the Babylonians began to snicker at their King and everybody kicked the golden idol and Ashpenanz bent over and began to whisper in his Sire's ear very very rapidly and the great Nebuchadnezzar, Father of Heroes, King of Kings, admitted failure, and commanded that they be brought out. And the Furnace was extinguished, and the Tremulously Radiant Princess of Salamanders was nowhere to be found. She had left him, left him, left him.

The Moral

Every part of creation deserves to have its worshippers, no matter how dangerous or evil it may seem to others. Hence Shadrach and YAWEH; hence Abednego and his eggs; hence Meshach and the Salamander; hence Nebuchadnezzar and the golden idol.

Fourth Interview with Nebuchadnezzar

"Evidently I was wrong," said the tyrant, passing round cigars of congratulation. "I will not conceal from you that that causes me some anxiety and dissatisfaction. I do admire you boys for having gone through with this; yes indeed, you were absolutely correct, and this YAWEH of yours (who isn't even listed in my Divine Registry) can deliver people from furnaces – which I freely admit that my golden idols can't do. But where does this leave me? I can't say I come off looking too good in front of my priests and counselors. To be frank, you boys are dangerous, and I obviously can't execute you, so what I'm going to do is promote you to the governorship of my most outlying provinces. Or, if you prefer, I can equip you with gold, slaves and radiation suits so you can go back to Judah to direct the reconstruction and have a swanky time in your very own bunker."

"Your Majesty," said Shadrach proudly, "we accept the promotion."

Their Dying Glow

Shadrach had known Noah and Methuselah personally – so he later told people when he was famous, and did little parlor tricks with tallow candles, through which he never came to hurt, thanks to the indulgent angels. He lived on, it is said, to the time of the Catacombs. By then his popularity had been half-eclipsed. Christ had told him that he might have the succession, but in the so-called "Secret Testament" discovered in one of the transepts or trifomiums of the Vatican, there are indications that Christ considered Shadrach to be too rude, too scheming. The mysterious circumstances surrounding Christ's death, and in particular the empty tomb – all this does implicate Shadrach, or at least make him suspect. He spent his declining years among the Goths, where the campfires cast long shadows in the woods, and dirty women suckled their infants at the same time that they defecated.

Particularly sad in the ruddy light of his somewhat undeserved good fortune is the fact that, out of the long roll of saints who were cast into fiery situations in subsequent ages, very few survived.* Saint Afra and Saint Apollonia were burned; Saint Cosmo, Saint Damian, Saint Ephesus and Saint Lucia were not, but died of other tortures; only Saint Christina can be positively said to have been as fortunate as the three brothers.

Abednego, still persuaded of the utility of reason over faith (he was the originator of the proverb "YAWEH helps those who help themselves"), could never be convinced to come close to fire after it was all over. In his view, rationalism had made a statistical blunder in preventing him from having burned in the Furnace. (Then again, he reflected, perhaps his clay armor had helped – for like many old men, he forgot that he had had no armor in his time of trial.) In any event, he did not want to chance it again.

The Problem Child

As for Meshach, despised by his brothers, left homeless, thanks to Nebuchadnezzar, but, like his brothers, presented with his freedom by the cringing witnesses of the Furnace miracle, he wandered into the mountains. From any one of those peaks, Meshach could look down into the crater where the fire and brimstone had overwhelmed Sodom and Gomorrah. The walls of that vast ruined bowl were smooth with reddish-orange powder. You could slide down them, all the way to Hell, through the hot white clouds that waited above the bowl, down, down, down, to where the ultimate Fiery Furnace was waiting for you. The steam rose slowly up the crater's defiles, not injuring itself on the rocks, creeping, creeping with mindless patience, each puff being a one-way messenger sent to remind us of the Fiery Furnace before merging with the streaky sky, like semen flowing into a sewer. – As Meshach went higher and higher, the sand clotted into scintillant orange pumice, which was so light that he could balance any gigantic boulder of it on his little finger until a gust of wind blew it off and it went tumbling down the scree with a dry clinking sound, and pretty soon other rubbly-wobbly rocks were dislodged and also clinked

* "... Signs of a growing feeling in favour of cremation," wrote Thompson prophetically (p. 14), "are evident in various parts of Germany."

tunefully and dislodged still other rocks and started a melodious avalanche that coursed down to the hot orange plain below playing the song "How Dry I Am," as meanwhile, on the peak, Meshach felt the wind and snow on his neck and kicked some empty orange rocks and waited for YAWEH (whose Name resembles the howl of a wolf) to come explain to him why He had made him love the color orange to no good purpose, but YAWEH didn't come, and Meshach said to himself, "All right, YAWEH, You don't even have to answer my question; just let me walk with You and show me a new Canaan where there are Salamanders who can kiss me without scorching me and toilet-seat covers are orange," but there was still no Answer, possibly because there were so many other rubble-peaks about that he would have been lucky to run into YAWEH, Who was pretty busy making sand blow and sparrows fall: – whether it was the glowing orange of the Furnace or the chilly orange of the mountain, it was all the same; Meshach was on his own.

Now more than ever before he was determined to marry the Tremulously Radiant Princess of Salamanders. What else was there for him to do? – Of course he had no home to bring her to, no perpetual flame in which to warm and clothe her, nor had he any method for entering the flame to take her from it, so anyone else would have given the project up as hopeless, but Meshach did not; he would go to her.

Liebestod

He crossed the salty plain from Ur to Susa, and then walked down into the unknown southeast, along the edge of the Eastern Sea. YAWEH had not yet finished blasting this region into dead sand and stones; He could "change times and seasons" at His leisure, since no one lived there yet, so it remained tropical. Treading high above the sea, stepping on stairs of red volcanic rock slippery with the slime of life (rainwater, mud, rotten yellow fruits), Meshach ascended the green mountain, since the orange one had failed him. Smells of coffee and pepper made him dizzy. The air was mist, so full of oxygen that he needed to take only shallow breaths. The ocean was bluish-green. The coastline was pleated and severe. He saw a rainbow over the sea; he breathed in the rich rich clouds. He passed blue flowers that smelled like fermenting apples. He ducked through a shiny tunnel of trees. The rain-forest

smelled of marmalade. Endless hills lay before him, crowded with
yellow-green trees as dense as green coral-reefs or bundles of green
pipe-cleaners, and a less bedazzled fellow might well have despaired of
finding any orangeness at all, but it is remarkable the way one can find
what one looks for, and Meshach knew this, so he continued on through
sun and rain, sun and rain, following a wall of trees so closely-spaced
that they seemed to be branches grown from one trunk. He descended
root-steps, clinging to root-banisters as fat and wrinkled as elephants'
trunks. Branches creaked in the wind. There were dozens of gnats in a
single white flower. The hot wet air was as natural as his own skin, and
the jungle became an extension of his skin as he continued downward,
the stairs becoming black lava boulders and the branches meeting above
his head in a cool green tunnel of unripe fruits; and the descent was
easy because in the jungle everything was easy, so in due time Meshach
passed between two dripping black cliffs and came to a grotto of
stagnant water, on the bottom of which heart-shaped leaves rested,
decaying very peacefully, and water dripped from the smooth blackish-
green overhang (for since everything is so easy in the jungle, the jungle
easily urinates and bleeds), and Meshach sat on the shore of that murky
lake until his eyes became adjusted to the darkness – and meanwhile
mosquitoes and disturbed bats flew around him – and he saw a narrow
fontanelle or fissure curving round behind the slimy stone of the cave-
wall, and from it came the same inescapable glow of scintillant orange
which he had found within the Burning Fiery Furnace. He swam across
the lake (his eyes now making out the translucent forms of blind
whitish-orange cave-carp), and pulled himself up to the threshold of
the fissure, where he stood for a moment looking back at the sun,
because he knew that this was the last time that he would see this earth.
For a moment he was baffled by the mystery of the sun, which contained
so much orange fire. He watched it sear the tops of the jungle-trees in
its descent, so that the leaves turned red and yellow and purple, and the
entire slice of world which he could see from the cave seemed to be on
fire. – If only he could have gotten to the sun! – But YAWEH had not
answered his prayers. It may be, he reflected, that beneath his feet was
some gateway joining the fire of Hell to the fire of the sun, and if there
were not, at least he had his Salamander, with whom he must be
content. He descended into the fissure. The glare strengthened; he
could see his face reflected in orange tones upon the back of his hand.
– Deeper and deeper. – The passage steepened; the rocks became

moist, then wet, as hot steam blinded him and he tumbled down into a sulphur-creek bursting with yellow bubbles, and the boiling current rushed him down boulders and into swirling slimy fizzing pools in which mangy orange rats dived for their brothers' boiled bones and came up scalded, the hair falling off them in pink patches so that the rats squealed and then their brothers could tell that they had been hurt and paddled over gleaming-eyed to devour them and *their* bones fell to the bottom still cooking, so new rats shook themselves and dived down to their doom, as meanwhile everything whirled round and round and the sulphur-river cascaded down slimy orange cliffs into an orange darkness which poor dumb Meshach was still naive enough to exult in, thinking that having survived the Burning Fiery Furnace he must be invulnerable and that the Tremulously Radiant Princess of Salamanders was expecting him when really she did not care, and the sulphur-falls roared down and down toward the scintillant orange magma that keeps the Salamanders toasty, and Meshach was already so far under the earth that YAWEH was indifferent to him – as He had always been anyhow, for the only reason that He had saved the three boys was to convert Nebuchadnezzar, who had considerable influence and would not stint to offer up millions of screaming souls in the burning sacrifices of ziggurat-building and cinder-raking and soldiering that YAWEH loved; as for Meshach, he had served his purpose, so let him die! Therefore, in a slimy tunnel far below the world, he met a scrawny, dirty-orange hound whose eyes were EMBERS deep inside burnt-out eye-sockets, and his snout was narrow but his jaws were wide. Dirty teeth grinned all along that mouth, which was smeared with blood and cinders, and the jaws creaked open a bit, and the dog growled once, a silky, knowing growl like a cat's purr, and slaver fell from his tongue in sizzling drops. This was the Orange Dog of Hell who had led the wolves against the sheep when Meshach was a shepherd-boy in Judah. But Meshach had never seen him until now, because he had never looked away from his sacred flames. He did not know how desperate wolves eye desperate sheep. (Still, he *ought* to have known, thanks to his own researches – for the heads of fancy matches may be dyed all the colors of the rainbow, but when struck they produce fire of a single color, the color of dangers and alarms.) Neither did he have anything with which to perform the proper propitiations; since he had not attained the Burning Kingdom below, he possessed no flaming marvels to bestow like biscuits, and of course the paltry nutmegs of the airy world would be of no more use than sheep-prayers (and every prayer is but a sheep-prayer); so the Orange Dog growled, and the Orange Dog GROWLED, and the Orange Dog glared at him with hair-trigger rabidness, as if he might or might not bite him (but the Orange Dog already knew that he would bite), and the Orange Dog circled round him and lifted a leg and pissed on his footprint. Then, before Meshach could call upon the Tremulously Radiant Princess of Salamanders (who was laughing so hysterically anyhow in the hysterical flames that she would never have heard, and if she had heard she wouldn't have done anything), the Orange Dog sprang and tore his throat out and ate him down to the bones.

Benediction

Catherine, lost among lions, had once fed a lion-cub on her own milk, and it grew up and protected her and walked beside her in the desert when she set out to find her way home. It was Shadrach who came across them. He was a bright-eyed youth in those days. The Babylonians had not yet invaded, and Judah was strong, and Shadrach had never been wrong. Knowing that the lion would eat Catherine any second, he raised his bow and killed it. Catherine wept. Had she done wrong in raising the lion so that it trusted her? Had Shadrach (whose courage no one can fault) done wrong in rescuing her? Did the Angel do wrong in exposing Meshach's perversion? These are questions which can be answered only as Saint Catherine answered them: – with silence.

For Seth Pilsk

YELLOW ROSE

For
Maureen Riordan,
partner in crime

I

When I put Jenny's picture up against my glasses her face fogs into a pale yellow moon mistily aswim in the darkness of her hair and high school uniform, because as ageing progresses (so I once read), the minimum distance required for the eye to focus on an object increases, which depresses me and incites me to strategies of avoidance, such as chewing psilocybin mushrooms. Two bitter grams of these infallibly "increase the absolute blue space/Which alienates the sky from my embrace," as Baudelaire said about something else. I still pretend that when this expansion takes place, easing my surroundings farther outward on the circumference of a wheel radiating spokes of isolation, then whatever I look at crawls beyond that fatal focal length of vision, like a dreamer fleeing through the molasses of a nightmare, reaching the end of the world at last and jumping into indigo where monsters can never reach. So Jenny herself moves farther and farther away into a freedom the more clear for being lonely; now, through the intergalactic telescopes of my widening pupils, I can decipher the *I love you* that she wrote on the back of her photograph, which before was a disquieting mammogram of blue-ink veins. To a bacterium upon the dot of an "I", no doubt, the meaning must be less distinct for being more closely embraced.

The night that I decided to declare myself to Jenny, I was at my connection's house, laughing until I ached (convulsions being a side effect of the drug) and drinking Coronas at the kitchen table with friends for whom I had much esteem. The bubbles in my friends' yellow beers as they tilted the bottles to their mouths one after the other seemed to me indescribably *COOL*, like jazz solos performed with glass instruments of perfect subtlety. I suspected that my friends were drinking that way on purpose, to show off to me, but I did not mind because I had never seen beer drunk so professionally. In fact, I admired myself for having such amazing friends. All of us slammed our bottles down on the table laughing. I was sure that we would come into some money soon and never have to work again, just sprawl around on the sidewalk drinking wine coolers and bloating ourselves with leisure. This thought circulated through my body like a bubble. While it was passing through my cranial arteries I remembered what it was and understood it down to its electrons; but as it left my head it became unknowable again, though I did not mind much because it tickled pleasantly down my neck, my thigh, the top of my big toe. Soon thereafter the open-eyed dreams began. It is needless to say that I retained control of myself, for I saw oddities only in the shadows, which were insignificant in the context of the golden kitchen and golden beers ripening with light. My friends were now playing more than their Coronas; they had added their lips and teeth to the orchestra, scattering sparkles whenever the light struck their gleaming incisors, and pumping their lips in bellows movements against the necks of their beers. I tried not to look at their mouths too much because what they were doing was dangerously complicated. But when I turned my head away I saw prickly greenish entities in the darkness beneath the table. Studying the sink for relief, I was stunned to find that the drainboard was not a drainboard at all, but a *Helmet Rack*, for steel mixing bowls gleamed upon it with dull military efficiency, as they had when I was three and my father had pretended that I was a German soldier and put a bowl over my head and shouted "*Achtung!*" – My friends whooped at this discovery and slapped my back, yelling, "Helmet rack! Helmet rack!" until I could see their tonsils palpitating like a colony of cherry-colored mussels, even after they had closed their mouths. Presently we all lurched to the living room, watching spots of various hues, but primarily lavender, crawl upon the rug like spiders. At first I considered the spots to be hostile eyes that might destroy me, but as I became acclimated to the living room I saw that I had simply lacked confidence, as was my fault with strangers, and that the eyes were delightfully friendly. For this reason I started feeling good as I walked upon the carpet, which struck me as being a meadow in bloom; – never before had I realized that the distinction between inside and outside was but an invention of the academicians. The ceiling, for instance, could easily be a white sky without heat, expressing neutrality for me and all that I stood for. This was how it would feel to be the narrator of Wells's "Time Machine," strolling moodily on the beach at the end of the world and watching the giant crabs. My friends had vanished. As I traveled across the plain of spots, perfectly aware that it was still the living room, I began to feel a desire to go, although where I wanted to go I did not know; yet as I thought about it I felt a secret glee that indicated that I did know where I wanted to go after all; I just didn't know that I knew; and once I had deduced this, flattening the dough of concepts into substance with strenuous use of my biggest rolling-pins, it became clear that I was going to see Jenny. Then I put on my coat, laughing until I cried.

The night was marvelously clear, as if varnished in epistemological peppermint. I walked up Haight Street faster and faster, until I almost thought I was running, but the street unrolled block after block of ultramarine shops, dreamy cafés and humid window-fronts, in order to besiege me with options, confused as I already was, first by the multiplicity of bars, next by the comic book stores, then by the record stores where millions of disks chafed inside their cardboard sleeves. Streets radiated from me. But I knew that all of them except Haight Street were streets that I should not take. As for Haight Street itself, wide and bright though it was, like some interstellar boulevard, it would have an end; and though it was expanding faster than I could run, my urgent purpose would empower me to traverse it somehow, just as an insect can travel many times its own length. The sidewalks swam with shadowy crowds going counter to my direction, as if pulled by an undersea current. Their hair floated; I thought I saw bubbles coming out of their ears. Were I to stop or even hesitate, I would be ingested into that remorseless stream and fall backwards past the blackness of Buena Vista Park and down the steep hill behind it, so that I might never see Jenny again. But I kept smiling. (Sometimes I had to stop to laugh into my hand.) A pale woman with cropped brown hair drifted mockingly toward me and waved her fingers in my face. I walked on, but for hours I felt the presence of her fingers still twining themselves over my eyes like seaweed. Then I knew that if I were not careful I might lose myself forever in this unknown world. It was essential that I devote my mind to Jenny, the goal, enfolding my brain-lobes around her in tightest concentration until her edges cut into the cerebrum and cerebellum, the same way that when I was a child going to buy candy I used to squeeze my dime in my hand to be sure at every step that I hadn't lost it. The silver dime of my determination ached behind my forehead. Deliciously (I now had to laugh for a long time, hardening myself against the fishy stares of the fish-people), the knowledge began to bubble up inside my chest, where I had kept it secret from myself out of fun, that I was in love with Jenny. Whenever I forgot about her I began to drift into the painted side-alleys where the skinheads lounged in their ultraviolet jean jackets; or else that current of flitting faces pushed me back step by step, draining silently out of theaters and late-night delis; but before any harm came to me I always felt the star of Jenny glowing in her second-storey flat to bring me to her. Naturally she did not know that I was coming; she was studying. But I could feel her radiations. Of course she was awake; otherwise the tickling in my chest would have diminished to a drowsy tingling. So I strode on, block after block, not letting myself feel panic that I had not yet reached the end of that vast wide street, the thoroughfare of a chess empire, where up ahead Golden Gate Park occupied a greenish-black space in the night. More hours went by, though Jenny's energy transmissions refreshed my tissues like mint-tingling lymph; and finally I passed the ice cream store and reached Stanyan, which was a sloping grey ribbon of a street that stretched on north of me for several thousand miles, all the way to Geary with its diesel dragon-buses. Now that I had come to Haight Street's last block, the night-people roiled behind me like minnows in an eddy; but they were not a menace anymore, since my buoyancy alone would win the fight, carrying me beyond the headwaters, past source-springs and strata and water trickling down sewer gratings; and at precisely this moment, as I saw that Haight Street had been a subterranean river, I emerged from it into the thin air of the wilderness. I was now in the Sunset district. The windows of the apartments were all laughing at me. Every few steps I had to turn aside and laugh into my hand. But there were windows on every side to see me. I felt Jenny not far away, studying calmly like a light bulb. I turned alternately right and left, in hopes of finding windowless walls where I could laugh, just as a drunk will look for a peaceful place to urinate. But there were none. So I continued on my way, turning left, then right, my footsteps very loud on the streetlit sidewalk, until I reached the block where Jenny lived. The darkness was playing dominoes with the housetops. Into my mind came a variety of aphorisms, since I was now in the fiendishly loquacious stage of the drug, and I was eager to see Jenny and express them to her: pins are just like hyphens if you cut the heads off; love is two crickets hopping in the same direction. Clearly there had been no effect on my PK, that is psychokinetic functions.

I stood across the street and looked up at the second floor. Her light was on behind the curtains. She was preparing for her medical boards. I wondered if I should leave her alone. I could go up to the third floor, where my own flat was, but then if I went to my bedroom and turned on the light there would be nothing in there but Jenny's vacuum cleaner (which I had borrowed), alert, but, like all appliances, opaque in any discussion; and it was not for the sake of the vacuum cleaner that I had successfully gamed these complex turns of streets; and I also knew that if I did go upstairs and turn on the light just to see Jenny's vacuum cleaner watching me I would begin to laugh, and all the neighbors across the street would hear and see through their windows, which my windows were transparent to. I could avoid this publicity by taking off my shoes and leaping around my flat in the dark, chuckling very quietly, but inevitably the darkness itself, though it easily subsumed Jenny's vacuum cleaner and indeed the whole apartment, would despite its impressive range not be as good as Jenny (who did not know that I was in love with her) because I would begin to feel restless and so would go eventually to the window to see the lights outside. Then I would start laughing. That would be defeat. And, bubbling up inside me, as I stood on the doorstep, was the knowledge that whether or not these considerations were valid I was going to show myself to Jenny anyway. Gleefully, I rang her doorbell. It was one in the morning.

2

Jenny was Korean. She came from a very traditional family. If her mother ever suspected her of being involved with a Caucasian, Jenny would be cast off. Her mother had just booked her a ticket to Seoul for her vacation so that she could get engaged to a nice Korean boy.

3

"So, will you be upset if I get engaged to somebody else?" said Jenny, looking at me with her flat black eyes.

"Yes," I said.

"Why?" said Jenny.

I didn't say anything.

Jenny had a beautiful round face like a sun or a golden coin. She had chubby arms because she loved cookies and ice cream. She eternally wanted to lose twenty pounds. Whenever she called home her mother told her that her legs ought to be thinner by one-third. She had studied biochemistry at Harvard and graduated with honors because she worked with diligence – "No-Ryok" in Korean, which has ideogrammatic roots in "strength" and in "slave," which latter in turn breaks down into "woman" plus "hand."*

Jenny was Soon-Jin (innocent), "Soon" being a fresh shoot sprouting from the ground on the right of the ideogram and a string of twisted silken fibers beneath a cocoon on the left to indicate purity, while "Jin" was a man's head nodding, meaning "genuine." One often sees "Jin" in Korea on the labels of liquor bottles. My pretty Jenny was always smiling and loved to go to Macy's. She kept her room perfectly clean. For me she symbolized above all rest and happiness, an escape from my own gangrened calculus. I wanted to have children in her womb.

"Do you mind that I don't love you?" she said.

"No," I said. "Do you mind that I love you?"

"Don't say that," she said.

We sat on her couch together, and I rubbed yellow marker all over my face to show my resolve to be acceptable to her family. They would not like it at all if she married a white boy. Maybe her brothers would beat me up. That was why Jenny had done her best not to love me. She saw no future in the affair. But I myself still hoped for Kyeol-Hon, matrimony (that is, lucky tie-up woman clan-name day). This must have been why I was awakened in the mornings by the anxious beating of my heart. I do not believe that I have ever cared for anyone as strongly as I did for this Korean girl, because I knew that she was not right for me. In California, where I was born, where I have lived most of my life, wants are satisfied so easily, so cheaply, for the Boo-Jas (rich people) and the bourgeois, that stagnating lusts vent themselves in gambles with fortune. If one is so unfortunate as to win, one moves on to other drugs, to art films and absurdly expensive Kiwi fruits, each one personally picked by a Maori chieftain in New Zealand. Or so I sometimes told myself – that my affair with Jenny was only a shrink-packed novelty like a new compact disc. And yet later, when she said she loved me I felt a

---

* For a glossary of Korean words, with their ideograms, see page 234.

funny weakness localized three inches above my liver. I soon found that I would do anything for her.

4

"I just picked up a really cute guy," said Jenny, down in L.A. "Boy, it was so hard to ride the windsurfer out there; he had to help me. Actually, he's not that cute, but he has a cute personality. It's really difficult trying to tack. Also, wind died out. Well, here he comes. All right, all of you get lost. Just kidding."*

The man came across the sand, scrunching his golden toes. Jenny gave him beer from the cooler and he thanked her easily and was gone.

"Where's the windsurfer now?" said Martin in his deck chair.

"Over there," said Jenny, pointing at the buoys.

We were at Marina del Rey, the five of us: Jenny, Martin, Lilith, Anna and myself. Lilith was out on the windsurfer; far away she could be seen riding, riding in her blue and green bathing suit, freed from the land and its problems, more or less as she was on the beach, curled on her towel, Japanese eyes almost closed, a soda in the sand beside her as she lay tanning herself like some golden honey-plant, nourished by her personal stereo, which was Thoreau's different drummer that only she could hear, rocking her beautiful head (which was more beautiful still than Jenny's) in time with that intimate music which we others had never been privileged to hear or hear of, her face swimming through her long black hair in a coolly masturbatory rhythm, not unfocused ecstasy as I had first imagined, since Lilith was still capable of tabulating the land's ill-conceived interactions behind her eyelids, so that whenever anyone ate a chocolate Tootsie pop she'd slowly open her eyes and say, "Mmm, it looks like you're eating shit on a stick!", and smile brilliantly and almost close her eyes again. Her face was sensuous,

---

* Jenny spoke the sweetest English that I ever knew. Whenever it came time to tidy her room, she'd announce, "Gotta tighten up now!" – Every minute that she was not studying saw her rushing on errands, saying to herself, "I'm gonna – I gotta – ", until it was time for dessert. "I'm so bad!" Jenny cried. "I've been eating chocolate truffles till they came out my tears!" – At the fish store there were turtles and there were frog-legs. Fat banded shrimp glistened like resistors. Jenny's eyes went wide with excitement. She saw some squirting clams. – "*Ooooh!*" she said. "They're *alive!* They're trying to hide. Ooooh! I wanna *eat* them."

cruel, well cared for (she made a lot of money). She would be frightening when she aged. Jenny went to Macy's and bought Clinique makeup but forgot to use it, while Lilith had her compact with her at every moment and took every measure possible to preserve her skin, rubbing ice cubes on it in the living room and no doubt bathing herself in fresh blood like that fifteenth-century Hungarian vampire-countess. Martin had been interested in Lilith the previous year, but other girls had manifested themselves to him in a sweet whirlwind of skirts; other coconuts had fallen off the tree, cracking open just right for Martin so that all he had to do was suck the juice and wait for the next one to drop, just as we now waited for the windsurfer to blow Lilith back to us, no one caring that much about taking a turn; but not opposed, either, to sailing out in a chilly mist of salt sea-droplets, seeing that the day had to be eased through somehow; there was no sense in rushing it because if we did we might get tired or sunburned and then we wouldn't want to go out drinking that night, and if we didn't go out drinking there would be nothing to do except a movie or the television in the hot living room; for we did not converse, considering each other compan- ions of convenience with sweet-smelling playdough souls unsuitable for interactive entertainment; bluntly, it did not matter if we never saw each other again (for my wooing of Jenny was a secret thing which embar- rassed Jenny, so that she had forbidden me to give others any indication; mute lovers tell no tales). At night Lilith hung around me by the TV, wanting to take me for rides in her Porsche past the used car lots and pizza parlors of Santa Monica, where I was born, but I never went with her because Jenny was the only one for me. And in the mornings I'd whisper every new secret thing to Martin, while Jenny and Lilith and Anna changed in the bedroom, rubbing suntan lotion beneath the straps of each other's bathing suits for luck; and it was another hot perfect morning, the beach anyone's only conceivable destination, and Jenny (whose real name was Ji Yun) asked somebody to help her carry the windsurfer out to the car, and I got up fast to be the first one to lift an end of the windsurfer, walking backwards with it out the apartment door to look into Jenny's eyes, Jenny my giggly love, my yellow rose, my Korean girl, my butterfish, my kimchee delight; and this was California, my glorious California, where I would never want for anything. Martin felt much the same. A native of Orinda, he knew how it was to be tanned and wear pastel-colored shirts. In San Francisco, Martin and Sheila, Martin and Sherri, Martin and Shoshanna went off to the symphony in formal dress. Once Martin and Jenny went. Martin was pretty sure that he could seduce Jenny whenever he wanted to, but so far he had not gotten around to it. Shoshanna was always bringing him flowers and baking him cakes; and Lilith called him on the bedroom phone, but he had to work late that night at the lab. – "You know, I feel a little guilty," he said in his softhearted way, for he never wanted to hurt girls. And outside in the fog, Sherri honked her horn. – We were, in short, Guk-Mins; that is, citizens; literally, if one researches the source ideogram, walking eyes with obstructed vision. The ancients were cynical about mass thought.

"Do you think Lilith will fall off the windsurfer?" I said.

"God only knows," said Jenny, bored. "I swear."

Lilith's figure receded slowly among the other brightly-colored sails.

The hours went by slowly but effortlessly, as if we were in a convalescent home. Jenny was in a giggly mood. She shook the seawater out of her curly black hair, spraying me. "Windsurfing is a good way to do this, to pick up these guys. Don't worry; he's a nice Caucasian guy. Not all that cute. Very nice guy, nonetheless."

When one lies face-down on a beach mat, the whole world is nothing but yellow and white stripes framed by blue sky. Martin's hairy knees were in the periphery of my view. Jenny's feet were chubby and pinkish-gold. She lay back in her beach chair, chewing gum and dangling her hands from the armrests. Her white teeth were the color of the expensive boats in the lagoon, as could be seen when she laughed. Her heavy round face glistened in the sun. I looked at her and felt Ae-Jong, sincere love, or, to be more precise, a blue heart crowded with slow movement. More than anything I wanted to settle into habits of well-fed intimacy with her. Over and over I told her that I loved her. Our conversations on this subject continued for months, in the shade of various apartments. Sometimes the whole business seemed futile, like attempting to sleep with a bad head cold, but I could not stop. Unbeknown to Jenny, I had decided that if I failed to make her love me I would shoot myself in the left eye.

"I love you," I said. "Sweetheart."

"Don't call me sweetheart," she said.

But we screwed in the back seat of her car.

"Let's do it again," she said.

"As many times as you like," I said.

"Don't assume anything," she said.

We fell asleep together on her waterbed.

"You're my first man," Jenny said. "I hope the others will do it this well."

"Why do you want the others?" I said.

"Kiss me goodbye," she said, and gave me her innocent tongue.

"I love you," I said.

"Oh, never mind," she said. "Another thing I said in my letter. Don't love me too much. It's bad for your health."

"This is the last time," she said.

I sat imagining the cool barrel of the gun against my left eye.

"I see no future in this," Jenny said.

"I love you," I said.

"I'll have to think about what that means," she said.

"I love you," I said.

"I care for you," she said very softly. "My heart is breaking for you. It's my heartbreak that I cannot love you more. I am not going to marry you. I just can't do this to my family. So you have to be lighthearted about this. Otherwise, I'm not gonna come back here. I'm not kidding. You're going to be lighthearted about this. Promise me you will."

"No," I said.

"I am not worth it. I am not worth it. I am not worth it. I am not worth it. Tell yourself I am not worth it. Seriously."

I cried.

"Do you promise not to love me too much?" Jenny said.

"Sure," I said.

She sighed. "You're so transparent."

"Baby," she said. "You're so good. I love it when your legs go all over the place."

"I'd do anything for you."

"Do you like it when I hold you like this?" I said.

"Kind of!" she whispered with a giggle.

"Mom would stab me with knives," said my Korean girl. "Mom would fry me alive if she knew. I'm becoming steel-faced, as my mother said these days."

"Well," I said, "I hope someday I can get on Mom's good side."

"No way," said Jenny. "She'll never accept you. Not your fault, kiddo, but you're never gonna be acceptable. I just can't do this to my family. That's why I'm gonna leave you."

"Oh," I said.

"Don't look at me like that with those glassy eyes!" she commanded.

"Sorry," I said. "I didn't know I was looking at you that way."

"I don't know what to do," she said.

"I love you," she sniffled. "How could you do this to me?"

"I love you, too," I said.

"Oh!" she cried in exasperation. "Suck my tit! At least that way you'll shut up. And I can't believe you tried to screw me when I was on the phone. You are so bad!"

A month later I was living in her room, as Jenny looked at big red pictures of eyeballs in her ophthalmology textbook, lying cosy on the waterbed. "I'm recharging my little eye thing," she said to me. "Then I'm gonna want to practice on you because you have blue eyes, you know." Every evening she came home in her white medical smock, smiling at me. "Hand me my Board scores," she said on the bed. "Actually I'm kinda glad you're around so you can get me things." – But we never held hands where Koreans might see. If we drove to Chinatown she might have me put my hand up her dress, but we both had to look straight ahead so that the crowds outside the windows would suspect nothing. Jenny had Chinese friends, too.

5

Jenny loved taking trips, so in the summer we either went down to L.A., stopping at the Carl's Jr. in Kettleman City, the halfway mark, to cool off from the desert while Jenny ordered soft drinks and fries; or else we drove north and east for the weekend, tenting by a picnic table fifty feet from Jenny's car so that we could get whatever we needed (and Jenny always had everything imaginable in the trunk, having worked for fifteen hours the day before to make salad and salsa and Korean barbeque which went into her cooler with the beer), but we never went by ourselves for a trip in those days because I made Jenny nervous; she did not want to be my girlfriend or to marry me, so often my flatmate Martin came along, talking about genetics and opera with the latest girl from the lab whom he was trying to screw. Martin was always sincere. Each time he believed he'd found true love. But true love seemed to transfer itself with austere completeness from Martin to the girl he'd just mounted; and then there was the agony of getting rid of her, the

phone ringing for Martin every evening, every weekend, with Martin
not returning the calls because he was up at the lab working late,
meeting and recruiting other girls; and the harder he had to work to
screw a girl the more and the longer he loved her. So Martin motored
along with us to the north, he and his new girl up front, while Jenny
and I hung the back windows of her white car with towels and white
sweatshirts to keep out the sun; and Martin drove steadily down the
freeway, his foot pressuring the fuel injector with the same care he
devoted to pipetting one of his genetic liquors; and around noon we
checked in at some manmade lake resort. – "So hot!" exclaimed Jenny.
"I swear." We carried Jenny's cooler down to the water, and Martin
and the new girl waved and proceeded to an adjacent cove, the new girl
wary but potentially tender, while Martin secreted the maximum doglike
sincerity into his eyeballs. We did not see them again for hours. –
"Don't lie there! Come on – swim, swim, swim!" said Jenny, and I
waded in slowly as Jenny, already immersed, burst out of the water and
splashed me, and we made our progress across the uninterested lake, I
hugging a yellow air mattress and she breast-stroking beside me like a
seal puppy. The channel was about a quarter-mile wide. Jenny was
going slowly for my sake, being a much better swimmer than I. She was
a very strong girl. Sometimes I would kick fast and hard to catch up
with her, and I'd pull her to me over the air mattress and turn her wet
face to me so I could kiss her. She'd laugh and splash me.

I invented conversations with her in my mind:

"Someday I'll show you Korean thing, a total intimacy kind of thing."

"What kind of thing?"

"I'm not gonna tell you. First you have to marry me, buy me things."

"But what is it?"

"I don't know."

(There is something to be said for attaining the end goal of one's
passions as slowly as possible, lingering over each stage: the first kiss,
the declaration of love, the progressive sexual exercises; because there
is in life a continuous urge to escalation, and it may well be that after
you have her and she has you there is nothing else to do.)

Being in love unloved is not unlike rowing in a glass-bottomed boat,
which allows you to see both the shimmering green light of the pond
and the muck at the bottom; unimpeded in your love by her virtues and
vices (since she is indifferent to you), you proceed across the surface of
your beloved, leaving behind you the shortest-lived ripples imaginable;

and flowers and pine-boughs dance upon the breezy bank. You are alone. – How much more difficult it is, unloving, to have *her* in love with you. The boat weighs on you and exposes to her gaze your private depths, until there is nothing for you to do but work in concert with the next available storm to capsize her. When, on the other hand, you love her and she loves you, in your desperation to reach each other you will forget who is in the boat and who is in the water, and one or the other of you will break through into the green light and SEE EVERYTHING with rapturous drowning eyes before tumbling slowly into the muck.

When we got to the other shore Jenny wanted me to screw her on the air mattress. I was nervous because I could see passing speedboats through the trees, which meant that through the law of reciprocity they might be able to see us; and besides we were within a hundred steps of the rest rooms – but I did not want Jenny to think me timid. (That was another reason that I took psilocybin.) – "Come on, silly boy!" she giggled. "Suck my tit!" – I could not understand why she was suddenly so much rasher than I, I the Mushroom King. How afraid she had always been that Martin and the others might find out that she was my secret girl ... and now, in front of anybody who might amble by for bowel or bladder relief, she was taking off her bathing suit. I was her boy; I pulled my swim trunks to my knees, holding her wet brown body in my arms to protect her from whatever it was that I continually watched for even as Jenny's hips and my hips did the necessary. But nothing happened within my visual range (which was bounded on the near side by ballooning focal length and in the distance by haze and nearsightedness), though I surveyed the water like an Aztec apprehensive of Cortez. – "Once you told me I was too shy for you," said Jenny, kissing me and kissing me. "Am I too shy now?" – I felt the same fear that even the expert drug abuser has when the dose is too great, and controlled consciousness disintegrates, the soul whimpering as it senses that it is now strapped to the electric chair of destiny. I didn't realize that she wasn't screwing me out of brazenness, that I had not corrupted her and made her into a jade, but rather that she loved me desperately.

6

Regarding Jenny's mother, I reminded myself that "there need not be proof of the emission of semen; proof of penetration only is necessary to constitute proof of sexual intercourse. Nor is it necessary that penetration be full and complete; but the slightest penetration of the male organ of the man into the female organ, or vulva, of the woman, as penetration sufficient to rupture the hymen, will constitute sexual intercourse, or carnal knowledge." I am, of course, quoting from the decision of State v. McCann, *18 Ohio Dec 64, 5 Ohio Law R. 388, 389, 52 Wkly. Law Bull. 563*, as interpreted in *Words and Phrases*, published by West (St. Paul, Minnesota, 1953). As yet, however, I have said nothing regarding sodomy res veneria in ano, per os and per anum.

"Oh!" said Jenny. "I don't *believe* I tried oral sex. It wasn't so bad, though. It's like a slippery lollipop."

Jenny's father, whose picture I never saw, had died after they had immigrated. Spinal meningitis had killed him. Because he could not walk, the doctors told Jenny's mother that he was lazy. His final coma, which lasted a year, had destroyed the family savings; and Jenny's mother, who now stood silently in her kitchen frying meat and watching me, had the look of someone who had worked hard for life, a strained slenderness of hands and features, and black curls going grey. She ran a grocery business (in Korea she had been a concert pianist). It was clear to me at once that what I was doing to Jenny would hurt this woman, that I had less right to be in her house than she had to be in my California, where, in the words of Hassan the Assassin, "Nothing is true; all is permissible," when back in Korea it had been so well understood what her daughter was to become, even when Jenny was the class leader of her elementary school back in Seoul, deciding who among the other pupils had to sweep the classroom, who had to get coal for the stove in winter; and then when she was eleven Jenny was picked by a magazine to be a child model, and Jenny's mother had to buy her a whole new outfit, but she told none of the relatives because she didn't want Jenny to be spoiled, and Jenny wasn't spoiled; and when Jenny's mother came to school to greet the teachers she looked so young then, so pretty, that everyone said to Jenny, "Who's that? Is that your sister?", and then Jenny went to high school and graduated with honors and was accepted by Harvard and then medical school, her mother thinking that she was still Soon-Jin, but there were to be no full-blooded Korean children out of her; already her womb was being ruined by a Caucasian with no rights to her; and though Jenny cried sometimes she did not entirely comprehend the spermatic tragedies nightly enacted; but Jenny's mother surely would if she knew the case. Then she and Jenny would both hate me. – "Thanks for the shower," I said. "It felt good after the ride through the desert." – Jenny's mother laughed politely, as if I had made a joke. Jenny told me that her English was not good.

The house overlooked a golf course. It was very hot there. "Do you ever get golf balls in your back yard?" I said, considering this to be a charmingly casual, even witty question that would solve all difficulties. – "All the time," said Jenny's younger cousin politely. Later I found that Martin had asked the same thing when I was in the shower.

Jenny snapped her fingers and gave orders. "Carry my clothes up," she said. "Hurry up! Wash my clothes. Clean my room. Make two gin and tonics." She was the darling of the family. She could do whatever she liked.

7

"It was an outdoor Sunday service kind of thing," my Korean girl was saying in the car as she drove us all to the beach. "They had about five thousand foods."

We got to the beach and set up the windsurfer. Jenny ate plums and fanned herself. "What a weather! My Mom's about to eat me alive because of the little tan I got. She goes, 'You stay out of the sun!' She's pissed 'cause I'm so dark."

When Martin went out on the windsurfer, Anna took a shower and Lilith went to the bathroom, we were alone for a minute. Jenny lay on Anna's towel. I slid my hand down the top of her bathing suit. She opened her eyes slowly. "Well well well well well," said my Korean girl.

All of us lay on the beach doing nothing for hours. "I love sun!" laughed Jenny. When it was dark we drove through Westwood in her little white Nissan, the windows all the way down, while Jenny chewed her sugarless gum. The sidewalks were crowded with teenagers trying to pick each other up, anxious to clasp each other like sea anemones in beachfront bedrooms. Jenny shook her head at them. "These kids are so bad!" she said. "All my friends were pretty much virgins when they married." – But she added slyly, "They got married early."

After this, Jenny took us to her favorite bar, "Yesterdays." Jenny and Anna had sweet pink drinks. All the rest of us had beer.

8

Having been previously disappointed in love, my flatmate Martin had become very confiding of all romantic developments, feeling, doubtless, that in the act of telling his love to the indifferent world he could reassure himself that he *was* loved. Anyone who encouraged him was his friend. I was almost the same way.

Martin and I were flatmates because we had gone to an experimental school together in eastern California, where females were excluded for the sake of strong libido development, making us Trustees of the Nation in a very real biological sense, as our founder had desired. Acting upon these principles, Martin and I used to go off together to smoke pot beneath the green desert moon. We'd roll out our sleeping bags side by side in the marble canyons, drink beers and talk about girls, thereby inculcating in each other a constellation of expectations which winked and blinked nightly as we lay staring up and thinking; so it was inevitable that when we graduated we would go chase all the women we could, in a low-key sort of way involving valium and Sonoma wine. I enjoyed telling Martin about my high school girlfriend, who had dropped me, but whom nonetheless I had laid beneath her father's desk, which made me, I believed, quite special. The first girl that Martin screwed was named Virginia Lemmons, in a dome house in some commune or other that Martin was hitching through on his academic break. Such episodes used to be as common as measles, back in the days before Acquired Immune Deficiency Syndrome, Martin not grasping that promiscuity is a failure to understand the basic sameness of vaginas, of women, of oneself, of one's own deliberate entrapments. Virginia Lemmons wrote Martin, but he never answered.

There were days, months in our twenties when Martin and I had such good times talking about women that I loved the grin of his big white teeth as we sat on the beach, Jenny and Martin's new girl out swimming; or Martin and I loitered around our dining room table, eating a chuckling granola breakfast right over the heads of Jenny's roommates. Then I knew that Martin and I would be successful with our girls and marry them, and have terrific extramarital affairs.

"Are you going to marry Sherri?" I asked.

"It's not inconceivable," said Martin in a tone of academic through-ness, so that I knew that he was about to scan every phenomenological side of this Moebius strip. "I know the real and imaginary blocks, and I've discussed them with Sherri, so I think, yes, there's a chance. But I wish she'd clean up her room, and she should brush her teeth before she kisses me. Also, she's always borrowing money, which I find annoying. I tend to count my pennies. But I went to this party for this professor who got tenure, and this girl from the other lab was there; she was drunk, and it was so tempting to just sort of walk her home and . . ."

"Was she pretty?" I said.

"Oh," said Martin, "I think she's pretty enough. She's actually about Rhonda's height. She can look pretty, yes, kind of a coy little-girl expression, you know how it is . . ."

And that pleased me, that Martin knew that I *KNEW HOW IT WAS*.

Martin and Jenny and I sometimes went sailing in the Bay. Jenny kept failing her licensing exam, so she had to continually go out, never quite learning how to bring in the jib or how to tack. Martin had to do all the work. – "I know how to tack," she insisted. "I know how to bring the boat in the Bay and out of the Bay. It's just like driving. It's just a matter of confidence. I also have very little sailing experience compared to Martin. He's sailed Sunfish, and I don't know what else. But someday I'll get it down. But before that I need to do reading for a couple hours, on points of sail and things like that." – It was peculiar watching Martin metamorphose from a hanger-on at Jenny's Korean meals (which she cooked for everybody) to the omnicompetent skipper, shouting at Jenny to take in sail or take out sail. – "There isn't much wind," Jenny said defensively. "We're just putzing around for a long time. And we keep getting close to Angel Island. I keep telling Martin to put the motor on." – "Jenny, get ready to come about," said Martin. – "Oh, give me a break!" cried Jenny. – I lounged on the stern side, squirting Jenny with my plastic replica of an Uzi pistol. We floated on the blue Bay until the fog came. When it got rainy, Jenny huddled in her slicker with her hair frizzing out from her hood, as if she were a poor wet Eskimo (Eskimos, being Mongolian in type, are closely related to Koreans, I once read), crying, "I want to go home, I want to go home," down in the hot cabin that reeked of diesel, and Martin and I sat companionably at the ropes, rain gear zipped up to our chins, winking at each other like old sailors.

It was Martin who first got Jenny to smoke pot. She never thought that she would do it. Martin persuaded her that it would be a good scientific experiment. Jenny smoked too much the first time and got dizzy and Martin had to hug her. That was O.K. with him. Martin enjoyed hugging girls. After Jenny became my girl he kept hugging her. Sometimes he'd rest his head on her shoulder for a very long time, or kiss her cheek while I watched.

Martin genuinely liked Jenny. He told me that her breasts looked really good. He often borrowed her car. He liked going on trips with Jenny because he could use her car and she would usually make something to eat. Jenny was very convenient for Martin.

Down in L.A., Martin gazed like a lord at Anna and brown-skinned Jenny carrying the hull of the windsurfer into the water, like a pair of Melville's Pacific island women with an outrigger canoe. Then they unrolled the sail and snapped it to the mast. ("Where's the batten?" said Anna. – "Maybe we must have forgot that ropy kind of thing," replied Jenny, endearingly.) – "Martin, you go first," Jenny said. – "Actually," said Martin, half-asleep on his deck chair beside me, "I don't feel like it." – "I'll go," said Anna. "But I want you all to watch me. As long as I'm going to hurt myself I may as well entertain others doing it." – "Lilith, help us push her off," said Jenny. – Lilith disconnected herself from her headphones and raised her eyebrows and stood up, hugging herself so tenderly that she seemed her own lover. For a moment I myself almost loved her, so confident was she of her own splendor that her faith moved me, amorous agnostic though I was; but then she turned to Jenny with a little sneer, and I was released. – Martin and I watched the three girls walk slowly down the beach to the windsurfer. They slid it into the sea. Anna stood upright on it, clutching the mast and looking diminished by her assignment. The three girls stood in the water as if they were having an oceanography seminar. Jenny was a dark brown figure in the water, which came up to her knees. She extended her arms, as if to help Anna magically before Anna fell. Anna toiled with the sail and drifted, Jenny wading after while Lilith stood in the water watching. I could see Jenny following, her arms ready. Jenny pointed and pushed off. Anna sailed a short distance and fell.

"You notice that she's moving and hasn't ever gotten the sail up," said Martin from his deck chair. "It's a lot of work. Still trying. Still trying." Martin, being a scientist, habitually observed and commented on the phenomena around him. When something happened, he could not help but take notice (Ee-mok, literally, "ear-eye"). – Jenny swam out to help. – "Well, she's standing up," said Martin, surveying things through his white-framed sunglasses. The hot breeze stirred the hair around his nipples. "I always forget whether you move the sail forward or back," he said.

"Well," said Lilith, who had just reached us, "it's all a matter of getting used to things. Could you pass the fifteen lotion? It's going to be a rough day in the sun." Lilith was an engineer at a nuclear plant, because, as she quipped, she had a glowing personality.

9

"Mom says, 'Jenny, why are you getting as brown as a nut? What are you doing windsurfing today? Remember, Jenny, white is beautiful.'"

"Right," said Lilith in a world-weary tone.

Jenny knew all the department stores in town. On Sundays she liked to sit in the living room, eating blueberries and reading in the paper about sales. "These blenders are so cute," she'd tell me. "Macy's is having special. But here they are at this other place. Probably a better place to go than Macy's, no matter sale or not. Anyhow, I already have a blender."

One night I lay in her bed watching her get undressed. When she looked at me I waved. – "You're so silly," she giggled, removing her earrings. "Any case, I'm so tired, I can't believe I have to write this goddamn pediatrics case out. Very big head circumference. Pulse is fifty-six. In the playground she buries a lot of toys in the ground. What's wrong with this TV? This TV has funny problems at times."

"I want you," whispered the actress on Jenny's TV. – "Dana, I've found the traitor!" said the male firmly. I swam in Jenny's waterbed . . .

10

Concerning psilocybin, we must not forget that even the love of Tristan and Iseult, as admirable an achievement as it seems, was only the result of a potion, and can thus hardly be credited to the two songbirds. This being the case, we should be fair and admit that negative emotions may similarly have chemical causes, preventing us, however much we would like to, from assigning blame.

Lifting her plump wrist, she squinted at her watch in fascination. "I don't believe it!" she cried. "It's all opposites!" – Jenny and Anna lolled back in their chairs, screaming with laughter. The straps of the beach chairs dug into their fat thighs. Jenny's face was purple. She was laughing so hard that she was gasping for breath. She clutched Anna's red and orange towel and kept twisting it and chewing on it. To me in my own drug state, the towel glowed fatefully, investing the entire beach with sullen hues of lava and vomit, no matter how I turned my head away from it. – Jenny kicked her legs in the air. – "I see your gums!" she said to Martin. "Oh, this is so weird!"

Now she was getting the mushroom sweat. Her round head fell back helplessly, and I thought of the way she had stroked my face and said, "I love your sunken Caucasian eyes." Fat drops of moisture ran down her cheeks and arms and legs. Then, as I lay on the sand watching her, the mushrooms took me also, and she began to change in my eyes, her body getting redder and older until I saw her as she might be twenty years from now: heavy, indolent and shameless, sitting out on the porch screeching and laughing and yelling day and night so that I got no sleep because she was MY WIFE, the kind of wife who would be the shameless laughingstock of the awful neighborhood that we had to live in thanks to my cruddy income, for I would never be either Boo-Ja or bourgeois; and Jenny sat rocking on the top step, whisking away the flies and bellowing for me to bring her things and tidy up the house; while my own kids, a platoon of half-Asian youngsters with serious faces, organized the household as directed by her, passing me by silently as a worthless lump of white meat ridden with the maggots of a bygone empire; as well they should in a culture where the word "Pu" (father) was derived from a picture of a hand holding a whip; I did not live up to that; and Jenny's mother ("Mo," a woman with nipples), now so old as to be just a grey stick with glaring eyes, hobbled down the stairs once a day to beat me for having degraded Jenny; but I didn't care about any of it because I still loved Jenny, because I remembered how she had been that night when I first rang her doorbell, high on mushrooms, and Soon-Jin Jenny came downstairs in her nightgown and she opened the door not really knowing me, and she had never seen anyone on drugs before. – "You're drunk," she said tolerantly. "God only knows. You want me to unlock your door for you?" – "No," I chuckled. "It's not that." I beckoned her very close to me and began to whisper to her a secret story which I knew she would find irresistibly funny. – "Jenny," I whispered. – "What?" she said, shivering in her nightgown. – "Jenny, when I was at my friends' house ..." and I began to tell her how the rooms had been different, all about the helmet rack and the spots on the rug, "and the spots were watching me," I explained, leaning right up against Jenny's ear. She was staring at me. – "At first I thought they didn't like me, but" – I was already beginning to grin, because the punchline was so good – "then I realized that they were very friendly!" – I laughed so hard that I almost fell down. And dear Jenny looked me up and down and shook her head and laughed, too. I really loved her then.

"Kiss me with your tongue!" she commanded. "It makes me feel kind of nauseous, but I like it! Because, you know, I'm kind of a flittery girl."

I kissed her.

I I

While Jenny was in Korea I went down to Haight Street to smoke hash and watch rock and roll videos. Late at night I met a blond addict who appeared surprisingly clean-cut until I got close and saw how pale he was and he pulled me into a dark storefront doorway and showed me his skimpy slimy filthy little joints. – "They're covered with hash oil," he assured me. They looked as if he'd spat on them. – "How much for one?" I said just to get out of there. – "Two dollars," he said, "just two dollars, and if you give me three I'd really appreciate it because I need my fix, man; I've just gotta get cranched." He was trembling. I gave him two and a quarter in disgust.

A guy was yelling outside the record store. "*HEY!*" he said. "I'm new in town. Where do I get to *MEET* somebody?" – Everybody laughed.

Although every day I craved Jenny, within me I think I already saw the days so soon to come when she admitted that she was ashamed of me, and when I put my arms around her in the bed she cried, "Get the hell out, I hate you! I hate you! I'm gonna go to church and pray." And yet, even granting that she might be perpetually ashamed of me, I still knew that our life together could be almost seamless. One day in Berkeley when I sat waiting for her to come home from Korea, I got ribs at Flint's Bar-B-Q. One might as well do something while waiting. (I eat.) We are always waiting for something new to happen. So time passes, and so do our opportunities. – I sat under a tree in Ho Chih Minh Park, eating. Two dogs came up to me. I told them to go away, but one stayed, and I kicked him. He looked at me very patiently. Finally I decided to give him the bone that I had just finished, because he was being very patient and dignified; and anyhow it seemed a waste to drop the bone in the trash can, from where it would only be conveyed to some contaminated landfill. I threw the bone to him. He picked it up very quietly, hunkered down, and began to grind it in his mouth. Every now and then he snarled, and I hypothesized that he was either (a) pretending to kill it, or (b) engaged in an irregular war with the barbeque sauce. I had ordered the hottest kind they had. It occurred to me that even if Jenny kicked me and yelled at me, I would be satisfied with whatever bone she threw me, even if it hurt to eat. So I made my peace with myself.

12

Dust to dust and lust to lust: Suppose I died, and when I got my post-thanatonic bearings it turned out that the dead were passionless, after all, as has often been postulated, but I wasn't, because I had killed myself out of yearning for Jenny despite the fact that as she lay there in her death-waterbed she made me promise to remarry and screw other girls, but her last words were, "I love you," so I decided to shoot myself in the head in order to remarry HER in Ghostland; but once I had done it I found her aloof, so I still couldn't have her even though I was dead along with her, and I felt terrible, like one of those dumb petulant poltergeists trying to get attention, and Jenny offered to take me to a dead doctor like Martin who could fix my brain so I wouldn't mind anything, and then that way I'd get reincarnated faster, but I wouldn't do it; I just stood in a corner of Hell getting more and more transcendently miserable because secretly I had the idea that maybe if you got more miserable than anyone thought possible you might achieve a special transcendence superior to whatever dumb transcendence this dumb Zen renunciation stuff offered; and if I did that I'd triumph over everybody; and then Jenny, who like other Asians was status-conscious, would come back to me.

13

"I don't care about solidarity; I care about commonality. It's so much more *immediate*," as I heard a Haight Street anarchist say.

Jenny and I, I decided, were going to make love on her waterbed, wearing separate but equal headphones plugged into the same tape deck, so that we could go up and down in synch to the Eurythmics doing "Sexcrime" at maximum volume, and then we'd dance around naked shooting my air pistol at pictures of Kim Il Sung and his appropriately named Yook Goons (army military), and then we'd get back in bed and do sixty-nine and I'd leap out of bed and flip the cassette so that the Eurythmics would sing, "Plusgood, doubleplusgood, plusgood, doubleplusgood!", and finally we'd walk through Golden Gate Park on psilocybin, talking and talking to each other like birds, endlessly expressing our love to each other in the greenness.

(Sublimely perfect communication, like the bird-cries, would actually be imbecilic, would be blissful cries that meant nothing and might even be mistaken for cries of pain, would accompany tropical colors, like those of the slate-blue birds with fan-shaped crests, swiveling their heads in martial increments, while rain ran off the leaves, and the birds (blue crowned pigeons, *Goura cristata*, New Guinea) puffed themselves up and marched through the mud, glaring with their red eyes; and green-banded black talking-birds uttered baffling cries in the branches of trees; and the water wavered with green reflections stirred by ducklike birds (Layson teal) that swam in fleets, leaving V-shaped wakes; they drank the water eagerly; and other birds sang with resonant metallic

sounds.* Plump white birds banded with black and red eased themselves into the water silently, paddling with fat orange feet, and then
sauntered through the rain like tourists, glancing round idly in the mud
beneath the trees; and blue-bellied brown hens pecked at worms under
stones. Yellow-and-black birds swooped down from round-leaved
branches like tigers glorying in their own colors; and grey-green birds
roosted in the trees patiently. Great needle-leaved palms stabbed the
sky, but the birds did not fly to them. The blue pigeons picked at their
own chests and shook their feathers. When alarmed, their wings shot
up darkly from their backs. Other birds were golden-beaked, rearing
tarnished heads and showing brown belly-feathers that looked like
shingles; while the flamingoes bent and stabbed down in the streams
like mosquitoes; and bridal-white birds veiled with trailing feathers
stood in shallow pools. Overhead, birds cried like groaning fan-belts.
The saffron-colored ones turned their backs and hunched, like high-
shouldered Buddhist monks. Egrets coiled their snaky necks and flexed
their twiggy feet . . .)

"You've got me hooker-sinker line," said Yellow Rose.

"You mean hook, line and sinker," I said.

"That's what I mean. Any case, you sure got me now. In Asian
tradition, when a man penetrates a girl he's gotta be responsible for her
for the rest of her life. I hope you're feeling responsible."

"I'll try," I said.

"You have upper hand now," she said. "I'd do anything to keep you.
My heart is aching for you. Oh, dearie, my heart is dying for you."

Now began the happy time when Jenny spoon-fed me ice cream and
bought me chocolate bars, and we lay in bed all day and I rested my
head on her shoulder listening to her talk on the phone. "I feel so
stupid compared to you," my Korean girl told me. "I want you to tell
me all about those philosophers – Aristotle and Pluto and those Greek
kind of guys." In the living room she lay on top of me on the sofa, her
skirt unzipped. "I'm not just a steel-face, I'm an iron-face!" she giggled.
"Mom would die." Whenever I went anywhere Jenny came to the top
of the stairs in her nightgown, begging me not to go. I tongue-kissed
her and stuck a finger up her golden ass.

---

* It was these sounds that Jenny seemed to me to imitate when she talked Korean
to her mother. I once transcribed the alien syllables that I heard her say: "Omja, kumi-
ja goo-o, gooey-gooey! Handala! Kulego kulegrum. Gahio." – But when I read them
back to Jenny she could not understand them at all.

The ring was a wavy gold band crowned by a diamond. Examined through the jeweler's loupe, the diamond itself seemed a transparent bud, comprised of a hundred tight-clasped petals of crystal veined to the core with yellow refractions from the gold below. I could not determine whether the diamond was yellow, blue, purple or perfectly colorless. – This was the engagement band. – The wedding band was a golden circlet of the same wavy shape, made to interlock with the engagement ring.

It was going to be a surprise for Jenny. I had obtained the complicity of her housemate, Margaret. Margaret was a shy gentle girl with a freckled face. All the girls downstairs were Soon-Jin. Margaret, when asked by Jenny for a rope with which to lash her sleeping bag onto her pack, furnished a pretty red ribbon, at which I smiled, while Jenny and I went backpacking in the Olympic Rain Forest, Margaret's ribbon flying from Jenny's pack as the trail took us through Spanish moss and maidenhair. Water glistened on the toes of our boots, making them brown and shiny like champignons. Secret Creek was hidden under tall cinnamon ferns. We peered through them to see black water glinting with cold gold light. Jenny grinned, climbing up the mountains. But since she was a city girl I had to give her my hand to help her across brooks. I had been with her for so long that I had what Asian-Americans laughingly call "yellow fever," for when I closed my eyes I still saw the gold light from her; and the autumn leaves in their oranges, browns, yellows and golds could almost have been butterflies born from her, each leaf fixed with a particularity of gold derived from her shimmery skin, the blood pulsing in her cheeks when she looked at me and told me that she loved me; and Margaret had watched the courtship smiling, so now when my pillow burned me at night and my dreams were of golden Jenny I turned to Margaret and confided in her, telling her that I had to marry Jenny at once; and Margaret, astonished that matters had gone so far, but trusting me, drove me down to Post Street, where the shop windows shone yellow with gold. Margaret and I were both nervous. Neither of us had ever done this before. – The jewelers all thought that Margaret was my fiancée. They put the rings on her finger one after another, while she held out her hand, blushing slightly. In the second store we found the ring that was perfect. The jeweler was an elderly man, plump and benign, who waited on us with attentive courtesy. There was something about the cut of his suit, the smell of his cologne, that reminded Margaret and me of distant exotic places where jewels come from; and I imagined him traveling to the De-Militarized Zone, writing out a check with his liver-spotted hands, unperturbed by the *PHWWwwwinnnNG!* of bullets, as his contact, a North Korean private, came leap-frogging over the barbed wire, on his head a conical hat stuffed tight with gold (for gold, too, was a drug; and no doubt its purchase and manufacture was attended by the usual risks). – As the after-image of my treasure-buying imaginings faded I looked at the jeweler's tie and let my heart pound at the romance of my own absurdly expensive purchase, Margaret also goggle-eyed; and Jenny was going to be astounded. The jeweler waited out my silence patiently. When I told him that I was unemployed he did not lose his gentleness. He got out the padded pews of diamonds and placed the rings on Margaret's finger for us to see. One of Margaret's fingers was bandaged. For some reason, the sight of her hardworking hand (she was a night waitress, carrying trays of cruel gleaming cutlery and heavy wine glasses that could shatter into a million dangerous jewels), with its Band-Aid and all its temporary diamonds, filled me with tenderness.

The fourth ring was the right one. Both of us knew it. – "Oh," said Margaret quickly, "it's really cute. I mean, but maybe cute's not the word for something this important." And she looked timidly down at the ring, in case she had offended me. – "Yes," said the jeweler. "See how pretty it is." And he withdrew the ring from her finger and gave it to her to hold.

There was a sapphire ring at the Shreve Company that Margaret and I liked almost as well, but we knew that Jenny was a traditional girl, and sapphires were not traditional, although the saleslady tried to convince us that they were mainstream now that Lady Di had gone with one. – "Let's get the diamond ring," I said.

We went back to buy it. When Margaret saw it again she nodded. "You have good taste," she said.

"Of course I do," I said complacently, "because I have Jenny."

From my shabby pants pocket I counted out the sum, in a great heap of tens and twenties on the glass counter, with a solitary hundred thrown in for garnish. Margaret told me on the way home that the jeweler had smiled just a little at my youthful display of cash. I did not see his face because I was looking at all my money for the last time. – "When's the big day?" said he, anxious, no doubt, to distract me from considerations of poverty. – "It hasn't been set yet," I said. "I'm about to ask her. When she sees this nice ring, I guess she won't be able to resist." – "Yes," said the jeweler in his stately manner, sweeping my money off the table. He gave me two clean copper cents in change. I gave one to Margaret for a luck-penny.

"Well," I said, "that's done. Let's hope I never have to do it again."

"You can't say that now or the ring will be cursed," Margaret said. "I know it's going to be your lucky ring." She smiled at me. She loved Jenny.

Jenny was home. "Where have you two been?" she said.

"Oh, just around," I said.

Margaret winked at me behind Jenny's back and left the house.

I gave Jenny the two little packages. I had even figured out what to say. "Jenny," I said, "once I told you that I wasn't worth your little finger. After you put these on that'll certainly be true."

"Oh, no," said Jenny, sitting down on the bed as if she had just discovered that she was ill.

She unwrapped the boxes and opened them. "There's so much tissue paper in here," she said. "Christ sake. I'm never gonna get to the bottom of these little things. I sure hope you didn't get what I think you got."

"That's the engagement ring," I said, "and this is the wedding band. Margaret said you're supposed to wear the wedding band nearest to your heart."

Jenny put the rings on her finger. "They're beautiful," she said, looking down at the bed. "You know I am not gonna wear them. You know I can't accept them."

"Oh," I said.

"Why are you putting this pressure on me? You know I'm not about to marry you. If I were head over heels with you, I'd say, hell with the whole world. I'd marry you right now. But I don't love you to that degree. You're so impractical. You've made me so unhappy." She put the rings back in their boxes and wrapped the boxes up again. "You've made me so unhappy," she said. "I can't believe you did this dumb kind of thing. How unhappy are you, on a scale of one to ten?"

"I don't know," I said.

"Ten would be all my family killed in an airplane crash. One is, you know, slight disappointment. That's the scale, Mister."

"I don't know," I said.

"You've put such a big burden on me. I'm a six. No, I'm a five."

"I see," I said.

"How about you? I've told you; now you tell me."

I considered. Ten would mean that I was ready to kill myself. I had already loaded my guns upstairs. "Seven," I said. "No, seven point five."

"I want you to return the ring right now."

"No," I said.

"Return the ring."

"No."

"I know! I'll tell you I don't like it. I hate this ring. I hate it. It's so ugly. Return the goddamn ugly ring. Now you'll have to return it, won't you?"

"No," I said.

"Boy," she said, popping her gum. "I tell you."

I turned away.

"Fine, fine, fine, get away from me," she said. "You just don't want to be near me anymore."

"That's not it," I said.

"I want you to return the ring. You are so impractical. Do you hear me? I say, return the ring. Anyhow, what finger's the engagement ring supposed to go on?"

"The ring finger," I said.

"Anyhow I never wear rings," Jenny said. "With all the scrubbing and scrubbing of my hands in the operating room, soon it would be worn down to nothing." She put her arms around me. She had never held me so sweetly. "You know I love you, you silly boy," she said.

That night Jenny tucked the covers of her bed around me gently and went out. I had dreams of severed heads. After a long time I woke up with Jenny's arms around me. – "You're having a terrible night, aren't you?" she said. – I said nothing, pushing my face hard against the cold wall. When Jenny finally fell asleep, I got out of the bed as quietly as I could and put my clothes on. She said something in her sleep. I opened the door and closed it behind me without looking back. I walked past Margaret's room and went downstairs. Outside, I unlocked the door to my apartment, went up to my room, and lay on the floor. My stomach squirmed in its acids inside me, and my chest was so tight that I could hardly breathe. After a long time it was still dark. But I could hear cupboards slamming in the flat downstairs; I heard a voice in Margaret's room; I heard streetcars rattling by and birds singing. No doubt ageing had set in with a vengeance, overcoming my many doses of magic mushrooms, increasing my focal length of vision further and further in the course of this night so that I would never again be able to see anything closer than Jupiter.

A Korean Glossary, with Hanja Ideograms

努力
No-Ryok
hard working

愛情
Ae-Jong
sincere love

國民
Guk-Min
citizen

父
Bu
father

富者
Boo-Ja
rich

結婚
Kyeol-Hon
marriage

純眞
Soon-Jin
pure, innocent

耳目
Ee-mok
to take notice

母
Mo
mother

陸軍
Yook-Goon
army military

THE YELLOW SUGAR

A Tale of Infamous Righteousness and Righteous Villainy

"As Thou hast adjudged me to be erring,
I will certainly lie in wait for them
on Thy straight path."

A PASSAGE FROM A DECAYING BOOK

Jhora Naek – A celebrated leader of the Multan Thugs, whose name they mention with reverence during their rituals. He was a Musulman and he and his servant [**Koduk Bunwaree**] are said to have killed a man who had in jewels and other articles property to the value of 160,000 rupees (£16,000) laden upon a mule. They brought home the booty, assembled all the members of the fraternity within reach and honestly divided the whole as if all had been present. Jora Naek, his wife and slave were all canonized in consequence.*

Sir William Sleeman, *Ramaseeana* (Calcutta: G. H. Huttmann, 1836)

---

* As this extract shows, Sleeman spelled these names as the mood struck him. I have done likewise.

A thief is a contemptible being, but a Thug – rides his
horse – wears his dagger – shows a front!

The Thug Buhran, to Sir William Sleeman (1830s)

I

I would like to retell here the tale of Joorah Naig, the gracious old
Thug from Multan, about whom enough has been forgotten for me to
embellish the account as is proper for a storyteller to do. In early life he
was a sensualist, and inhaled whenever a woman passed by. But close
upon forty years of marriage found him climbing other rungs of the
ladder of slippery pleasures. He still enjoyed his life, but even more did
he admire treasure, and more than treasure he loved rectitude, for he
was a sincere Muslim. When I first read this of him, I was astounded: –
How, I wondered, could a Jemador* in a cult of stranglers count
himself a believer? But then I recalled the pious whom I myself have
seen in Landi Kotal, an infamous low-roofed village in the Khyber,
whose people have forsworn liquors because the Prophet smashed the
wine-jars at Mecca, but who think nothing of hawking hashish, for they
are well-meaning, but a trifle literal-minded – hashish, you see, is not
specifically proscribed in the Sacred Book. So it must have been with
Joorah Naig. He was a Thug, it is true. Yet he was not wicked in his
heart, as was 'Abd Allah ibn Ubayy, leader of the Hypocrites, who
prostituted his own slave-girls when they wished to remain chaste. For
Joorah was wise and righteous, like an old banyan tree growing above
the water to shelter his own. I do not deny that the Qur'an condemns
robbery on the highway (XX.29.29). Yet let us be fair to old Joorah.
Who are we to say that he ever read that passage? Certainly he gave to
the needy, and prayed seven times a day. And he was considered a most
honorable man.

* For a glossary of Hindustani and Ramasee expressions see page 275.

He had a longish face, narrowing drastically from the cheekbones to the chin. In rest, it conveyed reserve or grim indifference; but he could put himself at pains to smile, which he did charmingly. "Who is that dignified old man?" people would say. "Is he a scholar, or does he perhaps travel on business for the Emperor?" – His lips were thin and almost grey, shadowed as they were by the bluish stubble of his moustache; and the close grey hair at his temples, flush against the yellow dome of his forehead, created a nearly hideous impression; but at first his victims perceived only the mild blue eyes crinkled up in a beam beneath the heavy brows; and the soft beard, purer in its whiteness than the turban whose immaculate coils crowned his head. This beard of his reminded people of a cloud. Clouds were rarely to be seen in summer in the Punjab.

As a group his Thugs resembled a class at a men's finishing school, such as existed in the days of the Moghuls to train court officials of perfect refinement. They were mostly young, those Thugs, and smiled at the approaching traveler with guileless sadness, like waiters on a holiday, their hands on their knees or else rubbing their precocious moustaches. They wore their white cotton clothes loosely on account of the heat. One saw them sitting around a circle of teacups in some wayside grove, the elder gurus among them glaring and nudging when they were not sufficiently jolly. In the rear squatted the apprentices, who held the horses during those moments of crisis which are inevitable in a Thug's career. These boys, often no more than eight or nine, peered over the shoulders of their companions, or hid bashfully behind the boles of the peepul-trees; while old Joorah sat conversing in the front with his chief confederates, Noor Khan, Lal Khan, Bhodi and Keema. Most highly of all he esteemed his Khansamah, or private servant, a man of the Lodhee caste named Koduk Bunwaree.

One day the band was captured on suspicion of murder. A merchant's caravan had disappeared not far from Lahore, and government approvers* found the gobba, or round grave. Joorah Naig and his assistants were placed in a strong jail to await their trial. – "We have no hope," said Bhola, one of the apprentice Thugs; "let us strangle ourselves with our silken roohmals and at least control our own deaths." – "Never," replied Joorah Naig. "Let us rather regard this time as a means to test

---

* Judicial investigators. They had their name, perhaps, because they were likely to approve whatever verdict would make them rich.

our philosophy. Everything happens by Allah's grace." So in prison, exercising an almost Socratic control over their shrunken destinies, they "ate out" once a week – that is, they spooned their bowls of rice, sitting cross-legged beneath the bars of the window, enjoying the sun. They could have done so every day had they liked, but upon old Joorah's command they wisely restricted themselves, and by so doing created a privilege which was no less enjoyable for being meaningless. In due time, being taken to the courtroom, they engaged the best lawyers to pluck at the judge's sleeves, entreating him for the love of Allah to save the innocent. Grandfathers came on camels, strewing rupees to the functionaries of the court. And the judge, after listening well to the whining swarms of lawyers, looked into the serene blue eyes of Joorah Naig and acquitted his band. "Yes," said Joorah Naig, "Allah is truly compassionate, merciful." For he was a Baroo, or Thug of great respectability.

II

They marched to faraway Oudepore then, breasting yellow dunes and dusty desert hills to see the Rajah, who was dressed in blue, with a collar of pearls around his neck, and sapphires marching down his chest instead of buttons. Between his eyes was painted the upturned white crescent of Shiva. The Thugs enlisted in his army, blinking their tattooed eyelids as they made him gifts. The Rajah for his part was wise, and so bestowed upon them the highest rank. Beside themselves with gratitude, they expectorated still more jewels from the mouths of their leathern bags and praised him until he yawned upon his throne. Thus all were satisfied. And later, when the police came after, timid Bhola cried out, "Surely we are overtaken." – "By no means," said Joorah Naig. "Surely Allah is with us." And Allah guided them into a dark place in the forest where they were not found.

They stayed in the Rajah's army a month longer, to be safe; and Bhola capered through the drills and standard-wavings. The Rajah liked him, and requested his purchase, but Joorah said that the boy was like a son to him, and his leathern bag wept two blue apologetic tears into the Rajah's hand. Then the band returned across the barley-fields and wheat-fields of the Punjab, to earth-baked Multan, where they had

been born; where the women stood in line for the wells, with their faces
veiled and modestly downcast. Bullocks trudged sweating in the fields,
dragging the ploughs, while the sweating men trudged alongside. The
young boys worked in the orchards, wearing the baggy clothes of the
region. If any strangers came to steal fruit the boys shot them in the
eyes. – All these were the people of Joorah Naig, for he, being a most
powerful Jemador, could summon them and command them to stand or
to sit. They protected him from the approvers, and he remembered
them when he distributed the autumn's booty. Yet they knew him not
as a Thug, nor as a Phansigar (as they are called in the south), nor even
as an Ari Tulcar, which in the Tamul language means "Mussulman
nooser," for from their point of view it was better to know him only as a
rich farmer. As with the rest of us, if they found dead bodies in their
wells they buried them in the fields and went about their business like
upright men. After all, Thugs never killed in their own district.

III

Old Joorah and his wife had been married, as I said, for almost forty
years; and so one might well expect dissension to have gnawed away at
the husk of love. But this was not so; the fidelity of Thugs' wives is
proverbial. Padma was modest in her gaze; for her he brought the heavy
gold jhumkas, or bell-shaped earrings of Rajasthan, and a mass of
enamelled jewelry (and back along the road from Oudepore travelers
had disappeared, and the village watchmen went around at night crying,
"Kaber-dur! Kaber-dur!" – Have a care! Have a care!). Old Padma
admired the jhumkas. She did not hang them from her ears, because
that would not befit a woman in her stage of life, but she held them
against one grey tress, where they glowed like scorpions in the dust.
Then she locked them away. – When other women came to visit, they
would show their treasures to each other. That was the principal
amusement of women.

From Padma's girlhood on she had prepared the curries and the milk
curd for her husband. She rarely emerged from the household except
in the evenings, when she went down to the Sind to wash their clothes,
staring across the chocolate-colored water at grasses growing in the
rocks like fingers from a hand. At those times she always wore her veil.

Stretched out to dry on the stones beside her, the clothes shone translucent in all their wet patterns.

Old Padma knew that she was the wife of a Thug. This horrid word, like the croak of a frog, had haunted her ever since she had reached the age of marriage. Wives of Thugs might be killed if they gave evidence of suspecting their husbands' professions, so Padma kept silent.

IV

That summer the Thugs worked in the fields like other zemandars. Every month on the last hot night of the moon's decline, Joorah set up an image of four-armed Kali in his house and adorned her with silver and delicious gold to the value of one hundred rupees. Then he made his prostrations. Outside, fat ants swarmed beneath the dirt. These were the nights when everyone wanted to be under the stars, but under the stars, as under the roofs, there was nothing to do.

When October came, Joorah tested the omens with Koduk Bunwaree. Just as, in the text of a speech reported in *Pravda*, it may be crucial whether there is "strong applause" or "stormy applause," so for the Thugs the way the dust blew, the cries of animals, the timing of rain – these and other matters were of great importance. (Sleeman reports, for instance, that "A Thug never moves without his turban, except in Bengal, perhaps. If a turban is set on fire it threatens great evil, and the gang must, if near home, return and wait seven days . . .") The auguries being promising, Joorah assembled the gang in the coolness and darkness of his house; and they drew the curtains, although only the impure of heart would have watched or listened.

"O you who believe," said Joorah Naig, stroking his long white beard, "whether you do a thing openly or in secret, surely Allah is ever Knower of all things. So says the Holy Qur'an.* This being the case, my friends, we may as well act in secret. Just as your doings with your own wives are veiled, so must our doings here be veiled. And if you disturb our Mother's veil, she will certainly punish you." – The apprentices trembled at these words, as they were meant to do, and old Joorah was pleased. – "Now for the *goor*," he said. – Koduk Bunwaree brought in a

* XXII.33.54.

lacquered tray, on which stood the cups of green tea that Padma had prepared. At the bottom of each cup was a lump of yellow sugar. The Thugs drank their tea and sucked on their sugar, each one thinking about the season ahead. And the bhutotes, or chief stranglers, laid down their pickaxes before the goddess's statue, scattering her feet with flowers and little cakes.

Afterwards Joorah went to the fort of Ibn-i-Qasm Bagh to make his customary presents to the Moghul soldiers. These being accepted, his Phansigars could resume their holy Thuggee. – "Kali Markey Jay!" they cried out, meaning, Victory to Mother Kali! – The streets were watered to lay the dust on the day that they left the gates of Multan. As they looked back they saw the grin of a rotting waterwheel.

V

First they set out from Bahawalpur, across the Great Indian Desert to Ganganagar. Not a cloud could be seen, and not a blade of grass. Their bodies were covered with red blisters from the heat. Sometimes ancient forts rose up like brassy mountains, or loomed tall and yellow-white with bone-ivory, their arched windows as dark as black tongues. At the base of the forts, hunched against their ruined ramparts of sandstone, were tea-stalls. Here the Thugs rested, drank green tea with sugar, and discreetly inquired whether any wealthy travelers had proceeded this way. They flattered the loquacious when they could. – "Truly your knowledge is a marvel!" smiled Joorah Naig, licking his lips as rapidly as does a frog. "They paid in gold, you say?" – Up in cow-dung huts upon the dunes, women shaded their eyes with their hands, looking at the strangers. Black goats barked.

Old Joorah led them on, his hands folded over his belly. In the mornings Koduk Bunwaree massaged him. The desert gradually became a broad steppe, with pale bushes, long grass, and ruins of villages ingrown by mulberry trees. Crocodiles bathed in the yellow streams. At certain landmarks the Thugs winked at each other. "Yes, here lie the merchant and his wife," they said, stamping on the ground. Palm trees grew sparsely on the plain, and there were mosques on the horizon like white bulbs.

They traveled by delightfully easy marches to Abohar, Bhatinda,

Nabha and Patiala, hiding their purpose in diverse assortments of smiles, just as stones may be hidden in cities, for the Qabba stands at the heart of Meccah, covered with black cloth embroidered in gold. Joorah continually instructed them with wise sayings. "'It is no sin for you that you seek the bounty of your Lord,'" he quoted from the glorious Qur'an. – "Yes, yes!" cried the Thugs. – "'Allah provides without measure for whom He pleases,'" he quoted. "'And those who disbelieve, their deeds are as a mirage in the desert, which a thirsty man deems to be water. And Allah is swift at reckoning.'" – "We will punish the disbelievers!" cried Bhola, dancing in the dust. – "'Surely thy Lord makes plentiful the subsistence for whom He pleases,'" Joorah quoted. And Koduk Bunwaree, his most favored servant, smiled woodenly.

Often they entertained wayfarers about whom no more was ever heard, following the advice of the Qur'an: "We give them to enjoy a little, then We shall drive them to a severe chastisement" (XXI.31.24). Closing their eyes in prayer, the Thugs saw those words in letters of blue fire, encircled in blue flowers as in certain of the illuminated Holy Books. For they were not at all vulgar, differing in that respect from European murderers such as the Frenchman Dumolard, who was brought into court on January 20, 1862, to a horrified hum of voices: "There he is! There he is!" – "Yes," said Dumolard with a greasy sort of swagger, as he waved his hat. "Here he is!" Or consider the stranglers Gabrielle Bompard and Michel Eyraud (1889), who killed an usher for his money. Gabrielle lured the usher into an abandoned house and began kissing him. Soon her arms were around his neck. He did not see that she had undone her waistcord and was holding the end of it in her hand. Lovingly she slipped it around his throat. Michel, who had been hiding upstairs, his face as pale and sweaty as the moldy walls, now made his appearance. The police documents do not say what the usher thought while Gabrielle twisted his hands behind his back and Michel tightened the noose. They threw the cord across a pulley which Michel, with true foresight, had installed at the top of the stairs, and then they hanged their victim and dismembered him. – These two, alas, were actuated by no religious motives. That is presumably why they wilted on the scaffold of justice, whereas condemned Thugs showed no such failing. (They had the yellow sugar to sustain them.) Brahmin Thugs even mounted the ladder and put the nooses around their own necks, so that no man of a lower caste, such as an executioner, might touch them; then they threw themselves off. For they were not only devout, but also well-mannered, as it behoved them to be.

So Joorah instructed his Thugs, and while the lessons were given they continued on to Jodpore and further east, stopping often in the cool groves. Under almost every tree was a secret grave. Sometimes travelers approached them on the road and dismounted to rest for a little from the heat of the day. These persons were victims thrown into their hands by divine power. They had to be strangled. There was nothing to be done about it. Joorah received two shares of the booty, being Jemador. In a leather sack on his mule he carried pearls, diamonds, doubloons, gold bangles, necklaces, earrings, rupees and engraved daggers, all in a disinterested heap. Behind came his lengthening string of ponies. He regarded the amassing of treasure with the same ironical satisfaction as he had watched the sunlight through the prison bars in Lahore. – "This world's life is only a sport . . ." says the Qur'an, "and a vying in the multiplication of wealth and children." Sometimes the bodies would have nothing of value on them. Then the cutters would be enraged, and after ritually stabbing the eyes, knees and armpits they made great irrelevant gashes to take revenge on the corpses for their disappointment. But Joorah Naig never lost his gratitude to God. "You who believe," he cried, "follow not the footsteps of the Devil!" So he reminded his fellows always of their duty.

VI

Yet, being wise, he took thought of their material as well as spiritual good. Three days into the jungle, they sighted a party of holy men coming round a bend in the road. No one else was near. Holy men, like the blind, like metal-smiths, pariahs, women and other lepers, were taboo to murder, but the Thugs were impatient, and clamored for an exception. At last the old Jemador, considering well his knowledge of these matters and consulting with Koduk Bunwaree, ruled that in this instance it would be permissible to kill, because in this way the holy men would reach Paradise that much the sooner. When he explained the reasoning, all the band cried out with delight at his wisdom. The holy men were strangled in a trice.

Next, three sisters appeared in a horse-drawn cart, escorted by their attendants. The women were of the Brahmin caste, and wore jewels. They had oval faces and long black braids. As the cart creaked closer and closer, the women caught sight of them and spoke to their attendants. The eldest, conscious of her responsibility, looked round her frequently, shading her eyes, and the middle one cocked her head and smiled anxiously, but the youngest sat still, staring sadly at Joorah Naig from the cart as if she were accustomed to being mocked or ill-treated. Her garment was patterned with black stripes and crimson flowers. It was of some value, but not as much as those of the eldest, which had golden buttons across the breast. The old man thought them all fine girls. Young girls sometimes became enamored of Bhola on long journeys; he had such high spirits. Once the boy had become close to a beautiful Brahmin maid. It never could have worked, of course.

In signs, Joorah's band begged him to allow the Thuggee. He considered, stroking his lamb-white beard.

"They are pretty," sighed Joorah. "It would be easy to fall in love with them, to let them go. To do otherwise would be sacrilege. You know that it is forbidden to murder women."

"Yes, Joorah Naig Jemador," said the Thugs anxiously. "We know."

"But it is clearly our fate to do so," said Joorah Naig. "Upon you be the sacrilege."

"Yes, Jemador!" cried the Thugs. They smoothed their garments, and obsequiously, like pimps of death, they bade the party rest with them during the hot hours of the afternoon. Keema went to help the four attendants unharness their horses, while the other Thugs seated themselves comfortably in the shade, smiling and stroking their moustaches.

The women were seized by their hair. Out came each Thug's roohmal, "a certain slip with a running noose," says the seventeenth-century traveler Thévenot, somewhat inaccurately, "which they can cast with so much sleight about a man's neck, when they are in reach of him, that they can never fail, so that they can strangle them in a trice." In fact the roohmal is not a noose at all, but a strip of white or yellow silk, like the waistcord of Gabrielle Bompard; with a silver coin consecrated to Kali knotted in one corner, as a weight. This is hurled round the victim's neck with one hand; the other hand seizes the knotted end, and the hands are firmly crossed to tighten the band across the throat. The aesthete tucks the end into the knot for elegance's sake, whereas the tyro leaves it out for a better grip. This does not, however, matter to the result. – The sisters perished after a short struggle, their necks marked by purple excoriations, and were buried in a gobba. Then the Thugs dispatched the four attendants. They sold the horses and cart separately. Each share was one hundred and sixty rupees.

Next came a solitary traveler on horseback. The Thugs hid in the jungle. The horse sniffed as it neared them and suddenly bolted, rolling its eyes, but Zolfukar leaped forward and seized it by the bridle, while Bhola and Dost Khan took hold of the rider's arms and pulled him backward. In a twinkling, old Joorah had slipped the roohmal around his neck and dragged him off the saddle by it, so that he strangled as he fell. "His destiny was written on his forehead," said Joorah Naig. "Yes, yes," said the Thugs with cunning smiles. They stabbed the corpse and buried it.

VII

Last night I saw the cadavers in the dissecting room of the hospital. They lay on the tables, each one tied under a vinyl sheet. Beneath the vinyl they were wrapped up the way that meat is wrapped in butcher paper. It was very hot in the room; and the smell of formaldehyde was biting. The heads were wrapped up separately, so that the first-term medical students would not have to see them right away. – "This one," the doctor said. There was something especially horrible about the *tightness* of the head-wrappings; the corpses could not breathe. – It was Khotub, the time between midnight and sunrise. I watched in a sick suspense as the doctor lifted the swathed head and began to unwind the bandage (upon which a fly was walking). Round and round, round and round; and gradually the shape of the face began to be ascertainable. Perhaps only one layer more veiled it, or perhaps three. I could now distinguish the pressed contours of the nose, and the concavities of the eye-sockets. A wisp of hair protruded from the edge of the bandage, like grey grass. Round and round, round and round; I prayed that the damp bandage would not stick to the skin of the dead face. The smell made me step back. – At last the face was exposed. It was yellow-grey and wrinkled, with a sort of drowned quality. The eyelids were bulbous with fluid. The thing had been a man in his sixties. Dead! Dead! He should have been left to rot in his grave. The formaldehyde had kept him for two years. It leached out of his eyes like tears.

VIII

Mud-hut towns shaded themselves under the many-stemmed peepul trees. The Thugs stopped in one of these to get some bananas. The vendor wore a red kerchief to protect his head from the sun. (In my mind's eye I can see his dead face tied up in meat-cloth, secured from flies by a plastic bag tied with rubber bands.) The Thugs filled a basket with fruit as he squinted at them, and they paid him with a silver coin. His young sons leaned against each other on the wall behind him, staring at the travelers. At this, Joorah Naig smiled and gave the boys a piece of sugarcane.

Soon thereafter they met a man with a grievance, who was on his way to the law courts. Old Joorah, having discovered his purpose, quoted to him a Persian proverb: "Speedy injustice is preferable to tardy justice," and when the man agreed they speedily strangled him.

They came upon a mother and her son, both dressed in green. The little boy wore a silver bracelet. When the Thugs came near, the mother hooded herself and drew a fold of her robe across her mouth. There was no one else in sight. When Joorah Naig raised his hand, the Thugs rushed upon them and killed them. The bodies had on them some gold mohurs. On the mother was a small box containing four hundred rupees. "Ho!" cried Bhola at this unexpected treasure, but Koduk Bunwaree and old Joorah surveyed him stonily, for he was desecrating their ritual by his impudence. In matters of this type, the two always acted in concert. They did not like each other, but esteem has little to do with liking; and Thugs, like our businessmen in this respect as in others, must put personal feelings aside for the sake of their enterprises.

They threw the bodies into a well at the roadside. There was hardly any water in it.

IX

This Koduk Bunwaree had been alive as long as Joorah could remember. The strange relations of those two had begun when Joorah, then a boy of nine, was first given the yellow sugar. – A new saint had just died. – In those days some villages in the Mianwali district had no saints of their own, so that the inhabitants lured Sayyidim inside their walls in order to kill them; then these towns too could boast their martyrs. In great Multan, however, this procedure was unnecessary, there being already a whole cemeteryful of saints, to say nothing of the renowned tomb of Saint Rukni-i-Alam, built by Tughlaq Shah, its dome rising above the bazaars, seducing penitents to come stroke its cool glazed tiles; or the tomb of Shams-i-Tabriz, the murdered Sufi; or the numerous shrines whose pattern-inlaid walls resembled Parcheesi boards.

One heard so many reports of these saints, peace be upon their names! Still talked about, for instance, was the fourteenth-century miracle worker Nizam Oddeen Ouleeah, who was a Sunni, and dwelled in Delhi. The Shiites called him a Thug, though the Sunnis denied it. In any event, he had a "supernatural purse," which he spent from wisely and discreetly. Joorah's father had lately begun telling the boy many tales of Nizam, for it was time to guide his beliefs into those of the profession. He spoke also of far sights, of the white balconies of Oudepore City Palace, birds flying past its domes and blue-tiled windows (for it was important that the boy desire to travel); of the Lake Palaces with their windows of colored glass, the blasphemous paintings of angels on the mirrored ceiling, defying the injunction against images – for they had gold-flaked faces, and they swished about in blue dresses and green dresses bordered with gold. Their shoulders were as symmetrical as double-bladed axes; for wings bloomed from their shoulders with endearing childishness. They gazed at the world in saucy profile, out of a single painted eye apiece, both hands held out to the sharp-leaved flowers of plants that grew in the sky like eagles. Young Joorah was excited by these images, but his father made him look into his ascetic old face, which was as brown as earth, with the eyes and beak of a hawk, and he said, "Those Hindu princes are idolaters, mocking Allah with their representations of his creation; upon them is a grievous punishment, which someday I shall teach you to execute." Seeing the excitement in his son's face then, he fed him the *goor*, or yellow sugar, which changed human nature to the point of destroying the capacity for pity.

X

I am reminded of the Afghan boy, Gholam Sayyid, who sat in the red dust of our guerrilla camp continually chanting from the Qur'an, and he was cross-eyed, and he did not like me because I was not a Muslim. It was Ramazan. "But whoever among you is sick or on a journey, he shall fast a like number of days" (II.2.184). So says the Qur'an, but nonetheless Gholam Sayyid would not permit my friend Suleiman to take medicine, even though Suleiman was very ill from bad water. It was a hot day, and the Mujahideen sat cleaning their rifles. They were going to attack a Soviet airfield in Jalalabad. Suleiman, who had helped me across the mountains and down a rotten glacier, who always let me lean on his shoulder, Suleiman was sick and Gholam Sayyid would not let him take medicine. I do not know if Suleiman is alive or dead now, but if I ever learn that the Russians shot him or dropped a bomb on him or gassed him, if I hear of a baby girl that he could not save, I will think despite myself of Gholam Sayyid.

XI

Because it was summer, Joorah slept in the courtyard, in a narrow charpoy. His father slept on the terrace above, and the boy could hear his snarl of dreaming breath; while from the interior of the house came the butterfly rustling of his mother and sister in their uneasy insomnias; for inside, where the women slept, it was much hotter; even out here by the garden where round mangoes swelled beneath the moon with cold sweet juice, and flowers clutched to themselves their dewy treasures of coolness, it was still too hot to put head to pillow, and the boy lay on the bare ropes of the charpoy, hoping that a breeze might blow to cool his naked back and send away the flies, when all there was was the humid midnight breathing down his back; that was when he felt a golden light behind his eyelids. It was almost a relief. He did not dare to open his eyes, because he felt breath on his cheek, the stale breath of the demon bending over him, like Shiva with his giant yellow eyes watching you, his cheeks puffed up as if he were about to blow you out like a candle ... It was clear that this was a demon, not a saint, for "if this is a saint bending over me," he reasoned (he was always a great reasoner), "why am I so afraid?" Of course it could not be Shiva, because Shiva was a Hindu superstition, and, as already demonstrated, it could not be a saint, but just in case he said trembling, "Peace be upon you." – "And upon you, peace," replied the demon ironically. Joorah knew the voice then, and opened his eyes. What he had supposed to be a demon was none other than his father's servant, Koduk Bunwaree.

He had a face of callous ruddiness. It was a lump of a face. He had a reddish moustache and big ears, but curiously enough his most noticeable feature was his wide ruddy forehead, which seemed to ascend forever into his white cap. There were long creases in his cheeks. He did not have the pinched triangular features of the born horse-holder; nor did he wear the long-chinned sneer of an old dacoit; yet he did not seem to be entirely carefree. His eyes were set deep in his head. Those who did not know him might have thought him stupid. In fact, however, he was a servant of considerable alertness. He had broad sturdy feet, which had almost more character than his face. As he went about the house sweeping rooms and cleaning lamps, one noticed the swish of his bluish-grey trousers; one watched his patient grimy feet bearing him here and there on his errands; one saw his muscle-strung forearms (he was an excellent strangler); his fingers accomplished their tasks; and all of this was so interesting that people often did not notice his face. There was a peculiar *obtuseness* in that face, an obtuseness not of stupidity but of its own granular matter, stubbornly denying while it pretended to acquiesce. Centuries later, you could see this quality in the faces of the poor old men who waxed the cars for the American consulate. Joorah had sometimes perceived a naked stoniness in the faces of village boys who disliked him; and Allah must have it to a greater degree when He met with the sinners and mockers who implored Him when He was already implacable, and He punished the sinners according to their sins, clothing them in garments of burning pitch; and His curse was on them to the Day of Judgment; and darkness covered their faces.

"What do you want?" the boy said angrily.

"I saw you taking the yellow sugar," said the servant. "Now you think that you will be alone. But remember throughout your life that I will be a guide to you, and a warning to you, and one day I will show you your appointed place."

"Have you been given a special Book so that you hold fast to it?" said the boy ill-humoredly. "Or have you been set above us?"

"I know more about the *goor* than your father," said Koduk Bunwaree. "Many times he has asked me questions on its properties. I remember one day that your father came home angry from an expedition. You were an infant then. He sucked on a lump of the sugar. Then in his rage he took you by your heels and threw you down."

The boy had nothing to say. If Koduk Bunwaree had spoken to him in this way a day ago, he would have reported the matter to his father. But he had eaten the yellow sugar for the first time. He had been changed. – There was now an implicit understanding between them. Just as Padma knew not to ask her husband where he went on his profitable autumn trips, so Joorah knew not to ask Koduk Bunwaree what he would be shown later in his life.

XII

As Joorah became older, he was always stopping at the stalls of sweetmeats in the bazaars, at which his father smiled knowingly. His mother wept. At this she was considered harmful, as if she were having her menstrual discharges. "God's light is ineffably white," his father said, but Joorah always saw golden-yellow beams behind closed eyelids. With the other boys, Hindu and Muslim, he became for a time seduced by the cult of the yoni and the lingam. Often they attended the fairs among the red- and green-striped tents of Multan, where the meaner sorts of dacoits and robbers had to be watched out for, but where there were certain women who sat on the window-sills of nearby houses, smiling and waving their emblems of white cloth.

"Remember," his father said, "Thuggee is not only a means of knowledge, but also of punishing the blasphemer and the oppressor."

The other boys drank lime-water only, but in Joorah's beverages there were always rose squeezings and yellow sugar added. So his faculty for mercy weakened. His father took him through the dusty alleys, between the tall, tottering houses, teaching him of the world: Here were the bookshops; here, in tiny arched openings in the street, sat the tailors sewing boots; here pounded the hammers of the smiths ("You must never touch them," his father said); and low-caste women squatted in doorways, holding out trays of sugarcane pieces.

His father was one of the principal leaders in the district, and he went away with certain men once every year and came back with presents. And every year these men would gather at the house to share out their treasure, looking contemptuously at the zemandars driving their beasts in the fields, and Joorah's father would weigh a jeweled brooch upon his scales and say, "Yes, we are different; we are not as eunuchs, to be flapping away the Emperor's flies with peacock tails . . ." – Koduk Bunwaree stood by, serving water and mango juice.

"The men are coming again," his mother said sadly, and young Joorah felt almost the same emptiness that his sisters felt on those sunny afternoons when they had to stay indoors, being females, and tidied their father's bales of cloth over and over, but couldn't get them right, their father sitting daily in the shop, within an arrow's flight of Chowk Bazaar, different cloths in front of him for the sake of show to be fingered by dirty bejeweled traders who had wandered in from the Silk Route. In the streets, flies screened the cauldrons of milk curd. So the scrolls of the afternoon continued to be turned. But everyone knew that the men were coming. Joorah's mother, who usually indulged him, made him go to bed early. But he lay on the charpoy waiting until his mother and sisters had retired. He wanted to see the men. In those days he had already begun to steal from the pile of rupees his mother set aside in a chest to be drawn from whenever the servants went on errands in the bazaar. At night Joorah searched in the chest, running copper coins through his hands until he found a silver piece to take to the sweetmeat vendors. The coppers which he received back with his candy he kept, and later returned to the chest. When his father gave him money on the holidays, he secretly dropped it back into the chest. A confusion of mind had come to him. He was no longer certain whether he had contributed more to the chest than he had pilfered, or whether the situation was reversed. His obligation, therefore, was not clear. When he took from the chest, he came to feel that everything belonged to him, but when he got a gift from his father it seemed to him that he had stolen it. So his senses were perverted against him. It had something to do with his father. But the men were coming here tonight. Now perhaps he would be illuminated, forcing his sensations to surrender to his moral intelligence.

He hid behind a screen and listened to the men talking with his father in a dialect which he had never heard before. His father went to a closet and got out a box of pearls. These he distributed among the other Phansigars. Joorah, peeping through a fold in the screen, saw this, and understood then that this property, obstinately opaque in its brute Thing-ness, had an even more uncertain relationship to him than he had imagined (where had the pearls come from?), and so his sensibilities became still more attenuated. That was why in later life he acquired a reputation among the vulgar for extreme liberality, when he was merely obeying the law that his nature and his father's nature had promulgated: Whatever belonged to others was his by right, and so he Thugged, but whatever was his must be stolen, and had in large measure to be given away. Thus he retained his humility.

So in time Joorah became wise, and was ready to go on Thuggee with his father.

XIII

At the end of that summer his father gave him a pretty pony, and they rode with Koduk Bunwaree to Lahore, where he was initiated. He received the pickaxe upon a white cloth. He swallowed the yellow sugar. He raised his pickaxe to the sky and swore that he would kill all the victims that Kali sent to him. He heard the screams of men and saw them strangled. For an instant he trembled upon his pony, but then he reminded himself that he had undertaken the duty, and he must have food. For a time the cries of his victims oppressed him, but progressively less so, until in the end he felt them only as little scratchings and scrabblings against his caramelized heart.

In time, Joorah's beard was upon him, and he established himself as Jemador of the Thugs, believing that all had been revealed to him. As for his father, he brought back many fine slips of merchandise, but in time the old man transgressed. Or so he must have done, for Kali punished him. He got worms in his body and died barking like a dog. Joorah was grieved, but said that Allah must have ordained it, so that the fault could not be his. In fact, what was going on was the cleaning up of the Punjab, which was to continue for half a millennium, until *The Hindu* (international edition) could report in its issue of Saturday, April 6, 1985, that ". . . the Punjab situation had shown considerable improvement as a result of action taken by the security forces . . ." Joorah's mother burned herself at the funeral.

So the decades passed. Koduk Bunwaree stayed on with Joorah, as faceless as he was faithful. The man washed the house and kept the lamps in order. His features seemed to become more vacant as time went by. He must have been as old as the toads by now, and yet he never failed in his strength. There was an occasional flickering in his face, like beetles crawling in the manure pile of old grudges. It could not be said that anybody liked him. He hardly ever spoke, and when he did his words were innocuous; and yet people got a sense of menacing irony from him. Not that it was his irony in particular that bothered them, or his reticence; it was his unpleasant woodenness of character and behavior. Everyone has major flaws. We forgive their minor flaws the better to condemn the major ones undistracted. (If *this* didn't bother me, the other thing would.)

As for Joorah, he distributed the booty, like his Emperor, Shah-Jehan (King of the World, grandson of Akbar), "with liberal and discriminating hand." – Then again, perhaps all this took place in the reign of Aureng-Zebe. Much of his own gold was wasted, of course, in fabricating bracelets, earrings and nose-rings for his wife, daughters and daughters-in-law; and then there was the brocade which Padma's postion required her to have, the striped silken stuffs with gold embroideries . . . But a quantity remained to be stored and inventoried, which task his wife performed, this being one of her few wretched enjoyments, since when the women of the household met together their discussions principally concerned the number of ornaments that each possessed, how well they became her, and how much they would sell for in the bazaars, which the poor pallid female creatures never got to see, being forbidden to emerge from their sanctum into the streets where they might be *seen*, and Joorah Naig did not care to spend his money on closed carriages. For security's sake he continually studied methods of looking indigent.

XIV

The sun burned their backs on the road. They longed for cool water. The hardy Koduk Bunwaree strode on stolidly, and the others cast him long glances shafted with dislike. They felt that a man who could go on without rest mocked them; for most Thugs were lazy, and unworthy of their Thuggery. Had they been leaderless, they would no doubt have seated themselves in the nearest grove until they took root. But Koduk Bunwaree walked ahead, and old Joorah walked behind. The other Thugs hunched their shoulders against the loo, or dry wind of the Punjab, and followed Koduk Bunwaree, brushing the dust from each other's backs. Even old Joorah looked at him askance, for though his carriage was alert, his strides were determined, and his powerful body carried itself with deliberate intelligence; though the sweat flew from him in his exertions, and his hands swung at his sides doubled in fists, yet on his face was a blind vacancy, like a stone. The Thugs might stare at him all day, but then in turning away for an instant they forgot his features, as if he were naked of them; and when they returned their glances to him, whispering, they saw again his coarse lips, his round sweaty nose, his half-closed eyes – an unexceptional middle-aged farmer's face; but when they turned away again it seemed to their recollections that there had been a smooth nothingness from his brow to his chin, like a round brown river-pebble. So more and more they stared at him and turned muttering away, but he stared ahead and marched along with piggish or ruthless unconcern.

XV

Joorah Naig saw what the others saw. "But surely he has always been like this," he said to himself. For he saw him as he saw other persons – as fungible quantities for his intended use. As he was the Jemador, it was necessary that he calm his men also.

"You are sullen," he said. "Let us halt and learn Kali's signs. Perhaps then you will be uplifted."

They waited for omens. A doneky brayed on the left, and then, after a long time, on the right. This was excellent. Bhola regained his spirits, and stuck out his tongue at Koduk Bunwaree when Joorah did not see. The others laughed.

As they walked mildly through the forest in their sandals they met an old man. He was taboo to murder. The Thugs turned expectantly to their Jemador, who stroked his beard. "If it be sinful to shed the blood of such a person," he said sternly, "then may the sin be visited upon his own snowy head." – Bhola capered with glee, and even the wooden face of Koduk Bunwaree expressed itself in a gaunt smile.

"You are an old man," said the Thugs. "We will aid you in carrying your burden, since you come from our district."

"How do you know that I come from your district?" said the grandfather suspiciously.

"What district do you come from?" said Joorah Naig.

"Hyderabad."

Joorah spread his hands and beamed. "Well, then," he said. "That is where we also began our travels. Of course we will help you. But first, let us withdraw to these trees for our evening prayer."

The old man became alarmed and began to reproach them for taking him into the jungle. "No, no," said Keema, "we mean merely to avoid the heat." – At the first convenient place they deprived the old man of his life.

XVI

The following evening they ascended a rise, where the high fort, carved with floral patterns, overlooked a white-roofed town from its green hill. At the edge of the town were resting-groves. They had strangled many travelers there. The Thugs gave the riderless horses to the town in exchange for its silence.

Seven travelers were encamped in the bazaar. Next morning the Thugs followed them and encamped outside the town. But their intended victims were leery of them when they saw Koduk Bunwaree.

"We do not care to travel with you," they said, "for you keep company with a man without a face."

To the Thugs, nothing was more miraculous than encountering opposition. Bhola squealed with rage, plunging his dagger again and again into the sand. At old Joorah's command, the band rushed ahead to find a suitable spot for ambush or decoy murder, which Dost Khan soon descried in a recess close to the wall of the fort, by a well in a thicket of jujube trees. – "Gunga ram!" hissed the Jemador, meaning, Caution! – His Thugs scuttled behind the trees, unwinding their roohmals. Yet they seemed to him uninspired, their glances downcast, so that even if they had not been so patently lurking there, any passerby who slapped his sandals step by step along the dusty road would perceive their guilt. He became increasingly irritable with the gang, with the boys' nervous twitterings, with the warning glances of the old gurus. Just then they heard the *Bees*, or call of the small owl – a terrible omen. Lal Khan sighed and cleared his throat. The others were silent. Presently the travelers came around the bend. Joorah did not give the signal. With pain he let them go on their way.

XVII

They fell in with five Sikhs. They were journeying from Kashmir, carrying yak-tassels, saffron, lead and copper. "Where are you bound?" said the Sikhs. – "We are on our way to Bombay for a supply of linen," said Joorah courteously. "And you?" – "We go on to the north," they said. – "Boundless and infinite is our desire to go to those parts," said Joorah Naig. – They brought him a melon from his native Multan; when he ate it, he was all tears. Soon the Thugs became intimate with them. At midnight they strangled them and cast away their bodies in a river among the hills.

At the next town of size, Gumboo, Laljoo and Wuzzee went off to spy in the bazaar. They found a likely party of seven men and a woman, whom the Thugs followed on the road. They watched them being detained at a customs house. "They must be wealthy, then," grinned Koduk Bunwaree. Bhola and Lal Khan were deputed to go forward, pretending to be beggars. Joorah made up a small party of imitation

Sepoys, and Koduk Bunwaree followed behind, leading a group of bogus merchants. So the comedy unrolled for several days.

One afternoon Joorah found the two supposed beggars waiting for them by a stream. "They camp within an hour of here!" chuckled Bhola. "Tomorrow you will give the order to kill them!"

"You are eager," said Joorah. "That is commendable. Go, then, to Koduk Bunwaree and tell his men to join us tomorrow morning where the road meets the river."

"Yes, Jemador!" said Bhola, but he slunk away, because he was certain now that Koduk Bunwaree was bad luck.

Joorah's men took a detour, walking quickly to pass the party unseen, then rejoined the road at a likely looking grove. The young Thugs were quickly established in a circle by the river. (And Bhola sharpened his dagger in a ruined temple.) They were excited at the part they had to play. The gurus marshaled them into an array of disarming smiles.

"The road is dangerous," old Joorah inveigled the strangers.

"Yes," they replied, "shall we then travel together?"

"You are wise men," said he. "In token of our friendship, kindly drink some tea with us." And he snapped his fingers at Keema, who began to prepare the kettle. But he was already brooding the murder.

Now Koduk Bunwaree arrived with his merchants. "Ah," he cried to Joorah, "you are a large group. Were we to travel with you, the road would offer no terrors. May we do so?"

"We would be pleased," said the victims. "We also," said Joorah.

Now that the Thugs were superior in number to the other party, the business could be settled. Koduk Bunwaree went ahead to find the murder place. That was his office; he was the *Beylha*. The travelers seemed anxious when he left, and were quieted by being told that in this region there were many tigers; it was always necessary to send someone ahead. (Still, there was something they did not like about Koduk Bunwaree.)

He returned soon, saying, "Yes, there are tigers. But I have found a fine clearing where we may rest until nightfall, when tigers must sleep. Let us go."

When they arrived at the spot, the victims were induced to make themselves comfortable. They were now in the last hour of their lives. – What a happy hour it was! – The younger Thugs commenced a game, playfully competing with each other in the speed with which they could dig a hole. Bhola raced between the diggers' legs, screaming and pelting them with dirt. The other travelers chuckled at the boys' energy, not knowing that what was being dug was their own grave. The Thugs took joy in their companions' pleasure and made them tea. Later, they put the entire party to death.

"Oh," cried Lal Khan in a rage, "your neck is too strong; may your sister be defiled!"

XVIII

"Are all the bodies here?" said Joorah Naig.

"Yes, yes!" cried the vile Thugs.

"Then in with them!"

Laughing, Bhola stabbed the corpses and threw them into the pit. They had begun to hurl rocks down upon them when Joorah Naig, peering into the grave, suddenly started. – "Halt!" he said. "Look, that one moves his hand."

XIX

Sometimes I feel so sick of myself that I almost shoot myself, but the truth is that I never have, because I might partially destroy my brain without achieving death. Worst of all would be retaining enough consciousness to know that I was damaged. Most likely I would be paralyzed, or under observation, so that it would be impossible for me to raise up my gun again. – Old Joorah felt the same way about his victims; the thought of their being incompletely strangled was abhorrent to him. Most Thugs buried their half-strangled victims alive without a care, even hurling screaming infants into the pit on top of their dead mothers, but Joorah Naig despised such bungling, which contradicted both the letter and the spirit of Pukka Kurna: – namely, burial in a deep and *secure* grave.

"Who was the strangler?" said Joorah Naig in an awful voice.

"I was," said Koduk Bunwaree.

"Surely your hand has been smitten with evil!" cried the Jemador, chastising him. "For before this you always made your kill."

The others murmured like bees, but Koduk Bunwaree turned neither right nor left. His face was as blind as a wooden shield.

"The man is dead," he said slowly.

He strode to the pit and pointed. They could all see that the neck of the corpse was black with the marks of his fingers. The face was swollen and purple. Blood trickled from the limbs, for Bhola had stabbed under the arms and legs. The life had been wrenched from every bone; yet as Koduk Bunwaree gestured, the broken neck began to twist like a snake. – "You see, he is dead," said Koduk Bunwaree, grinning.

They ran from the grave, leaving corpses with legs, heads and arms severed under the open sky. (From Kali's point of view, it must have seemed that little white-garbed ants were scattering from the pit; for as always the Thugs wore their white garments.) The birds and beasts of prey devoured what had been abandoned. Later travelers saw bones and scattered shoes.

XX

Old Joorah, being wise, had often felt fear before, so that now he did not lose his faculties merely because the taste of fear was in his mouth. And he had known Koduk Bunwaree all his life, so that he could not believe that the fellow meant to harm him. "There is no God but one God, and Muhammed is His Prophet," he muttered. When the others had fled, he stood facing the faceless one across the grave.

"Why does it seem that you have no face?" he said.

Koduk Bunwaree smiled. (Still it seemed a distant sort of smile, as if a stone was smiling.) "In the Book it is written, concerning the Devil, that 'he surely sees you, he as well as his host, from whence you see them not.' So at times you see my face not. Yet my face is always turned to you. And I am sent here to try you, old Joorah, for you have murdered thousands in your life. And for you has been prepared a severe chastisement."

"Surely it is not against our faith to put some to death," replied the cunning Jemador, "since it is also written: 'And kill not the soul which Allah has forbidden, except for a just cause.' A just cause may always be assumed. This I know. Everyone is a sinner worthy of death." For he was a niggler to the end.

But Koduk Bunwaree merely replied, quoting the surah which Joorah remembered from his boyhood: "'Surely We have prepared for the iniquitous a Fire, an enclosure of which will encompass them. And if they cry for water, they are given water like molten brass, scalding their faces. Evil the drink! And ill the resting-place!'"

Old Joorah began to stammer and clutch his beard, weaving speeches on the loom of his brain, but Koduk Bunwaree raised high the sacred pickaxe, or kassee, and shouted: "I am the pickaxe! I call now upon the *infernal inspiration of the pickaxe!*" And he threw the kassee against the ground, point first. There was a noise of groaning and grinding. The earth sprang apart around a grave.

As a corpse's wrist may move through the accustomed pivoting action, but without volition (when, for instance, the gases of putrefaction change pressure within the swollen arm), so this corpse exercised its hand, but in a curiously tentative, mechanical manner, like a starfish hesitantly sucking an oyster out of the shell. The chalky hand began to strain upward at the sky. Joorah Naig stared. Even the hair on the knuckles was not still, but commenced an unsteady rippling, like grass blown in some slight breeze. There was no sound except the humming of flies. – The back of the hand had collapsed, like the crackly skin of a roasted chicken, yet the sunken flesh remained hard and rubbery, like pickled meat. The tips of the fingers flexed. They were much whiter than the rest of the hand, so that the purple blood behind the fingernails stood out with gruesome distinctness. Slowly the hand groped upward, and then it slapped heavily back to earth, the fingers scrabbling in the dirt almost imperceptibly. – At this, Koduk Bunwaree softened. – "He is trying to draw a flower," he whispered.

"Ah," said the old Jemador. "He was an artist, then?"

Koduk Bunwaree shrugged. Seizing the sacred pickaxe, he raised it above his head and brought it down to pierce the ground. There was a hollow sound, like the beat of a drum. Then the dirt cracked open with a great stench and exposed an old woman's face.

"Yes, I remember her," said Joorah after a moment. "You were there. She was a widow. Bhola was the strangler. She was no trouble."

"If you do not find her troublesome now, then you are a dedicated man," laughed Koduk Bunwaree.

The yellow skin had cracked like a field in drought; the nose had hardened into a beak. From one of the nostril-pits, a red beetle regarded them. The mouth and cheeks especially were crossed by wrinkle-tracks. The ear alone had preserved its taut, glossy skin, supported by faithful cartilage which had not yet decayed. The entire face was tasseled with her grey, moldy hair, like a rotten corncob.

Her lips were tightly drawn together. They were the same color as her skin. Her face had sunken flat, like a continent weary of bearing the burden of a mountain range. Even the nose had begun to sag. There was dried mucus in the nostrils. The face was not at peace, but distant; it held a curiously considering expression, as if it were about to act. The dead yellow-grey slits of the eyes seemed sly. There was a translucent film over them, through which the hardened pupils could be seen.

"But we stabbed her eyes, as we did with the others!" cried Joorah Naig.

"Yes," said Koduk Bunwaree, "they heal. Slowly, but they heal. See, there are no longer any bruises on her neck where Bhola strangled her. As is written in the Qur'an, 'And if We pleased, We would put out their eyes; then they would strive to get first to the way, but how should they see?'"

XXI

"Allah is absolute," said Joorah Naig. "What I do, I do by His will. I kill nobody."

"You say you are a Muslim, but you worship Kali, not Allah. You know that what you do is unlawful. In the Hereafter you shall have a grievous chastisement."

"Allah created all things," replied old Joorah. "Therefore, Kali was created by Allah. Since He created her, He must be pleased with her. Otherwise He would not allow men to worship her. Surely what Kali orders in this world Allah will not punish in the next."

"You do not even trick your own slyness," said Koduk Bunwaree. "Shall I show you your appointed place?"

"No!"

"Behold!" cried Koduk Bunwaree. The pickaxe flew into his hand, and he cast it against a stone. There was a clang, and the dark earth split open, disclosing white skulls secreted there like stars. It shut, and opened almost at their feet. Here was a grave of younger men. Their faces were cold and set. Whereas the old woman had been sexless, these still looked masculine. Their eyelids were purple; their foreheads receded in a vaguely apelike manner, jaws outthrust, bloody lips clenched. Koduk Bunwaree chuckled at this sight and began to describe to old Joorah what was in store for him.

XXII

His fingers shone in myriad weblike flickers, like flames; and in his speech Joorah could hear the continuous irregular sounds of a fire — the same noise, really, as the noise of clothes or rugs flapping in a wind, rugs of woven souls upon which Koduk Bunwaree might sit at his ease, smiling at the burning he looked upon, as the flames burned yellow around the screaming adulterers, blue-green upon the charred mineralized bones of the murderers and hypocrites who were allowed by Allah to retain the miracle of sight, that they might *see* their own skeletons crumbling and glowing orange like lanterns in a night forest; and the flames rose and met in prayerful arches over their bones like the clasped hands of the faithful; and they cried out in the flames that consumed them age by age, until after nine hundred and thirteen thousand years their faces were black, sinister relics, the skull burnt away from the little naked nerves that Allah had left there so that the souls would continue to feel pain; and the flames met and crackled and flared away for another nine hundred and thirteen thousand years, until arms and legs burst and fell off; and after another nine hundred and thirteen thousand years their crackling rib-cages glowed red-orange and folded together very very gently, and their gall bladders fried; and after another nine hundred and thirteen thousand years their vertebrae became charcoal; and after another nine hundred and thirteen thousand years they had burned down to oozing octopi of sentient nerves baked in bitter ash; and at the end of this, the fifth age, Koduk Bunwaree reached into the embers with his tongs and pulled out the soul from its shell of cinders, and (this was what the soul had been most dreading) he held it directly in the flames, and it twitched and shriveled for the entirety of the sixth age (namely, another period of nine hundred and thirteen thousand years); and at the expiration of that time there was nothing left but a bright thread of pain to be woven into his rug, which was comprised of many floral designs. This, the seventh age, was

endless, and extinguished each thread's consciousness without dimin-
ishing its suffering. Sometimes Koduk Bunwaree got up and beat the
rug against the embers on the hearth, to fan the flames and thereby
increase the torment of the newer souls still lying in the fire; and then
the colors of the threads brightened still more unbearably. The carpet
cracked smartly against the hearth-stones; and this was the sound which
could now be heard in Koduk Bunwaree's voice.

XXIII

"You know who I am," said Koduk Bunwaree. "I am commanded to
show myself to you through the mercy of Allah. For Allah takes back to
Himself all who beg forgiveness from Him."

"What!" cried old Joorah in a fury. "Cannot fifty years in the service
of Allah give me my own foundation for judging my actions? And if
what you say is true, if I have sinned, then are you not two-facedly
working for my downfall? You do not wish me to beg forgiveness from
Allah! You are more sinister than 'Abd Allah ibn Ubayy, enemy of the
Prophet, slanderer of A'isha, leader of the Hypocrites!"

"Surely," said Koduk Bunwaree, "a hypocrite is one who has enough
morality to see the errors of others. I see your errors. You can still
repent. Recite the last surah with a sincere heart: 'Say: I seek refuge in
the Lord of men, the King of men, the God of men, from the evil of
the whisperings of the slinking devil, who whispers into the hearts of
men, from among the jinns and the men.'"

"Yes, yes," sighed old Joorah. "It is all the fault of the yellow sugar."

"Ah," said Koduk Bunwaree thoughtfully, "the *goor*. Well, let us
see." He bent over the old woman's grave and sprinkled a few grains of
it upon her lips. At once her jaws began to work; her black tongue
licked the corners of her mouth, and she sucked with animation. And
yet in time disappointment slackened her face. The black tongue
retracted itself; and scattered upon the old woman's mouth, cheeks,
and chin were the glittering golden crystals, dry, desolate, undissolved.

"You see that it is useless to her," said Koduk Bunwaree, turning
away. "The *goor* has no power. You are not addicted to murder because
of it."

Joorah could say nothing. He stood still, and his eyes shifted in his head, and he clutched at his beard. Koduk Bunwaree watched him for a moment and then struck the pickaxe against the ground, handle first. The graves closed sullenly, returning their souls to darkness. They were in Barzakh, the intermediate state between death and resurrection. Each soul was in constant fear of Hell. Allah had decreed that they must spend their time reckoning the difference between the sum of their sins and the sum of their good deeds. Even a merchant would have had a difficult time of it. They would thus be well-occupied until the Day of Judgment, when Allah would look into their hearts to find the final number, which would determine whether they went to Paradise or Hell.

XXIV

Death naturally screens itself with superstition. I remember being taken to see Fort Ticonderoga by my parents when I was eight, and my sister Angela was five, and discovering a glass case containing two children's skeletons, with the legend TWELVE-YEAR-OLD GRAVE. For a long time after this I dreaded becoming twelve. But there was nothing that I could do about it. I kept getting older. In point of fact, I lived past becoming twelve, and Angela died at six, so there had been nothing to worry about.

XXV

"I have now done my duty to Allah, and I am well satisfied," said Koduk Bunwaree, his face as old and empty as the desert. "You will not turn from me, and I accept you as servant. I do not like ungratefulness in my servants, but I reward gratitude. And I am higher than you, so I will always know what is in your breast."

"After all," replied old Joorah, "what is our trade but the transfer of treasure from one fool to another?" He said nothing more. He had realized by now that all he had to do to save himself was to strangle Koduk Bunwaree. In a neutral universe, where bad luck balances out good, where one's wife is unfaithful to make up for the happiness she once gave as a present, where one dies to cancel out being born – in such a universe, it ought to be possible to compensate for the odium in which Allah held him by strangling the Devil. But he thought that if Koduk Bunwaree had power over the dead then his neck might be too thick for him.

"I reckon as you do," said the other. "And in this life I will remain your bonded Khansamah, to avoid complications."

XXVI

That night they camped in a grove near the town of Murdhee, in Bilsa. "Do you see how the birds fly through the air by Allah's grace?" said Joorah Naig to his servant, instructing him as of old. But Koduk Bunwaree said nothing; either he had no face or else his face was made of wood.

They slept over the grave of a Pandit and nine attendants killed two years earlier. They had been no trouble. The next day they set out on Thuggee, with Koduk Bunwaree walking in the footsteps of his master. The gang followed them like scavengers in the jungle, not daring to rejoin them, nor to flee, nor to kill them. Often old Joorah heard their rustling. His servant smiled. "They will not abandon you, master," he said. "They will do nothing without you."

They saw a rich man riding in the trees. "Now surely Allah's is whatever is in the heavens and the earth," quoted Joorah Naig. He felt the thrill of stalking, of pitting his cunning against that of the bald rich beast.

"I will help you," said Koduk Bunwaree.

"Praise be to Allah!" said Joorah Naig. "Your face is bright in my sight." (But Koduk Bunwaree had no face.)

XXVII

In those days the green jungles extended almost to Lahore, and tigers competed with Thugs in their murder of the defenseless. (When in the jungle, people say, one must not speak of tigers, or tigers will come.)

The rich man had ridden his camel through the forest for many days, fancying sometimes that there shot through the trees the yellowish gleams of tiger-eyes, or that the shifting sun-dapplings between the branches behind hid a leopard about to pounce. But to deter misfortune he looked round him blandly, as if he had paid his way even into the confidence of Bengal tigers. (At night in his tent, with the camel browsing uneasily nearby, he dreamed of being pursued by tigers who had already massacred his family.) With his thighs he stilled the jingling of his money-bags against the saddle. He rode alone. No one could have understood what made him so bold, unless he had been seen removing his cotton shirt to bathe or to sleep; for round his neck was tied a bag that rested against the skin; and in the bag were the relics of a pir, or Muslim saint: – in particular, the joint of a finger, cunningly mummified by means of various spices; and a shard from a skull-plate. These things gave the rich man confidence.

But suddenly two men emerged from the trees and grabbed his camel by the bridle. One of them had no face. The rich man jerked back, grasping his dagger, and the camel arched its head up and gaped, spittle running out from between its yellow teeth. Behind the foliage came other whisperings and chucklings. The rich man was afraid. But old Joorah stroked his white beard, and said, "Fear not, for we are two litigants with our friends, and we want you to arbitrate. I say that Allah, no matter how merciful, has bound Himself to chastise certain crimes; whereas this man insists that Allah forgives all if the heart repents."

"But why do your friends hide in the forest?" said the rich man.

"They are ashamed to be quarreling over sacred matters," Joorah replied. "They dwell amidst the red-ribbed sands of Bikaner, where all must hide their faces from the dust, men and women alike; and so they are timid."

"I do not wish to arbitrate," said the rich man, but Joorah and Koduk Bunwaree caught at his sleeves, importuning him to stay and listen.

They sat together in a choultrie, or wayside grove, in the shade of lime-trees, with a sweet well at their feet, and monkeys playing all around them. The rich man pitched his tent to relieve them from the insects. He came from the town of Sehora, he said. He was a merchant who traveled with gold and silver across the land to wherever the exchange rate was best. He stopped in the villages only to buy food, which he cooked by himself. Joorah Naig listened carefully, pleased with all that he heard. Koduk Bunwaree nodded woodenly. It would be very hard to trace the rich man if he disappeared.

XXVIII

In the old days, we had no need to bury the bodies, because Kali swallowed them herself. Later, we had to use the pickaxe to hide them; and nowadays we must engage lawyers and go through countless forms.

Like all true Thugs, Joorah Naig loved to ingratiate himself into the trust of his victims – not just for information, but for the sake of the game he played. He loved getting them to tell him their plans for the future, as if they had decades of life remaining instead of hours. ("Can you not imagine," whispered one of the last Thugs, during the trials of the 1830s, "the joy of seeing suspicion change to friendship, until that wonderful moment arrives when the roohmal completes the shikar* – this soft roohmal, which has ended the life of hundreds?")

In this case, however, stealing the victim's trust was not easy. The rich man was uncomfortable. "I am half of a mind to leave you as deceitful robbers," he said. "I am told that these regions are infested with Thugs of infernal cunning. Last night in the bazaars they related to me a tale of a Moghul prince who was destroyed by Thugs. He had decided to refuse the company of all travelers, in order to protect his own life and that of his manservant. On his first day out of Delhi he met a group of Thugs disguised as Hindus, and denied them leave to travel with him. So the Thugs disguised themselves as Muslims and accosted him again on the second day. Again he refused them. That night the Thugs ingratiated themselves with his servant. On the following morning they attempted to accompany him, their tongues rolling in their mouths, and the servant assured him of their friendship, but he ordered them away. Even then they did not give up, but rode ahead of him, strangled another traveler, and met him wailing over the dead body. One of their number had died of disease, they said. As they were all illiterate, they begged him, an educated man, to read the burial service. There was no possibility of avoiding this duty without dishonor,

---

* I never found out what a shikar was.

so he knelt down by the corpse and they strangled him. – How then am I to know that you do not have similar plans for me?"

"I too have heard of these Thugs," said old Joorah. "They are reputed to live in the forest. They are made of wood, and have no faces, for they are born of the union of tigers and trees. They eat men down to their bones; that is why the missing travelers can never be found. They keep immense hoards in the jungle. I can take you to one if you desire. The light from their gold is so blinding that birds flying over it fall from the sky, and darkness never comes there at night."

"So you wish to lead me into the jungle!" cried the rich man. "I say once more, I have my suspicions that you yourself are a Thug, for you thrust yourself upon me, and seem intent to lead me into dubious adventures."

"I a Thug?" laughed Joorah Naig. "You flatter me. How could I hope to overpower a strong man like you?" And he smiled behind his hand.

"Swear on your pickaxe that you are not a Thug," said the rich man, for he thought he knew something about the Thugs, since he speculated in their profits.

"Certainly," said Joorah, knowing full well that an oath upon a consecrated pickaxe was more binding than one upon a Qur'an, but an oath over an unconsecrated pickaxe meant nothing. The pickaxe had to be purified every seven days. Its power could be lost if it were dropped, or set in a spot, where a woman in her period had been. His pickaxe was presently unpurified. So he made the required oath. "I swear it," he said. "Be it not so, as the Pathans say, may I never ascend the throne of Delhi!"

But the rich man was still suspicious. "You claimed that these wood-demons have no faces," he said. "And look, the man who disputes with you has no face!"

Joorah Naig drew the back of his hand along his chin, from the throat outwards. This was a Phansigar sign indicating caution. "I have no knowledge of what you claim," he said. "It is only revealed to me that he *sometimes* has no face, like a rock tumbled smooth in the river."

"Yes," said Koduk Bunwaree. "It is an old deformity."

XXIX

The rich man had done his part for wealth, blindly but surely. He was the son of a rich man. As a boy he had been taken by his father to see hunger and disease. "You understand now," said his father, "why it is important to accumulate gold coins." This was a lesson that he had never forgotten. Those saffron-colored disks were for him the yellow sugar, the excuse for his existence. Just as a monk of Hare Krishna, however yielding he might be in private life, became *institutionalized* by his yellow-orange robe and might commit innumerable unkindnesses to avoid defiling it, so the rich man suspended his sluggish code of ethics when he lent his money at interest, in despite of the Qur'an, as he well knew; but the coins maddened him, crawling upon his back at night like cold heavy beetles so that he became ascetically devoted to them and justified any measures which aggrandized them, for they were his brood, put into his care by Allah; and there were long days when he sat at some poor villager's door laughing until the women stopped up their ears, and his debtor shuddered as he brushed past the rich man on his way to the fields in the morning, on his way to supper in the evening, and still the rich man sat in his doorway laughing and fanning himself, and his chuckles waxed throughout the night so that the neighbors could not sleep, and as the yellow spears of dawn shot him through the trees he was still there laughing, and when his debtor came out on his way to the fields, the rich man plucked his sleeve and whispered in his ear, "When I laugh, Allah laughs," and as he said this he really believed it, and the debtor, stunned by this monstrous power, would sell everything he had to pay the rich man. So the rich man prospered in his life. He was capable, and he struggled endlessly for the good of his helpless trusting wealth.

Old Joorah recognized his type without undue cogitation. The Jemador knew that as long as the discussion was concerned with theoretical purity, he would be safe, for rich men have a love of the abstract. As it happened, both he and Koduk Bunwaree had a talent for full exegesis, in which every word, every letter of the Qur'an is commented upon.

As the sad embarrassment of places where we used to live reminds us of our failures there, so the bending of the grasses in the evening sun brought a melancholy to the rich man. The grasses waved and bowed themselves low, as if better to listen to some secret being told them underground.

But the rich man was not swayed. "I hold my own purpose," he said, "just as the Emperors guard their Ganges water. Even when they come to the Punjab, they bring it with them in sealed jars."

The rich man thought them handsome dreamers. He did not notice any longer that Koduk Bunwaree had no face, because in his transactions he was used to having no face himself.

The rich man was, unbeknown to him, almost saved by a kite's cry, which is a dreadful omen to Thugs, but just then the kite, its mouth distended in preparation for a screech, got a butterfly in its throat; and it swooped far away to choke.

Old Joorah opened his hand and dragged it across his mouth and down, to indicate to the other Thugs that the time for caution had passed. At that, Bhola crept shamefacedly out of the jungle, for he badly wanted booty. The rich man did not see him. He crouched upon an overhanging limb.

XXX

They talked until night, and the rich man slept in his tent. In his dreams he was riding a fast horse, but someone was galloping behind him. He knew that the worst thing in the world would happen if his pursuer overtook him. He reined in his horse at a turn in the path and fed the creature many brown pills of opium. As soon as he was back in the saddle, the horse snorted and shook, foaming at the mouth from the drug. He galloped much faster than before, thanks to the stimulant, but his enemy was coming closer and closer.

XXXI

In those days, people told time from the sounds of the day. Caravans departed at dawn, and dawn was made known to them by the twittering of birds. It was a matter of faith that birds did not lie. Even the zemandars, who had to lead their bullocks into the fields at dawn every day, did not question the voices of the birds because they had not been given the possibility of knowing them. I remember my friend Major General N., of Peshawar, who once told me that not until his middle age had he learned that butterflies come from caterpillars. Yet he knew the fields. Many travelers, of course, were merchants, and spent their lives in high-walled towns. They marked dawn only at Ramazan, when it was forbidden to eat or drink after it was light enough to distinguish a white thread from a black. When birds sang, then, travelers awoke from their nightmares of the road and prepared to go as quickly as they could, since the heat of the day would not wait upon them. Most Thugs were adept at imitating these sounds. When Joorah made a warbling through his pursed lips, Koduk Bunwaree proceeded barefoot through the wattlings of the grove and began to shake branches in order to awaken the birds. They stirred in their nests and began to chirp sleepily. At this, Bhola caroled to them in their language, questioning them about matters of interest to birds, such as twigs and tigers, so that they answered him in concert, and the rich man awoke believing that it was dawn.

XXXII

The rich man felt the shadow of Bhola's soul falling upon and chilling his own. Yet he did not know that he felt it. What one fears in death is the skeleton advancing down the darkened hall, bending over one with an awful desire – for what, one does not know – and the matter is rendered more uncanny by the self-evident fact that the skeleton ought to be blind, as you are blind to its purpose and nature. How can it see you? There are no eyes in its sockets. And why does it want you? It must have a life of a sort, to have desires, to be drawn to life. But such postulates do nothing to the murk. That is the real horror, that this yellow-white, unclean thing is possessed by a mystery. In certain Nazi concentration camps, persons sentenced to execution by hanging were kept waiting in front of a black curtain, to make the punishment more terrible.

So he began to look over his shoulder, but old Joorah quickly distracted him. "You are saved," said the Jemador. "Even if I were to have all the treasure you possess, still I could not hope, as you do, to own the treasures of Paradise. You will live in gardens of perpetuity. There you and your family will be adorned with bracelets of gold. You will wear green robes of silk and brocade. Houris will come to you; they will be pure, beautiful, like pearls. Their breath will be as musk perfume."

"Of course you are saved," said Koduk Bunwaree, "since, as I have insisted, Allah forgives all to him who repents."

"Punishment cannot be averted," quoted Joorah Naig from the glorious Qur'an as he flicked out his roohmal.

The whole was conducted like a medical operation, as the three grinning Thugs went to their assigned places in a twinkling, Koduk Bunwaree holding down the feet, old Joorah, the bhutote, kneeling on the rich man's back and applying the roohmal, while Bhola held the rich man's hands and rubbed turbans slyly with his fellows. The rich man was not even able to struggle before he became pale and still. Then they stripped him and stabbed his eyes and body.

XXXIII

When he had been safely buried in his own gobba, Joorah Naig Jemador trod upon the grave and laughed with his men. Yet he laughed not unkindly. "I recall the tale of Timur-Lang," he said, "when he captured the great Sultan, Bajazet, in the heat of the summer, and kept him in an iron cage until he died the following spring. (In those days nobody killed mercifully, suddenly, as we do.) When the prisoner was entering his final torments, Timur-Lang commanded that he be brought to him. And when he saw the Sultan in the cage, he laughed. Bajazet was angered at the insult to a helpless enemy, but Timur-Lang replied, 'No, no, I was not laughing at you; I was but observing that you are missing an eye, and I have a limp, and the world calls us kings!' – So it is now with us, my Thugs. We laugh, but only from amusement at our own imperfection."

Most of the Thugs still hid shyly in the trees. Old Joorah let his fingers play among the jewels and yellow coins that now belonged to him. He smiled more than a little sadly. Koduk Bunwaree began to count the booty. Presently he reported that the total value was in excess of a hundred and sixty thousand rupees. – "We may as well divide it as if all were present," said Joorah after a time. "Clearly it was not their fault." And so they bore the treasure home and distributed it among the others when they came abashedly into the village. And when that was done, and Koduk Bunwaree went about the business of cleaning the lamps, old Joorah sat holding a single piece of gold in his hand, and staring deeper and deeper into its stamp, and he thought that for a moment the image of the Emperor smiled at him . . .

XXXIV

Even while being strangled, the rich man, like Job, had remained patient, trusting himself to God (since he could trust himself to no one else); but he died. So he went to his Paradise, having been virtuous in his own way, though his business had caused many to starve. Who knows what his Paradise was? Could it have been the India of today, the computerized India, where all accounts can be billed and paid across muggy phone-wire networks that sag in the heat; and the courtliest Thugs do not have to kill anybody, just have their programmes debit their accounts from rinky-dinky swivel chairs, faces pockmarked; and everyone flatulent from eating too many betel nuts?

But now, as then, it is certain that Iblis keeps the promise which he made to Allah: **"As Thou hast adjudged me to be erring, I will certainly lie in wait for them in Thy straight path"** (VIII.7.16).

For Ken Miller

A Hindustani/Ramasee Glossary

Barzakh – The state of the soul between death and resurrection.

Bees – An owl's call. A bad omen.

Beylha – Thug appointed to scout out the murder site.

Bhutote – Strangler.

Charpoy – Rope bed.

Choultrie – Wayside grove.

Dacoits – Bandits. Inferior to Thugs in subtlety. Perhaps it is for that reason that they are still extant.

Gobba – Round grave.

Goor – Yellow sugar. In 1982 I saw Afghan refugees sucking on sweet brown lumps which they called *gura*.

Gunga ram! – Watch out!

Jemador – Leader of a gang of Thugs. (Literally, a colonel.)

Kali – Hindu goddess of destruction.

Kassee – Consecrated pickaxe.

Khansamah – Most favored servant.

Khotub – The time between midnight and sunrise.

Loo – Dry wind of the Punjab.

Pir – Muslim saint.

Pukka Kurna – Secret burial.

Ramazan – The month when Muslims abstain from eating and drinking from sunrise to sunset.

Roohmal – Strangling-cloth.

Sayyid – Holy man.

Shiva – Hindu god of transformation. Sometimes called "The Destroyer." Kali's husband.

Thuggee – What Thugs did.

Zemandar – Farmer.

AUTHOR'S NOTE

The "Passage from a Decaying Book" is virtually the only information on Joorah Naig which I have found. Apparently the Thugs used to conduct a horrid gloating ritual in his name after every murder (cf. Sleeman). Sitting on a blanket, they dug a little grave in the sand and sprinkled the yellow sugar upon the sacred pickaxe, calling upon Kali to reward them as she had done for Joorah Naig and Koduk Bunwaree. And that is all that I know about our Jemador.

The apologias for wrongdoing are grounded in Thug conversations recorded by Sleeman. The rich man's story of the Thugs and the Moghul prince is genuine. Thugs from Multan used bullock-cords instead of roohmals, but that is just too bad. The tale of Timur-Lang is told in Thévenot. Citations from the Qur'an are loosely based on the revised translation by Maulana Muhammad Ali (Lahore: Ahmadiyyah Anjuman Isha'at Islam, 1973). I hope it will be clear that this story is an attack upon hypocrisy and Thuggery, not upon Islam, a religion for which I have the highest respect.

THE GREEN DRESS

A Pornographic Tale

Hermetica

There are women so reclusive as to seem perfect. It is not that they hide themselves, or (less likely still) that men avoid knowing them, in order to tinge their faces with spurious mystery; but it does please us to believe that there is a secret world of women. Uncloistered contact deforms the image in men's eyes. This is why we love each other best when we do not know each other. Engaging women, helpful ones, aggressive ones impress us sooner and then fall away. The retiring ones remain. – I am thinking now of the woman who was defined almost entirely by her *Green Dress*.

The Panther's Glance

I had lived above her for nine years, the better to consider her green dress, so I glimpsed her through my living room window whenever she went out, clutching her coat around her shoulders to cover herself from my chilly purpose, although she never looked behind and upward as a more reasonable person might have done if suddenly, for instance, the greengrocers came running from their shops to exclaim at a multitude of parallel vapor-trails in the sky. Possibly she knew that I was at my window, but she did not want to prove it, because then there would be the annoyance of changing locks and of acknowledging to herself that someone was spying on her in the unfriendly fashion of the National Zoo, where a hen is placed inside a little barred walkway along the perimeter of the panther's cage, to make him lively for the Olympians who stroll upon the grounds, so that the panther slinks round and round in his cage with the hen's image reflected in his eyes, and the hen struts nervously, pecking at green grain, with the panther's breath and the panther's smell on her, aware that there is nothing that she can do about the panther, so she keeps marching (rather more quickly than a hen in ordinary circumstances would do) and disregards the fact (if she knows it) that at the end of the day she will be the panther's dinner; – thus from the cage of my apartment I stalked my neighbor for her green dress, and my eyes were yellow and unblinking in my head; and I knew that if she had ever looked up at me she would have taken alarm and fled me, not being confined like the plump brown hen. Yet the truth was that I meant my neighbor no harm: – if I could take her green dress without murdering her I would happily do that; and if it had been possible for the panther to eat the hen without injuring her, I am sure that he would have consented; for none of us are bloodthirsty when we hunt our green dresses, merely intent, as I was when I closed my eyes and saw a green triangle on the inside of each eyelid, knowing by that token that I was fated to capture the green dress and make her love me for myself, giving me freely of her inexhaustible greenness, while my neighbor would not miss her much because my neighbor frivolously wore dresses of every color. At certain times I loved my neighbor and thought her virtuous solely because she had the green dress, just as a possessor of the Grail must be virtuous; but I could never look into her face without boredom, so at last I concluded that she did not have distinction. Following my green duty, therefore, I set about weeding out friendly feelings, saying to myself that, after all, possession was an accident – although of course that meant that if I myself were ever to seize the green dress I would have to be as watchful as a dragon afterward, since anyone with sufficient strength or cunning could take her away from me, even if I had her in an ivory closet, with locks of gold. The green dress herself seemed increasingly thrown out of ease in those latter years of my window-study. She clung sweatily to my neighbor's haunches on every walk; she did not entirely trust me. – Well, how could she? She did not know me. Trust was not an issue for me, however, because I knew that I had to have her no matter what injury she might do me.*

---

* It was this clear discrepancy between my courage and hers that led (I am

(I have read, by the way, that if a mouse is placed inside a snake's cage within a screen-armored cube, the snake, learning that he cannot have his prey, will in time become accustomed to the mouse's smell, and then if that mouse is taken from his fortress and dropped naked into the cage, the snake will not molest him – but panthers are smarter than snakes.)

I watched my neighbor, then, through the glass, disregarding her oval face in its setting of hair – all that was for me but a mirror, a zero – and smiling at the ringing confidence of her naive high heels (by rights she should have muffled her steps in nervous sadness); while I snugged down the toggles of my concentration upon her scoop-necked green dress, which had three-quarter-length sleeves and belled tight around her legs, so that the legs had to move in small helpless steps – yes, they would be happy to be freed from the green dress; I would be doing the legs a favor. And how tightly she took in my neighbor's waist! – How divinely diminutive my dress would be if there were no flesh and stubborn bone to keep her from maximizing her minimalization. – Even in the shadow of Stelling's Market she glowed like a green ghost. No matter how quickly my neighbor walked, the green dress clung to her faithfully, hugging her legs and lending her the sparkle of her pert black buttons. She endured even the vulgar grazing of my neighbor's simulated crocodile-texture purse, which brushed against her in a series of insulting pendulum-strokes; my dress was that patient; and when my neighbor folded her arms, the sleeves of my sweet green dress touched each other and their ruffled hems exchanged rustling compliments; and her collar-ruffles endured the dark weight of my neighbor's unbound hair or smiting braids, as my neighbor dictated, but when the wind freed them for a moment, how expressively they danced, like flowers ringing my neighbor's neck-tree; and my neighbor's shoulders became sloping green meadows of polyester crêpe satin, and the draped bodice of my sweet dress flowed upon my neighbor's body like a rainbow-green oil-slick in a sunset puddle . . . She was certainly not a *wild* green dress, even though she was made to be tight; no, it was those other dresses who were lascivious; they were the ones whose skirts tripped and danced behind the buttocks that swung them. She was so subdued

---

convinced) to our later falling out, because once I had her I could not forget that she had not been willing to go as far as I; she was a little tainted with the commonplace.

and well-behaved . . . If I were to ask for her help, she would not refuse me.

The Green Light

To avoid being known in the neighborhood as a peeper, I first sent my imagination after her from behind drawn curtains. When my neighbor had her on, I knew it as surely as if an agent had reported the case to me, and then I looked out to observe with many secret sighs her green dress, my green dress, carrying my neighbor down the sidewalk, wrapping her, protecting her, but above all giving off nourishing green rays which I could feel even at my second-storey window like weak winter sunshine. Every night I heard my neighbor coming up the stairs; then there was a pause during which I supposed her to be finding her keys in her purse and unlocking the door. Soon I caught the breathless slam of the door, and if I were to creep down the back stairs in stockinged feet I would see the light coming on beneath the door. Surely one bond for so many of us is the memory of that golden hallway light when we were young and made to go to bed before we were ready, and we lay there hearing laughter, music, mysterious sounds which would have been silenced forever by the time we were older; so as I stood in the dreary darkness of the stairwell I became even more determined than before to learn the secrets behind her door.

When my neighbor was wearing her green dress, the light beneath the door was green. At those times I could go out into the street and see greenish beams spreading from her living room lamp, even when she was in her bedroom with the door closed; but when she had undressed, the green light faded. No one else could see it, because they had not specialized in greenness from an early age, as I had; so that the green light impinged upon their rods and cones, but so did beams of other colors, so that for them the colors blended into a muddy sienna, which defeated inspection as solid earth will do. But I saw it . . .

This green light occupied my attention more and more, being so deliciously shy in the way that it stole under the crack in my neighbor's door that I became certain that the green dress had never thrown herself at anyone, that she was full of love to lavish – not necessarily on me, since she did not know anyone but the other dresses in the closet (my neighbor, her wearer, did not count as more than an animate coat hanger, owing her sole function to her bones); but whether or not she would love *me* I could feel that affection distending her, as if she were a boil; soon she must be pricked. I spent hours on the back stairs, never tiring of her light, and never understanding it. I hoped someday to unbutton that beautiful green dress and let my kisses travel like slugs upon her emerald inside seams.

One day when my neighbor was coming home with a carton of milk in the crook of her arm, I, knowing from the buzzing of my imagination that the green dress was there, went so far as to open the window and lean out; and my neighbor did not look up at the sound, but the green dress fluttered her sleeves, and I knew that she was aware of me ... Alas, I saw her far too seldom; weeks went by when she was kept in the closet, although she needed to be put on *daily* in order to glow; compassion told me to free her and keep her near me so that she could glow forever. My neighbor, not appreciating the treasure that she slipped around her insipid hips, was starving her. As yet, however, I did nothing except to stand longingly on the back stairs for still longer periods (always comporting myself quietly, of course, so that my neighbor's alarms rested untripped).

During those years my opportunities to speak with my neighbor accumulated arithmetically, like the scars upon a woman's ovaries from cosmic rays; but meanwhile my desire *not* to say anything to her rose in the same proportion, for she was the Keeper of the Dress, and I now ardently believed my postulate about not turning over pretty stones. Twice she knocked on my door to borrow something, and I obliged her, but with the fewest possible words, so that she conceived a disagreeable impression of me and left me alone to color her image as I would. Those were the most temperate years of my life. I knew well that my interest was best served by distance. Yet in time her very inaccessibility, which I had so artificially maintained, became tedious to me; and I decided to escalate matters. The green dress occupied me like a second soul. Here was an entity whose consciousness could never be known, no matter how much I might torture my reason to dream up brilliant thought-experiments; for a dress cannot speak. Being now content with nothing less than the impossible, I fixated myself upon that dress with deliberation, like a purple fly who, seeing full well the carcasses of his desiccated brethren, descends rapturously onto the sticky paper. So I decided to make love to her green dress. (I was not interested in the perpendicular smile between a woman's legs.) I had occasionally wanted to commit adultery before, but had always felt constrained by fear of my wife. She having happily died, I buried her in a black dress, held a funeral party, and set out to commence operations. – Yes, I was emboldened to rescue her from my neighbor and from the other dresses who must throng inside the closet like massed knights of darkness.

Having thus accepted the principle of my solitary conspiracy, I began to draw up timetables of the woman's comings and goings, not for the sake of their windy rush but in order to congeal my plot. So gradually I came to know her habits, which were as apodictic as the natural law that rouge should only be applied from the middle of the nose to the turn of the cheek. My inspection was rewarded on many an afternoon when, pressing my nose against the window, I saw my neighbor in her green dress. She was beautiful, but only because of it.

Greenness of the Absolute

When I was young my favorite color was always "garden green" (that was the name of a particular crayon): – a yellow-green like a field full of mustard-flowers and dandelions after a rain; and garden green reminded me also of Sundays, especially Easter Sundays, when my family would let me go out to the yard to find chocolate Easter eggs hidden for me in the wet grass; but the green dress had a different hue altogether, a darker green, though not as sombrely pure as an evergreen tree because she possessed a hint of blue in her. – How can I triangulate upon this lovely green? – At one time the forest must have been women's green dress. But now the leaves are scattered; and only one leaf of all the billions contains the vanished forest. This green dress of hers was the leaf. From its template the primeval ferns could have been reconstructed, the great green trees with raspy sticky bark, the emeralds in the moss, the long afternoons after the dinosaurs when we hid our faces behind our translucent-webbed hands, and the very weed-sap was green and sweeter than maple. – You must understand that I am not easily fooled, for I have seen green dresses buttoned and greaved, green dresses squiggled with decorations like marzipan cakes. These green dresses, though woven from fancy silk, were not much moved by the girls inside them (though the hems might sometimes be moved by raised thighs); they could, in short, do no better than *hang* suspended from flesh, like felons sagging and swaying on the gibbet on a rainy day. Could that be construed by any pair of green-going eyes as fitting? But this green dress moved by herself. Rapt with the rustle of oxygen, she sang upon my neighbor's shoulders with the voiceless song of dead birds. The texture of her fabric encompassed both the softness of berry-whiskers and the glossiness of foliage. The buttons, though cast from black plastic, could have stood for unpolished ebony-wood, ringed with the years they had lived. My neighbor's arms became the beautiful branches; her breasts were the fruits of the forest. Her eyes were the distant blue planets that illuminated the trees at night. – But what the green dress embodied most of all was *trimness, pertness* and *readiness*.

The Pimp

There was a grey dress who was distinguished in no way other than that she loved me. I had tested her many times when my neighbor wore her, and she always prayed to me upon my neighbor's thighs, like a faithful pensioner who had no hope of my love, whose highest hope was merely that I should know of her constancy. It was understood that I would use her services ruthlessly.

One evening when my neighbor went out, wearing the grey dress, she began to close her front door, when at the last minute the grey dress caught her sash inside the frame, and the door slammed, so that my neighbor was trapped. She could not unlock the door, because my good grey dress had jammed it. This was my time; for the next few minutes she would not be able to enter the building. I rushed upstairs to sweeten my breath; then I proceeded to her back door and smashed it in.

The Hour of Tafrac

The occultist Francis Barrett, in his infallible treatise *The Magus, or Celestial Intelligencer* (1801), assures us that every hour of the day and night is ruled by its own peculiar angel. I have no reason to doubt this.

It was in the eighth hour of the night, then, ruled by Tafrac, that I gained entrance to her flat, with its clock, its dark hall of antique furniture, its closed rooms.

I stood outside the bedroom door listening, and heard nothing, so I looked through the lace curtain behind the glass in the door and saw nothing but my reflection; and I bent to look through the keyhole, and saw nothing but a black keyhole-shaped darkness framing a line of tiny glittering white buttons or spheres which might have been part of the locking mechanism inside the door or which might have been something else inside the room, and I felt time passing to validate my belief that there was no one inside, so I turned the cool glass doorknob slowly counter-clockwise and opened the door as quietly as I could, seeing the reflection of my arm in the door glass like a long black branch . . .

Through the doorway could now be seen her bed, her desk, a sweatshirt lying on something, all dim and quiet. I reached into the room and turned on the light. There was a calendar on her wall, still showing last month's page, and a ball of socks on her desk. The sweatshirt was on a laundry basket. I went in sideways to avoid opening the door any wider. To the right, past the armchair, was the closet. As I opened that last door I breathed in a strengthening greenish light . . .

Reading the Bride

First I must tell you how much I admired the slope of her sleeve. It hung down from her shoulder in a relaxed but almost rakish arc, as if she were about to wave to me.

When she hung in the closet, bowed like a wrist-tied prisoner proudly standing away from the firing squad, she remained aloof among the other dresses. It was tempting to see her wire hanger as a straight, aristocratic neck, holding an invisible head firm and high, but I knew that the hanger was no more *her* than any other woman's accessory made a woman into herself. To one versed in palmistry and mime, the inclination of her sleeve might have meant something. She held her invisible arm a little forward, as if she were about to push someone back or raise her hand imploringly. But she had no hand; there was only a forlorn, intelligent darkness in her sleeve . . .

For a long time I did not dare to touch her. She waited in profile, in line with the other dresses to take a turn at the closet mirror. But I crept up to her, begging her pardon, and stroked the tiny ruffles of her collar. My first kiss fell upon her sash. Presently I succumbed to my craving to bury my face in her armpit, and the odor of her was the fragrance of fresh green limes.

An Accounting

I am still not sure if I was justified in asking her to run away with me. At the time I did not consider what might happen to her. She was a living nineteen-fifties-style dress, and other dresses, dead dresses, had eclipsed her in fashion. She was not used to much now except for the odd promenade or trip for milk. So this new life was bound to be difficult for her.

And I suppose I should have been ashamed of the way that I kept hugging her and sitting her on my lap, but I had wanted to do it for so many years that all I felt was satisfaction. No doubt she got rapidly weary of sitting on my lap, since I always had to ask her and bodily *place* her on my lap, but I never harmed or insulted her. When I had my arm around her, or when I carried her in my arms up and down hills in the Park, I was so happy as could hardly be conceived, but my feeling had nothing to do with what most people called beauty; for she was ageing rapidly; and I knew that I would be just as happy holding her when she was vermiculated and moth-eaten. I believed that she loved me in her way, and that was all that I could ask for.

The Pharisees

I took her in the street, in my arms. If anyone asked, I was taking her to the cleaners. There was in my attitude an incorrigible mixture of shame and defiance.

As I walked along I noticed people averting their eyes. It made them uncomfortable to see me, a man, carrying something that did not rightfully pertain to me. Either I was a homosexual, or else I was running some woman's errand, in which case I was obviously not my own master. I was a disappointment to everybody. To say that I did not care would be an understatement of my views. I welcomed the shame that I felt in holding her against me, her heart naked against my heart in public, because irrevocability bewitched me. Since I had committed this indecent act, I could never go back again to what I had been. And this was good; I knew that I could not get a firm footing in her kingdom unless I stepped completely out of my own, for there were many streams and daisies to leap across (when actually I saw only the debased green tongue of the Panhandle, with its seventy-four discrete dog turds per square foot – but one must have faith).

As I carried her down to Fisherman's Wharf, I saw her shadow on the concrete wall. Tourists stood atop it, the wind blowing through their hair, and the waving branches blessed them, but looking up I saw the tourists raising bony fingers, not to bless us in turn, but to point us out and mock us. The ladies sneered and turned towards their men, who made concise staccato replies which convulsed the assembly, so that my dress and I were drenched with their spittle, which did not seem to be coming from any one of them, their faces being as serene as if they were a convention of curators discussing some pair of spoiled specimens; and the green trees moved more than they, so that for a second I doubted that we were spattered with anything other than the milk of oleanders.

The Bed of Furious Hope

That evening she sat beside me on the passenger's side of my black '59 DeSoto, the kind with little lozenge-shaped windows out of which we could view the Stalinized buildings at a speed and smoothness suited to our twelve miles per gallon.

I sat her in my armchair. I opened the window. A breeze blew in and stirred her, so that she raised her sleeve to me for me to kiss. Now I thought she smelled a little of sweat. I did not want to admit to myself that that smell was the smell of the woman who had worn her. And yet I knew that she was alive. She billowed gently at me; I threw myself down at the foot of the chair and her hem caressed my forehead with indescribable gentleness. Her movements in the fresh breeze reminded me of the days of my childhood, when my sister and I used to have ghost shows in the basement. We took a sheet, raised it at its center, and tied a string around it just below where the head was. Being taller, I flung the free end of the string over a beam, and my sister pulled it down. We now had our ghost. My sister turned out the light and trained a flashlight on the ghost, while I pulled on the string so that it swooped up and hovered over us in the darkness with its sad white trembling folds ... But sometimes, being little, my sister would let the flashlight wander, exposing the string, and then it was all ruined. So now the odor of woman's sweat was an insistence that my green dress was not alive. But even as I looked up at her, beginning to feel that great grief which inevitably follows every great faith, she whispered at me; her hem frothed up high and silky like lacy flowers springing in the wind, and she leaped into my arms.

"Oh, let me suck your breasts!" I said, "please let me" – knowing that I was not being articulate, but feeling from her the heat of whores on a rainy day, when everyone else is inside or in transit from A to B, and only the whores have time for you, as the green dress always did, my green dress that walked so thin and hourglass-shaped, toward me, away from me, crossing the street throughout my life; she was mine. – She did not stop me from doing what I wanted to; she made no criticisms. Into my head came the following words:

I come as full as I enter.
I leave as empty as I tremble.

"Now move over," I told her, getting into bed, "move over like a good green dress when she's got company."

The sleepy dress put her sleeves around me as I entered her, but she couldn't feel me; she was too big; her cunt was the size of any other woman's waist.

The Honeymoon

Sometimes it seemed that there was a woman inside her, a smiling happy woman with long green hair whom I was carrying in my arms, and this woman let her head loll back as I carried her, running up and down hills across Golden Gate Park to show her my strength; but as I came to know her better I was able to reject this beginner's anthropomorphism, just as I had advanced beyond the idea that Jehovah had a white beard. My green dress was vitally alive in her pleats and seams, in the way that she rippled in the wind; she had weight and substance, like a woman, but her substance was phlogiston and interstellar ether, perceptible only to the gauges and instruments of faith. Her sleeves fluttered like the wings of a Luna moth. As I ran round and round holding her, I believed that she was the green sun that centered my orbit, penetrating me with green rays as soft and warm as cat's fur. Then we went to a Vietnamese restaurant and sat in front of two beers. Someone turned the fan on, and she fluttered mischievously . . .

At that time I hoped to be the Champollion of her embroideries, deciphering her stitches like phonetic hieroglyphs until I knew firstly the purpose of Him that made her, and secondly her own thoughts and designs, but I had not understood then that in love there is never, cannot be, any Rosetta Stone, and that anyhow flesh and fabrics warp as they sag (no matter whether you firm them with iron-on Vilene), so that what might once have been a snake or a water sign becomes in time a double reed. Perhaps my neighbor had some Turkish spectacle-case in her closet, or something of the sort, which had once laid out in the exposition of its patterns every last correspondence between the stitch-homilies of my green dress and the noble thoughts of the Iznik philosophers; no matter, the moths and the ageing fabric molecules had destroyed the equation. I did not yet know that it was better so.

I got her a bird in a cage, and in time the bird sang to her. At night I sometimes laid her down upon the birdcage when we had finished kissing, and the bird slept, and she slept, and for awhile I think that she was diverted in greenish dreams (though imagining so is more difficult than you might conceive, because the silent watchfulness implied by the forward slant of her shoulder might in fact have been a reproach).

Revenge of the Grey Dress

These beginner's spasms were quickly gotten over.

Just as a dress may be suspended from the shade of a hanging lamp, so that it goes spinning, spinning and its shadow reels across the floor, so I hooked my green dress to me. Sometimes we embraced fully, my naked skin inside her naked skin, which was translucent; my arms in her sleeves; and I buttoned her close around my shoulders. Yet it would have been happier for us if our love had been set obstacles to test us: – for instance, if she had been found by my neighbor and indignantly locked into the closet once more, so that every night I must tie a cord around my waist and lower myself from my bedroom window, shrinking from streetlights and automobile headlights; until I brushed against my neighbor's bedroom window as softly as a leaf, hoping that I had not awoken her when I blotted out the moon; then it was necessary to apply a few drops of mineral spirits to the window-tracks, so that the pane would rise silently in its well; and I raised it, permitting myself only a quarter-inch per quarter-hour, for haste in courtship is just as fatal as cowardice; and if I heard her stir I would stay perfectly still there on the window-ledge, with the fog seeping around me into the warm room; and once I heard my neighbor's slow calm breathing resume, I would dig my fingernails into the sash of the window again and recommence the raising of the glass until at last I could slip into that bedroom, like a deep-sea diver entering the porthole of a sunken ship, uncertain as to whether he will find a giant cuttlefish waiting inside for him with slimy sucker-cup arms and a murderous beak, or whether a reddish-brown stew of decomposing bodies will insinuate itself around him, and skeletons will wag their heads with the hair still on them; but for me, entering my neighbor's room would be even worse because I could not shine a diver's lamp around and thereby put faces upon my unknown perils; so, in stocking feet I would alight upon the carpet, listening to my neighbor toss in her bed uneasily, maybe seeing her white arm; and at her bedside I would halt and listen, and perhaps she would sit up suddenly and say, "Who's there?" and listen and start breathing very quickly, and I would crouch down on the rug and unplug her bedside lamp from its socket just in case she tried to see me, and I would hold my breath for the sake of the dear green dress who was waiting for me, and after another hour my neighbor would sigh and decide that she must have imagined the sound, and lower herself back into bed, and I would hear the heavy sounds of her bedclothes that raved to drag her with them into dreams, and I would see the orange dial of her alarm, telling off the minutes and seconds with electronic disinterest, and finally she would begin breathing slowly and steadily again, and I could proceed to the terrors of the closet . . . But I possessed my green dress, and she possessed me, so that our love, having nothing else to reach for, lost the yearning which had given it its strength.

I no longer sat day and night with her in my arms, my face buried in her. I preferred to sit by myself, looking out the window – although I still hung her from the lamp beside me, so that from time to time I would start at suddenly perceiving a reproachful green darkness above my left shoulder. Although I could see the light through her, she seemed to me very severe. I had not wanted or expected our elopement to cause her such suffering. The shadows that streamed upon her from waist to hem had once been very companionable in their mystery, but the longer I gazed upon them the more similarity I found between them and the imbecilic folds of the drapes. As for her very real virtues, knowing them I exhausted them: – her faithfulness, her patience impressed me as dullness. (It is possible to never know how much you love someone until she no longer loves you.) – There were now times when I sickened of her flimsy nature, and wanted someone who did more; and then I would mistreat her and we would quarrel; next, with the predictability of a recurrent disease, I felt ashamed, since she was so pitiful, so pure in having nothing but a beautiful skin – what did she have to do with my rolls of fatty guts? – Then, from the guilt, a meager gladness sometimes came – for she was glad that I still cared for her enough to be guilty, and I was glad that she was glad, and so our love continued to button and unbutton itself every night, and I stroked her civilly, not knowing that civility will not prevent conflicts, only stifle them temporarily until a proper provocation is found; and meanwhile her collar was limp and soiled, and there was a stain on her hem, and it seemed to me that every day she felt less at home with me.

We sometimes had friends over, at which she seemed to become very stiff and silent, and when my friends and I sat at the table, drinking beer and listening to the dogs barking outside, I forgot her, and my friends never addressed a word to her – nor she to them; and she was as still as the pretty pictures hung upon my wall. At the end of such visits I felt almost as stifled by her reticence as I had once felt lonely. I wanted to shout and hit her for being so withdrawn, but I knew that if I had done that she would have gone sickeningly limp, to roast me in salty guilt. And I sat at the table turning a glass round and round in my fingers, already alone as my friends went down the stairs. Outside, my men friends paced back up and down the block admiring each other's briefcases, while my lady friends sat at a round table beneath the trees, their dresses whispering to one another in the happiness of summer, but I could not wear the green dress outside, because I was not female; nor could I carry her outside without urgent cause, since I had stolen her and enslaved her, so I must hide her; meanwhile the ladies sat outside among the greenness of life, while I was confined to watching my green dress who was like a green patch of mold on the wall. So gradually I felt alienated even before my friends got up to go, and I stopped having any company but that of my own true wife, whose color you know, and I sat with her watching bird-flights and bird-fights through our window's blue sky. When I carried her around the house with me, she trailed upon the floor.

In the autumn, the trees grew in the parks like chicken-legs, and the grass was like sparse hairs; then in the rainy green winter everything came back, but hid in the fog's breath, so that from our living room it seemed that translucent grey dresses were piled up against the windows, but I knew that winter had come anyway because my green dress seemed darker and moodier to me. Then the spring came, and the trees sent forth their messages written on white blossoms, and blue air flowed from the sun, so that the fog drained into the sea and the days were hot and bright. I reminded her that even though we could not go out she was better placed now than she had been before, because her closet must now be a hot wretched place full of the smell of varnish – only in the winter was it cosy, a refuge where snow and dampness never came – and how dark it must be in there now; surely (I said) she was grateful that I had rescued her.

She said nothing, at which I was sure that she was angry; not that I was surprised or considered myself undeserving of her green and bilious temper, because my love for her had so plainly decreased that for the first time I was asking her to be grateful. That is what she must have thought. I tossed anxiously in my bed at what she must have thought. Then dreams of *faces* pressed down upon my shoulders, for it is generally what we lack that we are required to dream about. I had never had any use for faces before, and was, if anything, pleased that my love did not have one – but here they were, grinning and staring and pouting and smiling . . .

I woke up in a fresh rage at her. – What of other dresses left cast off in the woods, blouses once given to hospital derelicts who threw them away because they didn't fit; dirty underpants; old coats blowing around under trees? – Had I not saved her from *that*?

Yes, there was a bitter cutting streak in her.

When I embraced her now, I could not help thinking, is she in love with me or with my coat? It was my coat-sleeves that held her, not my arms. These thoughts made me almost faint with jealousy. Many times I almost packed them both out the window.

"She Never Told Me"

And yet I had *chosen* to carry her out of that closet, with its forests of silk and gingham, into the grey desolation of my home, where the walls and the ceiling were like rock, and I had not looked backwards into the closet when I took her, so I did not see the depths of perfect greenness that might have kept her for so many years, and I did not see whether sleeves swelled out of the closet door like supplicating branches, nourished by the balsams of that same mysterious past: I *must* have walked away sullenly unseeing, with her slung over my shoulder to see that forest for what she thought was the last time, and we emerged from the fissure in the wall and passed my neighbor's neatly made bed, now rounding the corner and ascending the back stairs, but to her (though she never told me) it must have been a sensation of descending the slope of some stone-white mountain whose cedar crown had been cool alone of all the mountains, and we wound down dirge-gorges and dry screes to that endless colorless desert (no matter that the desert was fog).

Once, upon waking up from a fearful dream, I was certain that the apartment had been burglarized, and looking out I thought I saw someone running down the fire escape with my green dress, and I lost sight of him behind trees and roofs and water-pipes, but I stood watching still, expecting to momentarily recover the silhouette of that robber, like a black fell foulness beneath the grey sky, but he did not reappear and he did not reappear and I *did not care* – I was happy; then I wept to see how much of a torment my festering love had become for me; and I felt free until I looked beside me, and there was the green dress, "until death do us part."

I could tell, as I said, that she suffered, and because she was so quiet I began to suffer for her. At first I considered it a relief whenever the pangs stopped, but because they came back again, regularly, inflexibly, the space in between them gradually became less comforting; and ultimately they were a worse torture than the pain itself, because I had to sit there tense and sweating (the green dress never sweated), waiting for the pain to come back and complete the moment.

The Closet-Death

So I began to consider the closet that I had found her in. Late at night, lying beside his innocent sleeping wife, a man may be delighted to imagine her with her pretty friends, performing for him; for while he can never sleep with her friends without betraying her, if *she* were to do it (so it seems to him at the time), not out of licentiousness but only out of desire to please him, then she would be the legitimating bridge to the forbidden island; then, too, by the act she would be dressing herself in the colors of novelty, thereby regaining the enigmatic appeal of all new women – and yet the sad truth is that if she were to wake up in the night and recount a dream about rubbing her girlfriend's vagina (she telling her husband this only because she trusts him), he would become jealous; he would not like it at all. So it was with the closet. I imagined the other dresses that she had brushed against. (At least I did not commit the ultimate infidelity of imagining a woman's white arm in her sleeve, a woman's black tresses spilling down her breast, a woman's skeleton to hang her on.) When we argued on windy nights, and the moonlight made her seem greenish-white, and she struck me and whipped me with her angry pleats, and her sash curled in the dark bedroom like a poisonous sea-snake, then I could not help but suspect her capable of lesbian thrashings in the closet.

Yet I felt that I had to take her there. In those days she seemed to be losing her life, like a weak grave-spirit sinking slowly back into the ground. I laid her down on the sofa, stroking her ruffles by the hour, and yet she did not say a word. She was gravely ill. I laid her down in the bed. When I closed my eyes I could see a swarm of grey dresses hovering like doctors around our bed; this gave me the idea that she might need to be with her own kind. Perhaps the closet, where she had been brought up, might revivify her; and yet my jealousy delayed me from going back there with her. I invented dress-plagues, horrid brown winds of moths that blew in the hot season and settled on the shoulders of the dead dresses, eating them until they putrefied. With these as my excuse, I avoided the closet; while every day she became a milkier shade of green, until I could not deceive myself. I had to take her there.

So I went walking with her in the darkness of the closet. It was winter. She brushed snowflakes or moth repellent crystals from her sleeve, and we skated across the glassy darkness past where old frocks still hung, in all the hues of autumn's leaves; and the bare coat-hangers depended from the beam. Her round empty collar was her mouth, her laughing, laughing mouth as we skated across the ice, I in ecstasy mingled with terror that some wind might blow her away. I did not dare to embrace her too tightly for fear of crushing the fragile breath out of her.

Then I saw that I was alone in the closet with a dead green scrap . . .

The Tomb

I buried her at the edge of the sea. Every night I went to that little mound of sand whose importance only I knew. There I sat on the rocks looking at her grave, while the waves rolled behind me, black and green in the moonlight, and the fog rose and the night became blacker and blacker, the fog black and clammy against my neck, and the blackness of the shadows between the rocks was so deep that I could lose myself in it and forget her grave until my eyes began to yearn again, and I looked at that low white stretch of sand, now so dull in the moonlight, and I could not believe that she lay buried only a few feet from me. On the nights when I wanted her back most desperately, and overruled that aloofness which was so valuable to me, I sent my imagination, which was ordinarily accustomed to expeditions of many green light-years, to complete that short sad journey, and as it left me behind I saw my own sleeves darken; I felt them chill, and my imagination made itself into a little colorless ball and rolled onto the grave; and then my imagination dispersed itself into little droplets and leached down into that clammy grave; the sand was wet for a moment, and then the moisture vanished, sucked downward by the dead presence that I had come to commune with; and then I waited for a long time for my imagination to come back to me, hours at the oceanside with a clammy pressure on my empty heart, while I stared at that unmoving grave, and the cold black shadows of the rocks elongated themselves and caressed my knees, and the sea-sounds went on behind me like rattling gravel, and the tide rose higher and higher until the waves soaked me, but I never turned to see if her spirit was hanging behind me because my imagination had gone; and finally her grave began to quake as if a panicked rodent were coming out, and a hole burst out in the sand and my imagination came rushing back to me in cold and terror, and I rose indifferently to smooth over the grave, my imagination not having affected me yet, and then, just as I finished, I began to feel that icy screaming in one of my auricles, and my blood pumped it all over me until I understood the putrid green stench of that mindless decay . . .

The Lazarus of Desire

Nobody contemplated my grief in the twin museums of my eyes – not that they scorned me, but they were very busy driving to Macy's and back; and politeness dominated their delight at the whole affair – delight is not too strong a word, because this death of still another person who had never impressed them confirmed their own imperviousness to natural selection; but, as I said, they did not want to hurt me by displaying the triumph that had carved their faces into a multitude of smoothly parallel lines (for lusts of all kinds will shape the flesh, just as my own desires had poisoned the green dress). To help me speed my mourning, they suggested to me that I could improve upon her. Certainly there were other dresses at Macy's, they said.

It was already becoming hard for me to remember exactly what she had looked like. Before her death, the latter grey reaches of love cast a fog upon the hindward glow of remembered infatuation; and now even the fog was behind a black curtain. Foggy nights perished and were succeeded by foggy mornings in which the white houses outside my window could not be distinguished from the orange houses, yellow houses, grey houses. As far as I could tell, my neighbor had never noticed the disappearance of her green dress. I still saw her going in and going out, but now her movements had even less meaning for me than when her skeleton had been a scaffold for my purpose. Sometimes the fog was so thick that I would not have been able to see the green dress even if she had still been alive, so that she would have struggled to accommodate my neighbor's legs as she walked, but my neighbor would not have cared and no one else would have seen. – But once she had crowned my attentions with her silk. – The insinuations of my acquaintances, however, made me wonder whether perhaps she had been like the others, and we had argued, the dream being of walking hand in hand along a pretty path, when what had actually occurred was a futile shuffle of stubbornnesses, back and forth against each other's rigid hips. But, no, she had never resisted me; she had been as light as air. I had carried her over my shoulder; she was bent double over me, her neck kissing my chest; and the spring air fluttered her. These gloomings made me absent-minded almost to the point of senility, so that sometimes my tailor would say something complicated or disagreeable to me, and I would forget that it was he who was on the phone now, and I would think, boy, I'll have to ask my tailor about this. Even Yule, which was so green a holiday, failed to cheer me. The Christmas ornaments seemed like hanged midgets dangling from the branches of a gallows-tree. – In the end I had to marry a proxy.

A Grateful Wife

As the studio lights and light stands came out of their Zero Halliburton case, I knew that I could not duplicate the romance with my dead green dress, but, having learned the perishability of ideals, I would be more suavely considerate of my new lover; the relationship would be shallower but more harmonious. And I so needed a new green dress . . .

I never would have employed a proxy if I had been able to find any one else. Leafing through the illustrated magazines, I sometimes saw the meaty globe of a breast, the less-than or greater-than symbol formed by a beautiful arm cocked upon a beautiful hip, or some other feature which I would have liked to send away for, but I distrusted their smiles; and most of all I distrusted that loathsome pinkness. It seemed so unreasonable to have to put up with the day-to-dayness of glands, hairs, tissues, fluids and moles, when all I wanted was a Companiom to hug, and to hang in the closet when I did not want to hug her. – Why, then, all this warmth and breath?

The newspaper advertisement brought me letters from many young ladies who appeared at my door holding bouquets. In time I found a tolerable stranger, one who would not speak unless spoken to, and she powdered her face to a very pale complexion for me until I was satisfied with her effacements and promised myself that she would be good enough to carry my green dress. I had had an exact replica made, and although it was not alive as *she* had been, it would at least serve to dupe my willing fancy for a space of two to three days . . .* I would not say that the proxy liked me, but it is the business of proxies to be unfeeling; they are the hands, the strong shoulders, the animated cunts of the world; their sensations are irrelevant. Since the shallowness of child-dancers can be ignored, one can as easily ignore the dancers themselves, seeing only animated dresses; for all that was wanted is a pale face, a chin raised and lowered on demand: – dark eyes, a white chin, and white hands. My hands touched her and left marks on her.

Women put their faces against each other's shoulders to see me. "Oh, my *God*," they said. "How *funny!*"

The wedding photographer untelescoped his pair of backdrop stands against the concrete wall so that they grew taller and taller like bamboo ejaculating new segments, and then he slung the roll of paper across them. (He used the same apparatus to frame executions.) His assistant unrolled the paper across the floor. Every aspect of their preparations was inconceivably grand; for a moment I floated in a green suspension of rapture. The paper shimmered under the basement bulb. People's shadows made little lakes on the bottom of the paper. From my point of view, namely, the dark, the paper was magic because it was bright, empty and clearly delineated. The photographer and his assistant attached umbrellas to the lights. Little girls came, skipping around the cords, trying to give the photographer their mother's checks, but he was too busy. "This is the first time I've used this reflector," he explained to the crowd.

The proxy also sat, watching. I thought I saw bitterness in her mouth.

---

* Just as one may choose to study microscope-slides of one's wife's tissues to verify where she has been, so with my new green dress I inspected her cable stitches and Vandyke stitches. – How grave that Inquisition! (And yet all the while I knew that I must accept her, no matter how compromised she might be. Even if my tailor had taken the grey dress and dyed her green – an envious, bilious green – and if my hand lens had shown me the deception, so that I recognized that pirate ship of threads, overcast with grey, scudding through fog and yarn-waves to a bad end, even then I would have paid with fresh green bills. I report this fact not as an angler for pity, but only to part for you the foliage of my once verdant mind, so that you may see the birds' nests and spiders' webs that ruin me.)

All her life, she had studied and hoped to be a green dress desired by everyone; now she was only wearing one. It must feel like this to be a surrogate mother, mercilessly illuminated with legs spread, while somebody injected something that would be grown inside her and harvested from her and taken from her forever.

"Your accent sounds French," I said to her, to make conversation.

"Even in my language I have a slight speech impediment. People are always asking me if I am French."

"The way you speak English sounds very nice."

"Yes, it is a sweet impediment."

I looked into the moss-grown pits of her nostrils, like a men's entrance and a women's entrance into the marble temple of her skull. When she inhaled, breath went inside her in those two parallel but isolated channels, going deep inside her head to a place where everything met. (But any search for *greenness* inside her would have been as profitless as an expedition to Hyperborea.)

The makeup man came in to begin his work, using a kit valued at five hundred dollars. The proxy sat chewing gum and looking into the mirror. She wore the green dress, my green dress, to which I was going to be married. I suppose there was no good reason not to love her. The layers of powder made her face successively pink and white, coarsening her into some kind of geranium with a green stem. Her eyes became darkly outlined. The makeup man had a special golden comb for her eyelashes. He rouged her cheeks; he curled and folded her hair. In the looking-glass I saw her trying me on. (We know from mannequins that if someone looks straight into your eye it does not guarantee candidness.) I decided again that I did not care in the least what she thought of me. When the makeup work was completed she returned to the study of herself in the mirror, gripping the counter with both hands, just as a green fly pulls itself slowly out of a puddle of filth, goggling its eyes with an expression of infinite satisfaction.

"Put your hands on your hips and relax," the photographer said. "I'm shooting just your face."

"My beautiful face," the proxy said.

"That's right," the photographer said. "You're *easy*."

The proxy danced for me on the white paper; the world rotated; the photographer took pictures for my wedding album. – How pleased I was with him! – I had seen his prints many times. Most memorable was a photo of a twelve-year-old in a black tutu, the line of the sternocleidomastoid perpendicular to the line of the arms, the wrists curved like water plants, the face absorbed in its own rapture of parted lips, all brought into focus by the horizonless blue of the background. When a hundred sheets of film had been expended, the proxy went up to the main stage to complete the ceremony.

Surrender of the Proxy

The stage was like a smooth blue floor of scratched ice. Great sheets of blue material hung as backdrops. The ballet dancers bowed and straightened their crenellated bodies like ferns or sea anemones. Their clothes, their silken stuffs sparkled blue and gold like mica. Until then I had never realized how after all a dress *could* hang almost livingly upon an arm, a hip. But as for the dancers waiting in the wings, though their costumes were lovely and the light came in upon them in beautiful blues and greens through the serried curtains, their dresses were alive only when shadows brushed across them. There was a look of sinister or imbecilic exaltation on their little heads, and exaltation is the beginning of abstraction to Dress-ness. Their eyes were as big and blue as marbles. Some girls' necks were as white as paper, but still the girls had flesh; still they sweated; after each performance their dresses had to be washed.

Sometimes the ballerinas would be dancing mockingly for each other in the wings. Their rouged cheeks almost glowed in the dark. Across the stage I could see other tall blue dresses waiting upon white forms. I wondered if the women hanged themselves upon the old grey beams, the mechanical cages, the wide screens of the wings, when their bodies became old and gross. When it was time for two dancers to go onstage, they took each other by the hand and smiled at each other before entering in a flying embrace. As they receded from the wings, their costumes came alive and made them dolls, and they danced until the sparkle of their sequins became indistinguishable from the sparkle of their sweat.

Little girls, their pudgy arms clasping their own shoulders, looked down at their stockinged feet with a modest blankness that accentuated their costumes. Their faces were like sweet little plums. Their hands swept the air.

My proxy danced in the center of the stage. She was small, and had eyes with the marbled dreaminess of cat's eyes. Only she was allowed to wear a green dress (it was not the Green Dress, but I could not believe that my green dress was not alive and could not love me). At one point I felt someone behind me and turned round, and a golden floodlight was in my eyes, and an Asian ballerina was looking into my face with wide black eyes, and I almost desired her for my own, but I turned back to see my proxy dancing, my green dress dancing, and at last the proxy spun on her heels and whirled the green dress over her head and held it to her for a moment. Underneath she was wearing a black leotard that made her white arms flow like streams in moonlight. She brought the green dress to me in her arms and let me hold it. When I kissed it, it smelled like her sweat.

She pulled the dress back on; she spun upon the stage; she lifted her leg; I could have looked up her dress, but, oh, I did not want to; I only wanted to see that green dress spinning round and round, a translucent disk in which Galileo might have seen the trajectories of Jupiter's moons, and others might see the scale of their own desires; as for me, what I saw was pure greenness. (How pale the page on which I write this!)

Until the Divorce

And so we were married, in approximately the same number of minutes as it takes to accomplish the steam-destruction of two dozen unsuspecting clams. I had wanted to dance with my proxy and marry the green dress at that moment, in front of the audience, kissing it all over as she pirouetted; then, coming offstage, the proxy and I would hold each other's hands for a moment, kiss and say, "Thank you." But I could dance no better than a teleost.

The Marriage Knife

Many of the other green silk dresses at Macy's had flowers and ripples patterned into the sleeves; they were flaming green women lacking in substance, and I passed them by indignantly. – "This is a nice dress," my new wife said. "Oh, I like this. Oh, I love this!" – From far away the green dresses in the Impulse Department could be seen on their rack, at some remove from their spurious cousins of aqua and blue. Night rested in the shadows between them, infinitely soothing to me, like a forest bivouac at the bank of some rushing stream, with colored pebbles luring me to wade across its sandy bottom. – The pretty young girls were leaning, entirely at home, against the racks of shoes which were all the colors of automobile bodies in a parking lot. "I think this is exciting," they said to each other. "I love it when you actually buy things." – The insolent yellow sweaters (especially the leopard-dotted ones) infuriated me; the red and blue shirt-skirts drooped on their hangers like last year's leaves; the pink scaly blouses jangled at me like blood vessels bursting inside my eyes; there was but one small patch of green – four green dresses crowded behind two white dresses and two blue ones. These expressed reticence, gentleness and modesty; but it was not enough. They offered their shoulders to me in supplication. How could people buy and sell them? – "See that thing sticking down beneath your skirt? It's *authentic*," said the woman at the shoe department, which was not so different a place from the bus station, people just sitting waiting (but *here* they waited for each other to choose things), or pacing around (but here the pacing was to try new shoes); the women handing their candidates to their husbands for inspection, the husbands invariably turning them over to study their soles, as if doing so would reveal some secret: – the new husbands, who still loved their wives, studied the soles reverently, as if they were in an art gallery; while the older husbands stared at each shoe-sole with open suspicion, no doubt worried about the price; as all the while gentle music played. Only the salespeople moved briskly; the others walked dreamily about, fingering shoes they would not buy, enjoying a little foreplay previous to the transmutation of an alien thing, prized precisely for its separate being, into a possession conquered and thus despised, the whole catalyzed by money.

Just as a real Macy's woman will spend hours picking out the ideal Young Collector Shoes just across from Jennifer Moore where two olive-skinned mannikins watch the shoes very seriously, as if they expect at any moment for some missing third, perfect or at least perfectible in every detail, to slip on a pair of purple size 8's and then come to join them forever; and just as each Macy's woman hopes that *she* will be that third woman, so I myself still spend hours of hope and fear among the green dresses. How strange it is to see the women make off shyly with their new blouses, or wander, noses uplifted, from shoe to shoe. One can sit very close to the bright wall of shoes and listen to them try to breathe. One can smell the pornography thickening here; it is so much less innocent than mine. The women shoppers so often travel in twos, their gazes converging on each treasure under consideration; for they too want their completing third. Sometimes I see one of them emphasizing what she says by pressing her palms to her cheekbones. – I have always been fond of women.

For Alyssa Rose Bernstein

THE BLUE WALLET

The thing you dislike or hate will surely come upon you, for when a man hates, he makes a vivid picture in the subconscious mind, and it objectifies.

Florence Scovel Shinn, *Your Word is Your Wand* (1928)*

I

I loved Jenny most when, sitting beside her at sentimental movies, I would look away from the big screen where the beautiful actress was about to leave her lover forever, and see Jenny sitting upright in her chair, her black button-eyes concentrating so hard on the film, while she chewed and chewed her gum so earnestly, and I ran my forefinger below her eyes to verify that her face was wet, that Jenny was crying for the people on the screen, crying in perfect placid happiness over this debacle that had never happened; and I knew that after the movie was over Jenny would forget that she had cried, but she would feel refreshed by her tears. – How harmless it all was! Sometimes I myself, reminded by the actress of my own failures, would be scalded by a single heavy tear; but this would not be a good feeling, and I would have to stroke Jenny's wet eyelid again with my finger to be soothed.

2

"I got in a fight with this fucking *fat woman!*" cried Bootwoman Marisa, who was now a bicycle messenger. Her legs were covered with bruises like rotten apples. "Right when you get to the end of the block you go up onto the sidewalk. And there was like a Mack truck coming right at

* Marina del Rey, California: DeVorss & Company, p. 74.

me, and it was *totally obvious* that I was not gonna to be able to fucking avoid it unless I put on my brakes to *skid* to like avoid this woman. And I told her, I go, *MOVE!* I *yelled* really loud; I go, *MOVE!* and she goes, *No!*" – and, imitating the woman's voice, Marisa expressed this determined negation in a birdlike screech – "and she *stands* right there, and I go, *Fine!* I'm gonna *hit you!* – So," she laughed, "I hit her, straight on. – And she *throws* me off my bike! She fuckin' throws me off my bike, an' my bike is goin' that way; I'm goin' this way, and I just got off and *punched her in the face!*"

"All *right!*" yelled everyone, with enthusiasm as blue-white and glowing as the most powerful cleansing powder. This enthusiasm could have eaten holes in walls.

"Jesus! *BAM!*" screamed Marisa, so loudly that the dog began to bark. "And I start screamin', '*Bitch*, what in the *fuck* you think you're doing? *Bitch!*' And she's opening up her little purse, and I'm just *waitin'* on her. *Bitch! Bitch!* And she goes, 'Well, you were in the wrong! You were in the wrong!' – and this black guy steps between us and goes, 'Come on, don't get in a fight,' and I go, '*BITCH! YOU NIGGER-FUCKING WHORE!*' – and she turns around and she goes, 'You got *that* shit correct,' and I go, 'Of *course!* You're too fuckin' *fat* for a white man to fuck your lousy ass!"'

3

Marisa never liked me as well as I liked her, partly (I suppose) because I wore glasses and did not know how to fight hand-to-hand, in the knightly fashion of skinheads and other street-conquerors, but partly also because my girlfriend was Korean. She did like me enough to be polite to Jenny, it being one of the rules that if somebody was your friend you did not fuck around with his lover, as was demonstrated when Ken's girl Laurie went up to Dickie at a skinhead party and touched his shoulder to ask him for a cigarette, and Bootwoman Dan-L appeared from nowhere and warned Laurie to stay out of her territory unless she wanted to get beaten up. So because Jenny was in my territory Marisa tolerated her. – After all, Marisa did like me O.K. – This must have been why she sometimes came over and cooked me breakfast: huge omelettes with mushrooms and cheese and bacon and red onions, while in a subordinate frying pan her home fries sizzled obediently, becoming the golden-brown of Jenny's skin, at precisely the moment when the cheese melted and the mushrooms were done and the steam rose from the titanic omelette like a chord from some cathedral organ, and Marisa would start doing the dishes that had piled up in the sink and say, "Boy, your girlfriend doesn't take very good care of you, does she? What a mess this place is," and I'd stand beside her at the sink and feel good that Marisa was *being* good to me; and meanwhile I'd be drinking whiskey out of the bottle because I was hungry, and the sun swam through the fog and I felt dizzy and Marisa shook her pretty bald head at me and buttered my toast. Whenever I asked her to, she'd tell me stories, such as how the Pretty Boys who peddled ass on Polk Street moved into the Pink Palace and then the Sleazy Attic and became the Bootboys so that they could die early because the Bootboys were such *severe* skinheads ("Almost *all* the skinheads are already dead," sighed Marisa, "all the good ones"); and while Marisa went back into the kitchen to finish doing my dishes, her bootsister Thorn told me about how when she was in London her boyfriend Luigi got his eye popped out by the Italian Fascists, and then Marisa came back and told me about how when she was a thirteen-year-old girl in Chicago she started going with a skinhead named Sean, who was eighteen or twenty, and Marisa loved to hang out in Sean's apartment, which must have resembled the workshop of a medieval armorer because scattered through its dark dirty chambers was a Camaro in pieces – hubcaps under the bed (so I imagined it), bucket seats emplaced against the living room walls for conveniently screwing Marisa and other girls, the shiny silver exhaust pipe by the door to hit enemies with, the carburetor serving to deploy old socks and dirty underwear and a black leather flight jacket to best advantage, while the gas tank was actively poised beside the window, still full of gasoline and ready to be hurled down onto the dirty icy street like a flying bomb; and presumably Marisa and Sean must have always been stepping over screws, and the windshield was in the cold dark moldy bathroom, covered with grime; and buckler-plates of chassis hung overhead in Sean's bedroom, and the battery slowly leaked its acids through the floor; and now I have come to the end of all the auto parts that I know (except for the fan belt) – and Sean also possessed a stolen stop sign still in its cement base; possibly this was his hatstand. Although Marisa had not become Bootwoman Marisa yet, she loved and admired

Skinhead Sean, so she tattooed Sean's name on her body and started unrolling her secret capabilities by piercing her ears half a dozen times and doing fucked-up things to her hair, none of which things Marisa's mother cared for, which was an incentive for Marisa to do them because Marisa's mother treated her like a baby; when she used the leftover batter to make a final tiny pancake she'd say, "Oh, there's a *Marisa-sized* pancake!" – and that *really* bothered Marisa. At that time, going to school started to bother her, too. Since she liked Sean better than she liked that listless two-hour commute from the North Side to the West Side, through cold dirty snow, with the cold wind blowing through the rusty railings, Marisa began sneaking down to the basement on those dark winter mornings instead of going to the bus, and when she heard the door-slam of her mother going to work Marisa would run back upstairs and dive into her warm bed and wait for Skinhead Sean to let himself in and hop into bed with her and watch TV until her mother came home at the end of the day, and then Marisa and Sean would go back to Sean's metal-happy apartment. – Sean was very strong. One time after she and Sean broke up, Marisa was at this AOF show, and there was this skinhead band named The Alive going *dwuuunggg!* on their bass guitars, and one of the guys in the band picked up on her, and Sean slammed his head against the wall. *BAAAAAM!* until the blood spurted out, and Marisa thought that was the coolest thing, and then Sean threw him off the stage, and Marisa *loved* it. – Years later she met another Sean in Marin County when she and Thorn were over there trying to pop some virgin boy-cherries, and wily Marisa bet the new Sean two hundred dollars that she had his name tattooed on her body (which of course she did). Sean went for it. – Poor Sean! – Since he didn't have the two hundred, he found himself under a universally acknowledged obligation to get her stoned on his dope for the rest of her life.*

"Now, tell me about how you decided to become Bootwoman Marisa," I said, eating my eggs (eggs very lightly done, Marisa told me, are called "scared eggs"), while Marisa and Thorn sat at the table to keep me company, Thorn smoking and staring out the window and

* Of course this was not quite as good a scam as the one perpetrated by the bum in the Panhandle who comes up to you and bets you that he has your name tattooed on the head of his dick *regardless* of who you are, so of course you fall for it and he unzips his jeans and flicks his thing, and there on the head of the glans, sure enough, are tattooed the words YOUR NAME.

crushing her cigarette butts into a mug while Marisa drank tea (she never ate what she cooked at my house; she cooked it only for me).

"Well, I didn't decide to be Bootwoman Marisa," she said, "it was sort of like a gift." (At this remarkable commencement my mouth fell open, and I was in such a state of suspense that I almost became incontinent.)

"How's that?" I said. "They invited you?"

"Okay. I don't know if you knew me 'way back when, but when I would hang out on Haight Street and shit, I used to wear like really funky makeup. *Really* funky makeup. I don't know. I guess I had a much different attitude back then, about a *lot* of things. One day, Dee was like walking Rebel, right? And I saw her. So I was like, 'Hey, why don't I go with you?' And so we went, and we sat in the Park for hours and we talked. She was just like, 'You look like a *freak*, Marisa!' She just laid it right out, and she said, 'You look like a freak, and none of us want to hang out with you if you're gonna look like a freak.' So, we went back to her house, and she sat me down, and she took off all of that freaky makeup, and she said, 'Now that's *it*. If you want to revolt against the world, you know, I hate the world, too, but it all comes from inside, and if you do it from the outside, people aren't gonna respect you at all and you're never gonna get anything you want.' Then I sat down, and I took off all my stupid jewelery and shit, and the other Skinz were like, 'That's *good!*' " – Marisa pounded on the table. – " 'You have the potential to become a *Bootwoman!*' " – She pounded again, so that all the silverware jumped. – "And that's what it was."

"You must have had your feelings hurt a little at first, when she said that about your makeup."

"Well, no," said Marisa. "I didn't really have any reason for doing it. I never did. I just did it. What the fuck. It's just one of those things, you know."

"Did you feel *different* when you got your head shaved?"

"Well, *fuck*, yeah! It was cool. It was pretty cool. People started treating me with a little more respect. I stopped getting like black eyes every other week," she laughed, "and Spike started teaching me how to fight. That was fun."

"Why did you use to get black eyes?"

"Because just everywhere I would go, people would look at me and just think I was some sort of fucking weirdo, and punch me in the face. That was *lots* of fun!"

"What would you do then?"

"I'd punch them back, naturally. But I didn't know how to fight for shit. And I'm still not like the *best*, but I can defend myself a lot better than I could back then. See, now I'd rather fight with a *large stick*. Like last night."

"What happened?"

"When, last night?" she said nonchalantly. "See, I went out looking for this girl, right? There's this girl on Haight Street, and she's a total lily. *She's* a freak now, and I wanna . . . *change her mind*. I wanna let her see *my* side." She chuckled. "And I'm gonna do it with a stick!"

"How do you know her?"

Marisa and Thorn hissed contemptuously at me for this idiotic question. "I don't know her," said Marisa patiently.

"You just know the way she looks, huh?"

"Yep." Both girls laughed. "Yep," said Marisa. "She's definitely got like an attitude problem. I was *really* freaky looking. She's a nothing. She walks around in this *leather* that's big enough for her to fucking *live* in. And it's got like DROOLING IDIOTS written on the sleeve and all sorts of punk rock shit written all over it, and she walks around and she like hangs on all the guys. She's a total bimbo. Definite bimbo. So, *I think we need to send her to Boot Camp!* What about you, Thorn?"

"Mmm," said Thorn boredly over her toast.

4

I had been Jenny's lover for more than a year. She had never told her family about me. The fact that I was white was a problem, although Jenny and I both struck each other with bludgeons of the heaviest loyalty whenever one of us was so unguarded as to consider swimming away from the attachment like a slippery fish. Jenny laughed and laughed whenever the sun came out, whether it was the sun in the sky or the less reliable sun in my blue-steel eyes, for, as her cousin Alice explained to me, there are many different suns; as evidence, Alice cited the tale of the great Korean poet who got drunk in front of His Majesty and composed the following lines: "I see three moons: One in the sky, one in your eye, and one in your cup." – When Alice stayed over, Jenny and Alice slept together in Jenny's waterbed and I slept on the living room couch, because although Alice knew that Jenny and I usually shared Jenny's bed, Alice had not actually seen *evidence* that we did; if she had, she would have had to tell her mother, even though she loved Jenny and knew that Jenny would suffer when Alice's mother (who was so conscientious as to place folded tissue paper inside the family's shoes to keep them from accumulating dust overnight), was obliged by reason of that conscientiousness to call Jenny's mother on the phone; in the meantime Jenny and Alice and Alice's friend Ivy went out with me to a Korean restaurant on Geary Street; while I sat at a corner of the table stirring the raw egg and raw beef around in my cold metal bowl of Yuck Hwe Bi Bim Bop, the others laughed and talked in Korean and conducted symphonies with their chopsticks, turning hunks of marinated chicken and beef and tripe on the little grille which the unsmiling waitress had placed in the center of the table, and the meat sizzled and the yellow flames shot up and warmed our faces; and every now and then Jenny would take a wet lettuce leaf and shake it down onto the grille to discipline the flames. – "Ooh!" she cried gleefully, holding up another chunk of smoking meat. "Intestines!"

The Korean girls all had tiny mouths and smooth taut faces. When Jenny smiled, her face was like a wide golden shield. They talked about movies which they had seen. "It was such a comedy," laughed Alice. "I couldn't believe it." – "I heard it was really bad," said Ivy. – "I just liked the title music," said Alice. – They talked about Jenny's brother Richard, mostly in Korean so that I did not obtain a lengthy catalogue of his imputed qualities, but the way the Korean girls sighed through pursed lips made it clear that Richard had lapsed into error, and from the occasional English phrases which were thrown to me in afterthought I gradually came to understand that he was seeing a Korean-American girl who had Caucasian ways. "He's so serious about her," said Alice in melodious surprise. "But she knows nothing about Korea. I don't think she wouldn't fit too good in with the family." Alice saw me looking at her and took an earnest unsmiling bite of her tripe.

5

Sometimes when Ice was too drunk to take care of himself, Marisa and Thorn had to help him piss. Thorn would lean him up against a wall and hold his shoulder and grip the seat of his pants. Marisa would tell him to put his dick back in his pants, and if he couldn't do it she'd do it for him.

6

In the summertime Jenny took me north so that she could splash around in cool lakes, and she'd coax me in, too, so that we'd be holding hands and wading deeper and deeper, trying not to walk on the pointed stones, which pricked our feet almost pleasurably, like spicy food; until when the water was up to Jenny's thighs she'd jump in and then I'd jump in and the water was cold and the sun was hot and Jenny would be laughing and calling to me, "Come on! Make big swims! Big swims!"

7

"Have you ever made watermelon punch?" said Marisa, and I said no, and she leaned forward confidingly and said, "All you've gotta do is take like a watermelon, remove the rind, and put it in a blender – not for very long, though, just because all it is is water. You don't want to chop up the seeds. And then you put it through a strainer to get the seeds out, and you can put as *much* alcohol in it as you want, and you'll *never* taste it. It's pretty cool."

"I'll have to try that," I said.

"You should *do* that!" growled Marisa with a hoarse friendly kind of toughness.

"On Jenny and her pretty roommates," I said, eating my scared eggs – and there was one of those transitional silences, as Bootwoman Marisa came to herself and remembered that I was not as pure and wholesome as I had pretended to be, because I stooped to racial shame with Jenny, and she turned to Thorn and said dryly, "Jenny is his girlfriend."

"Oh," said Thorn, knowing enough from Marisa's tone to take on an air of distaste, although she did not yet know Jenny's sin.

"And," grinned Marisa, screwing her voice into a cheerful singsong, "she's going to look really *gross* by the time she's *forty!*"

I laughed, but as I recall my laugh now it seems to have been a somewhat insincere, wooden laugh, my empire of humor already riddled with termites, and Marisa moved in for the kill, saying, "I'm warning you, Bill, dump her while you've still got the chance!" – and to Thorn she explained my shameful secret, in the parentheses used by two people speaking of a third's terminal disease: "(She's Oriental.)"

"I'll pass that on to her," I said, still laughing in my loud insincere way, and Marisa said rapidly and coolly, "You do that, Bill. You just do that."

8

I had a party, for which Jenny made artichoke dip, kahlua cake, sweet-and-sour chicken and a variety of other foods, abetted by her house-mate, Margaret; and Marisa and Thorn were invited. Most of the other guests were Jenny's Korean friends. When Marisa came in, she cried out, "Hey, Bill, I brought you a present. We were at the St. John's Grill, and we stole you this ashtray fair and square!", and I was touched and thanked Marisa with a big hug, but Jenny's friends contracted, and I took Marisa and Thorn into my bedroom, away from the drinks, and closed the door so that we could shoot my airgun, and the girls laughed at the target and yelled, "That's Cougar's head! – That's Rona's face! I'm going to *kill* that slut!", and Marisa shouted, "*KEE-lore!*" – meaning, "KILLER!" Thorn and Marisa mainly stayed in the kitchen after that, helping Margaret mix up drinks, since this affair was a little quieter than the skinhead parties which often started in early afternoon when you pulled your boots on and buttoned up your black jacket nice and tight and took the bus down to the Tenderloin or the Fillmore where you knocked on the door of a garage and two beefy Skinz looked you over and took a dollar for beer and one of them stamped your hand with a dinosaur stamp to verify that you had paid, allowing you to go on through the garage and up a passageway that took you into a barren courtyard of stamped-down dirt with rickety apartment buildings towering around you, and skinheads and bootwomen permeated this snakepit, some ascending the fire escape to the first-storey terrace, the second-storey terrace, the third-storey terrace where things were dark and rotten, and at any point a skinhead might block your way and you'd have to be awfully polite to get past him and keep climbing to the fourth-storey terrace where Bootwoman Dan-L yawned and scratched her new-shaven head, and Marisa sat on the stairs with other skinhead girls in a pool of beer, which trickled slowly down the stairs in a nice uncaring way, like Ice's piss, losing itself in Marisa's jacket and under Marisa's leg and behind Bootwoman Kim's shoulder and so on to the ocean. For the most part Marisa said nothing, because she was already very stoned.* She stared out across the world; you could see clouds here, and dirty windows, and laundry hanging from distant fire escapes, and at any time you could look down on the yard as if from a low-budget watchtower, to see the Skinz lined up at the beer keg to pump Bud into plastic cups for themselves, their buddies, their girls; and in the middle of that grey sad space there was a grey sad tree that rose three storeys; and the Skinz tied a rope around a cupful of beer and threw the rope up around a branch of that tree and caught the free end and started raising the cup very slowly and carefully until it was about thirty feet high and then they began to swing the rope back and forth, back and forth as they raised it, the beery pendulum whizzing merrily over everyone's faces, and then the Skinz got excited and started really yanking with their big tattooed arms and the cup upended at about fifty feet and rained beer on everybody and some girls in black frowned and said, "*Fuck* you," and some Skinz laughed, and some individuals were not noticeably affected. Everybody was getting a little drunker and louder now. Some guy ambled up to Nazi Joe and asked him what his boot size was. Nazi Joe stopped talking to his friends and turned around very slowly and said, "Why, do you want to *steal my boots?*" He knocked the guy's head against the wall and punched it hard five times! Blood

---

* This was not too long after Marisa lost her job at the bakery on Castro Street because the owner read an official government report that skinheads were racist and sexist. – What a surprise! – "I don't have anything to say about that," said Marisa defiantly. – "Well, I can't have someone working here with those opinions," said the owner, whose boyfriend was Jewish. Marisa told her to fuck off.

burst out of the guy's ears. After that, my friend Ken kept going up to Nazi Joe and asking him what his boot size was. Nazi Joe only laughed, I guess because it mattered who asked him. Later on, it got dark, and things *really* got going; Ken got drunk and took a girl whose face he never saw into the basement and porked her against the wall. – So Marisa and Thorn, in short, were not entirely at ease in the more ideologically flabby surroundings of my party where Jenny and her friends talked about Macy's and other topics which Jenny forgot about later, and everyone else stood around the living room table and sipped the Chivas Regal which Jenny had bought me down in L.A., or else they sat on the sofa and talked about new innovations in computer programming, such as the UNIX chip that was due on the market for micros, and with two of my favorite mechanical engineers I discussed the possibility of printing books on plastic paper, and I took my schoolmates Paul and Nancy into my room to show them the 1902 Tamerlane edition of Poe that Jenny had bought me for my birthday for a hundred and fifty dollars, and Jenny came over to make sure that I was eating the food that she had made for me, and Nancy and I discussed five books for five minutes, and then Paul and I each had another drink, and Jenny had another drink, and I went back to the kitchen to visit Thorn and Marisa and joke with them about the size of my dick. – "*That's* nice!" they chorused laughing. I leaned up against the refrigerator and they leaned up against the sink, and I drank tequila and beer and tequila and beer but Thorn drank lightly in order to make sure that Marisa drank lightly, because Marisa got violent when she drank too much. – "San Francisco used to be the skinhead capital of the world," sighed Marisa by the sink. "Now it's so pathetic, it makes me want to puke." – My flatmate Martin came in and grinned at us uncertainly. – Meanwhile my other guests drank margaritas and walked around the living room table and stood up and sat down and talked and avoided Marisa and Thorn, while Marisa and Thorn avoided *them;* and Jenny drank Old Bushmill's and got very dizzy. Thorn told me about her drawings (she has since been accepted by a fine art school), and Marisa told me about the time she had belonged to a ballet troupe in Australia (which I have never visited and therefore enjoy imagining), getting picked up on wherever she went, not that she cared since she knew she'd never see those men again; and at the Hotel King's Cross in Sydney she played strip poker in the boys' room until the Director came back, so freckled Marisa had to get her clothes back on real fast and crawl out on the window-ledge to get back into her room, and the Director saw her, so she bitched Marisa out for that and then Marisa had to be watched for days and days, until finally there was a free day when members of the troupe could go out in groups, but Marisa said *fuck* this shit; she was going to hitchhike, so she set out for a fleamarket to buy her San Francisco friends some stupid Australian T-shirts and the Director saw her sneaking back and wrote up a report on her for that, too, but Marisa, who at that time had greenish-red hair which was short in some places and long in other places (and in other places still it just went *tiiing!*), didn't care because at the fleamarket she'd gotten picked up by some guy who was *really* good looking; meanwhile everywhere they traveled around the circumference of this reddish-brown continent, a more faithful admirer still followed Marisa in a chocolate-brown Rolls Royce, and she would always get mixed up and try to get in on the driver's side instead of the passenger side because the roads and cars were opposite from the ones in America, but Marisa's admirer just laughed; he was about forty, and the Director, who was seventy-two, had a *big* crush on him, not that it did the Director any good; and then the troupe danced at the Sydney Opera House and another man fell in love with Marisa and took her out to dinner, but the Director caught her sneaking back into the hotel late at night, totally fucked-up, so Marisa was barred from dancing for the next two performances, and in the next city the guy in the chocolate-brown Rolls Royce gave Marisa enough pot to get the whole company completely stoned, which she did, so they had to call off the next performance, and Marisa got expelled from the company, although they couldn't send her home early because that would have cost too much, so she got to stay on and get into as much trouble as she wanted. Finally the company had to stop boarding her with families who had sons. The people were *cool* in Australia, except that they spread Veg-i-mite on toast.

9

At the party, Jenny's blue wallet disappeared. She did not notice until the next day because she had drunk too much. Jenny was very careless with her belongings, and had lost her wallet several times before. Once we were coming home from a movie, and just as we got out of the car Jenny realized that she did not have her wallet. We drove back to the theater and did not see it; we went to the bar where I had bought Jenny a drink and it was not there; then we saw it lying in the middle of the street, miraculously unrifled. Evidently Jenny had dropped it while unlocking the car. So I was now certain that the wallet would soon be found, but it wasn't. Jenny was in a frenzy of anger and panic. Her keys were gone, too. Evidently she had left her wallet and keys on the table all night, beside the drinks and potato chips.

"It was your friends!" shouted Jenny in my ear. "*You* invited them here! This is your fault! And they took my keys, so they can break in to your apartment and my apartment and my car! And they have my goddamn credit cards! You're responsible for this! I bet Marisa's down at Macy's right now, buying bluejean things. Oh! I got a headache that just won't go away. I told you not to invite those Nazi Skinz, 'cause they're delinquents!"

"Let's look for it downstairs," I said. "Maybe you left it there." At that time, still convinced that the wallet would turn up at any moment, I still did not understand how angry Jenny was. I preferred to be entertained with her ludicrous image of Bootwoman Marisa going to Macy's.

"In this instance, I just remember it so vividly," Jenny insisted, "'cause what I did, I left the wallet in the car, then I went to your room directly, thinking I had the wallet with me, but I didn't, so I went back and got it, and I sat down and I put the wallet there. As it is, the only places I could have put it is in the kitchen or in the living room. Who else would do it? It had to be your goddamn skinhead friends!"

"They wouldn't do anything like that," I said.

"They came in with a stolen ashtray!" Jenny screamed. "Maybe they wouldn't steal from you, but they don't know me. Far as I'm concerned, you can forget about me if you ever see them again. Sometimes I hate you so much. I don't know why I ever hung around with you. You don't ever care about me. You think your criminal friends are more important. Top of everything else, I bet you're glad they stole my wallet and keys. I'm telling you, I don't ever want to see those bad girls again."

"Jenny," I began, but she hit me and said, "Don't say 'Jenny' like that to me! They have my wallet and my keys. What am I supposed to do now? I want you to look all over the house again. Look through the trash. Maybe somebody threw the stuff away by mistake. I'm not gonna be able to sleep tonight."

We did not find the blue wallet.

"I told you they were like that," Jenny said. "You better promise me right now that you're never gonna see those skinheads anymore."

"No," I said.

"Then you're not gonna see me anymore," Jenny said, tears rolling down her plump golden cheeks. Jenny did not mean exactly what she had said; she meant only the worst thing that she could think of.

10

"At first I thought they were really funny," said my flatmate Martin, preparing to embrace the views of his class. "But then I decided they were kind of frightening when I realized that they were serious."

"I don't think they did it," I said.

But Martin was certain that they had.

11

There are times when you know that something is not right anymore or that something is over, but with that knowledge comes a sick premonition of what it will mean to you, as if you suddenly realized that the ground was dissolving under you, and under *that* was darkness and dirt and crawling bugs, and you want the comfort of solid ground back so much that you will keep to the thing that is not right, willing it to be right for another day's journey, a few thousand more steps, because you want to not think about the dark hole waiting for you, and if you *can* delay the collapse of the ground you will certainly do it. I had felt this way toward my relationship with Jenny on many occasions, and I felt it now regarding distrusting my friends. I could not believe that Marisa had taken anything, and I could not believe that anyone else had taken anything.

Jenny hardly slept for two nights. – "These skinheads, these Boot-women," she said, "I wonder if they disapprove of me. I wonder if they hate me 'cause I'm Asian girl. Maybe they want to hurt me. I mean, they're Nazis!" – I had not told her what the skinheads said about her, but even so she knew that one night a month or two from now, when we had forgotten the incident, Marisa would come sneaking up to the door and unlock it with the stolen keys, and then Dickie and Mark Dagger and Chuckles and Blue and Yama and Hunter and Dee and Spike and Nazi Joe and Ice and Dan-L would then come charging up the stairs and Dagger would shatter the banister with one kick of his Nazi boots and Yama would smash in the curtained glass door of Margaret's room and start hitting Margaret over the head with a chair and the rest of them would come back into Jenny's room and find Jenny and me sleeping on her waterbed and Dickie would slit the waterbed with a sharpened tin can and the skinheads would yell at us, "All right, where's the money? Where's the money?" – and Marisa would tell me I had one minute to get out and leave Jenny to her fate, and then Yama would hit her in the face and say, "Shut up, bitch! We're gonna carve 'em all!", and Chuckles and Blue would piss into our faces and Ice would begin to dismantle the living room stereo with tender care.

12

After two weeks, Jenny became resigned. We took to locking her door and my door with the deadbolts, which had not been used before, and which Jenny had not had keys for. Her face was still puffy with tears. For Jenny, who loved clean things and neat things and organized things despite her own carelessness, the loss of the wallet was an aesthetic disaster as well as a security risk. "I wish I misplaced it," she said mournfully, "though it really doesn't make any difference, 'cause I still have to go through all the hassle. It's been so many days now. Get me a new bank card. Call about my driver's license. I'll cancel Macy's card. Now, today I want you to eat a good lunch 'cause I'm gonna cook the Mom's meat for you. Promise me you'll eat a good lunch. Do you promise? And you want frozen chicken nuggets?" A little later she was humming a Korean song about barley fields.

13

Meanwhile, Jenny's other brother Adam came up for a visit. He was a slender self-confident young man who liked to wear polo shirts. Jenny adored him and was always calling him long-distance late at night to give him advice, which I am not certain that he consistently followed. The look of a baby brother still clung to him. He and his friends from Yale carried in a bucket of giant clams which they had gathered on the beach. Jenny dumped the clams into the sink at once and began scrubbing their shells with soapy steel wool to get rid of every subversive germ; in Jenny's world, as in Marisa's, every alien must be sterilized. She steamed the biggest ones, who sighed futilely through their excurrent siphons; the rest I popped into the freezer for five minutes to weaken them so that their numb adductor muscles would be unable to resist my knife; already sick from the long oceanless ride in the trunk of Adam's car, they cracked open in easy surrender to their sushi doom. I carried them out on a plate and set them before Adam, who sat at the dining room table loudly laughing with his friends, these boys evidently respecting him as their leader, much as Izutsu and Sagara respected Isao in Yukio Mishima's *Runaway Horses* because Isao was going to turn them into rightwing extremists and then become divine by cutting open his belly in a ritual rapture that would most likely make the sun explode behind his closed eyelids; I imagine that Adam's clams felt this way when I slit them open; but Adam accepted them without seeing either them or me and passed them to his disciples, who cried, "Adam! Adam!", and Adam gave one clam to Jenny and then ate one, and passed the clams to Izutsu and Sagara again, who doubtless were learning how to become divine with him at Yale. – "Well, Adam, do you need anything?" I said. He went on talking to his friends. But when he saw me in Jenny's bed, his jaw fell and he shook his head very slowly and went out, leaving the bedroom door ajar, and before driving home the next day he taped a note in Korean to Jenny's door. The note said: "Elder Sister: I was very disappointed about your boyfriend. I was ashamed of you. Please think of Mother and Grandmother." – How to explain this revulsion that the colors of the rainbow feel for each other?

In her nightgown, biting a juicy peach, Jenny sat down on her

waterbed and called Adam. I had made her do it. "I'll be there late,"
she said. "Can you do me a favor? Tell Grandmother not to sleep in my
room. Margaret and I will be sleeping there. Another thing. Rent me a
couple movies. And tell Mom to take the big car to work. And tell
Richard not to go out with the big car early."

She swaddled herself in blankets. "Now, I keep forgetting to tell you
this, but you're really rude leaving that letter. What do you mean,
honest opinion? And you were really rude. He kept trying to talk to you,
be nice to you. You acted like a brat. – What do you mean? – Adam,
you really have to behave. What is honest opinion? No. Listen to me.
Listen. Bill's my boyfriend, and you have to – Adam! – Listen! *Listen!*
LISTEN! You say you love me, but if you do, you have to respect . . . –
Listen! LISTEN!

"Adam, I don't understand why you think things that way. I want to
know why you came to that kind of opinions. You have to defend your
opinions. – No, you have to provide a reasonable cause. You can't say,
I just don't feel good. Adam. Adam. *Adam!* I know you're upset. But
you cannot just act on first impressions. What do you think now? What
do you think now? You see, you don't know him and you said things
that really hurt me. I want to understand why you wrote that letter, why
you behave that way. – Just because of appearance? In what way? What
do you mean, you don't remember? I'm not criticizing you, I'm asking
your opinion. Just because one's different? That note you wrote said
you're ashamed of me. Why, why, why, *why?* What type? What type is
he? He didn't do anything to you."

She made her little brother cry on the phone (which gave me
satisfaction), but he still hated me.

14

If this had been a Chekhovian story, or a tale from de Maupassant, the
blue wallet would have turned up eventually, proving by its determined
refusal to be elsewhere that all suspicions had been reified to the point
of logical and moral death, so that now, as all the thought-chains
strained inside our brains, and the little homunculi downshifted the
thought-gears to provide maximum mechanical advantage in their futile
attempt to drag the blocks of leaden trust back to safety, those corrupted

metal concepts hung upon the summit of that black waterfall that everything goes down eventually, and the homunculi did their dwarfish best but the chains snapped and the trust careened down the waterfall and fell into the spray below and we never saw it again, but the blue wallet remained to remind us of our limited beings.

In fact, I did find Jenny's wallet eventually. It had fallen into a paper bag under the living room desk, along with her keys.

We went to other movies, and Jenny sat with her knuckles pressed raptly against her cheeks, happily crying at the spectacle of a newly imagined romantic disintegration.

15

A month before Marisa's seventeenth birthday, Jenny and I met her at a party on Haight Street. In the doorway it said: *S.F. BOOTWOMEN – THEY'LL ROB YOU OF YOUR MONEY, YOUR PRIDE AND YOUR MAN!* Marisa did not have her bicycle messenger job anymore because she'd come riding into some Bank of America office tower with an urgent message, and a secretary or petticoat executive had looked her up and down in a sneering sort of way, so Marisa called her a bitch or possibly a fucking bitch, and the bitch had complained and the messenger service had lost the B. of A. account and so Marisa was fired. – Jenny and I were sitting together on the sofa listening to the Supremes going, "*Ba*-by, *ba*-by! Where did our *love* go!", at a volume suitable for launching killing vibrations through our tympanic membranes and into our bony labyrinths and so into our membranous labyrinths to cause special damage; and Jenny was trying to get me to dance with her.

"Come and dance," she said.

"I don't feel like it," I said.

"Please dance with me," she said.

"No," I said.

Marisa came into the living room and started dancing by herself, looking very soft and furry with her sweater and the grey downy stubble on her head, and Marisa's eyes were closed, and she danced and danced on the rug, and Jenny said wryly, "Marisa! Pull him up and make him dance. I've never seen him dance" – and Marisa came over and stared expressionlessly into Jenny's face, and said coolly, "And you never will."

For Jacob Dickinson and Janis Kibe Dickinson

THE BLUE YONDER

A Tale of Cleanliness

Functioning as a 𝔐𝔬𝔯𝔟𝔦𝔡 𝔞𝔫𝔞𝔱𝔬𝔪𝔦𝔰𝔱, the pathologist
seeks for organic abnormalities – traumatic, natural,
or both – whose presence is incompatible with
survival.

> Lester Adelson, M.D., *The Pathology
> of Homicide: A Vade Mecum for
> Pathologist, Prosecutor and Defense
> Counsel* (1974)*

Sunny Days

Sometimes I saw Evangeline and Indian Mary sitting together on a park
bench, with Mary's radio playing loud sunny songs in the grass behind
them, and Mary's smile seemed even more winning now that she had
lost one of her teeth. The sky was blue, and the sky was blue, and the
sky was blue. – "Look," chuckled old Evangeline, who never took off
her dirty parka no matter how hot it was, "here's George!" – and she
showed off her pet, a green foam-rubber lizard who lived in a mesh of
puppet-strings as a Portuguese man-o'-war must inhabit its cloud of
paralyzing tentacles – except that poor George was not a predator but
rather one of the paralyzed; for a stupid happy smile had been painted
on him, so that he must always be stupid and happy; most likely he
thought that cigarettes fell from heaven. Of course, since Evangeline
and Mary did not have friends in high places, a stupid happy pet was
what they needed to help them pretend that the sky would stay blue.
George, therefore, was perfect for them, being capable of so many
cheery pseudo-voluntary activities that it was astonishing, considering
the cranial trauma which he had evidently undergone at the jaws of
malice unknown (for not all of George's head was there): – he could
skip when Evangeline pulled his strings, he could struggle, he could
hop until the strings got tangled, and he could play dead. – "We like

* Springfield, Illinois: Charles C. Thomas, 1974, p.15.

George, 'cause he *protected* us last night!" cried Mary sincerely, and she
told the story of how she and Evangeline had been drinking on the
bench in their private darkness when the police came and were going
to bust them until they saw George and leaned on their nightsticks
laughing and told them to just take their bottle somewhere else, and
one of the cops even gave Mary fifty cents! – The day they got George
had been a lucky day, too. Mary panhandled enough change to buy
three-fifths of Night Train; at the same time Evangeline got half a
cigarette and three slices of pizza. – "Look, poor George has half his
head bit off," sighed Evangeline. "I think a dog must've got him." The
dog, then, would be the *proximate* cause of George's decease once
George finally died. Those things happened, because the innocent
always fall short of the advantaged, and those who live in the Wild Blue
Yonder are doomed to be devoured by the monsters of the place.

A Nice Fellow

If you have ever seen meat gone bad and green, with mold-fuzz on it,
you will know what The Zombie's face looked like. He was a pale
creature whose neck leaned forward, in the angle favored of old by the
prehistoric lizards, but whose head was not correspondingly lowered.
It was as though he wanted to thrust his jaws as far ahead of him as
possible, so that he could prey upon the smaller reptiles almost before
he saw them. Darwinians and Lamarckians would have made identical
projections of the future of his species (of which, at present, The
Zombie was founder and sole proprietor): – the neck would lengthen,
the head would become armored with knurls and knobs of bone, the
nostrils would widen, and so would the jaws ... He had blond hair
waving on his forehead like an overgrown wheatfield, and his hair grew
down over half his ears, and he had soft blond stubble growing from
cheek to chin to cheek, and his face was pale, and his lip was hairless,
and his eyes were half-shut, as if his long blond furry eyelashes had
grown together, and between his blond eyebrows and his hair there was
nothing but a smooth sickeningly white wall of forehead, and there was
not a line in his face. There was, however, a black slit between his fat
white lips, and his eyes were two slits of candid putridity. As he walked,
tapping ahead with his cane, you were sure that he did not see you,

because it did not seem possible for him to see anything with those eyes, and he rarely turned his head or modified the angle of that extruded neck. Particularly horrifying was the fact that he combed his hair. It was as if a corpse were to somehow be capable of spraying deodorant under its arms. The little vanities of those whom the human race has excreted are so sinister because we know by them that there must be *consciousness* in those skulls.

A Church Social

It was a warm greasy meal at the free food place, the foodless folks queuing at the counter so that their trays might supplicate for lukewarm zucchini that had been boiled so long that it squished apart when you put it on your fork, and irregular lumps of yellow and black bread, and salmon that might have been rotten salmon jerky. The next step was to proceed to any foldout chair at any long dirty table. People talked in low voices, or inspected their food like suspicious Borgia-guests, and some even ate, but most sat hanging their heads because they soon must shoulder the wide streets where it was raining and would keep raining loneliness into their hearts, while the air, which was already the shade of aluminum, continued to tarnish until it was triumphantly black. There would be no moon. The Insiders would sit by the fire eating whatever they pleased as they relished the raindrops running down the far side of their windows, dissolving streetlight to become yellow beads, and the Insiders heard the leaden noise of the rain on the streets and were content to be inside although they did not think much about it. For them, the night was a lullaby of the uncared-for Unknown. The puddles gleamed golden for them in the street. But those who lived outside did not admire the gasoline-rainbows or oil-rainbows upon the puddles, even when it was not too cold since the aluminum afternoons had not yet completely tarnished. They did not see the rainbows, since their eyes were closed and their hat-brims were low on their faces. They did not even see the gleam of raindrops crawling down their crutches. So in the free food place their heads fell forward as they were used to doing, and they were quiet.

A black man in army clothes sat down at the piano and started to play, nodding to himself, and his music sounded sunny, so that fat old

Ruby, who sat stuffing herself with Evangeline's dessert, was happy, and Evangeline unzipped her dirty orange parka an inch or two; while beside her redhaired Carolina (the first to die) sat muttering and polishing an empty paper cup. There were puddles of water on the floor. Rich ate his salmon very very slowly, bent over it so that his blond locks kissed it. Gypsy stepped in, dripping, and surveyed Rich's salmon in disbelief, finally muttering to himself, " I don't *give* a fuck!", at which Rich smiled a smile of incredible sweetness, but Gypsy did not see it because he had already turned and marched back out to the Park, where the rest of the Wrecking Crew sat drinking in the bushes while rain trickled down their collars. – "Well," said Rich, "this here fish could have been better and it could have been worse." – A chilly wet wind blew through the doorway. At the back of the room, a man in a skullcap was thinking deeply, leaning on his hand as he stared at his coffee cup. Slowly his eyes closed. He held a book open with one hand, and as he slept his face continued to aim itself at the text with the right level of concentration.*

"I wish I could eat," said a girl wearing a striped blanket. "Today's fish day."

"You don't like fish?" said the guy beside her.

"I'd try, but it would give me the dry heaves."

"Bad attitude," scolded a little blonde runaway hugging a skateboard. "Lick my rose."

The Zombie came in.

Exits

Some people think that the worst part of life is knowing that they must lose everything. Those people are all rich! It is almost as if (difficult to credit!) they had never heard the outcries of a yellow leaf peeled *slowly* from its branch by the wind's untiring fingers, whirled still living into mud and mold, crawled on by snails, stepped on by uncaring muddy boots, until at last some miserable drizzle washed it down along the gutter and into the sewer. In the Park, not far from where the Wrecking

---

* In the Blue Yonder it is sometimes essential to look awake when you are sleeping, and to appear unconscious when you are anxiously listening and watching.

Crew used to sleep, is a bad black pond in which leaves float, or sink, or are suspended; not all these leaves are dead yet. There are so many on this earth who hate their lives; for them any losing is a lightening. But even they would rather die *before* they rot. An oldster quickly cut off, floating down the warm waterfall of a cerebral hemorrhage, is more fortunate than his sister who lingers through stroke after stroke as she sits with hands on knees in *sinking* vacillation from grief to dullness until when death finally sidles up with a thousand sadistic grimaces, she looks on in speechless indifference. (Anyhow, a happy death is as difficult to imagine as a happy life.)

But however much horror we may excite in our lifetime, the changes which occur thereafter are of a nature which will cause the most gregarious cadaver to be shunned. The reclusiveness of coffin-inmates shows decency; *they* do not torture their successors, the living, by displaying their egregious alterations in color and shape. – Truly unfortunate, therefore, were The Zombie's victims, who died in agony, then were hidden with insulting superficiality, so that in days or weeks the living would find them, and be afflicted by their presence.*

Carolina's Last Night

It was a cold moonless night. Some cold nights are translucent by reason of their coldness, so that you seem to see the cold empty spaces between the stars, until your gaze falls farther and farther into the blue-black deadness of the beyond, and the stars themselves begin to sink away, like winter's first snowflakes landing on the surface of some black pond which has not yet frozen, and the snowflakes spin down, down into the water, which is so murky that no one can tell whether they will melt or go all the way to the rotten muck at the edge of galaxies. In Chinatown, however, the decline of the stars was obscured by closer lonelier lights. Headlights streaked toward North Beach like tame meteors. Jewelry stores and restaurants made light in signs and shallow windows, attracting most those appetites which ought to have been most

---

* Fortunately, as Adelson points out in *The Pathology of Homicide*, the serious aesthete "soon discovers that thanks to olfactory fatigue, he becomes less and less aware of and bothered by the unpleasant odor, and he can carry out an informative examination with a minimum of discomfort."

satiated by buying and spending, while the tramps turned the other way. The streetlights shone as imperiously as blonde whores with uplifted chins.

Carolina sat on her park bench and opened a pint of rum with her new friend (whom she did not know was The Zombie), and because he was clean she gave him permission to drink from the bottle, but she herself drank from her special paper cup, which she constantly rinsed and guarded with her most watchful love, in order to protect herself from poison. She couldn't take any chances. Last night someone had contaminated her water, which she knew for a *fact* because she had gotten dizzy and puked and sobbed and started slashing her wrists until somebody called the ambulance, but fortunately the poisoner wasn't alive today, since his fucking *head* got blown off as he *deserved!* Now that it was safely dark, she showed The Zombie her own precious drinking fountain that she brushed her teeth from because it could not be polluted and because the water stayed warm even in the middle of the coldest night, which proved that it must issue from a secret volcano ten miles underground.

Every few minutes, a drunk would start to piss against the side of the elevator. Carolina would call out to him: "Honey! *Hey there, honey!* You gotta pee?" – and the drunk would turn around in slow surprise, his hands still on his fly, and Carolina would run up to him and pat his shoulder and say, "Get in the elevator, honey, and punch 'M'. That's where the men's room is." – And the drunk would stumble into the elevator. Carolina pushed the "M" button for him. – This happened over and over. Carolina was the patron saint of such emergencies. – "It's a terrible thing when you have to pee," she said. "I know how it is."

Carolina and The Zombie sat close together on the park bench drinking her rum. She was sorry for The Zombie. She kept making him drink so that he would be warm. In fact The Zombie did not want to drink. He did not want to corrode his shiny concentration. But Carolina would not understand if he did not drink with her. He took small steady sips, hunched over the pint like a ragged blond bird. His fingers were numb. His toes were cold in his wet shoes.

In the shadows, two drunks were fighting over a woman, inspired far more by her than by the swimming greatness of the Transamerica Pyramid in the fog below them and the Empress of China Restaurant behind them. – "She's not for you, fucker!" one said. "*She's not for you!*" He pushed the other, who fell. The first drunk helped him up, and the woman looked back laughing. Then the three of them wandered amicably into the darkness, through the curtain of red lights that alerted and alarmed the night.

Carolina pulled her parka tighter around herself. "It's so cold," she said. "It's bitchin' cold. Do you have a place to stay?"

"No," The Zombie said. He stroked his cane, which felt like wet ice.

"Hey, I'll go see if I can bum ten dollars and get you something to eat," she said. "But first I'm gonna pee. You gotta pee? No? Then you watch my water and make sure that no one touches it."

The Zombie sat waiting for her in the cold windy night. The wind blew garbage out of the garbage cans. It stirred the wet grass. Against the dark-greenish sky the trees were like whisks. The fog had begun to eat at the glowing yellow squares of downtown windows, replacing them with its cold, smothering moisture that made the parkoholics start coughing wet coughs and swearing, while the fog devoured more and more lights until finally Carolina came back shivering. "I gotta do something to keep warm," she said. "You stay here while I go bum a cig from one of them tramps." As she set off into the darkness, something very important occurred to her. "Hey! Do *not* let *no one* touch that water."

The winos lay belching and fighting on their bench. Water ran down their faces. – "You're beautiful!" they yelled at Carolina. "Hey, spread your meat!" – The Zombie did not listen because he was considering what he would do with Carolina's corpse. But Carolina took her cigarette and stepped back. "You listen to me!" she said. "I'm *asking* for a cig; I'm not *whoring* for it. Can't you understand the difference? I thank you for the cigarette. If I ever have one, I'll give you one. But you deserve to have your heads bashed in. You keep your fucking mouths clean or I'll wash 'em out with lye soap." – The winos chuckled and burped. – "Shut up, bitch," they called. "Don't you want your pussy pricked?"

"I hate those assholes," she said to The Zombie on the cold wet bench. "They're so dirty. See, I always carry soap with me wherever I go. Not them. They're animals. Here, you want a drag on my cig?"

The Zombie shook his head.

Carolina looked at him sharply. "You're sitting all hunched up, like you're nervous or embarrassed to be seen with me or something like that. What's your problem? You got nothing to be afraid of from me. I'm very conscientious, mister. I'm pure and I'm clean."

"I'm clean, too," said The Zombie mechanically. He rubbed his hands, as if to wash them; then he played with the fastenings of his satchel. An intense, eager light seemed about to break from behind the wall of his face, and Carolina could see it and sense it but she thought it was from the rum.

A rich family passed by Carolina's bench on their way to the elevators. There was an extensive parking garage beneath (and, in truth, it was probably the parking garage with its steamy exhaust atmosphere and hot sweaty shoppers and hot greasy coins which heated the drinking fountain, not a volcano); that was where they must be going, since they did not punch "M." The boy looked at Carolina as they passed. It was a spoiled, lustful glance, expressing torpor, fear and regret.

"Did you see how he looked at me?" said Carolina. "He wanted me."

"You're very nice looking," The Zombie said, stretching out his head on his long long neck . . .

"Nice looking ain't *nothing* to me," she said. "Sex ain't *nothing* to me. I don't believe in sex without love. I wouldn't sleep with a man unless I knew him at least a couple of years. I want my man to be *clean*. If I could have anything in this world, I'd ask for no contamination *forever*."

The wind began to blow harder and colder. It was very dark. "Do you have any advice for me?" The Zombie said. "I sometimes feel distant from myself."

"You're a man," Carolina said fiercely. Her teeth were chattering. "Do you know who you are? Then be yourself! You're more than you think you are. I can see it in your face. Just live your life, and try to be happy. You have to be strong these days because the Devil's coming close. The Devil rules this world." She lifted her cup, but the pure water spilled out of her hand. "I'm not drunk," she sighed. "Not very."

Carolina, with her long tangled red hair, her stare, her narrow shivering shoulders, was a saint. It was for precisely that reason (because The Zombie rules the world) that something horrible happened to her that night. I saw the bloody parka in the trash can. But the water from her secret drinking fountain still comes faithfully and warm.

How the World Mourned

"The coroner's report said the girl already died, but it says she was born on the seventeenth and in fact she was born on the fifteenth!" said the legal secretary, in high exasperation. "It's just *crazy*."

Heaven on Earth

Sometimes at midday the sun would be so sweet that the Park People gorged on it, drinking it in and drinking it in – or, rather, *having* already drunk it in so that they had to lie in the grass with knees up or toes up to help them sleep while they digested that sweetness; and stunted brown sparrows with feathers like moldy shingles pecked in the grass and wandered between the sleepers, eyeing them brightly. Evangeline sat making George dance in his lizard-strings (while the shy wild mice danced behind her in the grass by a stagnant pond, loving the blue sky over them as they gleaned for bits of bread and cracker crumbs). Mary was sure to stroll out of the shady mystery of the public shelter, just as a police car was sure to roll almost silently down the sidewalk, though whether the police took the sleepers away or let them lie was as Fortune would dispose. Mary lay down in the shade next to Black Fox and slowly turned the pages of the newspaper, as the birds rolled their heads to let one black eye and then the other peek at the sun to make certain that it was still there, and the hot breeze carried the smell of french fries from McDonald's. Presently Mary went up to the next bench and put her hand on her hip and said, "Could you spare a cigarette?" and walked slowly back across the grass to her shade, with the cigarette dangling from her hand; and another police car rolled along the sidewalk from the opposite direction. All these things had happened in only fifteen minutes, yet it seemed that a long succession of nightless days had dripped by. Night would never come; the sleepers never moved. A man walked from trash can to trash can, chewing on the insides of rescued banana peels. Another man pushed a shopping cart full of blankets and papers. A woman walked in the sun, her multicolored shirttail flying above her flying hips like a swarm of butterflies. Mary read and smoked at Black Fox's side and listened to KFOG on her radio and seemed content. Her fate had not yet come searching for her.

A Sermon

What unlikely things we are, of course, with our voluntary locomotions, and our body heat which keeps our fat from congealing until death! – and how natural the inevitable downward course! (For it seems a wonder that our fleshly contraptions can endure an hour.) – How natural, then, The Zombie.

Ruby Among the Old Men

The Wrecking Crew had not known Carolina well, so they were not alarmed at her disappearance. Nor did they remark on Ruby's new friend. Ruby and Evangeline saw each other once or twice a week at the free food place, but their conversations were only about food. Barlow heard on the grapevine that Ruby finally had somebody who listened to her, but all he had to say was, "I sure wish I had a feather stuck up my butt so then we'd *both* be tickled." – As for Rich, he had not heard anything about The Zombie, good or bad (and of course The Zombie did not call himself The Zombie), for the truth was that the Wrecking Crew had its own problems, and was not so interested in Ruby. She did not sleep outside, as they did. Nor was she restless for God's blue sky. Yet among the inmates of her boarding care home, who resembled grey fenceposts or pier-pilings grimed to their grain, splintered and leaning, leaning, old Ruby was the best connected with the Blue Yonder, because she had wandered there for fifty years in shock treatments as uncountable as the rings inside a great fossil tree that daunt the gaze and blur beneath a hand lens into spectacles of dead wood without any meaning. The state hospitals had heard her screams for fifty years. Now that she was old and would die soon, they let her out. She tried to be happy and smile at everybody, because (I presume) she had heard the commandment to smile issuing from the blue mists that boiled from her anterior cranial fossa all the way to her parietal foramen, and, secondly, she was also not sure whether she had met anyone before or not, so she walked up and down Haight Street with the see-nothing goodwill most often met with in intergalactic ambassadors.

And yet people did not like her – particularly not Cory Smith and grey-faced Lenny Ezell, whose opinions counted almost as much as that of MR. BAUMEISTER. They thought her too anxious. But Ruby did not know that she was anxious, so she could not help her cause, and must be perpetually gobbling crumbs of old smiles. Then, too, she was stout – a failing particularly despised in California. When she sat in her room, her bulk made the room seem very narrow; the way she leaned forward reinforced the impression that she was straining at the toilet. She was as big across the hips as two ordinary women. Ruby often wore sweatshirts with wide white horizontal stripes, which accentuated her own width, and called attention to her level lips and eyes when she was scowling, which was often. She said that the antipsychotic drugs at Napa and at Agnews had made her fat. Once when she was at Agnews she had not wanted to be fat, and when the nurse got a phone call Ruby ran lumbering to the dispensary and gobbled half a bottle of diet pills. But it had not helped her. Some days she looked just like a pig. When she scowled and let her chin sag, her nose became a pig's snout, and she snorted when she talked. Her face was the shape of an olive. On a bad day it was like a pickled olive.

She lived uneasily among the Boarding Care Men, who leaned in their TV chairs and glared at the blue screen with eyes as brightly sullen as stars about to shoot down, down into the blue atmosphere; and when they fell asleep in the afternoons their flesh did fall into dimness; their chins doubled and tripled, their fingers dangled, and their hair grew down their shoulders with the airiness of hanging ferns. When they woke up again, life continued to fall out of them. They had crooked black mouths. Acid sweat ate holes in their stiff scaling socks. Their bulging bellies bloomed with hernias like immense chestnuts, and their tattoos faded from hour to hour. (If you have seen thousand-year-old Chinese paintings, you will know the blackish-green soot color of dying tattoos.) Their eyeballs rolled when they moved, as if their optic nerves were fraying and loosening like the wires in car stereos after the car doors have been slammed and kicked for years and the cars have gone in some junkheap caravan over fifty thousand miles of dead roads full of gravel and broken glass.

Doughnuts and Happiness

"I have my own activity to go to," said old Cory Smith. "I won't be called down and told not to. Other things that are not really an activity, but I consider it that way, is going to that there Hunt's Quality Coffee Shop on Twentieth and Mission, where everybody thinks that doughnuts is happiness. Well, that's the way they feel, especially for the guys that come and go with doughnuts. You know, they come and buy, buy, buy; and off they go with a load of doughnuts. Well, sure, anybody would go for a doughnut off of one of them guys, if they could spare it, but they don't feel that way sometimes. What everybody wants when they go there is at least a cinnamon roll, PERIOD. And I also like to go riding on the buses sometimes, at night when I can buy me a late-night transfer. Just ride around and get back home, that's all. But that's the only activity I look forward to, just looking into the dark, you know."

Pictures from the Deathmask Album

These pale old men lay naked on their beds every afternoon, wrinkling their necks and thinking. But they never told anyone what they were thinking about. Sometimes they went out, because they liked to sit on the steps in the morning as the wind blew their scraggly hair like patches of grass on crumbling seaside dunes, and they wrinkled their noses at the wind and sat cursing at the flies; or, if they felt as adventurous as advance mortar-shells fired haphazardly into the Blue Yonder in some losing engagement, while the artillery men were still trying to get the range (but it was already too late), they strolled slowly round the corner and watched Brandi suck money out of the Wrecking Crew ("You gimme those eight dollar worth of food stamps an' I'll be *right* back!" she said to Evangeline, and Evangeline waited and waited and finally reported to Barlow, "Now she don't even *speak* to me!"); and the old men viewed the tramps sitting pretty in Haight Street doorways, equipped with bottles and beards and outstretched hands; but then the old men's gazes fell slowly to the sidewalk, even on blue summer days, because they were too tired even to watch the newspapers blow, so they returned to their rooms and went back to sleep, pillowing head against wrist – and they slept, snoring and farting; and they slept, wagging their chins – or else they got their second wind and stood erect as admirals in the TV room, swivelling their birdlike skulls, which had weathered ceaseless apprehensions of death, although the flesh retreated between their neck-tendons from year to year, leaving gulleys and canyons scoured ever deeper by the caustic sweat that dripped down their chins when they dreamed of death; and when they grinned their teeth were like stained piano keys that somebody had pissed on long ago and somebody else had shot at half-heartedly from a good distance in order to produce the random black gaps with which their mouths were graced.

Courting Ruby and Lenny

Just as in the Fillmore you walk down the street politely limiting your gaze to your sneaker-toe in order to avoid looking into any face and thereby conceivably antagonizing its owner, until your eyes distinctly see the *shadow* of someone behind you, and the shadow comes closer and closer; whoever is following you must now be almost level with your right ear ... and then the man passes you without a look; and then another shadow goes evenly by, and so does another; but you know that someday one of these shadows will be the one to kill you; so now in the doorway of old Lenny's room Ruby preserved a watchful tragic attitude, expecting the inevitable, as no doubt she used to do before being placed on one or the other of those well-padded beds to await the convulsive, clonic and tonic phases. – "You look like you *want* me, stranger!" she said through a transparent wrapping of cheer.

"I saw you in the free food place," said The Zombie, staring down at his cane as he tapped it slowly up and down. "You reminded me of a friend of mine who's dead now."

Ruby chuckled. Her big belly went up and down until her face turned pale and she put her hand to her chest and gasped for breath. – "You're really cute," she said. "You're a cute one. What do you want?"

"You tell me what you want," The Zombie said. He blinked his long blond eyelashes and squinted. "If you could have anything in the world, what would it be?"

"*Oooh*," said Ruby. "I *know* now it's Christmas time. I want . . ." Her voice trailed off. She looked distracted, then peevish. She frowned until her cheeks bulged out. – "I need to escape from the police, 'cause they keep controlling my *ears* with their shocks. They make their buzzing in my ears to tell me they can hurt me. Last year they put two flies in there. You can say you don't believe me if you want, 'cause they're *listening*."

The Zombie spread his lips in a smile that was tight on the upper lip, but fat and protruding on the lower. "I'll help you," he said.

Ruby glowed because someone was paying attention to her. "You know," she said slyly, her big old tits bulging out, "when I came here I thought this would be a nice place. But I'm the only girl here. I think these guys might *rape* me or something." She giggled. "They're watching me, just like the police. I got my picture taken by the police. I don't know why. They thought I had a stick of dynamite, but it was only a candle."

"Get the fuck out of here, you bull-dyke bitch, or I'll beat your face in!" yelled Lenny Ezell as he came up the stairs. "Always hanging around, trying to jinx me up . . ."

Ruby cowered back and ran down the hallway crying. Soon, however, she was back again, peeping shyly into Lenny's doorway. – "Bitch!" Lenny yelled, and off she went. – And so The Zombie was left to himself.

Lenny's face had not yet gone slack. His skin had thick deep folds from nose to lip, but the flesh had preserved its tautness, particularly during his frequent rages, when his eyes were like flames inside agates, and his shoulders hunched. He had big shoulders. His face was always grey. – "What are *you* doin', messin' around my quarters?" said Lenny.

"I wanted to give you this naked woman picture," said The Zombie slyly, reaching into his pocket.

Lenny calmed down. "Well, thank you, sir. I'm grateful to you for bringing me that picture."

"What are you going to do with it?" asked The Zombie.

"What I gonna to *do* with it? Gonna keep it for myself."

The Zombie brushed his blond hair back across his forehead. "I'll give you whatever you want," he said. "Do you want something else?"

"What do you mean?" shouted Lenny, suddenly suspicious. "Stop tapping that cane! You need a cane *no* way! Are you coming on to me? Do you dare come on to me? Get out! What else do I want? To get you goddamned motherfuckers out of my face and have folks stop *worrying* and *bothering* me!"

"All right," said The Zombie. "If that's what you want, I know how to make the whole world stop bothering you." He smiled and tappy-tapped his cane.

A Eulogy

"I read the newspaper this morning," confessed Cory Smith. "You know, I always like to look at the obituary page, just like Mr. Baumeister. You see, Mr. Baumeister knows everybody that *ever* died! – But Lenny didn't make it into the newspaper yet. I certainly consider that he will, tomorrow or the next day, because they know they have readers waiting. – Now, as for the actual *case* of Lenny Ezell, I don't know how it stands. I can't say how long I was going from his presence. Either it was all morning long and I got back after supper, or else it was all night, until the next day, you know, when I got back to the room a little after lunch. Well, I think Lenny wasn't in bed when I went in. He was a-layin' on the floor, like *this*, you know: – knee up, and the thigh down. I don't remember if it was both legs; I didn't notice. (Didn't try to.) He was simply being AGONY, you know, in *pain* there. Making painful sounds, you know, *Oww, oww!* He was not happy, but it *did* look to me like his face was halfway dissolved. I *did* think that. And there were BLUE CRYSTALS on him. I decided to go to bed and nap, which I did. Then I woke up around suppertime because Mr. Baumeister came around announcing supper. That woke me *up*, see. So when I got up, there was Lenny still on the floor! I says, this is too much for me, I says, *I'm* not going to fool with him! I told Lenny, I said, 'Lenny, Baumeister came and told us to go and eat. Now get up and put your clothes on.' Well, Lenny was still continuing in pain, you know, and when he made his painful sounds there was thick dark *slime* coming from his mouth. – Yes, I myself would say that it was *dark* slime, PERIOD. But he didn't flinch; he didn't budge; he just kept saying, *Oww, oww!* So I said, well, I'm not going to try to pick him up. I can't do it by myself! – So then I went to supper. I was gone a long time, maybe forty-five minutes or a whole hour. I must have been one of the last ones out of that dining room, or else *the* last one out. I was down there enjoying seconds, and coffee, all I could drink. Smoking up. Coffee, and more coffee. Thinking some more about doughnuts and happiness. Then when I got bored of doing that, I said, well, I'm going up to the room to see about Lenny. – Yes, that's what I said. – I went up around eleven-o'-clock. When I got there he was still on the floor; he was in the same position, you know, *Oww, oww!* And there was also all this darkish stuff coming out of his mouth, and down to his chin he was greyish-white and kind of *dissolved*, like someone had come and DISSOLVED him . . . I said, 'Are you still doing this, Lenny? Christ sake! I ain't gonna bother with it; I'm going to bed. Would you get up and go to bed your own self?' (Lenny was *always* a sick man, I understood from Mr. Baumeister, you know. Noddy said that Lenny always *was* a *very* sick man. And that woman Ruby, Ruby Todd, the fat one, she was of the same opinion. Of course Ruby always was anxious. But not me! I used to tell them, oh, Lenny's just acting up, just putting on. Nothing's the matter with him, because he used to act funny, then get up, put his clothes on, walk getting into a goose-step. I think he was German. Then he would go on downstairs to eat. So I used to say, *what* is this? What kind of games does he play? Well, *I* ain't to know.) – Anyway, getting back to the point, I slept until two a.m. I looked at the clock. And Lenny wasn't layin' on the floor! He was layin' on the bed, like *this*, the feet down on the floor, and the rest of him from the waist up on the bed. I said, I wonder how that happened? He either tried to get there under his own power and didn't make it to lay straight, or else somebody helped him up, and just let him go. I don't know what guy might have done that. I'm stumped right there. – But the next thing I said to myself was, *I don't know if he's alive!* I'm gonna see for myself. It looked he was melting away, into *sewage* like Jesus Christ the LORD has ordained for us in our Judgment. I couldn't figure it out, though. I said, what does he want to do that for? I went near him, and I *yelled*. I said, 'Lenny, come *on*, get *up* out of bed; we already ate a long time ago. You missed supper.' And I told him what we *had*, see. I told him, 'Go to bed!' – No response. – I said, I'm gonna see if he's alive. I went near him, and I looked at his stomach to see if he was breathing. I said, well, I'm gonna touch his *tummy*. I did. It was *hard* as *stone!* I said, uh-oh! He might be DEAD . . . So the next thing I did, I went down to the public pay phone in the lobby, and I rang up the coroner's office, so they came over, a Big White Lady Police, and a Small Colored Lady Police, just the two ladies, you know, dressed in uniform with their weapons. I think I waited downstairs for them to appear. I must have looked out the door to see if they were coming. – They said, 'Are you the man that telephoned?' – I said, 'Yes, I am.' – Then the Small Colored Lady Police said, 'What's your name?' – I said, 'My name is Cory Smith. I *stay* here, you know.' – The Big White Lady Police said, 'Where's this here guy that you say had died?' – 'Well,' I said, 'he's in my room; he was my roomie; he's up in room nine.' – They went up the stairway, and I went after them. So they went into the room, and they found Lenny, and he was still laying in the same position. He was all *decayed*. The two Lady Police figured the same as I. They figured maybe he was dead, since there was *decayed* stuff from Lenny on the floor and they couldn't help stepping in it. I don't think they liked that. (Not that I *myself* ever disliked Lenny in particular, since he *was* a *sick* man.) – So the Big White Lady Police rang up the fire department. Two firemen (although they weren't dressed as firemen) came in with a re-*soos*-itator, to see if he was breathing, you know. They didn't so much as apply their re-*soos*-itator to him. They just said he was dead. They pronounced him 𝔇𝔢𝔞𝔡! Then one of them Lady Police rang up the coroners, and they came up, and they just started talking; they didn't start touching the body or anything. – They even called Mr. Baumeister downstairs, to see what he knew. – He didn't know *nothing*. It was the first time in our lives that Mr. Baumeister didn't know *nothing*. – They asked him if Lenny was taking medication. He said yes. So he came up here with all the bottles and the charts, and all that crap, to show to them. Then they asked him if Lenny had any relatives. And Mr. Baumeister said no. And someone mentioned something about funeral arrangements, so then they broke up and left me there. I went out, and I said, 'Mr. Baumeister, how long is it going to take for these morticians to get here?' – 'Oh, about an hour or so.' – Then Mr. Baumeister left, and I remained all by myself, with the body of Lenny Ezell, with the BLUE CRYSTALS glittering on the collar of his shirt. I was wondering if the morticians were *ever* going to get there, 'cause it was taking them a *long* time. – Well, they finally arrived with the stretcher. They put gloves on, and they took his body off of the bed, and they put him flat on the stretcher, and covered it up, and then they put a sheet around him. Dissolved stuff went right *through* that sheet! Then they put a blanket around the stretcher, and they took him out. And I went behind 'em, and they went out the front door to a *brand*-new hearse. A very marvelous-looking, BRAND-NEW hearse. And they slipped the body of Lenny Ezell into the *BRAND-NEW HEARSE*, and away they went! – And it never occurred to me to ask them where they were going to have the funeral arrangements! I never did check it out! I'll never know if they had a ceremony for Lenny Ezell, and a funeral procession, and where they might have buried his body! That beats me."

The Other

What The Zombie did in the daytime does not much concern us. The cleanest people are the deadest, as has been known since the time of Boltzmann, for perfect order is attained only by a perfect blue crystal at absolute zero. While The Zombie helped others into this state, he himself was a soul of higher entropy, containing *two* systems in hostile equilibrium with each other. Imagine two gases, each in its own vessel. Let the stopcock between them be opened. There is no law which says that they must now diffuse into each other; it is not impossible that all the molecules of Gas A might hold themselves aloof from the molecules of Gas B, or that after eons of mixing they might reattain that original state, perhaps trading vessels for the sake of novelty – but the probabilities are against this, because out of all the billions of states which those gas molecules may come to, the unmixed state is but one. That is why no one has ever seen it happen. Gas A must almost certainly marry Gas B, then. If they can react, they will do so; if not, they will merely envelop each other, as the lines of black and white stones do in the game of Go, so that the board becomes a confusion of black besieged by white surounded by black. Writhe though they will, the two gases must now forever pillow their heads on each other's bosoms. – How cruel it would be if Gas A did not want to marry Gas B! With virginity and divorce almost infinitely unlikely, Gas A's happiness could not be observed through the most powerful ultramicroscope.

Suffice it to say, then, that The Zombie was but one of two synchronous persons, The Other being ideal and monatomic, a blondish daytime fellow who resisted diffusion. The Zombie did not care. He had already diffused. For him, The Other was himself. But The Other hated The Zombie. His molecules clung together in a set of rigid contractions, thinking that they enclosed The Zombie so that The

Zombie could not diffuse into him, but he did not see that The Zombie was a dark blue cloud which extended around and behind him, so that who enclosed whom was debatable. He *would not* be folded into The Zombie, so he resisted dreaminess, and his thoughts were honorably separate. But though he had made himself unaware of The Zombie, like a gas shrinking back into its vessel, The Zombie had followed and was aware of him. Thus in their relationship The Other was blind and deaf, while The Zombie knew everything.

This equilibrium might have persisted beyond calculation, had it not been that The Other came to know of the murders. In his room on Turk Street he hid his terror from himself, but The Zombie saw his terror and began leaving notes for him, chummy hateful notes which made it clear (not that he had doubted it) that the Park Killer was himself. He found them on scraps of paper beside his bed when he woke up. And so The Other began to clean up after The Zombie. It was in their mutual interest for him to clean up after him, for although what The Zombie did was not The Other's fault, there was no reason to believe that the police would not hear such a denial without smiles of proud sarcasm. The Other applied himself, therefore, to the discipline of defensive forensics (also known as "covering one's tracks"). Having studied the illustrated works of Spitz, Snyder, Weber and the great Adelson, he felt himself as well able to read a dead body as a field of clues. After each murder it was necessary to clean up after The Zombie, for a single careless fingerprint might compromise his freedom – not, however, that he could hope to obliterate every last niggling error; that was why his long-range goal was to end The Zombie's crimes. If possible, he would do so without exposing The Zombie's *self*, which was a garbage can tightly sealed – and inside, everything was going soft and bad, stinking and bursting ... If there was rotten stuff in *him*, that was as it must be, but let The Zombie be the receptacle! – In short, he was not The Zombie; yet he was responsible for him. – He himself was and always had been a hateless being! But his superiority rested lightly on him. He did not want to insist on it. Even The Zombie, he supposed, had a right to his own thoughts, although he did not want to know what they were. Then, too, he himself was not blameless. His association with The Zombie must be the result of some negligence of his own. So he reflected, blinking his eyes and picking at his long eyelashes. He would have to stalk his brother heart with inductive sadness.

But how was he to come to grips with The Zombie? The sheer

impossibility of it maddened him. Where The Zombie was, The Other could never be. – What could he do? . . . And yet he sometimes had intimations that fighting himself, exhausting though it was, might be successful if he only knew the right sort of suicide-judo to flip himself out of his head . . . But he did *not* know it. – Of course there were all kinds of secret answers and solutions and connections and advertisements in those immense machines of facts which we call newspapers. But these could be used hardly at all. Newspapers did not comment when losers died. They might be banks of circumstantially relevant facts, but their significance became doubtful without a scheme for applying them, so were they clues or occlusions? – The very indifference of the world did, however, give him one material advantage. The Other could go about his investigative business without much nervousness of calling attention to himself; no one is suspicious about an issue he cares nothing about.

The Examination

The Other once dreamed that he was conducting an autopsy, in some grand dark place, he did not know where, in whose walls were set narrow observation galleries, each with its own black window. Looking through those panes were serene blue-black faces. – Strange that he had become such a famous doctor! But perhaps it was only this case that was so important. – He was bending over the dead body; with his probe he was tracing the abdominal aorta, which normally bifurcates at the lower trunk to descend into the legs in separately equivalent iliacs, but this aorta was an abnormality, whose expired life he must recapitulate for the sake of the cyanotic spectators; it was a cold bloody snake that had writhed for years inside that body as it struggled with itself – for it would not separate from itself, nor did it want to stay with itself! One branch, the thin one, the feeble one (and when he dissected it he learned that it was marbled yellow and white with fat inside, like scrambled eggs), wanted to become an iliac and had attempted to escape from the other, first seeking its appointed place in the left thigh, then, encountering its punitive brother already there hissing and striking, it doubled backward in a no less vain ascent to the chest cavity in hopes of hiding behind the beet-moist lungs . . . but the other branch considered itself the *stem*, which would not abet the diffusion of any isolationist shoots (a decision quite within its power since it was the stronger, being firm like a fibrous root and reddish-purple and ringed with subclinically horrible muscle), so it muscled its way determinedly after the weak branch that craved separateness; and it bored through the grey heart, snaked round the lung, and struck at the weak branch. The weak branch did not try to escape. It let its brother corkscrew tightly around it, choking it, lacerating it; and the strong branch maddened itself and lashed its tail against that skinny grey tuber that had sought to reject its own flesh; over and over it beat the weak branch with low weighty thudding sounds until finally something burst open, and at once the main branch insinuated itself greedily in, snuffling up its brother's stringy insides until it had absorbed the weakling. There was only one aorta now. When The Other cut it open, he saw that it was full of blue powder.

A Moral Embolism

"You know who killed Lenny?" Ruby giggled in the TV room. "*I* know! It was the police. They took my picture once."

Old Cory raised a finger severely. "No, Ruby, it was natural causes. Somebody said that. I think it was Mr. Baumeister. But everybody's got their suspicions if they don't want to believe in natural causes."

"If it was natural causes how come his face got *half-dissolved?*" said Ruby ironically. "Don't tell me *that* wasn't the police."

"If something happened in that house during the night, I don't know," said Cory. "Amen, PERIOD. But everybody's got their suspicions. I did hear this *tappy-tappy-tap* of somebody with a cane going down the back stairs. But nobody's come out and said directly, this guy might have been *murdered* and all that. Nobody says nothing. Not even Mr. Baumeister. We're supposed to forget their names, and not be harping on it, you know. Ruby, you're always bringing it up. It's always *die, dying, death,* and nobody likes it, and I can't correct you, because you'll turn on me."

Sunny Days

In the bushes, Evangeline sat on Barlow's foam pad. She had a beautiful old face. Whatever her wild blue past was, it had left its wildness in her eyes and lips. She unscrewed the cap from a half-dead bottle of Night Train, looked at the bottle, sighed, and stared through the trees, with the meditative concentration of some wise woman of the mountains who knows the ways of the sun (death comes in the sleep of the sun) – but there was no oblique red ray between two cliffs to tell her things; there was only Haight Street. Evangeline raised her shoulders, drank, and lowered them slowly. Grimacing, she unzipped her parka and rubbed her stomach.

"What's the matter with *you?*" said Barlow.

"Nothing," said Evangeline. "Nothing but too much drinking. Nothing that another drink won't cure."

Hints and Promises

The Other's fugue states often came on at night, but not always. He never remembered what The Zombie had done or where he had been. When he came to himself, it was after sleep. The Other woke up in his own bed; The Zombie covered his tracks. Occasionally he had a memory of some bluish-grey dawn which he must have seen through eyes not his own; and one day he found that whenever he closed his eyes he saw an image of coldly glowing red beads trailing one another against dirty black velvet. It was a vision of automobile tail-lights on the night freeway.

The Woman who Laughed

The Zombie had a room in a residential hotel in the Tenderloin, next to a "health club," and on Sundays he sat in Boedekker Park and listened to the whores say, "Wherever *you* be going, *I* be going," and he watched the dark grey pigeons fixed like statues on the roof-ledge of the building adjoining Big Red's Bar-B-Que, while old women sat across from him, combing their hair for hours. Here he whiled away the day, tasting blood as he licked his decaying gums. (The Other did the same.) – "If you ain't got nothin' else, then '*bye*," he heard a whore say. Pigeons gurgled and chuckled and waddled fatly. A man in a black hat leaned against the lamppost smoking, and the smoke was thick like milk. A woman in a tan coat sat bent over her knees, scuffing her tennis shoes to keep the flies away, and then suddenly raising her greying head, more or less as a jack-in-the-box will pop abruptly out of its gay metal coffin. The Zombie saw that she was weeping. Beside her sat The Woman Who Laughed.

He had found the rooming house when he cane-tapped down Turk Street past The Woman Who Laughed, and a lady on crutches was purring, "I smell *fire*," at which The Zombie swiveled his head up on his long stem of neck to see smoke coming out of one of the barred windows of a black brick building that looked old and dirty and hope-less, and there was a sign saying ROOMS AVAILABLE – LOW MONTHLY RATES, and The Woman Who Laughed came rushing up and sniffed the smoke like an animal, snorting and laughing. The hallway smelled like dead fish and never stopped humming with slow fat flies. There was a security camera in the elevator, under which some knowing soul had scrawled **RAPE BITCHES ANYHOW.** The Zombie lived on the eighth floor, a special place for special people, where the hall lights were burned out and the carpet was charred. The door to his room bore hatchet marks. Inside was a dirty sink which he used as a urinal, a three-legged bed with a greasy mattress, and a window that looked out upon a brick wall. It was very dark and still in that room. The Zombie hid in his bed and looked at the brick wall through the window. Perhaps it was this lack of a view which had impelled him to go wandering in the Blue Yonder. (Oh! Had he lived in a mansion on Russian Hill, then

he never would have become The Zombie; is that what I am saying? –
Not at all; I do not want to investigate causes and hypothetical has-
beens; The Zombie was a *thing* without a cause.) – He did not go
out much when he was The Other, either; – for more or less the
same reasons that blood in a dead body soon becomes permanently
incoagulable, The Other had never been a good mixer. Sometimes The
Zombie woke up with a fever headache, the chills racing up and down
his fingers like the arpeggios of a concert pianist, and there was a
meaningless throbbing in the soft tissues of his buttocks. He lay rubbing
his neck and staring up at a brown stain on the ceiling. An ammoniac
smell sometimes came to his nostrils then, caustic and clean, as if he
had gotten chlorinated water in his nose or sustained a sharp blow to
the face. This meant that The Woman Who Laughed was sitting
outside on the front steps with her dress hiked up, tapping her toes on
the concrete and laughing.

She had a very round pimpled face. She might have been Indian, for
her nose was flattish and she had black bangs and high cheekbones.
She stank. He did not know where the clean smell came from. Her
black eyes were tolerantly knowing, mocking you without malice, as if
she had seen every sort of death and found it funny, but if you tried to
look into her eyes she would cover herself with her arm and shake with
laughter. If you tried to talk to her, she ran away. (She dreaded the
warning-pangs of encounters which might poison her laughter, as
Carolina had dreaded the defilement of her drinking cup, for we all
want to keep something clean, no matter if it is a lump of ice dwindling
in our hotly protective hands.) Once a tweed-suited radical woman
came marching and smiling down Turk Street, distributing leaflets, and
The Woman Who Laughed accepted one politely and read it and
started to laugh so hard that her fat legs quivered, and The Zombie
heard her laughter up on the eighth floor, so he went downstairs and
stared at her through the bars of his golden eyelashes and held a quarter
in front of her to draw her inside, and she kept laughing and reaching
for the quarter as she followed him step by step, dragging her two black
garbage bags behind her through the hallway, and he pulled her and
her bags into the elevator in a familiar way, with his hand on her
shoulder, and she laughingly suffered his touch because she *knew* him,
so he suffered himself to breathe her stench all the way to the eighth
floor, while the security camera emitted its death-rattle and a drop of
dirty water slunk down the elevator wall, until finally the doors opened

and he showed her the quarter again to impel her down the hall, so that then he could unlock his door, sweeping moldy underwear off his one chair and sitting her down on it as he lay back on his bed like a crocodile floating on the surface of some dirty brown river. There he watched her nod her head and spread her hands and wave at the air, and then as her shoulders would sag she'd shake her head and begin to laugh helplessly. She *knew* him! Her feculence aroused his disgust and anger to a degree bordering on sexual pleasure. (How could she smell so bad?) Sitting in his chair, stroking her trash bags tenderly, she unwrapped a lifesaver and ate it. She looked at the wrapping and laughed and laughed. When she laughed on Turk Street or in the brickwork park, passers-by smiled slyly behind their hands, thus proving that humor is indeed contagious, especially when joy-wrapped in idiocy and stench; so she contributed some cheer to the world, although of course it was not the reward of the world's scornful merriment which elicited her good deeds; it could not be, because she kept laughing in The Zombie's room even though The Zombie did not laugh or smile or do much of anything. (All he wanted was to know why she smelled so bad, and where the other *clean* smell came from.) What made her so happy? (She smelled like rotten wharves, like tuna-canning factories, like a mass grave on a hot afternoon.) Sometimes the sweet smell of lifesavers on her breath would overpower her odor temporarily, like a soothing cherry coughdrop to put a dead woman to bed. Her hair was washed and done up in a neat mare's-tail; who could have helped her? – She laughed and pointed at the window. For the first time, The Zombie saw something there other than the brick wall next door: – Pigeons were tapping at the window with their wings; they wanted to get in. The Zombie got up and ran his fingers through his hair and opened the squeaking groaning window (he had never done that before), and The Woman Who Laughed peeked over her shoulder to make sure that no one would rob her or hurt her and then took a slice of blue-moldy bread from one of her trash bags and threw it on the floor, and the pigeons rushed down into the room jostling each other in a cloud of feathery dust, dirty-black pigeons and dirty-grey pigeons, and they crowded on the floor around the bread waddling fatly with downcast heads and pecked until all the bread was gone; then they pecked at each other, and the Woman sat there with her black trash bags clutched to her, working her mouth as the pigeons ate, and the smell from her got worse and worse. It was a sweetish rotten smell. Laughing, she opened the other bag to show him.

Inside were dead pigeons, so decomposed now as to be squashed fans of feathers stuck together by slime, and flies buzzed out of the bag and landed on The Zombie's underwear and some of them whined and went greedily back inside that dark stinking bag and settled between the feathers and on the sharp black pigeon-heads and walked into the black pits where the pigeons' eyes used to be. Looking at this made the Woman very happy. Oh, how she laughed! (Was she a murderess or just a collector?) The tears rolled down her cheeks. She laughed and laughed and shook her head in smiling humorous disbelief at the ways of the world. Then she sat still for awhile, resting her pimpled cheek in her hands. Heat and dust streamed in through The Zombie's window.

Ruby's Last Night

Ruby loved going out to collect her blue summer-wages, sitting in doorways or in the grass of Buena Vista Park or Golden Gate Park to take the air while she giggled and chattered to strangers with the affected childishness of a retarded person. She had a sad but not unbeautiful face, which seemed grateful to be bathed in her loose grey hair. Her eyes were dark, wet and deep. Lines radiated downward from them, like the rays of a setting sun. Each eye was in its own lined pouch, and the area between her nose and her mouth was subdivided into thirds. Ruby's pores had grown bigger and redder over the years, but her head retained its graceful shape. – In time she became more wild, fearing that the police were getting ready to swoop on her and carry her back to Agnews because she had missed her scheduled shocks, so she began sleeping in the Park on clear nights, curled beneath the bamboo tree on the shore of the pond near where the Wrecking Crew kept their headquarters, not that she could grow close to them because they considered her monstrously old, and, besides, she rarely drank, so they had nothing in common. In the darkness she could hear them yell and scuffle with the rats. She came back to the Boarding Care Home sheepishly at sunrise, half-expecting to be punished, because Ruby never understood that no one cared where she slept. And no one cared one morning when she didn't come back. Not even Mr. Baumeister.

"That Ruby, she loves to take a powder," Cory said. "She has a *history* of it. On the other hand, I myself have rarely known her to refuse a good meal. *Amen*. Who might have known her? Anyone who might have bought her lunch. We had a delicious beef stroganoff today, with spaghetti, and bread, and big chunks of ravioli, and was she there? *No*. I myself had seconds. *Yum, yum!* That's why I myself consider her absence conclusive, PERIOD."

Gypsy was certain that she was still alive, because she owed him money, and, besides, he saw the name "Ruby" written on the side of a #43 Masonic bus. Brandi said she'd never heard of her. Noddy, who had not yet heard the news, stood grinning and letting his paunch breathe in the fresh air outside the iron gate. Beside him, Josiah sat looking into space.

Sunny Days

Scrawny, greasy, unwashed, tramps strode down the street with their dogs. They had long flowing beards. When they drank, their mouths sometimes opened in wonder. Their eyes shone. In the bushes they upended bottles of Gallo Lite Port – hurray! two in each mouth! – while their young assistants stuffed cigarettes between their own lips to show moral support, and time went on and the faces of the drunkards broke out in sores, until finally the blue sky yellowed over the silhouettes of cold black houses, and then it was night.

The Caress of Gloved Hands

The Other awoke at daybreak. Not a sound came from the street, where the night had been extinguished and the morning was not fair begun, so that the houses were still tall black blocks of ice unmelted, between which were canyons of darkness – none of which The Other could see. He opened his eyes sick at heart, being certain that something unclean had happened, and there was a note to him in his own handwriting: *Go clean it up   i did it in the dirt at the parks edge.* There was lead in his heart. Dirty light began to spread inside his room. He rose; he rubbed cold water on his eyes and stared through the window at the chilly greyness of the brick wall, but the note was still beside him, so he pulled his rubber gloves on contemptuously. Into his pocket he slipped a rectal thermometer. The razor blade was already there. He took a #7 Haight to the Park and strode through the grass with pale unblinking assurance. The morning sky was pinkish-blue. Ruby lay under the bamboo tree by the edge of the stagnant pond behind the benches where Evangeline and Mary and the Wrecking Crew sunned themselves. – Her body was in the dirt, as The Zombie had promised. She had been decapitated. Only an inch of her neck remained, like a fatty collar enclosing the sawn-off vertebral column. There was brown froth in her glottis. – As he stood there examining her, he was grateful for The Zombie's cunning, for he was half screened by the shrubs so that no one could see Ruby or determine what he was doing; if anything, they would assume that he was relieving himself. He had to make his investigation quickly and get out. If there were traces, they would be his; how could he explain that they were *not* his? He would have to trust The Zombie to have left no fingerprints.

A dog was sniffing at her. He kicked the animal away. A drain was running near him like an endless piss.

The Lay of the Land

The pond was roughly star-shaped. It was about ten meters at its widest point. Melancholy brown grass grew in patches around it, like hair. In most places, the bank caved down into muddy grass and so eased into the water like a cautious wader, but where Ruby's body lay it was steeper, being composed of waist-high rocks with sharp soapy cleavages. There was a dirty island in the middle of it; gum-wrappers and toilet paper had washed up there. A willow tree had grown on it, and let its long green leaf-streamers dangle down listlessly. Styrofoam hamburger cartons were very still in the brown water, the surface of which was just greasy enough to streak like a dirty windowpane onto which dead leaves had been glued. Sometimes the water was foul with detergent foam, but on the morning that he found Ruby (who lay quite naturally on her stomach, with her jacket thrown above her shoulders as if to protect her face from cold, but of course the jacket was stiff with blood) the water was simply brown, like shellac, and he could see the reflections of the trees in it. The reflection of the island willow was a darker dirtier brown silhouette between whose branches could be seen the shimmering blue-green rottenness of the Blue Yonder inside the pond. A rotten board listed in a green froth of algae. A yellow beech leaf floated. Upon the surface scuttered nervous water-striders. A dead stump still clung to the mucky bottom, caressed by decaying leaves. Occasionally children threw pennies into the pond for luck, and since there were not enough of them to make their salvage worthwhile the tramps had left them there to turn murky and rusty and uncaring of their own lost brightness, so that they no longer resembled the moon. Sick grey tadpoles swam across their faces. Few of these tadpoles ever lived to become frogs.

The crime had evidently taken place in the shadow of the curvy wall that led into the tunnel of phony stalactites (brown plaster on wire forms), which stank and was spooky even at high noon when the street people wandered through it to reach the soccer field by the playground where it was warm and sunny and they could sleep on the grass or on benches; at night the tunnel was especially dark, like the naked old trees that crowded the pond; they were the hue of the blacktop path that led from Evangeline and Mary's bench past the trash cans and along the far side of the pond to the stalactite tunnel.

The mud was impressed with footprints here, and it was clear that something heavy – Ruby's body – had been dragged from the spot to the bamboo tree, where the dirt was reddish and crumbly with blood. The grass was smeared with mud and spattered with dried blood. There was a great deal of blood in jelly-clots on the rocky bank, and the pond water there was pink.* In the water was that fleet of open hamburger cartons layered with leaves. One of these lay directly below the bloody rocks. The leaves inside it were blackened and brittle along the edges, as if they had been charred by something. At the bottom of the carton was a blackish precipitate. The world of the pond continued in its ways: – the leaves floated on the water, and an old spiderweb between two ferns remained triumphantly unbroken. The reflection of the sun shone very small and white in the blackish water, as if it were in trans-Plutonian space. A penny submerged near the bloody rocks was very very shiny.

In the earth were several round holes. These could also be found

* "The following variables tend to decrease the clotting time," says Department of the Army Technical Manual TM8-227-4, *Clinical Laboratory Procedure – Hematology* (December 5, 1973). "Rough handling of the blood specimen, presence of tissue fluids (traumatic venipuncture), frequent tilting of the tube, and unclean tubes."

accompanying a set of shoe-prints which approached the spot, proceeded to the water's edge, and then turned back onto the sidewalk. Evidently, when he was The Zombie he carried a cane. He recognized the shoe-prints because they were his own.

More Clues

Rigor mortis was complete. The elbows, knees and fingers showed no flexion when he manipulated them with his rubber-gloved hands. She must have been dead for six to twelve hours. – There were no abrasions on her hands, and no blood under her fingernails, which meant that she had not struggled; she would have died quickly, then, unless she was already unconscious first. If she had been stupor-drunk when The Zombie attacked her, she might not have been aware when he opened her arteries.

Her pants and sweatshirt were smeared with dirt. Her sweatshirt had worked itself up under her arms while she was dragged; The Zombie had pulled it back down, but carelessly. Her back and waist were abraded and muddy. The neckline of her sweatshirt was black with blood. In spots, however, the fabric had been dissolved into weak starchy strands.

The Continuum of Chill

According to Moritz, the number of hours elapsed since death can be computed by subtracting the rectal temperature from 98.6° Fahrenheit, and dividing the result by 1.5. The Simpson and Rhodes-Gordon-Turner studies suggest that the average decrease in temperature for a clothed body in a 60° climate is 1.5° to 2° per hour for the first twelve hours. – How servile the dead are, in conforming so readily to the coldness of the world! I pray that when I am dead, I shall attain some defiantly anomalous temperature and maintain it for the duration of my putrefaction, blazing as I rot, or crumbling into crystals of sky-blue ice! – He took the corpse's temperature. It was 86.4°. The Moritz equation yielded a time of death eight hours previous, or approximately eleven o'clock at night, when life was dark and moon-washed, so that pale trees could leap out at you like lions from a crouch. (He remembered being himself until about eight-thirty, when the dizziness of his usual change came over him.) – He had killed her at eleven, then. – The Simpson rule produced a similar result, assuming the lower loss figure of $1.5°$, which seemed sensible considering the obesity of the victim.

Blue Pathology

Why must we now go back inside The Zombie's head? – The most authoritative reply is given by J. Gordon and H. A. Shapiro in their tract *Forensic Medicine: A Guide to Principles.** – "It is an advantage," say these oracles, "to open the skull first because observations which depend on the sense of smell will be interfered with to a lesser extent by competing odours from the body cavities, their organs and their contents."† – Let us then proceed to smell The Zombie's thoughts.

Sunny Days

When The Zombie was little there was an abandoned warehouse down the street, and when he could escape from his stepfather he ducked into the window of this old unhappiness factory, which now manufactured those scarcely less valuable products, mildew and gloom; and here, crouching among the mummified corpses of birds, he streaked finger-wide windows in the softly dusted panes; and sometimes saw the tramps striding by, for the trainyard was near and it was trains which preserved tramps in their freedom, their high times and low times; as for the bums that The Zombie saw perfecting the art of the jellyfish-float in occasional doorways, these folks traveled distances no less bold for the stillness of their bodies: – into what blue holes they tumbled, through what blue skies they fell screaming, only one who has daily

---

* New York: Churchill Livingston, 1975, p. 49.

† However, Adelson has the following caveat (*op. cit.*, p. 84): "The cranial vault should not be opened when head injury is suspected until *after* the cardiovascular system has been decompressed by opening or removing the heart."

endured "the spins" can say – that despicable condition in which we can no longer hide from ourselves the whirling of the universe, a rotation of diabolical regularity so that there is no question of an uncontrolled tumble into the Yonder; rather, we have the sick knowledge of deliberate torture. – Oh, when you feel *that*, you must look for local points of steadiness. The cold wet curb that pillows your head may help, although you pray that it might become colder, to pierce its freezing needles through the back of your head; that might distract you from your spinning for a moment! – Odors, on the other hand, are persistently unhelpful. The smell of food is as revolting as that of sewage (for what is the first but the unfinished state of the second?) – Meanwhile, you continue to fall. You tumble steadily head over heels through a space of fixed blue darkness, not in the least comforted by the fact that the curb, and the doorway, and the black narrow street of grinning faces are all falling with you; you are all falling between the stars. – It is the nauseous *desolation* of this descent which bloats the vagabonds' faces.

Once on a blue noon, a man lay whimpering in the doorway of the warehouse, and The Zombie was curious, and opened the man's eye with two fingers. The drunk screamed; his eye was red and lusterless like heated iron; when The Zombie let go of the lids they slammed together so tightly as to deny the existence of a chink between them. – It was not so much the eye as the denial of the eye which perturbed The Zombie. That drunk had insisted on keeping his brain alone inside a dark padded skull-world, either because light was agony, or because there was something in his world which he did not want the World of the Sky to see, even through the translucently deceptive windows of his eyes. Of course it was not this latter, as drunks are shameless, but The Zombie did not know better. (Truly he was unclean; he did not know the mysteries of sunshine.)*

---

* The Blue Yonder had its own deities of cheer and wandering cheerlessness, for everyone believes in something. But the believed-in varies according to the believer, and among the losers could be counted three species. First and brightest was the Wrecking Crew, for the whole world was remote to them. If Haight Street had run ten thousand miles, with a liquor store at every block all the way to Tartary, they could have panhandled up and down it ten thousand times without finding a home. They had been face to face with the sun, and could no longer endure the mean life of the Insiders. – As the adventures of the tumbleweed surpass those of the mushroom, so the Wrecking Crew surpassed the Boarding Care Men in *their* careers – but even the latter did not consider themselves much "at home," being a random ragtag lot beset by each other's accidental presences – and that, I believe, is why Cory Smith did not incorporate all his

Forensic Anthropology

Browsing through garbage cans is a must for the serious investigator. In his mind, The Other constructed three categories of garbage, in order of increasing interest: (I) First there were the non-unique items, which could be subdivided into two types: the ubiquitous, of which cigarette butts furnish so thought-provoking an example, and the locale-specific, such as bag lunches in a schoolyard dumpster. The general characteristic of this category would best be described as *anonymity*. (II) Secondly came items which were odd and individual, but most likely of random origin with respect to the murder at hand. An example might be a book of matches from an out-of-state restaurant: – the matchbook would be possessed of obvious if minor distinction, like some tourist who had been to Africa, but there was no reason to believe that it would furnish any information about the crime. The essential quality of this category was *miscellany*. (III) Finally there were items which were both *unique* (and therefore traceable), and also *hypothetically specific* to the crime. If, for instance, he were to find a hacksaw blade with a reddish-brown stain, he might well have the instrument used in the decapitation. Items in this category would possess *potential essentiality*. They might help him find Ruby's head. – You must see by now, brother officers, that The Other was a fellow of earnest motivation!

---

powers to save Lenny. If *you* saw a vagabond dying in the street, you would do nothing – not for laziness, but for sheer want of information. You would not know that he was dying; you would guess him drunk. You would not know what to do with him. You would not know whether you would have to pay. – Grant this, and imagine that you are Cory Smith, and the dying vagabond is forced upon you as your roommate. Does this break the case? – No. – Still and all, Cory Smith *was* a mushroom. And, as tumbleweeds surpass mushrooms, so mushrooms lord it over algae, and such, of a surety, The Zombie was. – So accordingly could beliefs be graded. The Wrecking Crew believed in Smackwater Jack (about whom more later), who must be considered the king of the tumbleweeds, and old Cory Smith worshipped that darkly majestic toadstool, Mr. Baumeister, so it is no wonder that The Zombie cherished his own superstitions uniting blueness and yonder-ness, and what he believed in was scummy and rank like algae.

The Scavenger Hunt

There were four trash cans between the pond and the street, but he did not bother to look within their separate cylindrical darknesses. What, after all, would he have seen? Of course they would be crammed with interesting things, which he could fit into any one of a thousand mental mosaics to dazzle him like some gorgeous stained glass window which is, alas, translucent, for The Zombie would not have used *those* trash cans at all. They were too near the benches where tramps slept every night. The Zombie – benevolent fellow! – never cared to disturb anyone but his victims. Knowing this, The Other became almost scornful as he regarded the trash cans; they were not worthy of his effort. (But I myself wish that I could go through every trash can in the world, for the life-mosaics which can be puzzled together from them are TRUE, even if irrelevant to *my* life; what could be truer? How many people deceive their trash cans? And if garbage is irrelevant, isn't that because *I* have made it so? In every trash can lives The Zombie, the Wrecking Crew. They live in *my* trash; they are *my* Zombie; *my* Wrecking Crew. – But of course The Other had a most urgent purpose in his heart. His logic and his knowledge were like acid, etching the glass of his perceptions which he thought so transparent; he was building his church-windows like the rest of us, but he did not know it.)

On the far side of the pond, the first garbage can awaited him. He lifted its lid. Stench and darkness rushed up around him. – Oh, how it stank! The stench was like that of dead frogs. You rarely find the remains of theories in the trash. You find the ruins of lives. – As a boy, he (or perhaps it had been The Zombie) had caught some yellow leopard-frogs and dropped them into a jar of water. The lid was screwed on for the night; and the next morning unscrewed. What a milky stench of suffocated frogs! – Breathing through his mouth, The Other investigated the garbage can.*

His gloved hands encountered first a tight-packed newspaper-

---

* All of the artifacts described here were recovered by me from a trash can in Golden Gate Park on the morning of November 13, 1986. However, the inventory is abbreviated, so as not to strain your patience.

epidermis which, when grasped anteriorly and pulled firmly away, exposed a mesodermis of crushed cans destined for Categories I and II – garbage in, garbage out! The endodermis consisted, as is customary in such cases, of slime. It was now time to remove the internal organs – ordinarily a more delicate procedure, for with human cadavers the aim is to disturb the tissues as little as possible, but here, thank God, the entire organism was random, and might be considered only on the basis of its separate parts, most of which would be discarded disregarded, and a very few of which might be fitted into another mosaic of pieces, which might or might not be random ... The Other next discovered a used six-pack of Kirin beer, whose six glass necks persisted in glittering very dully, like Lenny Ezell's dead eyes, still wide open in his face (although one eye was burned black and one was white like the mold that films on dead fish-bellies; and blue crystals glittered between Lenny's eyelashes). But the beer-bottles were Category I; everything of interest had been drunk from them. – Abutting them, as if they had previously operated in conjunction with them in some unimaginable way, were a plastic flip-top spaghetti sauce container full of dirt, and a paper cup crumpled around an empty bottle of Kuyper Cherry Brandy. Below this assemblage, the next layer of filth (which The Other suspected might prove less pleasant, for it is with garbage as with life: the deeper, the dirtier) was temporarily occluded by thirteen cartons which had once held grape juice. – The Other squashed them in his fingers – *krrrch!*; the autopsy continued. – Next came a shampoo bottle, a paper towel infused with puke, and five Night Train empties all together (for Paul Raven, member *ex officio* of the Wrecking Crew, liked to throw away things in batches), plus one Southern Comfort hip flask, not to mention twenty-two clinking stinking bottles consecrated to Thunderbird and therefore to the lips of tramps, and the necks of these bottles were smeared with that cough-syrup-like stuff which Mary, Evangeline, Sal, Rich, Barlow, He-Wolf, Gypsy, Paul Raven, J.J., Sky Boy and the rest of the Wrecking Crew past and present had all craved, so that yellowjackets, craving it too, cakewalked round and round the bottlenecks; and the stupidest yellowjackets got trapped inside and buzzed and stuck to clots of tramp-phlegm and drowned in tramp-spittle. I am not sure whether the death of scavengers within this great dead garbage-organism demonstrates autolysis or simple putrefaction gone awry; I can be certain only that bottles do not decay as we do, for we become earth, whereas they become sand. – Peering down into the darkness, The Other removed these bottles two by two. They clanked like bone-chimes. The last pair were beaded with condensation. When he lifted them out, a puff of hot steam with the odor of decayed excrement made it clear to him that he had finally reached the primary body cavity. (Here was yet another anomaly, for whereas dead bodies lose heat, dead garbage often gains it through fermentation and spontaneous combustion. It is a wonderful world we live in, where the Moritz equation will not always apply.) This cavity was partially filled with some dark-colored exudate or bile which he did not trouble to analyze. From the liquid he brought up something soft and heavy wrapped in paper towels with a rubber band over it. When The Other unpackaged it he found the corpse of a pigeon with a broken neck. But the sad little corpse did not teach him anything, because The Woman Who Laughed had revealed her secret lust only to The Zombie, so he threw it down and dissected out the succeeding item, which was a Mr. Submarine bag proving (when incised posteriorly with his razor) to contain greasy wrapping paper accompanied by the matching empty Pepsi cup lid-pierced by its straw – for the garbage-organism is conceived not all at once, but organ by organ, and every organ is born dead (how strange it would have been for The Other to discover a healthy Mr. Submarine bag-organ containing viable food!) and in the stinking darkness beneath that were three partially squashed Budweiser cans, and a top-sealed Colonel Sanders receptacle for piping hot fryer chickens (now digested, evidently, for what was in there now was a honey-colored turd). – Below the turd was a blue plastic wrapper for the *New York Times*, a snotty kleenex with the hardened texture of peanut brittle, and a Continental Yogurt cup whose scrapings had separated and partially liquefied and attracted bean-shaped maggots, and an advertisement section of the *San Francisco Chronicle*, dated yesterday, and a *National Geographic* map showing Columbus's route to the New World; the map had been torn neatly in quarters, and there were many neatly torn scraps of paper bearing numbers, such as:

x	2450	x
x	x	x
400	750	1100
2800	3200	3100
1250	x	800

plus a bumper-shaped piece of black molded plastic, which might conceivably have existed in some reified space far beyond and superior to The Other's categories, so that if he had not discarded it he might have won the war against The Zombie; and there were unheard of quantities of used toilet paper which crackled when he ripped them away from the wall of the garbage can, a smelly black sock with a hole in it, a Double Rainbow ice cream cup stained with something pink and sticky in which ants lived as thickly as hairs on a fur coat (how that sight would have offended poor Carolina!), eight Quarter Pounder cartons, a broken mirror, an egg carton stubbed half-full of cigarette ashes, a bent coat hanger with a brown stain on it (this Category II object he set aside), an issue of *Analog Science Fiction* dated June 1984, a black plastic bag containing grass clippings, a broken plastic strap faithfully accompanied by its wire buckle, and a pair of spot-worn dishwashing gloves, which he set beside the coat hanger. At the very bottom of the trash can he saw a bouquet of wilted dandelions. They were glued there by dried slime.

So he had a coat hanger which might have blood on it, and a pair of gloves which The Zombie might have used to avoid leaving fingerprints.

The Witnesses

In the grass beside him, two men were lying, breathing like band-saws. One of the sleepers rolled onto his stomach, and the other got up and sat on a bench and asked what time it was and wandered off, and then the first one got up rubbing his head and wandered off, probably for free food since it was now the breakfast hour.

"You know what time it is?" said a man who looked ready to run away.

"Eight-thirty," The Other said.

"Thank you. You wouldn't need any doses, would you?"

"No, thanks."

"Okay," the man said smiling, loping out of sight as quickly as he could.

Laboratory Tests

The Other went home and scraped some of the brown stuff from the hanger into a glass. He kept a sack of forensic props under the bed. He had used them many times before. He added twenty millileters of glacial acetic acid (vinegar) and one millileter of three percent hydrogen peroxide, and then he shook the glass gently. The solution did not change color. If the brown crust had been blood, a blue-green color would have come almost immediately. So the coat hanger remained a Category II item.

The Other swirled the suspicious gloves in the glass, one by one. The solution became faintly blue-green. Heartened by this, he dusted the dishwashing gloves for fingerprints, slitting the latter along the outer wrist. He opened his hand lens. The prints on the gloves matched his own. He was quite pleased. He wrote out a note for himself: *Gloves are Category III.* But when he read it over, he saw that his hand had written: *Its easy   look in the baseball dumpster you asshole   in the garbage bag.*

The Merry-Go-Round

He went through the stalactite tunnel and walked through the playing field and then the children's playground, where horses and dragons, stags, zebras and giant geese went up and down on their poles while the carousel rotated slowly to a patriotic polka. The plastic mouths of camels were taut in perpetual snarls. The merry-go-round stopped; the mothers came to seat their children, some of whom sat very still with their arms around the necks of their steeds, while others kicked at the saddles and fidgeted; and the merry-go-round recommenced its merry-go-round, round and round, up and down, but almost riderless, as always; and the children looked for their mothers as they went by and the mothers waved, scrubbing the air in wide effortful motions so that their children would be sure to see them, and the music never stopped, so that although the animals struggled up and down on the poles that impaled them they could not free themselves. The melody was an aerosol can containing concentrated essence of Austro-Hungarian Empire. – He passed, and went down the hill to the baseball diamond and up the next rise and started going through the dumpster. He found Ruby's head in a garbage bag.

Ruby's New Face

Some of her hair had fallen forward over her, like the grey husk of a coconut. It was bloody and burnt. He parted it with misgivings. She had a new blue face! From the mouth down, her face was partially dissolved, soapy and wet and shiny. To give himself time to become accustomed to her, he decided to begin the examination with the top of her head. Her eyes were closed. He raised one lid, and saw an iris that was round, glassy, and as vacantly perfect as a grey dinner plate. It seemed to see everything without knowing anything. The light glinted on that blue-grey iris, and the black pupil conserved its moist roundness, being shiny and fragile, with the integrity of a jellyfish. – There was a hematoma on her left temple. It had a small dark center, perhaps an inch in diameter. When he made an incision with his razor blade, hardly any blood trickled out, proving that it was a genuine bruise, not some caprice of post-mortem livor. It was still purple, which meant that it had probably been administered very shortly before death, otherwise it would have journeyed through the rainbow spectrum peculiar to bruises: bluish-brown, greenish-brown, yellowish-brown, tan and finally yellow. – The cheeks were swollen, puffy and slimy with mucus. There was dried blood and vomit in her nose. The mouth was a ruined cave. It was black and soapy with necrotic tissue. Flesh had sloughed off inside the cheeks, and what remained of the lips was black and crackly, like the chin and the lower cheeks and the flesh below the nose. She might have vomited; it was difficult to say. Inside the mouth was a great quantity of black precipitate. The odor of it was quite unmistakeable: it was Drano. He extracted it with a gloved finger and broke it into clumps, hoping to find a few unactivated crystals of the caustic, but there were none; it was all black and coarse, like sand. Drano powder was blue, but this might well be a carrier or byproduct. It might have been Drano which had left the worn spots in The Zombie's gloves. (This explained *why* he was compelled to wear the rubber gloves; his hands would have been very near her mouth, the Drano, and the water. He would not have wanted to burn his hands, and most likely he also suffered from the bourgeois prejudice against leaving fingerprints.) – In the dumpster was a paper pie plate with dirt on it. He shook it as clean as he could and folded it around a quantity of the wet black grains. This he slipped into a plastic newspaper bag.

Forensic Odontology

There was also a set of false teeth in the trash bag. The dark mud on them told its own tale; they must have fallen into the pond. The Zombie would have sealed them into the bag out of precautionary tidiness.

The Funeral Director

He enshrouded what he had found back in the garbage bag and carried it away. Later he buried it at the bottom of another dumpster on the other side of the city. Several tramps had seen him, but none had thought anything of it. He had bent low so that no one could see what he had seen. No one cared, anyway. But as he peeled off his gloves and hid them inside an empty Pepsi can, a black man came running and crying with hoarse desperation, "Stop there, boy! I'll *slaughter* you! Go away, boy! Gonna kill you, Lone Ranger!" But he ran on past. In the distance, his voice sounded: "I'm never – gonna be – a *way!* a *way!* a *way!* They're gonna *slaughter* me!"

Another Eulogy

"Maybe I myself did hear screams," said old Cory Smith when he heard that Ruby was dead. "I think I was passing by the Park at that time. It sounded like her. Well, I myself wouldn't call them the kind of screams of someone who was just screaming for the fun of it. They were more like, *Ooh! Ohh! Please!* – That kind of thing."

Confirmation

The Other cut off a lock of his hair and put it in a glass of Drano powder. He added water slowly. He watched his hair slowly thinning in the cloudy blue liquid. Something was being taken out of it, as happened when dry spaghetti-rods were leaned against the inner edge of a saucepan of boiling water, and the spaghetti slowly lost its rigidity and sagged and slipped further and further until it was all in the water, and then it got limp and mushy so that diners could prey on it. Within three minutes, his hair had dissolved, leaving a foul brown liquid bursting with oily bubbles. (Drano combines with protein and fat to form soaps.) There was a black precipitate at the bottom.

Remembering the one bright penny he had seen in the pond, he dropped a tarnished cent into the glass and watched it take on a golden sheen.

The Zombie's Penny

Once when The Zombie was young he found two pennies, one tarnished and one shiny. He took them both and kept them, but the shiny penny he kept for The Other, and when he went inside the cabinet under the bathroom sink to see Blue Lady and became The Other, he put the shiny penny into his pocket. (The tarnished penny he soon lost track of.) Gradually he became convinced that The Other was indifferent to the shiny penny. Either it was not shiny enough, or else it was not significant in the pure shiny world of The Other, where carpets were clean and clothes were fresh and everything was shiny with white diamonds; whatever the reason, the shiny penny was insufficient. Then he was ashamed, and knew that he was bad. The Zombie lived in filth, because his soul was what he lived in. Knowing this, his stepfather beat him with the electric cord, which was striped like a king snake; and in the kitchen were big rats that scared him, and in the living room his stepfather sat drinking and waiting with closed eyes to get work, but since he never got work he was angry, and if The Zombie went out there to scrape food from one of the bowls that his stepfather had dropped on the floor then his stepfather might open his eyes and chase him and beat him with the electric cord. So it was best to stay inside the cabinet under the bathroom sink. When he pulled the door shut, the little cabinet was as dark and dusty as a vault. His world's roof, however, was the underside of the sink, which was white and bright like a porcelain flower. The stem of the flower was a silver elbow of pipe that vanished into the wall. It was a flower of cleanliness, much cleaner here than in the world outside the cabinet. (Next door, a man hanged himself in woman's clothes. His pale stately face bobbed against the window.) Sometimes steps came, and someone turned on the water, and there was a cold rushing sound inside the pipe, which made The Zombie think that something important was about to happen, but then there came a rusty squeak and the water stopped and the footsteps departed. So The Zombie would think that he must have been bad because nothing had happened after all. But every now and then the rushing began without footsteps, and it was musical and shrill. That meant that Blue Lady might come.* He strove to be someone else, someone good, and if Blue Lady was convinced by the pretense then she would come; he had that hope to warm him. – But although his selves were divided as unmistakeably as if by a nasal septum, it did not occur to him that either self was not *his* self. (The Other, of course, being the good self, did not want to own the bad self – and that was acceptable to The Zombie, because a front for his badness must disown it to be a front.) The Zombie's life was spent satisfying The Other, so that he could satisfy Blue Lady; and if this sounds peculiar, so is the idea of a man's spending his life to satisfy his penis; but some men do it. If Blue Lady was deceived into coming, then the pale glow of the sink-flower overhead began to color like a pre-dawn sky. There came a blue reflection of clouds on that silver pipe, and a shudder of color passed over the wall-tiles. The pipe shuddered; the underside of the sink became brighter and colder. Blue Lady's face was there, smiling down at him. Blue Lady had black hair and white teeth. Her face was blue. She wore a string of white pearls. Sometimes, it is true, her cold tears ran down the white flower even as she smiled, for the sink leaked, but even when she cried she made him happy, so that when he came

---

* In his footnote to "Al Aaraaf," Poe says: "I have often thought I could distinctly hear the sound of the darkness as it stole over the horizon."

out of the bathroom to get food, his stepfather, seeing his face, would beat him again with the electric cord. Sometimes The Zombie saw pennies on the sidewalk. They made him feel guilty and angry. He never knew whether to pick them up or to leave them, so he gathered them and threw them into the pond where he killed Ruby and watched them settle into dull gold spots at the bottom of the brown water . . .

A Relief to All

The morning Ruby's effects were taken away by police, everyone on the first floor turned their chairs toward the front door and sat with crossed arms, bowing their heads slowly, while the flies buzzed and were silent and buzzed and were silent, and the blinds shimmered like the scales of a dragon, and old Cory Smith sat down on his neat but grimy bed and stared at his writhing thumbs. He had a mouth like an "S" that had fallen over. His skin was like raspy grey tree-bark. Every time he turned his head to look at you, you could hear something snap like a rubber band inside his neck. He sat on the bed for a long time. He smiled and whistled like a rusty hinge. Then he went and leaned against his dresser, which contained the rest of what he owned, while his new roommate, trembling Noddy, peeked at him in the mirror. Noddy had lost his mind some time ago. He would not cash his social security checks because he thought the numbers written on them were a secret wicked code.

The Blue Yonder

One day The Zombie was careless and Blue Lady saw that he was The Zombie and not The Other as he had pretended. – Her eyes widened. "You've *tricked* me!" she said in her soft voice. Her face – which was the underside of his stepfather's sink – assumed a dingy, disappointed cast as she penetrated his badness. Then those pure white pearls which she had always worn around her neck began to darken. They burst. They were nothing but drops of dirty water. – "You've *tricked* me!" Blue Lady cried again. How she paled; how she wrinkled her mouth in rage!

– An evil change came over her face. The boy had never seen so much darkness *inside* a face before. And yet (except for her mouth) it was not a dark face of itself; it was dirty-white and dirty-grey. Her flesh swelled and corrupted; her cheeks puffed up until he could no longer see her eyes, and her face had become sharply triangular. The features lost much of their definition as they decayed, but the concentrated pallor of hatred remained, so she became a stinking IT who was as he was; that was why she must hate him. Teeth smiled at him from her awful black mouth. – "*You dirty, dirty* . . ." Blue Lady growled, and her voice was low as she squinted at him through her pale puffy slits of malice. There was such exulting vindictiveness in that face as he would not have thought possible (and later his victims saw the same in his face); there was such *pale, steady hatred* in her face . . . She had become freckled with stinking putrefaction. Her blue pallor, the whitish rolls of flesh where her eyes used to be, and above all her CROOKED BLACK MOUTH gave her features a restless malignity. Rotten strands of hair had fallen into the creases of her neck. He closed his eyes in horror, but even then he could see the ferocious shining of her face and that BLACK, BLACK MOUTH . . . What testimony might the BLACK MOUTH give? Then, too, it was the unquietness of that rotting face that terrified him – for if this were Blue Lady, and she had died, what right had she to that hideous restlessness? – He heard her jaws working in the darkness above him, like a dog's. – Then her mouth opened; her cold breath offended his nostrils; her white lips curled, and a frothy taffy-colored liquid began to dribble down on him. He could not move. It dropped upon his eyes; it filled his mouth and nostrils; it stuck to his face with icy viscousness. He had a feeling of desperate suffocation – and yet he could not move! – in his utmost exertions his fingers barely twitched; and now he saw the moon before his eyes, over which the icy lacquer was hardening; the moon whirled round and round, as though he were seeing it underwater from the vortex of some whirlpool; and then, as asphyxia finally overtook him, the moon fell in on him, with a sullen viscous splash of black water, and he saw its craters grinning like hungry mouths. One of them ate him . . . He was in the Blue Yonder . . .

. . . Around him, as far as he could see, was a plain of bluish-grey mud, through which he must toil. Sickly blue flowers spread their flabby petals. Their circumference was immense. At their centers were perfect round ponds of foulness overgrown with scum. – He began to trudge toward the horizon. He could hear nothing but the pulse in his ears, as if he were submerged in a transparent diving bell. Presently he realized that indeed he was underwater, at the bottom of some blue ocean whose darkness he had taken for light. The horizon was in reality only a small distance away. With his realization of the darkness, the darkness increased. He could barely see in front of him. He strode on through the dimness. Ahead was a monstrous wall, barnacled and corroded with fissures. He began to ascend it. He pulled himself up by grasping great stalactites of rust ... He was climbing a blue mountain now, and the sky was blue above him, and in it were blue clouds that clashed with a noise like striking brass. He was in a meadow, and the flowers were blue like gas flames; they were pure and delicate, unlike the gross sea-flowers. – Here in the Blue Yonder, fear was asleep and dread was almost dead, for the country was in custody of that diving-bell silence. It was night, and he was traversing a bluish-grey plain of sand which stretched on and on, rendered no less dreamily empty by the grey scrubby trees, whose branches had never known any leaves, so that the trees were like scattered wire skeletons. There was no wind. Nothing stirred. There was a cottony pressure in his ears. The ground was scattered with smooth bluish-grey pebbles. When he trod on them, they slowly took on a blue phosphorescence akin in brightness to the glow of rekindled embers, so that, looking back upon his path, he saw a line of unwinking blue lights, the farthest brighter than the nearest, so that the horizon was lit with blue fire. The moon was blue and white above his head. Occasionally he thought he saw bluish-grey horses running among the trees, but he was always deceived; they were only clouds.

The Other's Inferential Case

He was on the verge of understanding it now. He must have dragged Ruby through the darkness, tightly gripping her long grey hair, which did not (as he had feared) come off in his hands. He would have come up behind her, hit her on the temple with his weighted cane, and dragged her toward the pond. Why hadn't she heard him? Perhaps she was staring into the water, hypnotized by its black swirls as she had once been by electroshock phosphenes. There would have been moon-light rippling on the pond like shoddy gold-leaf, because it had been a clear night. The willowy tree on the island would have fanned its

branches in the chilly breeze, so that to The Zombie it appeared to be
a huge dark spider hunched in the middle of the water, spreading its
long legs and hunching, spreading and hunching, crawling nowhere like
the trapped water-striders; and there would have been light in lines and
pools on the water, and the night would have been cold, like the cold
black dirt on the edge of the pond. In the silence of that darkness it was
likely that old Ruby had heard him after all, but was paralyzed with
helplessness and hopelessness, as she had been taught to be on the
electroshock table; when she struggled they simply brought in more
nurses to hold her down. So now her will would have waned, eclipsed
by her terror. – The impressions of his shoes were neither closely
spaced nor far apart; The Zombie would have approached in an evenly
inconspicuous manner. He did not feign a limp. Here he would have
raised his cane; the cane-holes stopped five paces from the bench where
she had been sitting. Surely she would have turned her anxious eyes
just then; if so she would have seen the cane held high above her head.
Just before he hit her, she might or might not have cried out – most
likely not, in spite of what Cory Smith said; Cory Smith was an old liar.
He would have dragged her no farther than was required to pull her
face underwater, because he would not have wanted to wet his shoes.
For the moment, of course, he would have permitted her mouth to
breathe just above the surface, as he stood over her gloating. Probably
he would have made his accustomed hand-washing motions. Her hair
would have floated on the water like greyish seaweed. He would have
bent her head back so that her mouth fell open, wider, wider (and her
false teeth fell out and gleamed through the brown moonlit water that
was speckled with dead leaves), poured the Drano into her mouth,
packing it down her throat with the end of his cane (this point was
verified by the black precipitate found in the cane-holes accompanying
his footprints going away from the pond). Then he would have
submerged her face entirely so that water came into contact with the
Drano (and perhaps it was now rather than before that the teeth would
have fallen out of her black and bleeding mouth). He would have
cocked his ear and listened to that slow, hideous fizzing. He would have
felt the heat on his cheek and smelled the fumes rising from her mouth.
Her lips would have been encrusted with Drano. Some would have
spilled into the water. All this would have occurred in the safe foggy
darkness. It might have taken place within thirty seconds.

Now, how would he have equipped himself? He would have wanted his hands free, so most likely he carried the Drano in a satchel or pack which supplied ready access; the can would not have fit in his pocket, and a satchel would make him look more like the street people that he hunted. Yes, it would have been a satchel. He could almost remember buying a satchel, so he must have done it. After Ruby was dead (or, it was safer to say, after The Zombie considered the Drano to have done its work – she might still have been alive), he would have sawed off her head. Most likely he would have first admired the black ring of dissolved flesh under her chin. Her lips would have been black and glistening; they would have been spotted with brown burns. He would have smiled down at the greyish-white corrosions of her face while he cut into her neck. He would have set down the satchel near the water's edge, although there was no trace of it; he would have wanted to hide her head away immediately. It had to be admitted that getting rid of her head was a brilliant step. In one stroke, so to speak, it disposed of the incriminating bruise on her temple, which could easily be linked to his cane; of the telltale Drano, whose black precipitate granules still slobbered out of her gaping mouth like Hawaiian beach sand (and a brownish pulp of dissolved flesh oozed and oozed and oozed); of the most identifiable part of his victim. – Most likely he would have put the satchel above and behind him, to keep it from getting bloodied. He would have had a trash bag already opened. He would have put the head into the trash bag, sealed the bag and probably (knowing him) rinsed it in the pond. – More hand-washing. – Most likely he remembered her dentures after that, because they were tangled in the long grey hair of her head, which suggested that they had been added afterward. It would have been more efficient to scoop them up first, place them in the bag, and then decapitate her. Maybe he had been anxious to kill her as quickly as possible. (The teeth, by the way, were speckled with the black Drano precipitate. He was not certain whether they showed signs of corrosion or simply wear.)

He would have put the garbage bag into his satchel. He would have dragged the body under the bamboo tree, hastily straightened her clothing, and thrown her jacket over the dead shoulders. Then he would have run through the cave of phony stalactites . . .

The Blue Yonder

Now he was in a blue country, and far off was a city of blue houses. People walked the streets dressed in blue. Day came, a glowing blue day. Then followed a night cut from blue crystal. The night had a ceiling which could not be seen from the city, despite its yellow lights and blue-windowed cable-cars, but The Zombie knew well the way nights looked from a window: – the sashes always sliced the darkness into a block. Here he was, then, in this dense blue world like the world inside a glass paperweight.

At a door in a blue wall, Blue Lady was waiting for him. Her face was shiny and blue, shiny and white, shiny and transparent. There was a childlike air about her. – "Do you want to be dirty or clean?" she said.

"Clean," The Zombie said.

"And I was *puzzling* over you!" she laughed. "When all the time you only wanted to be clean! How impossible! Do you really expect to get on with people?"

The Zombie did not know what to say.

"You're not going to give in to me, are you?" said Blue Lady bitterly.

"What do you want me to do?" said The Zombie at last.

"If you really want to be clean, you're going to have to kiss me!" – and her china-blue face literally split itself into a grin as it puffed back into that loathsome Other who had frightened him with her *black crooked mouth;* he could hear her tongue rasping and rasping inside that putrefied head, like some furry rodent rustling among dead leaves ... He would not kiss her, and she knew that he would not kiss her, so she turned away from him and he never saw her again.

Vectors of the Crime

The Zombie would have made his approach from Haight Street, where the roof-stripes of McDonald's and the window lights of Cala Foods glowed very white and bright, and the silhouettes of tramps on the street-steps were tall and dark against the streetlights, and from the park benches came the frog-croak night-noises of burping and snoring, and each tree cast a long thick-fingered shadow across the blacktop, and when cars drove by the streetside boundary of the Park was illuminated temporarily into a weary bright grey waste-plain; and there were stars feebly winking, and the last tramps clinked their nickels together to buy their last fifth of Night Train, and then the voices ceased. No doubt The Zombie would have been waiting for this. He would be sitting in front of a beer in the Nightbreak or Murio's Trophy Room, counting the time until it got quiet and the tramps slid their extra sweatshirts down over their shoulders and huddled together for the night. Maybe he would have eaten some stale sweet squishy candy bar for energy before setting off into the darkness (but where had he *come* from?).

As he came down the blacktop, The Zombie would have heard the sound of water before he saw that bowl of tree-crowded darkness. Seeing the first bench with clothes spread out on it to dry (so we may assume, for the clothes were there every night), he would have passed it up out of fear of someone's unwelcome return. He would have walked by the first trash can, and then the next trash can, and someone in fluorescent white sneakers sleeping uneasily on the next bench, his head on his knees. Cars went by. The Zombie moved silently. He would not have wanted to disturb this sleeper (whose presence is known without doubt, because he always slept there); that was the reason The Zombie would not have retraced his steps a few minutes later, when he had completed his business and needed a trash can in which to deposit that trash bag with its cannonball-shaped contents; as we know, he used the trash can further into the Park.

Ruby, then, as we know, was sitting alone on the rocks. How much taller the pond-trees seemed at night! The Zombie came down into the bowl, so that now the Park was a glowing rim behind him, surmounted by black bench-silhouettes, and the willow on the island hung its head so that he could not see the stalactite tunnel that he was going to walk through. The water pattered and pattered and was very black. The reflections of cars would have shed light across it in red and white speeding ovals. The water would have looked deeper and darker at night, but no less dirty. Most likely The Zombie would have used the trees for concealment, treading on grass in the soft-soled shoes shown by his footprints; he would have sneaked over the narrow dark lagoons and turned right to approach Ruby in a counter-clockwise direction (again, as his footprints demonstrated), and when he hit her the sounds would not have carried because the water kept running and the cars kept passing and the public shelter was at least two hundred yards away.

Search for the Lair

Where would he have gone then? He would have retraced his steps, and he would not have gone left, because there was a police station there, so unless he had wanted to go deeper into the Park for some reason he would have turned right and emerged from the trees at the #5 Fulton bus stop. The #5 ran east and west. He would not have ridden to the ocean with its failing possibilities and its conspicuousness (it was the End of the Line). – It was, of course, possible that he had an apartment in the neighborhood, but not likely since that would have cost too much. – So most likely he caught a #5 or a #38 Geary or some such bus going in the opposite direction, to some less fastidious quarter, such as the Haight, the Tenderloin, the Fillmore, the Mission, or the Potrero. It would not be where The Other lived, because The Zombie had to put away his tools. The Other had searched his hotel room, but there was no cane, no satchel, no Drano can hidden under a pile of dirty clothes. – Where, then? Maybe he could lure himself with something that belonged to him, some fetish or tool or dangerous bit of evidence. Something blue. But what? – Maybe he could provoke The Zombie into giving himself away somehow. Maybe he could lure him with a demonstration of some powerful new industrial-strength cleanser which would make Drano look like nothing. (But of course that was why The Zombie loved Drano – because it was Nothing.)

By Extension

So The Zombie would have loved Drano and made it into his signature on account of its coarse heavy crystals glittering in the sheen of topaz, yes! – that pure blue color, like tropical blue oceans, an aquamarine color, the hue of the Blue Yonder where few people went and none came back, the blue of poisonous salts and stars' hearts, the blue of sea-lights, the blue of sky, sky, sky, the blue of heaven. We know this with predictive certainty, with Carnapian logic. We know this because Drano is blue, and blue is ever so clean . . .

Ode to Drano

ALL-PURPOSE DRAIN-OPENER
Chews thru
Grease, Food & Hair . . .
as no liquid can.*

The Wrecking Crew

Or else their cooings came from bays of trees.
Like a contented wind, or gentle shocks
Of falling water. This and all of these
Were tunèd to one key and made their harmonies.

Hopkins, fragment (1864)†

The Wrecking Crew hid from the wind, wrapped in dirty blankets and dirty coats and dirty foam pads. They had hoarse voices. – "Evangeline, gimme a cigarette!" said He-Wolf. – "Ease up on that," goes old Evangeline, with her round red face and grey hair bobbing angrily like a fishing-float in a stream. – "What time is it?" said Rich. "Twelve o'clock?" – "'Bout twenty after one," said Evangeline. "I gotta babysit everything." – They grinned and chuckled like frogs, sitting smoking behind the wall of trees. It was another world back here of slimy leaves and orange peels and trees and flowers and dirt. (Through the chinks in the trees you could see the beginning of Haight Street and people walking on the sidewalks and shiny cars turning into the McDonald's parking lot.) It was a child's dream of running away from home and

---

* This message was copied from the side of a Drano container.
† Revised fourth edition of W. H. Gardner and N. H. MacKenzie (New York: Oxford University Press, 1970). The fragment I quote appears as item number 98(a)(ii), p. 134.

living in the summer woods. But there were no woods left. When I was ten they were still building houses on Rayton Road, which was a dirt road with dirt driveways like gangplanks to green lots where the new houses were going up, and if you went behind these houses the green woods were still full of mushrooms and porcupines, and you could keep going up the hill into the forever woods where it got greener and greener and after a dozen miles you got to Moose Mountain, and beyond that was the Blue Yonder. But those woods aren't there anymore. – The trees in Golden Gate Park were merely planted park trees; and as it would have been wasteful and dangerous to make the Park into a wilderness the Tree Department planted only a screen of trees so that city people could possess soothing if spurious greenness; and a bulldozer had been doing something in there, too. The Wrecking Crew lived about fifty yards from the bulldozer pit. When the wind blew, they hid their noses in their dirty sleeping bags.

"You have to fight every day to survive," Rich explained to The Zombie.

"On a *national* basis," mumbled skinny old Paul Raven. "It's been on an *experimental* basis in Michigan for five years. It doesn't deter me from picking up litter at all. Hell, I should have gotten started earlier." He saw two empty bottles on the ground and bore them slowly through the trees to the real world, where there was a trash can by the bus shelter. He wore a baseball cap and an army vest. He usually slept by the church. His dreams were more fluid when he slept outside. He never had nightmares when he slept outside.

"You have to panhandle to get something to eat around this place," said Rich to The Zombie, "'cause ordinarily you wake up too late to go for free food 'cause you drank the night before 'cause you panhandled. You also have to watch for these murderers and murderesses, 'cause last night I thought somebody was strangling my best friend, but it was a bad mistake 'cause he was only huggin' her. This idiot over here, he was goin' to try to pull a bar number on her."

They drank red liquid out of a Night Train bottle. Hearing the sweet gurgles, a vastly bearded fellow licked his lips and woke up. The first thing he saw when he stuck his face out of the sleeping bag was Evangeline glaring at him.

"Bitch!" he yelled.

"Yeah, fuck you, too, you bastard!" said Evangeline spryly.

"Fuck you, too, bitch!"

"I'm only a bitch 'cause you didn't get none last night."

"I don't get no pussy; I don't get nothing."

Evangeline shook her head. "Go back to sleep, Barlow."

Barlow sat up, his face copper-red. His curly beard was reddish-brown. He was missing teeth. His hands were swollen, and his eyes shone with a golden light that partook of sunlit distance. He leaned across and kissed the back of Evangeline's neck. "This stupid bitch bit me on the side of the head, slam-dancing," he said.

'And I got a fluffed-up finger outta the deal, tryin' to slam-dance *him*," said Rich. "Tripped over the log. Sure looked like you was chokin' her to death."

"I wouldn't choke her for the world," sighed Barlow in his tenderest croak. "Fucking bitch." He stroked her hair and picked the bugs out.

Evangeline looked crabbily down at her lap, clutching her cigarette and her Night Train bottle. Her face was pinkish-gold. "I'm not sayin' I lost respect for you as a friend or anything," she said, "but you don't know me."

'You don't know *me*," Barlow said. "You try my patience."

'Works both ways," retorted Evangeline.

"But I have a feelin' someday somethin' will break," said Rich to himself. He had long blond hair and gap-teeth as yellow as kernels of buttered corn. He wore Barlow's straw cowboy hat and a dirty jean jacket. There were blackish-purple scabs on his cheeks. "It'll be either for the better or the worse," he said. "I'm a pretty positive thinker myself. Might be a hole in the ground, might be a nice house up on the hill." – He took a swig of Night Train. – "This bottle might last forever, might last one more minute."

"Shut the fuck up with your dumb shit," said He-Wolf.

"You have the skinheads, you have the punk rockers, you have the hippies, the tramps, the bums and hoboes, and you have the rich," explained Rich to The Zombie, who stood smiling and screwing the tip of his cane deeper and deeper into the dirt. Rich thought that The Zombie wanted to situate the tramps in the world-political situation, when actually The Zombie wanted only to know what everyone's heart's desire was. (If most people knew what they really wished for, they wouldn't believe it.) Obligingly, The Zombie opened his black book of death, in which he recorded first names and last wishes. – "On the streets it's self-*survival*-ness," continued Rich. "But there *is* such a thing as a *family*, and it's called THE WRECKING CREW. Some days are *hard*, some days are *easy*, but one of these days it's all gonna be *queasy*. 'Cause, we all gotta fade away someday. By *ourselves*. Signed, RICHARD RAYMOND TISDALE."

"Oh, gimme a drink," said He-Wolf in disgust.

"It's not your turn," said Evangeline. "It's *my* fuckin' bottle."

"I can't even get a drink," said He-Wolf. He lay there and stank.

"Tell your story," said Evangeline, her arms folded. "Don't drink my bottle."

"You gonna give me a drink or what? This is pretty fuckin' stupid."

Evangeline gave him the bottle.

"Now, wait a minute, wait a minute," said Rich. "Gim*me* a drink."

"Naw," said He-Wolf. "I'm gonna give it to her." He pointed at old roundfaced Sal, who sat crying softly with her back to the rest.

"Don't give it to *her*," said Rich. "She's in outer space."

He-Wolf crooked his finger at The Zombie. "You know, I don't like to sit up so much," he said. "Sit down, sit down." When The Zombie was within his reach, he snatched The Zombie's black book of death and tried to read it, smearing it with dirt from his black smelly hands. (As I look at it now I see the black smudges.) "Kin you read what you write?" he said.

"Yes," The Zombie replied, rubbing his hands together softly. "I can read what I write."

"I said, kin you read what you write?"

"Yes, I can read what I write."

"Oh, you dumb shit," sighed He-Wolf. He lit up a cigarette.

"Save me shorts on that," said Rich, watching the burning butt.

"You're not even worth as much as a slug," He-Wolf said.

"Oh, he's all right, He-Wolf," said Rich.

"Tell your story," said Evangeline in her dirty orange parka. "He's here to listen to stories."

"Did you say you could read what you wrote?" said He-Wolf uncertainly.

"I can read it pretty well."

The True and Complete History of Smackwater Jack

"I'll tell you about the STP Family," said He-Wolf at last. He lay in his blankets like a rotting turd overgrown with black matted moss, and rarely moved because he had lost a leg trying to hop a freight. His eyes were swollen and yellowish-black. "Three brothers came out of 'Nam with it. One of 'em came out of New York. Two of 'em are dead. Only one's left alive. That's Mad Dog."

Young Wendy came running up with a piece of paper. "Hey, my Grandma died and they been trying to find me. I guess she left me a lot of money."

"Bishop Major," said Barlow, "that was the original STP Family. Bishop *M*. Major. Only one left. I bet I can tell where Bishop's buried at, 'cause he's buried in Boulder, Colorado. People that started it out, they got out of 'Nam. They fell in love with each other, and they started a family, and they migrated to Boulder, Colorado."

"And, say, sixteen years later, now we're in a recession," said Rich, smoking earnestly. "And Smackwater Jack, he's dead."

He-Wolf started and jerked and looked around. "Smackwater Jack, he's *dead*. Don't talk about the dead. Please. Come on, I don't want to talk about the dead."

"He died in Boulder, Colorado," said Rich.

"Don't talk about Smackwater Jack," said He-Wolf, seeing the Angel of Death. "Just don't talk about Smackwater Jack. There was this one chick, 'cause she was tripping, for a long time ago, I was He-Wolf and she was She-Wolf, and she was my old lady. I *was* He-Wolf. With Smackwater Jack. In Boulder. Yeah, that was Smackwater Jack. – No, he's DEAD!" – He-Wolf's eyes opened wide in horror. "He's *DEAD*."

"Yeah, he died on a bandshell," said Rich, the cheery pitiless voice of history. "He choked to death in his own puke. It was around October. Boulder, Colorado, 1982."

"Hey, Rich, you find my hat?" said Barlow, beginning to prepare himself for the day.

"Naw, I'm just wearin' it. It don't have bugs in it, does it?"

"You'll find out," Barlow chuckled.

"Run the jug, slug!" yelled He-Wolf. They passed him the bottle and he finished it and let it fall in front of his face. Old Paul Raven went and threw it in the garbage. – "Name's Raven, Paul," he said softly. "I like to think I look like Eisenhower. For *security*. Spiritual strength. *Security*."

"I gotta watch my hands," said Barlow, who had a slimy handshake indeed, as The Zombie had learned to his horror. "Don't wanna get them staphs on 'em again." – Evangeline took his hand in hers and stroked it. "So it's swelling up there, too?" she said. – "You know," said Barlow, "I don't even fuckin' *care*." – He leaned against the blue air, glaring down at the dirt he sat in, while Evangeline in her parka shook her head and had another drink. "Come on, snap out of it!" she said kindly, but Barlow would not hear her, and his headband slipped slowly down over his eyes.

"And that's how Smackwater Jack died," said Rich with triumphant finality.

"No," said Wendy. "He froze to death. On a picnic table."

"You knew Smackwater Jack?" said He-Wolf sharply.

"I never knew him, but I read about him in the paper," said Wendy.

"Now, what he did, he choked to death in his own puke," said Rich, with the persistence of a snail clinging endlessly to some cold wall.

"What do you mean?" said He-Wolf. "He fucking *froze* to death."

"Now, that's true, too," said Rich agreeably. "But there was barf on the side of him."

Still Another Eulogy

"So what *about* Smackwater Jack?" said He-Wolf. "Tell me one good thing about him."

"He was a GOOD MAN," said Rich, solemnly taking off his hat. "He was a bouncer."

"He was no bouncer!" yelled He-Wolf.

"I used to drink with him," said Rich.

"You used to *drink* with him; *big* whoopee. Tell me one good thing. One good thing he did for you. Anybody here say *anything* about Smackwater Jack?"

"Well," said everybody, "I never met him."

"He gave me forty cents one time," said He-Wolf. A tear trembled at the bottom of his eye. "He said to me, 'Hey, He-Wolf, where ya goin'?'"

"Hey," said Evangeline. "I wish I coulda met Smackwater Jack. That's one man I wish I coulda known."

"They used to have those auctions there, too," said Rich. "Ten speed bicycles."

"Smackwater Jack's DEAD," said He-Wolf. "We're all gonna rot. It was real nice till the FBI came. We was havin' a real bunch of gloms. FBI came, said, 'FBI!' – We said, 'STP!'"

Their Happy Rest

From the edge of the Park their silhouettes could be seen behind a bench, through a hole in the trees to their jungle world. In the summertime The Other sometimes saw Barlow sleeping on a hot brown patch of shaved grass, his shoulders steaming in the sun – but always behind a bush or a hedge. On a bench by the bus stop, a fat girl in a purple sweatshirt sat feeding the pigeons. She laughed and laughed. On a bench beside her was piled a bunch of knees and elbows belonging to Barlow. Life for this perpetually sleeping man was essentially a series of disturbances.

Sometimes various members of the Wrecking Crew waited out the day in their back yard, which was Buena Vista Park; and the pigeons rose into the air and landed in their own time; and from behind every rise the tramps could watch the fluffy up-springing of dogs' tails; and the dogs sat and panted and raised their ears and kissed each other; and Rich reclined on a bench, one leg on the bench and one on the ground, ready to kick anyone who might grab at his paper bag of liquor beneath the bench; and the orange buses went by, darkened inside by the silhouettes of standing passengers, while Rich's pal lay flat on the bench, his head on Rich's boot, and one arm, one leg hanging down; and another bus went by, and Rich pulled his foot away from his friend and tied his bootlaces very carefully, taking ten minutes to do it, and then he tucked the bottle under his friend's leg, and he walked away down Haight Street, and after awhile his friend raised an arm, a leg, and stretched out queasily on the bench, and the birds took wing again, and the sun came out, and another bus went by, and Rich returned with another paper bag; and he had a smoke with the black bum on the next bench and then disappeared, while the drunken man slept weightily, facing down toward the center of the earth where in the course of eternity his atoms might well make their way. – A dog trotted by. – A dandelion blew. – The afternoon was pretty; the Blue Yonder was here; the drunk was in the thick of it.

A fly on a flower crawled from petal to petal, tracing the perimeter of every edge in its careful pursuit of nectar. Meanwhile, no one went in or out of the Christian Science Church across the street, and bus #5263 stopped at the corner, but no one got on or off.

People walked along Haight Street. It seemed that they were moving very quickly and surely. No doubt their leaders were proceeding to and from the Financial District, which could be seen beyond the tennis courts and past the low cubes of the Western Addition, on the horizon where the Transamerica Pyramid, the Bank of America building, the purple towers and white towers with their columns of windows as regularly spaced as the holes on punchcards rose above the Bay, above the blue hills across the Bay, so far away that the hurrying cars could not be seen, and meanwhile the tennis racquets struck every five to ten seconds.

When Rich's friend had slept forever, he sat up. He put on his cap, he smoked, and he spat. Then he smoked some more. Surveying the world and reasoning upon it, he lay down and went back to sleep. After awhile he got up, scratched his ass, and pissed in a wide white waggly stream. He pissed forever. Then he, too, started back for home. It was late afternoon. His dog jumped up and licked his hand. The pigeons flew again, in a compact mass whose grey wings were like the faces and vertices of a moving sky-crystal.

The Death-Pond

Everything was aberrant at midnight when The Zombie came forth from the rooming house; the yellow-blue points of the moon had strained and strained to embrace each other and bitterly dissolve each other into a gooey orb like necrotic flesh so that the moon's lonely extremities would be taken into one putrescent ball of self. The lights were off, except for the supermarket lights which glowed all night like candles in skulls. What speculations the ants made within the cheesy porous rottenness of what we mistakenly call "the solid earth" will never be known, because the ants were quiet as the trees were quiet, and the leaves did not dare to rustle in that moist sacred time of midnight, and the tramps did not snore, holding their unconscious breaths in sleeping suspense because they were having nightmares about their murdered comrades walking stiffly back to them from wine-soaked graves, their faces black and horribly oozy from the Drano powder, which blew away from their carcasses glowing like blue star-crystals, falling from between their crackly fingers, falling out of their sad blind eyes, some of which were burned black and some of which were burned white, and the dead faces had no ears because those had also been dissolved, and the dead open mouths were black inside, and the dead heads had no hair, just black charred continents on their pinkish-black skull-globes which zoomed in closer and closer as the zombies came closer and closer and the very tramps who had loved them when they were alive now whimpered in their sleep, hoping they would not come any closer although all the dead ones wanted was to be loved so that they would forget how much they were burning and hurting and turning into slimy black soap-lumps, and they wanted to hug their friends one more time before tumbling back into their smoldering graves, although of course that embrace would smear Drano on the living tramps and sear their flesh and make them scream and burn and burn as it destroyed their faces. Whether or not The Zombie was aware of what they were dreaming is another unknown, but if he had been he would have felt pleased. He entered the Park and passed under the greenish-black trees that guarded his pond, and looked up at the bluish-black sky where the bluish-white stars flickered like dead little eyes, and water ran and ran with lacrimous viscosity into the pond. In that ugly pool was the same poisoned oblivion that a bottle of Thunderbird was drunk for. Sometimes The Zombie didn't kill any tramps. Sometimes he just poured Drano into that stinking water and smelled that smell of cleanliness (and the fish and tadpoles died), and the water almost boiled and he could feel the heat of it, and then he stood slowly combing his hair in the moonlight, as the grains of black precipitate fell to the mucky bottom like grains of shot.*

* The Wrecking Crew never slept near the pond, because they were afraid that

Concerning the Next World

Two old men were leaning against a newspaper machine. – "Well," said the one in the black cowboy hat, "I know wherever I'm going, it's gonna be better than this. Goddamnit."

The Dance of Death

With their long loose hair and long loose clothes, the Wrecking Crew were one with the medieval men in Holbein's "Dance of Death" (Lyons, 1538), who knelt to the Cardinal amidst tall flowering grapes, smiling like Rich; and the sky was clear, and there were leaves on their shabby coats, and Death came and stood at the Cardinal's side and pulled off his hat with bony fingers, while the Wrecking Crew continued to exist down in the wet grass, indifferent to the comings and goings of the great, as they were to the comings and goings of the #7 Haight bus; but when later Death came for *them* on a windy rainy day they shook their fat heads and cried, and Death pranced and grabbed the blankets in which they had feebly wrapped themselves, and led them gleefully into Hell; of course The Zombie was not gleeful by nature, but there was often a gleefulness of *circumstances*, and a gleeful mocking mystery to what had happened, as in the sad but indubitably true history of Smackwater Jack; so that the nature of Death was conserved; and the long lean tramps on Haight Street got caught, too, and they opened their mouths wide and turned to run after their growling dogs, but Death choked them by the collar and they fell, and their teeth broke against the hard cold sidewalk, and blood came from their mouths; but Cory Smith merely bowed his head, praying that Death would finally strike him on the neck, *Amen*, PERIOD.

Some people go halfway around the world to find their graves; others

---

they might roll down the bank and into the cold filthy water to get *drownded*. "Anyhow," said Evangeline, "it's not a pond, it's a sewage system." – "For who?" cracked Barlow, and they all laughed.

wander in the waste places and along the highways of their own nation; and the lazy, easygoing ones dodder wherever they are, cognizant that in due course their graves will open up before their feet.

"The Wrecking Crew?" a guy said. "The Wrecked-Up Crew, *I* call them."

Why They Didn't Have Jobs

The Job Track Workshop in the Tenderloin has kindly compiled a list of reasons why people are not hired. I quote from the appropriate ones:

1. POOR PERSONAL APPEARANCE.
4. LACK OF PLANNING FOR CAREER, NO PURPOSE AND NO GOALS.
5. LACK OF INTEREST AND ENTHUSIASM . . .
13. NO INTEREST IN COMPANY . . .
18. FAILED TO EXPRESS APPRECIATION FOR THE INTER-VIEWER'S TIME.
19. INDEFINITE RESPONSE TO QUESTIONS POSED BY EMPLOYER . . .

The Next Act

"I think He-Wolf's gone up to Seattle," said Rich, and that may have been true. "He said he had an itch to get out of here." That was why nobody ever saw him again.

Where the Dead Losers Went

The cemetery was on a hill. The tombstones were whitish-blue. At sunset, orange bars of light came across the sky. If you were intoxicated by the Blue Yonder and did not see how things were, or if you had been lost in the Blue Yonder for a long time and your eyes were not as good as they used to be, you thought that the place was just another park where you could panhandle and play cards and drink yourself to sleep, but when the right moment came, the gravestones levered themselves out of place and the restless drunks rolled into their ordained pits, and then the stones dropped back into place upon the living men who cried as they saw the black shape fall, fitting perfectly so that it would block out the light . . . Against the weight and hardness of those stones, who could prevail?

The next morning the cemetery looked like a park again. The fog was blue early in the morning. Every hill the streetcar went over had tracks that vanished in the fog. In the long ribbed streetcar tunnels, the light at the end was not a yellow bead or a white bead, but a blue bead. Most of the passengers slumped palely. Only the executives, who had definite places to go, stood jingling their keys, legs braced, as they avidly read *The Last of the Breed.*

The Sixth Street Men

One night two homeless drunks with bad breath stood talking in an alley, and a new friend was with them.

"We're comin' out of the Service," said Code Six sadly, "we're not trained for anything but KILLIN' . . ."

"And RECONNAISSANCE . . ." said the Chief.

"And SURVIVAL . . ."

"*Survival!* What *good's* survival?" sneered Code Six. He thought. "Well, survival does do you good out here. I will give you that."

"*Thank* you," said the Chief sarcastically.

"You survive, like him an' I down here, for EIGHT YEARS, y'know!" cried Code Six exultantly, but then he sighed and admitted, "which ain't really a real hell of a claim to fame. Now, you know that as well as I do. It's something like being the Captain of the *Titanic*."

"Yes, it was great while it lasted," their friend said – with what meaning they could not at that time appreciate.

"And they said the boat wouldn't sink!" said the Chief. "But people are sinking."

"That's 'cause everything we learn in the Service is *fucked* out here!"

"It sucks," said the Chief. "You know why? We have no weapons."

"So what would you do if someone tried to kill you?" The Zombie said, opening his black book of death.

"Plenty of things," the Chief said expansively. "Look here. You know what we do? I look at him, and all I have to do is move my shoulder like this. I don't know who trained him, but all he has to do is see my shoulder, and that tells him I'm in trouble. That's the *sign*. That's what we veterans know. And *turn* your fucking weapon on, and go *blazing!* – Of course, we have no weapons."

"Well, Chief," said The Zombie with a horrible smile, "if you could have anything in the world, what would it be?"

The poor stupid Chief started roaring and whirling his crutches in the air. "I'd have a *fight* to the DEATH!"

The Zombie smiled and made a note and tapped his white cane in the darkness.

Old John's Last Night

Earlier that same day, two tramps sat on a bench beside the old bum John. It was a chilly day the color of steel. The tramp on the left strummed his guitar. The tramp in the middle guarded a bottle on his lap. This was a perfect division of labor, which the two of them had engaged in for so long that each had taken on the name of his profession: Strum and Jug. Old John, grizzled and almost blind, kept leaning his head on Jug's shoulder and stroking the bottle. – "*Hey*, pass on!" Jug said. "Go piss on yourself!" When John bowed his head down and groped at the bottle, he resembled a senile fetus. – "You smell like piss," said Jug interestedly. "*Hey*, asshole." – Strum kept playing his guitar. "Hey, John," said Jug to the old bum with real tenderness. But John had fallen asleep. "You asshole," sighed Jug.

The air darkened and chilled, and it was night. When The Zombie came from Sixth Street, John was all alone in his spongy dreams. His friends had not abandoned him; they had gone to the liquor store on Leavenworth to get a pint of Thunderbird. – But motives never matter. – Old John slept with patient weariness; there was nothing else to be but sleepy and patient until the bottle came. He was almost used up. Even sleeping was an exertion which he could barely sustain. It did not refresh him; it was a swimming struggle just under the surface of consciousness, for he wished to go down deeper and deeper, with his head between his legs, but somebody was pushing him up with merciless palms. Old John had learned that if he let himself be pushed back to the surface, he would be rolled over on his back, and then the spins would have him. This was perhaps the only thing that John had learned in his life. He did not want to spin around and round, as he had done for so much of his life, so he hunched his head still lower and groaned.

The Zombie hit the old man with his cane. – "Wake up!" he said disdainfully. His face was so pale and smooth that it seemed almost to have been waxed. – "Wake up!" The Zombie said again. – John squirmed, but he did not open his eyes. One of his fingers extended itself slowly, with the laudable caution of an amoeba bulging its protoplasm into a dangerous sensory outpost in the great unknown, and ran itself around the rim of the empty bottle. Concluding through some occult means that the bottle was still empty, the finger withdrew and curled up safely in the bum's hand. The hand went slack and fell over the edge of the bench. Old John coughed tentatively, jerked once, and gave his head permission to commence the long slow slide back to his knees. He wanted only to sleep. The Zombie struck him repeatedly in the mouth with his cane until a tooth broke; then the poor old man, still not roused, whimpered faintly and began to suck on the end of the cane. The Zombie levered his cane sharply up and down, then poured Drano into the bleeding hole. Old John hiccoughed once, choked, and slept.

From the Coroner's Report

"An unidentified citizen reported that the deceased had been lying on a bench without movement for several hours ... An empty bottle was at his right side ... Atmospheric conditions were cold and wet due to the ongoing rains ... The deceased had been decapitated, but this was not evident to the witness because the deceased's upper body had been covered with a poncho ... No information regarding the identity of the assailant ... The deceased had had a history of heavy wine consumption."

Other Opinions

"He's just a human being that died the *hard* way," said beautiful Brandi, the Haight Street Whore. She was blithe because she knew she could handle *anything*. – But the Wrecking Crew had begun to fear The Zombie by now.

Sunny Days

The next morning was very hot. Indian summer held the pneumonia season at arm's length, for which everybody was grateful who thought about it. In the Park, the dead brown grass was warm to lie on, and trash cans were burning to the touch. No breeze took the heat away, but the sky was blue and blue and mockingly blue above, so that Brandi peeked up at it and shook her head, and Sal wanted to know how she could get up there. On her park bench, Evangeline sat very patiently in her dirty orange parka, waiting the day out in the ease of sunny freedom. There was a sore on her lip. She looked left and right and had a quick gulp of Night Train. She looked down at the ground.

A man came to her and mouthed something so quietly that the sound (if there was any) did not travel outside his mouth.

"How are you doing?" said Evangeline.

"You don't need to say that after what I said!" he shouted.

"I didn't hear what you said."

"*You* heard what I said! You *know* what I said to you!"

Slowly Evangeline looked up from George, who had lost the rest of his lizard-head and was so dirty now as to be almost black, but still basked obediently at her feet in a tangle of broken dirty strings. "I didn't hear what you said," she told the man crossly, "and I couldn't care less."

"That's it, then," said the man. "That's life."

People came and went beneath the shade tree where Black Fox and Mary held court. They sat down and shared their lunches, while the Wrecking Crew (whose composition changed every day) claimed the grass at a polite distance from the bus stop, some getting up to panhandle and take their dogs for a walk along Haight Street, others asking strangers hopefully, "Need some indica weed? Need a little bud? Got some change?", and the flies buzzed round and round in the trash cans, always unhappy, it seemed.

Sky Boy came ambling across the grass, his coat tied round his waist, swinging a quart of orange juice as if it were a canteen full of oxygen that he needed to treasure in his journey across the Mountains of the Moon. – "Hey, you stupid *sonofabitch!*" they greeted him from under their tree. More and more tramps came, but meanwhile their shade dwindled in the noon sun. It was a hot day, and like every other day it would be endless.

A Hypoxic Feeling

Truth to tell, The Other had made little progress in his investigations. He was not clever enough for himself. The case of Ruby had been typical. Had The Zombie not assisted him, he would have done no better than a decedent with cerebral parenchymal trauma. Yet he did not take the hint. There was a low door in his mind which he could not open. Had he been able to do so, he would have seen rays of logic crossing each other in the darkness. – The truth is that The Zombie had beguiled him as he had beguiled Carolina. He never thought, as he reviewed his categories of undisputed fact, that he had become interested in the murders for their own sake; he did not know why it was when, absently tinking the rectal thermometer against the razor blade, he suddenly felt pridefully happy. He really believed that some current of rigorous thought was bearing him effortlessly into the Blue Yonder, when in fact it was pervading him. If you know what The Other had in common with the Wrecking Crew, you will know what I mean. (But the Wrecking Crew was better than he was.)

Sometimes he walked slowly around the Death-Pond, his eyes searching in the darkness between grass-blades. Everything around him might be a clue. – "*Did* the blood on the soles of the victim's feet get there when he was moved by the funeral director or was it present before the body was disturbed?" asks Adelson rhetorically.* To The

* *Op. cit.*, p. 44.

Other, who, having murdered, must now play the part of funeral director, this question was by no means a rhetorical one. What disturbances had he left on the scene? And what evidentiary escort could he maintain? In the grass beside the body he saw a blue bus transfer, good until 3:00 p.m., and since blue was yesterday's color he knew, at least, that the litter had not been removed since before the period of interest (but he did not know anything). The rest could be effortlessly contained in the Platonic dumpster of Category I: scraps of plastic, cigarette wrappers, stained papers, bleached cardboard ground into the sullen grass . . .

"Well!" cried Brandi with a cheeky smile. "I seen *you* before. Where's your cane?"

"I left it at home," The Other said.

Brandi ran up close to him and whispered in his ear: "Gimme fifty cents."

"I'll give you a mouthful of Drano if you don't shut up," The Other said.

Nobody particularly liked him when he was The Other. The Wrecking Crew certainly did not like him as well when he was The Other, because he was less subtle then, and because The Zombie bought them Thunderbird.

"What would you do if somebody tried to kill you?" he asked Evangeline.

"Stop asking that!" she said. "Will you *stop* it, please! You just asked that last night. I don't want to think about that guy out there with the Drano, hunting us down."

"Oh, shut up and run the jug," said Barlow.

"That guy's gonna do whatever he decides he wants to do," said Evangeline. "Barlow, I need you always to sleep with me to check on me. I'm asking all of you to sleep within my distance in case I want to holler. I want you to be near me if I have to start yelling, 'Wake up, wake up, wake up!'"

Sal's Bedtime

It was dark, and in the darkness Sal's red old face was glowing with happiness, so that her gap-toothed mouth transformed her into a jack-o'-lantern. She had just panhandled ten whole dollars! At twilight she'd made five, and dark blue shadows were stretching across Haight Street when a man came up to her singing of springtime, O tinny bells and flowers! and she asked him for change and he said, "Why don't you sing me a Christmas song, dearie?", so Sal started singing "Jingle Bells" in her slow cracked voice that sounded like a rundown robot toy, "Jin-gull, all . . . th'wayyyyyy!", and the man chuckled and gave her a five-dollar bill. When Black Fox was apprised of this intelligence, he slapped an STP sticker to Sal's boot because he said she'd *earned* it. – "What does STP mean to you?" said the other tramps solemnly. – "It means, SAL TOP PANHANDLER!" cried Sal, laughing and laughing until she wheezed.

Sal had another reason for being happy: she had just gotten out of jail. Oh, lucky Sal, to have two independent causes for that fine feeling which our Declaration of Independence permits us to pursue! She had been sleeping on the corner of Haight and Cole when Officer Ferris, whose patience for sidewalk obstructions was no more abundant than naturally-occurring kurchatovium, woke her by hitting her across the bridge of her nose with a billy club. It was he who gave Blind Mary a black eye for committing a similar sin. I would that I had time to strap this fellow to my moral dissecting table, but he is too quick for me; there he goes, smashing Sal's nose once more for good measure and pushing her into his shiny black van. She was in the drunk tank for five days. Her nose kept hurting. She did not know her nose was broken until she started waggling it back and forth in her empirical studies of its aching, and she realized that it could move in ways it had never moved before! One of her eyes swelled, and the other one closed up tight. Then she got dizzy and sick. Finally they let her out.

"But I'm gonna make up for that now," Sal told her new friend, who had just given her a dollar and was standing listening to her. "I'm gonna have a little *drinkie*. This one man asked me how much I drank in a day and I said, 'Anywhere from four to six fifths.' He looked at me and said,

'You mean you're still *alive?*'" – Sal shook with laughter. "Of course I've cut down since then. What did I drink today? Well, between the gang of us, three to five fifths. But that's between the six to eight of us. There's none of us alcoholics that want to drink by ourselves. But so what. It may not be a holiday, but I want to celebrate. I'm going to get me a full jug and say, *fuck it!* What kind of bird don't fly? – *Thunderbird!*"

It was getting darker and colder. Sal stood on the sidewalk holding a long smoking cigarette in her hand. The Zombie thought that she looked lumpy in her white coat, with her plaid shirt-sleeves coming out of the arms, and the big furry white coat buttons like snowballs on her stomach. She had fat red dirty hands. Often she bent her red, blocky head down to rest it, and every part of her looked tired except for her perkily cropped hair. Underneath her eyes were sweet sad wrinkles.

"Let's go drink in the Park," said The Zombie.

"Well, of *course* we will!" Sal cackled. "But first I have to tell you this story before I forget, because *this* was the funniest thing that ever happened. See, I guess it was yesterday – no, maybe today – anyhow, there was four of us waiting to go the Haight Free Clinic to get antibiotics and Kwell* and all that good stuff. I had a bottle of Suave Shampoo sticking out of my pocket, and with the white cap, it looked just like a half-pint of vodka. (Actually, we had a fifth stashed behind us.) So this cop comes up, and he just *yanked* the bottle right out of my pocket! And there he was looking at it and reading the label to himself: STRAWBERRY SUAVE SHAMPOO. We were all laughing and laughing. Even *he* couldn't keep a straight face. Finally he just handed the bottle back and said, 'Move on.' – Speakin' of which, let's move into that liquor store on Masonic, 'cause I got *real money!*"

"We can't go to the one on Cole?" said The Zombie. That was more on their way to the Park; he wanted to murder Sal as soon as he could.

"No, that one's closed," Sal said. "Here we are anyway. – I want a fifth of old Thunder," she said to the men behind the counter. There were two of them; they seemed to be brothers. For a long time they looked her up and down. They must have known her, because she was a nightly customer, so it followed from their pretense of not knowing her that they despised her. – How strange, when the sellers looked down on the one who brought them business! Was it because Sal was dirty (which was why The Zombie hated her), or because she had no

---

* A compound which kills body-lice.

self-control? – But both those aspects of Sal were a result as well as a cause of her trade with them. And in a modest way Sal was making them rich. It seems to me they should have kissed the dirt she walked in.

"Who's buying?" said the clerk at last.

"I am," said The Zombie. – Sal turned to him smiling. "Well, thank you," she said. "You're a real friend."

"Two dollars and fifteen cents," said the clerk.

"Oh, don't I know it," sighed Sal. "Don't I know every last penny of *that* number!" – and she stretched out her skinny shaking arms for the bottle. As they passed it to her silently, she started singing. – "Isn't it just like Christmas," she said, "getting something all wrapped up like that, even if it *is* only a brown paper bag!" She put her arm around The Zombie and started creeping in her feeble old way toward the Park. It was cold enough now to see her breath. The sky was blue-black. Murky stars blinked, but there was no life in them.

Beneath those stars they came upon a starstruck figure living only in sadness, who stood beside a phone booth as if awaiting the ring of destiny (but he had no hope). – "Hey, Danny, come have some wine!" cried Sal. – "I can't," the tramp said. "I got money in the phone and I dropped a dime in the street." – "Come on! I'll give you a dime," said Sal. – But the tramp stayed in the cold, leaning against the phone booth, his face downcast.

At the next corner was tall, severe, grey-haired Captain Hook, who frowned at them with his hook-nose and waved his cork arm (he only put the hook in when he had to fight or play pool). – "Upon my soul!" he said. "My beautiful Sally, ha-ha-ha! My one true dolphin in this age of piss-cod and flounder! By my stun-sails! Are you drinking again?" – "I sure am, Captain!" chuckled old Sal. "Come have a drink with us." – Captain Hook surveyed the paper bag, with such lofty implacability that it seemed his nose must momentarily swoop down and stab it. – "As long as it's *white* wine," he said warningly, and there was such grimness in his eye as to enforce a respectful silence . . . "*Or* red," said Captain Hook. – Sal laughed so hard and loud that she almost dropped the bottle, and even The Zombie smiled and leaned on his cane and scratched his blond stubble. – "No," cried Captain Hook at last. "I cannot. I must raise anchor! (In fact, my friends, I cannot even swim.) – You see, I have just taken a hit of acid, and my friend across the street took nine. I must protect him, and I must protect AMERICA." – He turned to The Zombie. – "As for you, my friend, take good care of Sally. Cherish her. She is a legend."

"I'll take care of her," The Zombie promised.

At Haight and Stanyan, in the Cala Foods parking lot, a dark-bearded tramp with fiery eyes was standing. – "Have a drink with us, Stanley!" said Sal. – Stanley walked slowly towards her. – "Where did you get that STP sticker?" he said. – "The one on my boot?" said Sal, laughing already at the funny funny joke. "That means, *SAL TOP PANHANDLER!*" – But Stanley did not even smile. "You know you got no right to wear STP," he said. – "I do too have a right!" said Sal. "Black Fox put it on me!" – Stanley clawed his hands and lunged at her boot, but Sal pulled back with surprising speed. – "Don't try it," she said. "Somebody already tried that once, and you see I'm still wearing it." – Stanley stepped aside contemptuously. "You know if I want it, Sal, I'll take it. You got no right to wear that." – "Talk to Black Fox," said Sal, hobbling proudly past, but she was crying.

She led The Zombie across Stanyan and into the Park. Behind the screen of trees where the Wrecking Crew lived, it was dark and quiet.

"Barlow!" Sal called. "Hey, Barlow!"

"What?" said Barlow crabbily.

"I brought a friend along."

"Oh, good," said Barlow. "Oh, great. Suck my dick."

Sal chuckled and squeezed between the trees, with The Zombie following after like an obedient hound. In the dark blur of bedrolls on the ground, an empty bottle gleamed green in passing headlights. It was very dark. The shadows of trees were dark against the darkness. Forming a sort of railing on one side of the camp was a long low branch thick enough to sit on. In the night it had a strangely pale and desiccated look. The Zombie sat on it and made distracted washing motions with his hands and watched Sal squatting down by Barlow's bedroll to talk. He listened to the coarse, heavy breathing of drunken sleepers in the darkness. These vulnerable lives were his to extinguish one by one in the course of time. Yet, sadly, this thought gave The Zombie no satisfaction, perhaps because it was too dark here among the trees to see the dirt of the Wrecking Crew; the thicket was lit only by the solitary orange glow of Sal's cigarette.

"You gonna have a drink, or you gonna be grouchy?" said Sal indulgently.

"I'm not grouchy. I just want to sleep."

The streetlights seemed extraordinarily yellow and bright through the trees. They made a curtain of light, into which it would have been unimaginable to go, just as it would be impossible to exist on the surface of the sun.

"Sambo took over your bedroll," Barlow said. "That stupe went and passed out on your stuff."

"Hey," said Clyde indignantly, "that's *his* bedroll. I know, 'cause John found it in the trash can."

"No, it's Sally's," said Barlow gruffly.

"Oh," Clyde said. "It is?" He gulped down a drink, sighed rapturously, and stuck his head back into his bedroll.

"Never mind," old Sal said. "I can sit up till morning."

"If it was mine, I wouldn't *give* a fuck," said Barlow. "I'd say, get the *fuck* out of my bedroll."

"Oh, why are you such a grouch?"

"I been a grouch all my life," growled Barlow with relish. "I ain't never gonna change. All I'm sayin' is, Sambo's passed out on your bedroll. You think it's cold now, you wait till just before that sun comes up."

"I know it'll be cold then," said Sal. "I'll raise hell then." She struck a match to her new cigarette, and for a moment there was a yellow circle of brightness that revealed the Wrecking Crew to be twisted caterpillars in their fat wrinkled bedrolls, their eyes squinching shut against the light; and then the match went out and spots of brightness floated in front of The Zombie's eyes, settling slowly, like grains of sand in an ink-filled paperweight. Sal sat rubbing her broken nose in the darkness. "Yes," she repeated wearily. "I'll raise hell then." She seemed suddenly confused. "Will these folks stand by me?" she said, rubbing her nose. "I hope they will."

"Sambo!" said Barlow sharply. "Sambo!"

Sambo slept.

"Fuck," said Barlow. "I've had it. Well, I'm taking my shoes off when I sleep, at least. I'm sorry for everyone's bad luck when they smell my feet." – For five minutes he groaned and fumbled slowly with his boots. Suddenly the darkness was permeated by a stench compounded of sweat, toenails and turning vinegar. It was a stench of remarkable power, sweeping across the camp and taking The Zombie's breath away. – "Yep, I got the dry-rot," Barlow explained to The Zombie proudly. "My toes are coming loose. I already lost the skin. If you ever have a party and the guests won't leave, you just bring me over and I'll clear 'em out."

"And I've got to sleep beside you," grumbled Sal. "Anyhow, I'm used to it."

"I say, if you want Sambo to move, you better tell him."

"In a minute. I just got settled. Let a woman have an honest drink."

"I'm telling you! When it rains, don't say, 'Hey, Barlow, I'm wet, here's someone to *disturb* you!'"

Sal got up slowly and hobbled over to a snoring bundle at Barlow's feet. – "Sambo!" she said. "Sambo! Get your butt out of there! You're on my bedroll!"

"I ain't on your bedroll," said Sambo faintly, as if talking from some distant continent.

"You are!" corrected Barlow.

"You move on over, and gimme my own bedroll back," said Sal inflexibly.

"I ain't on both blankets," said Sambo.

"Yes, you are. You know what's right and what's wrong."

"I mean, what's *she* supposed to do?" cried Barlow in high exasperation.

Sambo stood up and tried to run away with Sal's blankets. – "*Uh-oh!*" cried Sal alertly. "That's *mine!*" – "I was just shakin' 'em out for you," said Sambo. "I was just sleepin', mindin' my own business . . ."

"Oh, shut up!" said Sal.

"Sal, get off his case," Barlow said. "He's showin' you some respect by givin' you your stuff, so ease up on him."

"Oh, fuck you, too, Barlow!" said Sal. As Sambo staggered about sullenly, brushing greasy grime off cardboard scraps from which he would construct a new bed, Sal crawled slowly into her nest, like a dumpy white animal.

Phhhrrrrrrrrrrrrrrggghhhhhhhh!

"Phew!" said Barlow in admiration. "That's a good fart."

"I did it," said Sal.

"Somebody's got to do it, girl," said Barlow.

The Important Question

The Zombie caned his way softly and carefully through the darkness
and sat down beside Sal. The bottle of Thunderbird, now almost empty,
was between them. – "Tell me," The Zombie said. "If you could have
anything in the world, what would it be?"

Sal lay smiling and staring up at the sky. "I'd have all the good friends
I already got. The friends that love me and help me and stand by me."

This was the first time that The Zombie had ever heard a wish that
he could not further. He stood up and leaned on his cane. Then he
tapped sadly away.

Mistakes

Had The Other understood less, he might still have consolidated his
position. (The Zombie wanted to be noble; The Other wanted only to
keep his finger in the dike.) He should have forgotten about The
Zombie and gone about his own purposeless business. Had he done so,
The Zombie might have forgotten about him. Instead, he intruded upon
The Zombie more and more, categorizing and plotting and memorizing.
He kept searching, rocking on his feet while The Zombie tapped his
cane . . . Certainly he could not have preserved the gains of his earlier
life, but he might yet have retained a not entirely dependent existence.
He was like a tramp camped behind a furnace who, not satisfied with
the heat, dared to expect light as well, and so opened the boiler door
and died in the explosion.

Paul Raven's Last Night

Skinny old Paul Raven wished to use his thousands of diplomatic and
social opportunities to achieve a central place in the Park where the
grass would be clean and families would come by on Sunday afternoons

and feel the grass to see how well-kept it was, and fathers would turn to their sons and say, "Paul Raven did this; Paul Raven kept this park *secure*," so Paul Raven accompanied the Wrecking Crew for the same reasons of ecological hygiene that a vulture removes the offense of a dead body from our world, bit by bit; bit by bit Paul Raven removed empty Night Train bottles from Rich's happy hands, from the space beside Evangeline. Late one afternoon The Woman Who Laughed came to the Park with her stinking black garbage bags. She sat in Paul Raven's grass, shivering and laughing until she choked. From one of her bags she took a moldy slice of bread and threw it into the grass, but the pigeons didn't come, and Paul Raven, after five minutes of extreme anxiety, finally snatched the bread and ran with it to the trash can. The Woman sat there laughing and laughing. – What an offensive stench! – Her round pimpled face bobbed blankly on her shoulders. She got another piece of rotten bread and crumbled it into a thousand crumbs and scattered them around her so that Paul Raven could never pick them all up, and he was neutralized into timid helplessness and walked very quickly round and round looking for some other piece of litter to throw away in order to distract himself. Finally Rich said, "Do you want to help her?" – "I do," said Paul Raven very softly. "I want her to be *safe*." – "Then just let her be," Rich said. – Paul Raven nodded very rapidly and blinked back tears. Then he started walking toward the pond.

"Hey, man!" yelled Barlow. "Don't go *near* there! That's where some fucked-up character's been *murdering* people! That's where Ruby died."

But Paul Raven did not pay attention. He waded into the pond and sat morosely on the island, dripping beneath the willow tree whose sad green fronds licked his face, and the Wrecking Crew watched him until dusk came and they could not see him anymore.

"You jerks understand he's not comin' back?" said Barlow in the darkness. "You understand he's not gonna be there in the morning?"

"Stop your gloom and doom," said Evangeline.

"Listen, bitch," said Barlow. "Don't you speak ill of the dead in that way. Paul Raven may not have been the man that Smackwater Jack was, but at least he was a man; at least he had balls."

"He could have been good, he could have been crazy, he could have been good and he could have been lazy," said Rich contentedly. The Woman Who Laughed sat shivering on the grass and laughed all night through. They never saw Paul Raven again.

A Definition

"The term 'loss' as used herein," according to that insurance standby, the *F. C. & S. Bulletins*, "shall mean with regard to hands and feet, actual severance through or above wrist or ankle joints; with regard to eyes, entire and irrevocable loss of sight; with regard to thumb and index finger, actual severance through or above metacarpophalangeal joints."*

The Police Save the Day

One afternoon The Zombie met Rich and Gypsy and Sky Boy on Haight Street, in front of the Red Vic where everybody was milling and leaning and watching because across the street they were making a comedy movie and the police stood guard around the bookstore and the crew set up a dozen director's chairs on the sidewalk and Rich and Gypsy and Sky Boy were heading away from the police, although not out of town as He-Wolf had already done and Barlow was soon to do, so The Zombie bought them a fifth of Thunderbird, and they were very happy, and he went with them to the Park to drink it but as they were walking toward the stagnant lily-pond they saw the black paddy wagon come rolling almost silently down the sidewalk, and it stopped at the place where they had been planning to go, and two cops got out with sternly raised nightsticks and flung the back door open and strode over to the grass and began to drag drunken bodies into the van: – one, two, three, four, five members of the Wrecking Crew they threw in there; and the four survivors dropped back to the glass-covered map for tourists, bowing their heads and studying it as hard as they could because the paddy wagon was rolling back toward them, and the closer it got the lower they bowed and the harder they stared at every detail of

* *Companies & Coverages*: Speciality Lines Kra-3, KIDNAP–RANSOM–EXTORTION (November, 1981).

the map of the Park, as if they were trying to make up their minds whether to proceed to Stow Lake or the Arboretum this afternoon, and the paddy wagon slowed and they felt the cops looking at the back of their necks, so they looked even harder at the map, and the paddy wagon finally rolled away, going around the corner to the station on Kezar.

A man came up to them and said, "See that guy on that bench over there, tapping his shoe so fast? He's a snitch. They pay him. Every day since he's been here, the wagon comes. He's a speed freak; that's what he spends the money on."

"Come on," rasped Gypsy, "let's go," and he hit Rich's arm, and Rich said, "God *damn*it, don't hit that arm; that's my fucked-up arm," and they stood around the map until Sal and J.J. came over. Sal was carrying a crutch and a bedroll; the cops wouldn't put those into the wagon, so she had to take care of them until the other Wreckers got back. J.J. was a black man with a lined face. The cops had asked him if he was drunk, and when he said no they let him alone.

Gypsy's Coon-Tail

Gypsy wore a dirty dark jacket that had **GYPSY** written on the back, and he had phony silver dollars and buffalo nickels (twice life size) on the tiestring of his bedroll, and he had a coonskin cap that went well with his wide silvery beard. He looked fifty; I imagine that he was about thirty-five.

"Gypsy," said Sky Boy, "you look like a squint-eyed Mon-*go*-lian!"

"My eyes don't look too bad, do they?" he rasped anxiously. He had a loud buzzing voice, which sounded like a noise a wasp might make if he had crawled too long over some delightfully rotten fruit, drinking the fermented juice until he was too drunk and weak to sting.

"They look fine," said Rich.

"You look like an old drunken lush!" sneered Sky Boy.

"I'm a Cossack!" buzzed Gypsy.

"If you're a Cossack where's your horse?"

"He must've forgot to steal one from the police," teased old Sal.

Gypsy Exercises the Dialectic

"I used to have a coon-tail on this cap," croaked Gypsy. "Got stolen."

"Who took it?" said The Zombie.

"Some bitch."

"I hope you fucked her good first."

"I didn't even fuck her," he buzzed in wonder. "She fucked me. She knew right where I lived. I trapped that racoon myself, up north. Up in Oregon. Up in Washington. Bitch came and cut the tail off in the middle of the night. Never saw her again."

A police car went by.

"I don't give a fuck," he said with finality.

"Yeah," said The Zombie.

"I said, I don't give a fuck."

"I don't either," said The Zombie

"I DON'T GIVE A FUCK!" Gypsy buzzed in his loudest rasp, like a proverbial saw, and people looked at him from the far side of the pond; and he sighed and said philosophically, "Well, maybe I do. I do and I don't, you know what I mean?"

"I know," said The Zombie. He wrote the name "Gypsy" in his black book of death.

"Anyhow, I don't give a fuck."

Gypsy Gets Punished

They all went into the bushes and sat down on their bedrolls. Gypsy started throwing branches at Sky Boy. "You shithead!" he said. He threw another branch. – "Leave off it," said Sky Boy. – Gypsy threw a bigger branch. It hit Sky Boy in the face. – "You'd better cut it out," said Sky Boy. – Gypsy picked up a big stick and threw it so that it hit Sky Boy on the side of the head. Sky Boy jumped up and shook Gypsy. – "*Stop fucking with me, man!*" he said in a low dangerous voice.

But Gypsy would not, so J.J. beside him, who had been trying to quiet him, finally got up and crouched down on the ground in front of Gypsy and rolled up his sleeves and spat on his hands to frighten

Gypsy, and started punching Gypsy very quickly though gently, and Gypsy, who was foggy as well as nasty-drunk, shook his head in bewilderment, but finally he got the idea and had another drink of Thunderbird (Rich, Gypsy, Sal, J.J. and Sky Boy drank the whole bottle in about ten minutes) and spat on his hands, too, and then J.J. started hitting him in the stomach and in the face, quick sharp blows that were intended to hurt Gypsy only a little, so that he would behave, and Gypsy tried weakly to hit back, but he couldn't, and J.J. kept hitting him until he moaned a little, and it was clear to the satisfaction of all that Gypsy had learned his lesson and would be good.

Why Gypsy Was Unhappy

Gypsy had been a P.O.W. in Vietnam. He was a Search & Destroy man, so the gooks didn't like him. One day he got shot twice from nowhere, right in the chest. He fell onto his back and passed out. His unit left him. They got in their choppers and breezed back to Saigon to fuck little gook girls. When Gypsy woke up, there were seventeen gooks standing over him, jabbering at him in their gook language that he couldn't understand. He was still holding his assault rifle; it was pointing straight up at the sky. They kept jabbering at him, so he said, "*I don't know*," very slowly, and one of the gooks kicked the rifle out of his hands, and the medic gook came up to him because he was bleeding, but Gypsy spat in his face! – They put Gypsy in a cage inside a concentration camp for two years. Every other day, they used to take him out and question him. What they learned, he didn't know. He didn't give a fuck. When he was repatriated, he still had the two bullets in his chest.* He lifted up his shirt to show The Zombie, and there, above the hard purple lesions that spanned his belly ("Agent Orange," he said), was the place where the slugs had gone in, and he had The Zombie touch the hot infected flesh, and as The Zombie stroked with a finger he felt the two bullets like hard cysts, at which Gypsy grunted and fell down moaning on his back. – "What was the POW camp like?" The Zombie said, rubbing blue shadows under his eyes, and Gypsy looked around at the Wrecking Crew hunkered around the bottle, with

* Forensic pathologists call them "souvenir bullets."

the fog blowing in and out of everybody's faces, and Rich sat scratching and J.J. turned up the volume on his yellow plastic tape player with the rainbow decal, and Sal was squatting at the top of the knoll, scratching herself through her parka while she pissed, and Sky Boy sat sourly on his bedroll, and Rich whistled to Kent's dog Grizzly, who had been hit by cars three times but had still been able to rape a coyote to sire the other dog, Red, whom Rich was taking care of for Kent because Kent had been taken away with seizures, and Gypsy said, "I was in my little fucking *cage;* it was just like being here." – "Hey, pass the bottle, don't babysit it," said Sky Boy. J.J. took the bottle away from Gypsy and had a swig. He passed it to Sal when she came back. She had a big glug and gave Sky Boy some. He sipped moodily and passed it to Rich. There was barely enough in the bottle now for one good drink. Rich laughed. "Well, your bad luck, Gypsy," he said. But Rich drank only half and passed the bottle to Gypsy. Gypsy did not look to see what Rich had done for him. He threw the bottle into the bushes. The liquor that Rich had saved spilled out onto the leaves in big red droplets. – "You don't *care* about me!" he buzzed. – "You asshole!" cried Rich, offended and hurt. "I saved you a little corner on that."

Gypsy lay down and began to snore. J.J. laughed. – "Oh, say, can you see . . ." sang J.J. in time to his snores. Everybody laughed. After awhile, Rich bent over Gypsy and gently tucked a bedroll under his head.

J.J.

J.J. had two problems. The first one was that he had to drink as soon as he woke up in the morning. The second one was that after he drank his problems didn't go away. But he didn't mind anymore, he said. He was immune to unhappiness. (The Zombie wrote this down in his black book of death.)

One time J.J. was in a private paradise of food and pot and alcohol, but some guy wanted to spoil it by lighting a fire in a garbage can, so J.J. asked him politely to put the fire out, and the guy said, "Who the fuck do you think you are?", and J.J. got up and turned the garbage can upside down, and the guy came over and hit him in the face, and J.J., who could never bear to be touched or hit or slapped, took out a little knife and stuck it in the guy and twisted it so that it snapped inside him. But J.J. didn't kill the guy.

"Life's pretty good, except that it sucks," he said.

"It sure sucks," said Sky Boy. "It really does."

Carved in Stone

On the wall of a boutique on Haight Street, somebody wrote the following, which I like no less for understanding none of it:

> WESTCOAST
>
> 12 JIMBO – 69
>
> F.T.W.
>
> S.W.P.
>
> WRECKING CREW

Someday soon, when they are dead, all of them, I will scrawl it on their tombs.

Fear of Death

As he went down the hall to his room one cold night, The Other had a bad feeling, and under the edge of his door was darkness. He put his key in the knob and turned it slowly. Darkness wailed out at him. Inside it was chilly and still. Darkness made the room much bigger than it really was, multiplying the hiding places for his evil conscience. For a moment he did not turn on the light. – Here, he said to himself, am I: I am a part of this darkness, and when I turn on the light I will destroy myself. – He turned on the light. – At once the room shrank into a yellow cell of wretchedness. But it was no less empty for being so diminished; if anything, it was more empty, for the darkness had had a potentiality for something greater than his own self, because, being darkness, it was unknown. – He turned off the light, and it came back again. There was a sullen yellow glow from the window (street-rays rising between brick walls) which seemed to have its own intentionality, as if, being bright, it was a *show* that he was supposed to watch – but in that case he was standing as it was *intended* that he be standing; and what if someone were standing behind his back?

How dark, how cold everything was! After awhile he began to hear sounds from the other side of the room, but when he turned on the light they stopped.

The Other's fear of the dark grew upon him, until finally he must turn on the safe lamp-radiance even in the first moments of twilight, when the blue air outside the front door had begun to congeal into a rectangular black clot of night, and The Woman Who Laughed sat on the steps, black against the blackness, and he took the elevator, but the light in there had burned out, so he rode the cage in darkness, and as he walked down the long dark corridor on the eighth floor he had to flip on the light switch, because in his head ran the words from the forensic pathology text of Spitz: "*a semi-skeletonized decedent . . .*"*

Gypsy's Last Wish

"I'm tellin' you, I want everyone to know *I don't give a fuck!*"

The Old Game

The Park shelter smelled like burning – a dirty smell, because there was a log on fire in the dirt; and dirty smoke blew slowly into the darkness inside. Some of the bench-boards had been burned away in other fires a long time ago, so that there was charred darkness where the seats used to be; and in that darkness old ashes twitched when the spiders scuttled in their webs. (Spiders spin over space, ashes fall, and emptiness is filled somehow – except in the Blue Yonder.) It was always smoky and shadowy inside. It was cold, too; the burning logs did not warm it at all.

The stencilled notices on the wall said NO GAMBLING. Every table had a deck of cards or two on it. Old men sat gambling at the

---

* Werner U. Spitz, M.D., and Russell S. Fisher, M.D., ed., *Medicolegal Investigation of Death: Guidelines for the Application of Pathology to Crime Investigation*, 2nd ed. (Springfield, Illinois: Charles C. Thomas, 1980).

back. Their necks were bowed; their noses drooped. They played their hands as if they were afraid of waking each other up. – What dreams did they suspect each other of in that darkness, I wonder? – Each old man was playing the old game by himself; they did not know one another. Whenever they looked up and saw each other, they seemed surprised. Sometimes the old men smiled when they saw their cards. They were cleanshaven, and all wore hats and coats. One who resembled the patriarch Abraham sat on the table top, his cigarette hanging out of his mouth.

After a long time, The Zombie came.

Barlow's Last Night

It was night. The Zombie walked down Haight Street, his trousers billowing like dark sails. Barlow was standing beside Cala Foods cursing because his feet were itching as they rotted and he wished they would stop. Because he was drunk, he did not remember that night sounds can be significant, and he did not hear the slow steady tapping of The Zombie's cane as The Zombie approached from Shrader Street, nor did he see the tall, thin shadow coming for him from under the awnings. There was no need even to stun him with the cane. The Zombie came up to him, looked quickly around, and took Barlow by the arm. He was going to take him into the darkness of the Park. Barlow started yelling and swearing, but no one paid any attention. The Zombie shot his left arm out, almost into Barlow's face, and then The Zombie's left hand rose to the vertical like the throat of a questing viper, and when Barlow stared down the dark barrel of The Zombie's sleeve he saw the hacksaw blade with which The Zombie was going to cut off his head. The Zombie smiled. Barlow leaned against the wall of the supermarket, sneering and raising two dirty fingers in a supercilious peace sign.

Sunny Days

"Take me with you," Evangeline moaned. Her tears washed the dirt down his cheeks. "Oh, please, Barlow, help me."

"Hush," said Sal. "Hush now, sweetie."

"Don't leave me," said Evangeline.

"Stop talking to him, honey," said old Sal. "You know he just don't have the power to hear you now."

Thanksgiving Day

Everyone who was anyone was sitting in front of the shelter, while brown crackly leaves blew around their feet, and Mary was grinning-drunk and Sal sat smiling and nodding with a flower in the buttonhole of her coat, and Evangeline was rubbing her stomach crabbily. – "Hey!" yelled two kids. "You wanna buy a knife?" – Nobody answered, so the kid who had it pulled it out and swashbuckled it around. – Black Fox spat very slowly on the sidewalk. "What the fuck are we gonna do with a paring knife?" he said. "What did you do, steal it from your mommy's pantry?"

George the Lizard's Last Night

Evangeline and Mary gave him away to a child without any toys. By then poor George had neither head nor legs.

A Resolution

The Other had now determined that he would NEUTRALIZE The Zombie or die. If he could, he would now have thrown open that creaking wooden bulkhead between his self and the Zombie-self, but that door had warped into place forever, and he must go round the long logical way to enter the darkness.

Fortunately, The Zombie had heard him and would help him.

The Zombie by Himself

The Zombie had a secret place. It was in the utmost Blue Yonder, beyond the pale, where no one else could go. It was a dark place where the sunlight could do no harm and rain could never leach. He had his blue treasures in there. The blue crystals waited in their cans. He kept his hacksaw and his stunning-cane there; he was happy there.

The Zombie was a monster, and he was not a monster. He wanted what we want. He wanted to own his whole self. Once he had been The Other. The Zombie knew that The Other had become dirty somewhere along the way and tumbled into the Blue Yonder, but he was not informed as to the circumstances. So The Zombie hated The Other for soiling both of them, although at the same time he wanted to be The Other as well as himself, in order to be *himself* completely. He knew that he was dirty. He hated The Other for being dirty. He hoped that he could become clean. (The Other knew perfectly well that he could never be clean.) Himself failing to find the straight path to cleanliness, The Zombie decided to clean up the world instead. To do so, he had to disguise himself as dirty. He was dirty also because, hating The Other as he did, he suspected The Other of preferring to be dirty, which meant that it might be necessary to be dirty in order to woo The Other as he was wooing the world.

The earliest memory that he had after The Other had come alive was of sitting by himself at a little round table in some deli, and there was an empty bottle of soda in front of him, and it was late at night, and outside it was raining. There were other chairs at his table, but no one sat on them. There were other people; they sat at other tables. The Zombie could hear individual syllables, but the words made no sense to him; they were speaking the one enigmatic language of all animals, as lost to him as the ultraviolet patterns on flowers are to us. He heard their slow, earnest, modulated sounds, which they produced inside their throats, and modified with teeth and tonsils and flickering tongues. From The Zombie's point of view, he might as well have been listening to cattle. He was the only sentient one in the world. Outside it was so cold and rainy and dark ... He looked at his sleeves, his knees; everything was wet. He knew that he should be doing something, but he didn't know what. So he sat there watching the people smile and eat and look at him. Evidently they thought that he was staring at them. Or was there some other reason that they were watching him? He listened to them to try to understand why, but he could not understand them. Outside, there were only rainy trees, the red tail-lights of cars, and shiny yellow crosswalk lines against the black of the street, which was so new and perfect that somehow it reminded him of blackboards and laboratories.

"That's my attitude," he finally heard someone say. "They should be *happy* to come to my office."

"Thanks to his pathology," someone else said, "I'm taking a vacation."

He walked around in Point Richmond. On one side of him, it was like Christmas in hell: – the city lights, red and green, converging along the industrial boulevards, becoming dingily yellow as they dwindled into the night distances, on trajectories aimed straight at the Richmond Hills (he could determine their summit solely from the line of winking yellow lights, dots connected by his eye); and beyond that was the main thing, the Freeway, with its glaring yellow lights monotonously spaced, yellow-white along the wide lonely concrete tongue of it that rolled on and on through the smoke of the night refineries. Along its edge, he saw a wall of closely-spaced cement cubes, veined with dinginess.

Eighty feet below his left shoulder, the water was calm and dark, with lights on the far side of the Bay making long clean lines right across it. Some lines were yellow, and some were white. They did not really touch the blackness and deepness of the water. Infrequent ripples hinted at the power of the water. What gave the water its true texture were the squiggles at the edges of the glare-beams; and the light itself seemed to be máde up of sub-squiggles, being neither fish nor fowl, neither matter nor energy, as I noticed once in Victoria, B.C., when the Empress Hotel was lit up for Christmas Eve, and the lights formed a pixel-image of the building upon the cold black harbor; and that was beautiful as this was beautiful, but The Zombie turned his back on it and went toward the freeway . . .

An Invitation

It was evening, and blue clouds mottled the sky's face. *You want to find me pal there are two ways you can find me*, ran The Zombie's note. *You can come over the freeway, or you can come under it if you come over it, you may find me and you may not but if you come under it, i promise i'll find you.* Then something had been written and crossed out, as if The Zombie had shyly hesitated, and at the bottom of the paper it said *down under the overpass near 16th & missouri st.*

The Woman Who Laughed was quiet whenever she saw The Zombie, but when The Other passed her that night she laughed derisively. He did not care; he was prepared. In the flask that he carried was a solution of chloral hydrate. When his hands began to make little washing motions he would swallow the liquid. This would take his consciousness away very quickly, before he could become The Zombie. When he woke up, he would have cycled back into his non-murderous existence. This could be assumed with near-predictive certainty. He walked up and down Haight Street, waiting for darkness, and it was cold and Sal was crying on the sidewalk and saying, "I'M HUNGRY!" in her slimy rasp,* and no matter how much money anybody gave her it wouldn't do any good.

---

* Street alcoholics know that if they say they are hungry somebody may take pity on them, but if they say that they are in agony from Thunderbird withdrawal nobody will give them a cent.

The Other's Last Night

It was cold and dark. All along the freeway the cars went, shining wearily in the night. They saw billboards and exit signs illuminated from beneath. The darkness was a vast ceiling over them, infinite because featureless. It was high enough so that they could never reach it; yet it was all around them. That is why it was God. The cars passed through tunnels of yellow light whose radiance was dulled against the corrugations of concrete. To their left as they rode was the black water; to their right was the city. They sped above the skyscrapers, with their closely spaced tiles of light, past the Transamerica Pyramid and the radiant necklaces of the Bay Bridge, and they crossed the tail-lights of other cars ascending onto the freeway, headed for Emeryville and Berkeley and thence who knows where. They sped like frantic red beads falling off a string, none knowing that beneath them was a long hollow darkness. That was where The Other was.

He walked deeper into the darkness. The night acquired a grey belly, hurtling from sky behind him to ground before him: – the freeway. The place in which he found himself could almost have been a railroad yard, because there were so many train tracks growing out from under the overpass like fern-fronds. The Other could not really see them, so he had to step carefully from tie to tie, wondering where The Zombie was. He looked up at the concrete ribs of the ceiling (above which were two tiers of interstate traffic, so that there was a faint rushing as of a wind outside a cathedral), and for a moment he wondered rather madly if The Zombie might somehow live in one of the black rectangular cavities which occurred regularly between those ribs, like vertebrae of emptiness; in the darkness he could not ascertain whether these dark spaces were fashioned cleanly, like hollows in a honeycomb, or whether each might have its little ledge on which The Zombie could crouch with his Drano. – No, that would be impossible. There was no way to get up there.

Presently something hooted, and he saw a Southern Pacific engine approaching on a track twenty feet away. Two close-set eyes blazed unwinkingly on its narrow front, illuminating the tunnel ahead through which it must trundle, and it creaked slowly by. In the swatch of light, he saw grey gravel, dead plastic bags, and milk cartons squashed as flat as dead white leaves.

The Other stepped to the next track and began walking toward the tunnel. Clouds were blowing across the yellowish sky, eating away at the tall buildings so that the city shrank momentarily. The tracks were crossed by broken paths of golden light. These light-paths were too ethereal for the gravel and dirt between the tracks; they could live only glancingly, striking in parallel perpendiculars to the long double-sweeps of polished silver, silver metal in the moonlight, silver perfection visited by perfect gold. Between the rails, the ties were stubby cutouts of black velvet. The freeway lowered ahead of him, so that the place he must go became increasingly dark, low and mean. But the windows of warehouses still shone like cracked gold foil. – On his left were two lockers side by side. They were probably used by Southern Pacific. In any event, they were bolted, so he kept on. As he drew level with City Electric Supply, a double-decker passenger train pulled by, heralded by the same high narrow-spaced lights. It must have been one of the last trains, for they stopped running at ten-o'-clock. The windows were yellow inside. The train was full of faces, but not one of them saw him. The train went by.

His footsteps echoed round him in a spiral of sound, as if he were recklessly casting lantern-beams into the darkness. He did not yet feel that *there was someone else with him*, but potentiality seemed to be increasing and concentrating ahead of him like mist. The whole place was thick and grim with darkness. The air was heavy with it. With every breath, he inhaled darkness. He had not been prepared for this. It was as if he were an ant, walking inside the lonely blackness of a dead body. – Something flickered blackly. – He suddenly sensed the presence of fence on either side of him, although he could not see it; he was trapped now, like a steer in a narrowing slaughter chute. The freeway continued to descend. He saw something at his left shoulder like a gallows. It was a high-necked train beacon. There was a ladder, each rung barely wide enough for one foot, and he ascended it to escape from his feeling of claustrophobia and to see what he could find out about the black spaces above his head. But he could not really see anything better. The black spaces were larger, but no less black. The beacon hummed and clicked above his head. The full moon rested on the roof of City Electric Supply, and the clouds swarmed around the moon.

A brakeman walked steadily past, swinging his light, and The Other did not move. The brakeman did not see him. Ahead were two low signal lights, a red and a green. The Other watched as the man swung them around to face the tunnel, and presently another freight train came by from that direction. When it had passed, the brakeman turned the signal lights around again and retraced his steps. For a long time The Other could hear his boots on the gravel, but his little light soon disappeared into the darkness. When he was quite gone, The Other clambered down and continued toward the tunnel.

In the sky to his right, a billboard wore its authoritative message, illuminated by unsleeping advertising lights of such power as to expose the pale hill of rubble below. Yes, he was fenced in now. There was a smell like stale coffee-grounds. The tracks went on, dull and silvery, into the archway of darkness beneath the Eighteenth Street/Mariposa exit. The moon was glowing through a swirl of spilled clouds.

He picked up an empty bottle of Gallo port and let it drop. It did not smash. (Did The Zombie hear?)

Beside the train tunnel was a long gallery with empty black windows. It was as though he were entering a buried amphitheater with many stages and pillars and dead dark sideshows. He could not tell whether the dark spaces were blind or whether they were open to the night. Most likely they were blind, because the atmosphere was close here, despite the vastness of the place. Perhaps he was breathing in The Zombie's breath. It occurred to him that if he were to see The Zombie now he did not know what he would do. – In that instant his heart stopped still, and then began to pound, because in one of the side-galleries he saw a whitish oval face! The face was watching him. He saw the thin lips, the awful black mouth, the black eyes. The face did not cease from watching him. It regarded him with phosphorescent malice. Presently he understood that it was a painted face. – The pupils of his eyes had dilated, and now he could see the night-paintings all around him. On his left, on the long smooth dark wall that stretched ahead as far as he could see, was depicted the silhouette of a black-hooded skeleton aiming a gun into the darkness; beneath that long, long arm (an arm is long that ends in a gun) was a decapitated head, glowing dirty-white in the scarce moonlight that reached it; it was crying. Another whitish figure stood beside the skeleton, staring out at him with a dim uneasy face, but what it was he could not tell. On the other side of the gallery was written the word WAR. Had The Zombie so decorated his quarters? The Other thought not, and as he reached his conclusion he felt a moment of pity for that monster (which was his last pity for himself), because he understood then that The Zombie, still more than the Wrecking Crew, was never at home, that he would do nothing to harmonize his environment to him. Had he loved the darkness and sought to propagate it, had he surrounded himself on purpose with dark things, he would at least have embodied something, but The Other comprehended that it would have been all the same to him if he had lived at the Hilton Hotel or at a school for smiling clowns. One empty space was as good as another for The Zombie to hide. As for The Other, he would not have wanted a flashlight and a mirror at that moment. He was afraid of the darkness in his own mouth.

Darkness, darkness! He took his slow and careful steps through the ooze of seconds and minutes. As he proceeded through that overly still darkness, he felt anxious that someone might be behind him, about to strike at him. It was the still *obscurity* of the darkness that most alarmed him: – the darkness itself could strike him with its darkness. Maybe the darkness was The Zombie, in which case The Zombie was at this moment bending over him and fondling him and kissing his mouth. Just as someone awakened late at night by a threatening phone call, as he has been on random nights over a period of years, will find his heart pounding and his viscera slopping in their own corrosive acids, because he knows that he is trapped, so The Other realized that he was trapped. It was a dingy feeling. He strode on, in an angry nausea against the darkness that was at least preferable to fear. – The freeway continued to lower. As he walked between the twin rows of pillars, which reminded him of concrete legs, and everything exclusive of the freeway was more and more blotted out by that lowering, he felt as if he were crouching beneath the underbelly of an immense lizard. The monster was not yet aware of him. – As he proceeded deeper under the hill, he sometimes encountered places that were very brightly lit from overhead, where the off-ramp was. Very sharp trapezoids and triangles of light occupied the floor. When he strode into one of them, he was blinded for a moment, and felt a sense of exposed vulnerability. – Yes, it was light, too, that he feared, not for itself, but for what it revealed to the night. – But these zones were extremely narrow – a step or two, and he had returned to the safe darkness.

The gallery came to an end. On the right was a bright steep upward way. Because he had been inside for so long, it took him some time to understand that he was now in the open air. (In fact he was not in the open air at all, because there were several other freeways in the yellow-lit night above him.) He undertook this narrow rubbly path. The slope was so dry and crumbly with sand that he had to use both hands and feet in his ascent. As always, there was a quantum of *sterile improbability* in this night world, which made everything clean because nothing was real. He might have been in some crumbling dream of ancient Rome. He passed desiccated scraps of newspaper, bricks, squashed dark garments disposed like dead dogs. He was coming closer and closer to the belly of the lizard, where the overpass met the dirt. He could not see into the darkness of that same hill two feet to the left of him, because he was in light. Overhead, he now saw that what he had taken to be the dull sky of a greyish-yellow night was still another ceiling; he watched horizontal bands of light go speeding on it from the unseen cars. He clung to the guardrail to help him in the final few steps of his ascent, and pulled himself up until the dark hill at his side had become the merest crack, capped at last by the freeway. He stood at his ease. The noise of traffic was all around him. Then suddenly he began to feel light-shy again, so he stepped down a few steps, ducked under the freeway (whose cold belly was only an inch above his head), and sat on that dry dark hill, with the bright hill glaring a few inches away from him, and had a clear field of view as he looked down into that long low gallery where he had been, with light shining on the train tracks. From his high darkness he could peer further into the dark side-galleries than he had been able to before; they were like cutaways of graves.

He turned his face toward the ceiling of that cold dark world, but still could make nothing of the black squares between the concrete runners. He reached up and could not touch the depths of them. He sat thinking for awhile. Then he started digging with his hands in the rubble about him. Presently he lifted up a piece of cardboard and found the satchel. Inside it was a cane, a black book, a box of garbage bags, and three cans of Drano powder. He opened the black book and saw the long list of names in his own handwriting.

Something broke inside his head. It seemed to him that he saw a figure coming toward him through the gallery. It was his own figure. He almost started crying. How could this be? Was he so distant from his other self that the two selves could not even share a body? – And yet, when he became certain of what he saw, a feeling of suicidal intoxication came over him. He wanted The Zombie to come to him, because The Zombie *must* come to him, after all. It was so much better than the waiting and the hunting. – The Zombie approached, remote and unhurried. From far away he could see that cheese-white face in the darkness, and the thin white blur of the cane (but he had the cane beside him!), and now he could hear The Zombie's steps and the slow steady tapping of that cane. He could see the eye-slits now, looking at him. The head craned forward on that pale white neck. One shoulder was raised; he could see the dark satchel swinging below it. The Zombie passed through the first narrow triangle of light, and in that revelation he seemed to The Other quite insignificant. Then he achieved the darkness again and became grand. His white wall of face loomed whiter and larger. – Oh, that evil face! Sadistically he swished his cane in the air, and The Other had a desire to yell at him . . . what? – but he did not, because although he knew that The Zombie saw him and was coming for him and that was exactly what he wanted, still now he hoped against the proof of his senses that The Zombie had not seen him (although he stood atop a hill of light), and it seemed slightly plausible to him (there was no hope of greater plausibility) that if he made no sound then nothing might happen to him. A flower of blood was going to blocm in his throat.

There was a steady quiet scrabbling sound as The Zombie's cane tapped toward him in the rubble. He saw himself hunching closer and closer to himself. – How sad, to fear and despise one's own reflection! – He thought to himself: I am ugly, but my eyes cannot be *those* dark vacant pits.

The Zombie's figure was getting larger very quickly now. As he approached, a cloud momentarily changed the quality of the light, and The Other saw that he was not so white after all, but grey, grey, grey – the color of the moonlit dirt. Their meeting was very near now. The Zombie had come irrevocably into the moonlight and was ascending the hill. It might still have been possible for The Other to pull himself up onto the freeway with his hands and pray for help from the streaming red cars, but he was still. And his chloral hydrate? He did not see it anywhere. Probably he had never had it.

There was no doubt anymore that The Zombie was going to hurt him. He could see The Zombie's face close-up now. He could see the shadow beneath The Zombie's lower lip. He could see the dark places behind The Zombie's eyelashes, and the stubble on The Zombie's neck. And yet there was not the hellish eagerness that he had always imagined when he told the murders to himself. Here was only sadness, seriousness. Perhaps there was yearning, too, but not lust. – The Zombie had turned his head to one side, the better to watch The Other as he neared him, but The Zombie's head was extruded forward nonetheless on that long, long neck. That slit of darkness was very narrow and even between The Zombie's lips. There was a weary scorn on his face, which glowed so white against the darkness below and behind him; and yet The Zombie's face was whitish-blue with *pain*, because it wanted him so very much.

"But what do you want from *me?*" said The Zombie

The Other stared at him with hate and horror. "I just wish you were dead," he said.

After the Orgasm

The Zombie went home. It was very late when he got to Turk Street. Everything was very dark and quiet; the police were making their 2:00 a.m. sweep of the nightwalkers. But on his front steps The Woman Who Laughed was waiting for him. – How she stank! – Dumb beings, it is said, often have the talent of discerning evil in others. Cats will run away from sadists. But The Woman Who Laughed had no fear of him. He bent over her in the darkness and whispered to her. The Woman Who Laughed heard every word. Her shoulders started to jerk. For several seconds she held the laugh in, but it was bound to come out, like a rush of black vomit, and she sat shaking her head and laughing until the tears rolled down her fat dirty cheeks. – He led her upstairs. Laughing, she threw off her coat. She was wearing a dead pigeon around her neck. She lay on the floor and spread her legs for him. The Zombie pretended that she was already dead, that she was Blue Lady, that the soles of her feet were stinking and livid red and yellow.

Out of the Yonder

By day, the underpass seemed very bright and spacious. (He had never seen it except at night.) The train tracks rolled steadily on (there were five of them), and the freeway was high enough to admit the blue sky to its foundations. On one stained concrete pillar someone had written **PISS TEST**. On another was a drawing of a vampire bat with the legend C.I.A. Across the street it said *THE NIGHTSTALKER EATS JUNK FOOD*. But as The Zombie kept walking and the freeway lowered, things became cooler and shadier. Once again he was walking beneath the belly of the lizard. A train went by, jingling its bells. It bore diagonal orange stripes on its face. The commuters frowned over their newspapers; no one looked out at him. He saw clouds reflected in the windows. Then the cars vanished into the tunnel.

Between the concrete runners he could now see a finer texture of perpendicular beams where last night there had only been darkness. Those spaces resembled textured bathmats. Above the tunnel's mouth, behind the guardrail, local trucks went by. The echoes traveled in reverse direction.

In the daylight, the gallery was still vast. Its walls were a variety of soft greys. The painted black figure which had seemed to be pointing a gun was only pointing; and the decapitated head was almost *smiling!* How happy and sunny everything was! What had looked dirty white in the darkness was actually semi-fluorescent orange. There was a dead woman painted on the wall, beside the pointing figure. He did not know why he had never seen her before. Her shadowy face was haughty and blue. She stood, hands on her hips, watching him from far away, far certainly from the dirt commensurate with life. Of course it was very difficult for anyone (let alone The Zombie) to imagine what she was thinking. Whose lives did *she* seek to rip from living flesh? – Somebody had painted a hula skirt and a bra over her nakedness, but it could still be seen through the flat translucence of her clothes.

The sun streamed narrowly in, where the freeway light had fallen before, in the same long, narrow triangles and trapezoids. These patches of color made the underpass seem wretched, whereas before it had been grand and melancholy. As for the side-galleries, shafts of light had reached even those walled graves, in each of which was buried a pigeon-corpse, which darkness, earth and ignorance had kept invisible from The Other, just as injected formalin will render cyanide undetectible in a cadaver. The sun shone on the railroad tracks and on the weeds. Flies were suspended in the golden air. Were *they* happy? Smoke fell slowly from the freeway, exhausted by diesel trucks. On a flight of concrete stairs leading nowhere, whose edge was starkly white in the sunshine, someone had written **BLOOD** and **VOODOO**. An engine was canted on its side in one of the crawl-spaces. It had not rusted; it had only become enshrouded in sand.

He looked up the slope once more, but The Other's body was still gone. So he turned back the way he had come.

The shade was very chilly. Bits of broken glass gleamed greenly like gems. He stared fixedly at those green points of light, admiring their beauty, perhaps, although it is difficult to be sure, since now that he had drowned half his brain in black blood his thoughts were even more conjectural than Ruby's had been, for he must go mute. – Ahead of him were the consecutively lengthening patches of sunlight corresponding to the freeway's rise into the Blue Yonder. The side of the City Electric Supply building was warm and tan. The sky was blue and the sky was blue and the sky was blue. As he walked back into the sunlight, abstractedly looking down at the single set of footprints, his shadow preceded him. He stepped over a dead battery; he passed swollen yellow pieces of melted rubber that resembled fried grubs. The dirt was packed down flat before him, and the rubble was warm.

One of the railroad tracks turned off into a narrow shady passage between two buildings where someone had written *U ASKED FOR IT*, but The Zombie was not tempted; he kept walking into the light.

The Zombie's Last Night

And now The Zombie, having put off his disguise of evilness, owned himself for the good being that he was, but he knew that the world would not see it that way, so he swallowed liquid Drano and died in agony – alas!

Rich's Last Night

Rich and his buddy Kelly died in a fire in Berkeley. They broke into an abandoned building to sleep, and one of them lit up a cigarette, and the building burned down. They had only wanted to be warm. I remember Rich because he had such honest loving eyes. It could have been better and it could have been worse.

A Sixth Street Memorial Service

"They fell asleep," said the Chief, who had been missed by The Zombie. "So they burnt their *own* asses up, and *fuck* 'em! If I had 'em over there in Nam or Korea with me, I'd 'a' put my goddamn A-One Nine-One Eighteen-Oh-Three right up their goddamn tushy and pulled the trigger!"

"Yeah, but you know what?" said Code Six. "I can't exactly say that, man. I can't exactly go along with that, because anybody – me, you – we all can fall asleep with a cigarette or sumpin' like that, have some kinda tragic *incident* occur."

"Okay, dummy," said the Chief. "Now, look. With your military training, you *knew* you're not supposed to light a goddamned cigarette up – "

"*Fuck* that!" said Code Six.

"*Fuck* you, too!"

"Okay. Okay. Training is good, okay?"

"*Thank* you," said the Chief sarcastically.

"*If* you're sober and have a right mind, you got *presence* of mind and all that shit, training will do you good. But you enter alcohol into the picture, you get drunk enough, fucker, you're gonna burn up, too!"

"You're *goddamned* right!" the Chief growled.

"Alcohol alters your fucking sense of *being*, you know."

"No, not being, but *timing*."

Evangeline's Last Night

One night just before the fall rains started I saw Mary on Haight and Shrader, and she did not look very pretty and there were a lot of drunks behind her and she was drunk and so she rocked very slowly back and forth on her heels at the edge of the sidewalk, with a periodicity approaching the exactitude of a laboratory pendulum, and eventually she was going to fall down into the street and hurt her face. She did not recognize me. She had only known me for three years. – "Do you have some change?" she said, swaying and swaying. I looked at her, and it was clear to me that Mary in her long soft coat, smiling her smile of gap-toothed sweetness framed by her long soft hair, Mary in her ski cap was not reflecting on THE END*; and she thought the pause was longer than it was and looked guilty and said, "I didn't mean to be rude," and I gave her twenty cents. – "I've got to go get my sister some water," she said. "She's not feeling very well." I saw another Indian woman sitting on the sidewalk, looking down at her knees. The woman had a round unhappy face. Like Mary, she seemed to be engrossed in the long slow process of forgetting who she was. She began to retch.

"How's Evangeline?" I said.

"Evangeline's in the hospital," Mary said in surprise. "It was her stomach. Too much drinking."

"And how's Luke doing?" Luke was her man.

"Luke?" she said. "I haven't seen him." She spread her arms. "I haven't seen him. I haven't seen him. Last I heard, he was in Santa Barbara. But I haven't seen him. I haven't seen him."

To Be More Specific

In the Necropsy Suite it was very bright and clean. The steel tables, scratched but dauntlessly silver, shone in the sunlight that crept through the frosted windows. On one table there was a long mound under a white sheet. There was an unaccountable bulge near the far end of the mound. What could it be? She did not have a big belly. She did not have big breasts. I could not understand it. Of course it was easy enough to wait patiently unwondering, since the mystery would come off with the sheet.

Against the wall were three steel trolleys, each one housing its own pulleys and cranks. What could *they* be? They were reminiscent of slaughterhouse winches. – "We don't use them anymore," said the pretty blonde pathologist. "They're awfully antiquated."

By the refrigerator were shelves of pickling-jars, each with its own brittle bits of meat.

---

* "Remember the end," says Ecclesiasticus (VII.36), "and thou shalt never do amiss."

The pathologist went into the shower room to change into gown and pants. She slipped the paper covers over her shoes. Then it was time for the disposable hat, and the surgical mask, so that all I could see of her was her pale face and big spectacles. "I've been finding the gowns soak through with blood," she said. "This worries me because I have a number of open cuts from dermatitis."*

The pathologist put on two pairs of rubber gloves. Just before she raised the sheet, I experienced a revulsion of feeling.

"Yesterday I looked at this guy who was fifty-eight, a boozer, and I had this feeling he must have kept resolving to stop, and put it off and put it off and put it off, and finally he was dead. You only have one chance," the pathologist said. "You only have one life."

Evangeline looked quite small and naked on the table. Her head was thrown back so firmly that a block of wood had been placed under her back. It was her breast and shoulders that had been the lump. Her reddish hair flowed down onto the table. Her chin was a huge fatty bump. There was hardened pinkish matter inside her nostrils. Her eyes were screwed shut; it looked as if she were biting her lip. Her face was red, and there were mottled red and purple patches of livor mortis. Purple excoriations were stamped on her flanks and thighs. As yet, Evangeline's blood was still inside her.

A flower was tattooed on her thigh. Had Barlow ever seen it?

The pathologist held Evangeline's breast up with one hand and began to cut around it. The first drops of blood came. If Evangeline had been alive, this might not yet have been a mortal wound that the pathologist was inflicting, but *now* . . . or *now* it would have been. – She was red and yellow inside; the red was her blood and the yellow was her fat. – The pathologist's scalpel swam downward, through the fat of chest and belly and almost into the pubis with its pitiful treasure of reddish hair. The blade was wet and scarlet-black. When it reached the bladder, a beautiful golden liquid began to run out onto the table. Second by second, it became more orange as it mixed with the blood, undoing all the work that Evangeline's kidneys had performed so unremittingly for fifty-two years (although with less and less success).

The pathologist's assistant began to cut behind Evangeline's ear. (Was it still Evangeline's ear?) He sliced around the back of her head,

---

* "One does *not* get 'cuts' from dermatitis," Adelson remarks here. "One gets *fissures.*"

with the steady care of a man proceeding on a long journey, and in time, thanks largely to this painstaking attitude, he had reached the other ear. – Evangeline's hair was wet. They had hosed the death-sweat off her face and wiped her down before putting her in the refrigerator to await this event, but they had not dried her hair, where the cold clear droplets hung suspended in hair-grease like grapes. The assistant seized her clammy hair in his hand, pushed firmly down on the forehead, and yanked. (It was his aim to turn her inside out.) There was a slow wet crunching sound, like teeth in sugarcane, and the flesh on the back of Evangeline's head came off, still hinged to her head by hair and skin. The face had not yet been destroyed. He pulled this visor of wet red flesh down over the eyes, and Evangeline's long wet hair fell down over her face, covering her chin. At the back of her head was the bloody skull.

By now the pathologist had opened the body cavity. She and her assistant palpitated Evangeline's fat wet intestines, which were as brown as link sausages, and the assistant cut a loop of them out and started skinning the fat off. He let them dangle on her thighs. They left fine blood-points there. – How the living labored over the dead! Sometimes their energetic motions stirred the wasted arm, and the hand with the wedding ring still on it twitched, although it remained closed as tight as ever. – "There's so much fat in a woman!" the pathologist muttered to herself. As she scooped out that congealed yellow tallow, the breasts lost their fullness. They sagged; they became flat and wrinkled and white. The musculature of the chest was striped with red, like beef, but there were thick yellow stripes.

Slowly the assistant hacked Evangeline's intestines out, and the smell from them got stronger and stronger. He cut through the diaphragm and probed with gloved hands. – How red and yellow she was inside! Now the blood began to come out. He stuck an aspirator into her belly and sucked it out. It whirled down the long plastic tube and drained forever into the sink. He sutured the intestines and set them into a bowl to wash them. For a moment the smell of Evangeline's urine was almost overwhelming. (I had loved Evangeline.) He lifted the bowels in his hands and hosed water inside them, so that reeking brown liquid flowed through them until the bath in which they lay became reddish brown. He rinsed them and rinsed them. When they were clean, he put them into a tray which he rested on the dead woman's naked ankles; it was no inconvenience to *her*. He kept hosing down the blood on the table, to keep it wet, because dried blood can be inhaled, and may transmit disease.

Her head was now hinged in several places. Between the wedges of flesh, which the pathologist turned musingly like the pages of a rare book, were bookmarks of hair. Her assistant started cutting through the skull with his bone-saw, producing smoke and fine white bone-dust. Sometimes that pink fleshy visor slid upwards, like a skirt in a wind, and I could see Evangeline's face again. There was a smell like the smell of drilling teeth at the dentist's. Her hair was speckled with bone dust. As he continued, her face began to deflate. Evangeline was going away from us. Her features became sagged and wrinkled. Then I understood that our faces are masks, which must come off on Judgment Day. But for the assistant, the falling of Evangeline's face was only an incidental *effect*, not a *result*. He would not dissect that once most expressive part of her. The head-house had had its glorious windows, in which Evangeline's lighted love had lived, and even though the curtains had now been drawn upon that sad and empty house-front, it was his duty to enter humbly, from the back door, in respect for what had been. The bone-saw whined and whined. White dust powdered her wet hair.

At last he had slit her skull from ear to ear. He took hammer and chisel and began to pound against the skull's last and most formidable defense, its bony hardness. Calmly, slowly, he drove the chisel in. The skull continued to resist him until he had worked a hook into the widened crevice and twisted sharply. Something creaked. Blood dripped slowly from the back of Evangeline's head. Her face was swollen and wet. (He set the red wedge of skull on the table, where it lay, hard and useless, like a bit of coconut shell.) Light fell upon a membrane through which her brain could be seen. The tissue of this window was worked with red arteries. Behind it, her brain appeared hard and firm and bloated, like a basketball. He took his hook and scissors and slowly drew back that last envelope that kept him from her brain, with its deep blue-yonder convolutions.

Meanwhile the pathologist kept peeling the chest-flesh aside, working up under the shoulders; and the farther she went, the redder the meat became. She rolled the dead breasts up onto the chest. With bone-saw and hooked silver knife, she sliced through the ribs. Now came the more delicate work of peeling away the fat below the ribs. For the first time, the world saw the shady pink darkness under Evangeline's ribs.

There was a hollow space there, because when Evangeline exhaled her last breath the lungs had collapsed. They were spotted black. Evangeline had not smoked; it was only from the city air. – Now here was her liver, grey and pale with cirrhotic scars. The pathologist cut into the pericardial sac, and a tea-colored effusion dribbled out. It was blood-tinged, but not clotted. This was indicative of stress on the heart. She reached into the lower abdomen again to loosen the bladder. Yellow globules of fat slowly drifted down. She cut through a membranous sheath spangled with blood . . .

The first fly came, *en retard*. Evangeline had been dead for four days.

They bent over that poor dead belly, and their gloves were black with feces and blood. Worrying her shoulders, they threw her breasts back down where they belonged for a moment, and there was a heavy slap of dead flesh against dead flesh; for her breasts were like those lead-weighted lap-robes that one must wear while receiving X-rays. The assistant cut off a little cube of fat and dropped it into a jar. He added a strip of red meat. Those two flesh-gobs must now dwell together, floating, floating, while the virgin transparency of formaldehyde was slowly clouded over the years and tinged reddish-brown. – The pathologist made a final cut and eviscerated the cadaver, clutching those guts and organs with as much care as does an obstetrician performing a Caesarian delivery – and with as much reason, for if the latter must guard a new life, the former had in her bloody gloves the final judgment on Evangeline, the purple slimy things which would demonstrate what Evangeline had done to herself that she must die so early.

– What a pale pathologist! She was paler than her white mask because she felt the nauseating onset of some gastrointestinal disease. How could she have illusions about what was inside her? Of *course* it must be malign. She bent over the organs, her gloves stained with dried blood. Everything had its own protective sheath to be cut through.

Sunny Days

Evangeline's kidneys were a dark and royal purple, each cortex being deeply pitted, bruised with internal hemmorhages. How strange that we had once sought so far for Phoenician dye, when all the time it was inside us! – And there was also a certain fish which some Emperor ordered brought alive over many dry leagues to the capitol, because the Emperor loved to watch him asphyxiate. I can imagine the crowd that His Majesty must have permitted to gather (unless he preferred to view the spectacle in a private chamber, as I viewed Evangeline): the grinning courtiers – some grinning to make the Emperor grin, and the rest excited by the costliness, the novelty; the abashed fisherman, to whom the Emperor might toss a golden coin; the pale artist; the bored royal favourites. All his life the fish had lived in the sea. Then he was exclaimed over and thrown into a barrel of sea-water, in which he must now swim round and round, while men carried him across the desert, and the sky was blue and the sky was blue and the sky was blue; until, at the Emperor's nod, he was seized by his tail and drawn into the air. Still living, he was palely translucent, like Evangeline, whom everybody stared through, seeing an empty doorway where she sat. – But now the fish gaped his mouth! He flopped and flopped, strangling in that which we breathe – and the Emperor leaned forward searchingly, awaiting the first sign of what he pleasured to see. The fish was full in his torments, slapping the air with his head and body, since he could not do so with his tail; and droplets of sea-water sparkled on him and sprayed from him, and water ran from his mouth. A slow tinge of purple began to color his gills – and how the courtiers exclaimed! The further along he went in his dying, the richer was his purple – such a *lovely* purple color. And everyone thought, as I said, that purple was so rare, when they had it in their own kidneys all along. As for Evangeline, her kidneys were a more magnificent purple than her spleen, although the latter organ was more marvelous to us, being (as is customary in alcoholics) grossly enlarged, so that when the pathologist threw it down onto the pan of the butcher's scale, the pointer dropped as if she had punched it in the solar plexus and it trembled and quivered and finally came to equilibrium at 580 grams; whereas the spleens of most dead people weigh barely a hundred – for Evangeline had drunk so much Night Train in her life that she developed portal hypertension and then her liver began to fail, and the blood backed up into her spleen until it bulged and its white-cell spots died, and then it turned to purple pudding inside.

Her liver, however, was less hypocritically flattering to the royal preference, having become disloyally colored as, ruined by Night Train, it began to disloyally serve. I could have mistaken that swollen, cirrhotic organ (1660 grams) for her heart, such was its size. The healthy liver is soft and dark. This dead thing (Evangeline had killed it) was pale grey and quite firm to the touch, because it was now composed of little more than scar tissue. In texture it had a loathsome coarseness. Diseased nodules speckled it. – As the pathologist cut it open, she inadvertently slit the gall bladder, and it let loose its ropes of bitter green syrup, sandy with blue-black gallstones. – How like a book the body is! We each write our life story in it, describing to perfection what was done to us, what was done by us. Evangeline's liver was a chapter entitled: "What I Wanted." The text was short, but not without pathos: "I wanted to feel loved and warm and happy and dizzy," Evangeline had written. "I wanted to live in the Blue Yonder. I wanted to live in the blue sky and the sun. I wanted to be my own person. I got everything that I wanted." – The pathologist went on snipping and snipping.

The ovaries, which should have been pale, were black and encysted. They were bursting with blood. The bladder mucosa, which should have been white, exhibited red spots from some urinary tract infection. – "Not unusual with her sort of hygiene," said the pathologist, shrugging. There was nothing of note in that fat, grey, slimy uterus, and after slowly slitting it open with the big knife she dropped it into the trash, where Evangeline's dirty orange parka had already gone, where the rest of Evangeline would go piece by piece. What use, after all, did the world have for a dead uterus? It was only natural to throw it away. – The aorta was smooth all the way down to its bifurcation, as was to be expected; it would have been difficult for Evangeline, with her unenthusiastic diet, to roughen it with atherosclerotic fat. The pancreas was normal, but the trachea was raspberry-red inside. (It should have been white.) Evangeline, you see, had aspirated blood. She had been vomiting blood right before she died. She had choked to death in her own blood. – Oh, Evangeline, through what cruelty did you have to be born? – Blood had stained her red, red larynx. – The pathologist grasped the duodenum. (A fly settled happily on the rim of the organ jar, then on the edge of the tupperware tray that was so red and yellow with organs.) She slit the stomach open and hosed out the gastric content – mainly clots of blood, since you do not eat much at any time as a member of the Wrecking Crew, and you eat less still when you are on your alcoholic death-bed vomiting up blood. Surprisingly enough, the stomach was not ulcerated. It was a beautiful pink, like raw flank steak. Rugae were raised in pride along the inside tissue, like lovely leaf-veins. Here and there, however, were minor bloody erosions.

"Well, the pulmonary arteries look nice," the pathologist said. "And the coronary arteries are both open, so she had no occlusions." But there were blood clots in the heart muscle, suggesting a possible myocardial infarct. At least the heart muscle was nicely striated. As the pathologist cut, it fanned out on all sides like the undergills of a mushroom. – Evangeline's heart itself, as predicted, was grossly enlarged, being 470 grams, or almost twice normal weight.* It had had to work very hard toward the end, after the liver-chapter was written and her blood got more and more saturated with waste, so that her poor heart did not know what to do and tried to pump her blood *faster* through liver and kidneys as if that would somehow make it clean; – pumping, pumping, as the sun went up and the sun went down; but there was no way to make her blood clean anymore. Her heart swelled up, and later she died.†

It was clear, then, what Evangeline had died of, but for the sake of thoroughness the pathologist threaded Evangeline's small and large bowel through gloved fingers, looking for polyps. There were none. In places the intestines were hemmorhagic (engorged with blood), but that was a standard pre-terminal occurrence, so the pathologist said. She dissevered Evangeline's lungs and inflated them with formalin from a big plastic jug marked MORGUE. She had to do that to see them as they were in life. – The purple lungs floated in their thin red bath of formalin and blood. When they had "fixed" for ten minutes, she slit them open. One of them was bleached by pneumonia.

The Death of Death

Evangeline's body lay on the block, its skull empty, the breasts hanging down on either side of the skull. Her resigned face was covered with hair, and the pink skin-cap stayed low over her eyes. Only her downturned mouth expressed any displeasure at the situation. The pathologist's scalpel lay beside her in a thin layer of blood. If you looked into her cranial cavity, which was pink and blue, you could see the huge eye-holes where her brain used to see, and then a round hole with the

* I.e., 280 grams.
† "But why do the hearts of alcoholics swell up?" I asked. – "They don't know," the pathologist said. "It's a complete mystery."

pink brain-stem still in it, and finally a sort of cleft palate, now half-full of blood, where the cerebellum had been. Presently the assistant strode over to suture this last big piece of Evangeline back together again for the mortuary – not that it really mattered because she was a "curator case" with no relatives or friends who could claim her, so the state could do as it chose with her. (There was a urologist who collected penises from curator cases. He did not make a hobby of women's organs, so the carcass was spared that.) Sewn up, Evangeline still looked as if something had been taken out of her. Her breasts had sunk. Her arm hung off the table, as if in exhaustion at what had been done to her. Her matted wet hair concealed the suture in her skull. The assistant wiped the blood off. He hosed her face; he scrubbed her bloody legs. Then he laid out a new plastic sheet on a cart, rolled her onto it, folded her arms and wrapped her up. You could still see her shape. He wheeled her away.

The blood coagulated quietly on the steel table. On the shelves were jars full of bits and pieces of dead people – the rubble of organs, piled upon each other in the formalin like bits of exotic fungi.

"How long will something keep in formaldehyde?" I asked naively.

"Forever," the pathologist said. "See, there *is* immortality."

The Menu

"They serve us cornflakes," said old Cory Smith very thoughtfully. "Crip-sey rice. For breakfast. And grits, cream of wheat, corn meal and oatmeal. And pancakes. But seldom have they fed us French toast, which I suppose is too much for them, you know, to fix up for a bunch of guys like us. For lunch we have a variety of things to eat. We get chili and well-seasoned spaghetti, and we get tuna casserole – *Amen!* – and stews, and black-eyed peas – *yum, yum, yum!* – and short ribs, spare ribs, steaks, and pork chops. We don't get no – well, we do get rice. Principally on Sundays. We used to get rice with chunks of meat in it. And for supper we ordinarily have various kinds of sandwiches. Tuna of the sea. And liverwurst spread. Peanut butter. And CHEESE. Baloney, salami. You name it, they have it. Everything you wish. Everything in the whole Blue Yonder. And soup. Mushroom soup, chicken noodles, and chicken rice, and split pea, and minestrone – oh, boy, you name it,

and they have it! I thank the LORD that He has provided all this for us
guys that are on welfare, that are getting the money on welfare, if it
wasn't for the LORD. And I believe that deep inside each of these guys
they feel that way, even if they don't talk like that. My soul goes up with
the guy because they say they ain't got no one. But they got Jesus the
same as I have, so, *Amen.*"

Sunny Days

Sometimes the sky was so solid and even a blue that I wondered if the
ancients had been right, and it was in fact a vast dome of yonderness.
One day the birds flew by more freely. There was no one on the grass.
Black Fox sat under the shade tree, but there was no Mary, no bums
lying out or sitting out except for one man who sat with his chin in his
collar, his elbows on the back-rest, his hands in his pocket, staring
straight ahead. Sometimes he scratched his hair. He had been there
every day. Every day! The mind reels at it. If I had to live in the grass
forever, I would wish for The Zombie to come.

Rainy Nights

Some nights the fog would blotch together in the dim-starred sky like
the primeval continent of Gondawaland in the maps drawn up before
continental drift, and then a little while later the rain would come. The
wall of trees in the Park behind which the Wrecking Crew used to sleep
was now a rank of whitish trunks that seemed to wave in the rain like
underwater roots, and in all the black spaces between them there was
only a single yellow street-light shining steadily from far away. Once
there had been cigarette-tips and match-lights dancing there, when the
Wrecking Crew sat around drinking and arguing. Now there were only
a couple of members left, and they slept in the shelter with the rest of
the herd. The benches around the pond were deserted, of course.
Everything was sunken, black and clean.

On Haight Street a tramp was bowed over the hood of a police car
while the cop patted him down.

"Where were you bound?" said the cop.

"Haight Street," the tramp replied serenely. He was old, and had a long beard.

"Have a seat in the back," said the cop. "I'll drive you straight to the Greyhound terminal."

Sunny Days

The wind blew, and clouds curdled in the blue sky, and broken glass shone, but there was no one on the grass that I knew anymore. Even The Zombie was dead. Now the losers had lost everything.

The Last Word

The worst tragedies are those that take place in the sunlight.

For Jacob Bray, his wife Jeanine, and their son Ahab

AUTHOR'S NOTE

Three or four years ago, a number of decapitated bodies were found in Golden Gate Park. The murderer was never found. In 1985–6, the tramps in the Park told me that someone was trying to kill them off. They said that people were beaten to death or killed in other ways. I have yet to see my first dead body in the Park, and the Drano killings occurred solely in my imagination, but, after all, they could happen. To quote Dr. Adelson once more:

> Because malice, depravity and ingenuity take so many forms, cunning, evil and inflamed minds and imaginations conjure up unusual and unique methodologies of violence in order to maim or kill the objects of their hatred . . . One cannot categorize the huge number of ways in which people attempt to or succeed in killing one another [pp. 876–7].

THE
INDIGO
ENGINEERS

All stresses to which a material is subjected cause a deformation in it.

Machinery's Handbook, 13th ed. (1946)[1]

But Why do the Machines Fight Each Other for Possession of the Dead Flesh?

I do not have the strength of will to begin by describing the immense rust-orange wheels of Mr. Werner's Square-Wheeled Car. Allow me to start with the struggling, belly-crawling thing that pulled itself out of a thicket of steel thorn bushes one night, helplessly dragging its paralyzed legs behind. Truly, any good which I anticipated could not have been located with the most powerful electron microscope. Why had the belly-crawler not given up, like a rabbit that waits for its own predestined snake in helpless stillness shot through with shudders? – Because, my friend, it was a SNEAKY SOLDIER. (But to me it was only a human thing.) Its face was worried, sweating, anxious, but not hopeless. It *would* beat the cancer. It *would* escape the scalping party. It would *make* them give the job back. So the human thing worked its dogged and doglike way through the dirt; and arms creaked, legs hung; the set face stared dead ahead. The night was greyish-black. If you were buried alive so that you could see the dirt lying on your eyes you would completely understand this most unpleasant night which the human thing must sneak through. There were steady unknown noises in the darkness, like sonar-beeps or heartless cricket-songs. What gave the noises a particularly insidious character was their electronic purity, which pierced the air so evenly that it was impossible for the human thing to know whether they were coming closer. (The poor human thing could do nothing but

1 Comp. (New York: The Industrial Press), p. 345

continue sneaking and sneaking.) Presently, of course, the machine came racing after like an immense lobster. It was a tall machine with mercilessly upraised arms. Its claws were already shaking with tremulous need and glee. It gained on the human thing very rapidly. It seized the human thing, lifted it high into the air, and slammed it down, over and over. The human thing's body made a dull metallic clang; it was a robot, too. – Attracted by the struggling prey, another machine came racing up on long vicious screw-threads that left gashes in the ground. It was long and ribbed, skeletal and speedy, with hideous joints and angles. It held a Mummy-Cat's head in its claws; the head was still hissing and spitting feebly. It pinched the human thing's head in its claws (and then there was a dull resignation on the rubbr-mask face of that mutant, which had never had a chance), and from between the machine's long skinny metal arms a spiked penetrator-organ shot out and struck the human thing in the neck. Then triumphantly the machine turned its flamethrower upon the human thing, and the human thing's head burst into flames and the machine slammed its head off its neck and impaled the burning face on a pole, turned to the decapitated carcass, struck it over and over and over, then burned it with the flamethrower and slammed itself against the dead metal skeleton with sullen hollow sounds.

Concerning the Mummy-Cat

"The cat there is basically just a vehicle for my tank to show what a *real* victim is like, going down, kicking and screaming all the way." So said Matthew Heckert with a grin. "When it gets grabbed by my tank, it wiggles and tries to get away – although it *can't*, of course, since it's clamped in the sharp pincers of my tank. It's grabbed this hairy wiggling thing it doesn't know quite what to *do* with, since it won't stop wiggling and spitting."

The Master Plan

Winged like maple-seeds and insects, their thoughts fell to earth in a thousand ways – always verified by the smell of mchine grease. First there were the martyrized pigeons, then the posters, then the rockets and the crawling robots viciously battling for possession of decayed freeway underpasses or rubble-covered parking lots, while spectators cheered, fulfilling their own function of ghouls revelling in devastation,[2] and *then* the machines began to get larger and smarter and eviller. In those days they had flamethrowers and military CO_2 lasers. Meanwhile the Indigo Engineers,[3] concerned, perhaps, lest their machines become too complacent in their metallic strength, mated them to fresh or mummified carcasses, so that the robots were subjected to foul and stinking burdens. Dead rabbits became rabots when attached to devices which made them walk backwards in coy dead shudders; these worried and irritated the Mr. Satan robot as if they were vermin. The Indigo Engineers had by now begun to shatter glass in their festivities whenever possible. So punctuations were crystal-sharp in the expanding grammar of the Mechanical Hand, whose digits were so much more powerful than Mark Pauline's finger-stumps; and the stainless steel Walking Machine did its tormented part, at which the Mummy-Cat bucked and spat and the Witchy-Head expressed grave displeasure; but the Indigo Engineers (who called themselves Survival Research Laboratories) were not satisfied even so, and conceived the Screw Machine to massacre their Sneaky Soldiers (every predator is also a prey); and in the world we now had, therefore, the Spiky Roller Machine and the Buzz Saw, the dynamite-powered Shock Wave Cannon, the Walk and Peck Machine, whose pecks reduced the rabots and stink-dogs to bloody protoplasm, the Flying Rocket Powered Shark, the fifteen-hundred-pound Square Wheel Car, and of course the Inspector, "performing its contrasting functions of delicate manipulation and total destruction."[4]

2 Mark Pauline disagrees with my assessment of the spectators. But more on this later.

3 I call them this because they operate in the Beyond.

4 From a leaflet, "Previous Events by S.R.L."

Best of all was the Sprinkler From Hell, which sprinkled high-pressure gasoline in a truly illuminating fashion.

The Roster

MARK PAULINE (from 1978)

MATTHEW HECKERT (from 1981)

ERIC WERNER (from 1982)

Operation of the "Chain Thing"[5]

"Once engine is running smoothly, you may connect the previously disconnected battery lead. While carrying out this operation one *must* exhibit the most extreme caution and not place hands, body or clothing in any place where they may become entangled in chains, sprockets or cams of the moving machine. The three spinning chains on the front may come into action immediately when battery is connected . . ."

A Desperate Step

Andrea Juno, who was a senior editor at *REsearch*, the periodical of the peculiar, said that she and Mark and I could have dinner together on Sunday to discuss things, but if I called on Sunday and there was no answer, that would mean either that we were having dinner on Monday, not Sunday, or else that we were not having dinner on Sunday or Monday. On Tuesday it became clear that the latter case had been the operative one. Andrea Juno went out of town soon after. So I called

5 "When in operation," wrote the designer, Matthew Heckert, "it walks, taking steps which are constantly increasing or decreasing in length, and periodically rotates the three chains on the protruding shaft at approximately 630 r.p.m. It appeared in the performance 'An Epidemic of Fear' (Fort Mason, June 29, 1984, S.F., CA), and was fed a diet of whole raw chickens."

Mark Pauline myself. I had called him intermittently for months. I always got his answering machine. This time, however, I reached him on my second try.

My First Warning

"We don't like anybody over here when we're workin' over here," Mark Pauline explained on the phone. "National news people have offered us money to do it, and we've turned them down. They do their stories anyway, but they don't get what they wanted. Also, we're not interested in personality cults."

Mark Pauline, or, My First Personality Cult

Andrea Juno told me that Mr. Pauline drove slowly. This surprised me, because I had imagined Mr. Pauline as a loud fast careless person who did not scruple to break the speed limit, but I had to believe her, since I had not yet met Mr. Pauline. If one has only three points from which to extrapolate and one point is shifted, the graph may become quite different;[6] so, learning this new fact about Mr. Pauline, I now conceived him to be very slow and cautious and soft-spoken – and in fact the photographs of him in the *Industrial Culture Handbook* published by *REsearch* bore out this impression. He was a tall, gaunt, dark-haired individual with glasses and a frown. He seemed a little tense, a little sad, as he leaned against the post of some shed while superheated gases flared from his arm and shot across a vast distance and scorched a steel hoop. While posing with the Mr. Satan robot he appeared to have a

6 "I find it interesting," says Jacob Dickinson, a mechanical engineer, "that a single datum – one bit of information, perhaps two – can have greatly expanded significance depending on its context. One single lantern hanging in a church steeple could mean that the British intend to take a land route in their effort to destroy naval stores and round up subversives" (unpublished journal entry for 9/25/85). This interpretation of the lantern might indeed be the correct one. But a lantern is only a lantern, beaming forth light from its streaming eye with idiotic randomness. Perhaps the single light might mean nothing at all. Perhaps it might not even be a lantern, but the candle of some rustic arsonist . . .

lump in his throat. He was swallowing, shoulders hunched in melancholy. So I came to consider him a very measured person, particularly because in the *REsearch* interview he spoke as though he were slowly assembling paragraphs, bolting one sentence to the next with moderate redundancies in the grammatical design so that no matter what editing torque the transcript was subjected to, it would not lose its information value: – "Well," he said, "I've always liked to think that I can stir up trouble. It excites me to think that I can cause trouble. It's a very exciting thing and it still continues to make me excited to think that I can make trouble and annoy people . . . in a way that confuses them." So I now imagined Mr. Pauline to be slow, dry and unpredictable. But he was not that, either. He was *articulate* and *watchful*.

Note to Instructions for Setting Up Crawling Machine

"These instructions *must* be followed exactly. Otherwise the machine will function erratically, not at all, or most likely will be damaged in such a way as to preclude any possibility of repair."

Survival Research Laboratories

Following Mark Pauline's instructions exactly,[7] I came into a dismal neighborhood where some young men in leather jackets kicked broken

7 Exactitude is very important. I once set off to find Survival Research Laboratories, on a foggy morning, as a passenger on the back of James's motorcycle. James was a mechanical engineer. He had once seen a video of Mark Pauline performing a "Stink Dog" – the meaning of which soon became burningly apparent to him. – Vale, the other big co-cheese at *REsearch*, had told me that all I had to do was to proceed to Potrero and Twenty-Fifth, then walk down Twenty-Fifth to San Bruno, and turn onto San Bruno until it dead-ended in a warehouse courtyard; so we went up and down the Church Street hills, fog above us and fog below us, and followed Twenty-Fifth to near San Bruno, but Twenty-Fifth and San Bruno did not seem to intersect (actually, they did, but we did not understand the subtle collusions of that neighborhood's streets), so we swung onto the freeway, the wind grabbing our helmets with ghost fingers, and people in cars shook their heads at us, and the fog picked up and we turned off at the Silver Avenue exit and followed San Bruno over another big hill and down into Daly

glass and greeted me, "Fuck *you*, bitch." – Thus encouraged, I turned into a driveway between warehouses and turned right and was in an alley between garages. On my left was a stack of sinister machinery. There was an open bay door giving onto Survival Research Laboratories, where it was dark and creepy and filled with machines. A sign said: TRESPASSERS WILL BE SHOT. SURVIVORS WILL BE PROSECUTED.

Borrowing Things

"I'll take good care of them and bring them back," I said.

"I imagine you will," Mark Pauline said calmly. "I already put you down on The List."

Instructions for Setting Up Crawling Machine

"The yellow-brown wire leading to the power supply should be plugged into the first tab of the timing switch if it has fallen off during transit. note: Any mistake in the wiring will destroy the drive motor when power is applied."

City, but San Bruno still did not dead-end anywhere; in fact, it had now become Bayshore Avenue, and we saw a lot of decaying yellow-brick warehouses along the edge of the stagnant salt water but none of them could be verified as having anything to do with Survival Research Laboratories, and we came to another hill and gave up, so we swung back to Guadaloupe Canyon Road and went up into the fog, past San Bruno Mountain (where there was supposedly an Indian cemetery), and the fog got colder and the wind got stronger and the hills vanished around us and the air turned white and my hands went numb and we kept going until the road went downhill again; nobody was on it but us; and when we got to warm Mission Street we turned right and went back into San Francisco and stopped at our favorite burrito place, the San Jose Tacqueria, and that was the end of that expedition.

The Goodness of Mark Pauline

Heckert said that one night he was on the roof of Survival Research Laboratories, which is an extremely ugly sort of roof, rimmed with barbed wire, and covered with empty and broken beer-bottles, whose translucent brownness is reminiscent of dead Japanese beetles, and it was evening, and Heckert was in his bathrobe, and ten white punks from one of the Sunset gangs were facing him on the roof in what must be considered a threatening fashion, and one of the gang said, "Come on, you bitch, let's go for it," and Heckert was thinking he was going to have to hit the guy *really* hard on the side of the head, when just then his buddy Mark jumped in, pushed Heckert out of the way, and gave the enemy a short burst with a flamethrower. The guy screamed. He was not seriously hurt, but his arm was burned and his shirt was on fire. – "Hey, man," he said. "I mean, you didn't have to *flame* me!"

In the Shop

Mark Pauline was measuring things with his tape measure and the radio was playing "Oh, Happy Day" while Heckert was getting his work area reorganized and Malcolm the kitten was growing up second by second so that he would be able to fulfill his purpose: catching rats. The shop had a big lathe with seven yellow handles, two red knobs, and one black-sleeved indicator light in the corner next to the 440-volt controller box that said CORROSIVE and ! DANGER POISONOUS GAS and KENDALL GT-1 HIGH PERFORMANCE MOTOR OIL. The concrete floor was cracked and brown-stained. Mark Pauline was up on his ladder making smashing sounds. From my barely tolerated corner I could not see what he was doing, and knew better than to ask because at Survival Research Laboratories there was very little conversation (that is to say, none) for long periods of time, and one did not want to interrupt this concentrated industrial silence by asking questions. The lathe bin was bright with gleaming metal shavings. Mark Pauline went grimly up and down the ladder. A poster beneath him said, LET'S BACK THE

ATTACK – PREVENT ACCIDENTS. The shop was full of tool chests and benches and tall narrow carts and shelves of spray paint, gear lubricant, battery cleaner, ignition spray, brake fluid. Across the room was a black clock three feet in diameter. Its hands did not flinch when Mark Pauline began to strike metal with repeated ringing blows. His trained guinea pig, however, hid in the greasy box that gave it privacy in its cage. The guinea pig was a big animal with black markings. I sometimes saw it nervously eating its food. Its big black eye glistened sadly in the darkness. It had been inside a machine at one of the shows. Most likely it would be anxious for the rest of its life. Across the room, all was quiet in the place of different-hued wire spools.

We put huge rusty pieces of angle-iron into the Johnson reamer, which must itself be counted as one of the Indigo Engineers, and the sawbelt went round and round, slicing deeper and deeper into the metal and dripping coolant into the bottom tray, and finally a piece of angle-iron banged onto the floor, and Mark Pauline measured off another segment and slid it into the reamer's reach, and this happened over and over, while the sawbelt turned and smoked, and the coolant bled, and the reamer's heavy green head slowly nodded down, down, down, and the saw cut deeper, and another piece of angle-iron fell. Mark Pauline stood meanwhile, frowning and drilling. – And Heckert was making new hydraulics cables for his nasty machine, the Inspector, which had been blowing (cable pressure was 800 psi); he cut the new lines clean with the cut-off cell and then he threaded the lines in and tightened them with a crescent, his big right arm going round and round; and Mark Pauline was out in the courtyard making something hum, and as we went out he went in and began to hammer on something, and Heckert had brought the Inspector out onto the sunny concrete driveway and fitted in the new hydraulics with the crescent, and his hands were black-wet with molybdenum disulfide. (Now Mark Pauline was under a steel cabinet, flinging hammers and sockets and other jetsam over his shoulder so that they slammed against the floor.) Heckert wiped his hands and checked the oil supply. "Half-stroke," he said. "I need oil *there*" – and inside, Mark Pauline was soldering something, and a fierce white light blanked out his face beneath the visor; and Heckert went in and came out with a big yellow can labeled HYDRO and gave the Inspector its honey-colored blood through a funnel. He opened the air supply which activated the remote control. *Mmmm!* went the Inspector. *Mmmm!* – It spread its horrid metal hands.

But blood was leaking out. Heckert had built the lines out of used tubing, and one of them was leaking. He went in, past the reamer, past Mark Pauline, who stood glaring down at the grinding wheel, which was whining and pissing a wide stream of orange sparks; and Heckert got some more line and cut it in the Sever-All, which also emitted sparks, and then he ground it on a belt sander, while up on the ladder Mark Pauline performed some operation which I could not understand, the singing sound of which was in the key of one of the piano's black notes. – Patiently, Heckert began to assemble the replacement lines. He would not know until he finished them whether or not they leaked, too. – Mark Pauline put a drill bit between his teeth and thought. He climbed up the ladder.

"Can you hand me that hammer there?" he said to me.

"Which one?" I said bewilderedly.

"The one right in front of your face."

Mark Pauline had me lift one end of a huge filthy old beam. First he wanted me to unhook the yellow cable, but I couldn't tell which hook or which cable, even though he got mad at me and yelled, "Can't you SEE it?", but I could not, so I took an end and hauled it up while Mark Pauline unfastened the cable and I carried my end out into the yard, forced to lift with both of my relatively weak pipe-arms while Mark Pauline sauntered along holding his end in one work-gloved hand. (I did not have work gloves, and my hands were soft. The beam, therefore, cut into my palm and made it bleed.)

The Wit of Mark Pauline

"Looks like you're about twice as strong as I am," I said.

"*That* wouldn't amount to much," said Mark Pauline.

He let go of the bar without warning me, and my end slammed down on my finger, and blood burst forth from the tip.

Heckert's Office

was a vast concrete room left of the shop floor. The first thing you saw there was a café booth with a napkin holder on the table and a book of matches and a little juke box built into the wall so that if you kept your gaze low and did not look away from the wall you might believe that you were in some cool dismal very old pizza parlor, but then you raised your head a little and caught sight of the refrigerator in the corner with the gruesome red plastic hands stuck to it, and then you might notice that the counter, with its catsup and toaster and microwave and dishes, was not quite clean enough to come up to Health Department standards, for the wood beneath the countertop was black with machine grease; and then there was a big expanse of concrete floor, with Heckert's desk like an island in the middle of it, and then more floor, and then shelves with gauges and things on them, and a big poster that said FROZEN ALIVE FOR 20 YEARS. Next to the café booth was a loft, above which was a mattress roofed with mosquito netting draped over a framework of steel bars, and below which was a darkroom. Heckert lived here, just as Mark Pauline lived in his office, and Werner in his. It was here that Heckert had designed the Inspector.

Instructions for Setting Up Crawling Machine

"*In addition*, make certain that the electric eye bar is *far enough away from the machine's mechanical hand so that it does not cross the beam when fully extended*. This can cause the machine to operate continuously and must be avoided."

Heckert's Drawings

I see two nested compass-sweeps, in which would-be radii inch out in parallel increments upon a diameter's good foundation. In successive drawings, I see more points and triangles upon the arc. The lines are elegant, ghostly-thin. I see squares and numbers; I see the caution: DISC TO MACHINE MUST BE 250 OVERSIZE. Then the circles are gone, and we have a blocky mechanical arm, with the thunder-suddenness for which Demiurges are noted. There are in these last drawings, smeared with machine grease, all the signs of art and intelligence, but the grime, the absence of captions, and my own mechanical ignorance makes everything seem irrevocably *lost*, cross-hatched and aged, the purpose never to be comprehended.

The Inspector at Rest

It was a cold greasy metal thing which, at home among sheet-metal scraps and rusty bars and cranes and curvy cages (some of which were also alive, although I did not yet know it), was camouflaged by them and seemed to dissolve into its parts. The Inspector's elbows were drawn in close against its body, and its hands (each of which had eight two-foot-long spikes for fingers) also faced inward. Survival Research Laboratories sometimes pretended to be only an auto repair shop, and Eric Werner was in blue overalls inside saying, "If you *do* want to try that steel wool . . .", and hammering was going on from the other shop across the courtyard, and the sky was indigo and the rusty cars rested and the thick black axle at the back of the Inspector was still, which meant that its three half-inch-steel Z-shaped blades were still, too (when they rotated, they formed into a vicious whirring swastika that could chew a cardboard box or a sheet of plywood or a dead animal into fragments that rained down as sawdust or meat, as the case might be), and on these days it seemed quite impossible that the Inspector was really what it was. Perhaps it was just a wheeled cart that somebody used for hauling tools. But why the claws, and why all the hydraulic hoses connecting those long jointed cylindrical arms to the pipes and pressure gauges beneath the trapezoidal platform of the Inspector's thorax? And why the greasy bicycle chains and motors mounted to the hands? What did those hands do? What *happened* when those horrible fingers "inspected"?

(It was shocking how quickly the Inspector could move. It was shocking to see the "massaging" capabilities of those cruel fingers.)

The sun shone on rusty sheet-metal warehouses, and power wires flapped in the sky, and the freeway noise was a steady rushing, and behind a fence at the end of the courtyard were tall trees. Werner's old white Pinto in front of Survival Research Laboratories had the following windshield message: THE ENEMY IS LISTENING.

Instructions for Setting Up Crawling Machine

"Before startup *be certain* that the grease supplied in the coffee can is spread under the wheels on the legs."

The Inspector at Play, or, How a Rabbit Died Twice

The rabot struggled so hard. The Indigo Engineers had killed it and put a struggling-machine inside it, so it had to keep struggling whether it wanted to or not. In ecstasy at such marked and prolonged pain, the horrid Mechanical Hand rose in its bath of oil and clenched its long sharp fingers and then, unable to stand the rapture, it submerged into the dirty fluid and bubbles rose up to tell the ecosphere that the Mechanical Hand was chuckling. Meanwhile the Inspector zipped around and brought its claws together and paused for thought and then discovered a Witchy-Head spinning around on a post, and at once the Inspector sped over to the Witchy-Head so as to vacillate delicately and then grab it and stab it with its thruster, but unfortunately a metal crab scuttled out from behind a curtain and jealously blasted the trophy with its flamethrower, so the Inspector had to drop it, and the crab got on top of it and then the machines fought and paused to think and then fought until finally the Inspector got away and grabbed a struggling Mummy-Cat, its second choice, but the cunning crab (which was the Walking Machine) rushed over to torch the Mummy-Cat, too, and the Mummy-Cat spat and struggled and burned as the Inspector crouched on its treads watching so raptly, and when the dying Mummy-Cat tried to escape it fell and broke into pieces and kept struggling and smoked and burned and stank, still struggling in singed pieces on the ground. The rabot died the same way.

Instructions for Setting Up Crawling Machine

"When facing the front of the machine, the square bar which forms the backbone of the arm *must* fall to the left of the lever protruding from the gearbox. *Attempts to attach the arm onto the opposite of the lever will result in the irreparable destruction of the arm and motor assembly.*"

The Mechanical Hand

Beside me at my desk I have Mr. Werner's Mechanical Hand, amputated from its hydraulic heaven so that it has a diminished, grasping aura, as if it could do little harm anymore but would still like to. Unlike a severed human hand, it has not relaxed its grip. Its springs and hard metal flesh sustain it. In fact, I can operate it manually, grasping in my own hand a gleaming silver tube which emerges from its hydraulic wrist. I pull the tube out of the cylinder, working against increasing spring pressure, and doing this pivots an angled silver bone downward, which tightens five linkage cables, one for each finger, and as they tighten they spin a groove-ridged cylinder around, and that extends the long tubular fingers, whose terminal joints taper into points capped by sinister black rings. The hand opens against spring pressure; let the wrist-tube go, and the fingers snap instantly back into their horrid curl. The thumb is a flat and hyperarticulated affair, with so many screws in it, so regularly spaced, that they seem to be a feature of its flesh, like pores. Its final joint is very sharp. I can easily draw blood by rubbing my own thumb against it.

Perhaps the skeleton of a human hand would look just as cruel. – Let me see. – Well, the human fingers spread over a proportionately wider angle. This gives them a less ambitious character than the mechanical fingers, which reach and reach and reach in tall almost parallel lengths. Secondly, the human fingers are fluted quite beautifully at their joints, as if some sailor had been hours a-carving them from their yellow ivory to give them their impractical loveliness. The silver fingers are tubes, pure and simple. They are no less complicated, but they gleam with a singleness of manufactural purpose which is rather daunting. Finally, the human skeleton-fingers hang free from the flexor carpi ulnaris, all in a plane unless they actively grasp, so that their natural state is a hail or a wave, but the natural state of the mechanical fingers *is* grasping. This fact, combined with their inhuman size, makes them seem formidable and ferocious.

Instructions for Setting Up Crawling Machine

"Caution. *Do not remove* the lower bolt [of the Mechanical Hand], which attaches the U-shaped mounting brackets to the square backbone bar. If removed, the washers could be mixed, or other parts incorrectly assembled, resulting in the destruction of the drive motor, the arm, or both."

In Werner's Office

"What's this thing here?"

"Oh," said Werner, "that's something I've got to finish one of these days. It's called the Torture Machine. It's a table that you sit at at.

You're strapped in the chair, and then your head is held in this steel frame. This thing here is a kind of indexer. There are six different *tools* on this carousel. This thing comes down, like *this*, and then it goes up to *here* and it pecks and drills and goes through a lot of infamous tortures. So it's going to have a lot of mock horror-drama. The head is going to be made out of plastic shell, in the shape of my actual skull, based on a computer picture. And we'll put a latex skin on it, with veins and everything like that. And this thing keeps going away at him, you know. What it does is, *here* it goes down to *HERE* and then turns ninety degrees after each operation, and then there's six nozzles that spray oil and solvent at high pressure to rinse it off. Also, all the way around it there's little tubes that'll be mounted and will have little streams of oil going up, like it's underwater."

"Sort of like the Mechanical Hand."

"Yeah," said Werner. "I really enjoy things that sort of like live in oil. – See, here's the old Mechanical Hand."

"What happened to it?"

"Oh, it's just been busted up over the years and stuff like that. I have this thing where after I do something I just kinda lose interest, no matter how much time I spend on it."

It was very gloomy and dusty in Werner's office, like some greasy garage-grave.

"And this is my version of a ten-barrel twelve-gauge shotgun," he said. "It shoots all ten barrels at once. What you do is, you put two guys in a Volkswagen and you don't like 'em, you drive by with this thing and stick it out the window. It'll blow the doors off, kill both people, and blow a hole right through the Volkswagen. You shoot Triple-O buck out of it, and each barrel's shooting eight thirty-eight-caliber bullets."

Instructions for Setting Up Crawling Machine

"With the threaded holes in the base aligned with the corresponding holes in the mounting plate, proceed to thread in allen head screws through the holes in the plate and into the threaded holes in the base. Do not overtighten these screws, as the metal in the base of the drive unit is a zinc alloy and is weaker than most other metals. However, undertightening will result in *irreparable damage* to the drive motor due to improper alignment with the black tubular sheath."

Mark Pauline's Crawling Machine Diagram

This resembles nothing more than a drawing of some crab or giant spider with stubby knee-cylinders in which electric eyes and reflectors are embedded, and the cables could be weird insect tendons, and the pump motor appears to be an esoteric venom-organ on the back of the spider's head (which houses the drive motors), and the on-off switch forms a horn which it would be easy to imagine as being made of chitin; and looming forward into an eyestalk is the stainless steel ball-and-drive unit with its black shroud. Not immediately noticeable, and more sinister for that reason, is the diabolically skinny hand of the claw-motor.

The Frightmaster

"How would you say that cruelty enters into your work?" I said.

Sourly, Mark Pauline chewed his Mongolian beef. "Cruelty is one of those kinda words that you hear repeated so much that it doesn't make any sense anymore," he said. "Cruelty the way I use it is just one aspect of the shows. It's like a tool; it's one way that we use to make the shows really happen. We're talking about shows with MACHINES, you know. It's kind of like in silent movies, actors tend to overact to get the same point across. You know, when sound came along, it settled down to the point where acting became a much more subtle thing. Well, I see what we're doing now as the very beginnings of trying to understand how people relate to the sight of machines interacting. In the old days, when philosophers talked about identity, it was never an issue for inanimate things. Inanimate things could not recognize in each other any kind of identity. You had to be alive; you had to have an intelligence in order to have an identity. And you had to have an identity in order to be able to understand either other identities or inanimate objects. Well, in these shows, what we're trying to do is bring inanimate objects to a level where they can act, and people can relate to them as identities. Towards that end, everything we do in the shows is very, very, *very* overplayed. But I just see the cruelty as one angle, an intensification. I mean, where do you draw the line? What's fondling and what's caressing? Kind of like that thing, you know, in child molestation. What's cruelty and what's like some sort of a personalized interaction between devices? It's hard to say, and in *fact*, how can *you* even ask? You say a machine can be cruel to another machine? How can that be? That's a weird question to ask, and it just suggests to me that what we're trying to do here to a degree succeeds."

"What if the machines *were* conscious and *did* recognize each other? What would they think about then?"

"Well, you have to infer that they think in the same terms that a person thinks: pretty much in terms of their limitations. You think in terms of what you have awareness of. Of course with people, the way that their mind works, they have an awareness that's cumulative. That has its limits, though. These machines are very limited in comparison to that. There's a very limited amount of functions that they can do. There's a potential that they have, and we are able to bring out that potential and operate them, but still, there's a limited potential that they have in some ways. I think that if they could think, and whatever they feel, if they do feel – there is that argument, that every single thing has consciousness, although it's such a speculative sideline that it's not worth bringing in – I think for a machine it would be just a question of *fulfilling the range of its potential possibilities in the best way possible*, and that's all a machine thinks about. A machine has no concern for whether its actions are right or wrong; a machine has no use for morality in the human sense. All it wants to do is . . . Well, it's like a *missile*, you know, with one of those high-explosive warheads. Think of the High Explosive as like the BRAIN. All it wants to do is *explode*. It's telling all the other parts of itself, 'I've gotta explode, I've gotta explode! You've gotta help me! We all have to work together so that I can BLOW UP;' And then like the Guidance Thing says, 'Wait a minute! You can't just blow up; we've gotta find a *target!*' and the Explosive just says, 'I don't care, I don't care; I'm just gonna blow up right now!' – and then the Rocket Motors are going, 'C'mon, c'mon, c'mon, you guys! Like, get it together 'cause I wanna like *get going*, you know!' You have to kind of look at it that way. All these machines – the complicated ones, at any rate – are made up of all these different systems that interact. You can sort of imagine all of them . . . *wanting* to get in on the action. When they don't get in on the action they get sick. – But these machines are still at a point where they can only express their personalities through people, which I'm sure is very disconcerting to them. But that's just the way it is. Just like *I* can only express *my* ideas through machines. It's too bad, but it's the way it is."

Instructions for Setting Up Crawling Machine

"Loosen the small hose clamp on the black tube which secures the tube to the fitting. *This is extremely important.* If the fitting cannot spin within the tube, attachment to the pump motor will result in kinking of the tube and burnout of the pump motor."

Two Weeks Before the Show

One night Mark Pauline was in his office watching the six-o'-clock news, which was all disasters, and Heckert looked up from a machine-in-progress and said to his assistant, "You know what it is, these *tabs* are too goddamned wide. I think some fucking Communist built this thing," and he bent back over his open-frame creature, whose wheels were turned cautiously sideways. It was not alive yet, but it soon would be. "It'll be like a figure-skater in full body armor," Heckert told me. The shop was humming and glowing, and it was dark outside. Later the Indigo Engineers would pull their corrugated door shut, so that intruders could see the skull-sign upon it that proclaimed NOTHING IN HERE IS WORTH LOSING YOUR LIFE FOR.

When the news was over, Mark Pauline emerged from his office and went back to work on his Worm machine. He was in a good mood; Werner said it was because he had gotten free food. According to Andrea Juno, he lived on three hundred dollars a month.

"So this is the machine that's going to bulldoze the mass grave?" I said.

"Yup," said Mark Pauline.

It was angled and bluish-black. I cannot easily describe it (how would *you* describe in plain language a machine which no one else has ever seen?), but its most conspicuous feature was a tall black A-frame elbow which grew taller and thinner when the Worm was bunching itself up, and shorter and wider when the Worm inched forward. It did not yet possess its excavating attachment, but it would soon. The relays had been cannibalized from a 1970s drilling machine. The Worm had three different voltages: six, twelve and eighteen. "That thing goes in the front there," Mark Pauline explained, "and this first valve is called the jump valve. It has to go on before anything else can go on. See, *this* has to fit every time."

Whereas an embryo grows on all fronts, the fingers becoming articulated at the same time as the brain becomes more brainish, a machine comes to life in modules and pieces. Treads can turn before the cannon is mounted. – Or is this a distinction, after all? People can play the piano before they learn French. – Perhaps it is best to say, then, that a machine's physical attributes develop like a person's mental attributes. – But is *that* true? A person can add various snap-on accessories to his being, such as watches, eyeglasses. The naked flesh-thing just happens to be the main module. – What *is* the difference, then? – Ask the Worm.

"I'm gonna do some things to it that'll make it move quite a bit faster," Mark Pauline said. "It's just a general purpose machine." He chuckled. "I like it, 'cause people can watch it and wonder what *else* it can be doing."

Werner's Principles

"See," he said, "everything I make is a version of something that already exists. Like the ten-barrel shotgun. I just change the rules a little. And everything I do's real streamlined, real condensed. It can't be made any smaller than it is. Every part's gotta have a balanced relationship to every other part. If it's really important to you, you know, you have to take the time until you know it's the right move, and at least here, when I make something, that's where I'm allowed to feel that."

"And, Oh, the Destruction!"

It was a dark and chilly night. Everywhere around me I saw stubbly faces and black coats. Had expressions been despondent, had the coats been a little less new, I might have fancied myself in the midst of a midnight evacuation of workers during the London Blitz. But in fact these pale punk people were vampires. How the Sinister Women's eyes shone! (And how the Ghouls smiled.) Every head was styled. I saw a tall man-woman with earrings and orange hair; I saw shaved heads; I saw high translucent rooster-combs. I saw a pale face, a mouth with a cigarette coolly uplifted . . . There were so many cruel spoiled faces waiting to be entertained. Three thousand people besieged the parking lot. They laughed and cheered as the Indigo Engineers tested the flamethrowers.*

On the concrete, H-shaped towers had been erected from fifty-five-gallon oil drums painted garish colors, and klieg lights glared down, and I saw Heckert pacing there, very serious in his blue-grey jumpsuit, and assistants with orange armbands ran from cable to cable while old music played, spunky upbeat songs like "The Flight of the Bumblebee," and the loudspeakers kept saying things like, "*Report to the Control Room!*" and the towers were harshly blue, white, red and black, and all around me were black leather shoulders and black velvet shoulders and black spiked hair.

"So, have you seen them before?" said one pale powdered face to another.

"Yeah," the other said, in such a way as to convey that he knew everything about EVERYTHING (of which the Indigo Engineers were only a small part), and he had not the slightest interest in ANYTHING.

"What's it like?" said the anxious face.

The face who knew all looked coolly away. "You'll see."

"It was like this *cannon*, you know," a pale girl narrated excitedly to

---

* NOTE TO FLAMETHROWER SCHEMATIC *Never* activate electronics while valve F is open and there is little or no pressure in fuel cell!

her embracer, "that shot these fluorescent light bulbs. That's what I saw last time. And, oh, the *destruction!*"[8]

* * *

The Miracle of the Pit (1944)

My friend Pawel was born in Poland in 1938, so that it was tautologically evident that his boyhood must have been a succession of miracles. One night when his wife was present he told me the tale.

"So, you know, the story was, they took us to the forest, which was the other place, and we were *waiting* for something, and I didn't know what we were waiting for. And there was a kind of machine gun on the special stand, and I was really curious and interested in this piece of equipment."

"I bet you were," I said. We both had a good laugh.

"You know," Pawel said, "I was a small boy. I was five years old. We were waiting for our *execution* there," he told me in astonishment, "and I didn't *know* that! But I had this *feeling*, because of my parents' behavior. They didn't tell me anything."

"They didn't want you to feel bad?"

"I don't know. Maybe they had also some hope to avoid this. But we were waiting, and there was a long discussion between the German officers, and they said, well, eventually they decided, 'We are not going to be involved in this situation; let's send them to Gestapo.' So eventually, after another few hours, they took us in those trucks again. They took us to Warsaw, to the center of Warsaw. And there was a famous, a very bad-famed prison, which was a Gestapo prison in Warsaw. For the sound of this name, people would get white. And we were taken to this."

---

8 Mark Pauline prefers to believe that people are more primally affected. – "So how do you feel when your audiences cheer over the destruction?" I once asked him. – "I don't think that's what they're doing," he said. "I see it more as a mass laugh track. There just is that human gut reaction to things happening in real time. You just cheer and scream."

To Reiterate

"When it gets grabbed by my tank, it wiggles and tries to get away – although it *can't*, of course, since it's clamped in the sharp pincers of my tank."

The Miracle of the Apple

"I spent one night in this prison," Pawel said. "I remember that very well because all people were sitting on the benches, and they were not supposed to turn round. There was one entrance, and a grid of solid rods on one side, and they were sitting like that, and they were not supposed to move all day and all night, sitting like that on hard benches, row by row. But I was young, and I was allowed to go around, and I approached this grid; I was looking at the corridor. In the corridor were all those *beaten people*, you know, or Jews, or others who were sent to the concentration camps . . . and that was the night I spent. I remember that I slept on the floor, on the concrete floor."

"Were you happy because it was an adventure for you?"

"It was an adventure I didn't understand, but I felt something was wrong, you know, and I remember in the morning there was a terrible noise, and those German officers were running around shouting, and I was looking at this kind of coffee, it was ersatz coffee; I remember the *taste* of this coffee! And I was *looking* at those people, those frightened people; they *knew* that was their last moment. So this officer was *shouting* at them, and moving and so. I was looking at this officer, and he approached me; the German officer looked at me and gave me an apple." He laughed. "So I *remember* that apple."

Form Follows Function

"Our machines aren't monsters, as far as I'm concerned," said Heckert, who was designing a ninety-horsepower calliope.

"What are they?"

"They are what they are: various. You have a Walk-and-Peck Machine; you have a Spiked-Roller Machine, whose function is to spike and roll."

(And now, reflecting on Pawel's story, I see a Guarding Machine, an Execution Machine, and an Apple-Giving Machine.)

Dead Souls

When the seating on three sides of the parking lot had filled to capacity, the black-clad passengers were permitted to file across the concrete, under the bright white glare-lamps, as if they were crossing the runway to board some spaceship of cruelty which would blast them off into the indigo regions where things are black and black and almost black; and the night got colder and the yellow plastic streamers which marked the perimeter of the show area fluttered between the barrels which upheld them, and small furry mummified animals which had been impaled at each sentry post bared their brown skulls and watched the crowd with tiny black eyes like raisins and grinned with their white teeth.

"How do you like that animal?" said a man in a paternal, caressing voice, as if he personally had trapped, killed, mummified and impaled it for the benefit of his companion, a woman in black who wore a necklace of bleached rodent skulls. – "*Ohhh*," she said. "I *really like* it." I wondered whether Mark Pauline would have to cram it into her mouth before she understood that she was not supposed to like it.

The Miracle of the Interrogation

"Then my family was interrogated," Pawel said, "and we went upstairs to be interrogated in the special room. Again we were extremely lucky because they usually interrogated people in *other places*. Now there's a museum of this place."

"You know," said Pawel's wife in a voice of wonder, "this room was so small!"

"It was so small," said Pawel, "it was called 'Tramway' in slang. If someone was in this 'Tramway' he had no hope. If someone entered this building, some Pole, there was no hope to be alive. So my family lost their hope. They were talking about the name of the concentration camp to which we were going to be sent. The first place where we were was Pawiak, and then would be Oświęcim, that was Auschwitz. So we were waiting in there, but there was a miracle, because my uncle, the brother of my mother, was in the Polish Underground, and he organized an out for us. It was extremely difficult, but he had a friend who was working for the police, for Germans. This guy was an undercover agent. So he was taking the information for Home Army from Germans. He was oficially an interpreter with Germans. He was eighteen years old. His German was excellent. So my uncle's friend said, 'Okay, I'm going to save these people.' And during the interrogation he came to this prison as an official. He had all our documents, because Germans wanted to know what we are, and the Germans were surprised with this intervention; that was very suspicious, so he risked a lot. This guy really was very brave. My mother didn't know him. My mother even didn't know where her brother was. She knew he was in the Underground, but it was too dangerous to know for any member of the family where he was, and so this guy came, and during the interrogation the German interrogator went somewhere from this room, and he said to my mother, 'I'm from your brother!' – She was so surprised in the center of German Gestapo headquarters to hear about her brother! She knew he was in Underground; it was beyond her, and so she thought, *everything* German knows, and she thought her brother must be killed and we were doomed, but he said, 'Don't be afraid, everything's going to be okay.' So that interrogation, *I* was asked for something even by the interrogator. I was eating this apple all the time. And then we were interrogated, and after that they decided to release us. My parents couldn't believe about this, and neither this German officer who led us from the building. He said, 'You are extremely lucky; I don't understand why we are releasing you.' And that was something for *him*, even! Nobody could leave this place alive. That's why this place is a museum now. So this intervention was a miracle. And I was so stupid that I asked my father, 'Where's the truck?' I think I liked this truck! My father said, 'Be quiet and don't ask any questions.' So they released us from going to Pawiak."

The Prettiest Thing is the Darkest Darkness

"Everybody always assumes the worst, y'know," said Mark Pauline in the Chinese restaurant. "I just use that as a rule of thumb. Most people just assume that there's a lot of leeway in what we do, and things could happen that would be very bad. But people don't understand that what we do – while it is really violent and really intense – is still just a very very lively representation of Other Things that kill people every day."

"Do you think the world is that way?" I said.

"You mean, is *my* world that way? Well, sure," said Mark Pauline, a little testily. "It wouldn't have happened if it wasn't that way. We never would have made that film if it didn't relate to something that *happened*. We have a very pessimistic outlook. I see things like that all the time in everything, probably in places where they don't even exist."

Indigo Mythologies

The patient, craning people, the lights, the tawdriness and above all the gay music made me think I must be at some country carnival which had run late so that it was cold and dark and all the rides had closed and the freaks had gone to sleep and only the technicians and their indigo ringmasters were left.

"You've never seen their show before?" said the knowing blonde.

"No," said Old Baldy.

"Ah," she said compassionately. "You'll like it."

Mark Pauline strolled across the concrete, waggling his elbows to the music. The audience began to cheer, but since he kept walking, they shut up.

"You know," a professorial vampire explained, "if you were about to die, you could will your body to this guy and he could reanimate it as a MACHINE."

"Oh, he doesn't do *that* anymore," yawned his companion. "He hasn't done that for *years*."

Everyone cheered as Mark Pauline ran a hand through his hair and raised his hands in commanding upwellings so that they cheered louder – and then he smiled rather sneeringly and said it would be another ten minutes.

The Miracle of the Tank

"And can you imagine," Pawel said, "that my father remembered one guy who was very badly beaten in the same place, and this guy was sent to the concentration camp, but before he was sent to the place in Warsaw which had a very bad reputation, this place called Pawiak, and my father met him after the war, and this guy survived. He couldn't recognize my father because he couldn't see at that time, but my father met him on the street and he said, 'We know each other, we met over there in this transport.' He said, 'Yes, I was there. I was sent to Pawiak, but then, during the Warsaw Uprising, Germans used prisoners to attach them to the tanks when they attacked the people, the Home Army in Warsaw. They had a tremendous problem. First problem was, they couldn't use tanks because that was narrow streets; there was always one boy with a bottle of gas! They were furious! So they attached some women and men and children to their tanks, just to stop Home Army from attacking their tanks so they could attack. And I was one that they attached. But, well, Home Army shouted me that, escape now, and then they'd shoot at tank. I managed to escape and reach them, you know. Other people were killed.' That was in May '44, four months before the Warsaw Uprising."

Tanks

"The wheels are the medieval part of my Square-Wheeled car," Werner said. "They're the translation from the past. I got a lot of dreams about World War II. When I started illustration when I was a kid, that's all I really drew, excessively exotic battle scenes."

"So, would you like to build your own version of the T-34?"[9]

Werner laughed. "Whatever, yeah."

"If you could design the prototype of something, and you had a lot of assistants who could just turn out fleets and fleets of your machine, would you want that?"

"Probably not, just for humanitarian reasons. These things for me are exercises. They're frivolous in nature. They're toys. They're dreams. I enjoy life. I got a gun, but I hardly ever use it.'

The Machines

At last the motors started (I remember an account I once read of one of the earlier tests at Auschwitz, when the condemned had to wait in the gas chamber for hours and hours until the engineers got things working).

The Vampires and the Mass Grave

The machines sounded like titanic lawn mowers. You could feel the vibrations of their motors in your chest. Smoke gushed out of the twin towers of the highest barrel-H, and then the Worm emerged. It had a high stern narrow chest, buttoned up with horizontal metal fingers. It turned its wheels; it sashayed its ass (and meanwhile there was an explosion from somewhere else and dirty orange flame soared high into

9 A Soviet tank, regarded by many as superior to the Panzer for most of the war.

the darkness, leaving the pallid lights and the concrete behind them, like true filthy sunlight ignoring the glimmerings of a dentist's aquarium). The Worm hissed and wriggled and rolled unerringly toward Mark Pauline's mass grave, and its front section bent down horribly and the steel fingers swiveled outward, becoming tines of an immense excavation fork, and the Worm began churning up the disturbed earth beneath the glare of the lights, and the night was very cold and dark, and presently we began to smell an odor of decay, and the odor got stronger and stronger as the Worm rooted in the dirt as directed by its masters, the Indigo Engineers, and the Worm speared something white and thin upon its tines and quivered and growled and hissed pneumatically as if it had studied the gloating behavior of dogs toward buried bones, and the Worm straightened itself and telescoped toward us, and we saw that the prize was a prosthetic leg, and the grave-stink continued to increase and everybody smiled and said, "*Neat!*" but when the smell did not vanish immediately upon being praised they wrinkled their noses.

Desperation

Heckert and I were at the Tu-Lan, a Vietnamese restaurant on Sixth Street, and we were talking about machines. (I forgot to mention that Heckert's handshake reeked of metal-smoke and machine-grease. He was Heckert-the-Armorer.)

"Well," I said, chewing on my chicken salad, "the function of an animal, or I guess any being, is to live and reproduce its kind and extend its territory, but it seems like in these videos I've seen of your performances these machines are always after dead things, like they really want to get them and destroy them. And if one has prey, another will come up and flame it and destroy it."

"Mmm," said Heckert coolly. "Yeah. As you say, occasionally there's a bit of that. But to see that the only thing going on is a free-for-all over some dead animals, well, that's not the only function. Some machines have animal parts on them, and they are more or less a type of extension of the combination of machine flesh. They're only functioning as that machine would, with its desires and wants and needs – attempting to fulfill those needs in any way it can, sometimes in a more desperate manner."

"What makes them desperate?"

"Here's the hot sauce," said Heckert. "It's a little bit on the bright side."

"So what makes them desperate?" I said.

"What makes anything desperate? We're trying to create the most immediate and intense situation for the audience as possible. Therefore, the only way we can get that across is to create the same sort of situation for the machines."

"If these machines were intelligent and they could think, do you think they'd consider it cruel what you did to them?"

"If they were intelligent, they'd be doing it themselves," said this Indigo Engineer.

The Miracle of the German Officer

"My brother was born on nine of August, 1944," Pawel said. "And my brother was born when the entire Russian army approached Warsaw. We were on the other side of the river, closer to the Russian army, and Russian army approached, and Germans evacuated all the people from the area, but because we couldn't move we hid in a small laundry. The front stopped at that time. And it stopped for six weeks. And it was a no-man zone we were in. And we knew there were patrols, German patrols around. But we were hiding. And in this situation we had almost nothing to eat for six weeks, and at that time my brother was born. The problem was, first of all, he was hungry, and he was crying and shouting, and that was the problem, because they could find us. So we were trying to cook only at night. I was the only person who could watch whether the Germans were coming or not, so I used to sneak from the place we were to look for someone coming. I remember that moment very well when I noticed German patrol coming, and we were already in desperate position, so my parents decided to cook something. There was a little cooking place over there. And they saw the smoke, and they immediately came, and I reported this to my parents. I was pale, very very white when I said, 'They are coming,' and you know, those guys couldn't believe! They said, 'You are still here? Everyone was evacuated from here!' And there was an officer and two soldiers. And my father spoke German, so he could communicate with them. They said, 'Unbelievable! You should be evacuated immediately; you know this is the front zone.' But my father said, 'But this child is born and I can't move.' – Oh, well, that was not true, because child was born four weeks or five weeks ago, but, well, that was an excuse. – This German said, 'The mother will be taken to the hospital, and you'll be sent to somewhere THERE,' and we *knew*" (here both Pawel and his wife laughed) "what perspectives we had, and my father told them, 'No. You can shoot us on the spot. There's no other way. We are not moving. If you don't like us here, it's your decision.' And this officer was *thinking* a little bit. And he said, 'I wish you good luck.' And they left. That was a very critical situation. Then I remember my father wanted to offer him a bottle of spirit we saved for disinfection, but everything was okay, and they left. They didn't tell anybody that they found us."

"Because he showed them he's brave," said Pawel's wife.

"*No*, my father was desperate!" Pawel shouted.

"It is easier to persecute someone who's afraid of you, 'cause they are not – "

"*No*, between those Germans, you also had some human feelings, even though . . ." He stumbled for a moment. His voice caught. *Even though . . .*

A Commentary on Why the Germans did not Liquidate Pawel's Family

"What's the difference between being a machine and being a good German?"

"That's what a lot of the machine is: following orders. – And then occasionally disobeying them," Mark Pauline added slyly. "When the possibilties arise."

"When do they disobey them?"

"Well, when you exceed their limits they just don't work right. They malfunction. When you try to make 'em do something they can't do, then they break."

Previous Events by S.R.L.

"*Saturday, May 24, 1986* . . . 'FAILURE TO DISCRIMINATE; DETERMINING THE DEGREE TO WHICH ATTRACTIVE DELUSIONS CAN OPERATE AS A SUBSTITUTE FOR CONFIRMATION BY EVIDENCE' . . . machines of immense power and complexity . . . were brought to bear on each other in an eerily-white chalk lot, where the action centered on a steepled log cabin. Highlights of the performance included an out-of-control Square Wheel Car weighing 1500 lbs with 5-foot-*square* wheels accelerating to 35 mph and colliding with the Shock Wave Cannon, a Flying Rocket Powered Shock, and a drunkenly waddling 2200-lb Walking Machine . . ."

Machines Brought to Bear, or, The Miracle of the Craters

"And then it was another week or two when eventually the front moved," Pawel said. "But that was even worse, because we were in a very little shed or something like that. And then, when they started to attack, it was a lot of bombs around, but you couldn't avoid bombs, so we were laying on the floor. I remember that of course the windows were closed and the blinds were closed. Everything was closed, as this place was inhabited. We put a lot of quilts and blankets on us. My brother was between us. We didn't know what to do because there was such a terrible smoke and – "

"And noise," said Pawel's wife timidly.

"And bombs, and my father was afraid that they would drive a tank through the house . . ."

Pawel's wife moaned. "My God!" she said.

"Because you know when tanks attack, there is no problem to – to – you know . . ."

"Yes," said Pawel's wife.

"And eventually they hit us with a shell. And this shell burst exactly on our floor!" he laughed. "So immediately it was a light around us, and a smoke around us, and all those parts of the shells, they hit the quilts we were covered with, and the quilts were really in pieces! But we were not hurt. You know, the entire window was broken – the entire window just went on the opposite side, on the wall, and we were covered with glass! It was really a miracle. And my mother was afraid that everything was burning because of the smoke, and we were afraid of leaving, and then after that, in a few hours, the front passed, and we were *saved*, you know!

"We were not hurt," Pawel said. "We were not hurt, and we went out, and we saw seven big craters on each side of this place! Craters! Each crater was the size of our house. And I remember we were *playing* in those craters, because you could *hide* there; they were big craters."

The Lingering End of the Egg-Man

Pretty soon the Inspector came out, and then a machine with a low mean ramp lifted itself and thought and began spinning and grinding louder and faster, and it puffed blue smoke and then zipped rapidly away to perform its premeditations in the darkness. Meanwhile, the Worm growled over its mass grave. The low-slung machine came back and was whining and shaking and swiveling its wheels. It swiveled between the towers. Then it began to stalk the Worm. The Worm loomed and bowed like a Tyrannosaur. It hunched over the other low-slung machine. Its head was two squat gears surmounted by a wide thin wafer of a gear, all of them sideways so that they were nothing but cog-grins. The low-slung machine backed off. The Worm dropped the artificial leg into a spittoon full of water and cigarette butts and dead animals. Then it sidled up to a tower topped with something white. There was an explosion. The white cover blew off. Atop the tower was a man in a chair. The man was made out of eggs. The Worm growled and tilted his tower, and he began to drip and bleed egg yolks down onto the ground, which was illuminated by dreary red flares.

Germany

"Basically, it gets down to Germany," said Werner. "I'm from German descent. I have a lot of – I guess it's called *Kunst* or something – about the nationalism, about the feeling. You know, the Italians were ROMAN-TIC, but when you look at anything that's been made in Germany over the last forty years, it *stinks* of something awful. It just has a LOOK to it. It just reeks of excessive inbreeding, this certain way things are shaped. You don't see it that much today, but all through the 'fifties and 'sixties, and especially through the war. The very way the planes were shaped. And this encapsulates it all. This is a dream I had when I was sixteen." He rolled up his sleeve to show me a tattoo. "See, the Z goes through the 7, and the 7 goes through the Z, and it makes a whole. I always thought to myself, how come nobody else thought of that? It's the same kind of shape as the ⚡⚡. When you go to Pennsylvania, the Amish have these hex signs on the sides of their barns. It's this sort of Teutonic tribalism. Northwestern European tribalism at its best. Like, look at the Messerschmitt 205 jet, the first jet that really made it in the war. The way that cowling's shaped around the engine. It's just got a look like a *skull*. Or aviator sunglasses. That's the kind of imagery I'm interested in."

Further Opinions

"Hitler hated himself," said Richard the homeless veteran.

"All great politicians have hated themselves," said Heckert.

Sneaky Soldiers

"I remember the first night after that," Pawel said. "The front passed, and there were Russian soldiers and Polish soldiers over there, and they came, and they said, 'It will be counterattack this day, this night. You have to leave this place. There is a shelter over there.' We went to the shelter. And we had the rest of our belongings. It was ridiculous, you know, what you can take with you when you have to escape from your house in fifteen minutes. You can imagine what you can take! – Everything was stolen at night, by soldiers," he laughed. "Because we were in this shelter. And there was no counterattack."

Instructions for Setting Up Crawling Machine

"The side of the pump motor opposite the front of the machine has a green hose attached to it. This hose extends into a one-gallon can strapped to the side of the backbone tube. [Before operating the motor] this can must be full of the white liquid supplied for this purpose . . . or *the pump motor will be destroyed*."[10]

The World Around Him

"That was in September '44 till January '45," Pawel said. "The front stopped only fifteen kilometers from the place where we lived, and it stopped for many months. And then we were attacked by Germans from Warsaw, so we went to a new place, because then we came to the place where we lived, and that was almost normal life, but with everyday attractions because there was a lot of shells, so our parents called us not to play around. There were Russian soldiers close to our house, and I was playing around and there was two big Katyushas, you know, those rocket things, and they had a big hose, and you know those trucks where Katyushas hide, they put eight rails on them, and for each rail they had one missile on the bottom and one on the top, one on the bottom and one on the top. When the Russians loaded them, they moved to a close place on the other side of the road, and they fired. Then they came back, they loaded them again, and they fired. I was

10 All instructions on assembly and operation of Survival Research Laboratories' machines are excerpted from information sheets kindly loaned me by S.R.L.

told by my parents not to touch anything, so it was forbidden for me to touch anything. But a lot of my friends, they loved to play, so they lost their legs, their hands, their eyes, or they were even killed. There was Scouts working in our town, because it started to organize after the war. Scouting was very famous in Poland, and scouting participated greatly in the underground activity. (But after that it was real scouting, because they tried to change them as the Pioneers.) I remember at that time I was always looking for my friends, but I was not in scouting. And they went for scout trips. That was a tragic thing; they were choosing the place for their camp somewhere, and they found mines. They were killed. I remember that event, and I looked at them in the church before the mass. Well, I was too young for scouting."

In Search of a Mineless Zone

"Do you have any recipe for a life that would avoid what those machines represent?" I asked.

"Well, I don't think there's any way to really *avoid* the bad things in the world," said Mark Pauline. "What you *can* do is, you can either choose to mete those sorta horrible things out to yourself, or you can have someone else do them *to* you. You can control your fate as it relates to the limited possibilities of people on earth, or you can let someone else control it. I just chose to be able to control it myself. And towards that end I had to come up with this system. That's the only way that my life would be worth living, enclosed by that world. Punishment is never so bad when you mete it out to yourself. When you let other people do it to you, then you lose your pride."

Nobody and Ruins (1945)

"I remember the period when eventually in the winter Warsaw was liberated," Pawel said. "I remember that, how Warsaw looked like. You know, eighty percent of buildings were completely destroyed. So you can imagine how it looked. Ruins, ruins and ruins. That was one million people in this town, and when we came there, me and my father, there was nobody. Nobody and ruins. That was a terrible thing, and we were watching Warsaw fighting, because Warsaw Uprising was on first August '44, and we were on the other side of the river, and we were watching each day this *tremendous light* from fire over there. They resisted heavy bombs for only two or three days, because they were not prepared. They resisted more than two months, exactly sixty-two days. They had no supply. Soviet army was on the other side of the river, and they did not allow Allies to drop some equipment. That was something terrible; that was a Stalin idea, to just let them be destroyed by Germans; that would be nice. So, Polish air forces started from Brindisi in Italy; they were crossing the entire German territory, which was more than a thousand miles in order to drop something to Warsaw and to go back when they were subjected to attacks of German artillery and German fighters, and they were not allowed to land on the other side of the river. Hundred thousand of people were killed over there in fight against Germans, and they had no equipment. They had pistols, you know, and bottles . . ."

In the Parking Lot

Flames shot fifty feet into the air. Painted oil drums whirled round and round a tower, and a cannon shot at them and set them on fire and the Worm inched up to grab at them, and the cannon kept going BANG! and the cans burned and whirled and dripped liquid flame and smoke blotted out the sky and the Worm crouched happily over the flame, warming itself in this destruction as the audience was doing, but then it hissed suddenly; it had caught fire; the Indigo Engineers rushed in with the fire extinguisher (oh, shameful!), and the other machines came and tried to topple the towers, but they couldn't, not even the Square-Wheeled Car which came rushing and thumping, so the show ended and the vampires shook their pale, pale faces and said, "He's lost his motherfuckin' touch."

Dead Flesh Again

"Why is it," I said, "that in that video I saw, in the first scene, where the Sneaky Soldier was creeping along, why did a machine come over and prey on it, and then another machine fought the first machine for the privilege of flaming this dead flesh?"

"Mmm hmm," said Mark Pauline, poker-faced. "That was a rubber mask. It wasn't dead. It was part of a rubber tree. – Why were they fighting it? Well, that was just sort of an underlying theme of that tape – you know," he shrugged, "endless pursuits and inevitable captures and merciless punishments. You see that in all our shows."

Werner's Complaint

"I've never had the time to develop my machines to their fullest potential," he said. "I'm always two or three weeks behind the show deadline, so towards the deadline I always have to make excessive compromises. Also, to this point the way the machines have interacted with each other hasn't excited me, because there has never been any of what I call FULL-BLOWN VIOLENCE. That's what I'm *waiting* for."

"What would that be like?"

"That's what I'm setting up for New York, to have the Whirly and the Ram Car go at it, maybe not even head-on, but cat-and-mouse style, until one highly developed machine really just *dominates* another highly developed machine, to where the aftermath is considered a loss. One machine that was beautifully crafted, and had a lot of hours and thought poured into it, is just DESTROYED beyond any reason to even *bother* repairing it. It's just fucking *gone*."

Why You and I are not Good Enough to Destroy

"I mean," said Werner in disgust, "how can you root for a *prop?*"

"Such as a Sneaky Soldier?"

"Yeah, I mean you *can* in a way. They get CRUSHED. But it's just an *imbalance*. Naturally, Sneaky Soldiers are easy to make, and they're *beautiful* and so *funny*. You see 'em in the tape; they're just crawling along, and the big machines just come along and pick 'em up. But the thing is to have HEAD-ON-WAR."

My Judgment

The Indigo Engineers are geniuses of a peculiar and most unpleasant order. Just as one would not want to draw the envy of the halogens by producing some new blue-green gas which eclipses the rather meager menu of blue-greenness which is set out on the periodic table, so I myself would not alert our Secretary of War to the possibilities implied in these machines, which resemble what I might see if I let three inventor-torturers set up shop in my garage; for those ominously revolving spiked drums take on true seriousness when spectators *laugh* and *cheer* at the performances. They laugh because there is so much hatred inside them that it makes them happy to see things hurt and destroyed, and that is the way that people have always been and always will be.

Reader, do you consider yourself a Sneaky Soldier? I know that I am one, plodding, sneaking, sneaking across my concrete days, while something big and bad comes after me. I know that I must admire myself and every other Sneaky Soldier for trying, however unsuccessfully, to sneak away.

When I see an infant clutching for his shiny plastic toys, or sucking at the breast, I am sad, because I know that he will die, and the manipulations which he is learning can do no more than help him get through *life*.[11] At these times I myself manipulate things to console myself. When I activate the squeaker, the baby becomes excited and kicks his fat feet and shakes his head and tries to suck at his shirt, looking for the Platonic Form of a Breast; watching him I am consoled by his involvement. This is the most important function of engineering.

AUTHOR'S NOTE

The Indigo Engineers are always seeking donations of money, equipment and expertise. "Part of what we do involves debunking the whole myth in the art world perpetrated by lazy artists, lazy people, that less is more, because, you know, we believe that more is even MORE," said Mark Pauline. "We want to continue to expand, as long as we can maintain our ideals."

SURVIVAL RESEARCH LABORATORIES
1458 San Bruno Avenue, Building C
San Francisco, CA 94110   USA
(415) 641–8065

11 "Life is nothing but an embalmed *mummia*, with the mortal body preserved from putrefaction by some solution of salts." So said Paracelsus in 1590, anticipating the rabot, the Cow Bunny and the Mummy-Go-Round.

VIOLET HAIR

A Heideggerian Tragedy

... the reader will find a totally new table of Martyrdoms, in alphabetical order, so that pictures of saints undergoing torture, or being executed, may be immediately understood ...

Major Arthur de Bles, in the Foreword to *How to Distinguish the Saints in Art by Their Costumes, Symbols and Attributes* (1925)*

Saint Catherine of Siena

They say she was broken on spiked wheels, and then, since she miraculously remained alive, they decapitated her with an axe. When I see her in the paintings, studying at her Book of Devotions with such sweet concentration, it is hard for me to understand why anybody would have wanted to interrupt her. Of course I cannot ask her; nor can I ask her persecutors, since they died in the desert long ago and thorns have grown up on their graves. Therefore I have chosen to record the tale of Catherine O'Day, who is also a martyr; and if I fail to achieve my purpose may God have mercy upon my soul.

Saint Catherine of San Diego

Catherine had violet hair. The sun wanted to tell Catherine something golden, but since she had such violet hair she could not hear any other color even in the might of summer when dark green tree-shadows cooled the emerald grass, and other women wore white summer dresses because they knew the meaning of summer which even the dogs knew in their tongue-lolling ambles and waggy-tailed sprints which made

* New York: Art Culture Publications.

music with the clinking of their identification tags like ice in cocktail glasses, and everyone else under the sun was caught in summer immensities which made their morning shadows strong and faithful as the shadows ran at their heels and swerved through enormous angles unimpeded by houses or walls or the scorching gleam of silver mica stars in the sidewalks, because summertime is above all immunity from pain. Summer was in the Berkeley T-shirts with clouds and colored music-notes on them, and it was in the tanned milky-smooth faces of the lovers skipping down the sidewalk hand in hand, and summer could be perceived (in its deficient mode of Being)* in the prances of the gawky freckled girls who wore shorts and had big round glasses that made them resemble summer owls trying to be happy and forgetting the cruel needs of moonlit nights when they had to swoop down onto desperate mice and bear them high and devour them in their horrible beaks while watching them with their big expressionless eyes, which were painted on their feather-masked faces out of the same evil trickery that makes cosmic rays shoot across the sun's face like the bars of a visor so that summer is dimmed and confused by entities which want to keep the sun's true nature hidden – except to the Elect, which included Catherine, and that was why the sun was trying to reach out to her, but Catherine would have none of it because she was not a summer person. Summer people did not know that pretty soon they would turn their backs on everything that they now thought was so important. It was not that they were hypocritical; it was simply that someday summer would be over. Meanwhile the new Berkeley students streamed across the concrete, offering each other string cheese, turning their class schedules round and round in their hands, saying "Okay okay okay," and the freshman boys told the freshman girls how primordially they needed them at their parties, and the freshmen girls said they would see what they could do, and Asian girls sat cliquishly on the steps, tapping the toes of their silver shoes, and Catherine in San Diego lay on the bed reading Heidegger as she had been doing for almost seven years.

---

* For a glossary of Heideggerian ontifications see page 532f.

Her Earthly Unearthliness

Much of her life, Catherine had been reading, sometimes taking her book to visit me in Heaven where it is cold and foggy and she must lie on the couch wrapped in a thick Canadian-Indian sweater and a reindeer skin. Sometimes she rested her temple against two fingers and stared straight ahead at her book or manuscript with the same strenuous fixation of gaze as a competition shooter; in truth her thought traveled like bullets along the violet beams of her gaze, exploding every concept she met into a plasma of minute distinctions, and her silky hair seemed to be three different colors of violet. The strands of Catherine's violet hair lived together in beautiful braids or beautiful tangles, as Catherine dictated, and they visited each other when the wind blew; and although her lips were pinkly lovely, like the customary pink-streaked rose-petals to which so many other describers of lips have rightly resorted, her hair was even holier than her lips, being violet, since violet light will cause potassium metal to fling its electrons out in worshipful offerings, which no amount of red light can ever do. (Violet has the highest frequency in the visible spectrum.) Catherine's hair was a violet meadow that laughed at the rigid violet bars of mercury's and calcium's emission spectra; in this violet place Catherine's spirit waved like a searing wind which made hearts ache. Her hair was almost translucent in the sunlight. It was persistent and inescapable.

The Boundaries of the Catherine-Horizon

It is known that holiness is localized. Thus, a weaker ectoplasmic field is reported to exist on automated ranches, whose green alfalfa-beds are enlightened only by the random rainbow dews of sprinklers, than in desert ghost towns where tall thin phantoms hoot in chimneys like apes of justice, laboriously attempting to imitate their mentors and masters, the summer owls of whom I have already spoken, and although they scarcely possess the resonance of flesh, which would be of value to them in achieving their dark-livered endeavors (actually they do not have livers either), their reedy efforts are indulgently applauded by the owls in feathery wing-beats; thus encouraged, fat ghosts now roll tumbleweeds back and forth on Main Street with translucent smiles of vacuous delight; if the owls are amused then they will clap their claws together in mid-air with the savage elegance of clashing antlers, in the process, perhaps, letting slip some squeaking dying rodent-ball whose bloody dews the ghosts can inhale, but since this happens no more than every hundred years, if at all, it is fortunate for these freeze-dried souls that they have no tibial collateral ligaments to shrink or spasm, and can therefore flex their shimmering knees all night in the pursuit of their summer sport, vainly hoping to incite the owls' beaked praise. The truth is that they cannot propel a real thing a single inch, nor could ten thousand ghosts united (be happy that you are not yet a ghost!); it is only wind that blows the tumbleweeds about, whistling through their weed-bones while the stagnant ghosts swirl in the night-dust behind, indefatigably pretending to push them, not only to propitiate the owls, but also to keep from considering themselves even more superannuated than they already do when, knowing the outcome and hence snarling in such despair that they expose their clacking teeth, which resemble those icicle-like fangs of the deep-sea fishes, these revenants lay their heads upon each other's breasts and listen for a heartbeat, as is customary at the termination of a deathbed scene; if even one soul were to have within his chest the pulpy mechanism which emits those dull and bloody thuds, they would be soothed, just as a puppy taken from his mother will stop whimpering when a loudly ticking clock is placed against his belly; but of course the ghosts hear nothing and furiously rake each other's non-existent chests with their non-existent fingernails, and then, afraid of the owls, return with increased anxiety to their delusional project of the tumbleweeds; meanwhile, more mathematically-minded sprites play "Musical Chairs" between the tombstones, trying once and for all to solve the problem which eluded Leibniz: how do you put ten bodies in nine graves while adhering to that monadist doctrine of one body, one grave? – for they want privacy when they rest their cool cheeks against the cool cheek of the earth; and meanwhile young ghosts creak doors beautifully, ingeniously, as they are expected to do. Thus every spirit does its part. – But turn your back and walk over the dunes for two dozen steps, and the night is depopulated.

So the holy presence of Catherine could be felt only from Tijuana, half an hour south of her, to Mount Shasta, thirteen hours north of her.

This point having been clarified like ectoplasmic butter, we will now enter the Catherine-horizon and begin the story.

A State of Grace

I am the Holy Ghost. As I descended from Heaven, I presently reached that violet-black sea of storm-tossed mortality, and at the bottom of the ocean was a little blue bubble, and I shrank my form into a discrete particularity in order to make myself available to the people there on a one-to-one basis, believing as I did in the religion of good manners, the trajectories of which are usually as carelessly plotted as those of champagne corks. As I continued to fall, the ontic world loomed bigger and bigger. It sparkled with cities and airplanes and fireflies. Presently it took up my entire field of view, and continued to enlarge, the horizon becoming less and less curved until at last it was the standard Being-horizon in its average every-nightness that we experience in our freeway relatedness, speeding southward toward Catherine in San Diego (or rather, to be more concrete, Solana Beach); and the smoggy moon got bigger and bigger every hour until it was like a beautiful yellow ball of superprocessed glow-in-the-dark cheese. The air pollution smelled like coconut macaroons. The following morning, continuing south through Los Angeles, Long Beach, Seal Beach, Leisure World and other points upon this continuum, I found that the smell was like smoke, rusty metal, asphalt and rotten eggs, in that order. This part of southern California was defined by its four-lane gas stations, its speeding blondes, and above all by its grey-white sky through which the desert mountains were hardly visible. Once I completed my journey through those low sea-passes, Catherine was attained.

However

Half an hour south of Catherine, in Tijuana, Beelzebub (whom we will see again) was buying a stiletto. – How much?" he said. – "Twelve dollars," said the man gently. – "How about ten?" said Beelzebub. –

The man spread his hands sadly. "Okay," he said. "I wrap it up for you."

My Materialization

"I actually have this peculiar feeling that something in the air is trying to talk to me," Catherine said.

"I've never been afraid of spirits, but I know that potentially you *can* be," said her sister Stephanie. "For American Indians, fear's a big thing. But one finds that the spirits are usually very *strong* and *guiding*."

"Well, let me see," Catherine said, hiding her mouth behind her hair. "What comes to mind is that I'm very skittish about spirits. *Extremely*."

"In the Ghost Dance religion it's almost universal that people resist," explained Stephanie. "They don't want to go in to where the spirit takes them. It's often the Elders that convince them to open themselves. The skepticism and resistance are really a part of the *process*."

Catherine didn't say anything.

"When you close your eyes, what does it look like?" asked Stephanie.

"I immediately got an image," Catherine reported, "but I don't know if it's a good one. It could be improved. Well, for some reason I just see a face – well, let me try to get a second one and *then* I'll describe them both." – She was still for a time. – "Well, okay," she said finally, "I have two images now, and they're very different. The first one . . . I was hesitant because I had a feeling that it's from some memory of some painting that I've seen, so it's a little suspect . . . I just see a face, and I'm pretty *sure* I've seen this face somewhere. It's yellowish. No, the hair is yellowish. Pale yellow. Long face, long hair, sort of high cheekbones with . . ." She paused to think again. "Large features. Let's see. I wouldn't say . . . Sort of *sad* and *somber*. Okay, that was the first image. But again, I think that came from a painting I saw once. – The second one was very diffferent, and . . . young, handsome, smiling." She laughed a little embarrassedly. "Sort of sensual, and *colorfully* dressed, very colorfully dressed. – But it's difficult to concentrate."

"Do you think they're two approximations of the same thing?" said Stephanie interestedly.

"Of the same thing?" said Catherine. "I *think* one's the true one, and one's the false one. I think the true one is the second one."

"Just because it came later, or because it's happier?" Stephanie said.

"Because it's happier."

"My first image of myself," I announced, "was this sort of green clammy thing, a bunch of vapors with these two black eye-holes full of greyish fog. I'm the Holy Ghost, you see. I'm kind of a sad thing, but I'm not an *evil* thing."

"Mmm hmm," said Catherine cautiously. She had already begun to withdraw from the conversation. There were days when she was very very tense.

"How about you, Stephanie?" I said. "How do you see me?"

"Well, you know," she said, "from the first time I became aware of you, I always got a visual image, and it was the same one. It's grey smoke, in a sort of thick column that *ripples* the way water ripples if you toss a pebble in a lake. So you're this sort of ripply column of grey vapor that I can't quite see through. In my peripheral vision I can see what's behind you, but if I look at any one spot I just see opaque smoke. But it's funny; sometimes your image fades out, and there's just this black shreddy raggedy tophat and a black cane appears below and beside it, and it doesn't occur to me *why* that happens."

"Do you two want to talk to me, or are you afraid of me?" I said.

"As I said, I've never been *afraid* of spirits," said Stephanie. "I personally have never experienced that. You spirits have always been a lot more *powerful* than I am, but you're stronger and guiding, and it's always very *light* and *uplifting.*"

"How about you, Cathy?"

"Am I afraid of you? Well, let me see. What comes to mind is no, I'm not afraid. However, I know I'm still a bit skittish. But if you want to stay over for a few days and it's all right with Stephanie, I would certainly *love* to have you."

At the Dinner Table

"Well," said Stephanie, "I don't think Beelzebub is *all* negative, but he has his *quirks*. Cathy, you have such *different* friends, like night and day. The Holy Ghost, for instance, would never exploit you, but the Devil has always exploited you."

"What do you think about all that, Catherine?" I said.

After a long silence, Catherine hung her head and said, "Well, I don't think the Holy Ghost would exploit me."

"Cathy and Beelzebub operate hand in glove," said Stephanie to me brightly. "She really goes for it. There's something so vulnerable inside her. Somewhere inside her there's this passive, insecure creature."

Catherine smiled tremulously, looking definitely the younger sister.

"Does the Holy Ghost know about Magog?" said Stephanie.

"Yes," said Catherine.

"Does the Holy Ghost know about Beelzebub?" said Stephanie.

"No," said Catherine, smiling and clenching her hands.

Authentic or Not?

Stephanie took the wishbone out of the duck. "Why don't you two break it," she said, "since you know each other *so* well."

Catherine and I began to pull at the bone. I wished that Catherine would love me and that I would love her, so that we could go to Heaven together. – The wishbone snapped.

"I think you won," Catherine said.

"I hope so," I said.

Stephanie looked at the two halves. "Never have I seen a wishbone in two such equal halves," she said, smiling at us.

What the TV Said

"You know, I still don't believe this," said the TV.

A Summer Night

That night it was too hot for sleep. Putting on my grave-clothes at 3:23, I crept past the open door of Catherine's room and went out toward the beach. The moon was so bright that I could see for miles. As I walked along the sidewalks, I saw nobody except one long black car in the final block, and when the black car saw me it turned around very discreetly, so that I was alone. There was one house with its light on at the top of the Solana Vista stairs, but as I began to descend those steps it winked out its light, and as I approached the pale lavender ocean my worst fear was that there was Someone standing and looking at me from the top of the stairs, and that the Someone would presently come after me. But no one did. I sat on the deck of a lifeguard station to get my bearings. Above me, the California houses extruded their wide black roofs over the edge of the precipice.

It was low tide. Low waves crawled back and forth along the shallow beach. Directly below the moon (which was too bright to look at), each final wave-crest was gold, but the rest of the sea was featureless, excepting only those long hummocks that spanned it in regular monotonous parallels, like rolls of cloth. It was terrifying to walk upon the white white sand, especially where the cliff curved back into a sort of amphitheater, because the night was so bright that I, the Holy Ghost, could not hide.

Next Morning

"Cathy," smiled Stephanie over morning coffee, "your horoscope says that a visit from fascinating friends will prove *invaluable*." – But Catherine said nothing.

My Fundamental Being

My reason for seeing Catherine was to persuade her by my example to become a martyr so that she could live in Heaven with me forever and I would get her pregnant with spirit-children by immaculate conception and take her for long walks in the icicle-woods. It was my purpose to leap ahead of her in my solicitude (H.122)* in order to help her

---

* I.e., Heidegger, first edition of *Sein und Zeit* (1931), p. 122. See Glossary, page 532 below.

authenticate her cares; thus I had materialized as a ghostly example of divine wonder; but she suspected me, perhaps rightly, of leaping in *for* her instead, so that she was displaced by whatever she needed to do, and no matter how well I did it for her by being perfect for her I could not be helping her.

The Cathedral of Saint Catherine

The curtains were always drawn in Catherine and Stephanie's living room. They were printed with buttercups, bluebells and red poppies; and where the daylight came in and superimposed its luminous window-squares upon the curtains, the flowers were lit as if they were lantern-slides. I sometimes wished that Catherine and I, instead of having to go to Heaven, could simply be flowers together in this illusory world. Ferns waved in the lower lefthand quadrant of the screen door (the street door was generally left open in hopes of some factic breeze); next there was a wall of cool green leaves; and the upper half of the door was backed by high flowers: – white flowers on the left tree, and full pink blossoms on the right. Catherine could probably see them from her bedroom window, but she never talked about them. – The living room was hot and dim and sleepily sloppy. Here no one died or came to life, even in the burning mornings when anyone could feel a thrilling quality in the sunlight, deriving from Mexico as did vanilla extract. The living room remained quiet. Its quiet was in fact a buffer against the profane world (remember that the boundary of the Catherine-horizon was not very far away): – after all, the ghost never gets you as soon as you open the door of the haunted house; he waits until you have come inside and looked around and shivered, and you mount the creaking stairs, nervously playing with your violet hair, and there are goosebumps between your shoulderblades and the proverbial chills run up your spine, for there is something rather unpleasant about being alone when it is cold and dark and suspecting that something is preparing to hurt you; and it is getting darker and colder the farther you go up the stairs (you are closer to Heaven; that is why); and the rotten banister begins to glow like long cold comb-teeth, and *then* suddenly the front door slams inexplicably behind you and you see the Holy Ghost smiling and shimmering like foxfire at the top of the stairs . . . For similar reasons,

Catherine lurked cautiously in the house whenever possible, aware that someone or something wicked could always rush in from Mexico to destroy her in a harsh clap of sunlight. This did not prohibit her from going out in the sun, because Catherine was an exercise *fiend* and she supposed that she always *would* be; but when the sunlight was strongest she preferred to lie indoors. There was a Navajo rug on the floor, and a brown Tongan *tapa* print subdivided into squares, each square being patterned with diamonds or other squares, some of which were filled by intersecting lines, others bearing suns at their centers, stripes at the periphery; but the squares containing individual figures were always separated by squares of dense crisscross patterns, so that the *tapa* seemed to comprise all subspecies of everything, which of course it did, as I did.

The TV lorded it over us from its throne at the end of a reception hall formed on one side by Stephanie's work table, which rose high against the window thanks to its stacks of notes and journals, and on the other side by a grinning piano. Seen from the floor, as the sisters saw it, this corridor seemed a monument to towering constriction, with the flower-curtains a sunny uncertain escape and the TV at the end of it, the one sure thing. Here every day Catherine and Stephanie spent an hour of their lives. Every afternoon, when the TV came on, barefoot Catherine leaned against the pillows, in her striped shirt and sweatpants, with her hair tucked back, and Stephanie lay on her side on the mattress, clutching her shoulders, two feet away from the loud bright screen. From this corridor, the TV's revealed truths departed with the speed of sound. (Just as Mount Shasta is heralded first by manzanita and snowy cherry, so the discourses of the TV were announced by colors so effusive as to be almost fragrant.) – As for Catherine and Stephanie, those two had their innumerable secrets, which thrilled me because I could never know them any more than I could keep up with the TV's astonishing reversals, so that their persons and characters seemed strangely and distantly colored, as if in some fresco from the fourteenth century. Occasionally the TV would let them in on some new ontic twist which they had never suspected. At such times Catherine sat very still, almost smiling, her dark eyes peering wide beneath her lovely curved brows.

They sometimes spent the day in their nightgowns, watching TV and discussing the new tax law or foreign aid and other comparative religions. They munched animal crackers and drank booze and cooked diet TV dinners and were happy.

What the TV Said

"You weren't suppposed to make me feel desperate, because you weren't supposed to love me," said the TV.

"Now, he's said that before," explained Stephanie, "but this time it might be a *hint*. I think he knows he's going to die."

"It's conceivable, yes," said Catherine skeptically.

"Our *favorite* character got killed," sighed Stephanie.

"Yes, he did," Catherine said. "At least when those things happen, they happen *tranquilly*."

"You always hated me," said the TV.

"Is that true, Catherine?" I asked.

Catherine didn't answer for a moment. "Not *completely*," she said, spreading her hands.

Being-Towards-Death

The *not-yet* of the sun setting cast a sinister shimmer over the steadiest heat of any average afternoon at Catherine's house; this could have been concealed and tranquilized beyond the Catherine-horizon because north of Mount Shasta Catherine was already gone and was therefore merely present-at-hand with the leaden listlessness of her absence; but in Solana Beach, where I existed *in relation* to Catherine, the *not-yet* of darkness possessed its own horror, like the black pages of a black book slowly turning as burnt pages turn in the fire.

The Overheard-Being of Catherine

"I don't think the Holy Ghost is very direct," I heard Catherine say to her sister after supper when they both thought that my omnipotence had slipped. "Somehow It can't say what It thinks very directly, and I find that very oppressive. I would normally deal with that either by removing myself or by feeling angry, but because It's come all the way over here I don't feel like I have the whole range of feelings available – which I don't appreciate."

"I'm sorry you're feeling upset," said Stephanie.

"Well," said Catherine, "it isn't so *good*, but it isn't that *bad*."

"Because before, I couldn't have felt anything that *hurt* this much," said the TV.

"Well, *that's* sound," said Catherine.

Complications of the Second Night

At dinner, passing to refill her wine glass,* Catherine put her arm around me. But after dinner, she said, "Well, I'm going to go to bed early. What are *you* going to do? Are you going to stay *up*, or . . . ?" – "Well," I said, "what do *you* suggest?" – "*I'm* not suggesting anything," she said. – "Well, I guess I had better go to bed," I said.

Stephanie's Morning Meditation

"I'm just waiting to get used to the kitchen," Stephanie said. "Now that the refrigerator's been moved, I have this feeling – which is probably

---

* "Nature has provided the female with an adequate storeroom in her liver," says R. H. Smythe, M.R.C.V.S., *The Female of the Species* (Baltimore: Williams & Wilkins, 1960) (p. 62), "where she can accumulate fats, sugars and vitamins, but before she can fill the storeroom, she, herself, will require extra food."

erroneous – that the *space* has been changed in some way which is small but not insignificant."

"I feel things now that I never used to feel before," said the TV.

Another Meditation

"So what the reader is asked to do, after considering all the available clues, is merely to decide what the role of the female really is in the scheme of the Universe. It is simply a matter of deduction."*

"I don't know," Catherine said. "Well, I think that's mainly when you make a certain *choice*."

How to Study Heidegger

Catherine lay on her bed, ankles crossed, white arms behind her head, and her long hair hanging down. She seemed imprisoned in some summer reverie about whether sunlight is essentially present-at-hand because it is there in itself or whether it is ready-to-hand† because Catherine discovered it and felt it on her through the window and related it to her on her bedspread; and meanwhile the morning and the afternoon passed in such pleasure that the sunlight itself, the proximal cause of Catherine's pleasure, became subordinated to that pleasure, because Catherine had been existentially thrown into the sunlight and could take it for granted, so that for her it became present-at-hand simply by creating the climate for her to have this idle argument with herself; so the poor sunlight lost out. And Catherine's summer mornings rushed into those summer afternoons, rushing, rushing into the violet as the earth turned away from the sun.

"The organization is there," said Catherine to herself, "but it's not something you want to *schematize*."

---

* Smythe, *op. cit.*, p. 32.
† "Anyone may dream in the sunlight which is so ready-to-hand," says Heidegger (H.71).

Spirit Stuff

Meanwhile Stephanie transcribed her field notes and taped interviews. Through the open door of the study, I could hear her tape recorder telling me exactly what she had said. – "If all Indians were terminated, would you continue to dance?" asked taped Stephanie. – "Yeah," the taped Indian said. "I would."

What the TV Said

Catherine shut the door that afternoon when the soap opera came on, because, she said, she wanted to make the living room look like a movie house where nothing but the image was real. Coolly she settled herself against a mabel and lit a cigarette. She had spent all morning in a panic about Heidegger. (Partly it was that southern California always *laid* her *low*.)

"I'm going to ask you a question," said the TV. "Will you be honest with me?"

Catherine looked round equivocally.

"I'll have everything that used to be mine, and everything that's *still* coming to me," the TV warned her.

Catherine smiled and laughed, with her cigarette cocked at a forty-five-degree angle. Her head was cocked against her hair. She was wearing a stunning black top and red shorts. I wanted to kneel before her and kiss her knees, even though I knew that that would not be appropriate since she was only a saint and I was the Holy Ghost.

"Well," said the TV, "once again you've allowed yourself to become seduced by the promise of feminine favors. When are you going to learn that your body is a temple?"

This was clearly directed at me, and I resented it, so that I turned away from the TV and looked Catherine full in the face.

"Well," said the TV somberly, "I understand the temptations of the flesh all too well."

Catherine raised her beautiful bare arms above her head. I patted her shoulder, and she peeked at me with an inquiring smile, as if she were gently perplexed that I had bothered her. The smoke of her cigarette blew horizontally past my face in bluish-white helices and corkscrews, like the ocean's golden ovals translucently interleaving with each other upon the purple wave-billows of sunset – purple like her violet hair, which flowed around her sweet pink ears in motion no less real for its motionlessness, for the following eye saw that it moved; and her hair framed her head and shoulders like an arch inset in the top of an arch; and violet shone in her hair, which had lines of motion like mahogany-grain.

"I don't care what either of you say," announced the TV sourly. "I'm calling the shots, and I won't take any chances."

The Third Night

At that time I still believed that authenticity and fulfillment must be the same. When one's circumstances and opportunities diminished, for instance, one's upper limits of authenticity must diminish, too, for the sake of consistency. I advanced this thesis to Catherine, but she said, "Well, suppose that, um, an innocent girl marries a *deceiver*. And he takes her away with him and makes her very unhappy. That would be *authentic* for her at the time but it wouldn't actually be very *fulfilling*, would it?" – so I countered with a metaphor of a bowstring being drawn back infinitely, in infinite time, so that from moment to moment it was increasing in taut authenticity, but could it fulfill itself before the never-to-come moment of release? – Yes, by my definition it would have to, so I said to her that if an innocent girl married the Holy Ghost and the Holy Ghost really was a slimy ghosty sort of thing and not the man in bright colors that she had imagined, then the marriage would be not only authentic but also fulfilling, because I had defined it so, and I was the Holy Ghost and had unlimited powers at my discretion, so everything would work out, but Catherine only hung her head at the kitchen table while Stephanie's black dog Jessica cried softly in the portion of hot night that had been allotted to the back yard, and there was an oval of white light beneath Catherine's right eye and the bridge of her nose was illuminated with light.

"I'm not talking about that kind of love!" cried the TV.

Mount Shasta Again

"It's so hot in here," Catherine said.

"You can cool me off," said Job, who paid most of the rent. "Just use your goddess powers to chill me."

"Well," said Catherine with nervous amiability, "think of *icebergs*, Job."

"I'd rather think of mountains," said Job. "Icebergs are too desiccated."

Assessment of Holy Progress

In the morning I asked Catherine whether I was being good. – "Of *course* you are," she said. She considered. "Although ghosts . . . well, they make their presence *indirectly* felt. So I would think, but then it's hard to say what would motivate a ghost to do *anything*. They're existing, but in an obsolete way, going on in a certain *inertia*."

"Like a commuter," I said to her.

"I think we're all ghosts in our daily lives," said Catherine tactfully. "At least we're *carried along*."

What the TV Said

"I don't *need* help," said the TV that afternoon, and at this Catherine lit up a cigarette, and a lovely violet-black corkscrew ringlet dangled below her ear.

"Well, I think it's very sad that they separated the two of them," said Stephanie.

"The last I saw," Catherine explained to me, "she was at a plaque at this church and suddenly got dragged away by a Ghost in white high heels. Then these *owls* swooped down. You almost think that she may be . . . being written out." – Catherine said this with real sadness.

"You *could* plead diminished capacity," said Stephanie.

"Facticity's going to get involved in her defense," Catherine said, and she brought her ashtray beside her and stretched out in her red shorts and her striped shirt. "That's why I wonder if they're going to bring Guilt back today."

"They *have* to," said Stephanie in surprise. "I mean, they *haven't* killed him *off.*"

"Are you ready for that, sweetheart?" said the TV.

The Smile

After the soap opera, Catherine went back into her bedroom to work on Heidegger, and I sat in a rocking chair facing the blank green depths of the TV, watching the unmoving blade of the fan, the exercise bicycle, the quadrilateral of sunlight by the dining room table. Presently I heard Catherine talking in the shower to some unknown inner interlocutor, and then she returned to her room, and every quarter-hour I heard the soft sound of a page turning, and in the golden quadrilateral on the rug a tree's shadow flickered, and I saw the young smooth oval of my face in the mirror, though my features seemed to be far underwater, and the aching feeling which I had in two perpendicular zones of my torso did not go away, and some object was now shifted in Catherine's room, where she had one of my pictures on her wall and one of her second sister's pictures wrapped up by the closet door; she had shown me the picture; it was of a man holding a woman's likeness in his hand, and staring at it; meanwhile children played across the street, and in another house someone was vacuuming, and it was almost cool inside the living room; the temperature was in fact very pleasant, and Stephanie's file cabinet stood by the door in a rather supercilious stance, each drawer smiling a silver unenthusiastic smile with its handle, and looking at nothing through its cyclopean rectangle just above, where a label could be inserted; and just then I heard Catherine moving inside her room, and she went past me into the kitchen; she had put on blue trousers with white stars, and she stayed in the kitchen for a moment; and from the filing cabinet I got the idea of the *smile.* If I were to smile at her, a smile of love and friendship and reverence perfectly conceived, then that smile would eventually draw Catherine out of the kitchen and across the quadrilateral of sunlight, which had by now become a definite diamond, trapping one side of one leg of the china cabinet in its field; and Cathy would next walk across the carpet itself and then she would take her first step upon Stephanie's Indian rug (upon which the exercise bicycle and the fan were standing), and she would cross the Indian rug's white border, which was V-marked by black and some faded color; and then Catherine would step over two intermediate zones, and onto the central region of the rug, which was essentially a rectangle with a beak on the top and the bottom; and she would cross this zone, whose mere perimeter I have failed to satisfactorily describe, much less the patterns inside it; it is only a black box of finitude to me, whereas Catherine in her spiritual power would see the glorious and indescribable patterns within *as they are*, and not care about what they should be or whether they are good or bad; and she would be able to name every shape by its true Being-name which I do not know and could never keep straight, can barely even wonder at, as Catherine does not because she wonders at nothing and says nothing and thereby does not hurt the Forms which truth has woven for its own reasons, and we must make our own reasons which Catherine cannot communicate to anyone except in the most elusive terms, or maybe it just seems that she cannot communicate them because we have not read the Source Book carefully enough to understand her fine hesitations, her laughs and silences – yet sometimes she does speak in ways that I can understand, so then I think it must be that there are things which she does not *choose* to say.

Anyhow, my smile would bring Catherine closer and closer across the rug; that was my intention, and so I theorized, wanting them to believe in sympathetic magic. But I stopped smiling, I think now too soon, and dared to speak to her as she came out of the kitchen:

"Catherine, is there anything I can do to help you with your work?"

"Oh, not now but perhaps *later*," she said, and I cannot even remember anymore whether or not she smiled.

An hour later she went to the kitchen again, but this time I did not dare to speak to her. What had been delicacy on my part was now timidity. And meanwhile the golden quadrangle continued to narrow as it grew southward.

The Fourth Night

I had begun to suspect by now that Catherine did not want to become a martyr and go to Heaven, but I was too polite to say so. The issue of unredeemed suffering did, however, arise.

"It's my belief," Catherine began, laughing, "that you will not feel guilty over suffering which you *encounter* and over which you have no control, *if* you have learned by experience – by experience I mean, having given your *all* to *compensate* for the suffering over which you have no control. After you experience *that* for a *long* number of years, you realize that it's an aspect of *finitude*."

"Hmmm," I said foggily.

"I mean, what *can* you affect? What can't you affect? I mean, if you can't affect something – it has nothing to do with *willingness* to sacrifice – it becomes a different issue, and when it becomes a different issue, guilt is just an *indulgence*."

"Would you sacrifice yourself if you thought it might bring about utility?" I pursued.

"Yes," said Catherine.

"Would you?" I said.

"Well, I think I've *done* that," said Catherine angrily, "and I've seen it *hasn't* brought about utility, and it *frees* me from feeling guilty."

"What's giving your all? Would giving your all be giving your life?"

"I think life is less than *all*," said Catherine.

"Yeah?"

"Yeah."

"What's your all then?"

"It's *much* worse," said Catherine simply.

Friendly Advice

"If I wanted to lure someone into martyrdom," said Stephanie at the table, "I would *lie* to them."

The Long View

At night, clouds seen through an airplane window can be either black or white or violet, depending on whether or not Catherine is beneath them. Often, however, they shine sullenly even when they are violet; it is the cities seen through them which overpower Catherine's presence. These moonlit battlements become more sullen still when seen from Heaven, because then we must deal with additional secret factors. But the violet emanations of Catherine's hair still register on my celestial oscilloscopes.

What Heidegger Said

"There's this quote from Heidegger: 'You are what you do,'" said Catherine the next morning, "although I don't think he wants to talk about explicit intentions."

What the *Great Soviet Encyclopedia* Said

"As a whole, Heidegger's irrational philosophy is one of the acute manifestations of the crises of modern bourgeois social consciousness."

What the TV Said

"Take off your clothes," said the TV.

"That's our *least* favorite character," scolded Catherine.

"I've always been ashamed of you, too, daughter," said the TV.

This stymied or neutralized poor Catherine for a moment, and the TV gathered up its irresistible blue rays, and chilly blue laughter gurgled out of it like a creek running down from the snowfields of

Mount Shasta in the spring. "Well, now that we're alone," said the TV, "let me ask you that burning question. Did you sleep with her?"

"*Yes!*" cried Stephanie.

"That's it," said the TV. "The one I want to take off you."

"I *told* you it was racy," said Catherine.

"And my *breasts*," said the TV.

Catherine inhaled cigarette smoke in a nervous laugh, jerking herself back and shaking her head.

The Fifth Night

"Do you idealize women?" Catherine said to me very softly.

"I try to," I said.

She was like a gracious tree shading some clear pool in which her own reflection was almost unvaried, and she was perfect in every part, even to bearing her hard green fruit which sustained my ontological expectation by virtue of ontically disappointing me from moment to moment, never refreshing me, never decaying – and it was not until I had known Catherine for years that I realized that refreshment must always be vulgar; only in the *not-yet* which Catherine exemplified could I hope to give witness to a purity far less fragile than anyone who did not know her might have suspected, because her green fruit had a thick waxy rind which kept disease at a distance for years; it was as durable as if coated in polyurethane; thus her betrayals served not only to nourish the continual evasions which she required, but also as nervous stitches in the tapestry of a larger fidelity which she wove – not necessarily for me; it was completely incidental whether there were anyone in particular whom she wanted to be pure for (a flower does not care which bee pollinates her) – a tapestry depicting a birch tree with a trunk as slender as a girl's waist, and fragrant white arms more slender still, growing upward in a rich fragrant ray, showered by its own green leaves between which, in a thousand tiny windows, the blue sky and white clouds changed, and the leaves changed and the tree grew taller and greener from summer to summer – but this was a Canadian birch which I once saw, existing beyond the Catherine-horizon, which rendered the image still more appropriate because Catherine alone existed by projecting herself beyond her own horizon of damaged violet hair (which would someday be grey), her demeanor of worn velvet,* none of which would ever matter because Catherine did not live where she was, not even being a birch tree, for instance, but a fruit tree whose fruit would never Be-there, making her wonderful in the mystery of what she was, so much more beautiful than a woman who kept her promises; the only danger, the point of entry for the termites of doom who must eventually destroy her sweet trunk, was that she made promises at all; even at the San Francisco Center for Perfect Enlightenment, where she had been a saint for eleven years, she would have had to promise things; if she lived on her own island or existed somehow in the violet sunset of outer space she would not have to make promises but then I imagine that Catherine would have gone mad; her perfumed sap would have become more and more acid and eaten through her from her heartwood to her rusty bark; so perhaps she was best as she was, although the severe requirement placed upon her of projecting herself beyond herself left her strained and weakened, particularly at night, when her eyes sometimes looked weak and hunted, while for longer and longer periods of time her hair gave up being violet at all and was simply black or reddish-gold as the light struck it, and Catherine put her hand to her throat and smiled in a rather forced way because any smile was as *beyond* as birch-fruit, which I have been looking for all my life but never saw, and that is why in photographs of Catherine's smile it seems as if the corners of her mouth are continually trembling on the glossy paper and the smile is contracting, contracting, without actually getting any smaller; in one picture she was smiling with her head cocked and raised, her white hands clasped before her neck in a praying blur like the blur of her violet hair through which the green leaves behind her could be seen; and when I took this photograph and burned it the blue sky turned violet and then diminished behind an advancing border of black ash; and the flames next played among the foliage in such a living way that for the first time I could imagine a Tree of Flame growing higher and higher above the black cinder-plains, its

---

* How did I feel about her growing old? To tell the truth, the thought of those high Seminole cheekbones becoming more prominent, skull-like; her violet hair going grey once and for all, her eyes becoming moist and weak, her skin ashy-grey as indeed it already was on her bad days – these things concerned me very little. It was chiefly the thought of her reduced mobility in her eventual grandmotherly state that chilled me. She would no longer be able to flee. But compensating for that would be her inevitable retreat into death or vacancy; thus there was some hope that her distance would always be maintained, so that my presence would never shatter the mirror of her perfection.

trunk and branches black, its leaves orange and red and changeable, consuming itself and offering the ashes of itself as its fruit; so the flames lived among the leaves over Catherine's head without seeming to hurt them, but then I looked at the leaves where the flames had been and there was nothing but black ash; and Catherine's white face seemed to flush in the flames as if she were finally in love, and the flames came closer and closer to her; at last her violet hair took the first flame and her head was suddenly crowned with the flames but her face was still untouched, and then the first flame reached her forehead; immediately the flames destroyed her eyes and nose, and only her smile was left unchanged but since its context had changed it did not seem to be a smile anymore but rather a grimace of unendurable hapless pain. – I did not tell Catherine any of this.

The Courtship of Catherine

Over dinner (steak, mushrooms, champagne, beer and brandy) we discussed the afterlife. I maintained that there was no such thing, because I could not remember what had happened to me before I existed, and so had no reason to think that anything would happen to me after I stopped existing. (Of course I was being sly here, since, being the Holy Ghost, I knew that I would never stop existing.) Both Catherine and Stephanie (who sincerely loved Catherine) were both surprised at me. Pragmatic Catherine believed in some sort of continuity of vitality but not of self or memory – which struck me as no proper afterlife at all; and Stephanie believed in the unity of all things, which unity (so I construed her) must be like a pie composed of infinite slices of all dead, living, lost and hypothetical particularities; because this was necessarily conceptualized timelessly, every possible thing would always be. (But what if Beelzebub ate a slice of the pie? Why should that ontological goodness just sit out on the stove forever to cool while the sun shone through the kitchen window and outside I ran endlessly in a sunny chasing game with Stephanie's dog?) – Stephanie said that it was not like this at all. Unity was not a pie; she considered me a poseur who insisted on my little dichotomies, such as life *versus* death, when in fact everything was one. Because language necessarily expressed itself in particularities, it was impossible to talk usefully about what she meant.

Only when death is conceived in its full ontological essence, said Heidegger (H.248), *can we have any methodological assurance in even asking what may be after death; only then can we do so with meaning and justification. Whether such a question is a possible theoretical question at all will not be decided here. The this-worldly ontological Interpretation of death takes precedence* (sneered Heidegger) *over any ontical other-worldly speculation.*

Stephanie and Catherine had cooked dinner for me in their negligées; both of them were transparent dinner bundles of marvelous things, and now Catherine came and stood behind me and began rubbing my shoulders as I reached behind me to embrace her. She kissed my arm. Catherine stood behind me still, and Stephanie said she must be an angel whispering into my ear, and at this Catherine breathed very gently into my ear. She had never done that before. – "Cathy's standing on your right," said Stephanie, "that means she's your good angel." – She and Stephanie began to sing the song "Froggie Would A-Courting Go," and they wanted me to make up some verses about Miss Mouse or Miss Bluejay or Froggie's other women, but I did not want to because I was as shy as a ghost ("I think it would be *upsetting* to a ghost to have a person there," said Catherine) and also because I wondered *what if they really were frogs?*, and Catherine began to play songs from her favorite old 1960s records, sitting very severely on the floor by the piano, smoking and drinking wine; and I put my arm around her; and she leaned against my shoulder (she had already said that she hoped she was not making a mistake); and then I kissed each of her fingers one by one, at which she laughed a little and kissed me on the lips, very quickly and very lightly, and I started kissing her until she pulled her head away; then I stroked her back while she sat there so seriously, changing the record after every song and leaning forward to read the lyrics on the covers, her features a little more sharpened than when I first knew her, at which I felt for her even more, and I lay beside her holding her small light hand, and she said nothing, so I kissed her knee, and played with her toe. – "Catherine," I said, "I'll never do anything bad to you." – "I'm *depending* on that," she replied. – The songs were all in a major key; they were from that ancient time before Catherine had entered the Center for Perfect Enlightenment when everyone zapped each other with super-love, and mocha-chip octopi kissed raspberry octopi in the gardens beneath violet oceans, and every octopus was in love, and every tentacle could taste and supply its own peculiar pleasure; as to what happened to that loving Octopus's Garden in the end, my friends, the answer is blowing in the wind. – Catherine's hair trailed behind her like the violet trail of a meteor. I was undone by her hair. "If you want to describe an indescribable thing," said Stephanie, "my avenue would be to *feel* the thing and then describe my experience of feelings," so I felt Catherine's hair and hid my face inside it and kissed it, drinking violet from it because no matter how much I drank there was always more, and I kissed Catherine's face and nervous mouth. I gave her honey-kisses, sugar-kisses, fire-kisses, flame-kisses, bride-kisses, ghost-kisses and other displays of ontology. Catherine was my violet summer. (To Beelzebub, watching from underneath the floor, the sight must have brought inexpressible grief; he cried hoarsely, and his tears fed the thirsty moles.) I kept hugging her, and occasionally she kissed me or stroked my arm, but mainly she just smoked and listened to her songs. – Earlier that day Catherine had said, "In the ready-to-hand Heidegger's talking about behavior at a level you're not aware of. When you reach for the pen, you're not aware of reaching for the pen. What you're thinking of is writing with it. Although in his prescriptive mode I think he thinks choice is very important." – So now I found myself unaware of inclining my face toward Catherine's lips; what I was thinking of was kissing her; her pale freckled face was always a fresh surprise for me. – Finally she said she would tuck me into bed. She turned down the corners of her bed for me. I started to close the door, but she said, "Don't touch *anything*," and so I didn't, and she commanded, "Now, lie down," and she said, "You'll *never* be more comfortable than this," and she patted the covers over me and said goodnight, but I asked her to sit with me, so she kissed me, but then I still would not let her go; poor Catherine was being possessed by a Spirit; she had to kiss me three more times.

A Flat Joke

Reading the paper the next morning, Catherine said in a rather academic tone that she favored arranged marriages, and at once I took this chance to say, "Well then, Cathy, let's *arrange* one," but the response to this was only silence.

What the TV Said

"All right!" cried the TV. "I failed."

"I do not know why I cannot find a sweet-natured woman," said the TV.

"I hope you get her," said the TV. "It would serve you right."

Loss, Diversion, Deficiency and Projection

I was in a state of constant torture, which I do not think that Catherine was entirely unaware of (the highlight of a day was when she touched my hand); and of course I was happy in that state. But I was like the black dog Jessica, who sobbed in the back yard every hot night because of the fleas. I did not want to be an unwelcome guest. Already I had heard Stephanie say, "Somehow the Holy Ghost has some relevance *here* on *this* plane, and yet It *really* belongs on the *Other Plane*."

Why Catherine Became a Saint

"As I remember," said Catherine to me in Heaven, lying wrapped in my best Finnish reindeer skin, "my life was pretty *difficult*, particularly from the age of eleven or something, so that by the time I was eighteen I was pretty *exhausted*, I mean just *exhausted*. And it was really appealing . . . the idea of a monastic retreat, somehow, too – a form of absolution, you know, because I've always been so self-critical . . . Intensely *so*. So anyway, so that was the beginning. The middle – well, let me see. What was the midway point? – Two sides. You know. On the one hand, you know, things were sort of positive, and certain people liked me a lot, so I was receiving some sort of *love*, like an *infant*. At the same time, too, things started happening; I mean, there were sort of certain *obstacles* to sort of relating to that kind of community because I was too sort of *individualistic* and the other side of that became manifest in terms of the *self-criticalness* and since this wasn't a channel there was a reversion to the old channel: self-destructiveness. So that was the middle *phase:* accepting a love or rejecting myself which meant that I *couldn't* accept a love, because I was sort of skeptical about the whole thing. Then the *end* phase I think was . . . sort of realizing the whole thing wasn't . . . *workable.* You know, I deeply *wanted* it to work, and it *wouldn't.* You know, it just *wouldn't work.*"

For a long time she lay by the fire without saying anything. (Because Heaven is very cold and high and dark, we must always have fires.)

"Because I actually *left* more than once, I mean, it seems that the entire time that I was *there*, I was always *leaving.* That was my *mode*," she said smiling.

A Visit

"I don't know if it's changed or not," Catherine said in the car nervously. "We'll see."

Coming into the Center for Perfect Enlightenment's reception chamber, which managed to be dim, chilly and gracious, you removed your shoes to proceed to the room where services were held, a wide rectangle which was also dim and chilly with its white-ribbed ceiling like a cold skeleton, its brick floor that chilled your feet as if you were wading through a pool of carp, the carp being the one- and two-dimensional spirits upon the surfaces of the floor-bricks which shone with underwater dullness, and you squatted on the rectangular island of tatami mats in the middle of the floor and chanted sutras, which Catherine once thought might ultimately make a *little* bit of sense, but returning into this cheerless room after her years of absence, Catherine, who was a box of secrets, felt that there were many different truths in the world and found the sutras rather *dogmatic* with their talk of the right way and the wrong way, and she raised an instrument like a lacquer-handled leather baseball bat and said, "I don't remember this exactly," and struck a big black bowl so that it rang, and a crabby C.P.E. woman came to the shut door and looked at Catherine through its little window, but Catherine could not get into trouble for making music because she had been there for eleven years, so she struck the gong again, kneeling on a black mat in front of a black music stand that bore

the Song of the Jewel Mirror Awareness (Baojing Sanmeike), which I
do not pretend to understand as I do not pretend to understand poor
tortured Catherine who had been an inmate of the Center for Perfect
Enlightenment for so long that her every breath was a ghost; ghosts
were in the very smoke of her cigarettes, and meanwhile the traffic went
by in a muffled mode of Being as it must have done for Catherine in
her eleven years of sainthood, and the windows of the services room
gave onto a garden where the green leaves waved indifferently; again I
could almost see the old golden carp swimming among those leaves,
cold and beautiful and long-lived, and carp swam between the lines of
the Song of the Jewel Mirror Awareness, which began:

> The teaching of ghostness
> Has been intimately communicated by buddhas and patriarchs.

[But some C.P.E. feminist had crossed out "patriarchs" and substituted
"ancestors."]

> Now you have it
> So keep it well.
> Filling a silver bowl with snow,
> Hiding an owl in the moonlight –
> When you array them, they're not the same,
> When you mix them, you know where they are.

– so that it was evident from the profusion of images and rules that the
Center for Perfect Enlightenment prized the ontic, and Catherine must
have believed in it, too, as when she used to strike the *mykugyo* upon
the crown of its head to make a dull wooden sound while the *mykugyo*
expressed serene astonishment from its golden goggle-eyes, which were
actually the scales of interlocking Zen fishes, and the *mykugyo*'s wooden
mouth now smiled for Catherine exactly as it used to smile for her and
as it had smiled for others before her and would smile for others after
her, for the *mykugyo* valued everyone exactly the same. On the altar,
which was cedar and severe, and which Catherine had had to bow to
for eleven years, was the Gandhara Buddha, who bore a tombstone
between his shoulders, and beside the altar the Golden Guardian
(whose name Catherine could no longer remember) closed his eyes and
inclined his head toward the red candle below his feet and the cup
where Catherine had once offered him incense, though not, she said, to
him *personally* but to some great Being which had failed her; and beside
him the Black Guardian (whose name Catherine had never known)

scowled and folded his arms and brandished things in other arms and shook his finger at me. The silence became heavier and heavier, until the room was grey with gloom, uncushioned even by Catherine's Being-There, although the stones in the garden through the window were sunken deep into moss and delicate clover like a beloved's pubic hair, and the ferns were so soft and graceful; of course they were *outside* the Center for Perfect Enlightenment, into which new Elect inmates were at this moment carrying their packs and suitcases and boxes. The ghost of the founder, Mitsubishi-roshi, was in a corner at the bottom of the stairs: – a grey silhouette on silver mesh, with a bald head and big ears, and he held the ghost of the stick which was used at the Center for Perfect Enlightenment to hit people who fell asleep at the services; and that ghost watched you with his stick at his shoulder until you had descended another flight of stairs and gone around the corner through the priests' entrance to the underground meditation room where everything was grey and dim, the windows covered with rice-paper to dully diffuse each day like the Cimmerian fogs of the Sunset District; and along the walls ran the tiers of wooden *tans* where Catherine used to have to bow to her cushion and then bow away from her cushion and after that she was required by Zen to swing herself up onto her *tan* without grazing its edge and sit down upon the cushion in full lotus position, facing the wall, which was painted brown to reduce glare, and then she had to meditate for forty minutes and then stop for ten minutes and then engage in walking meditation for ten minutes before returning to her round cushion to meditate for another forty minutes, from three-thirty in the morning to ten-thirty at night except during Meditation Weeks when Catherine had to stay upon her cushion staring at the wall day and night, although she was permitted to turn round for meals. In the middle of the room were other pallets facing long white dividers like computer cubicles where tired minds must work amidst still wearier abstractions until they reeled at the 68020-assembler language of Zen, the Zen of one lobe meditating, and everything inside this vast room was so cold and pale; it was a *wan* room, perfectly suited to propagating the gospel of nothingness. The pallets went on for rows and rows; – of course those of the Abbot and his assistant were reserved for them *personally;* Catherine would never have been allowed to use them. (As Stephanie once said, "Any benefits to be had from martyring yourself will be strictly *worldly* ones that you'll get in the process of martyring yourself." So Mitsubishi-roshi and his successor Beelzebub-roshi martyred themselves in order to receive their private pallets.) Through a doorway and down a long dark hall around the corner from where Catherine had endured her years of wall-torture, were the timekeeping instruments of that place of sullen ritual: – the *han*, which was a block of wood to be struck fifteen minutes, ten minutes and five minutes before commencing meditation; the great drum, which re-related Dasein to temporality at the end of meditation, with one beat for every hour which had passed; while the bell beside was struck once for each quarter-hour. Proceeding upstairs, past a stone frog which stared at her in a sunny window-niche, Catherine went to see her old room, but the door was closed and there were different shoes outside it.

Catherine went up to the roof to light a cigarette. "You know," she said, looking out at San Francisco, "it's like you're in a desert and you come across this *writing*. But after trying to decipher it for years, you find out that it was only the alphabet, the *English* alphabet."

Catherine's Alphabet

The California volume of Stephanie's *Handbook of the North American Indians* assured me that San Diego County had a lot of petroglyphs and pictographs. Stephanie said that we could go visit some if I wanted. Of course the Indian-horizon has contracted noticeably in the last three centuries; as for the petroglyphs of southern California, they had long since been appropriated by secret leagues of anthropologists, and to locate them you first had to call Triple A (assuming that you were a member) to get a special number at the Museum, and then when you called that number if you were good the Museum would give you the number of Professor Glyph at home, and Professor Glyph would interrogate you over the phone for twenty minutes but if you lied or if you put Stephanie on and Stephanie said that she was a graduate student and had seen all the petroglyphs on the Ute Reservation and of *course* she had read his article, then Professor Glyph would trust you and reveal to you a certain secret spot off the freeway, requiring only a half-mile walk through rattlesnake-infested poison ivy.

The petroglyphs (they were pictographs, actually) occurred in faded red maze-patterns upon a high white rock overgrown with bushes, and desert shrubs grew like golden barbed wire in the rocks above, and above *them* was blue sky, and below them were rustling lizards; and boulders of white feldspar rested and shaded their shoulders in the bushes, and below them were power poles and evening cicadas and houses in construction. The pictographs had faded, and it was clear that they would not be here for many more hundred years.

"We were only looking for petro*glyphs*," said Catherine brightly, "but we *picked* a *peck* of *picto*graphs!" And she looked round shyly.

She went down to a stagnant lake but was soon *attacked* by half a dozen crawdads in a line, and was forced to throw sand on them to *discourage* them.

The Sixth Night

When it was dark Catherine stood in the doorway looking at Venus and Jupiter and all the constellations she could see, while the dishes sat on the table, deplorably ontic in the way that they were chipped and had food on them and were not stacked in infinitely tall shrink-packed columns inside some ontological cabinet.

"I think I need just a little more wine," Catherine said.

"No, I think you need a *lot* more," I said.

"No, a lot more would incapacitate me. I don't *want* to be incapacitated."

A Subtle Distinction

The difference between Heidegger in the daytime and Heidegger at night was exactly as great as the difference between day and night. So Catherine believed, lying on her bed day and night in her Heideggerian panic. "To be closed off and covered up belongs to Dasein's facticity." In the daytime this seemed to Catherine to mean that being closed off was constitutive of stuffiness-in-the-World of her room while Stephanie sat far past the living room entering field notes onto the Commodore 64 computer with its wavery underwater-looking screen, and a low hot breeze blew up from Mexico, and Catherine was closed off or covered up by very listlessness; but at night when it was chilly and mists came up from the sea she was closed off from the darkness because she felt *safer* that way . . .

Catherine's Ghost Stories

"Well," said Catherine to me, as we sat at the kitchen table burning spirit-candles so that green flames illuminated our mouths and chins, and Catherine's hair was darker and softer than the hot soft darkness, "I remember one night when I was meditating at Half Moon Bay – which is actually very *pretty*, but in this foggy woods. Generally, if you're an older student you have a cabin to yourself – it used to be a summer resort – and there was this *young* guy (he must have been about eighteen) who was living in the cabin next to me; and I think I must have been feeling – you know, *tense*, because this young *man* was sort of emotionally disturbed, and he'd actually become *terribly* infatuated with me and threatened to *kill* me. He used to make these threats – you know, very vivid descriptions: – *crushing* my *skull*, etcetera, etcetera. So he was living next to me and it was rather late at night, and as I said I was skittish, since I don't *like* to be alone in the *dark* in the *woods*, so I came in, got into bed, and just as I was going to sleep I got this *very* strong sensation, and what it felt like was like a cat pouncing on my stomach. I had to really struggle to sort of *expel* it. It took a couple of minutes. I was reacting to it as if something was trying to take possession. That abdominal area, there's a lot of *lore* about that area, with yoga and things of that nature. So I *may* have encountered a spirit.

"You know," she said, "it's so *odd*, these things. I remember one time when I was walking on Haight Street to catch a 6 Parnassus bus – this was broad daylight – and I suddenly had this peculiar sense of some *enormous* presence, something sort of behind me and above me."

What Heidegger and Catherine Said

"The world has a *structure*," Catherine said very earnestly, "and when you look at how it's structured there are these sequences of *steps*."

A Dream

That night I dreamed that I was one of a number of children who had
been kidnapped by a giant woman who had chopped off all our arms
while we screamed (I cannot say whether or not her hair was violet),
and she kept us on a ledge on a cliff on Mount Shasta, which was
higher than Heaven, and she began pushing us one by one down a
steep structured sequence of *steps* that led down to the bottom of the
cliff (and of course we could not even throw up our arms to punctuate
our dramatic backward fall, as people did in, for instance, Eisenstein's
Potemkin when they got massacred and their baby carriages bumped
down the stairs into the ocean); and when we had tumbled almost to
the bottom of the stairs, then the giant woman shot us.

Another Dream

I sometimes dreamed that I was kissing Catherine, and my mouth was
on her mouth, and my tongue was in her mouth, and when I woke up I
found that I really had been kissing someone's lips, but she was not
Catherine at all. There are definite pecking orders in life; I am sure this
is why the relics of a saint have more power than a dead dog's bones.

Anxiety of the Ontic Rose

Returning from the beach the next morning, I took a rosebud off a bush
for my sweet Catherine. – "Oh, *thank* you," she said. – "I picked it five
minutes ago," I said, "and look, it's already open." – I guess it must
have thought *now* or *never!*" said Catherine gaily.

Another Subtle Distinction

"Who's your best friend, Catherine?" I once asked her.

"Why, *you* are," she cried smiling, flinging her arms wide. Then she qualified herself: "At least, you're certainly *one* of them."

My Rival

"Well, I'm supposed to meet this person in about four minutes," said Catherine, and she went down to the beach, but she did not know that I had followed like a wisp of fishy fog, so that I saw her standing ankle-deep in the waves beside a gentleman in a black coat whom I recognized as Beelzebub. He had his arm around her. "Cathy dear," he said, running his fingers through her long violet hair (and I was happy to see that Catherine shrank away from the touch of his swollen burned fingers), "*dearest* Cathy, if you don't like the Holy Ghost why don't you send It about Its business? Or, if you'd rather, *I* could send It about Its business," and out of his coat pocket he took a Tijuana stiletto, the body of which was cast iron with great antique square screws, and the message on it read NATO FRIENDS, and Beelzebub clicked the stud and instead of a blade of metal a blade of violet fire leaped out, and Beelzebub stabbed at the water with a devilish grimace, so that the ocean sizzled and steamed and evaporated all the way to the horizon, leaving swimmers and surfers lying on their bellies in the wet sand, and a beautiful fish flopped and flopped and flopped, but then Beelzebub put his forefinger back on the stud of his stiletto and clicked it the other way so that the flame-blade returned to its primordial state of hideous hiddenness and the ocean rolled back just in time to save the fish – at which I felt a certain kinship with my enemy, because that was exactly the sort of thing I would do if Catherine and I were walking through a dangerous part of Oakland at night to get to a liquor store and some character with his hat pulled down over his nose strolled over to make us buy his Thai weed, and I put my arm around Catherine tight and began to exercise my powers. But of course Beelzebub wanted to harm me. – "Well, you know," replied Catherine to this demonstration, "I become sort of emotionally bound to a person or a Ghost, and when you leave there's a certain shock. And there's also this *inertia*. I suppose those are the two reasons against it. And the *comfortableness*. Of course at the time you don't know those reasons. It then seems to be whether or not you *love* the person."

"Poor Catherine!" exclaimed Beelzebub, and he dropped a bloody tear into the sea.

"I *know*," she said enthusiastically. "I mean, *poor me*."

Wickedness

Beelzebub liked doing all kinds of things to Catherine. One time he got his Swedish girlfriend pregnant, and he decided to get her an abortion without paying for it. The Swedish girl, not being an American citizen, was but a lowly link in the Great Chain of Being, which stretched deep under the ocean until its slimy crusty barnacled links lost themselves in solid ooze; so she was not eligible for Medicare, but Catherine was, so Beelzebub took Catherine to have an interview with a social worker, and poor Catherine had to say that she was pregnant and she was very nervous because it was hard for her to lie, but, fortunately for the Swedish girl, the social worker interpreted that nervousness as desperation and felt sorry for Catherine and expedited the abortion, which the Swedish girl had the following day in Catherine's name while Beelzebub sat with Catherine in a Berkeley café drinking rather overpriced Espresso from a large number of tiny glass cups. Catherine looked very becoming in a blackish-violet sweater which matched her blackish-violet hair, and as she sat beside Beelzebub the poor thing felt much at her ease because Beelzebub carried on conversations for her, while sweet Catherine cocked her head and listened intently. By now he had hooked Catherine into a get-rich-quick scheme involving Infernotron personal computers. The State Department had banned their sale in Europe since they contained top-secret microchips behind their video screens and we did not want the Russians to get what the Russians probably already had, so Beelzebub told Catherine that she could buy the computers in California at a discount on her credit card (she didn't have one then, but Beelzebub made her get one by using a dummy

credit system which he had invented) and then sell them in France and
Italy for whopping profits (assuming that the CIA didn't catch her) and
then pay her credit bill just before it came due and *then* split the
difference with Beelzebub, who in the meantime decided to take a
Hawaiian vacation on a special deal with Catherine if Catherine would
just advance him the money, so Catherine advanced him the money and
then sat expecting Beelzebub to call her any day now.

Another Sad Story about Catherine

Once I called Catherine on the phone and asked her how she was, and
she said, "Well, I'm a little disoriented. Actually there's this demon I've
been seeing for two or three days and we just had a little argument,
well, actually about birth control. I've always been very cautious; I've
never gotten pregnant, and it turns out he's taking a certain chance he
told me he wasn't taking."

Still Another Sad Story

Once when Beelzebub and his new girlfriend were going to Paris and
Catherine needed a place to stay, Beelzebub said that she could stay
and then said she couldn't stay and then said she could stay but he
wasn't going and then finally decided to go. He was supposed to call in
twenty minutes to confirm that she could stay. He had gotten two
round-trip tickets to Europe for two hundred dollars because World
Airways was going out of business on Monday. But there were some
last-minute hitches. She waited for his call all day. When Catherine
called him, he said that he would call her back in twenty minutes. An
hour later, he called to say that he would call her in half an hour. He
left three days afterward. He had told Catherine that she would be free
to listen to his collection of compact discs in his absence, so he packed
them up and took them to Paris, and Catherine, although conscious
that severe injury was being inflicted upon her, got in the back seat of
his car because she was going to drive it back from the airport so that
Beelzebub didn't have to pay the parking fee, and as they approached

the terminal Catherine locked her nervous hands into praying position and asked if she could use his car to drive to San Francisco once or twice while he was gone, and Beelzebub said that she could, but she was not to drive the car more than twenty miles, and he turned to his new girlfriend who sat eating ice cream in the front seat (lying, convincing was what their operation was all about) and he said, "Succubus, my dear, check the odometer and write down the mileage," and poor Catherine was humiliated.

Dependency

"It's hard to be dependent, isn't it?" I said.

"Well, yes," said Catherine. "Especially to be dependent on Beelzebub. He's so . . . well, anyhow, I don't want to worry about it."

Never have I seen anyone as adept as Catherine at making the noncommittal statement. This was her most reliable defense guard. I once saw her in the Mixtec Indian ghetto of Tijuana, sitting on a folding chair in the sun, lips drawn back, with her brown boots peeping out beneath her blue dress, and she had little to say about the sights and smells. "All those *children!*" she exclaimed at last. "*Remarkable!*"

What Happened When Catherine Forgot to be Tense

There had been times when there was such tender delicacy between Catherine and me (so I imagined) that I was afraid even to raise her hand to my lips for fear of damaging her somehow as her violet hair had been damaged, which was why she braided it at home instead of letting it fall down her shoulders where it could torture me with its softness. – When I held Catherine's cool little hand, I was as happy as if I had done something good to earn some great reward. As we walked, her eyelids fluttered. – No doubt she had been just as uncautious that time at the Center for Perfect Enlightenment when she went for a walk with the angel Gabriel, and although it was night on Earth they wandered down the hill and into the Tenderloin without reading their supernatural compasses, and it was very dark and quiet there, and men leaned against the buildings watching them, and Catherine felt cold and buttoned up her white-knit sweater, and they heard a man cursing and there were scuttering sounds behind them on Turk Street, and then suddenly someone ran up behind them and grabbed Gabriel by his white wings and stabbed him dead for no reason at all. Gabriel fell to the sidewalk with the knife in him, and a little golden bubble blew out of his mouth with his soul in it. The bubble tried to ascend to Heaven, but there was a droplet of blood on it that weighed it down, and Catherine did not know how to help, and as the bubble struggled and shone in the night, Gabriel's murderer saw it and clapped it into his mouth and swallowed it. Then he ran away screaming. The feathers started falling out of Gabriel's wings and blowing away, and the whores on Leavenworth caught them up innocently because they were pretty and the whores laughed and put them in their hair, and Catherine was left alone in the darkness, with people watching her out from dark doorways and alleys and bars and second-storey windows, and the darkness drowning her violet light (that was the first time that her violet hair had gone out), so that when the police finally came, in a chuckling flash of red and blue lights, they saw only a dead angel and a young woman with dark hair and closed eyes, standing very very rigidly on the sidewalk clutching her temples. – Catherine did not much like to talk about it. – "I'm trying to remember the Tenderloin," she said cautiously. "It's sort of a kind of *patchwork* place, in a lot of ways – just *physically*, for instance; and the people are sort of – well, I mean, people are doing all sorts of things to just patch their lives together." It was difficult for Catherine to say anything negative, even about the people who had killed her friend.

What the TV Said

"Which is the real you then?" said the TV.

"You know," said the TV, "I actually feel like different people sometimes."

"You can't be *serious*," said the TV.

"It seems like the only way I could relate on a sexual level was pretending to be another person," admitted the TV.

"Oh, God," said Catherine, whose face was freckled like a robin's egg. "She's been *brainwashed!*"

"Part of me wants to have that power," mused the TV, "but you know I hate women like that."

"And we've already *watched this scene!*" said Catherine. "Well, hardly *anything's* happened."

Leaping-In-For

"What can I do for you, Catherine?" I said.

"You mean right now?"

"No, in the long run."

"Well, you already do *everything* I *ask* of you. You could read my Heidegger paper, maybe. That would help me."

The Being of Catherine-In-The-World

As Stephanie said in a footnote to her article on Tongan dance, "it felt very birdlike, and always on the verge."

Conjectural Physics

Catherine for her part came to be sick of me, more and more, or so it seemed, perhaps because I had been invited to her house in much the same fashion as the Soviet army was invited into Prague: – although actually it was the *heat* that made Catherine reclusive and forced me to the beach in mid-afternoon where I could meditate on her "conjectural past" (Melville), which, whatever it was, must be too finely wrought for even the ontological (which I was) to transcend it, Catherine being so far above me or beyond me in her inmost self, as demonstrated in everything about her from the pitch of her voice to her sad eyes, that I could never hope to know her even if she martyred herself for me and went to Heaven. It was as if I were in some seaside cave (which again I was), surrounded by flies and rotting ontic kelp, while in the limpid evening the ocean of Catherine's nature shone before me in its highest perfection of light and color, and I could have gone out into the evening sun to walk along the edge of that ocean, which was so violet that the sky seemed white, but I did not because that would have been too good for me. Even if I were to come out of the cave, my shadow long and thin upon the sand like an Egyptian figure, I could have stood in the sun but the water would still have been beyond me; and if I sent my sight flying into it with the speed of light, as afforded me by my binoculars, I could then have taken in only a tiny round slice of it, so concentrated now as to hurt me with its terrible dazzlement. Not that Catherine was terrible, but her beyondness was. (Here I must disagree with Plato, who was complacent that if we just waited and squinted long enough, we would be able to look upon the sun inside Catherine and understand her nature!) – And each little circular universe of running foam and golden traceries of glory upon the foam was impossibly complex to comprehend. And this was the best time, when the horizon was golden and the evening was urgently immense, while it was merely hot and dim within the screened-in houses. I could not merge with the ocean, but since I was the Holy Ghost I could at least become that lone white bird that flies above the hot evening oceans of our hopes.

Ontological Exposition of Futurity

It must have been those golden swirls which left their traces in the sand the following afternoon at mid-tide, when men borrowed my camouflage binoculars to watch the pretty girls, and the sand was specked with gold.

However

Be this as it may, I am not quite finished in describing my final evening at Catherine's house, a half-hour north of Mexico, thirteen hours south of Mount Shasta – in the center of the World, in short, where the bleeding drops of the afternoon became cool and golden with clouds, and it was clear that the day was almost over, like the summer, like my earthly life; and Catherine knew that I was leaving and she was relieved and her obligingness now rose, as it must in a hostess at the beginning and end of any visit, no matter how unwanted or protracted, so that she became as active as the volcanoes of Kamchatka, and in a positive frenzy she was making me margaritas and crushing ice and slicing limes to have with my tequila (which I was drinking steadily, in far greater quantities than she), and calling airlines and buslines and Sacred Heart railroad lines to get me out of there, but they would not accept me because I was not a person, and I drank more and more until I was sure that I finally understood Catherine and each eighth of lime which Catherine had cut for me was so green and fresh that the delusional World seemed to reach out to me to enhance my yearning relatedness, and although I really had not wanted any margaritas I made myself keep drinking them because Catherine had made them and it seemed an appropriate desperate mortification to squeeze the poor green lime-eighths and gulp them down as fast as Catherine could make them and smear the rim of the glasses with good coarse salt; why she wanted me to drink so many margaritas I really don't know, but at least I had found something to do which pleased her, and Catherine asked me why I had not been smiling very much lately, and I told her that I was in fact very happy and drank another margarita, although by now my major objective was to sit at the table at a very precise angle so as not to get sick, and I had another drink and tried to walk robustly about to prove my strength but Catherine told me to go to bed and I threw myself down on the mattress and Catherine bent to take my shoes off and tuck me under the blanket and I grabbed her and pulled her on top of me and embraced her and Catherine said, "You're not yourself," and the next time I happened to speak with her on the ouijaphone she said, "What was the matter? You looked quite *piqued* and *distraught* on the morning you left."

The Last Morning

Every morning at coffee, Catherine sat reading the paper in her white nightgown, her face pale against her violet-black braids. At that time she seemed altogether a snow-girl or plaster-girl, except for her dark hair. (Today my face, too, was ghostly ghastly pale.) – "Evidently there was this female drug agent who had alcohol in her blood and got into a car accident," she announced. Her hair hid her face from me in its sweep down to her thighs. When I rested my hand on her shoulder (intending to award her my holy benediction), she did not seem enthusiastic. She did not turn or tense, but her air of irritable resignation was no less palpable than the light that glowed in the ruffs of her long white nightgown-sleeve.

"What are you up to, Catherine?" I said.

"Breakfast," she said coldly.

She went into her sister's room, and they murmured for half an hour. Then Catherine emerged in a blue dress, and Stephanie appeared with wet hair, announcing that we were to leave in five minutes. "Well, *that* sounds good then," said Catherine.

What the TV Said

"I want you to be my own true woman," said the TV.

"It's *true*," said Catherine to me laughing.

"Because you should hate yourself *more*," said the TV.

A Metaphysical Drive

I had once asked Catherine to drive me to Heaven, but when she asked me how far away it was I had to say it was more than a hundred miles, and then Catherine said that that was awfully long. Another time she was definitely going to go to Heaven with me, but she sprained her ankle. So it was understood that she would drive me to Hell instead. She and Stephanie had to go there anyhow for business reasons.

In the car, she lit up a Virginia Slim, but when she did it I could not see all of her face; I saw only the freckle-clothed cheekbone, the violet hair sweeping back against her neck, and, in the rearview mirror, her frowning freckled forehead with its furrow just above the bridge of the nose.

"You know," said Catherine, "I know a quicker way to the border, if you want to try it."

"Well," said Stephanie vaguely, "you can always try it. If you don't get there, I guess you'll end up somewhere else."

"Let's see," said Catherine, "I think it's something about veering a *hard* right."

"Unless we make a *left* somewhere," said Stephanie.

"It's possible that we do," Catherine replied.

She made an abrupt left turn. "I don't think the guy in back of me *liked* me very much," she laughed. She merged into the freeway, saying, "Now, *this* is what I call a *drive*."

Retrospective: Catherine Decides Not to Go to Heaven

"Oh, I would really love to come," said Catherine.

"We'll probably have to hitchhike through the clouds," I said. "Is that okay with you? Since I'm the Holy Ghost, you should be pretty safe."

Catherine looked nervous."

"Have you done much hitching?"

"Not since I was eighteen. I was raped. But if you're sure it's safe, then I'll come."

I thought her unenthusiastic. "Well," I said, "it would be nice if we can go."

"Don't say *if*," Catherine said pleadingly. "When you said *if* my heart sank."

"All right. It will be nice *when* we can go."

A Metaphysical Drive (Continued)

"That's an interesting view," said Catherine, "can you see it through the trees? – Well, it *looked* interesting, but now I can't see it."

On long-distance drives Catherine found it essential to set intermediate goals, her first one being in this case the San Fernando Valley; and the smooth violet wave of her hair in the mirror was intermediate in its frozenness; for that wave was ready to break all over her but it paused to reflect upon the meaning of potential energy; meanwhile her inquiringly upturned face and her busy white-sleeved hands on the wheel in 12:00–3:00 position did not seem to know the concept of immediacy; they just continued and continued to be ready-to-hand as long as she wanted. Her thin-framed gold sunglasses gave her a pitiless but not inhuman aspect. Through them, her eyes seemed like violet-grey pools beneath a misty sky. When I closed my own eyes, I could see the violet hair of Catherine still flaming in the mirror like an ionized stream of some ideal gas. I felt as if we were going to drive through the entire rainbow.

"Little did that Border Patrol know," said Catherine, laughing and spreading her hands, "that we were carrying *con*traband!"

She enjoyed fast driving. I could not help recalling the time when Catherine was still at the Center for Perfect Enlightenment and she heard from the *das Man* grapevine that the Abbot had left his reserved pallet and incarnated himself as a fleshly god in order to seduce his students (the courtship accompanied, perhaps, by the romantic music of the *mykugyo*), and the anguish of Catherine at his unrighteousness can best be expressed by the fact that she had a drink, although you were not supposed to drink at the Center, and then she had several more, followed by a *stiff drink* or two, and when she was good and drunk she got into her car and started driving toward the Bay Bridge faster and faster without really knowing where or why she was going, and, enslaved by nausea and dizziness, she grazed the on-ramp in a shower of sparks.

We ourselves drove northward for thirteen hours at the speed of faith. It was desert all the way. Stephanie twiddled the tuner of the radio, and Catherine stared straight ahead while the car approached its

Heideggerian towards-which. I wanted to tell Catherine, like my famous precursor, that I would return to her, but I was afraid that she could not bear it. Soon I would never see her anymore. It was a good thing that I was not alive or I would have had to cut my heart into ten thousand little cubes. Presently we came to the foot of a Mountain that was tall and white and grand.

Golgotha

The reason that Mount Shasta bounded Catherine's Being-horizon was that, like her, it reached the limit of perfection and unknowability. In both of them, iciness was loftiness. Through the high green ridges could first be seen blue sky (not misty, exactly, but *strange*), no mountain yet, and then the dry hills. The ridges lowered, and then suddenly we could see the Mountain attended by its lesser cones, which were purple-grey – no, violet – unveiling themselves, standing naked with the clouds blowing away from them like their lacy underwear. Mount Shasta was dressed in blue-green trees and yellow-green meadows, but these were only at its foot; the Mountain too was stepping out of its clothes and rising rosy-naked into sheer violet breast-scarps which had the texture of pastel chalk, crowned by snow and kissed by a single sucking cloud.

To uncover the grandeur and essence of the Mountain was impossible, because it was necessary to climb higher to *see*, and meanwhile the day waned, Dasein failed in its finitude, and finally one could see nothing. Nothing helped. One could, for instance, focus one's binoculars on the one-dimensional blueness of other hills, but that only made them larger without revealing anything. – Catherine drove upward anyhow. – "How *beautiful!*" she cried, no doubt influenced by the purple inertia of the Modoc lava fields (but I did not even care because I had tried so hard to prove my devotion to Catherine and she would not come to Heaven with me). At first we journeyed through sugar pines and spruces, which became taller and lighter-green as we progressed. There were hot spaces of deerbrush, goldenrod and violet huckleberry bells. Purple clover rocked the dreaming bees, and Catherine rolled down her window as she drove, so that the greedy sunlight could taste her and try once more to send her its golden warning or appeal, defeated again by the violet darkness of her hair, which kept the interior of the car warm and even like a steady plasma-torch; and a strand of her hair waved out the window for a moment as we passed some purple lupine flowers. We passed by a crowd of silver firs, but, impelled by the crystal-rays of the summit, did not stop in our ascent (which a century ago John Muir called "a long, safe saunter").* Because Catherine had to concentrate on her driving she did not see the bright butterflies that danced so guilelessly upon this sleeping Fire-Mountain; and the long grass waved a little in the sun's breath, and Catherine's hair stirred inquisitively, but did not fly away to see the butterflies. Everything below us was hazy and blue-green, as if it were cushioned with meadows instead of desert. (These lower slopes, which were violet in the morning and grey at high noon, became green in the evening sun. Nothing about them was steadfast.) – How pleasant it would have been to live with Catherine in sunny mornings in the pine-shade of Shasta, hearing water rushing down the rocks – but we had missed spring and morning; even violet summer was in its decay. Every few seconds we crossed into another of the elevation zones drawn on the topographic map as a concentric series of complex polygons, their density increasing toward the center as Mount Shasta launched itself into its final steeple, so that the farther we went, the more rapidly we gained altitude, and Catherine became correspondingly more exalted. Superimposed on the map of the Mountain was a checkerboard of mile-squares; they clearly thought themselves ontological because they were uniform, ubiquitous – and yet they seemed quite invisible when I looked for them out the car window, for the ultimate refinement in an entity is Being-Not-There at all, like whiskey whose smoothness resembles water, like perfume without a fragrance, like eternally absent Catherine. We drove upward and crossed from square to square. But Catherine never said a word about the squares. By now the dwarf pines (which had had violet flowers in the spring) became paler still in hue, smaller, and rarer; between them only bare yellow dirt. Grasshoppers rejoiced in Catherine, but she did not see them, either, because the road made her tense. Clouds hung sadly above the trees. The cinder-cones, whose closely spaced contours resembled finger-whorls on the topographic map, were far below us now, veiling themselves in cool blueness so that it was easy to believe that they had never been violet

* The current Department of Agriculture pamphlet reports: ". . . it is a long and difficult hike, and will tax the strongest of constitutions." Thus far have we decayed.

and nothing was really violet; Catherine's hair was not violet but only blackish-grey. Hard by Horse Camp we could no longer see the summit; it was cut off by trees and ridges and hard roots. Around us grew the purple stalks of forest darkness. Moss-grown trees let their arms droop. The yellow earth was becoming white. When we looked downwards, it seemed that every green mystery of spruce had its blue mystery of mountain behind it. The distant mountain ranges where the owls lived were like worn translucent spear-points of some hypothetical or impossible blue glass, behind which unseen violet flowers shook their heads *no* and shrugged their leafy shoulders at the twilight breeze. The cracked bark of each tree became more dappled with newness as it rose higher into the sky. All the trees were rising, rising in their jumping-off places; to them it might seem that they were leaping into the sky, climbing higher as their roots aged and rotted behind them until they reached their bug-eaten climax and fell from the sky with a dusty crash. But big trees and little trees kept growing in the dry violet sand. – Catherine steered between Red Butte and Green Butte. The air became thinner. We continued to ascend, and after awhile there was only dryness and snow and silence.* The cloud had already gone away. Beelzebub was waiting for me.

Hell

"Well," said Catherine finally, "*here* we are."

Because I, William T. Vollmann, am the Holy Ghost, I am able to understand all tongues, as if the world were as it is portrayed in some World War II television series in which everyone from Italians to Germans to far-flung Arab potentates (each of whom is played by Omar Sharif) speaks English, but with their own accents and verbal particles, thereby conforming to the famous prescription: "Socialist content, but in a national form." In the bazaars of Asia they say, "How much this cost? One, two free!" – and in France they say, "Please do not derange

---

* An understanding of the Being of snow remained baffling no matter how close one got to it, whether one gazed at it from the bottom of the mountain at what seemed to be white featurelessness, or whether, hot, sweating, with pounding heart and dry mouth, one climbed up into a stretch of snow and stopped to survey it through a hand lens.

yourself, Madame," *und so weiter*. For to me everybody speaks but one language, the language of Being. For me, therefore, it was child's play to hear what Catherine said to Stephanie about me as she drove away: "*Well*, so I don't know how *cleanly* I *extricated* myself from that situation, but I did. I'm *glad*. I'm really so glad."

A Question

In the nighttime, when a single light shines through the dark window of Heaven, and the radio always plays the same California song, I, the Holy Ghost, wonder how Catherine knew so well that even when someone really loved her she could be no less alone.

What the TV Said

"Things could be different," said the TV.

"No, they couldn't," said the TV. "They never have been, and they never will be."

"I don't think there's anything more to *be* said," said the TV.

"I guess I'm going to have to leave you alone now," said the TV.

For Robert Harbison

A Heideggerian Glossary

Authenticity – Living rightly and appropriately. The Holy Ghost sees authenticity as fulfillment, whereas Catherine sees it as responsibility.

Being-towards-death – The orientation of **Dasein** towards its own finitude in time.

Dasein – Literally, "Being-there." The human subject (you and me), defined in terms of its finitude, temporality, and **thrownness** into the **World**.

Das Man – The "They." As a fish must swim through water, so Dasein must swim through the "They," the ontic neighbors who tranquilize Dasein with idle talk on the porch on long summer evenings while Dasein drinks too much and forgets that it is primordially guilty and must die.

Deficient – A shabby mock-up of what you *should* be doing.

Factic – A fancy way for saying "factual"; or **(factically)** "in fact."

Hiddenness – The natural state of an entity. Dasein must *wrest* (Heidegger's word) things from their hiddenness in order to make them disclose themselves to Dasein's understanding.

Horizon – The limiting compass of knowledge and vision.

Leaping-in-ahead – The authentic way of caring for someone. Showing a possibility, example or method which the other person can act upon. An example would be encouraging the other to become a martyr.

Leaping-in-for – The deficient version, in which the Dasein who cares appropriates the other person's way of Being. An example would be torturing the other to death to force her to be a martyr.

Ontic – Particular, specific, random. In *Being and Time* this adjective seems on occasion to be contemptuous.

Ontological – Universally inherent, which I sometimes interpret (as Heidegger would not) to mean divine.

Potentiality-for-Being – The various exits on the Dasein Freeway. You can put the cruise control on and just continue on, *faktisch* and *praktisch*, or else you can turn off at the Existential Hotel, the Existentiell Motel, or any of a variety of seedy ontic resorts, or end up on Deficient Drive, or you can despair of becoming authentic and project your potentiality-for-Being into space when you drive over a cliff and see the cold grey ocean coming up at you in your last **towards-which** . . .

Present-at-hand – The ontological state of an entity which merely *is*, without being *for* anything. An example would be the dead body that was once a Dasein.

Ready-to-hand – The ontological state of an entity which exists in relation to Dasein. An example would be a Mexican stiletto which Beelzebub is about to use.

Relatedness – One of Dasein's most integral characteristics. Dasein does not exist as an isolated quantity, but as an entity *in relation* to the constellation of ontic flotsam and jetsam in the **World**.

Thrownness – The condition of finding oneself in a pre-existing ontic situation, the random elements of which (culture, topography, etc.) one has no control over.

Towards-Which – The goal or direction for which something is ready-to-hand.

The World – The external Being and possibilities that Dasein encounters in its relatedness. I once read that the earth is so rich in roundworms that if everything else were taken away they could still form a ghostly outline of every mountain and steeple and skull. It is something like this roundworm-portrait which Heidegger attempts to draw, subtracting every particularity to see what is left.

X-RAY
VISIONS

We cannot even tell what force may be acting on us; we can only tell the difference between the force acting on one thing and that acting on another.

James Clerk Maxwell, *Matter and Motion*
(1877), § 103 ["Relativity of Force"]

Hymn

"I say the soul is then a free agent," cries the alchemist, "and has the power, spiritually and magically, to act upon any matter whatsoever; therefore I said the first matter is in the soul; and the extracting of it, is to bring the dormant power of the pure, living, breathing spirit and eternal soul into act."* At this my heart trembles: – how wondrously clear and truthful! – for consider the great X-ray camera, which extracts the gnawing miseries of the soul to serve our knowledge – the worms, the perforations, the diseases spread across flesh and soul . . .

The First Vision†

We have here a flight of stars, far whiter and purer than the spinal column with its ghosts of marrow, diffused throughout the print's blue-blackness like an expanding universe. Above is the vast vague corona of the skull, which in its fitful sun-storms has cast forth a long curved tendril of light, the esophagus, kissing the pale balloon of the stomach

---

* Francis Barrett, *The Magus, or Celestial Intelligencer* (London: Lackington, Allen & Co., Temple of the Muses, Finsbury Square, 1801), Book I, Part I, "Alchymy," Part II, Lesson XI.

† All of the following stories are true. They are based on patient histories accompanying the trauma X-rays which I describe.

at the bottom of the print; two stars are making love. But what is that galaxy of sharp little stars?

He was a seven-year-old boy who turned his back. He didn't hear the soft mad footsteps behind him. Now the balls of shot sign his name with the surety of metal. They will illuminate the darkness inside his body until he crumbles in his coffin.

The Second Vision

A round planet floats in space. It has sharp ridges and craters. We come closer, like astronauts about to crash-land on Mars, where our last minutes will hiss away with our air-supply, and we will fall down upon the rocks and lie bone against bone, for this is an old man's skull that we are holding at arm's length, with blue-black crosshatching already in the eyes, like cobwebs. How wide and deep and dark those eyes are! They remind me of two gun barrels. You can look into the barrel of a gun that is pointed at you, and not see into the chamber. Perhaps you can see the bullet that is waiting for you, and perhaps you are fooling yourself. These bone-eyes, death-eyes, are looking at you through the flesh. They can see you. But they do not mean you any harm. The old man was always kind.

When the homeless stranger approached him, the old man told him that he could stay the night. The circumstances of the invitation are obscure, like the blurred grey vertebrae on the film, with their silences and darknesses and interlocking crowns. If I do not know exactly what was said, it is because X-rays are transparent to words; only deeds show up in their piercingly skeptical light. If I do not know whether the old man and the stranger were brought together on Mission Street or Potrero Street, if I am unaware who spoke first, the reason is that no X-rays of motivation or place were ordered by the ward physician. And because the old man did not himself have X-ray eyes (although now he will have them forever), he did not suspect that within the arteries of his guest spurted jets of ichorous hatred instead of blood. This creature – who was so mindlessly innocent in his resolutions, like a virus; who usually spent his nights in the shade of dead buildings, dogging the footsteps of the weak – now waited in the old man's living room, listening to the ticking of the clock and grinning in spasms that bared his blackish-yellow teeth. When the old man was asleep, the stranger got up and padded to his bedside, leopard-silent in dirty socks. In this X-ray it is the knife-blade that is most prominent: – a thick white band, the width of two finger-joints, that spans the skull diagonally from the left cheek, a little below eye level, right through the nose and mouth to the right side of the chin. – Even now the eyes seem mild. But they are melancholy and knowing. The smooth grey forehead slopes away into the Martian north pole, and along it is a thin white halo of sunrise.

The Third Vision

How perfect is the symmetry of this male pelvis, with its wide mysterious tunnel at the back of which the spine dwindles, the twin eye-shaped holes below, the tunnel between the legs – all these caverns and ways, honeycombing the white bone-cliffs! On every side, misty grey bones blur away into a darkness so complete that nothing can be said about it; the pelvis is isolated in that night, unable to rely on anything but itself; and it hates itself. This refusal to *be* is stubborn, noble, heroic; these bones ought to become their own marble monument, instead of deriding themselves with their Haversian texture of webbed bat-wings. In the lowest abyss is a stubby pale penis, like a sausage skin filled with water. There is a safety pin inside it.

This man craved a sex change. – How strange that he wanted a vagina, when, as the X-ray shows, he already had such beautiful holes in his pelvis . . . But we are never happy with what we have. That white pelvis of his was a flower in the gardens of covetous Night, that Night who raises all our bones from seed and then plucks them – and then is not happy with them and lets them crumble. So nobody cared for the pelvis. The man himself could not do without it; the guts of his being were enclosed in its pearlswept forms; but it made him suffer. He wanted it to flare in that beautiful bell-shape given to women by God; and no doubt he wanted the bars of his rib cage to curve for the sake of his artificial breasts, those flowers of artifice in the same cold meaning-less garden where the fruits plucked themselves and each other, eternally unsatisfied; and he wanted a womb to bleed and to nourish his children inside him, but he could not have those things. It would have been theoretically possible for him to have a raw slit cut between his legs so that he could deceive himself and his lover whenever either of them wanted to be deceived, but he had no money and the hospital would not make him a vagina for free. Desiring to make the doctors repent and to prove himself worthy of his purpose, he gave himself a woman's name; and then, with the resolution of a master craftsman, took a razor and sawed his testicles off. He did this with a composure that I can imagine but not reconstruct. The X-ray gives no hint of the terrible wound. Of course he bled in a magnificent way, being above all a showman, a performance artist, whose pain must be made visually tangible in that reddish-black stream that clotted bedsheets and more bedsheets, but the doctors saved his life, being permitted to act in this instance because it was an emergency, not a frivolous sculpting which the government in its bone-palaces would not fund. He was now, of course, neither man nor woman, and he hoped that the doctors would bring him to the far side of this limbo, where nymphs of his own nature would welcome him, but the doctors had already raised him out of the puddle of blood he had made between his legs; they were allowed to do no more. So he opened the safety pin and thrust it into his penis, beginning at the base of the abdomen and working outward toward the glans, endeavoring to bury the pin so deeply in the despicable organ that it would mortify, and then they would have to amputate – and *then* surely they would be morally bound to give him his sex change. He was like a soldier who hoped that by shooting himself in the foot he would be given leave to go fight on the opposite side. But he had not been thorough enough; the urologist was able to straighten the safety pin and pull it out through the urethra. Having nothing else left to try, the man tramped round the hospital in the dotage of his ideal, collecting signatures on a petition that proclaimed his right to be feminized, but he was expelled from the hospital long ago, and all that remains of his history now is that grey and white cathedral of bone, standing in the searing X-ray blackness, hopelessly consecrated to the negation of itself.

Seeing Through the Colors

I have seen X-rays of intestines like worms in darkness, rearing in segments, translucent to each other; and within these naked bowels the white glow of a bullet, a shard of glass, a cancerous polyp makes the future clear: – you are literally seeing death. These plates are severely truthful. Upon seeing them, the will sinks. – We all know the story of the two frogs in the pitcher of cream – how the intelligent frog knew that they both would drown, and gave up the struggle like a speckled little Socrates, but how the stupid frog bugged his eyes out and kept kicking and kicking and kicking in a panic until his struggles had churned the cream into butter. There the story ends, with the living frog resting on top of the butter, and the dead frog on the bottom; and it is supposed to be a happy story but I know that the next morning the farmer's wife came and found the cream spoiled and killed the horrid slimy frog (a melanoid *Rama pipiens*), because farmers' wives are no more tolerant than the rest of us. So the intelligent frog was really intelligent after all. He had X-rayed the situation. For X-rays see through the RED of our blood, the ORANGE and the YELLOW of our fatty tissues, the GREEN and BLUE of our intestines, the INDIGO of our dreams, the VIOLET of our preoccupations – and only the black and the white remain.

For Janice Kong-Ja Ryu

A NOTE ON THE TRUTH OF THE TALES

I have not verified any of the claims, reminiscences, yarns and anecdotes told me. But neither have I altered their content. They are as they are.* Why should I care whether they are true or not? When someone tells me a story it is probably true for *him;* if not, why cannot I make it true for *me?* If I were perfect, I would believe everything I heard. – To reverse the dictum of Hassan the Assassin, "ALL is true; NOTHING is permissible." – In my scholarly edition of the Bible are footnotes explaining the Divine in terms of the merely meteorological. But it would seem no less admirable to explain the meteorological in terms of the Divine. Surely I can know more than I see. I did not see Bootwoman Marisa's tooth get pulled out with pliers. But I will believe her anyhow. – Neither would it matter to me if there were no Shadrach, Meshach and Abednego. The issue is what *I* would do if my King were going to cast me into the Burning Fiery Furnace. If you object to my gullibility, I envy you; you will build great steel logic-castles, I am sure, whereas my roof has been leaking for three years.

---

* I have, however, changed minor details when requested to do so by my informants. (I regret that for legal reasons I have been required to change most of the given and street names in this book. To those who look through these pages in vain for mention of themselves, I offer my sincere apologies.)

ACKNOWLEDGEMENTS

I would like to extend my grateful thanks to the following individuals, institutions and organizations for their help in showing me the colors of the RAINBOW: Dr. Lester Adelson, the Black Rose Bar, Brandi, Jacob and Jeanine Bray, the cadavers *R.I.P.*, Dr. Richard Chaisson, "the Chief," Christina," Ms. Veronica Compton #276077, the Coral Sea Bar, Mark Dagger, Dan-L and Dickie, Ms. Kate Danaher, Janis and Jacob Dickinson; Dino's Lounge, "Evangeline" *R.I.P.*, Mr. Paul Foster, who was of invaluable assistance in conducting Drano experiments at home and in the field: Dr. Sharie Geaghan, Professor Glyph, Ms. Susan Halein, "The I.V. League," Mr. Michael Jacobson, who assisted me in my browsing through the trash cans and dumpsters of Golden Gate Park; Ms. Helen Jakubowski, "Jamaika," Jen, Paul and Marlene Kos, Ms. Andrea Juno and Vale, both of *REsearch* magazine; Officer Dave Kamita; Mr. James M. Lombino, Bootwoman Marisa, Bootwoman Mari, Ms. Yuki Matsumoto, who permitted me to use one of her recurring dreams in my description of the Blue Yonder fairyland; Mr. Ken Miller, who introduced me to most of the eminent street personalities of the day; Mr. Craig Mitchell, who kindly permitted me to sit on his porch-deck one September evening to watch an apartment building burn down; Mr. Jack Lee Moore, Mr. Bradford Morrow, Ms. Eileen O'Connell, Opal, Mr. Dennis Osmond, Mr. Ben Pax, Pawel and his wife, Mr. Seth Pilsk, who accompanied me on a vain quest for wild salamanders: Ms. Stephanie Reynolds and Ms. Maureen Riordan, who sketched their version of the ideal green dress for me; Ms. Catherine Reynolds, "Ruby" *R.I.P.*, Dr. Janice Ryu, Mr. Gary Scott, Mr. Michael Sebulsky, Shizue, Ms. Patti Simons *R.I.P.*, the S.F. Nazi Skinz, Spike, Mr. Jock Sturges, Mr. Walt Sunday, Survival Research Laboratories (Mark Pauline, Matthew Heckert, Eric Werner), Mr. Scott Swanson, Mr. Richard Raymond Tisdale *R.I.P.*, two members of the Vice Squad, Thomas and Tanis Vollmann, Ms. Esther Whitby, Officer Jadine Wong, and the Wrecking Crew.

Above all I would like to thank those persons unnamed or unattributed here: the prostitutes, the doctor who let me see my first autopsy, the doctor who gave me the trauma X-rays, and all the others who trusted me. Needless to say, any errors or misinterpretations are my own.